The Bo

NO ESCAPE FROM LOVE

Cimarron didn't like the angry, determined look on Trace's face as she retreated, but she was up against a pile of hay and could back no farther. It was time to confess; no matter the consequences.

"Look, there's been a mistake," she said. "I'm not really—"

"Game's over, no more stalling," he said. "I gave you the extra money. Now you give me what I paid for!" His left hand moved quick as a gunfighter's as he reached and jerked her closer.

"Don't you touch me, cowboy, or I'll scream and—"

"And just see who comes runnin' to this lonely barn!"

Terrified, the blonde looked beyond him toward the ladder, wondering if she could move that fast or even beat him to the pistol. She took the chance . . . and lost. As she tried to run past him, his strong arms caught her, dragged her to him kicking and screaming.

Trace's hand twisted in her long hair and brought her face up to his as he pulled her body against the cold metal conchos on his vest.

"Now," he murmured just before his mouth covered hers so that she couldn't scream, "sassy miss, let's see you earn your money!"

MORE TANTALIZING ROMANCES
From Zebra Books

SATIN SURRENDER (1861, $3.95)
by Carol Finch
Dante Fowler found innocent Erica Bennett in his bed in the most fashionable whorehouse in New Orleans. Expecting a woman of experience, Dante instead stole the innocence of the most magnificent creature he'd ever seen. He would forever make her succumb to . . . *Satin Surrender*.

CAPTIVE BRIDE (1984, $3.95)
by Carol Finch
Feisty Rozalyn DuBois had to pretend affection for roguish Dominic Baudelair; her only wish was to trick him into falling in love and then drop him cold. But Dominic had his own plans: To become the richest trapper in the territory by making Rozalyn his *Captive Bride*.

MOONLIT SPLENDOR (2008, $3.95)
by Wanda Owen
When the handsome stranger emerged from the shadows and pulled Charmaine Lamoureux into his strong embrace, she knew she should scream, but instead she sighed with pleasure at his seductive caresses. She would be wed against her will on the morrow—but tonight she would succumb to this passionate MOONLIT SPLENDOR.

UNTAMED CAPTIVE (2159, $3.95)
by Elaine Barbieri
Cheyenne warrior Black Wolf fully intended to make Faith Durham, the lily-skinned white woman he'd captured, pay for her people's crimes against the Indians. Then he looked into her sky-blue eyes and it was impossible to stem his desire . . . he was compelled to make her surrender as his UNTAMED CAPTIVE.

WILD FOR LOVE (2161, $3.95)
by Linda Benjamin
All Callandra wanted was to go to Yellowstone and hunt for buried treasure. Then her wagon broke down and she had no choice but to get mixed up with that arrogant golden-haired cowboy, Trace McCord. But before she knew it, the only treasure she wanted was to make him hers forever.

Available wherever paperbacks are sold, or order direct from the Publisher. Send cover price plus 50¢ per copy for mailing and handling to Zebra Books, Dept. 2176, 475 Park Avenue South, New York, N.Y. 10016. Residents of New York, New Jersey and Pennsylvania must include sales tax. DO NOT SEND CASH.

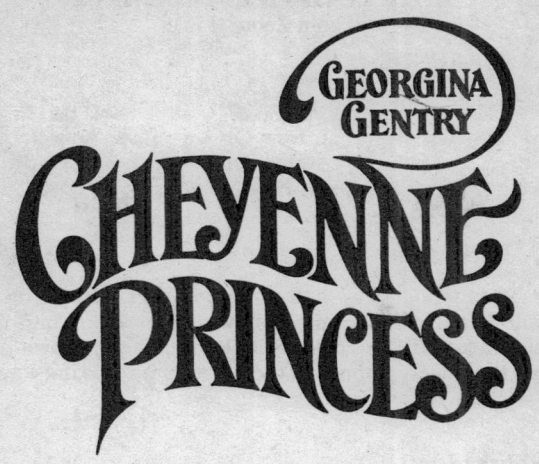

CHEYENNE PRINCESS
GEORGINA GENTRY

**ZEBRA BOOKS
KENSINGTON PUBLISHING CORP.**

ZEBRA BOOKS

are published by

Kensington Publishing Corp.
475 Park Avenue South
New York, NY 10016

Copyright © 1987 by Georgina Gentry

All rights reserved. No part of this book may be reproduced in any form or by any means without the prior written consent of the Publisher, excepting brief quotes used in reviews.

First printing: September 1987

Printed in the United States of America

For George W.

The poor, immigrant bricklayer who laid thousands of bricks year after year in summer's heat and winter's cold so his six daughters could have the education he only yearned for.

and

For Rachel W.

The incurable romantic who named her girls from novels she borrowed at the public library and who always dreamed one of them might become a writer.

Thanks, Mom and Dad. Because of you, I made it.

Prologue

It was called the "Great Outbreak" of 1864, that savage time when fierce Indians set the western frontier ablaze and blood soaked the ground.

Nowhere was it worse than Texas, where the Comanche realized that the white men had gone East to fight the Civil War, leaving their ranches, their livestock, and yes, their women, as prizes for the taking.

Texas was the only state to put secession to a vote of the people. Sam Houston and a few brave souls argued against leaving the Union. Not surprisingly, those counties along the Red River facing into the fierce Kiowa country and many of the western ones on the edge of Comanche areas voted "no." These citizens knew they would face the savages alone and defenseless should the troops go East. But the majority of Texans had a southern heritage, and they outvoted the others.

Knowing by bitter experience the ferocity of the Comanche, the Texans never intended to leave the western boundary open to their raids. But the three regiments left behind to defend that area went instead to invade Arizona, New Mexico, and Colorado, hoping to claim those areas for the Confederacy. Instead, the Lone Star regiments were shot to pieces and nearly destroyed by a combined Union force of Californians and Colorado Territorials, under John M. Chivington. He and his men would turn up later at a place called Sand Creek.

With the Texas regiments destroyed, the defense of the western frontier was up to a handful of ranchers and townspeople. The bloodthirsty savages soon discovered that there was a ready market for stolen horses and cattle among the Yankees to the west and the Mexicans to the south. The white captives were made slaves if they were not ransomed, and this was a terrible, living death.

And so began the "Great Outbreak," all along the Kansas and Colorado frontiers, but especially in Texas. The Comanche pushed the line of civilization back east a hundred to two hundred miles, almost to where it had been in the 1840s. They left a trail of blood and flames as they rode hard into the German hill country around Fredericksburg, raiding even into Austin, the state capital. The famous cowboy, Charles Goodnight, estimated that 300,000 Texas cattle were stolen and sold in New Mexico during the Civil War by Indian raiders.

The war parties were aided and supplied by the mixed-blood Spanish Comancheros. For a hundred years these ruthless renegades rode out of New Mexico to trade with the Comanche. These desperadoes had no qualms about the fact that the knives and guns they supplied would eventually cut a white baby's throat or scatter the brains of a feeble grandmother.

Now, down in a Texas hill country town called Fandango lived a beautiful half-breed girl named Cimarron, daughter to Cheyenne Chief War Bonnet and his golden-haired love, Texanna. "Cimarron" is Spanish for "Wild One," and it was an apt name for the smoldering, honey-haired beauty who could ride and shoot like a man and dared anyone to tame her.

The adventure started because Cimarron wanted to attend a party. She didn't expect to be caught up in a rape, murder, and the possibility of her own lynching.

Nor could she know she was about to clash with a mysterious, virile vaquero on a great ranching empire to the south. This dark-eyed *hombre* saw untamed women and wild horses as challenges to be broken to his will, expecting them to accept him as master.

Fate would sweep them both into the "Great Outbreak," and nothing would ever be the same again. . . .

Chapter One

September, 1864

Cimarron staggered from the bedroom. She closed her eyes to keep from seeing the blood on her bare breasts . . . on her hands.

But shutting her eyes didn't work. She could still feel the sticky warmth, smell the sweetness as she stumbled into the kitchen and grabbed the back of a chair. The horror of what she'd just done swept over her. Only sheer willpower was keeping back the sour nausea. Wave after wave of panic and revulsion shook her as she gripped the chair with white knuckles.

"Oh, no," she moaned, "Oh, dear God, no!"

Get hold of yourself, Cimarron, she commanded. *You have no time for the luxury of hysterics.* In a panic, she ran to the kitchen door, flung it open to stare out at the rainstorm outside. *She must go for the doctor. . . .*

No, it was too late for that. There was so much blood, Ransford must be dead. The echoing thunder outside might have been the pounding of her own heart as she gazed unseeing at the pouring rain, the dismal day.

The sheriff. Of course she must go for the sheriff. But even as she started out the door, she changed her mind. A Texas sheriff would never take the word of a half-breed girl on anything, especially when the dead man had been a respected pillar of the community. In a small, prejudiced town like

Fandango, she probably wouldn't even get a fair trial. These people, who had never forgiven her mother's love for a Cheyenne chief, might be eager to take revenge on the daughter.

Think, she ordered herself. *What are you going to do now? You've got to get out of here.* Slowly, her eyes focused on her trembling hands. She staggered over to the wash basin. She poured a bowl of water, plunged her hands in, mopped at the blood on her bare breasts. She stopped; stared at the white porcelain bowl, the scarlet ripples spreading to turn the water pale pink.

Closing her eyes with a shudder, she turned away, wiped her hands on her faded calico dress. There was only one thing she could do. Cimarron had to escape before Aunt Carolina and her two fat, homely daughters returned from the dressmaker's and found the body.

What was that noise? She stiffened and strained to hear. Did it come from the bedroom? She couldn't stand to go back in there. Maybe it was only the thunderstorm outside. The torrent seemed to be easing off, though. Could it be a delivery wagon with things for tonight's party?

There wouldn't be any party now. Not unless it was her own lynching party. With shaking hands, she pulled together the torn bodice. Her bruised body protested in pain as she limped to the pantry. She had been so naive and innocent, not realizing what he'd intended. . . . But she hadn't meant to. . . .

If she thought about it anymore, she'd fall apart and start screaming. Trying to force the images from her mind, she searched behind the cornmeal for the few coins she'd been saving to run away when the war finally ended.

Grabbing a hunk of leftover lunch cornbread off the kitchen table, and an old shawl, Cimarron stumbled through the ornate parlor. She had cleaned it so carefully this morning that the scent of furniture polish still hung on the air. Still, she imagined she smelled fresh blood.

If only she could go back and change the happenings of the last hour. If only . . . no time for regrets, she thought, it wasn't your fault. You acted in blind panic.

Cautiously, Cimarron opened the front door and peered up and down the deserted street. Ransford Longworth's bay gelding stood wet and forlorn, its California rein looped over the white picket fence. The rain had eased off to a fine mist.

She tried to look casual as she draped the shawl over her dark blond hair, closed the door and walked toward the horse. But inside, her heart hammered with fear. Pink Seven Sisters roses climbed the white pickets, their fragrance muted as they drooped in the sultry rain.

Oh, dear God, I didn't mean to do it! Cimarron sighed as she mounted up and her skirt slid up her long legs. She tried to pull it back down, wishing she had a sidesaddle as she looked back at the grand Victorian-style house. Where would she go? What would she do? She'd lived in Fandango all her life, but she had few friends. Life wasn't easy for a half-breed girl in a prejudiced Texas hill country town.

Señora Rodriguez would help her. . . .

No. Cimarron shook her head stubbornly as she rode out, tears spilling down her bronze cheeks. She couldn't involve others in this; they would be in trouble with the townspeople. Mrs. Rodriguez would surely help, but Cimarron wouldn't ask. She wouldn't endanger the kindly widow. Cimarron was on her own.

Just what did a naive, parsonage-raised girl do at this point? The rain fell in a fine mist on her face as she reined the horse around to the south. Cimarron had no idea where to go, but she couldn't ride north. That would take her through the town square, and she mustn't be seen. Her tense fingers gripped the one-piece rein as she kept her mount to a slow walk, thankful the sudden storm had driven everyone indoors for an afternoon siesta. If it hadn't been lightning and thundering, a neighbor might have heard Ransford's scream. . . .

It took all her willpower to ride out of town at a slow walk in case someone might happen to look out the window and see her. But her soul cried out to quirt the horse and gallop away as though the hounds of hell were nipping at the gelding's heels.

For at least a half mile, she walked the bay, listening intently for sounds of pursuit. All her ears heard was the echoing thunder of the fading storm, the gelding's hooves, and her own pounding heart. Finally she kicked the horse into a slow, casual lope. Only when Fandango was several miles behind did she quirt her mount with the Romal, the ends of the braided California rein. As she rode south at a gallop, she tried not to remember the terrible events of the past two hours. It had seemed so innocent. All she'd wanted was to go to the party. . . .

It had been almost noon when Cimarron took a deep breath for courage, smoothed her faded calico dress, and marched into the parlor of the elegant Victorian-style home.

Aunt Carolina stood surveying the ornate furnishings and gave her a curt, disapproving frown. "Oh, there you are, Cimarron. Did you get the windows washed? There's so much still to be done, with the guests coming at seven o'clock. I do hope it won't rain and—"

"I've finished the windows and beaten the carpets." Cimarron brushed back her tawny dark blonde hair, determined to keep her fiery temperament under control. "Everything's clean and most of the food's ready. If the girls would help me instead of sleeping late—"

"Are you criticizing your cousins?" Aunt Carolina's eyes expressed exasperation. "It's important they look their best tonight. After all, it's their coming out party, and while most of the eligible men are off at war, there's enough important, wealthy ones left that I thought it worthwhile. . . ."

Her petulant voice trailed off and her pout gave her pale features the look of a small, ill-tempered bulldog.

How like Carolina Longworth to think of the war only as an inconvenience, preventing her having eligible men come court her two quarrelsome, homely daughters, Cimarron thought, summoning up her courage to plunge in. "Aunt Carolina," she drew her tall, slender frame up to its full height, "About the party—"

"I don't suppose the Durango heir will come clear across the county, it's such a long way," her aunt mused, ignoring Cimarron. "But if he were to marry one of my girls, certainly his father wouldn't call our note next year when it comes due...."

"Aunt Carolina," she began again, trying to sound properly humble and grateful. How many times in the last two months had she been lectured about being properly thankful for the Longworths' generosity? "About the party—"

"What about it?" Aunt Carolina snapped, busily moving the knickknacks around on an ornate marbletop table.

Cimarron took a deep breath of apprehension, caught between her eagerness and the conflict she knew was coming. "I wondered if I might attend?"

"Of course, you'll attend," Aunt Carolina nodded, glaring out the window at gathering clouds. "Someone has to serve the sandwiches, and you and the other maid will have a lot to do to keep things tidied up tonight."

"No, I didn't mean as a servant." She hesitated and summoned all the courage of her twenty-two years. "Señora Rodriguez says she can handle the serving alone. I—I want to be a guest."

"A guest? To mix socially with Prudence and Patience's friends?" For a moment, Aunt Carolina's eyes widened. Then she assumed a pious expression and patted Cimarron's shoulder. "Dear, you wouldn't quite fit in, and you'd end up being miserable. You know how most Texans feel about Indians—"

"My father was a Cheyenne chief." Cimarron tried to hold her temper, but she could feel her dark eyes flashing.

"Don't remind me of my sister's scandal." The other woman's blue eyes flashed back. "To think Texanna would choose to go with him—"

"Is that what's really bothering you?" Cimarron let her temper and her stubborn independence run away with her. "Or was it that War Bonnet took her instead of you?"

Aunt Carolina slapped Cimarron's face. "I remind you that I was a respectable married woman!"

13

Instantly, Cimarron both hated her aunt and regretted her own thoughtless retort. As she rubbed her stinging flesh, two spots of bright red came to Carolina's pouty cheeks. Abruptly Cimarron saw the jealousy and unfulfilled passion in the woman's expression.

Her aunt sighed, turned away, and when she spoke, her voice was a whisper, as if she were thinking aloud. "No man ever noticed any other woman when Texanna was around. She could have had her choice of them, even . . ."

She sounded bitter as she stood looking out the window. "Pastor Schmidt and his wife did their Christian duty by you all these years, raising you until they died, and now, Cimarron, I am trying to do mine. What goes around comes around, as I always say, and surely I will be rewarded, if not on this earth, at least in heaven, for my good deeds."

Her voice had a decided edge as she whirled to look triumphantly into Cimarron's eyes. "I'm only thinking of you, my dear, not wanting you to be hurt and humiliated tonight by being rejected socially by Fandango's best families. You really should learn your place; be more humble. Besides," she gave her skirts a triumphant flounce as she turned to leave, "you don't even know how to dance!"

"But I can!" Cimarron's dark eyes flashed in her bronzed, high-cheekboned face. "I watched the dancing teacher from the kitchen as he gave the girls lessons, and I can waltz and polka as well as either of them."

She'd started to say "better," but her sharp mind gained control of her spirited retort. It wouldn't help to point out the clumsiness of her two plump cousins.

Aunt Carolina shook her head. "I'm afraid people would hurt you with their remarks." She smiled benevolently, but Cimarron saw the hard gleam in the ice-blue eyes. "Besides, you have nothing to wear."

"I do, too!" Cimarron tried to keep the spirited ring of triumph out of her voice. "I took Prudence's old green gown, took it in at the waist, let it out in the bust, and added some old lace around the bottom flounce to make it long enough."

"So you think you can just show up; a half-breed, a poor relative, in a faded, secondhand gown, and expect to mix with my daughters' friends?" Aunt Carolina's pallid skin went livid. Her dainty hands shook as she brushed her gray-streaked hair back.

Cimarron lost the last remnants of her temper. "I'm not ashamed of my heritage, but I know you are! And people shouldn't be judged by lack of money and clothes. But for the two months I've been here, I've been treated like an unpaid servant, and—"

"What a thoughtless niece!" Aunt Carolina looked toward heaven, as if beseeching divine help. "'How sharper than a serpent's tooth is an ungrateful child.' And to think I was kind enough to take you in when the Schmidts died. All the ladies tell me I've done more than my share, gone the second mile for my poor, misguided sister—"

"You took me in as a free servant," Cimarron said hotly, past caring and caution now as they faced each other like combatants. "And because you were afraid your snooty friends would talk about you if you didn't!"

"Of all the nerve!" Aunt Carolina blinked as she looked up into Cimarron's eyes. "This conversation is ended." She bit off each word. "I want to hear no more of your impudence. Now tonight, you and your Mex friend will be in the kitchen where you both belong—"

"Don't call Señora Rodriguez a 'Mex.'" Cimarron's loyalty to her friend made her lose all caution. "She's a respectable widow who can't find a decent job in this town."

She heard a noise in the doorway and her two homely cousins entered, still in their nightgowns and yawning.

"What is all the noise about?" Patience rubbed her pale blue watery eyes. "You woke us up."

"Sorry about that," Cimarron answered sarcastically. "I've been up since five."

"But you're supposed to be up then." Prudence brushed back her thin, pale hair. "Is there any coffee left?"

"Of course, we have coffee." Cimarron put her hands on her hips. "Even though it's scarce and costs a fortune, the Longworths don't do without luxuries."

"So?" Patience shrugged. "Why should we? If sister and I manage to marry rich, we'll be able to pay all our debts.

We're used to living well and don't see why we shouldn't." She scratched her fat waist indelicately. "What's the noise about, anyway?"

Aunt Carolina smirked. "Well, you're not going to believe this, but Cimarron wants to come to the party."

"So?" Prudence's prominent teeth stuck out over her lip. "Of course, she'll be there. Someone has to serve."

"I mean as a guest," Aunt Carolina said.

Prudence's mouth dropped open and the other girl looked horrified. "For pity's sake, Cimarron, you can't do that! Why, I would be humiliated to death, especially if that rich Durango fellow does show up. What would he think about us letting an Injun girl, even a poor cousin—"

Cimarron grabbed her then, even though she knew they'd make her regret it. She gave the thin hair a good pulling while Prudence howled and the other two stared in amazement at the plump girl's pathetic efforts to defend herself.

"Double damnation! Two months of this is long enough!" Cimarron declared as she attacked her other cousin.

Prudence set up a wail that could be heard probably down on Main Street.

Her aunt pulled Cimarron away and got right up in her face. "How dare you, after all I've done for you—?"

The front door opened and pompous Uncle Ransford came in, his florid face perspiring. "What in the name of Goshen is all that noise? Prudence, shut up! You sound like a sick coyote caught in a trap!"

"She pulled my hair and pushed me!" Prudence sobbed. "And I wasn't doing anything to her! For pity's sake! Not one thing!"

"That's right, Ransford," Aunt Carolina agreed smugly. "Poor Pru wasn't doing anything at all and my ungrateful niece attacked her."

Cimarron started to come to her own defense, then decided she was fighting a losing battle she would not dignify with an answer. If the Civil War would just end, she thought with angry frustration, she could run away and leave this hateful family and town forever.

The pompous storekeeper patted his sobbing daughter on the arm. "Now, now, my dear, I'm sure Cimarron didn't mean anything by it. Now aren't my two darlings due at the dressmaker's to pick up your new gowns for tonight's party? I see the buggy waiting out front."

Prudence nodded glumly, her round face tear-streaked. "I told her we'd be over about noon," she gulped.

"Well, it's almost noon now and it's sprinkling rain." Uncle Ransford sucked his teeth thoughtfully as he pulled out his big gold watch and chain that hung across his paunch. "Now you girls run along and Carolina, my dear, perhaps you should go with them. After all, you are the one with a sense of style and taste in this hick town."

"That's true," Aunt Carolina smiled in smug satisfaction. "But what about Cimarron? She has the nerve to want to attend the girls' party."

"Of course she'll attend," Ransford said mildly, "if she has a decent dress to wear—"

"Oh, I do," Cimarron's hopes rose. "It's one of Prudence's old ones, but it's nice enough."

"Ransford," Aunt Carolina's eyes flashed sparks, "you surely don't intend—"

"Well, of course she can wear the dress and be there at the party," he soothed. "After all, she and Señora Rodriguez are serving the cake and sandwiches. What's the fuss about?"

Cimarron's heart sank while the other two girls tittered with malicious delight. "That's not fair," she whispered, trying to fight back the tears of anger and frustration that came to her eyes and threatened to overflow those dark pools.

Uncle Ransford sucked his teeth. "We'll discuss this, Cimarron, while you fix me a bite of lunch and the girls go on over to the dressmaker." He smiled at his three women. "After we talk it over, I'm sure Cimarron will see the error of her ways and be ready to apologize when you return."

The two plump cousins smirked with triumph while Cimarron quivered and tried to hold her temper. What was she going to do, after all, if the Longworth family threw her out? She only had a few small coins saved and hidden away.

No one else in town would hire her if the uppity Longworth family passed the word around. She had few skills that she might use if she should get through the Yankee lines to try to start another life. There were almost no respectable jobs for women, although she wasn't afraid of hard work. And certainly she couldn't cross Texas and Colorado looking for her older half-Cheyenne brother, whom she hadn't seen since she was five.

More than anything, she wanted to attend tonight's party. She had spent her whole life looking after the invalid wife of Pastor Schmidt, and they had left their little horse ranch to the church. Even the congregation had not been overly warm or friendly to the half-breed girl and had been only too eager to evict her from the ranch on the Schmidts' death. In all her life, Cimarron had never attended a real party, the kind the Longworths were having tonight, and she wanted to desperately.

She decided to try and convince Uncle Ransford of that as she watched the three women get in the buggy and drive away. Then she fixed his lunch.

Uncle Ransford finished a bowl of her delicious homemade stew and belched loudly. "I don't know why such a long face," he grumbled. "After all, you will be at the party. What difference does it make which side of the serving table you stand on?"

"If you don't know, I can't make you understand it." She tossed her honey-colored head as she cleaned away the dishes. "I'd like to talk to you about it before you go back to the store."

He yawned. "So few goods to sell these days makes business slow. Damned war! Had to pay big bribes to get that fine cloth for the girls' party dresses and the food and wine. I told the clerk I might stay home all afternoon and help my wife get ready for tonight's party. Got to put away my horse, though, looks like a real toad-strangler coming." He scratched his jowls as he looked out the window at the growing clouds, the gray gathering storm.

"Uncle Ransford, about Aunt Carolina—"

"Poor Carolina, she'd give anything if we were one of old

man Austin's 'Three Hundred.' Those first three hundred settler families are the nearest thing to blueblood Texas has. Even more, she'd like to marry into one of the rich old Spanish families like the Durangos."

"Uncle Ransford," she gave him her most beguiling smile, "I have a really nice dress, and Señora Rodriguez says she can handle the serving alone. Aunt Carolina would let me attend the party if you asked her."

He looked at her as if really seeing her for the first time. "It's amazing how much you remind me of your mother," he said softly, as if remembering. "Texanna's hair was lighter, more red gold. But she was tall and slim like you."

He studied her for a long moment, and for some reason, the way he looked at her made her feel ill at ease and uncomfortable. To avoid his eyes, she busied herself with putting away the leftover stew.

He stood up and hooked his fingers in his vest. "Your hair reminds me of a tawny, honey-gold mountain lion I saw once lying on a big rock in the sun. That's what you remind me of, with your dark eyes and tawny hair, a lioness."

"My mother was white," she reminded him, clearing away the dirty dishes. "She couldn't have looked much like me."

"Well, she had fair skin and eyes the color of bluebonnets, all right. But the fire of her, the pride, her fine features," he answered softly, remembering. "Yes, I see that much of her in you."

His voice trailed off and she saw the sadness in his face and realized suddenly that Uncle Ransford had been in love with her mother. She wondered if Aunt Carolina knew it? Of course, she did, Cimarron thought, remembering the scene in the parlor. No wonder her aunt hated Texanna.

He must have seen the expression on her face, for he stood up and nodded. "Yes, I would have left Carolina for your mother," he said softly, as if speaking to himself. "But your mother wouldn't have me. Me, Ransford Longworth, one of the most important men in the Texas hill country."

"She loved my father," Cimarron whispered.

"Yes, damn her!" His eyes seemed to fill with pain and suppressed fury. "I offered to run away with her. Half the men in town wanted Texanna, but she would have none of us. She waited faithfully for that savage to come back for her. When he did, all the gold in Texas couldn't keep her from leaving with him."

"Aunt Carolina says she didn't care about me, so she left me behind."

"That's not true," the gray-haired man said sharply. "No one could have loved her children like Texanna did, but she loved that Cheyenne chief more than life itself. You were a sick baby, too sick to go anywhere. Moreover, the mob that was trying to lynch your brother was between them and you at the preacher's house. If she has never come back for you she must be dead; that's all that would stop her."

Cimarron bit her lip and clenched her fists at the idea. What a rotten choice, to think she was either abandoned or her mother was dead. Now she looked at the paunchy shopkeeper and tried to read his thoughts.

"Yes, all the fire of Texanna, but dark eyes and skin like War Bonnet's," the man said dreamily. "And you're not much younger than she was the first time I ever saw her. I suppose I owe her something for the way I treated her; the way this rotten town treated her."

He seemed to turn something over in his mind. "Is the dress you've got presentable enough that your aunt wouldn't die of embarrassment? Why don't you show it to me?"

Hope rose in her heart again. There was so little fun and excitement in her life. "It's really not too bad. Not as nice as the ones the girls are having made, but I'm handy with a needle."

There was something in his expression that she didn't understand, didn't like. "Yes, let's see the dress. I can probably talk your aunt around, convince her it's a generous, commendable thing to do. She cares a lot about what other people think of her."

"Uncle Ransford, you're wonderful!" she said happily, following him to the small, cramped room at the back of the big house. Ransford Longworth ruled the roost here like an old-fashioned dictator. If he said she could attend the party, she'd get to go no matter how angry her aunt and her two spoiled cousins became.

The paunchy man looked around at the small, dingy quarters and she saw the distaste in his face. "Land o' Goshen! I haven't been back here for years, I guess. Carolina ought to be ashamed when our two have so much. . . ."

His voice trailed off and Cimarron pulled the faded dress from the tall walnut wardrobe and held it up in front of her. "See? It's not too bad." She nodded to the pincushion, thread, and scissors on the table by the bed. "I've been repairing it at night when I finish the housework."

He frowned. "It's terrible. But even so, with your beauty, you'll put both our clumsy daughters in the shade and outshine every other girl in town. I have to admit that's probably the real reason your aunt and her friends might be upset if you attend. Their homely daughters can't stand the competition."

She smiled and felt herself blush. "Do you know you're the first person besides Señora Rodriguez who has ever said anything nice to me like that? The Schmidts preached against vanity."

"Now I haven't yet given permission." He shook his head hastily, and she felt his eyes sweep over her in a way that made her uneasy. "You know, you need to be able to dance—"

"I can dance!" she laughed, holding the dress up before her and whirling around. "I learned by watching the dancing master teach Prudence and Patience."

Uncle Ransford chuckled. "I saw some of those lessons myself. Both of them are as graceful as hogs on ice. But their mother is hoping she can marry them off to someone who has plenty of money, although we wouldn't need it if they weren't all so extravagant."

He held out his arms. "Let's see how well you dance, Cimarron, so I can tell your aunt you won't embarrass us."

"Well . . ." She laid the dress across the foot of the bed and went into his arms hesitantly, never having been held by a man before. Some of the boys at the small country school had tried to sneak a kiss, but she had pushed them away. Like her mother, there could be only one man for her, and she hadn't met him yet.

"Now," Uncle Ransford said, and he seemed to be breathing more heavily. "We'll just dance a little and see how well you do."

Cimarron complied, letting him whirl her around the small room. He was holding her too tightly and she could feel her nipples pressed against his checkered silk vest. The smell of his bay rum hair tonic was almost overpowering. His hand seemed very hot and moist holding hers, as did the one pressing into the small of her back.

Tense, she tried to pull back, but he pulled her closer as he danced her around. "I hadn't noticed how you've grown up since you moved in here." His face was so close to hers she could see the sweat on his florid jowls.

Outside, the sky seemed to break open, and lightning crashed as rain poured down.

"Uncle Ransford, your horse should be put away." She stopped dancing and looked up at him. The strange look on his face told her he hadn't heard her. "Uncle Ransford," she put her hands against his chest and tried to push him away, "I—I don't think—"

But he held her tightly and looked down at her. "You're almost as beautiful as your mother," he whispered, and his lips trembled. "You know, Cimarron, if you'd be nice to me, I could talk to your aunt; make things a lot easier for you around here."

"I don't understand what you mean," she began, feeling her heart beginning to thud a warning.

"Yes, you do. I can see it in your eyes, just like I see suppressed passion there. You're like a banked fire, Cimarron, hot coals glowing, waiting to burst into flames; waiting for a man's first touch. . . ." One of his beefy hands went up to stroke her long hair, and before she realized his intent, his moist mouth came down on hers.

She tried to protest, but her arms were pinned to her sides by one of his long arms wrapped around her. The hand that stroked her hair caught the back of her head so she couldn't escape from him.

Angry, but frightened, she tried to protest, but his tongue

was invading her mouth now as his greedy lips forced hers apart. She could taste the strong cigars he favored, feel his body straining against hers and the hardness between his legs rubbing her body.

As she struggled to break free, she stumbled back against the bed. It hit the bend of the back of her knees, catching her off balance. She fell across the bed with the heavy man atop her.

"Uncle Ransford, no!" she managed to gasp. "Have you lost your mind?"

But he was like a man possessed, holding her down by throwing himself half across her while his free hand pulled at the front of her dress. His mouth claimed hers as his hot, moist fingers fumbled with her breasts, jerking the bodice down. She could feel his sweat dripping on her bare skin and the reek of bay rum nauseated her.

"Cimarron," he gasped against her mouth as his hands pawed her ripe breasts, "be nice to me and I'll talk to your aunt and things will be better for you. You'll see! You'll go to that party tonight and be the belle of the ball."

"No!" she exclaimed, struggling to break free, more furious than frightened. If she could get one hand up to claw his face, he'd think tawny mountain lion!

"Oh, yes, Cimarron!" His wet mouth left a trail down her throat to her breasts. "I never got your mother, but you are just as pretty! Be nice to me, honey, and I'll get you your own little place over at San Antone. You'll live like a queen, lots of new clothes and everything. Your aunt won't need to know—"

Fear became a cold chunk of ice in her insides as she struggled, knowing he was determined to have her now no matter what the consequences. She could feel his fingers on her silken skin as he pushed her skirt up, fumbled with the buttons of his pants.

Out here on the edge of town, if she screamed, would anyone hear her over the storm? More than that, would anyone help her? Her heart sank as she realized no one would believe her if they came running; not when her uncle was such a solid, upstanding citizen. He would say she offered herself to him, tried to seduce him, then changed her mind. Besides, the thunder echoing outside would drown out any cry.

No, she couldn't expect help from the citizens, and it might be several hours before Aunt Carolina returned. Even innocent as she was, Cimarron knew this gave him plenty of time to enjoy her.

He had his pants unbuttoned. She could feel his hot, naked manhood against her bare thigh. That horrible sensation drove her to fight with renewed energy. But despite his middle age, he was a strong man, and he gradually forced himself between her legs.

"Be nice to me, honey," he gasped. "All you got to do is be nice to me. I'm gonna teach you what life is all about. It's time you learned, and you owe me for feeding and looking after you."

His mouth muffled her protests as she fought him, but she was determined he was not going to take her virginity. She would choose her own mate as her mother had, and if Uncle Ransford raped her, he would have to kill her to do it.

He had her wrists pinned above her head on the pillow now while he tried to force himself between her thighs and his mouth sucked clumsily at her taut nipples. "Be nice to me, honey," he murmured again. "Just relax and be nice!"

"Never!" she gasped as she struggled and twisted, trying to get away from his wet, seeking lips.

"Nobody'll believe you if you tell on me," he whispered as his damp hand went under the small of her back, lifting her; positioning her. "This is just the start, Cimarron, of a long, long friendship. Every time your aunt is gone, I'll come by the house and you won't dare tell anyone."

His tongue licked across her breasts as he came up on his knees, forcing her thighs farther apart. "It may hurt a little the first time, but maybe you'll get where you like it, not like your cold, frigid aunt. I've been going over to Miss Fancy's place in San Antone when I can't stand it no more. But now, I won't have to do that. I'll have you right here in Fandango and we'll keep our little secret."

His perspiration dripped on her bare breasts and his

clammy fingers stroked her inner thigh.

If she just had something with which to hit him over the head! Frantically, she freed one hand and felt along the edge of the table by the bed.

He was oblivious to anything now but his own need. "Be nice to me, honey, be nice to me," he whispered. She felt him reach down to position himself, getting ready to drive hard into her virginity.

Desperately, she fought to get out from under him as her fingers felt along the table, feeling for a hairbrush, a vase, anything. *She was not going to be raped!*

Her searching fingers closed on cold metal, not recognizing for an instant what the object was. Then the image of the dress flashed before her; the dress, the needle, thread. Still she was not fully aware of what she grasped as she made a last, frantic effort to save herself.

Her hand clasped the object tightly, brought it up to use against him as he made ready to rape her. She was past thinking, past anything but self-preservation.

The dim light flashed on the object as she brought it down. His eyes seemed to widen in sudden horror as he recognized it. He tried to raise one hand to protect himself but Cimarron's Indian blood instinctively made her as fast as a scorpion's sting.

"No!" He managed one small cry as her hand flashed down. She closed her eyes at the last moment, buried the shiny blades of the sewing scissors in his chest.

Chapter Two

Cimarron rode southeast at a steady lope, stopping now and then to rest the bay gelding. The light mist had ended, but her clothes were damp. What lay ahead of her she had no idea, and no real plans on where to go or what to do.

Her sire was the bravest and the greatest of the Cheyenne chiefs, War Bonnet. Her mother, the calm, serene Texanna, whom he had stolen from a north Texas wagon train. Now the bravery and the serenity in her bloodlines stood her in good stead. She tried to make plans as she rode steadily and the hours passed.

She had a brother, Falling Star, eight years older than she, if he were still alive among the Cheyenne to the north. But she would have to travel through both Confederate and Yankee soldiers to reach him. She wasn't sure if he would welcome her or if he were even still alive.

She fled southeast across the rugged limestone and granite, crossing the trail along the ridges called the Devil's Backbone. She rode toward the southern edge of the hill country. If she could make it to the coast, and figure out a way to pay for ship fare out of Galveston . . .

The bay was both blowing and lathered when she finally pulled up, dismounted, and walked a while to cool it out and rest it. The California rein made it easier to lead the horse, since it was a single leather strap that went from one side of the bit to the other. She had the advantage of not worrying about hanging on to two loose ends. Lots of times, she had seen her uncle drop the rein on the horse's neck and light his cigar while the bay automatically walked home.

All afternoon she headed across the cedar clumps and rocky limestone, stopping only to water her horse at Cypress Creek as she crossed it. The creek flowed from the mysterious hundred-foot-deep spring called Jacob's Well, to the east. She washed her feet in the icy water and ate the cold cornpone from her handkerchief. The bluebonnets and the scarlet Indian paintbrush that usually splashed the pale limestone with brilliant color had faded and disappeared months before.

The big sign in the ground was meant to be seen at a distance, she thought as she read: TRIPLE D RANCH. NO TRESPASSING. RUNNING IRON MEANS A ROPE.

Hesitating only a moment, she rode past the warning, wondering if the heir was coming to her cousins' party. Regretfully, she shook her head. There'd be no party now. She wondered again if she could have done anything differently. She hadn't meant to kill her uncle.

The Triple D, she thought as she rode. Some said it was only slightly smaller than the famous King ranch. A quarter of a million acres, she thought, knowing she had to cross this cattle empire that covered two counties, spread over the rocky Balcones Escarpment and down across the rich, rolling, coastal plains to reach Galveston. It would be a long ride.

Wearily, she sighed as she watched the gathering clouds blotting out the sinking sun. Thunder rumbled in the distance and a drop of rain splattered on her bronze arm. At least if it continued to rain, her tracks would be washed out and it would be hard for a posse to trail her. The sky turned the same lavender as west Texas sagebrush when the storm moved in again.

The breeze picked up a little. She smelled rain and shivered at the cool touch on her damp clothes. The gelding's ears went up and it whinnied suddenly and was answered by a whinny from over the next rise.

Cimarron stiffened, trying to decide whether to wheel her horse and make a run for it. But then she realized it was already too late. A man rode over the rise, a tall, lean man dressed in black, mounted on an ebony stallion.

For a long moment, she hesitated, torn with indecision. She gathered the shawl more closely around her, fighting her impulse to flee. But the man rode with the easy air of someone born to the saddle, and the powerful horse looked as if it could easily outdistance the bay should she try to outrun it.

She reined in and waited, trying to pull her skirt down over her legs, which was almost impossible riding astraddle. She knew the vaquero had seen her by the way his left hand went to his holster, his lithe frame tensing as if wary of a stranger. He wore a flat, black hat with silver conchos around the band. His ebony leather vest also gleamed with silver conchos. Even the stallion's black hackamore sported the shining silver ornaments.

He tipped his hat back as he approached her and she saw he was almost too rugged to be handsome. A lock of blue-black hair fell across his dark, high-cheekboned face. Spanish, she thought, or Indian. Maybe both.

How would she explain her presence on this ranch? Could she make up a story about going to visit someone and getting lost? Maybe he would believe. . . .

But he scowled and nodded. "About time you got here," he said as he rode up. His deep voice was a curious mix of Spanish accent and soft Texas drawl. "The boys up at the camp were about to give you up; expected you this morning. I thought there were supposed to be two of you girls?"

"Two of us?" Cimarron stammered, thinking he reminded her of a lithe, lean dark panther. His mouth was a thin, hard line. But in the dusky light she saw his eyes, and they were as large and soft as a deer's. "Oh, yes, there were." She thought quickly. "But you see, the other girl got sick, couldn't come. I've ridden for hours to get here."

Two girls for what? she thought, knowing she dare not let him suspect anything. Cimarron didn't know how far it was to the nearest town, but she didn't want this cowboy turning her over to the local sheriff, who might soon hear about the murder.

His eyes swept over her with a deepening frown and she thought again how their dark softness contrasted with the grim line of his mouth. "I don't think one girl can handle it, that's why I asked for two—"

"Well, if I'm willing to try," she answered with a spirited nod, "you ought to at least give me a chance."

He almost smirked and she had a sudden feeling that he hadn't laughed in a long, long time. But there was something about his gaze that made her breath quicken as it swept over her. She couldn't be sure of his age, maybe not much older than she herself, but his eyes seemed old and weary, as if he had seen too much.

"Darlin'," he answered, and she caught the irony in his voice, sensing that he didn't like women. "You are the sassiest little filly I've run across in a long time. "What's your name?"

"Cimarron," she blurted, without thinking.

"Cimarron." He drawled the name as if savoring it. "'Wild One.' Good name for your business."

She bit back a retort, unsure whether he was making sport at her expense or not. "I can handle the job," she insisted, with more confidence than she felt.

His eyes studied her again in a way that made her shift uneasily in her saddle. He threw his leg up across his saddle horn and she noted he had small feet for a man and wore no spurs. That was unusual for a cowboy. But then so was a gentle hackamore on a big, spirited stallion. As he studied her, he pulled out a paper-thin cornshuck and a small sack of tobacco.

She sensed he enjoyed making her wait as he twisted the cornshuck into a cigarillo Texans called a "quirley."

"Nightwind and I will take your word for it." He struck a match across the heel of his boot with an angry gesture. *"Si,* I'll just bet you're real good at what you do," he agreed with a defiant nod as he blew a smoke ring skyward.

"Of course, I am." She tried to sound both haughty and casual. What had he sent for? A cook? A cleaning girl?

He snorted, and she had a feeling he disapproved of her, perhaps of all women. Cimarron bit her lip, brushed back her damp, honey-colored hair. He was playing games with her, enjoying watching her fidget while he smoked and studied her in a dark, sullen way that made her uneasy.

"You look a little young for this, darlin'." He scowled and she felt his soft, moody eyes appraise her. "You been at this long?"

"Double damnation! Are you questioning my ability because of my age?" she huffed indignantly. It wouldn't do to answer too many questions, have him pry too deeply.

"Hell, no!" he snapped, and she thought she heard him sigh as he tossed away the cigarette. There was a trace of scorn, of disappointment in his deep voice. "I'll bet you're real good at it, just like the rest of them, after all. Doesn't matter who as long as the money's right."

She wasn't sure what he was talking about, but she didn't like the way he looked her over as he swung his leg back down to his stirrup.

"Speaking of money—"

"*Si*, darlin', money." He reached into the black vest and pulled out a small bag. "Although the Triple D's credit has never been questioned before. You're lucky I ran into you, because you're headed wrong. Good thing I was looking for a herd that seems to have strayed, or at least it's missing. If our paths hadn't crossed, you'd have ended up clear to the Gulf before you found out you'd missed the roundup camp."

"I guess I had bad directions," she murmured lamely.

"You see anything of a rider?" he asked. "Someone tried to ambush me a couple of hours ago."

She shook her head. "Lots of thieves and renegades running free with most men gone to war. You have gold instead of Confederate bills?"

He sneered as he held out the pouch. "Señor Durango spurns paper money. He says it wrecks governments."

Automatically, she reached out and took the sack. When her fingers brushed his, she felt an unexpected charge, as if electricity from the jagged lightning in the distance had touched them both. He must have sensed it, too, for his expression softened, but only for an instant. Then it was more guarded and hostile than it had been before.

"You little bitch!" His deep voice was a hoarse whisper as he appraised her again. She heard him take a deep breath. "Head out straight north and you'll reach the camp in half an hour or so, if you ride fast. You better get a move on, it's gonna rain."

"How dare you insult me!" She reddened at his epithet.

"You're right," he answered with the soft slur of Spanish-Texas accent. "I got no right to expect you to be different than the rest. But I keep hoping...." His voice trailed off, then came back brusque, businesslike. "Ride north, like I said. In less than an hour you'll see the smoke from the campfires. The old man's not doing well, I'm going to the hacienda." He looked at her again, smiled bitterly. "And darlin', remind me to look you up the next time I make it into San Antone. I want to find out if you're all you say you are."

"I am!" she flung hotly, furious at the implied insult in his tone. "Now I'll be on my way."

She wheeled her horse around, and the man shrugged and turned back south.

"Make my roundup crew happy," he called back over his shoulder. "And tell the boys Trace said he'd be back up in the morning." He tipped his hat over one eye. "And darlin', tell Miss Fancy we're pleased with what she sent this time."

Cimarron's face flamed as he turned and rode away into gathering dusk. Only now did it occur to her that he was speaking of the notorious bordello in San Antonio; that he thought she...

She had to bite her lip to keep from riding after him and throwing the money at his stiff, proud back. How dare he think she was a whore come up to entertain his men! Then she managed to control her fiery temper as she watched him disappear over the next rise. If she tried to explain that she was not the expected party girl from Miss Fancy's bordello, she was going to answer some curious questions about who she really was and what she was doing riding across the Triple D.

Besides, she was desperate for money. Hefting the bag in

her hand, she realized it was heavy with coins. Gold she could spend if she made it to Union lines, where the Confederate money would have been worthless.

Quickly, she decided on a plan. She would ride southeast as she had been doing, keeping well away from the ranch house where this Trace was headed. Thanks to him, she now had passage from Galveston. For just a moment, her conscience hurt her. Cimarron was an honest person, and she felt bad about taking the money. Someday, she decided as she swung her horse back southeast, someday, when she could earn a little, she would return every cent she had taken from the cold, hard cowboy called Trace.

The rain came now, first the occasional big drops on the limestone around her as she rode. Finally it began in earnest as dark settled across the high plateau created in massive earthquakes millions of years ago.

At first she gloried in the cool, wet rain, the smell of it, the feel of it on her bare skin. She even opened her bodice and let the cold drops splash on her bare breasts, washing away the last traces of dried blood so she finally felt clean again.

Hours passed, and the bay grew so tired that it stumbled several times. She found herself grabbing leather to keep from being thrown. The downpour grew steady and her clothes clung soddenly to her. She shivered, even though the night was as warm and humid as a wool saddle blanket.

Weariness overcame her, and several times she nodded off and awoke with a start, afraid she would go to sleep and lose her grip.

But she had to keep riding, she thought grimly, looping the rein over the saddle horn so she wouldn't have to hold it. Somewhere behind her a posse rode, and she didn't dare hope she would get justice in a town like Fandango.

Somewhere ahead of her lay the long border of cliffs that the Spanish had called Le Balcones, the balcony, that dropped away to the rich coastal plains. Even after she left the hill country, it would still be a long way to Galveston.

In spite of herself, she dozed in the saddle as the horse

splashed through the mud. Cimarron awakened a split-second too late as it stumbled in a prairie dog hole and went to its knees. She felt herself falling helplessly over its head, grabbing vainly for the rein, the saddle horn, anything to stop her fall.

She landed in a soft tumble in the mud. Realizing the danger of the spot she was in, she came up grabbing for the leather. But the California rein lay out of her reach across the saddle horn, and the bay backed away from her outstretched hand.

"Here, boy," she called soothingly. "Here, boy! Come to me!" Her heart began to hammer. She couldn't end up afoot in the darkness and rain of the desolate hill country. "Here boy! Good boy!"

But the weary gelding snorted and backed away from her. Silently she cursed the braided single rein her uncle favored. If she'd had regular split reins, the horse would have stood "tied to the ground" when the reins fell. Now he turned back the way they had come.

"Here, boy!" she called desperately. "Here, boy!" Cimarron made an agonized grab for the bay, but he snorted and galloped off. As tired as she was, she ran after him, but she was no match for the animal. He loped back toward Fandango, leaving her stranded on the empty prairie.

She stared forlornly after the departing horse as he faded into the darkness. Double damnation! Well, look at the bright side, she thought grimly as she turned and started walking south. At least, they can't add horse thieving to the charge, and with the rain washing out his tracks, the sheriff won't backtrack the bay and find me. Horse stealing was a hanging offense in Texas, just like being caught with a running iron that rustlers carried to alter a brand.

Could she possibly walk all the way to the coast? There was nothing she could do but try. Maybe tomorrow she could catch one of the Triple D horses. Then the moody boss of this cattle kingdom would be trailing her along with the posse from Fandango.

Keeping her fiery temper under control, she sighed and put one weary foot in front of the other. She slopped through the darkness while the rain soaked her clothes into a sodden mass. If she didn't get off this ranch by morning, that foreman, or roundup boss, or whatever he was would come looking for her. She remembered the suppressed anger of the man, and she didn't think she wanted to be around when he found out he'd been cheated and outsmarted.

It might have been midnight when she finally came to a barn that loomed like a ragged old sentinel on the landscape. There was no livestock in it, but a few horses and cattle grazed in the area. As Cimarron approached she recognized the giant semitropical shrubs planted around the barn: oleander.

Gratefully, she stumbled inside, glad to be out of the rain. In the darkness, she couldn't see much, but she smelled the sweet scent of hay, the masculine smell of leather. This had to be an extra storage barn for winter forage, saddles, and tack.

Cimarron hesitated only a moment as she shivered before stripping off her wet clothes and hanging them over a saddle rack in a hidden corner of the barn to dry. Then she rubbed her naked wet body with a clean feed sack until she was warm. Now she took her last soggy cornpone and ate it while planning what she would do tomorrow.

Deciding she was too weary to walk another step, Cimarron crawled up in the loft and lay down in a soft pile of hay. Its scented softness felt wonderful under her tired naked body as she spread a horse blanket over herself and dozed, thinking she would rest only an hour or two, until her clothes dried. Then she would check the barn for riding gear, catch a horse from the Triple D herds, and be on her way.

Since she was five years old she had lived the naive, sheltered life of a preacher's daughter. Now she had done the unthinkable and killed a man. Finally, she drifted into the heavy sleep of exhaustion.

Cimarron was awakened by a noise in the barn below her.

Alarmed, she sat up in the daylight, pulling the horse blanket around her naked breasts as she tried to figure out where she was.

Then her heart sank as the events of yesterday came back to her with a rush. *She had killed her uncle. Was that the posse coming into the barn?* Quietly, she wrapped the horse blanket around her silken body and peeked through a wide crack in the loft boards.

A man came into the barn below her—the same tall, lean cowboy dressed in black from yesterday evening. She moved ever so slightly, and a board creaked.

His left hand went to his holster in a flash as he looked up toward the loft. "Anyone up there?"

Cimarron flattened herself against the floor, hardly daring to breathe, knowing she was naked and totally helpless.

"Comprende usted, amigo?" he asked, this time in Spanish. Though he asked if he were understood and said "friend," she heard his pistol hammer click.

She tried to decide what to do as she stared through the crack at him. His upturned dark face might have been handsome had he smiled. His muscular form had the vitality and masculinity of a stallion.

But again, it was the eyes and mouth of the rugged face that drew her like a magnet, the mouth hard and grim, the eyes too melancholy, too tragic. He moved gracefully, like a black panther, toward the ladder. She felt like a small rabbit being stalked by a predator.

Her heart hammering, Cimarron held her breath and watched him put his boot-clad foot on the first rung. Should she show herself? Would he go away? Might he possibly shoot up through the floor and then investigate?

Now she thought of the money still tucked in her clothes. If he had already been out to the line camp, he was going to be furious with her for making a fool out of him, taking the gold under false pretenses.

There was no way down except the ladder, and he was standing at the foot of it. It would be impossible to get her clothes and run without getting past him. She was trapped! Her mouth felt dry and she licked her lips, wondering what to do.

She was saved from that decision by the sudden jangle of spurs outside. Another man entered the barn.

The man was a muscular, tall Spaniard; probably the most handsome man Cimarron had ever seen. His big Mexican spurs jangled as he entered the barn with the easy stride of a true aristocrat.

"I thought I saw that black devil of a horse outside. Trace, why aren't you up at the roundup camp?"

Cimarron sighed as she watched the newcomer, thinking he had the sophistication, the smoothness that only comes with money and breeding. He might have been in his late thirties, surely not more than forty. She watched him run a hand through black wavy hair, slightly gray at the temples.

The rugged cowboy frowned at the handsome man. "I might ask you the same thing, Luis. I'm headed for the camp right now. I went to the ranchero last night to see how the old man was doing. You'd know that if you'd ever spend any time there. Just how are the saloons of San Antone?"

"That's your area, not mine." Luis ran a finger along his pencil-thin mustache and flicked imaginary lint from his expensive cream-colored silk shirt. "Anyway, *hombre,* I don't worry about how things go when I'm gone. After all, you make such a good foreman looking after my interests."

"Damn you, Luis!" The other grabbed the front of the expensive shirt, "If the old Don only knew—"

"But he won't know, will he?" The handsome one sneered and disengaged himself from the cowboy's grip, smoothing the wrinkles from the fine shirt. "I resent your grabbing me as if I were some saloon bum instead of a Durango."

"Keep on prodding me and I may forget you're a Durango, forget . . ." His voice trailed off and his doubled-up fists turned white and trembled as Cimarron watched from above.

But Luis shrugged and laughed easily, and Cimarron marveled again at how handsome he was. So this was the Durango heir, she whispered silently to herself. No wonder her cousins had been so eager to meet him, even though he was a little older than Cimarron had expected. Still, she thought with her heart beating harder, many men were ten or fifteen years older than their wives in frontier Texas.

"You wouldn't want to tell the old Don anything that might upset him," Luis purred, and his voice was as smooth as the silk of his clothes. "After all, he is dying—"

"The doctor isn't sure." The cowboy sounded sad.

Luis shrugged and stroked his elegant mustache. "It's in God's hands," he answered softly, making a reverent ritual of crossing himself. "Although I grieve and do everything I can to make his last days comfortable. It is not I who have caused him all this grief—"

"Mention her name and you're dead!" Trace's left hand went to his holster and he advanced on the older man.

But Luis only smiled coldly. "I'm sick of your threats! As a Durango, I shouldn't have to put up with that—"

"As a Durango, might I suggest you take as much interest in this ranch as the old man thinks you do?" Trace glared at him and there was frustration in his voice. "I'm sorry if Texas and frontier life offends your delicate aristocratic sensibilities."

"Let's not talk bloodlines, shall we not?" the other sneered, his right hand going to his coat pocket. "I would think that's a touchy subject with you."

Trace's dark face went pale, his hand trembling on the butt of his pistol. But Luis Durango only laughed and strode out of the barn, his big silver spurs jingling.

Cimarron gaped with admiration. The handsome Spaniard had coolly stood up to the muscular cowboy even though Luis wore no gun. Then it occurred to her that the Durango heir was counting on that fact to keep the cowboy from drawing down on him. Somehow, she sensed the cowboy wouldn't shoot an unarmed man.

Below her, she watched Trace fighting for self-control. The cords in his neck stood out and his hand went again to the big Colt in his holster, then moved slowly away and clenched into a fist. As she watched, he slammed his hand against a post and she winced as he shook the fingers in obvious pain. She wondered what he looked like when he smiled. If he ever smiled. . . .

She almost felt sympathy, then thought better of it. Served him right, she thought, for trying to goad Luis Durango into a fight. There was a term for a man like this cowboy. Texans called it "on the prod." For only a moment, she wondered about his anger, his moodiness. What was it that had put Trace on the prod?

Cimarron bit her lip, crouching in the loft and thinking about it as she watched him. The dawn's light streaming through the ragged barn walls silhouetted the lone man digging tack and branding irons out of a chest. She tried to decide what to do next. There was no way she could sneak down the ladder and get her clothes off the horse stall until he left.

Her legs were cramped from lying in the same position in the hay too long, and without thinking she shifted her weight, causing a corncob to fall through a hole in the worn floor and land in the dirt at his boots.

Instantly Trace went into a gunfighter's stance, his big Colt coming out fast as a rattlesnake's strike as he looked up toward the loft.

"Whoever you are, show yourself or you'll breakfast in hell! *Comprende?*"

"Okay. Don't shoot! Don't shoot!" Very slowly, Cimarron stood up, clutching the horse blanket around her naked bronze body.

"What the . . . ?" His voice trailed off and his mouth dropped open in obvious amazement as he slid the pistol back into his holster. "What in the hell are you doing here? Why aren't you at the roundup camp?"

She took a deep breath, aware of the scent of hay and dust and old leather in the ancient barn. "I—I got through entertaining the boys early," she stammered, "and started back to town. But my horse threw me, and—"

He laughed then, a hard, mirthless laugh as he tipped the flat Spanish sombrero back on his head. "Women!" he snorted in a tone of derision, and she wondered again what made him hate them so.

"Well, it seemed like a good idea at the time." She felt herself blushing at the frank appraisal of his eyes. "Be kind enough to get my clothes and lend me a horse."

Her mind raced ahead. He hadn't been out to the camp, so he didn't know she hadn't been there, either. Most of all, she didn't want to give back the money. She needed it too badly for a ship passage to get away. Someday she'd return it with a note of explanation, but not now, with a posse probably only hours behind her.

But he didn't move to go outside. Instead, he mounted the creaking ladder. "Did you give my men a good time?"

"What? Oh, yes, of course," she lied, embarrassed at the images that came to her mind at his words. Still clutching the horse blanket to her, she looked away. Cimarron was too honest to be a good liar. "A very good time! Now, if you'll let me get my clothes—"

He was in the loft now, standing between her and the ladder in the dim, dusty light as he studied her. "What about the boss?" he asked softly.

"Perdone?" She felt a chill run down her back as his words sank in. "Well, maybe next time." She tried to smile archly, but there was a tinny taste of apprehension in her mouth. "You see, I really don't have time right now. Miss Fancy is expecting me back because we've got all these soldiers coming in tonight before they go East—"

"Now, darlin';" he smiled, but there was no mirth in the rugged face; "I don't know what kind of game you're playing with me, but I'm about to change the rules!"

She watched in growing consternation as he unbuckled his gunbelt and hung it on a rusty nail from a weathered beam.

"No, you don't understand." She clutched the blanket to her desperately and backed away through the soft straw beneath her bare feet.

"Nope, *you* no *comprende,* darlin'." His voice had a warning edge as he advanced on her. "Miss Fancy's sent girls out before and there's never been any disagreement. Now, you aren't going to service the rest of the crew and leave me out. It's always part of the deal."

"I—I want more money," she stammered, backing away, figuring he probably didn't have any more on him.

He stopped; scowled at her. "So that's it! I should have known. All right, you greedy little tart!" He took a gold piece out of his vest and flung it at her. "You're all alike, aren't you? One man's as good as another to you if he can buy you pretties."

She didn't like the angry, determined look on his face as she retreated, but she was up against a pile of hay and could back no farther. It was time to confess; no matter the consequences.

"Look, there's been a mistake. I'm not really—"

"Game's over, no more stalling. I gave you the extra money. Now you give me what I paid for!" His left hand moved quick as a gunfighter's as he reached and jerked the blanket out of her hands.

"Don't you touch me!" Her long, tawny hair half covered her full, high breasts and she covered her womanhood with her hands. Cimarron was as furious as she was frightened, and she knew her dark eyes flashed a warning.

But the man's gaze moved up and down her body appreciatively, and he sighed as he tossed the blanket away. "Whatever extra you charge, my sassy miss, maybe you're worth it. I'll admit this stallion never topped a filly with a body like yours before!"

"Don't you touch me, cowboy, or I'll scream and maybe Luis Durango—"

She had said the wrong thing. She felt it instantly as she saw the sudden fury in his eyes, the iron set of his jaw, the pulse pounding in his temples.

"Scream, darlin', see if he comes running! That damned aristocrat and I have been headed for a showdown for months now, so it might as well come today!"

Terrified, she looked beyond him toward the ladder, wondering if she could move that fast or even beat him to the pistol.

She took the chance and lost. As she tried to run past him his strong arms caught her and dragged her to him, kicking and screaming.

His hand twisted in her long hair and brought her face up to his as he pulled her naked body against the cold, metal conchos on his vest.

"Now," he murmured just before his mouth covered hers so that she couldn't scream, "sassy miss, let's see you earn your money!"

Chapter Three

His strong arms held hers useless by her sides. Still she struggled, as furious as she was frightened. "Let go of me, you coyote! I said 'no'!"

"Darlin', you're almost convincing," he whispered. "Try pulling this act on the soldiers tonight. Only a really skilled tart could put on such a good act!"

She tried to protest again as she fought him. But his lips covered hers, forcing them open to ravage the deep softness with his tongue. Cimarron was tall and strong for a woman, but he dominated her easily with his superior strength, forcing her slowly to the loft floor.

His mouth kept her from crying out while his hard hands stroked her skin. Cimarron tried to wiggle away but his lean body held hers down now, freeing his hands to stroke, to tantalize her skin. Every nerve ending seemed to come alive as his skillful hands teased and touched and his mouth burnt into hers like a hot brand. His kiss probed the depths of her mouth, demanding, dominating, delighting.

Her pulse started to pound with the sensation as she struggled. But the cowboy was obviously skilled with women, knew how to break down their defenses, make them forget their objections. One of his hard hands cupped her soft breast, catching the nipple between his fingers, stroking it into taut promise. Cimarron moaned aloud, unable to stop from responding to his hands, his sucking, seeking mouth.

She was afraid now, afraid of her own reactions to him,

never having been touched by a man like this before. She had never realized what passion lay smoldering like a banked fire deep in her own depths.

He was going to rape her, force himself deep inside her velvet softness. But was she being raped or seduced? She tried to pull away from him, but he stroked her now, as he would a small, wild thing. His touch made her skin come alive, goose bumps breaking out as every nerve ending cried out for another caress. She could feel his big manhood hard and throbbing with life against her leg, knew he was ready to pump his seed into her like some virile mustang stallion taking a mare in heat.

His left hand cupped her breast, fondled it, went down to touch her thigh. His fingers felt like live coals on her satin skin. She had to fight him off before it was too late. But as she struggled, his drawling, deep voice murmured, "Easy, darlin', take it easy. . . . Don't fight me. . . . Stop teasin' me. . . ."

She could not stop him, she realized that. The size and the strength of him easily dominated her. He was going to use her to satisfy his lust whether she fought him or not, and all she would get for her vain fighting were bruises.

Cimarron stopped struggling a moment, almost succumbed to the caressing kiss, the featherlike touch of his hands on her breasts. She shook her head to clear it, reminding herself she didn't want him as he pushed gently with his hand to spread her thighs.

"Steady, darlin'," he crooned softly, "you don't have to play games anymore. I'll pay whatever you want. . . ."

His lips were hot and sweet on hers, and she relaxed, let him explore her mouth. No man had ever kissed Cimarron like that, and she found her own passionate nature responding to an overwhelming, mysterious feeling.

The cold silver conchos of his leather vest cut into her soft breasts. She could feel the heat of his hands on the small of her naked back. The hay was soft and fragrant beneath her. Perspiration beaded on her skin in a fine, silklike sheen.

"No . . ." she gasped, fighting to regain her self-control. "No . . . stop. . . ." And some part of her was half afraid he would.

"This is getting old, darlin'," he whispered against her open mouth. "You know you want me as I want you. What are you trying to prove?"

His mouth was on hers, warm, sucking. A tide of rising emotions swept her that she had never experienced, and she was almost more frightened of that than of him.

Impulsively she bit his lips, and for a split-second she thought he would strike her as he jerked back. His powerful arm trembled as he seemed to struggle with himself, and blood trickled down his chin.

He muttered a curse. "So, 'Wild One,' now I know how you got your name!" He glared down at her coldly. "If you like to be treated rough, I'll oblige you!"

Before she could deny it, his bloody mouth came down on hers again as he held her head prisoner in his strong hands. She tasted the salty warmth of his blood and it both excited and repelled her.

Cimarron struggled, but he only laughed coldly, kissed her again, smearing his blood over her face and lips.

"Darlin', you got real talent, you do!" he gasped as he held her against the cushion of hay by the weight of his body half on hers. One of his hands pinned both her wrists above her head on the barn floor so that her back arched up, offering her taut breasts as a feast to his greedy, bloody mouth.

"Let me go!" she snarled through clenched teeth as she felt his mouth taste her nipples. "Damn you! Let me go!"

She tried to twist her body to bite his arm, but she was powerless with both her hands imprisoned above her head.

"That's quite an act," he smiled humorlessly as his free hand ran up and down her tawny skin. "I'll bet you make big money exciting men to violence. Are you going to charge me extra for the bites and scratches?"

She tried to tell him it was no act, that she was a virgin. But his mouth was on hers again, his strong hand still pinning both her wrists above her head. He didn't seem to listen to her garbled words. She didn't like the feelings his touch, his mouth were building in her. She felt helpless, vulnerable, and something else. . . .

Realizing she must break away before her own body betrayed her, she fought again to escape him. But he was very strong. His hands were like steel bands, and she could feel the hard muscle of his leg that was thrown carelessly across her body to hold her down.

"Come, little Wild One," he said against her ear. "Stop this phony act and earn your money!" His voice was laced with anger, bitterness. "How many men have you tried to fool with this? I know women! I know your lying, cheatin' ways!"

"Let me go!" she raged, struggling into a sitting position. "Let me go, you rotten—!"

He pulled her to him, kissing her roughly as he fell back down into the soft hay. She could feel him fumbling with the buttons of his pants now, forcing himself between her soft thighs. She felt the sudden hard heat of his manhood against the vee of her legs. Her traitor body seemed to arch up, wanting what he offered. Under the veneer of civilization, she was as primitive and passionate as her Cheyenne ancestors. The male, musky scent of him came to her, and the scent excited her; repulsed her.

Cimarron was torn by conflict, as angry with herself as with him. "You bastard!" she hissed. "You savage bastard!"

His face changed to a mask of cold fury. "Don't call me that! Don't you ever again call me that! You've gone too far with this little game!"

He was rough now, forcing her legs apart almost as if he were punishing her for something someone else had done. As he came down into her, she looked up into his dark, soft eyes and saw the tortured vulnerability there, some old scar she had torn open with her words. Then there was no more time to think as he drove deep and sure into her virginity.

She could not stop herself from crying out at the sudden pain as he rode her roughly; thoroughly.

"You little fake!" he gasped against her mouth. "What kind of naive fool do you take me for?"

But she could only gasp at the physical sensation of his hard dagger penetrating her velvet softness and wonder at the way her body began automatically to respond. He drove deep, throbbing with the life he had to give. With questioning wonder, she felt her depths tremble as her womanhood embraced his maleness.

She put her palms flat against his muscled chest, tried to push him away. But he was too powerful for her. Instinctively her body responded. Her arms went slowly around his neck, her long, tanned legs imprisoned his hard-driving hips. She felt her insides quivering, convulsing, trying to hold onto his hardness.

His mouth was on hers again, his tongue taking its softness as his manhood took her sheath. They were both damp with sweat and entangled in her tawny blond hair, but none of that seemed to matter anymore. The salty taste of his blood was still on her mouth. She felt the sinewy, lithe muscles beneath the shirt as she dug her nails into his back, clawing him with savage Cheyenne passion.

She tried to remember that she had pledged to kill him for what he was doing, but her body forgot as he rode her, making her submit to his male domination. *She hated him,* she told herself as she dug her nails into the back of the leather vest, feeling the silver conchos cold and hard cutting into her breasts.

His breath was warm and moist against her ear, making shivers run down her spine as his tongue flicked inside.

Cimarron trembled, on the verge of some great discovery. She knew it somehow, but was too innocent to understand it, understand what to expect. It felt as if she were standing on the edge of a precipice, the ground trembling and crumbling beneath her. Any second, the cliff would give way under her feet and she would fall into oblivion. But somehow, she could not back away. Whatever lay over the edge of this excitement was too wonderful, too exciting to miss. It called to her as a flame draws a fluttering moth. She was on the verge of discovering some great, primitive Truth.

It didn't happen. Even as she panted, feeling her pulse pounding harder, her muscles tightening, the lean cowboy in her arms gasped, stiffened, and lay still.

For a long moment, she held her breath, uncertain what had happened. He was dead! That was it! He'd had some kind of seizure, and she would be blamed for it. And yet, she could feel his breath warm on her neck, his heart thudding against her breast.

Regretfully, she mentally retreated from the edge of the invisible cliff. She forgot about the great discovery she had been about to make; forgot everything, except that she had just lost her virginity. She blinked, imprisoned by the weight of his immobile body. It seemed suddenly incredible that she had just been taken forcibly by a man in the loft of a barn, while a few miles away a posse searched for her.

She had to get out of there. She'd retrieve her clothes while he was unconscious, steal his horse and head south again. But even as she struggled to get out from under the powerful body, he stirred and his eyes flickered open. They were very soft, gentle eyes, she thought. The look he gave her was almost a caress. She had never seen such melancholy sensitivity in a male face. His left hand came up, touched her cheek tenderly.

Then, abruptly, his expression changed, as if he were closing her out. The deep emotion in his dark face seemed to be replaced by an easy, disarming smirk that he wore like a mask to protect himself. "I gotta hand it to you, Cimarron, you have to be the most talented lady I've ever chanced to meet. I'll bet you made my roundup crew so happy they've all offered to marry you and make an honest woman of you."

Her angry tears came then, and she reached up and scratched his face, causing him to tumble off her in confusion.

"What the hell—?"

"You rotten snake!" she sobbed, furious with herself that she couldn't control the tears. "I hate you for this! If I ever get the chance—!"

She scrambled to her feet and ran naked across the loft, grabbing for the pistol hanging from the beam.

But he was fast, too. Even as her hand closed over the butt of the big Colt, he jumped up and crossed the hay. His fingers closed over hers. They struggled for possession of the gun a long moment. His strength won out and he pushed her away. She fell to her knees, her long, tawny hair covering her ripe body.

She looked up at him through angry, tear-filled eyes, saw the telltale smear of her virginity on his body.

"Holy Mother of God!" he gasped, looking down, the hand holding the gun falling to his side. His expression was one of bewilderment, disbelief, horror.

"I tried to tell you!" she raged, throwing herself at him, beating him on the chest with her small fists. "I tried to tell you!"

He pinned her flaying arms with his strong ones and lifted her off the loft floor, looking down into her face with an expression she couldn't fathom. "Holy Mother of God! I've raped a virgin!" His face was shocked, as if the cowboy couldn't quite believe he had broken the code of the West, had forced himself on a chaste woman. And that was something a gallant cowboy would never do.

"My God, Cimarron! Why didn't you level with me when you had the chance? If I had even dreamed, I would never—"

"I tried to tell you!" she shrieked, clawing at his face. "I tried and you wouldn't listen!"

"You lied to me, Cimarron, led me on! Led me to believe—"

"I needed the money!" she raged, trying to break away. "I would have said anything to get it!"

"So you're a liar and a sneak, but not a whore!" his voice was cold, accusing. "Like all of 'em, I guess you're full of tricks, lies. What else is there I don't know?"

She paused, looked up at him, her mouth half open, suddenly afraid. He couldn't have heard this soon about the murder, could he? Did her guilt show in her face?

"Do you think the sheriff will care about anything except the fact that you raped me?" she bluffed, knowing that among the chivalrous Texans, even a foreman on a big spread like the Triple D could be strung up for taking advantage of a woman.

She was rewarded by the sudden consternation, shame, and guilt in his eyes. Then again, his expression grew guarded; his mouth a hard, angry line once more.

"So it's blackmail, is it? I knew, like all women, you were playing some kind of game. Maybe you planned this whole thing out, figuring I would be willing to pay you to keep your mouth shut. Well, darlin', I'm not the sucker I may look to be. I'm not paying blackmail, and you won't get to the sheriff to have me arrested. I reckon I'll just have to hold you prisoner; never let you out of my sight until you change your mind, you sassy, blackmailing cheat!"

He whirled her around suddenly, slapped her smartly across her bare behind. "Now, find your clothes and we'll wash up at the horse trough." His shocked concern faded as he seemed to convince himself she had been playing a cheap game, luring him with her body into some kind of trap.

The tender softness was gone from his eyes, replaced with hard disdain. "If you'd been honest with me from the start, I'd have protected you, would never have even tried to kiss you. Why in God's name . . . ?" He shrugged, gave her a cynical look. "I suppose, like with all women, there's a trick; a reason. . . ." His eyes looked her over and she saw consternation. "God, I didn't realize I was so rough, that I bruised you like that!"

She looked down at the bruises Ransford Longworth had put on her. "You animal!" she snapped. Why should she tell him? Besides, then he would ask what had happened.

"Okay, I'm an animal." His voice trailed off regretfully as he climbed down the ladder.

Grimly, Cimarron followed him down. She had never hated a man so much. He had taken by force the one thing that was hers to give. Whatever man she loved in the future, she couldn't give him that greatest gift of her virginity. It could only be given once, to one man in a lifetime. Now hers had been stolen by a rugged, moody cowboy, and she hated him for it.

She bit her lips to hold back her anger as they washed in the horse trough and dressed. Cimarron took her own few coins and tucked them in with the small bag of gold in her bosom, thinking regretfully what it had cost her. She brushed back her honey-colored hair as he caught a buckskin gelding from the herd grazing outside and saddled it for her. He still wore no spurs, she noticed, and the black stallion again wore the gentle hackamore. Dark ruby-red oleander bloomed around the barn, though the season was almost ended. She looked at the tropical flowers and turned questioning eyes toward him. He shrugged.

"The señora," he half whispered, as if the memory hurt too much. "Those damned flowers are everywhere!"

If he hated them, she would wear them, she thought defiantly, breaking off a spray to stick behind one ear. She was War Bonnet's daughter, proud and fierce, but as calm now and as stubborn as her mother ever hoped to be. Revenge was going to be sweet, she vowed. The first chance she got, she was going to kill him.

As she started to mount, he cupped his hands for her foot, as any western gentleman did to assist a lady rider. Pointedly, she ignored his hands and swung up on the mount unassisted. Trace mounted Nightwind and sat staring at her for a long moment as he tipped the black hat back. The perpetual lock of ebony hair fell across his dark forehead.

"Cimarron," he hesitated. "About what just happened . . ." His voice trailed off, as if he were not sure what to say. "All my women have been saloon whores. I've never had a virgin, so I couldn't know—"

"If you're trying to tell me you're sorry, it's too late!" she flung at him as she whipped up her horse. "You'll regret it if you try to keep me! I'm half-Cheyenne, and I can step as soft as silk. Sometime when you least expect it, I'll blow your insides out with your own pistol or stick a knife in your back!"

He smiled thinly, but there was no mirth, no warmth in his face. "Darlin', I'm a half-breed myself. You'll have to go some if you think you can catch me unawares."

"I'll take that challenge!" She tossed her head as she kicked the buckskin horse into an easy lope.

"Done!" he shouted behind her, and she was aware that her gauntlet had been picked up by the challenger.

What kind of strange contest had she gotten herself into? What kind of man was she dealing with? Her thoughts darted like the iridescent dragonflies the Texans called Devil's Darning Needles. The insects flitted among the bright wild flowers as the pair rode north. Slate-gray clouds built into low banks along the horizon. There was a good chance it would rain more, she thought automatically.

Because she had no sidesaddle, again she was forced to ride astride, her skirt hiking up around her naked thighs. She pretended not to notice the heat of his gaze as he looked at her legs. But she could not keep herself from flushing, knowing he was remembering those same shapely legs wrapping around his lean hips.

Angrily she jerked at the skirt, but there was no way to be modest. She could not cover herself.

She studied the lavender-gray clouds as she rode through the hilly fields of late summer blooms. The horses' hooves rang sharply against the rocks. Here and there were natural sinkholes, creating small watering holes for the wildlife. The limestone was honeycombed with caves.

If she only had a gun, she thought grimly, glancing behind at the silent cowboy. The hill country had a thousand places to hide a body. Even the clear rivers and artesian springs hid bottomless underwater chasms. Folks said there was an underwater cave big enough to hold a town at the bottom of Jacob's Well. She'd like to shoot a certain cowboy and toss him in!

He said nothing as he rode behind her. How foolish she had been to warn him so that he would be on his guard, she thought regretfully.

It was almost an hour before they saw a roundup camp, with a dozen or so cowboys squatted around a fire, drinking coffee and eating. Another, with a sharp knife, was doing something to a tied-up calf. She saw the flash of the knife; the calf bawled suddenly. Then the cowboy turned it loose, and with an indignant bleat, it trotted back to the herd.

The men were mostly too old for the army, or they were Mexicans, she thought. Even though cowboys were exempted from the war because the South needed beef to feed its troops, many of the cowboys had gone anyway. But the Germans, and many of the Spanish—those who sided with Sam Houston against secession—had not gone. Some had been lynched for their beliefs.

There were whistles and shouts of approval as the pair reined in. It was easy to see he was popular with his crew.

"Hey, Trace! Where'd you get that heifer?"

"Is that one of the fillies you promised us?"

"Oh, *compadre,* where you get those scratches?"

Trace nodded as he dismounted. "I rode under a limb and it caught me across the face."

Cimarron sat her horse, unsure what to do and holding her head up proudly, even though she could feel the cowboys' eyes looking at her bare legs.

A plump, middle-aged Mexican pulling at his ragged gray mustache grinned knowingly. *"Dios!* I begin to think you never get here, boss, and now I see why."

Trace smiled. "Cimarron, this is Sanchez, who has been with Don Diego since they were both young men. But he mothers all of us, including the Don."

Some of the cowboys chuckled, and an unshaven, hard-looking cowboy stood up. She saw he was the only one beside Trace who wore a gun. And he wore his pistol low and tied down, with the trigger filed away, as some gunfighters did. The man looked up at her with unblinking, hooded yellow eyes that reminded her of a poisonous Arizona Gila monster's.

"Hell's bells! Look what we got here!" the man exclaimed, tossing away the rest of his coffee. The man wasn't from Texas, she thought. She didn't recognize the accent. He set the cup on a stone by the fire as he came around to Cimarron's horse and grasped her ankle with his right hand. "It's been worth the wait, I'll say that. Come here, sugar!"

Her heart started to pound with apprehension and fury at the man's touch, but she didn't move. Trace frowned suddenly as his gaze took in the man's hand on her leg. His voice when he spoke was so low that Cimarron had to strain to hear him. "You right-handed, Holt?"

"What kind of a question is that?" The man turned toward Trace, but he didn't loosen his grip. "You and the old Don are the only lefties on this spread."

"Then you need that hand bad. Might say you'd have a

hard time handling that pistol without it."

"So?"

Cimarron held her breath, feeling the sudden tension between the two. Holt's hand felt very hot, very intimate on her ankle. The other men fell silent, waiting.

"So take your dirty hand off the lady, Holt, or I may break it off at the elbow!"

"You and whose army?" Holt's hooded eyes didn't blink as he spat to one side, then, very deliberately, he let go and turned slowly, his hand going to the butt of his pistol. "I thought you brought her up for all the crew. I didn't realize I was about to dip into expensive private stock."

"Very private stock." Trace stood with his feet slightly apart, his hands akimbo on his gun belt. His cold, hard voice challenged the other to draw.

This saddle tramp wasn't going to cheat her out of her revenge by killing Trace, she resolved suddenly. Even as she thought, she reacted, slashing at Holt with her reins. She seemed to take him completely by surprise as the leather stung across his face. He stumbled away, defensively putting his hands up to protect himself from her fury as the other cowboys slapped their knees and guffawed.

"Hey there, Holt, looks like you bit off mor'n you could chew! You couldn't ride a wildcat like that no how!"

Shoulders slumped in humiliation, his yellow eyes glinting, the humiliated gunfighter slunk back to the fire.

Trace came around to help her dismount. Defiantly she tried to avoid his reaching hands, but they were strong and almost spanned her slim waist as he grabbed her.

"Thanks," he said softly as he lifted her from the buckskin. "We're short on help now because of the war. I didn't want to have to kill him."

"Did it ever occur to you he might have killed you?" she bristled, jerking away from him, her dark eyes blazing.

"And do you out of the pleasure?" There was a touch of anger and grim humor in the brooding features as he suddenly reached up, jerked the oleander from her hair, tossed it into the fire.

"Why do you think I stopped him!" She whirled away

from Trace, flounced over. She couldn't ever remember being so furious. Men were fighting for possession of her body as if she were a pet, a possession, and the moody cowboy had laid claim to her favors. Well, she had a surprise for him! The pet was going to turn out to have a dangerous bite when he expected it to purr instead. She smirked at the thought as she knelt to pour herself some coffee.

The plump Mexican tipped back his sombrero and rubbed at his graying mustache again, and she realized two fingers were missing from his crippled right hand. "Señorita, our coffee is weak to save it—the blockade, you know—but let me pour you some."

She sipped the scalding liquid. "All Texans think it's weak if it won't float a horseshoe."

She smiled at his gentle manner, his face like old leather. Without thinking, her gaze went to his maimed hand.

He laughed. *"Sí.* I carry the mark of an old cowboy. Sometimes, señorita, a man does not move fast enough, *comprende?* His fingers are caught against the saddle horn by the rope if the calf moves too quick."

She felt self-conscious, embarrassed that he had seen her staring. "I'm so sorry—"

Sanchez smiled good-naturedly and reached over to turn bits of meat cooking in the red coals. "Nice lady, it is nothing. *De nada."* He shrugged as he turned back to Trace. "You two are hungry, *compadre?"*

In answer, Trace took a stick, raked some of the small morsels from the coals, bit into one with relish, and offered another to Cimarron.

Gingerly, she picked it up, blew on it, popped it into her mouth. The savory bite was delicious. Recalling now that she had had nothing but stale cornpone since yesterday, she grabbed a stick herself, raked more steaming morsels out, and gobbled them.

"Wonderful!" she sighed, wiping juice from her mouth, "Really good, Sanchez! What is this anyway?"

Trace snorted with merriment as he took another bite. The roundup crew broke into embarrassed, self-conscious laughter. Sanchez hesitated, warming his hands around his cup. "Señorita, you don't know?" He paused again. She ate and looked at him questioningly. Finally, he answered in Spanish.

"What?" Cimarron swallowed the meat and wiped her hands on her faded dress. Sanchez's dark face turned almost crimson as the flush started at his neck and worked its way up his lined face.

Puzzled, Cimarron turned back toward Trace, who was wolfing down the morsels.

"You must not know anything about cattle," Trace said as he ate another bite with aplomb. "Didn't you see the *capador* with his sharp knife turning little bulls into steers as we rode up?"

"So?" For a moment she puzzled, took another look at the small morsels roasting in the coals. "Oh, my . . . !" The realization dawned on her abruptly. Now it was her turn to flush brick-red while the cowboys watched. Trace was testing her, daring her, she knew that now as she looked into his sardonic, grinning face. He was proving she was fainthearted, weak.

If he expected her to get sick, to faint, he was in for a real surprise, she thought with a spirited toss of her head. Double damnation, she'd show him! With a very deliberate gesture, she took a deep breath for courage and raked more of the crispy morsels from the fire.

"Delicious, aren't they?" she challenged as she popped the meat into her mouth. Her eyes never left the dark foreman's face, and she thought she saw admiration there as she reached for her coffee cup.

Trace pushed his hat back and the slightest smile touched his hard mouth as he watched her. "Okay, *hombres,* let's get back to work. We got lots of calves to brand."

Cimarron frowned. "Even I know all this branding should have been done in the spring."

"It would have been if I wasn't so damned short-handed," he snapped, "With the war, I couldn't get enough men. I don't need your advice, sassy miss, I've been working cattle since I could walk!"

She saw the crew snickering as the men went into motion

like a well-oiled clock. They mounted up, roped calves, dragging them to the branding fire. A tumbador grabbed each calf, throwing it down for the hot iron.

"Easy," Trace commanded, "no use hurtin' the little fellows any more than we have to." He turned to Cimarron. "You can be the *atolero*." He handed her a bucket of lime paste and a stick with a rag tip. "Put this on the brand to soothe it, make it heal."

Cimarron heard the hooves galloping only seconds before she spotted the rider coming into camp.

"What's the rush?" Trace called out.

She watched the other men gather around the lathered horse as the old cowboy reined it in.

"Smelled smoke," yelled the man, gesturing wildly. One of his fingers was missing, too. "Think we got rustlers over on the east pasture!"

"Check your weapons and mount up!" Trace commanded and Cimarron blinked at the way the others scrambled to do his bidding. Most of the men pulled Spencers and Enfield rifles out of their bedrolls, but Trace and Holt carried Sharps. The Sharps was famed for its long-range accuracy.

The men mounted. Cimarron stood looking up at Trace as he swung easily onto the big black.

"Stay here!" he ordered, "No use takin' a chance on you're getting hurt!"

"Funny that should concern you now!" she snapped, mounting the buckskin defiantly. If it annoyed him, she'd go along.

"Suit yourself, darlin'." She thought she saw reluctance in his soft eyes as he turned toward Sanchez. "Is there a cottonwood in that pasture?"

"*Si*, boss. You know there is." The plump Mexican tipped back his sombrero. His crippled hand patted the lariat looped on his saddle.

Trace looked again at Cimarron. "You don't want to see this. Stay here till we get back."

Cimarron looked from the moody cowboy to the rope on the saddle as his meaning sank in. "You'd hang a man for stealing a few cattle?"

The men were silent, listening.

"It isn't that," Trace sighed reluctantly. "But it's Durango beef, and nobody takes anything that belongs to the Triple D."

"Anything?" she challenged.

"Anything!" He fired back. "The only way we can stop rustling is to make the price too dear! Let's ride!"

Chapter Four

Trace pulled his hat down over his eyes and urged Nightwind forward. The crew stuck spurs to their horses and rode out toward the pasture, each carrying a pistol or rifle from his saddle gear at the ready. Trace looked over at the drawn, set face of the girl riding along beside him. Obviously the thought of their stringing a rustler up made her stomach churn, but she was too proud to back down. He liked that, just as he liked the way she had forced herself to eat the calf fries even when she looked like she might get sick when she found out what the meat actually was.

What had he gotten himself into? He was chagrined and deeply ashamed that he had forced himself on her. As far as Trace was concerned, a rapist deserved to be gelded. He looked over, caught her eye. Yep, her expression was pure hatred. She'd probably like to take the *capador*'s knife to him. Now just what was a beautiful, chaste girl doing out riding by herself across the giant Durango spread? He'd detected just the slightest touch of a German accent, so he knew she was from somewhere in the hill country.

They topped the rise, and Trace gestured silently to his men. They spread out, surrounding the area. He smelled the faint scent of burning wood from beyond the cedar clumps.

"Stay back!" he ordered hoarsely to her. "It might be Comanche or Comanchero. They'd fight us all for a prize like you!"

He saw the sudden fear on her face, knew she had heard

the same horrible stories of Texas folklore. If only half the things they were said to do to women were true . . .

She rode up closer to Trace, seeming to realize he would protect her if need be. *Protect hell!* He thought bitterly, *he'd just raped her!* But she was obviously more afraid of Comanches, and with good reason. They would gang rape her, then torture her to death slowly. The renegade Comancheros would sell her to a whorehouse below the border . . . if they didn't keep her to amuse themselves.

The cowboys fanned out, rode at a hard gallop down the hill and into the green valley.

A dark-skinned boy squatted by a fire roasting meat on a stick. Even from this distance, Trace realized the boy was tall but very thin, and no more than thirteen or fourteen years old. He scrambled to his feet, pulled out a knife as they rode up and surrounded him. Consternation was reflected in his handsome face. A white knife scar marked his dark left cheek.

Trace swung off his horse, shoved the Sharps rifle into the boy's chest. "You little thief! Look around for the rest of them, boys!" Trace frowned at the sight of a butchered steer laying nearby.

The boy's gaze looked into Cimarron's as if he thought she might help him. Only then did Trace realize the kid had steel-gray eyes the color of a gun barrel. A half-breed like himself, he thought with sudden sympathy.

But the boy squared his trembling shoulders manfully. "I swear I wasn't rustling your beef—"

Trace snorted in derision, covering him with the Sharps. "The hell, you say! You think I'm blind? What are you, Comanche?"

The boy nodded reluctantly, as if loath to admit it.

Holt, cocky now that he realized the kid was alone, swung down off his blue gelding. "One damned Injun to pay for one steer! It ain't a fair price, but it'll have to do. Where's that rope?"

Trace snapped: "Shut up, Holt! Sanchez, check the kid's gear, see if he's packin' a running iron!" Trace was already sorry he had hired that saddle tramp. Holt was more trouble than he was worth.

Cimarron looked as if she were going to protest. The girl was right. One look at the thin, half-breed boy told him they'd find no makeshift branding iron, used to change or falsify a brand.

But the fat Mexican shrugged and pointed with his maimed hand. *"Dios!* The boy has not even a bedroll, Señor Trace. Much less a horse! What cow thief walks? Maybe he's just hungry."

The crew relaxed in their saddles and laughed. A couple rolled cigarillos or took out a plug of tobacco for a chew. It was a great relief to ride in thinking they were facing a war party and discover instead a ragged, Comanche kid.

Holt dismounted and reached over to take the lariat from Sanchez's saddle. "Running iron or no, that's a dead Triple D steer, I can see the brand from here. Where's the nearest cottonwood?"

Trace saw sudden horror in the girl's face as the kid's eyes blinked, and then the thin face hardened as the kid backed away. Comanche, all right, Trace thought, wouldn't beg if they tortured him to death.

"You're not really going to hang him over one old steer?" she asked in disbelief. "Why, he's just a boy!"

Trace looked from the kid up to her. "Boy or not, he's killed a Durango steer." He'd hanged a couple of tough cattle rustlers, but they'd been grown men. He had never faced this decision before. Easily, he feinted, grabbed the boy's wrist, disarmed him.

"Double damnation! I'll pay for the damned old steer myself!" She took out the small bag of gold coins Trace had given her the night before and flung it at his feet. "That ought to cover it twice over! Now let the boy go!"

The men fell silent, looking away in embarrassment. Trace felt the flush creep up his dark face. The girl had humbled him before his men. He had already decided he couldn't hang the boy, and now she'd humiliated him and he desperately needed a way to save face.

Trace leaned over, picked up the money, hefted the bag in his hand before putting it inside his vest. "The last I heard, I was still boss of this outfit," he said, frowning at her darkly. "Darlin', I always said any *hombre* who could outshoot me, outdrink me, and outfight me could have my job." His dark eyes swept over her. "I reckon you don't qualify on a single account."

Holt guffawed. "That's telling her, boss! Women belong in the bed or in the kitchen, not tryin' to play cowboy! Now where's that cottonwood?"

Trace frowned, wishing again he hadn't hired the man. "Shut up, Holt," he said again.

Cimarron looked around the circle of men. "For God's sake, aren't any of you going to do anything?"

But the men avoided her eyes uneasily. None of them seemed to quite believe what was happening as Holt took the rope, threw the loop over the boy's head. Trace saw the boy's eyes, looking about for a way to escape. Seeing none, he stood with the grace and bravery of a condemned warrior.

Her face crumpled. "Trace," she whispered, "I paid for the steer. Trace, please."

Trace looked at her. Distrust and suspicion were always in his mind, ever since. . . . "Why should you mix in?"

"You don't trust anybody, do you?"

"Not a woman." He shook his head with bitter finality. "Never a woman."

The boy said, "You don't have to beg for me, miss. It won't do no good nohow. Can't you see that one there can hardly wait to string me up?" He nodded toward Holt.

"That's right, you half-breed Injun pup!" The unshaven cowboy smiled evilly.

"Trace," she said softly, looking deep into his eyes, "who's boss at the Triple D? You or Holt? You're short of help because of the war. The boy could work—"

"No!" Holt exploded, disappointment on his tough face. He was evidently looking forward to the execution. "Hell, no! Luis said hang any man caught with a Triple D beef, so we're gonna hang him—"

"I give the orders here," Trace snapped, his hand going to his holster. It was a lie. Luis gave the orders, and Trace gritted his teeth and took them. "The lady makes good sense."

The silence hung heavy on the humid air. Somewhere he heard a mockingbird in a cottonwood tree, smelled the odor of burning cedar, of tobacco. A horse snorted, a saddle creaked. The breeze picked up a little, feeling cool on his perspiring skin. The wind smelled like rain. He ran his tongue over his cut lip, remembered the heat of her mouth, her sharp little teeth, the taste of his own blood.

"Hell!" Trace swore suddenly. "We've wasted the whole morning!" He stalked over, flipped the loop from around the boy's neck, tossed it back to the tough *hombre*. "Holt, I'm still the *caporal*, the ramrod on the Triple D. Don Diego wouldn't like it if we hanged the boy, and I'm bound to follow his orders . . . at least until he dies."

He looked up at Cimarron and had the sudden feeling she liked him a little better now. Or, at least, didn't hate him quite so much. "The lady's right. Sanchez, we can use the help. What's your name, kid?"

The boy sighed audibly, his steel-gray eyes bright in the dark face. "I call myself 'Maverick,' mister, 'cause I carry no brand, belong nowhere. I won't answer now to my Injun name. My father's dead, but I hated him like poison."

Trace tried to keep the pain off his hard face, not wanting to remember. . . . "That's not your fault, Maverick," he said almost gently. "Remember, nobody gets to pick his own daddy. If they did, lots would choose different than they got. Now, mount up *hombres,* we got work to do."

But almost as he swung up into the saddle, the swirling clouds darkened overhead and a sprinkle of rain fell. Trace swore under his breath and pulled his hat down over his eyes as he looked up at the gray sky.

"Hell!" he grumbled. "Had a drought for two straight years and now the skies are going to open up day after day and give us another toad strangler."

Sanchez nodded. "Can't brand in the rain, boss; wet hair makes a ragged brand."

"And the steam from the brand hurts the steer more," Trace muttered, almost to himself.

Holt snarled. "Who the hell cares if we hurt, 'em?"

Trace sighed and spoke slowly, as if speaking to a very stupid child. "Now Holt, listen and listen good. I'm the ramrod on the Triple D, *comprende?* When I make a decision, nobody questions it." His eye caught Cimarron's. "Except maybe a lady who figures she can get away with it. Now Holt, you don't seem like much of a cowhand to me, but when I hired you last week, you said you needed a job—"

"I do need a job," the other grumbled as a drop of rain splattered on the brim of his hat.

"You got one," Trace answered laconically, "Just take care of it."

"Luis Durango said—"

Trace glared at the man. "Nobody in this crew cares what Luis thinks. These men answer to me. I answer to the old Don. This ranch would fall apart if it were left up to our handsome aristocrat." But he had to take his orders, Trace thought, because of the secret they shared.

"All right, all right," Holt grumbled. "Don't get a burr under your saddle. I didn't mean no harm."

Trace shrugged. "No offense meant, none taken. Judging by your accent, you're not a Texan, Holt. Reckon you should learn Texans don't rile easy, but when they do, you better be ready to defend that big mouth of yours."

The rain started, dimpling little puddles and running off the men's hats as they mounted.

"Sanchez, *compadre,*" Trace said, "looks like we've done all the branding we'll do till at least tomorrow. Take the crew back to the bunkhouse for today. They can mend bridles and rigging. Always needs to be done, anyhow."

"*Si,* boss, shall I take the boy?"

Now just what was he to do with that starved kid? Luis wouldn't be happy about having another half-breed on the ranch. The thought cheered him a little. "*Si,* take him." He gestured to Maverick. "Catch a ride with Sanchez."

The boy went around to the wrong side of the horse and started to swing up, but Sanchez cried out a warning as the horse snorted, backed away. "Hey, *hombre,* we don't ride Comanche style, *comprende?* You better learn to mount like a gringo, or you'll get bucked off!"

Maverick grinned sheepishly as he went around to the left side of the horse. "I keep forgetting. That's how I lost the horse I stole west of here."

Trace grinned as Sanchez pulled the boy up behind him on the saddle. "If you're going to live among whites, you better learn we mount on the opposite side from Indians."

He twisted in his saddle to look at the tawny blond girl as they all rode out. She gave him a look of pure hatred. His men would follow him into hell, he thought, do anything he asked of them. But he didn't have much experience dealing with women, except the saloon tarts. He could read her face from here, guessed what she was thinking. Sooner or later, when he least expected it, she would try to get his gun, take the gold back, maybe even try to take Nightwind, and kill Trace for stealing her virginity.

As they rode away he watched her, knew she was toying with the idea of lighting a shuck for parts unknown. But the horse she rode couldn't outdistance the big stallion. He'd run her down in a few hundred feet. She must know that. There wasn't anything she could do right now but accompany him back to the ranchero.

He felt in his vest. He had the gold. She couldn't leave without money, wherever she might go. Somehow, he didn't want her to leave, and yet. . . .

He studied her as she rode. She gritted her teeth, glanced sideways at him. If he was smart, he'd give her the money and a horse, get her off the ranch and hope she didn't go to the law about the rape. Sooner or later, that ornery little Cheyenne half-breed girl would either try to escape or kill him. Maybe both.

Two Cheyenne half-breeds pitted against each other, he thought grimly. It should promise conflict and trouble, neither of which he needed right now, with the cattle disappearing off the ranch and Trace afraid the old man might find out about it, afraid someone would slip up and tell the old man the secrets. At any cost, Trace had to keep him from finding out.

* * *

The rain had been only a fine mist, after all, and it ended as they rode back to the hacienda. Trace sneaked glances at the girl as they rode. Just who in the devil was she and what was she hiding? Beautiful women with strange names just didn't ride in unescorted out of nowhere. 'Wild One' fit her in a way, but it wasn't the usual kind of name. The women he had known had ordinary names like Kate, Lily, and Rosa.

No, that wasn't true. The lovely face of Señora Durango came to his mind, and aloud he used the name the adoring old Don had given her, the name even Trace had used. *Ojos de Pana;* "Velvet Eyes."

He had not said the name, tried not even to think it since last spring when she had driven away from the hacienda. He would never have believed she would leave him or the old Don, especially for another man.

But it was the other thing that had shattered Trace forever and made him hate Luis Durango.

Trace muttered a curse under his breath. He would kill anyone who told old Diego de Durango the secret. Velvet Eyes, he thought with pain, Velvet Eyes, how could you, when I loved and trusted you so? Now Trace would trust no woman ever again. No faithless bitch would hurt him as the beautiful dark señora had done. He thought of the dignified, white-maned old man slowly dying in his room back at the hacienda. She could write a letter once in a while.

No, that wouldn't do at all. He shook his head. He had agreed with Luis to tell the lie to protect the old man's feelings. What if a letter arrived from New York . . . ?

Trace would never feel the same about women after that, never trust them. He would use them and throw them away, just as he intended to do with this tawny lioness who had turned up so mysteriously.

His stallion snorted, and Trace shifted his weight in the saddle and yearned for a cigarette, but he wouldn't stop to roll one. Was the girl a spy for the Yankees? The Confederates? He scowled, dismissing the idea. The Civil War was staggering to an end, and Texas had never been in the midst of the battles anyway. Mostly the state tried to get beef to the starving South, but with not much luck since

Vicksburg had fallen last year. The Yankees now controlled the Mississippi. So here the Triple D was almost sinking under the weight of thousands of cattle and nowhere to sell them. When this war ended, Texans were going to have to figure out some way to move their beef north.

He watched her ride, admiring the way she handled the buckskin. No, if she were a spy, there were no big military secrets in this state she could carry for either side.

Trace remembered her warm softness in his arms. She couldn't be running from a husband, Trace had irrefutable proof she was a virgin. Maybe she had been about to be forced into marriage with a man she didn't want.

He nodded. That made sense to him. What if her future husband was rich and powerful, maybe almost as powerful as the Durangos? Not that Trace might be able to count on Luis for help; Luis would be delighted to see Trace on the run or in jail, or even hanged for rape.

The girl's sweetheart would want Trace hanged for what he'd done, of course. So the answer was simple, Trace must not let the girl go to the sheriff. Somehow he must keep her away from the nearest town and stop her from filing charges. He knew how to protect himself; how to stop this trouble with the girl before it went any further. He half smiled, thinking how simple it was; he'd make her fall in love with him. Yes, he nodded, that would solve the problem. Then he'd figure out what to do next.

Trace wasn't quite sure what a man did to make a virgin he'd raped fall in love with him. In truth, here on the isolated ranch his contacts with respectable women were few and far between. The women he knew he'd met mostly on Saturday night trips to the wild bordellos of village cantinas, and once in a while to San Antonio. All the women he had mounted in his twenty-four years had been secondhand, paid whores. The question of money came up more often than a discussion of love.

Women! He spat contemptuously to one side as he considered the sex as a whole and how little he thought of them. Don't trust them, just lay them, he reminded himself, don't think of her as a person, just a convenience for a man when he gets that urge. But again he remembered Cimarron with the scarlet oleander behind her ear, just the way Velvet Eyes always wore it in her long black hair. Even now, he could close his eyes and see the Cheyenne wife descending the curved stairway of the hacienda into the arms of her proud husband.

Gritting his teeth as the ranchero came in sight, he thought of Luis Durango. Someday, he vowed, I will kill the arrogant Spaniard. But not yet. I must do whatever Luis orders for a while, because he has threatened to tell and the knowledge must be kept from the old man. Don Diego must always think his wife was faithful. When the old man finally died, he would deal with Luis.

But those problems lay in the future. Today's problem was to make the girl fall in love with him and pretend he was in love with her. Then, when he was sure she wouldn't cause him any trouble or go to the law, he'd give her some money, send her on her way. What happened to her after that was not his concern.

Yes, little filly, he vowed, all you need is a firm hand on the reins to master you, a real man in the saddle. I'll gentle you; make a fawning pet of you so you'll happily lick my fingers like little Tequila does now.

What an unlimited potential for passion she had, he thought, and no man had touched her before him. A sad-eyed saloon whore had told him once that no woman ever quite forgot the very first man who took her. If it were true, he'd use it to his own advantage with Cimarron.

Still, he'd never had a virgin before. Cimarron was his in a way no other man could ever claim. Now that he thought about it, he didn't like the idea of another man's touching her, making love to her. Like any Texas cowboy, he was gallant, protective of women, and deeply, sincerely ashamed that he had raped her.

But she had played the whore, he reminded himself, glancing sideways at her as they rode. How was he to know she wasn't a whore just trying to make a better bargain for herself? Riding astride pushed her skirt up, showed her slim legs, and he begrudged the other men the view.

Those slim legs. Trace remembered them wrapped around him, the feel of her soft breasts yielding against the cold metal conchos and the leather of his vest. She had arched her hips up against him instinctively, as if urging him to drive deep. Her femininity had been too narrow, he'd had to force his way in. That alone should have given him the clue that no man had ever entered her. But he'd been too hungry for her, too driven by his own need to realize that what he lunged against and finally tore was the thin silk of her maidenhead.

Wild One. He had never experienced a coupling like that. He looked again at her open lips as she rode, remembered dominating her mouth, forcing her to accept his probing tongue, the taste of her taut nipples as he rubbed his rugged face against them. Her waist was almost small enough to be spanned by his two hands and her skin felt like satin beneath him when he took her.

Trace would be ashamed to face the old man's fury if she told him. Don Diego de Durango was a gentleman of the old school and had once run the Triple D with an iron hand. But now that he was dying, Trace did what Luis told him and hated every minute of it. Still, he must bide his time until the Don died, then Trace would deal with the elegant rake.

Luis. Trace frowned, thinking how handsome the older man was, how women were smitten with his good looks. He would want this fiery blond beauty in his bed. Any man would. And Luis had manners and charm to go with his handsome face. If he wanted the girl, he could probably take her and Trace would have to let him.

Well, hell, Cimarron was just another female after all, pretty, unfaithful . . . like Velvet Eyes. . . .

Trace imagined Cimarron lying on Luis's bed, naked, yielding, reaching up to help him take his fine clothes off . . . no, he wouldn't think about it. It made an emotion build in him he didn't like. It was a new emotion for Trace. He had a feeling it would be called jealousy.

They crested the hill and he saw the hacienda, low and white on the next hilltop, as they started down the valley. The crew reined off to the bunkhouse, corral, and barn by the ranchero. Trace jerked his head at the girl to indicate they would go to the house, and she shook her mane of hair back like the fine-blooded palomino filly that grazed in the big herd on the nearby pasture.

He enjoyed the awe, the excitement in her face as he asked, "Like the place?"

"It's breathtaking. Any woman would want to be the mistress here."

Her words brought back the pain. "Not every woman. Some have a bad streak that just can't let them stay...."

He made a decision then that Luis would not have the girl. She belonged to Trace by right of conquest. In fact, as he dismounted and tied his stallion to the hitching post before the big courtyard, he decided he didn't like the idea of any man touching her, looking at her hungrily.

He went around to help her but she tried to avoid his hands. "I'm perfectly capable of dismounting," she snapped, but he reached up anyway because he liked the feel of her small waist in his two big hands. As he lifted her slowly down, he noticed for the first time the bodice of the faded fabric was torn, so that by looking down at her, he could see the swell of her firm breasts. He had to control himself to keep from reaching out, stroking the satin skin in the neck of the dress.

She had made him want her as he had never wanted another woman's body. Already he could feel the ache in his groin, wanting her again. When a man cared too much, a woman always used it to her advantage, used it to hurt him.

"Don't be a fool, Trace," he whispered to himself without thinking, and the girl looked up at him.

"What did you say?"

Her lips were parted and he put both hands on his gun belt to keep from grabbing her shoulders, pulling her to him. That soft, open mouth seemed to be begging for him to cover it with his own. Trace had the most overpowering urge to reach out, stroke that shining gold hair. "I said you'll stay here as a guest for a while."

"Suppose I decide to leave?"

He put one hand on each side of her as she leaned back against the buckskin. "You don't have any money or a horse," he said slowly. He was leaning so close to her he could feel the heat of her, smell the clean scent of her skin. If he leaned much closer, he would be rubbing against her nipples. . . .

She realized it, too. He could tell by the guarded, hostile look in the dark eyes. "I earned that gold the hard way, you rotten—"

"But you decided to buy a steer with it," he reminded her. "You never did tell me exactly what you were doing out unescorted riding across nowhere at dark."

"I—I was going to visit relatives."

He saw the uncertainty, the fear in her eyes, and he knew then he was right. Somebody was after this kid. He'd sensed it all along. Someone or something she'd left behind.

He hated women, didn't trust them, he reminded himself, because what he suddenly wanted to do was take her in his arms, tell her no one would hurt her. She was safe under the protection of Trace's big Colt. *Safe?* he thought. *You sorry snake! You're the one who raped her.*

"We need to work on that story, sassy miss," he said easily, stepping away from her with a sigh. If he stayed that close to her another second, he was going to swing her up in his arms, carry her to his room. "Nobody would believe that tale. Women don't travel unescorted with the Comanche raiding close to the settlements." He took her elbow and started across the courtyard toward the house.

She looked up at him, her voice full of irony. "Are you a liar, too, or just a rapist?"

"Don't get sassy. I'll think up something to tell everyone." Damn her! Why did she keep looking up at him with her lips half open? He'd had her by force, now he found himself wondering what it would be like to have her kiss him, have her come into his arms wanting him? The thought made his breath quicken and his groin ache. This sassy little bit of skirt promised nothing but trouble for him. Big trouble.

Chapter Five

As the riders topped the crest, Cimarron had caught her breath at the view spread before her. Across a small, lush valley rose another hill. Sprawled atop that hill's summit lay a magnificent Spanish ranchero. Its white adobe and red tile roofs gleamed as the sun came out momentarily from behind clouds, reflecting on the outlying buildings and main hacienda. A rainbow formed a pastel arc from hill to hill, giving the ranchero a fairy-tale effect. As they rode toward it, Cimarron had stared in wonder, thinking it looked as elegant as a story-book castle.

It loomed even larger and finer as they rode closer. She wondered about the señora of this grand home, who must live like a queen, or at the very least, a princess. What would it be like to be mistress of the Triple D? No wonder her cousins had been so eager to meet the rich heir!

They rode into the paved open patio, surrounded on three sides by wings of the house. French doors led from all three wings out onto a low veranda that opened onto the courtyard. The ornate fountain in the center gurgled and splashed into a small, low pool where cooing doves flew in for a drink. Cimarron reined in her horse and gaped at the giant oleander bushes growing around the house. Their ruby and pale pink blossoms bloomed everywhere, in bright contrast to the white adobe. A low, flat, red-tiled roof made a porch for the second story, with other French doors leading out to it from the upstairs rooms.

For a girl reared in a humble village parsonage, the display of wealth was almost overwhelming.

A small brown chihuahua ran through an open French door into the courtyard and scampered toward her, barking madly. She hesitated and bent over, snapping her fingers. But the tiny dog ignored her as it raced toward the moody cowboy.

Don't hurt it! she started to protest but the words died in her throat. Even as she watched in disbelief, the chihuahua danced around the tall cowboy's legs, yipping and wagging its tail.

A rare smile crossed the dark features. Trace knelt and scooped the tiny pet up in his arms. "Tequila! You scrappy little rascal!"

He strode over to her, struggling to keep the excited dog from licking his face.

"Tequila?" she sniffed. "Funny name for a dog."

"Not for this dog." Trace put it back down on the courtyard and it continued to dance around his feet. "Tequila, like his namesake, has a sudden, unexpected bite." He almost smiled as he took her elbow again, steered her toward the house. "Runs in the blood, I guess. His sire was called Pepper, and if I remember the stories correctly, I think his Granddaddy, Poco, bit people, too. If Tequila doesn't like you, he's notorious for unexpected attacks on the ankles."

"He must not base his opinion on character," she answered coldly, allowing herself to be steered toward the open French doors. "I see he adores you."

"Dogs, horses, and women always do, darlin'," he answered with a sarcastic raise of his eyebrow as he tipped his hat over one eye.

"I said he must not base his opinion on character," she emphasized, jerking away from his grasp.

"The señora always said Tequila had an uncanny sense of character." Trace watched the small dog, which now danced around Cimarron's feet, its tail wagging happily. "Funny," he mused softly, "I never saw Tequila take up with a stranger before. In fact, he was always her dog alone. It was surprising that she didn't take him with her...." His voice trailed away. The moody frown returned as if he did not like the images that came to mind.

She said it without even thinking. "You loved her very much, didn't you?"

For a split-second she thought he would strike her. Muscles jerked in the lean face and his eyes were as dark as a summer storm. She had reached in and touched something deep inside his troubled soul; his face told her that. The facade had fallen away and it took a long second for him to compose himself, to return to the easy, wisecracking mask.

"Velvet Eyes was a whore!" he whispered softly. "If the old Don only knew...." Trace shuddered. Taking her arm, he gripped it so tightly her flesh stung. "Never, ever mention her to me again," he snarled through clenched teeth.

"But you are the one who brought her up. I only wondered—"

"Never, ever again," he emphasized and jerked her toward the doors.

Even though she was tall, and long-legged, Cimarron almost had to run to keep up with him. They entered the house, the brown dog scampering merrily around her feet.

The inside of the hacienda was so large, so richly decorated that Cimarron gasped with admiration as Trace gave her a tour of the lower floor. There was an elegant entryway with a Victorian pier mirror. The entry opened onto an enormous room with the biggest chandelier she had ever seen and a stairway going up to the second floor.

"Like it, darlin'?" She could feel his eyes studying her and she wondered if he were being sarcastic.

"Who wouldn't!" She sighed, "I never saw anything so fine in my whole life. All this dark Spanish furniture, the thick rugs, the paintings."

Even in the early autumn heat, the thick white adobe walls made it cool inside. The ceilings were high, and the giant room with its great chandelier seemed to be perfect for large parties or even a ball....

He chuckled and gave her his rare smile, obviously delighted with her naiveté. They stood at the foot of the wide stairway, the small dog dancing around their feet. "I'll find Rosa," he suggested. "She'll get you some clothes. Yours seem a little worse for wear."

"Thanks to you," Cimarron reminded him acidly, looking down at her frayed calico.

"I said I was sorry."

"That doesn't change things, does it? Do you have a right to treat me like a whore?" She glared up at him, remembering the taste of his grim mouth.

"No," he answered, so gently that she was surprised. "Nothing gives a man the right to force himself on a woman against her will even if she's a paid slut. I've never done that before, but I thought you were leading me on, playing games—"

"And my virginity was the prize," she snapped.

"I said I was sorry, Cimarron, what else can I say now that it's over and done with?" He looked deeply saddened, regretful. "Shouldn't I notify your father or someone that you're all right?"

She felt the sudden chill run down her back. It wouldn't do to have him ask questions. Even now, the sheriff might be scouring the countryside looking for her.

"I—I've got no family," she blurted, not looking him in the face, terrified to tell him the truth. If she told him, would he help her or turn her over to the law? She couldn't, wouldn't trust him with her horrible secret. "I was headed to the coast to visit my cousin."

She could feel his hard gaze studying her, appraising her. "You're either a liar, sassy miss, or you've got a bad memory. You just got through telling me you have no family."

Cimarron gulped. "Well—"

He reached out, tipped her chin up so he could look her in the face. "Women!" he snorted. "Who are you really running from, Wild One? Some would-be suitor?"

"Yes, that's it." She pulled away from the warm touch of his hand that was so unsettling. "I have no one, no money. A man tried to force himself on me," she flinched, remembering Uncle Ransford. "I was scared of him, and I decided to run away."

"He try to rape you, put those bruises on you?"

She felt the blood rush to her face at the frank question. But now she could stare him in the eye truthfully. "Yes," she whispered and she couldn't hold back the tears that gathered. "Yes, he tried."

Trace swore softly under his breath. "I believe you, darlin'. Why didn't you level with me to begin with? You run from a rapist, and I finish the job."

He sounded remorseful, saddened, but she didn't trust him. Cimarron reminded herself that he was just like Uncle Ransford, only wanting one thing. She hated him for taking her innocence. "Since you used me like a whore," she said bitterly, "the least you can do is give me the money."

He looked at her, but she couldn't read his closed, hostile face. "You bought a steer with your money, remember? Regretting being so noble already, my sassy miss?"

He was taunting her, she realized, both of them knowing that without money she was stuck at this ranch, couldn't escape. Was he afraid she'd go to the sheriff?

"Double damnation!" she swore, tossing her head in a fury, "I would think the Triple D could afford to lose one old cow without taking a poor girl's money to pay for it." It was all she could do to keep from attacking him with her fists, scratching his arrogant face again. And as she looked up at him, she remembered the taste of his kiss, his hard muscles hot against her bare flesh.

"Then it looks like you may be here a while." He pushed his hat back with satisfaction.

What kind of game was he playing? Why would he want to keep her here against her will? The obvious reason came to her, and she felt both furious and vulnerable.

"I'll ask Luis Durango for a small job or a loan," she announced loftily. "I'll bet he'd help a lady in distress."

She saw the anger cross the rugged face. "You just do that, darlin'," he challenged softly. "Luis is such a proper Spanish gentleman, it's too bad he wasn't around to ride on the Crusades—"

The tiny dog interrupted his words with a low growl. Cimarron heard footsteps on the stairs behind her and turned to see a pretty Mexican girl in a bright skirt and low-cut blouse at the top of the landing.

"Ah, Rosa," Trace motioned her down. "We have—a house guest for a while," he said, catching Cimarron's eye.

The girl descended the stairs, her face alight with curiosity. "What happened to your face?"

His hand went to the scratches, the swelled lip, and he gave Cimarron a piercing look. "I rode under a tree and got caught across the face by a limb."

Rosa looked Cimarron up and down several times, her dark eyes hostile. "Who is this?"

Cimarron looked back levelly, determined not to be intimidated. The girl was older than she, perhaps in her middle-twenties, and pretty, except that her mouth was a little too wide, too full, and her waist was beginning to thicken. Rosa reminded her of some exotic jungle flower, no doubt in full bloom at the age of fifteen or sixteen, now already starting to fade. By the time she was thirty, no man would look at Rosa twice.

Trace glared at the girl, and in the look Cimarron read some secret that they shared between themselves. "Be more polite, Rosa. Señorita Cimarron is a guest in this house, and you overstep your place."

"I am head housekeeper." The girl's nostrils flared.

"And *only* the housekeeper," Trace said softly. "I think sometimes you think you are the señora herself."

"Don't get smart with me," Rosa flared, "or I'll tell Luis or Don Diego—"

"Get Cimarron some clothes at once," Trace snapped with sudden authority, "or I'll tell the old man myself! And put her in Dallas's room."

The girl was at once humble, wheedling. "I meant no harm," she simpered, "and Trace, the old man has been asking for you."

Trace straightened. "Is he worse?"

Cimarron saw the worry, heard the concern.

"No." The girl shrugged. "Much better, I think. You know how it goes with this cancer, one week seemingly in perfect health, the next close to death. Already, people ask what are the funeral plans—"

"Damned idle vultures!" Trace swore. "When the war ends, Luis and I'll take him back East, and he'll be cured, you'll see!" He took the steps two at a time, leaving Cimarron standing at the foot of the stairs with the sneering Mexican girl. They both listened to his footsteps fading down the hall.

Rosa sighed sympathetically. "Trace is the only one who won't face the diagnosis Dr. Hastings made last spring. But personally, I think part of it's in the old man's mind." She tapped the side of her head with her finger. "Since Dallas ran away from boarding school and disappeared, he's blamed himself. Velvet Eyes begged him not to send her—"

Cimarron could contain her curiosity no longer. "Is Velvet Eyes the señora?"

The girl looked her over with hostility. "What do you know of my señora?"

"Well, Trace said—"

"Maybe I should ask, what are you to Trace?" The girl looked at her keenly.

"And what are *you* to Trace?" Cimarron fired back, remembering the veiled look that had passed between them.

Rosa drew herself up proudly. "Señorita, I am a married woman."

Cimarron was immediately contrite. "Oh, I'm sorry, I thought. . . ." What had she thought?

"I am Rosa Sanchez—"

"Oh, of course," Cimarron brightened. "I met your father-in-law today, old Sanchez—"

The girl gave her a murderous look. "If you speak of the *caudillo,* the chief vaquero, he is my husband, not my father-in-law."

"I'm so sorry," Cimarron sputtered in confusion, trying to remember the man she had seen. He must have been in his fifties, at least. "I guess I thought—"

"I can see we are not going to be friends," the Mexican girl said coldly.

Cimarron glared back at her. "That's for you to decide. I'm the stranger here. But I assure you, I am no threat to your position in this household."

Rosa snorted. "I know that better than you! No one can take my place here. I was the señora's personal maid for almost ten years until she went away."

Cimarron burned with curiosity, but she knew better than ask any more questions about Velvet Eyes. "And what are you now?"

The girl drew herself up proudly. "I have been head housekeeper ever since last spring when old Juanita fell down the stairs and broke her neck. You'll find nothing happens in this household without my permission."

"I don't intend to ask your permission for anything!" Cimarron fired back. "But as I remember, Trace did ask you to find me something to wear."

Rosa seemed to decide she might have met her match. "Very well," she said coolly. "You may have Señorita Dallas's room but she took most of her clothes when she went off to school back East. But maybe I have a castoff." She wheeled and led Cimarron toward the back of the house, past the kitchen.

"What has happened?" Cimarron blurted without thinking, "are both the women of this household gone?"

Rosa whirled on her, her voice and manner scathing. "I punish the servants for gossiping. What have you heard—?"

"Trace told me." Cimarron stood her ground, bluffing.

The other's indignation faded as she once again headed down a hallway. "We try to keep the old señor from hearing the gossip," she flung over her shoulder. "We tell him Velvet Eyes has gone back to her people."

They entered what was obviously the servants' quarters, but well furnished and spacious. Cimarron looked around with a trace of envy, realizing for the first time how cramped and dingy her own room at the Longworths' had been.

Rosa dug into a wardrobe while Cimarron leaned against the door. She remembered the anguish on the foreman's face when the señora was mentioned. "Was the señora very beautiful?"

Rosa came out of the wardrobe with a faded gingham dress. Her voice, when she finally spoke, seemed to tremble.

"Velvet Eyes was more than beautiful. So gentle. So kind. Her eyes, if you ever saw them, you would not forget. I never thought she would leave without me, without her little dog. But then, there were things happening I never dreamed of. I still set a place for her at the table, because any time now, she'll return...."

Her voice faded away and Cimarron waited eagerly for her to go on, but instead, the girl thrust the dress at her. "You ask too many questions. Here, this should do for the likes of you."

She seemed to be almost daring Cimarron as she offered the ragged dress.

Cimarron obliged her with spirit. "I'm sure you have something better than that!"

The Mexican spitfire smiled coldly. "You can complain to the old Don, if you like."

"I might just do that!"

"I don't think you will," Rosa said. "I think you have too much pride to go tattling like a whining child. Remember, I am in complete charge of the house."

Cimarron accepted the dress with a frown of reluctance. "And where is Dallas's room?"

Rosa put her hands on her hips. "At the top of the stairs and to your left. You'll know it by its bright colors. If it were up to me, I'd put you in with some of the housemaids—"

"I don't know what you've got against me, Rosa, I represent no threat to you—"

"Don't you?" The girl asked, and Cimarron was not sure what she meant.

"I'm willing to help with the work while I'm here," Cimarron volunteered, "I'm an excellent housekeeper and a good cook—"

"So that's it! You think to take my position!" Rosa went almost livid. "No one comes in my kitchen, you hear me, gringo? I do all the cooking; I run this household. If you think to gradually take over, you are mistaken. I'll see the servants don't even speak to you."

"Suit yourself," Cimarron shrugged. "But remember, I did offer."

And with that, she withdrew from the Mexican girl's room and went exploring upstairs, the worn dress over her arm and the tiny dog following along behind her. The second story of the giant hacienda was as sumptuous and magnificent as the downstairs. She paused to admire the rich paintings, the Spanish antique furnishings, the oriental rugs. Throughout the house she saw large bouquets of the bright rose and pink oleanders. A hauntingly sweet scent seemed to drift from them as she stopped to admire the exotic blossoms. A thought nagged at her, but she couldn't quite remember what it was as she inhaled their perfume.

On the wall at the top of the landing hung a large painting of a dignified old señora, complete with lace mantilla and ivory combs in her gray hair. The wife of the old Don, she thought, standing before it: Luis's mother.

She knew immediately when she found Dallas's room. She liked the bright yellows and greens. The room faced south, with French doors opening out onto the upper porch overlooking the fountain. She walked across the woven oriental rug on the bare floor, examined the painting of a running horse hanging over the bed. Dallas was evidently an outdoors type, a tomboy. No wonder she had run away when the old Don sent her off to school.

With a sigh, Cimarron examined the faded dress over her arm. Rosa was determined to humiliate her, she thought, by having her show up at dinner looking worse than a servant. The dress wasn't any better than the one she had on.

Double damnation! She was tired of being humble and mistreated. Maybe Dallas had left a few things Cimarron might be able to wear. The wardrobe was empty, but in a small dressing room next door, she found lovely dresses and shoes. Even Aunt Carolina had never owned such fine things. Cimarron clapped her hands with glee like a small child at Christmas as she rummaged through them.

Should she be so daring? She hesitated a moment. Somewhere a sheriff with a posse might be searching for her. She faced an uncertain future, unless someone with power and money for lawyers came to her aid. Her thoughts came back to handsome Luis Durango. Now there was a gentleman who had both. If she were under his protection, no one would dare hang her or send her to jail. Durangos were a force to be reckoned with in the Texas hill country.

She thought again of Luis's good looks, his elegant manner. A girl could do much worse. Her face wrinkled into a frown. Yes, she could do worse; a girl could end up with the rough, moody foreman.

She clenched her fist, thinking of his impudence, his insolent attack upon her body. Idly, she imagined herself as the new señora, daydreamed of Trace begging for his life when Luis challenged him to a duel. Cimarron played the scene in her head several times and it always ended with the sardonic foreman begging humbly for his life while Luis waited patiently to see if he was to kill the rude cowboy. There were two problems. The way she'd seen Trace handle a pistol, no doubt he could outshoot any man she'd ever met. It also occurred to her that the rugged cowboy probably wouldn't beg if Comanches were holding hot coals to his body. No, he wasn't the begging type at all. Something about his sardonic manner told her he expected women to beg him for his caresses, his attention.

She played the scene again in her head. This time, the dark cowboy fell madly in love with her, but she slapped his face while announcing coldly that she was about to become Señora Luis Durango, and by the way, Trace was fired.

Cimarron liked that scene even better. She imagined it several more ways. In one, Luis took a quirt to the arrogant cowboy, who clutched Cimarron's skirt, begging on his knees to be allowed to stay on as her lowly slave and stablehand. Could even Luis get away with taking a whip to that virile stud?

The chihuahua had curled up and gone to sleep while she daydreamed. What dress would she wear to catch the elegant Spaniard's eye at supper tonight when they met? She looked at gown after gown, and then she saw it.

The dress was that popular color, clair de lune. Moonlight. Yes, moonlight might be romantically described as that color, she thought, a pale greenish-blue-to-lavender-gray hue. There was something unusual about the dress. She couldn't put a name to it and decided she was mistaken as she put it on. The fabric was sheer, delicate, almost like fog, like wisps of dark amethyst clouds wrapped around her tawny bare shoulders. The dress accentuated her tiny waist, and the full hoop skirt whirled over the little delicate slippers as she walked up and down before the mirror. Her full bosom and tawny skin were shown off well in the low neckline. The fabric had an unusual sparkle, a shimmer almost like star dust strewn across its full skirt.

Her hair. What should she do about her hair? She selected a lavender-blue ribbon from a drawer and put her dark blond hair up in a mass of curls on her head.

The small dog yawned as it uncurled itself, one ear flipping over in a comical manner as it surveyed her, sniffed at the dress. "Do I look all right, Tequila?" she asked and its tail thumped in seeming agreement. Somewhere a dinner bell rang, and Cimarron took one last approving look at her reflection before gliding down the hall followed by the scampering dog. The dress was a good fit, except that it was a little too short for her. Cimarron took a deep breath, her heart beating loudly as she went down the stairs and paused in the doorway of the large dining room.

For a long moment, the other people at the table didn't seem to see her, and she stopped uncertainly, surveying them all. It was an elegant table lit with silver candelabra. The host and hostess chairs at either end sat empty, although there was a place set at each, with the finest crystal and china, the heaviest of silver.

Along the length of the table sat Trace, Luis, old Sanchez, Rosa, and a beautiful little girl with black hair, exquisite ivory skin, and pale turquoise-blue eyes. Two young Mexican servant girls scurried up and down serving. The chihuahua ran around and positioned itself next to the child's chair.

Cimarron took a deep breath. "Good evening, all." She managed a tremulous smile, suddenly shy and uncertain as all eyes turned toward her.

The men half rose from their chairs. Cimarron started forward. But now, all eyes seemed to see her dress for the first time, and everyone reacted with frozen horror.

She stopped, her hand on the back of the empty hostess's chair at the end of the table. "Is something wrong?"

Rosa came up out of her chair with a shriek like a Comanche's, turning over her chair as she stood up, her face red with anger. "How dare you?" the girl seethed, coming around to face Cimarron, gesturing wildly. "How dare you wear Señora Durango's favorite dress?"

"Perdone?" Cimarron stammered in confusion at the open-mouthed, horrified expressions looking back at her.

Rosa rushed to confront Cimarron. "The dress!" she said, her face dark with fury, "How dare you wear Velvet Eyes's dress?"

Trace's face looked both angry and shocked, but the color came back to Luis's face as he got up, came over, bowed low before her. "Excuse our manners, señorita," he smiled, and she thought again how handsome he was. "Probably someone should have warned you—"

Rosa gestured. "Just helped herself to my señora's things! How dare you do this?"

Cimarron had had enough. "Well," she snapped, "if you had offered me something decent to wear, I wouldn't have been rummaging around in the wardrobe upstairs for something. I didn't know whose dress it was."

"Touché!" Trace said with a grim smile, leaning on his elbows, watching her. "This is Señorita Cimarron, everyone. I've persuaded her to visit for a while."

Luis looked at him, then glared at the Mexican girl, and she subsided. "As I said, señorita," he continued smoothly, "a thousand pardons. Someone should have explained that there are some things that some of us feel . . . rather sensitive about." He looked over at Trace, who glared back at him. "Anyway, we are happy to extend you the hospitality of the Triple D." He pulled out a chair. "Do sit down. Rosa, have a girl bring the lady a plate."

Cimarron warmed toward the gallant gentleman immediately as Rosa gave her an annoyed look and went off to the kitchen in a huff. Within moments, she slammed down a steak before Cimarron, a steak so big it hung over the edges of the plate all the way around.

"Oh, my!" Cimarron sighed, awed by the outlay of good food, the elegant china and silver. "I can't eat this much meat, and it's such a shame to waste it—"

Trace snorted. "If there's one thing we got, it's plenty of beef!"

"Señorita Cimarron," Luis put in smoothly with a nod toward the others at the table, "permit me to introduce Sanchez and his daughter, Turquoise."

Sanchez's leathery face smiled as he nodded. "I met the lady this morning when Trace brought her out to the roundup camp."

"Oh?" Luis looked curiously from her back to Trace.

Before she could answer, Trace did. "You might say we're very close friends," he said wryly, running his finger over the scratch marks on his face.

Cimarron cut into her thick steak, horrified at his remark. "Actually, we—we knew each other when we both went to school in San Antone." She tried to remember the story she and the moody cowboy had made up.

"Oh?" Luis said, "isn't it a little unusual for a lady to be traveling alone with all the Comanche raiding?"

"The señorita is a very unusual lady." Trace leaned back in his chair, pulled out tobacco, began to roll a cigarillo. "She was headed to the coast to visit relatives and got separated from her party."

That answer seemed to satisfy the elegant Spaniard. "Anyway señorita, I'm delighted you're here. I hope you'll extend your visit a long time. Life gets dull on a cattle ranch when you're used to Madrid, Paris—"

"Some of us are working too hard to think how dull it is," Trace said sarcastically, lighting up, blowing smoke rings in the air.

Luis glared at him. "It's customary for a gentleman to ask a lady if she minds if he smokes," he said with ice in his voice.

Trace glared back at him. "Should we ever have a *real* gentleman at the table, I'll be sure and remind him."

Was there going to be trouble? "I—I don't mind if he smokes," Cimarron put in hurriedly as she reached for cornbread to go with the huge steak.

Rosa reentered with a wild plum cobbler, serving it around the table with abrupt, angry gestures. "Turquoise," she snapped at the little girl, "how many times have I told you not to feed that dog at the table?"

"I forgot, Mama." The child looked a little frightened, as if she feared stern punishment.

The Mexican girl frowned, but before she could speak, gentle Sanchez gestured pleadingly. "Please, Rosa, don't scold her, you make too big a thing of this—"

"And you spoil her rotten," Rosa snapped.

The chihuahua came around by Cimarron's chair, sat up and waved its front paws as it begged. Cimarron gave Rosa a defiant look, deliberately took a bite of steak, handed it down to the pet, and winked at the delighted little girl.

They finished their meal. Luis offered Cimarron his arm and escorted her into the study for an after-dinner drink. The dog trotted after them. In the study, when Luis walked close to it, Tequila growled.

Luis frowned. "Somebody do something about that mutt," he complained. "He's already torn ten pairs of my custom-made trousers." The pretty child grabbed up the pet and began to play on the floor with it.

Luis went over to the crystal decanter on the desk. "Señorita, would you like some Madeira? It's fine imported stock. I choose it myself."

"*Si*, thank you," she smiled at him as he handed her the goblet, acutely aware of his fingers brushing hers.

Trace walked over, poured a glass of tequila. "Here, *compadre*." He handed it to old Sanchez, who nodded his thanks. Then he poured himself a glass, shook a little salt on his fist and licked it off as he drank the way cowboys did.

Luis frowned at him. "Your behavior is always common and vulgar."

"Inherited it from my parents," Trace answered lazily. "You know what Texans say, 'blood will tell.'"

Luis opened his mouth as if to retort, then seemed to think better of it. He admired his reflection in the large mirror on the wall by the bookcases. "Señorita, do you mind if I smoke?"

She shook her head, charmed by his elegant manners, his handsome face. He was only fifteen or maybe twenty years older than she was, and girls often chose more mature men on the frontier. What would it be like to be married to this aristocratic gentleman, have the Durango money, prestige and power? She frowned suddenly as she looked over and realized that Trace was studying her as he fingered the scratches on his cheek. The first thing she'd do would be to have Luis fire that ornery foreman.

Luis got himself a cigar, lit it, exhaled with a sigh. "Ah, nothing like fine imported tobacco."

Sanchez drained his glass, stood up, looked at Rosa. "I'm tired," he yawned. "Dear one, shall we go to bed?"

"I'm not quite ready." She looked about, as if afraid to relinquish the field to Cimarron.

Trace nodded. "Yes, stay, Rosa. I want to see how long it takes you and Cimarron to go at each other again."

Luis stiffened, looked at Cimarron, and shrugged helplessly, as if to say, "You see what I'm up against?" But to the Mexican girl, he said, "You may go, Rosa. We won't need anything else."

"But—"

"I said, you may go, Rosa," Luis emphasized in a frosty tone. She grabbed the child by the hand and they exited, the little girl still carrying the dog in one arm, although it turned back toward Luis and growled.

Sanchez looked appealingly at Cimarron. "Please forgive my wife's behavior, señorita," he apologized with a touch of embarrassment, his crippled hand fumbling with his mustache. "She hasn't been the same since the señora ran away—"

"Has anyone?" Trace snapped, draining his glass.

Sanchez hesitated. "No, I guess not, *compadre.*" He left the study, leaving the trio looking at each other.

"Well," said Luis uncertainly, "here we all are. Have you met the old man yet, señorita? And do you have comfortable accommodations?"

She sipped the delicious wine. "No, I haven't met him,"

she said, "but I'm looking forward to it. And the room is lovely. I'm looking forward to a good night's rest in that antique bed."

Trace raised one eyebrow sardonically. "There's really nothing like sleeping in the hay for real comfort."

Cimarron froze, glaring at him. Luis looked from one to the other, puzzlement etched on his features.

"Well," Cimarron said, "it's been a long day. I think I'll retire for the night, too."

Both men stood up, but Luis got to her before Trace did. He kissed her hand and offered her his arm. "Allow me to escort you, señorita."

She took his arm and glared at Trace. "It's so refreshing to meet a gentleman, Señor Luis," she said. "You can't imagine what clods ladies have to deal with these days."

Trace winked at her, running his tongue over his split lip. "I think I'll stay and have another drink, maybe read a little." He nodded toward the shelves of books.

She didn't give him the courtesy of an answer as she swept from the room on Luis Durango's arm.

Up in her room, one of the maids had laid out a delicate, very sheer nightgown for her. What would happen now? What plans should she make? Yesterday she had killed a man, this morning she had lost her virginity. Cimarron yawned, suddenly very tired. She wouldn't make any decisions yet. For the moment, she was safe from the law on the Triple D, Luis Durango seemed to be very interested in her, and she hungered for revenge against that damned cowboy. Cimarron blew out the lamp and climbed into bed.

She came awake abruptly, listening intently. Something had awakened her. The house slept quietly in the dead of night. What had disturbed her? She heard that slight sound again and realized it was her door squeaking ever so slightly as it opened. Cimarron lay very still, her heart hammering with fear. *Someone was sneaking into her room.*

Chapter Six

Cimarron tensed, ready to defend herself. Straining to hear another movement, she held her breath, listening.

Was that a sound? Had her imagination created the slight squeak of the door? The brush of movement of someone, or *something,* crossing the carpet?

Her heart pounded so loudly she was sure the intruder must hear it, too, as she gripped the coverlet with perspiring hands. Should she feign sleep? Boldly ask who was there?

She heard the intruder breathe, brush against the bottom of the bedpost. A sudden movement startled her as something landed on the bed with a small thump. Even as she started to scream, the small object whimpered and scampered across the bed to nuzzle her with a wet nose.

"Tequila!" She laughed with relief as the tiny dog snuggled up to her, licking her face with its warm tongue. "You little devil! What awakened you and sent you wandering the house in the middle of the night?"

As if in answer, the pet whimpered, trembling in her grasp as it stared toward the French doors.

"What is it, boy? Is something wrong?"

The chihuahua trembled more violently and wiggled from her grasp to jump down, still looking toward the door. Even as she watched his shadow, he scampered up to a chair and pressed his nose against the glass. She could see his silhouette against the sudden light of a full moon that peeked out from behind a cloud. Cimarron felt the room go chill, even though it was a hot, sultry night outside. Abruptly the scent of perfume drifted to her, a fragrance so overpowering that she gasped in surprise, knowing there were no flowers in her room. And yet, the Presence was reassuring. She felt no fear.

The tiny dog pressed his nose against the glass, whimpering more frantically, scratching against the pane.

"What is it, Tequila? What is it you see out there?"

In answer, the little dog threw back his head and howled, a long, heart-wrenching howl that echoed through the silent house, the midnight stillness. It was the saddest, most agonized sound she could remember.

Horrified, Cimarron sprang out of bed, raced across the carpet and grabbed for the dog. "Double damnation, Tequila! Be quiet! You'll wake everyone over some silly cat!"

She jerked him up out of the chair, holding his muzzle to silence him as she stared out, peering to see what had attracted his attention. Then she saw it, too.

For a long moment, she stared wide-eyed, shaking her head in disbelief as she clutched the tiny dog to her bosom. Her brain denied what her eyes told her, and yet . . .

It was her imagination, she told herself as she stared; her wild imagination coupled with a few wisps of clouds, maybe fog, shadows, and moonlight.

Along the black rim of the distant hills, a horse galloped in slow motion, as in a dream. Its hooves drummed along the trail, but somehow, she knew it made no sound.

Those were wisps of trailing clouds, she thought. But her eyes saw a long, floating mane and tail. The image swung its beautiful head wildly and the mane seemed to shake and sparkle, as if touched by stardust. The galloping specter appeared transparent, shimmering as it raced through the night along the purple rim of the world.

Cimarron stood petrified, holding on to the struggling, whimpering dog. She stared out at the ghostly apparition floating across the crest of the hill, outlined by bright moonlight.

I'm asleep and dreaming, she decided. But the tiny warm body in her arms, the oriental rug beneath her bare feet seemed real enough.

It was fog, she thought desperately, *wispy fog, or smoke.* Then why did the image of a magic unicorn or the legendary flying Pegasus come unbidden to her mind as she stood transfixed? The shining phantom galloped now to the highest crest, where the Milky Way spilled out of the night like a white satin ribbon thrown carelessly across endless space, touching the hilltop. At that point where the ribbon of light touched the cliff and led up into the sky, the image hesitated, rearing up on its hind legs. It shook its fine head wildly, the long mane of stardust sparkling with the motion. Or was what she saw a meteorite, a comet's fiery trail through the darkness?

The steed neighed silently and pawed the air as it reared. For a long moment, Cimarron felt its frustration, its disappointment as it plunged, trying to sink its front hooves into the ribbon of clouds that led up into Eternity.

Cimarron tensed, sympathetic to its mighty effort. She silently urged the magic creature on as it struggled to leave the earth behind, gallop away through the sky where it so obviously belonged. Throwing back its beautiful head, it neighed silently, and Cimarron felt its plea deep within her own soul even though she sensed it made no earthly sound. The deepest longings of the heart are often screamed in mute silence.

A second more it reared and plunged where the sky touched the horizon, struggling valiantly to mount the star-strewn trail to Forever. Then it seemed to realize the task was hopeless. Something was holding it back, keeping it bound to the earth. It could not leave. Not yet. . . .

With a final, resigned shake of its exquisite head, the ghost horse turned and galloped slowly along the crest of the purple hill and was lost in the hazy shadows of the night.

Cimarron stood there a long moment, staring out at the bare outline of the distant crest, unsure of her sanity, of what she had just seen. Perhaps it was all a dream, and any moment she would awaken snuggled down in the pillows of the big four-poster bed in the yellow room.

The small, warm body in her arms wiggled and brought

her back to reality. Trembling, Cimarron realized she stood staring out the door. Was it a dream and she had walked in her sleep? Could it have been her own wild imagination?

Very slowly, she leaned over, put the scampering dog on the planks, wrapped her arms around herself. Now she felt the bare floor cold beneath her feet, the slight breeze through her sheer nightdress. Cimarron took a deep breath and the scent of flowers seemed to fade away. The chill of the room dissipated slowly, the atmosphere grew warm and sultry again. Had it been a sleepwalker's dream or only her imagination painting the phantom across the landscape?

Well, whatever it was, she wouldn't be able to sleep now. In annoyance, she shushed the tiny dog whimpering and licking her bare feet. If she couldn't sleep, she might as well go down to the study and get herself a book. If nothing else, she'd curl up here in her bed and read a while.

Lighting a candle, she found her slippers and pulled a sheer negligee about her. The chihuahua danced ahead of her down the hallway as she tiptoed toward the stairs.

No, she wouldn't tell anyone what she had seen or thought she had seen, Cimarron decided. People would laugh if she told them about the dream horse. At the worst, they might question her sanity. That thought made her shudder as she descended the stairs. The Schmidts had told her there had been some talk of committing her mother, Texanna, to an asylum after she was returned from the Indians. Texanna kept trying to run away to go back to the Cheyenne, and of course, all her relatives in Fandango had thought her crazed. Cimarron sighed as she paused outside the door of the study. As she opened it, the dog bounced ahead of her, its nails clicking across the floor. She paused, feeling suddenly apprehensive in the shadowy doorway of the big room. Her tiny candle flickered feebly, catching the eyes of the stuffed heads on the walls. The glass eyes gleamed, and all the stuffed buffalo, longhorns, and panthers seemed to be looking down at her balefully. For a long moment she paused, fighting an urge to turn around and run back up to her room where she could bury her head in the covers.

Tequila whimpered from somewhere inside and it gave her

courage. "Double damnation!" she chided herself aloud as she moved across the room, holding her candle aloft. "Once you get the lamp by the fireplace lit and get yourself a glass of Madeira, you'll be glad you came down." Encouraged by her own brave words, like one who whistles in the dark, she moved gingerly through the shadows, holding her tiny candle high. The glass eyes of the stuffed heads seemed to follow her. It was stupid to be afraid, she thought as she stumbled through the dark toward the fireplace.

Again she heard the dog whimper, and she scolded him so that she wouldn't have to listen to the pounding of her own heart. "Tequila! You little rascal!"

The words froze on her lips as she abruptly sensed another presence, someone or something lurking in the shadows by the fireplace just outside the tiny circle of candlelight. As she stopped, a breeze blew the French doors open. Her candle flickered, went out.

She was not that brave. Cimarron gasped aloud and then opened her mouth to scream. A hand shot out of the darkness and clamped over her mouth.

"Don't wake the whole house, darlin'," he murmured. "I didn't mean to scare you."

She almost collapsed with relief as she recognized the big cowboy's Texas-Spanish drawl. At least this was an adversary she could see and understand. Very slowly, he took his hand away, then padded over to stare out the open French doors.

"Of course you scared me!" She scolded.

The moon came out from behind low, scudding clouds and gradually lit up the room. His rangy form stood silhouetted against the light as he looked out. A match flared as he struck it against the door jamb and lit a cigarillo. He wore nothing but his pants, she realized as she watched the tiny dot of flame from his smoke and smelled the pungent tobacco. He was bare-chested, his lithe muscles catching the light, his tousled hair black as a bat's wing.

The moonlight spilled across the dark floor like carelessly thrown liquid silver around the blackness of his shadow. Tequila hopped up in a chair and cocked his head, watching them both.

She put her candle down on the table with a bang. *Damn that arrogant cowboy!* "I wish you'd learn to keep your hands to yourself!" she scolded, moistening her dry lips, tasting the memory of his hand. "What are you doing prowling the house in the middle of the night?"

He leaned against the door jamb, staring out at the night and smoking thoughtfully. "Sassy miss, I might ask you the same question."

"I—I couldn't sleep," she blustered, too aware of the magnificent maleness of his half-naked body. She didn't dare tell him about what she had seen or dreamed. Cimarron winced, imagining him throwing back his head in laughter, in scorn. "And you?"

He hesitated, smoking slowly as he stared out at the night. She saw the light reflecting off his sinewy muscles, smelled the scent of smoke. The tip of his cigarillo glowed in the blackness.

"I—I was awakened," he answered, so softly that she had to strain to hear. She saw his expression in the shadows of light on his face and knew he was fighting a struggle, as she was, over whether to open up or remain aloof and invulnerable.

"You saw it, too!" she exclaimed, moving across to confront him. "You saw it, too!"

He whirled to face her, the forgotten smoke halfway to his lips. "You know about it? You've seen it?"

She paused a long moment, wondering if he were declaring a fact or questioning her before she nodded. "Yes, I saw it. What in God's name was it?"

Trace turned to stare at the night, took another puff. For a long moment he smoked, looking out, and she wondered if he had heard, or if he had, would he answer her? His voice when it came, was a whisper or reluctance. "The Mexican vaqueros would tell you you've seen *la luz del llano,* the light of the prairie."

"La luz del llano," she echoed. "I've heard Señora Rodriguez speak of it, but what is it?"

He took one last drag on the cigarillo, tossed it out the

open door. "No one can explain it, except by folktales, although I suppose there's an educated, scientific answer. Out on the range at night, a man will sometimes see a ghost light moving. Those who have seen it say it looks like a lantern, but when they follow it, it gradually disappears into thin air. *Le luz del llano,*" he whispered with a nod. "There's lots of old legends about it."

She moved closer, looking up at him. "But that's not what I saw," she said firmly. "And obviously, not what you saw either, or you wouldn't be prowling the house."

He shrugged, hesitated as if he were afraid she might laugh. "What I saw was a spirit animal."

"A what?"

"A Cheyenne spirit animal," he repeated softly, looking down at her.

She was abruptly aware of how close she stood to his half-naked body, of how sheer her nightdress was. Impulsively she wrapped her arms about herself, protecting her breasts from his gaze. "I—I don't know about that."

He seemed to frown. "You don't know the legends of your own people? Some Cheyenne! You don't even know their stories. Only those with Cheyenne blood can see it."

"I can't help it," she said defensively, hugging herself closer as he peered down at her. "I was raised by whites. I never heard of your spirit animal."

He paused, as if trying to decide whether to share his knowledge with her. "The Cheyenne people believe everyone has a ghost animal that brings them good luck and looks after them as long as they need it. Sort of like a guardian angel. They say it warns them of danger, of trouble."

She almost laughed, looked up at his serious face, decided against it. "And does this ghostly horse gallop across the skies to warn you often?"

"I've seen it only once before this. The night the señora left. And the next night, old Juanita, the housekeeper, missed her footing and fell down the stairs. Maybe it's a warning for you, Cimarron."

"Against what?"

He moved closer, so close his chest was almost brushing

against her crossed arms. Now Trace threw back his head and laughed. Once again he was mocking, sarcastic. "I don't know, my Cheyenne princess. Maybe against me!"

His protective shield was back, and she felt suddenly put off, defeated. The big cowboy had been about to open up to her, share something magic and wondrous. That tenderness, that sensitivity she sensed behind the tough facade had drawn her like a magnet. Now it was replaced by the hard, cold mask.

"You can unfold your arms," he grinned, raising one sardonic eyebrow. "I promise I won't grab you."

She felt the blood rush to her face, knowing he had read her thoughts. But she backed away from him before lowering her arms. "Tell me about the spirit animal," she insisted as she nervously brushed back her long hair.

He sighed. "The Cheyenne call the Milky Way Ekutsihimmiyo, the Hanging Road to the Sky. Their idea of heaven is running wild and free through the stars forever."

She tried to remember what she'd seen. *There was something familiar....* "It tried to mount that ribbon, run up the Milky Way and into the clouds. It tried, but it couldn't go. Why does it stay if it wants to leave?"

"I don't know, darlin', I really don't know why it stays." His drawl was serious, thoughtful. "Maybe it's not finished yet, maybe it can't leave because of something left undone. If I could talk to a Cheyenne shaman, maybe he would know." His voice trailed off, and very slowly, his hand came up to touch her cheek.

She didn't pull away, knowing she should. She hated Trace, she reminded herself. Sooner or later, she had vowed to kill him and yet....

His fingertips moved down across her cheek like a feathery caress, cupping her chin up toward his face. Her emotions were a tumble of indecision, of hate, of passion. His dark eyes looked down into hers.

"Cimarron?" he asked, and he must have taken her silence for assent, for his free arm went around her suddenly, pulling her hard against his bare chest.

She started to protest, but his hot mouth covered hers, the

hand on her face went to tangle itself in her hair. With his great strength he swept her to him, and she could feel the hard muscles of his chest through the sheer nightdress as her taut nipples pressed against him.

How dare he! Her small fists came up to beat against him, paused there. His lips caressed her open ones and now he claimed the hot, moist depths of her mouth. She tried to protest, but his seeking kiss stopped her words even before she spoke. Her breasts swelled and strained against the soft fabric, rubbing against his wide chest. Gradually the small fists that had gone up to strike at him unclenched and went up around his neck, pulling his rugged face down to hers. His two hands felt like smoldering branding irons burning through the sheer fabric of her nightdress as they slid slowly down her back to cup and caress her small bottom. She could feel his rigid, throbbing maleness against her belly through both their clothing.

Her breath came in a ragged sob and she tried to tell herself she must pull away and run before it was too late. But his tongue was invading her mouth now, darting, demanding, dominating. Cimarron clung to his wide shoulders, swaying on her feet as he pulled her to him so tightly she gasped for breath.

And oh, how her traitor body suddenly wanted him to take her, to mate her! She felt the sudden warmth and moisture as her secret place begged for his entry. She was no better than a mare in heat, readying herself for some big, rearing, plunging stud. *She wanted him. Oh, yes, her body wanted him!* But she had sworn vengeance against him for violating her the first time. How could she want him and hate him simultaneously?

For a long, dizzying moment she swayed limply in his arms, letting him mold her soft curves against the hard planes of his sinewy body. His fiery hands gripped her small hips, caressing her as he pulled her against him. She couldn't stop herself from rubbing her taut breasts on his great, naked chest. They seemed to have desires of their own, and she gasped and moaned at the sensation as she pressed her engorged, swollen nipples against the hard nubs of his. He was bending her backward, rubbing his manhood on her through the sheer nightdress as his mouth claimed hers. With a soft sigh of surrender, she stopped struggling, letting him force her lips even farther apart, letting him lick, suck, and caress the moist velvet interior.

"I'll start with your mouth," he gasped, "but there's another place I want to kiss this way!"

She shivered at the delicious, forbidden image his words brought to her mind. Would he really do that to her? It sounded so naughty, so wonderful. Such a thing had never even occurred to her. His warm lips moved slowly down the graceful column of her neck as he lifted her to him. She could feel her nightdress sliding down her shoulders and she didn't care as she trembled with passion, uncontrolled and uncontrollable. She arched backward in his arms, letting her hair fall free, almost brushing against the floor as his lips kissed the hollow of her throat. He lifted her up so that he could reach her nipples. Her pulse pounded so hard she was sure he could feel it beneath his lips as he pressed himself between her thighs. She could not keep herself from rubbing against his hardness, wanting him. Wanting him. . . .

And now he swung her up lightly in his arms, looking down at her in the moonlight. His face was shadowed but she could see desire written there. She felt her long golden hair spread across his arm, falling like a fountain of spun gold toward the floor.

"God! You're the most beautiful thing I ever saw!" His voice was ragged, almost a sob as he carried her toward the shadowy leather sofa.

Cimarron gasped, knowing he was going to lay her on it, take her again as he had in the hayloft. He would force himself between her thighs, ride her with savage abandon until he spilled his seed deep within her.

And she was suddenly afraid, remembering the pain and the terror of the other time. He must have felt her stiffen in his arms, because he paused, looking down into her face. When his voice came, it was a ragged, husky whisper of passion. "Cimarron, I won't hurt you. I'd never hurt you!"

And while she hesitated, his mouth took hers again as he

laid her on the sofa, slid his pants down, lay down atop her on the narrow couch. His bare skin was molten fire covering hers. Now she could feel every inch of his hot body, his pulse beating through her sheer nightdress, but his lips never left hers. She could not keep her body from arching against him as his hard hands caressed her thighs, stroked her secret place until she shuddered with delight.

His tongue claimed the depths of her mouth, so that she could not have protested if she had wanted to. *I must stop him while there's still time,* she thought regretfully. But she couldn't force herself to push him away.

His rigid maleness throbbed against her thigh. She felt the wet smear of his seed there and instinctively regretted the waste of it as her body moistened itself, wanting his. His fingers stroked her breasts until she gasped. Instinctively, her tongue darted between his lips.

She had to stop him, she thought. It was crazy to allow herself to be taken on a library sofa by a man she hated. But her body didn't hate him, and she couldn't control it now. She felt her hips tilt up as he slid one hand beneath her, positioning her. *This has to cease,* she thought wildly. But all she could think of was the feel of his hands caressing her nipples as his mouth dominated hers.

Without even realizing she did it, she dug her nails in his back, pulling him down on her, into her. He was built big, and she gasped at the sensation as he tilted her hips up, filled her.

"Easy darlin'," he crooned against her mouth, "I don't want to hurt you this time."

She had to tell him to get off, she thought in dismay. What kind of tramp was she to accept this stud between her thighs? And then he began to ride her, and she knew neither one of them wanted it to end. His fingers were tangled in her hair as he cupped her face between his calloused hands. Dimly, she touched blood on his back, knew it was because her nails dug into his dark, rippling muscles.

Her legs wrapped around his hard, driving hips so he could not get away. Cimarron was horrified that her body was arching up, begging for what he had to give. She did not understand the new feelings that swept her, had never experienced such emotions before. *Something earth-shaking was about to happen.* He rode her hard, the intensity and crescendo increasing as his hands slid beneath her lean hips, tilting them up so that he gave her every inch he had. His maleness was hurting her, stretching her, but she wanted even more, and she locked him against her with her long legs.

"Darlin'," he gasped against her open mouth, "oh, darlin'!" Then he drove into her so hard she could feel his maleness throb within her before he shuddered, then lay deathly still.

His heart pounded against her breast, and she felt his pulse rapid under her fingers. Otherwise she would have thought him dead as she ran her hands across his perspiring back. And as he finally stirred, she didn't know whether she was angry at him or at herself. Furiously she pushed at him, tried to wiggle out from under him.

He pulled away from her, looked down into her eyes, puzzlement written on his dark features. "Cimarron?"

Her traitor body had made her react like a harlot, she thought, her face burning with shame. No doubt, he'd laugh later at how he'd made her want him, what a tramp she was. "How dare you?" she seethed, "how dare you just grab me up and throw me on the sofa, mount me like a common whore?"

He jerked as if she'd struck him. "I thought you wanted me! You sure didn't act as if I was forcing you!" He got up, buttoning his pants with angry, jerky movements.

She felt the flush creep up her face and she'd die before she'd admit she'd wanted him, too. "You never gave me a chance to say no," she blurted, pulling the thin nightdress down to cover her nakedness.

"You rotten little tart!" he swore, looking down at her. His voice was hard again, hard as his face in the shadows. "I never had a woman show me that kind of response before. I thought you were one in a million, warm, passionate. And you were just teasing, tormenting me, weren't you, darlin'? Just tantalizing me?"

"No, I-I'm not that kind of girl." She stood up slowly, reaching out to him despite herself.

But he slapped her hand away. "Just what kind are you, sassy miss? You ride in out of nowhere, tease me till I rape you, when I've always thought a rapist was lower than a rattlesnake's belly! Now we play the whole scene again!"

"Well," she began, and stopped as she pulled her disheveled nightgown back up her shoulders. What should she tell him? She could hardly tell him she was on the run for murder, and she'd die before admitting she'd lost control over her own desires. She wouldn't give this moody, sarcastic stud the satisfaction of knowing he had driven her body wild with passion.

"No answer, darlin'?" He smiled cruelly, went over to lean against the stone fireplace where he stood, still studying her. "You must think I'm a gelding, rubbing yourself all over me, half-naked as we both are, and not expect me to want you, take you when you responded."

She saw his lithe body trembling in the moonlight, a light sheen of perspiration on his hard muscles. And the truth of it was that she wanted him again, wanted to feel him mount her, dominate her. She hated herself as much as she hated him for this need she couldn't deny.

"Damn you!" She moved closer, looking up at him. She was fully aware of how the moonlight silhouetted her slim form, her full hips, and jutting breasts through the sheer nightgown, as if she wore nothing at all. But she was too angry to care. "You shouldn't have—"

"Get away from me, darlin'," he warned, and his voice was tense, tight. "It's all I can do at this moment to keep from grabbing you again, ripping that little scrap of silk right off you, throwing you down right here on the floor—"

Frightened by the intensity of his gaze, she took an involuntary step backward. He sighed loudly, walked over to the desk, rolled himself a cigarillo, and went back to the fireplace, struck the Lucifer match against the stone.

In the sudden flare she saw the heaving of his sweat-drenched chest, the desire and frustration on the moody face.

"Damn you!" she said again.

He laughed coldly. "I don't know what your game is,

Cimarron, but I'll tell you one thing. If you don't go to work at some place like Miss Fancy's, you've missed your calling! I never saw a girl who instinctively knew how to make a man want her, make them fight over her. Is that what you're doing on the Triple D?" She watched him inhale and blow smoke like an angry dragon. The tip glowed brighter when he pulled on it.

Cimarron bit her lip. "What do you mean by that?"

He snorted with derision. "Maybe I underestimated you, little Wild One. Maybe you're after bigger game. Maybe you're after our handsome rake, Luis!"

"Why, you impudent jackass!" she fumed as she faced him. Without thinking, her hand went up to slap his cheek.

But his free hand reached out and caught hers in midair. "Don't ever do that, darlin'." He bit off each word. "Don't you realize I'm twice your size? I could break you in half if I wanted to!"

She stood staring up at him, her small wrist still imprisoned in his grasp. And she suddenly felt triumphant because she knew who had won this round. Abruptly she sensed that he would never hurt her, would kill any man who tried. "But you won't, will you?" she said softly.

He let go of her then, swearing long and low as he took another drag from the cigarillo, tossed it into the empty fireplace. "Don't press your luck, sassy miss! Only one woman ever dared slap my face, and she was trying to keep me from killing a man!"

"Did she?"

"Did she what?"

"Keep you from killing him?"

"You've seen Luis walking around alive and well, haven't you? If you're using me, Cimarron, using me to make him jealous, it won't work. You aren't going to be able to yell 'rape' and have the gallant Luis come running to the rescue, because I don't ever intend to touch you again until you beg me. Until you say, 'Please, Trace.'"

She laughed, hard and angry herself. "That'll be a cold day in hell! You conceited idiot!"

With a flounce, she turned on her heel and stalked from

the study, the tiny dog scampering ahead of her up the dark stairway as she ran through the darkness toward her room. But she got no sleep that night, alternating between the desire to kill Trace . . . or kiss him.

When Cimarron finally dropped off into a troubled sleep it was nearly dawn, so she slept later than she had ever slept in her life.

It was almost ten o'clock when she put on a bright calico dress Rosa sent up by one of the maids and went down to the dining room. Luis was having a solitary breakfast.

He stood, rushed around to pull out a chair for her. "Ah, good morning, señorita, you are more beautiful than ever this morning."

Cimarron blushed at his gallantry, the thought crossing her mind that it was very pleasant to have such a polite gentleman around after her encounter with the rough cowboy.

"Gracias, señor, you are so kind. Where is everyone?"

Luis shrugged. "Breaking broncs in the cool of the morning, I think. Trace gets up earlier than the birds. But then," he smiled easily, "someone has to, I suppose."

He turned his head toward the kitchen door. "Rosa, some coffee for the lady!"

Cimarron felt the Mexican girl had been lurking just behind the door, eavesdropping, because she came through it immediately with the china and slammed it down in front of Cimarron, sloshing the coffee into the saucer.

Cimarron glanced sideways, saw Luis's annoyed frown, and decided to head off the scene she thought would be forthcoming. "*Gracias,* Rosa," she said quickly, taking a sip. "Your coffee is delicious."

Rosa frowned. "Will the lady be having breakfast at this late hour or is she early for dinner?" She emphasized the word "lady" and "late" in a way that was unmistakable.

Luis pushed his own plate back. "Of course, she will," he said, a slight edge to his voice. "What would you like, Señorita Cimarron? May I recommend Rosa's chili pepper omelet with fried steak on the side? We also have a special treat. One of the traders managed to get through the blockade with real flour, so we have biscuits."

"Certainly," Cimarron nodded, as she sipped her coffee, warming to him for his masterful handling of the situation. It not only would float a horseshoe, it might float the whole horse. She thought about asking for cream, decided not to irritate the housekeeper any further.

Rosa made a slightly annoyed sound and flounced out.

Luis stroked his penciled mustache and gave Cimarron a dazzling, charming smile. "You must forgive Rosa," he said softly. "She resents anyone she feels might be trying to take the señora's place, and good servants are hard to get in Texas. People are so democratic here. Now, France," he sighed, "or Spain, or England. The wealthy there have good help. I'd import a butler, but these crude ranchers would laugh loud enough to be heard in Nachodoches."

Cimarron smiled back at him, thinking how handsome he was, how sophisticated. A well-traveled man of the world. "You don't strike me as the type of man who would be intimidated by the laughter of rough cowboys." Trace's hard face came to her mind and she brushed it away.

Rosa came through the swinging door of the kitchen and slammed an omelet of hot chili peppers and melted cheese down before her. The steak, Cimarron noted, was big, and done to Texas taste, fried well-done and very thin.

"Would the señorita like biscuits or tortillas with her breakfast?" Rosa asked, slightly impudent, but not enough so to be scolded, Cimarron thought.

She glared back at the girl. "Why, biscuits, of course, unless you're saving them."

Rosa left the room in a huff and returned to place them before her before stomping back to the kitchen.

Luis gave her an admiring look. "Bravo, señorita. I like a feisty woman with a little fire to her."

"Don't all Texans?" Cimarron looked up at him through her eyelashes as she ate.

"Do you mind if I smoke?"

"Not at all. I like the smell of a good cigar."

Luis sighed as he sniffed the one he pulled from his silk

shirt pocket and lit it. "Mine are imported, of course. Never have understood how Texans can smoke those quirleys."

She smiled fetchingly at him. "Because they don't have your taste and education."

He smiled at her over his cigar. "That's true," he said. "I was educated in Spain, you know. Texas is such a barbaric place by comparison. My father expected me to be a doctor, but I wanted to be an artist."

"Oh?" Cimarron said. "Are the paintings throughout the house yours? I think they're lovely."

"Some of them. But I'm afraid I lack the drive, the dedication to be truly a great artist, so I play at being the gentleman rancher."

She finished her food and laid down her fork, and he stood, came around to pull out her chair. "Come, señorita, let me show you the Triple D this morning. Do you ride?"

"Yes." Cimarron took his arm and they went to the foot of the great stairway. "If I can find something proper—"

"*Sí*. No problem." He gave an authoritative gesture to one of the maids scurrying past. "See that the lady is properly attired in riding clothes."

"After last night," she blanched, "I think I'd better not wear Señora Durango's things again."

"Nonsense. I must apologize for all of us, it was such a shock, you know. . . ." His voice trailed off, and when he spoke again it was so soft, she barely heard him. "Except for the yellow hair and the lighter shade of skin, it was amazing. . . ." His voice trailed off again and he gave a gesture of dismissal. "While you change, I'll go visit the old man and see if he's better this morning."

"I have not yet met him," Cimarron said, "perhaps—"

"If he is feeling up to it, perhaps we'll have coffee with him this afternoon," Luis said. "I think the old man would like you very much." His face grew thoughtful, sad, as some memory crossed it. He stood there a long moment, lost in thought, then shrugged. "See you out on the veranda in a few minutes, señorita."

The young Spanish girl led her upstairs and dutifully laid

out several riding outfits for Cimarron to choose from. Cimarron tried to strike up a conversation with the girl, but she seemed as shy as the gentle armadillos of south Texas. The servants must all be terrified of Rosa, Cimarron thought. No doubt Rosa's new position had gone to her head, making a petty tyrant of her.

Cimarron had never seen such fine clothing. Certainly Aunt Carolina had not had such things. She finally chose a chocolate-and-fawn faille riding outfit with chocolate braid on the jacket and a matching brown hat. She tied her yellow hair back with a brown velvet ribbon. Yes, she looked pretty in it, she thought with wonder, seeing that the colors emphasized her large, dark eyes. She looked self-consciously at her small hands, still rough and red from all the housework at the Longworths'. But the fine leather riding gloves hid the marks of toil nicely, she decided as she dismissed the shy girl and went out onto the veranda.

She heard the jangle of spurs and turned toward the door as Luis came out, handsome in an expensive Spanish-style riding outfit, big silver Mexican-style spurs on his handmade boots. He carried a small basket over his arm.

The Spaniard's eyes widened at the sight of her. "Señorita Cimarron," he breathed, "you are indeed breathtaking."

She reddened prettily as he took her arm and escorted her with a flourish toward the stable where a boy waited with two saddled horses—a tall chestnut and a smaller sorrel.

"You flatter me, señor," she smiled, her pulse picking up a little at the handsome Spaniard's admiring gaze. "I'll wager both the señora and Dallas are great beauties."

He looked pensive. *"Sí.* Before today, I would have said no woman in Texas could compare with them. The señora has a soft, gentle beauty, but Dallas is a tomboy."

"Dallas Durango," Cimarron mused. "Strange name for a young lady. Was she named for the town, or Polk's vice-president?"

Luis laughed. "I'm not sure. Both the vice-president and the Dallas brothers of the Texas Army were friends of the old man's. It means 'spirited,' you know, and it suited her. Even the Don had a hard time dealing with that high-spirited young lady, so he sent her off to school."

"And?" Cimarron prompted. Luis gallantly offered his hands for her small booted foot as she mounted.

Luis shrugged as he swung up on his chestnut. "Dallas hated the elegant finishing school in Boston. We got letters begging to come home. The señora thought she should be allowed to return, but the Don was adamant about turning Dallas into a young lady. He demanded she stay."

"So she took matters into her own hands," Cimarron guessed as she clucked to her horse and started away at a walk. "It must be terrible not to know her whereabouts."

Luis frowned. "Dallas was always too independent for her own good. And her running away caused trouble between the old man and Velvet Eyes. In fact, they argued the morning before the señora left."

Velvet Eyes. An image came to Cimarron's mind of a hauntingly beautiful woman in the moonlight dress. The kind of woman all men would fall in love with, even if she was married to the powerful Don. She thought again of Trace. Had he been fantasizing about Velvet Eyes as he raped her?

"Your horses are fine-blooded, señor," she said quickly, not sure whether it was the thought of the rough cowboy's forcing himself on her or the idea that he might have been thinking of another woman that upset her. "But must you use such cruel spurs and a spade bit?"

She glanced over at the big Mexican spurs and the sharp metal cutting into the chestnut's mouth.

"Some horses are like some women," he said jokingly. "They need a firm hand to show them who's in charge." He winked at her in a flirting manner and she half smiled, uneasy as to whether he was joking or not.

"I'm sure a gallant Spanish gentleman such as yourself could charm a woman into doing anything he wished."

His white teeth gleamed in the handsome face as he smiled. "A señorita as lovely as you could charm a man into doing anything *she* wanted."

She felt her pulse quicken. He was a bachelor and obviously taken with her. She began to imagine again what it would be like to be the señora of the whole Triple D empire, very rich, with a handsome, gallant husband such as Luis Durango. She could have clothes, jewels, and when the war ended she could travel to all the capitals of Europe. And she would have the dark, moody foreman at her beck and call. . . .

Double damnation! She thought with annoyance as she rode. Could she never get that rough foreman off her mind?

"You are very quiet, Señorita Cimarron," Luis ventured as they rode out across the rolling countryside. "I hope you do not find my company dull."

Cimarron started guiltily. She had the richest, most eligible man in all Texas riding at her side, and her thoughts were on his foreman. "Not at all, señor." She smiled prettily at him. "I was just thinking about the quality of your horses."

Luis nodded. "Only the King spread has any finer. You know what Texans say: 'Blood will tell,' and it's as true of people as of horses, I think."

Next he would be inquiring into her own bloodlines and background. "You know Colonel King?" she asked quickly.

Luis nodded. "I wonder if he's still in hiding? The Yankees did control the area along the coast near his ranch, and he sided with the South. The Triple D sided with the Union because of the old man's friendship with Governor Houston." He frowned in disapproval. "The Don was one of those hotheads who offered to bring in armed men to help Sam hold the capital when he was forced out of office for refusing to swear allegiance to the Confederacy."

She enjoyed the sun and the slight breeze as they rode. "Well, most of the hill country sided with the Union because of the German population. You remember what happened at Nueces two years ago?"

Luis nodded. "If a bunch of them wanted to leave the state and go fight for the Union, it was not gallant of the Rebs to ambush them, then shoot the wounded."

The thought brought tears to her eyes. "It's cruel of the Confederates to lynch protesters."

"Si, I agree. I was in Gainesville that day and I tried to stop

it, but the mob was in control. . . ."

She didn't want to think about the forty men lynched at Gainesville. They hadn't been the only ones.

"I'm enjoying the ride immensely." She changed the subject as she smiled at the handsome face, then thought of a face that was almost too masculine and rugged to be good-looking. "Where's the crew?" She asked without thinking and was immediately angry with herself.

Luis shrugged. "Somewhere in the valley pasture up ahead, I think, rounding up some mustangs. Would you like to see the herd? You seem to know horses, señorita."

Was he probing, trying to figure out her background? She would not tell him about Pastor Schmidt's small horse ranch, how she had helped raise and train the colts when she wasn't taking care of Frau Schmidt. But it hadn't occurred to them to leave her the little ranch. Obviously they had expected her to marry and let some man look after her. Or maybe they hadn't loved her, after all, because of her Indian blood. It hurt too much to think about it.

"Certainly, I'd like to see the herd." She kicked her horse into a lope, thinking of the expression on the foreman's face when she rode up dressed like a fine lady and accompanied by Luis Durango. She imagined the scene in her mind. Would he be jealous? Sneering? Uninterested?

Did she give a damn how that ruffian would react? Of course not. She gave Luis her most fetching smile as both horses loped easily across the rolling limestone hills.

September in the hill country was often hot, and it might be late December before the first frost killed off the wild flowers blooming in profusion among the cedars. The limestone hills were too rocky, the soil too thin to ever farm it. Cattle and fine-blooded horses were kings here. Cimarron took a deep breath, enjoying the smell of leather, of horses, the creak of saddles, the sight of quail rising up before them. The sun felt pleasant on her back.

Luis smiled at her, and she thought what a superb horseman he was, such a noble, handsome figure of a man. "Señorita, I had Rosa pack us a lunch so we can picnic at a grove up ahead. What do you say to roast chicken and a fine bottle of wine chilled in the creek?"

"Delightful!" She laughed lightheartedly, feeling almost guilty because she wasn't slaving away doing housework. So this was how the rich lived! She liked it. She liked it very much.

She thought she saw a flash, a reflection from the crest of the hill they approached, and her face wrinkled in puzzlement. "Luis—?"

She never finished. The rifle shot echoed through the hills as it took Luis's hat off. Her gelding reared up in terror at the shot cracking like thunder, jerking the reins from her relaxed fingers. Even as she grabbed for them, the sorrel whinnied and bolted away across the prairie.

Chapter Seven

Cimarron screamed, grabbing for the reins that the horse jerked from her grasp as it threw its head up at the crack of the rifle. The sorrel bolted, taking the bit in its teeth as it galloped away. Only the fact that she was an expert rider kept her on the sidesaddle.

If she fell, she might be trampled under its hooves or hurt on the sharp rocks. She swore a silent curse at the sidesaddle as the horse ran away, wishing she were wearing a pair of men's pants. If she'd been astride, she would have been impossible to dislodge from the runaway's back. That was what she got for trying to be a high-class lady.

"Cimarron, I'm coming!" Luis shouted behind her. But glancing back over her shoulder, she saw he would not be able to catch her running mount even though he slashed at his chestnut furiously with the reins, dug the big spurs into its heaving flanks.

The limestone rocks she raced across were uneven and her horse stumbled once before running on. For a panicky moment she imagined going down beneath its weight as it fell, but it righted itself and kept running. She had managed to get one of the reins back now, but the other dangled between its galloping hooves. If it stepped on it, it might stumble and fall, and she would go over its head. The sudden motion dislodged the little chocolate riding hat and she grabbed for it, but it was carried away, falling on the ground behind her. As she looked back, she saw Luis's horse trample the hat as he galloped in hot pursuit.

She could taste real fear sour in her mouth now as she realized that the ground was getting rockier, more uneven. There might be a cliff or a chasm up ahead of the blindly running horse.

"Hang on, señorita, I'm coming!" Luis shouted, right behind her. She didn't need encouragement. Grimly she hung on to the saddle, feeling the heat of the chestnut when its head pulled up beside her. Then Luis's strong arm reached out, lifted her from the running horse.

For an eternity she seemed to hang over fast-moving ground, before the Spaniard lifted her to the saddle in front of him and pulled the lathered gelding to a halt. Its sides heaved, red with bloody ridges from the big spurs, and its mouth sprayed pink foam from the spade bit.

Then he dismounted, lifting her to the ground, where she swayed on her feet in his arms. "Cimarron, are you hurt?"

His handsome face looked down into hers as he supported her limp body. She heaved a sigh of relief, thinking how strong and brave he was. Why, a man in his late thirties or early forties was not so old, she thought, remembering how he had plucked her from the back of the running horse.

"Señorita, are you all right?" he asked again, and she was dazzled by his masculinity, his concern.

"I—I think so. Did someone shoot at us?"

"Not us. Me." His aristocratic face grew tense, angry. "But God forbid you should be an innocent victim." His hand came up to brush a wisp of hair from her eyes. "If you had been hurt, Cimarron, there would be terrible revenge when Luis Durango finally caught up with the *hombre* responsible for this outrage!"

For a long moment, as he looked down into her face, she thought he might kiss her, wondered if she wanted him to. She never found out. Even as she swayed, she heard a running horse and turned, afraid it might be the gunman.

"Now, if this isn't cozy!" Trace's voice dripped with sarcasm as he rode up, leading Cimarron's lathered runaway horse. "I heard a scream, this horse came galloping past me. What happened, Luis?"

The elegant Spaniard frowned, went over to take the sorrel's reins. "Someone took a shot at us. Her horse bolted and ran away. I rescued the lady—"

"So I see. Looks like I arrived just before you were about to be rewarded for your daring." He threw his leg up over the saddlehorn, pulled out a smoke, and grinned at Cimarron as he struck a match on his boot heel.

She couldn't stop herself from flushing, then felt anger rise at her embarrassment. "One wonders just how you happened to be so close by. And especially, carrying a rifle on your saddle." She didn't say what else passed through her mind. *Only a Sharps rifle could carry that distance.*

"Si," Luis's face furrowed thoughtfully. "Now that you mention it, señorita, it does seem unusual that when some *hombre* shoots at me, Trace happens to be on the scene."

The cowboy paused, the match halfway to his lips. Then, very slowly, he lit the quirley, shook the match out. "I don't want to make any mistake about this," he said very coldly, deliberately, tossing the match away. "Am I being accused of trying to drygulch you, Luis?"

"You'd deny it anyway, wouldn't you?" Luis's voice had a decided edge.

For a long second she saw Trace's hand tremble in fury, then he took a deep puff and exhaled like a devil blowing brimstone smoke. "I do deny it, you elegant bastard. Begging the lady's pardon, of course." He tipped his hat to her as he apologized for the epithet, as any Texan would. "I'm a better shot than that, Luis, and you know it. The day I take a shot at you, they'll find you out on the prairie with a hole between your eyes. I don't know who's doing the shooting or why, but day before yesterday, on the way back to the ranch, someone took a shot at me, too."

"How convenient," Luis sneered, "that you suddenly now remember this attempt on your life."

Cimarron looked into Trace's face. He had mentioned it to her when they'd met on the trail that night. Maybe even then he'd been building himself an alibi for today's attempt on Luis. Would he wreck her reputation and tell Luis about meeting her two days ago, about yesterday morning?

Trace paused, took a long drag on the cigarette as he looked into Cimarron's eyes. "Nope, I don't have an alibi, didn't tell anyone about it," he said finally. "Never saw a soul from the time I left the line camp until I got to the hacienda."

She heaved a sigh of relief and looked away. Was he expecting her to provide the alibi, to speak out about meeting him on the trail? Whatever the reason, she owed him nothing, and she didn't believe him anyhow. She had seen the confrontation in the barn. She had no doubt that for some reason Trace hated Luis enough to take a shot at him. Besides, she was suddenly afraid that Luis might find out about the rape. For a moment, she enjoyed the thought that the fine gentleman would probably call Trace out over it. But on the other hand, she had a feeling Luis wouldn't be interested in a girl who was not a virgin, even though it wasn't her fault. It would be a matter of pride to him.

Luis took out a silk handkerchief, wiped his face. "Just who besides you would want to take a shot at me?"

Trace shrugged, puffed the cigarillo, blew pungent smoke rings that drifted on the warm air. "Don't know that you could win a popularity contest with the crew, Luis, but I don't think any of them hate you enough to shoot you." He looked genuinely puzzled. "Maybe Cimarron's intended?"

Luis reddened. "Watch your mouth, Trace. Cimarron is a lady, and as such, I will protect her reputation. Of course, I know the class of women you run with would hardly fit that classification."

"At least mine are honest whores," Trace said softly, and his eyes seemed to challenge Luis.

Luis blinked, nerves twitching in his face. "Oh, *perdone*," he said coldly. "I didn't know we were discussing the women of your family."

Trace jerked as if he had been struck. Cimarron tensed, saw him tremble violently, knew he was about to come off that horse right on top of Luis. For a long moment she was not sure what he would do. His face contorted, and then he seemed to regain control of his emotions as he tossed the cigarette away. She was aware that something terrible was being hinted that she couldn't understand.

Trace took a deep breath. "Someday," he whispered, and Cimarron realized that his fists were clenched. "Someday, Luis, someday . . ."

Luis turned to Cimarron triumphantly. "You see? Would you doubt that threat? I for one have no doubt—"

They heard the running hoofbeats first and then another horse thundered across the ridge. Luis's voice trailed off as they all three turned to see the rider. Sanchez and Maverick came over the rise, and off to the east and west other riders rode down the crests toward them. Holt came from an easterly direction. "Hell's bells! I knew I heard shots!" he said as he rode up. "What happened?"

Trace waved the men in. "A little excitement, *compadres*. Seems someone tried to take a shot at Luis."

"*Dios!*" The old Mexican pulled at his mustache, his leathery face grim. "Comanche, maybe."

"No, I don't think so." Luis frowned as the other riders rode up and circled around. He seemed to look them over, Cimarron thought, as if trying to decide whether the sniper might be anyone in the crew.

She frowned, looking at the foreman with his leg still thrown across the saddlehorn. As far as she was concerned, she'd already decided who the would-be assassin was; she just wasn't sure why. As far as Trace's claim that someone had done the same to him day before yesterday, she decided he'd been laying his alibi out in advance.

Holt rubbed his mean, unshaven face as Cimarron felt his eyes sweep over her. "I was over there rounding up strays," he gestured off to one side, then pointed. "Sounded like it might have come from over that ridge."

Cimarron shook her head. "No, I saw the glint of the barrel in the sun. "From the east, maybe."

Trace laughed. "Well, we've got plenty of clues, haven't we? Can't even decide which direction the shot came from, much less whose rifle. Maybe it's renegades stealing cattle again and thought you were about to spot them."

She looked around the circle. Every man there had a rifle on his saddle, except Luis. Abruptly, she felt very weary after her narrow escape. "I'd like to go back to the house, Luis, if you don't mind." She wiped her hot face. "I couldn't enjoy a picnic after all this, anyway."

"A picnic!" Trace exclaimed with a broad wink around at the crew. "My, I do hope there's potato salad enough for all of us! And here we were planning on cold cornpone and beef jerky! Have we a vintage wine?"

Luis drew himself up stiffly. "You wouldn't fully appreciate the imported wine I chose anyway, so I won't waste it on you. Come, señorita."

He walked back, picked up her crushed hat. Then he came around and gallantly offered his hands to give Cimarron a lift up to the saddle. "Allow me, my dear."

Trace swung his leg back down to his stirrup and spat to one side as Cimarron mounted. "Dammit!" He swore suddenly. "Luis, look what you've done to that horse! I ought to beat the living daylights out of you over those spurs and that bit!"

Cimarron turned to look too, noticing for the first time the bleeding cuts and torn mouth on the big chestnut. "Oh, my, the poor thing!" Her hand flew to her mouth.

"I couldn't help it," Luis said defensively. "Her horse was running away and I had to overtake her."

She had never seen such anger in a man's face as she now saw on the rugged cowboy's. "You better hope you get that horse taken care of before the old Don sees it." His voice was low with barely controlled anger. "And if you don't quit using those damned big spurs, someday I—"

"Someday you'll what?" Luis sneered. "I'll explain the circumstances to the old man. I'm sure after he sees the lady, he'll feel it was worth it."

Cimarron reached to stroke her own exhausted, lathered animal. She felt badly about the horse, but also annoyed that the foreman was being so rude to Luis, making him look bad before the men. "It's too bad you don't care as much about people as you do about animals," she snapped. "You're more worried about the horse than whether I was hurt or not."

He tipped his hat back and she couldn't read the look he gave her. "Animals are a man's responsibility. A man can depend on a good horse like that chestnut, but he can't always depend on people, especially women."

Holt snickered and she felt herself go brick-red. "That's telling her, boss!"

Trace frowned at the man, started to say something, stopped. She wondered again what it was that made him hate women so?

But the boy, Maverick, turned on Trace. "You got no call to speak to her that way."

Luis sneered slightly at the half-breed boy. "Keep out of this. I can protect the lady without any help from a wet-eared half-breed kid."

Cimarron felt compelled to rush in, seeing the boy's humiliated face. "He was trying to help, Luis."

But Luis frowned at both Trace and Maverick. "I'm perfectly capable of protecting you, señorita. Come, let's go back to the ranch."

They reined around.

Trace called after them, "Walk those horses back, and have the stableboy give them a good rubdown and cool 'em out before watering them."

Luis turned to give him a withering glare, not favoring him with an answer.

So they rode back to the ranch at a walk, and in silence. Cimarron felt troubled, torn with emotions. Last night she had been in the cowboy's embrace, this afternoon she had been in Luis's, and Trace had seen it. *So what?* She thought defiantly. *What did she care what the moody wrangler thought?* She ran her tongue over her lips absently, almost seeming to taste his kiss. What would Luis's kiss be like? More gallant, of course, not brutal and demanding like the cowboy's. Luis was older, handsome in a refined way. She couldn't keep herself from wondering what Luis looked like without clothing. Were his muscles as hard and sinewy? Did he have scars here and there from the hard life of a ranch? Her eyes went down below his belt and her face colored as she wondered if he were as virile. . . .

Luis cleared his throat, interrupting her thoughts. "I'm sorry, señorita, that our picnic was interrupted."

She favored him with a flirtatious glance. "We surely know each other now well enough for you to call me Cimarron," she smiled at him.

He brightened considerably. "I have to tell you, Cimarron, back there, when I pulled you off that runaway horse, held you in my arms. . . ." His voice trailed off and he cleared his throat. "No, it's hardly proper to say such things to a real lady whom I hardly know."

She was touched. "You're such a gentleman, Luis. It's so refreshing after that rough cowboy. Why, it was amazing how you restrained yourself in dealing with that ruffian. I don't know why you take any guff off that Trace. Why don't you run him off the ranch?"

"What?" He looked dumbfounded.

"Well, after all, he is just a foreman, and you could surely find another. Maybe old Sanchez—"

"Hardly." Luis grinned at her as if enjoying a secret joke. "The Don thinks nobody can do things as well as Trace, so nothing can be changed around here as long as he is still alive and in control of the Triple D. Besides, if Trace goes, the whole crew would probably leave with him. Remember, cowboys are impossible to get right now, they're all off fighting the war."

"Well, double damnation!" She was incredulous. "You mean you have to put up with that sass because help is hard to get? I'd at least speak to the Don about him."

Luis shrugged. "And risk making the old man furious with me? He wouldn't believe anything bad about Trace."

Cimarron felt indignant. "But if I told him how rude and impossible Trace is—"

"Cimarron," Luis said gently, "the trouble between Trace and me . . ." He hesitated as if loath to hurt her feelings. "Well, I hope you will not ask too many questions. It was . . . a private matter."

A woman, she thought. They were both in love with the same woman. She looked at Luis thoughtfully. The man was old enough to be Trace's father. What woman could it have been? Then a thought came to her. "Luis," she said slowly, "tell me about Velvet Eyes."

He winced, looked away, and those gestures told her everything. Luis had been in love with Velvet Eyes, too. The son had been in love with his father's beautiful young second wife, just as the foreman had been.

"*Si*. What do you want to know?" His tone was guarded, which told her nothing and everything.

She shrugged, a bit jealous. "Whatever you think I should know."

They rode at a walk for a long time before Luis spoke again. "Has someone else told you about Ojos de Pana?"

Velvet Eyes, she thought, Ojos de Pana, an apt description for the beautiful girl she could see in her imagination. "No," she said truthfully, "I mentioned her to Trace, and he acted as if I had struck a raw nerve."

"For him, she is."

She knew she shouldn't, but she couldn't control her curiosity. "And yourself?"

He gave her a long, thoughtful look. "I'll admit what you're thinking. Somehow I trust you, Cimarron. Why do you think I never married? I'm a hell-raiser with the ladies, anyone will tell you that. I wanted a woman I could never have. Velvet Eyes was the most gentle, beautiful woman I had ever known, the only one I thought I could ever love enough to marry, until you showed up in the dining room last night. . . ." His voice trailed off as they approached the ranchero, and she waited in vain for him to continue before realizing he would say no more.

They rode up before the house. An old buggy with a sleepy horse stood tied out front.

"Dr. Hastings must be here," Luis said as he dismounted.

"I hope the Don's not worse," she said.

"Sometimes he just comes by to have a drink." Luis came around to lift her down. For just a quick moment, his hands lingered on her waist. As she looked up at him, she thought the handsome Spaniard would bend his head and kiss her, but he only looked into her eyes. "How much do you know of Trace?"

"Not very much." She tried to remember the story she and Trace had agreed upon. Could Luis look into her face and know that her lips had already been kissed by the rough cowboy, that his hands had caressed every inch of her silken skin? Would Luis be interested in her if he knew the cowboy had claimed her body first?

He let go of her waist, almost reluctantly. "Señorita," he said softly, "Someday, this ranch and all that goes with it will be mine. When the war is over and the old man has finally died, I'll deal with that rude cowboy. Then, when I become Don, I'll choose a bride, the mother of the future heirs of the Triple D."

She looked away, abruptly aware of his nearness, the warmth of his hands on her waist. "I'm not sure I know what you mean, señor."

He handed the reins to the small Mexican boy who came running from the stable. "Forgive me for being forward, señorita, but I think you do."

She turned to the small boy to keep from looking at Luis. "The horses need a good rubdown and that one needs some liniment," she said to the stablehand. "Señor Luis was forced to ride it hard to rescue me from a runaway."

The boy looked over the pair of horses, disapproval evident in his features as he led them away.

Luis took her elbow, walked her across the courtyard, past the bubbling fountain. His big spurs jangled in the silence. "Where are you from, Señorita Cimarron?"

"Uh, northwest of here," she gulped, then chided herself silently for not being fast enough to make up some fictitious relative in Victoria or Galveston. "I do hope the Don isn't worse," she said, to change the subject.

Luis said, "Oh, sometimes the doctor just drops by to visit, but the attacks do seem to be happening more often since they first started last spring. "I suppose it's just a matter of time—"

As he opened the door, the tiny chihuahua bounced out into the courtyard, barking madly.

Swearing under his breath, Luis tried to sidestep the dog, but it attacked, grabbed his pant leg, snarling.

Luis looked more annoyed than angry. "I swear, sooner or later . . ."

But Cimarron knelt, scooped the dog up, and it licked her face happily. "Now Luis, you wouldn't hurt the little rascal, would you? He really didn't bite you."

Luis swore in Spanish under his breath. "This makes eleven pairs of my best riding breeches. Fine-quality, custom-made pants are hard to get as the war drags on."

The dog licked her face again and growled at Luis. Cimarron couldn't help but laugh at the Spaniard's dour expression as he glared back at the chihuahua.

"You little scamp!" she scolded, hugging him to her, "Whose dog is he anyway, Luis, I figure Trace's—"

"Tequila belonged to Velvet Eyes," Luis said slowly, regretfully. "I wish she'd taken it with her when she and her Yankee captain . . ." His voice trailed off, and then he seemed to remember Cimarron's presence and did not finish the sentence.

"Luis," she asked, remembering Trace's pained expression, "where did she go? Why did she go?"

Luis shuffled his feet, looked away. "She was Cheyenne," he said, "She decided to return to her people." The answer sounded too pat, too rehearsed.

"Why don't I believe you?" She patted the dog's head.

His aristocratic face grew pained. "Don't ask, Cimarron. Things are bad enough around here with the old man gradually dying—"

"What's wrong with him?"

Luis shrugged. "The doctor says it's some kind of stomach tumor, or cancer that's gradually spreading. If you ask me, a broken heart and mind is speeding it up."

They entered the study. She put the small dog on the floor. "Then someone should reach her, let her know—"

"Cimarron," he said, "if you left your husband for another man, would you come back because he was dying?"

The enormity of his words sank in as she stared up at him, remembered Trace's bitter words. *A whore,* he had called her, *a whore.*

"Maybe you're mistaken about the broken heart," she said, suddenly jealous of Velvet Eyes, her hypnotic spell over men. "Perhaps even the doctor doesn't know what he's talking about. You should get another opinion."

Luis crossed himself reverently. "I pray God you are right, señorita, that he will live a hundred years, but I see him going downhill every day, in spite of everything the doctor can do."

"But another doctor—"

"What other doctor?" he chided her gently. "Cimarron, there's a war on. Nearly every doctor has gone to take care of the wounded. Hastings is not very good, I'll admit that, but he's the only one left in the county right now."

He ran his hand through his gray-streaked black hair. "I don't think the Don can make it, but believe me, I light candles and enlist the padres' prayers when I'm in San Antonio. If he can last until the war ends, I'll take him back East to specialists."

"That's what Trace said, too."

Luis frowned. "He'd better pray the Don lives forever," he said, a glint of anger in his eyes. "When I finally take over this ranch, I'll deal with that arrogant cowboy at long last. We've had a showdown coming for months now. Until then, I'll not upset the old man over it."

Cimarron patted his arm sympathetically. "You are a good person, Luis, to think about what might upset the Don. But I agree the cowboy needs to be taken down a notch."

He looked at her curiously. "You don't like him? Strange, I seemed to sense a chemistry between you. I was afraid you might be smitten by his rough charm."

The memory came back to her, the sweet-scented hay, the warmth of his arms, the sweetness of his demanding kiss. He was an animal, she thought, a dominating, hard-driving male animal who had forced himself between her thighs. She blinked, trying not to remember his mouth covering her nipple, making her arch up against him despite everything she could do. And again, here in this darkened study, she had rubbed herself against him like some wanton tart, eager to feel his male hardness throbbing within her, mating her, making her surrender to him. . . .

"How silly of you," she lied, angry with herself for the images haunting her. "I can't imagine what any woman, even a saloon girl, would see in that unsophisticated brute when there's an elegant gentleman like yourself around."

He brightened, took her hand, kissed her fingertips gently. "Do I dare hope . . . ?" His voice trailed off, as if afraid of offending her delicate sensibilities.

"We've only just met," she put him off with a wave of her hand, "I—I'm not sure I will stay."

"Stay! Of course you'll stay!" His eyes looked down into hers anxiously. "You're our house guest—"

"That's just it, señor, how long can I impose on the Durango hospitality without—?"

"Oh, is that all?" He seemed to breathe a sigh of relief. "I'm sure I speak for the old Don when I say you're welcome as a house guest indefinitely."

She frowned. "You don't understand, Luis. I suppose you would call me proud. I feel I have to do something useful, you know, earn my keep, to be able to stay."

He leaned against the desk, fiddling with a button on the sleeve of the fine shirt. "Very well, I'll find you a job to do, if you insist." His tone was light, bantering, as he opened the desk and took out some accounting ledgers.

"Don't make fun of me," she flared. "I hate men who are condescending. I really am quite capable."

He didn't look convinced but he said, "All right. I don't suppose you know bookkeeping? The señora started keeping the ranch's accounts a few days before she left. But I don't suppose a pretty thing like you—"

"Oh, but my Uncle Ransford was teaching me to do accounts," she said impulsively. "He thought someday I might be able to work in his store—"

She stumbled to a halt. *Double damnation, Cimarron!* she thought, *you have just given him clues to your family background, should he be interested.* But Luis did not seem to have noticed.

"Wonderful, señorita." He reached into the desk, got a small strongbox from a drawer. "We keep some gold right here, which is silly. It all should be in our bank. But the Don is old-fashioned and likes to have cash available."

He smiled as he put the small box back in the drawer and closed it. "Then it's all settled! I'll let you help me with the ranch's bookkeeping, to the best of your ability."

His condescending tone told her he didn't take her abilities seriously, was only thinking to humor her, save her pride. Would he be in for a pleasant surprise when she showed him she really could balance books and do accounts.

He looked at her, a cigar and match in his hand. "Do you mind if I smoke?"

Such a polite gentleman, she thought with warmth as she shook her head and watched him light the cigar. And such a contrast with his foreman.

"Luis, I've wondered about the children of this ranchero," she said pensively. "Is there no school?"

He snorted. "School for a bunch of ranchhands' brats? The señora and the *padre* from the village had started one last fall, but when she left . . . well, that ended that. She taught right here in the study, using my books." He gestured toward the many expensive leather-bound volumes.

"I'd love to continue the school," Cimarron said, looking around the study. "It would make me feel more like I was earning my way, being of some use to the ranch—"

"But teach Mexican kids to read?" he scoffed, blowing smoke as he walked over to the big mirror and studied his reflection with a smug, satisfied smile. "They'll just work cattle or be servants the rest of their lives. It's throwing pearls before swine."

She frowned, not quite liking him so much as before. "I don't consider it a waste to teach any child to read," she answered. "One never knows where a seed, once planted, might grow and bear fruit."

Luis laughed, blew smoke toward the ceiling as he came back over to her. "That's just what Velvet Eyes would have said." She was not sure if he was making fun, being critical, but she was annoyed, and he must have seen it in her eyes because he crushed out his cigar and bent to kiss her hand. "For you, my dear, anything. If you wish to start a little school for the ranch children here in the study, I will help. But only because I admire you so much!"

Cimarron felt his lips linger over her hand. Besides being handsome and rich, Luis Durango had power in this state. If the law should ever track her down, no one could hang her or even send her to jail with Luis Durango's protection. Luis and Trace. Trace or Luis. Which one of the two had Velvet Eyes preferred? The thought came to her suddenly, even though she didn't want to think about it.

There was a noise in the hall and Luis dropped her hand suddenly, as if afraid someone might see him kissing her fingers. An old gray-haired man stuck his head through the door.

Luis crossed the room, shook his hand. "Ah, Dr. Hastings! How is our patient today? Come into the study for a glass of Madeira."

Cimarron saw a man with gray hair and a yellow-stained mustache that drooped under a red-veined nose and watery eyes. She thought he looked like an elderly walrus.

Luis steered him over to her. "Señorita Cimarron, may I present Dr. Hastings?"

She inclined her head slightly, and he bowed low. "Charmed, my dear," he said in a nasal, Yankee voice.

"How nice to meet you," she said politely. "Judging by your accent, I'd say you're not a Texan?"

"Hardly." His hand trembled as he set the small black medical bag on the desk. "Connecticut, actually, I got caught down here when the war started." He looked over at Luis and licked his lips. "It's very warm today. I believe, señor, you offered a drink—"

"Oh, a thousand pardons," Luis said, reaching for the crystal decanter. "Cimarron?"

She nodded, accepted the wine glass, tasted it while she watched the slight, stoop-shouldered doctor gulp his. A drinking problem, she thought sympathetically, and being from Connecticut, no wonder he was not in service.

"Dr. Hastings," she said politely as she sipped the wine, "how did you come to be in Texas in the first place?"

He smiled ruefully and held out his empty glass to Luis,

who refilled it with a shrug of his shoulders to Cimarron.

"I was an army doctor for many years." He accepted the glass eagerly. "First I was stationed up at Fort Smith in '58 and '59, then transferred to Texas just before the war started." He laughed bitterly. "Fact of the matter is, I was drunk the day the troops pulled out when Texas declared for the Confederacy, so I'm trapped here till it's over."

Cimarron glanced helplessly at Luis, embarrassed at the confession and unsure what to say as Dr. Hastings gulped the second drink.

"The good doctor is sometimes too candid," Luis said smoothly, trying like a perfect gentleman to gloss things over, Cimarron thought gratefully.

The doctor finished the drink, picked up his bag. "Perhaps I am," he admitted. "Now I've got to get over to the Rocking R; both the little Rowland children are down with the croup."

Luis nodded, offered the man a cigar. "Tell us, Doctor, what's the news in the western section of the county?"

"Not good." The man bit off the tip, spat it out. "Comanche raiding further this direction than anyone can remember since the Forties. At the Bar X, I heard the rumors the Comancheros are back supplying guns to them again."

"Those heartless renegades." Luis swore softly under his breath. "Some men will do anything for money."

"They're animals, all right," the doctor sighed as he leaned forward to allow the other to light his cigar. "Hanging's too good for Comancheros. But they're dug in so deep in the New Mexico mountains, no army'll ever manage to invade their stronghold."

Cimarron sighed at the thought of Comanche raiding, the slaughter, the burning. "The Comancheros are in Texas, then?"

Luis's face was dark, foreboding. "I heard that myself; didn't want to believe it, though. Trading guns to the warriors in exchange for livestock and captives, no doubt. I wish I could get my hands on some of those devils!" He clenched his fists in a choking motion.

The doctor inhaled his cigar. "You may get the chance yet,

señor. The combined group is raiding west of here; some think they may even finally get into Fredericksburg and the capital, and some of the areas close by."

Cimarron felt a shiver run up her back. "That close?"

Luis saw the expression on her face. "Now, Doctor," he said gallantly, "we are scaring the lady."

The doctor smoked, rubbed at his red-veined nose. "Sorry to do that. It's just that there's something afoot; the Comanche seem to be restless, from the reports I'm hearing. Folks are saying it may be leading up to a big raid, bigger than anything we've ever seen—"

"Let's speak of other things," Luis broke in with a concerned look toward Cimarron. "I'm sure it's all just talk. Now, how is our patient?"

"Much better." The old man paused in the door of the study. "It just amazes me how a couple of weeks ago I thought him almost at death's door. Today, he seems in excellent health."

Cimarron bit her lip, put down her glass. "You're saying you might have made a mistake in your diagnosis?"

The doctor frowned, scratched his head. "I didn't say that, miss. Matter of fact, I'm only guessing at my diagnosis. Don't remember ever having a case like this before, deep depression, vomiting, diarrhea, rapid pulse, sweating—not quite like what I would expect from a malignancy."

Luis gave Cimarron a knowing look and she wondered how much the physician knew about Velvet Eyes's breaking the Don's heart. "Anyway," he said, taking the doctor's elbow and escorting him to the hall, "we are planning a big party for the old man's sixty-fifth birthday late this month. I hope he'll be in fine shape for that."

The doctor nodded. "Hate to see September and October. We always called it harvest time back home, but in Texas, it seems to mean Indian raids."

Cimarron shuddered. Anyone raised in the Lone Star State knew the Comanches used the bright, moonlit nights of autumn so often for raiding that they were called "Comanche moons." She didn't want to think about it. "A party?" she asked.

Luis looked at her sadly. "I wanted to give the old man's many friends one last chance to visit with him before..." His voice trailed off, he crossed himself, swallowed hard.

She felt tears come to her eyes at his tender concern. "You are a good person, Luis," she said softly. "Not many people would be so thoughtful."

Dr. Hastings nodded. "Everyone is saying what a nice gesture it is, Luis. When they ask me how the Don is, I've been telling them they'd better make the party because the next time they see him, he will probably be in his casket."

Luis looked pained. "He's not dead yet," he said with conviction, "and the old man's a fighter. I pray your diagnosis is wrong."

"I hope so, too," the doctor mumbled as he puffed his cigar and hiccupped.

Luis took his elbow and the three went into the hall, out into the courtyard.

They stood there a moment under a giant rose-pink oleander bush, looking toward the house.

"You won't stay for dinner?" Cimarron asked politely as she broke off a twig and stuck it absently in her mouth.

"No, thank you just the same. I've got to get to the Rowlands' place." He noticed the blossom and smiled as he untied his buggy. "Such a pretty flower," he sighed. "We don't grow these up north, too cold, you know. Oleander is one of the few things I'll miss if I ever get back to Connecticut."

Luis frowned, reached over to take the twig from her lips, tossed it away. "There might be a bug on that," he smiled.

She laughed and turned toward the doctor. "You'll be at the birthday party?" she asked as he climbed into the buggy. "I'm really looking forward to it."

"Of course, my dear. I'm so glad you're here. They'll all need emotional support when..." He rolled his eyes significantly, clucked to the horse, drove away.

With a sigh, Cimarron watched him drive off down the road. "He's a pathetic little man, isn't he?"

Luis nodded. "He really doesn't belong here; Texas is much too savage for him. When the war's over, he can go back to Connecticut and maybe he'll stop drinking."

He took her arm. "Let's go have some dinner, my dear. I apologize that we didn't get to have our picnic, but we can spread it out here on the courtyard by the fountain, pretend we're out on the prairie."

"Of course. That'll be fun."

But about an hour later, she began to feel a little nauseated. It occurred to her that the cold chicken might have become a little tainted in the heat. She didn't say anything to Luis, knowing how shocked and apologetic he'd be.

She went to her room while he went to visit the old man. Cimarron lay down across the bed, thinking what a fine person he was, how much she liked the Triple D. She had never found a place where she felt so at home, a place that drew her so much. She could live happily on this ranch forever, without any regrets.

She slept an hour and felt better, went down and got herself a glass of milk from the kitchen. No one seemed to be about but a girl polishing silver.

"Where is Señor Luis?" she asked.

The girl yawned, *"De nada.* Out in the barn or taking a nap, perhaps."

Cimarron tapped her nails against the table. She was not used to being idle. She started to offer to help the servant polish the silver, then decided Rosa might punish the girl for being friendly to her. She looked forward to her little school, despite Luis's lack of enthusiasm. Even doing the accounts would be interesting. But for now . . .

She decided to explore the house a little while she waited for Luis to show up. If the old man were feeling better, perhaps Luis would introduce him to her later.

She stuck her head in the study door and the little dog came out from under a sofa pillow, yawning. With a friendly wag of his tail, he trotted along with her companionably. She explored most of the house. Upstairs, she tiptoed past the door she knew was the old man's so she wouldn't disturb him. She opened one door and knew immediately it belonged to Trace. There was something masculine, rugged about it, like the man himself. A bottle of tequila stood on the chest of drawers, a pair of chaps were thrown carelessly across a chair. A painting of the hill country hung over the bed. An Indian rug lay on the bare floor. Everything looked slightly scuffed and worn, as if the owner did not care too much for possessions and spent little time indoors, anyway. The room smelled very slightly of tobacco and leather.

Out in the hall, the little dog went to another door, whined as it scratched at it.

"Here boy, here Tequila." She snapped her fingers. It cocked its head, wagged its tail, then fixed the soft brown eyes on her and started scratching frantically at the closed door. Deep grooves in the bottom of the door told her the dog did this often.

Curiously, Cimarron opened the door and followed the dog inside. Dim light through the closed draperies half hid, half illuminated the large bedroom's massive Spanish furniture, crouched like specters. Cobwebs hung from the bedposts, mute evidence that no one had entered this room in many months. It smelled musty as a tomb. The tiny dog searched and sniffed every corner, whimpering as it looked.

"What are you looking for, boy?" she asked.

The small dog cocked its head at her, hopped up on the big canopy bed, and burrowed in under the pillows with a satisfied sigh.

Cimarron ran her hand over the furniture, looked at the telltale dust. On the dresser was an ornate silver comb and brush set, a crystal perfume bottle. A slight fragrance seemed to invade the stale air, and she looked around curiously for a vase of flowers. She felt the hair rise on her neck as she had the sense of being watched. She turned slowly. Then she saw the large portrait hanging slightly crooked on the adobe wall. Cobwebs draped the ornate frame. The evening light cast eerie shadows on the girl's face in the portrait.

She was Indian, Cimarron thought, studying the beautiful

features. The girl wore a rouge-colored dress and dusky-red oleander in her blue-black hair. In her arms she held a brown chihuahua dog. The eyes in the portrait were luminous, gentle. They seemed to follow Cimarron's every move, almost as if the portrait were alive. There was something familiar about the eyes. Yet, as Cimarron searched her memory, she was sure she had not met the girl.

The scent of perfume was almost cloying, yet the only flowers in the room were those painted in the portrait. The longer she stared at the picture, the more it seemed to her the woman almost breathed, almost seemed about to speak. *Was she losing her mind?* Automatically, Cimarron reached to straighten the frame. But before she could touch it, she heard a slight noise from the doorway and whirled around.

Rosa stood there, arms akimbo, eyes blazing.

"How dare you enter this room?" she challenged. "Already you imagine yourself in her place, taking over, using her things!" She gestured toward the dresser with its crystal perfume bottles, the silver brush and comb.

"No, I don't—"

"Don't you, *puta?*" Rosa snarled, advancing on her, "don't you weigh a decision between the men while they all pant after you? You think to take Velvet Eyes's place."

Cimarron turned slowly, looked again at the portrait. Again the woman in the picture almost seemed to breathe, to speak to her. "So this is Velvet Eyes," she whispered with a nod. "So very young, so aptly named . . ."

When she glanced around she saw the Mexican girl's eyes glittered with tears. "She'll be back," the girl said desperately. "Someday, the señora will return, when the cruel Don is dead, and until then, I'll protect her things, her position from those who would steal them, like you."

She went to the portrait, stood looking at it almost reverently. "I never come here," she whispered, "not even to clean. The room seems almost haunted." She glared accusingly at Cimarron. "And now you defile it—"

"No matter what you think," Cimarron said gently, "I'm not trying to take her place—"

"You couldn't in a million years, half-breed *puta!*" the girl spat at her. "And I'll protect everything for her until Velvet Eyes returns!"

Cimarron started to say something, decided she was wasting her time. The girl hated her for more reasons than Cimarron could fathom. Gathering up the small dog, Cimarron swept past the housekeeper and out of the room.

Chapter Eight

Rosa glared at the blonde as the girl swept out of the room. How dare that Cimarron snoop about, defiling the beloved señora's things with her touch! Well, that *puta* didn't fool Rosa. That half-gringa girl had been looking over the men of the Triple D, trying to choose one for herself. Already that blonde was thinking of herself as señora, imagining herself in Velvet Eyes's place, enjoying the good life of mistress of this rich ranching empire.

Hah! That puta *had better think twice!* Rosa ran her finger through the heavy dust on the low chest below the painting. *Velvet Eyes.* Oh, how Rosa adored her and missed her. She studied the painting, thinking it did not do her beloved mistress credit. No, Ojos de Pana was much more lovely than the portrait. It had been hanging here even before Rosa came to the ranch. She studied the chihuahua's face. Poco. That dog was dead long ago. Rosa did not resent the fact that the artist had loved the señora. Everyone did.

With a sigh, Rosa reached up to brush away the festooned cobwebs on the ornate frame, then drew back uneasily. There was something frightening to her about this room, as if it hid some secret. *Si,* even the room was sad that Velvet Eyes had gone away. It was a shrine that must not be touched or cleaned until the message came that her beloved señora was returning. Rosa knew she would someday, as soon as Velvet Eyes heard the old Don was dead.

Closing the door carefully, Rosa went down the hall,

inspecting critically as she walked. She did not manage the servants as well as her mistress had. Maybe it was because the others didn't like Rosa. Those lazy servants! Rosa frowned with righteous indignation. The hacienda was not as efficiently run as it had been before, but that would all change when the señora returned. Rosa could not fault her for running away with a handsome captain if the Don had been as cruel to her as Rosa's lover hinted he was.

That and a little greedy ambition had made her decide to help her love with his plans. With the Don dead, Velvet Eyes would return. Sanchez. Her husband was the very last block between her and what she wanted. She smiled secretly to herself. The reason she could see through the blond one so clearly was that she herself had often dreamed of what it would be like to be a member of this family.

Rosa went down the stairs, paused before the big pier mirror in the giant entry hall. She was running out of time. All she had were her looks, which would soon be gone, like an early-blooming, fast-fading flower. Critically she leaned into the mirror, studying her face. Were those tiny crow's feet about her eyes? Were the lines around her mouth any deeper? In less than five years, she would be thirty years old, and she would look every day of it by then.

Rosa had only a little time to make a secure niche for herself in the Durango family. She was not fool enough to think she could hold her love's attention forever. But if she were married to him in the church, she would be a Durango, with money and power. Rosa was no fool. She did not even care if he took a mistress later, once her place in this family was permanent.

Rosa prepared supper, thinking how nice it would be when the señora returned. After the war, they would search for Dallas. Rosa had always been a little jealous of the high-spirited tomboy, and that made her feel guilty, because Velvet Eyes loved Dallas so. Maybe Dallas had met some nice young man up north and married and would only come home for a visit now and then. *Si.* That would be perfect.

She laid out a tray for the old Don, remembering not to use the pepper mill. His food must be kept very bland so he would not be ill for his big celebration. The doctor said chili peppers and spices were bad for his stomach, but he was such a stubborn old man. Still, it was up to Rosa to make sure he did not relapse and miss his own party. The fact that he was still alive was amazing, but then, he had the courage and heart of a lion. Idle gossip had been planning Don Diego's funeral for months.

Rosa could not help but notice that blond *puta's* expression at dinner. The girl had a smile like a cat with cream on its whiskers. Both Trace and Luis hung on the girl's every word, ignoring Rosa completely. Even Rosa's own child, Turquoise, was captivated by the newcomer's warmth and personality. Only stupid, faithful Sanchez seemed unaffected by Cimarron. Rosa could feel her husband's eyes on her continually, as sad and faithful as the dog that sat under that blonde's chair, begging for food.

That was her señora's dog, Rosa thought grimly as she ate. How dare that Cimarron take over the whole house and Velvet Eyes's pet, too? That girl had to go.

Rosa retired early, unable to stand the competition in the study when the others gathered for an after-dinner drink. Cimarron had such bright, lively conversation, and Rosa could barely read and write her name. The señora had taught her that. Finally, everyone retired.

Rosa still lay sleepless as Sanchez came to bed, but she closed her eyes.

"Rosa?" he whispered. *The fat old fool.* Grimly, Rosa kept her eyes shut, knowing he was too hesitant to wake her. She had let him mount her two months ago for the first time in ten years. Now, every night, he came to bed hopefully.

She lay very still, and finally he sighed and turned his back. If he only knew why she had finally let him make love to her. She almost laughed, suppressed it as his sonorous snoring began. Rosa had thought she was pregnant, knew there would be a scandal if she were, since she hadn't let her husband touch her since the night they married.

Ten long years ago . . . Rosa sighed, remembering. It was

too sad, too tragic to remember the past. She had missed becoming a Forester, and now, her sights were set on becoming a Durango. But this was her last chance at money and position. All she had to offer was her beauty, and she was losing that fast. . . .

Even now, she could remember the stink of the adobe hovel outside Austin. Her parents were Mexican peasants who could neither read nor write. Like Sanchez, they were patient, uncomplaining, always praying to the saints for enough tortillas to feed the brood of hungry children, which grew larger every year. She saw her future, and it was just like her mother's. But Rosa was ambitious, determined to do better. At fourteen she ran away, intending to find herself a position with one of the rich gringo families of Austin.

But she was too ignorant to know how one did this. She starved for a few days, rifled ladies' purses when they weren't looking, stole fruit from open-air markets. Then one day as she hid and watched, a young man on the finest horse Rosa had ever seen rode up to the market. "Señor," he inquired of the Mexican shopkeeper, "might you know of a good personal maid who needs a position?"

The fat shopkeeper wiped his hands on his apron. "Señor Forester, has your sister run off another servant then? How many does this make?"

The blond man looked embarrassed. He was not much older than she herself, Rosa thought. "Six since last year." He flecked a speck of dust off his fine coat. "Emily's reputation is getting around, I'm afraid. No girl seems poor or desperate enough to work for my sister."

Rosa studied the handsome boy. He had an aristocratic manner, with eyes as pale aquamarine as turquoise stones.

Rosa stepped out. "Please, señor," she begged, "I would like very much to have the job."

The shopkeeper scowled, waved her away with his apron. "Off with you, you bit of garbage! Anyone can see you know nothing of being a fine lady's servant."

"I can learn." She rubbed one bare foot over the other.

The shopkeeper laughed, ran his tongue across his gapped teeth. "If she knew Señorita Forester, she would not offer, would she, Señor Edwin?"

Both of them laughed. Edwin Forester looked sheepish. "I'm afraid he's right, small one. My sister would eat someone like you for dinner. No one can deal with Emily, not even Mother, and the Iron Lady once stood off Indians."

Very slowly, she let her blouse slip down one shoulder so that the young gentleman could see the swell of her young, ripe breasts. "Please, señor," she begged. "I will wash myself and work very hard. Winter is coming on, and I have no place to go."

She saw him squirm uneasily in his saddle. "Well, perhaps Mother might be willing to give you a try, since no one else wants the job...."

The shopkeeper frowned. "Señor Edwin, the Iron Lady will be annoyed with you for bringing this *puta* home—"

"I am not a *puta!*" Rosa whirled on him, "I am poor but respectable, and I am willing to try very hard to please the Señorita Emily."

Rosa lifted her skirts a little so the gringo could see her trim ankles. "Please, Señor Forester, give me a chance."

"I don't know; Mother said to find someone with references." His voice trailed off and he pursed his thin lips. For the first time, she saw he had a weak chin and jaw line. Señorita Forester must be as frightful as a she bobcat, Rosa thought, seeing the fear and hesitation on the young man's face.

She leaned over a little so he could see the swell of her young, ripe breasts from his saddle. "Please, señor. I will try very hard." She would try very hard to entice the young man, she thought. Could a poor Mexican girl from the slums of Austin marry into a rich, gringo family like the Foresters'? Stranger things had happened.

And so it was that arrogant Edwin Forester took her home and presented his mother with the new personal maid he had found for his sister, Emily. Miss Emily and the whole Forester family turned out to be worse than she expected.

Rosa thought about the Foresters now as she lay on her

bed, listening to Sanchez snore next to her, to Turquoise move in her sleep in the next room.

Rosa had found out very quickly why Emily Forester had gone through six maids in less than a year. If Rosa hadn't been desperate, she would have quit herself.

At twenty-five, homely Emily was on her way to becoming Austin's richest spinster. Emily needed more than money to snare a man, Rosa thought grimly a few weeks later as she tried to lace up the heavy girl's corset. "You'll have to take a deep breath, señorita," she suggested gently, "Or I'll be unable to get you into that new dress."

The girl cast a baleful eye on her, her face so close Rosa could see the slight blond mustache on the girl's upper lip. "Are you saying I'm fat, Mex?"

"No, no," Rosa answered quickly. "Perhaps I shrank the dress when I washed it. It is all my fault."

The horse-faced woman nodded. "Exactly right! I have a lovely figure." She primped in front of the mirror, peeping at herself over her fan. "Don't you think so?"

For a brewers' carthorse, Rosa thought, but of course she only gave a nod. "A young gentleman is coming to call?"

Emily played with the fan. "Well, no," she said, and Rosa immediately regretted asking. "I wasn't terribly interested in that last one, anyway. But when my new dress comes in from New York, Mother plans to introduce me to a wealthy young man from Galveston."

Pity the poor young man from Galveston, Rosa thought but she only struggled to button the plaid dress.

Señora Forester, dressed as always in dove gray, entered the bedroom just then. "Emily," she scolded, "I believe you've gained weight again. I'm counting on your being able to get into that new dress I've ordered from New York. After all, you aren't young anymore, and that man from Galveston may be your very last chance!"

Emily fanned herself furiously, her plain, horsey face red with annoyance and anger. "Now, Mama, I hardly eat anything at all—"

"Emily," her mother glared coldly, "I know you pay the servants to sneak food up to your room. You are the oldest of my children, and I want all of you married before I go to my reward—"

"Mother," Emily sneered, "you will outlive all your children, to make sure none of us gets a moment of happiness, then you will try to intimidate Saint Peter. We know why people call you 'The Iron Lady' behind your back."

Harriet Forester fixed her with eyes as sharp as bits of broken glass. "Don't be rude, Emily. I only want what's best for all my children, and that means proper marriages. Remember, my family was one of the original three hundred."

"How could I ever forget?" Emily fired back. "You make it sound like we came over on the *Mayflower*."

The Iron Lady looked down her thin nose at her daughter, reached up to pat the steel-gray braids done up on top of her head. "To a Texan, being one of Steven Austin's original three hundred families who settled here is better than coming over on the *Mayflower*. Now, because I control the money, you will do exactly as I tell you, just as everyone else does."

Rosa tried to make herself as inconspicuous as possible while the two argued. Life at the Forester home had been more difficult and degrading than she could ever have imagined. And she soon found out why the homely girl couldn't keep a maid.

Emily Forester had a habit of picking at her food before company, making little noises about how she was so dainty that she ate just like a bird. Then the cook was bribed to send huge plates of leftovers up to Emily's room. The plain, raw-boned girl would gorge herself until she was sick, then stick her finger down her throat.

The first time it happened, Rosa was horrified at the sight of Emily Forester gagging and retching as she hung over a chamber pot, throwing up all the food she had just gobbled. But it soon became a common sight for Rosa. Worse yet, was the fact that it often splashed the bedroom floor around the slop jar.

Emily wiped her mouth, smiled evilly at Rosa. "Now clean it up," she ordered.

"But señorita—"

"Clean it up, I said," Emily's pale face blotched red with anger. "You're nothing but a Mex whore. I'll bet you sleep with Edwin and all his friends from school. If you want to keep your job, clean that mess up!"

Rosa took a deep breath of the sour smell, closed her eyes to the revolting sight. If Emily fired her, where could she go? Already the first blue norther of the winter season had blown in. She could go to work as a whore in a cheap saloon, maybe. Or she could go back to the hovel she had grown up in.

"*Si*, señorita," she said humbly, hating the grinning girl with the most terrible anger she had ever felt toward anyone. It wasn't enough to be humble; Emily would not stop until there was no shred of pride left. As Rosa swallowed hard and cleaned up the mess, she saw the girl watching her with a calculating smile.

"You Mex whore," she sneered. "You're not so pretty crawling around on your knees cleaning up after your betters. I'll teach you to know your place!"

It happened time after time now. Once she had discovered the enjoyment of stuffing herself without worrying about gaining weight, Emily seemed to delight in the game, especially forcing Rosa to get on her knees and clean up after her.

There was only one thing to do: seduce the hesitant Edwin. When he was so enamored of Rosa that he married her, she would get plenty of revenge on her homely sister-in-law. It was difficult to seduce him. He was so terrified of his mother that he was sometimes impotent, but she persisted. One rainy evening, he finally took Rosa's virginity, with awkward fumbling. He pushed her down across the trunk at the foot of his bed. They didn't even take their clothes off, she remembered now. When he had exhausted his own desires, he wiped the stains of her virginity off himself with her skirt and left her sprawled there aching and unsatisfied. Quickly, she learned just how to increase his desire, how to make him want her. But his boyish groping never got any more satisfying. But what did that matter, if he would finally give her his name?

But as she lay in bed one day with him and complained, she found out Edwin was not going to be much of an ally.

He raised one eyebrow and shrugged. "So what? That's the way my sister is. It goes with the job. You'll find the Foresters have a reputation for running roughshod over others, especially if they're poor or socially inferior."

"But Edwin," she whispered, "it's a game with her, so degrading."

Edwin yawned. "What do you expect me to do? I wouldn't dare get involved in a fuss between you and Emily by complaining to the Iron Lady."

"But if your mother knew what Emily was doing—"

"Emily would call you a liar." He looked shamefaced. "Frankly, I'm afraid of Mother. She wouldn't believe it, and we'd both be in big trouble if she finds out about us."

"Someday, Edwin, you'll have to stand up to your mother—"

"Someday, maybe." He looked away, avoided her eyes. "She'd cut off the money, which she controls just as she controls everyone in the family, including my father. Why do you think everyone calls her the 'Iron Lady'? I don't control my share of the money until I'm thirty."

She felt her hopes sink. "You have nothing until then?"

"Only what Harriet Forester gives me. There are two kinds of people in the world, the Iron Lady says, lions and lambs. Eating lambs is what's made our family so rich and powerful that everyone in Austin fears us."

Maybe a grandson would influence the Iron Lady, Rosa thought desperately. If she gave Edwin a son, maybe Rosa could move from the status of lamb into that of a Forester lion. So Rosa planned carefully over the next few weeks as winter came on. The younger children had been sent off to visit relatives for a while, and everything centered on the eligible young man from Galveston who would be arriving to meet Emily. But life in the household got even more humiliating for Rosa as that time approached. She sensed Emily knew of Rosa's ambitions, was determined to thwart them. And Edwin seemed bored with Rosa now.

Then Rosa discovered she was pregnant, about the time a new, pretty kitchen maid came to work. Would Edwin still be interested in Rosa when her body thickened, her breasts swelled with milk? She could see the ambition in the eyes of the new kitchen maid, ready and eager to move into Rosa's spot, accept the extra coins and small rewards such as hair ribbons from the arrogant young heir.

Rosa finally faced her problem the day she couldn't control herself and lost her own dinner while cleaning up Emily's mess. Emily was so enraged that she beat the sick girl about the head with her fan, kicked her when she fell down.

"You idiot!" She raged, her horsey face mottled with color, her pale blond mustache wiggling. "You think you're smart throwing up on my floor?"

So Rosa had to clean up two messes that night. Her bruises ached as she lay in her tiny cot in a back room of the mansion, listening to the cold wind howling around the corners. What would she do? Perhaps when she told him about the baby, Edwin would be pleased.

He was not pleased, of course. He slapped her face until her ears rang. "What do you expect me to do, *puta?* The brat's probably not even mine! Emily told me she'd seen you slipping around with the stableboy, the butler!"

She was horrified at Emily's cruel lie. "No, Edwin, please believe me," she begged. "It's yours! I swear by all the saints it's yours! You know I was a virgin. No man has touched me but you!"

Edwin yawned, boredom evident on his aristocratic face. "You're calling my sister a liar? Even if it were mine, so what? Half the men in Texas have little half-Mexican bastards running around."

"I thought you might want to provide for the child," she said weakly, "I thought if I gave you a son—"

"A Mex son! You must be joking!" His handsome face was pinched with anger, a blond wisp of hair falling down over the pale turquoise eyes. "Surely you don't think a Forester would acknowledge a Mex brat!"

"But a son—"

He laughed coldly, pushed her away. "I'll marry within my own social circle, of course. Some pale-skinned bitch my bossy mother picks out to continue the Forester line. I told you from the first I couldn't cross her, the Iron Lady controls the money and therefore all her children's lives." He took a few coins from his pocket and tossed them on the floor at her feet, not looking her in the face. "You'll have to leave; I don't know what else I can do."

She shook her head, still unbelieving. "I have no place else to go, and no one will hire a pregnant servant girl."

He looked angry that she had created this problem for him. "You should have remembered what I told you about lions and lambs. The Foresters are lions, remember that. Lions don't take pity on lambs. They eat them!"

And with that, he turned and was gone.

Rosa's hands trembled so badly, she could hardly gather up the coins. Her pride almost made her leave them there, but she knew she would need the money. Emily was partly responsible for this. . . .

It was almost dusk as she returned to Emily's bedroom. The delicate pale blue gossamer dress from New York had finally arrived and was spread across the bed. Rosa's legs ached from standing on her feet all morning pressing it.

Emily had just finished gagging herself and throwing up her dinner in the chamber pot. "Oh, there you are, you stupid girl." She grinned maliciously as she wiped her mouth. "Have you forgotten this is the night my beau is arriving from Galveston? You've got to fix my hair and then clean up this mess!"

Rosa sighed, too exhausted, too worried to argue with the chunky girl as she combed Emily's hair, piled it up on her head. But she had to use fake switches to make it look like anything. And finally, she laced the stocky woman into the delicate dress.

"Be careful and don't smudge it," Emily snarled. "Mama says the slightest speck will show on this silk, and there's not another dress so fine in all of Texas."

"Yes, señorita," she answered dully. She could hear the wind picking up outside as the shadows lengthened. *Where was she going to go? What was she going to do?*

"Hurry up, idiot!" Her mistress smacked her smartly with her fan. "The young man will be here any minute now."

A dog barked faintly out front and there were sounds of a carriage arriving. Emily laid down her fan as she fussed with her wispy hair. "You clumsy Mex, help spread my dress out so I can make a nice entry."

Rosa did as she was told and watched as Emily swept from the bedroom like an overloaded ship moving out from port. She heard the girl pause in the hallway, the Iron Lady's voice. "Emily, your fan! Where's your fan? It's so clever to flirt with, you must carry it."

Rosa looked over, saw the fan on the dressing table.

She heard Emily's faint voice. "I guess I left it in my room, Mama, I'll go back for it."

"Be careful of that dress!" Harriet Forester's voice ordered. "The slightest smudge will ruin it! I'll go wait in the parlor for our guests."

Rosa sighed as she looked at the fan, then at the chamber pot. She heard Emily's heavy step coming down the hall. There was one last gesture Rosa wanted to make.

She positioned the fan on the dressing table where it was just barely visible in the dim light of dusk. Then she held her breath as she picked up the chamber pot with its sour mess and climbed up to balance it on the half-opened bedroom door.

She heard Emily clomping down the hall toward the bedroom as Rosa climbed through the window and leaned against the house exterior, listening.

"Rosa, you stupid girl—" she heard Emily's voice as the door creaked— "Where's my—?"

There was a resounding crash, the sound of china shattering against the floor and the most ear-splitting, horrified scream she had ever heard. "Mama!" Emily wailed, "Oh, Mama! Come quick! My dress! My beautiful dress!"

Emily screamed and screamed again while Rosa leaned against the house outside the window, convulsed with bitter laughter. Then she turned and sneaked away into the darkness, knowing the Foresters would be looking for her. . . .

* * *

Sanchez muttered in his sleep and Rosa blinked, staring at the ceiling. Ten years, she thought, ten years ago. . . . She had had a terrible time the next couple of weeks after her few coins ran out. She picked up men and let them climb on her in dark, dirty alleys for a few pennies. But as her belly began to swell, the men were not as interested. Then she stole wallets, ladies' purses, food from markets. The winter was coming on, she had no place to go and no money. She could not go back to her family's hovel. There was not enough food for those already there.

Then the Holy Mother must have taken pity on her, because at the point when she was starving and the police had caught her stealing food, Señora Diego de Durango entered the picture. *Ojos de Pana.* Velvet Eyes. Loved by everyone, but worshiped by the grateful Rosa.

Tears came now as she stared sleeplessly up at the ceiling, listened to her child, Edwin Forester's daughter with the turquoise eyes, stirring in the next room.

Oh, Velvet Eyes, she thought, why didn't you take me with you when you ran away? My husband and child mean nothing to me compared with you. I would have gone East with you and your Yankee Captain to be your maid. No one can do your hair as I have always done it. No one could press your dresses as carefully as I did. I would have walked through hell for you because of your kindness to a starving, pregnant girl. . . .

She wondered if her lover were still awake. She sat up quietly on the edge of the bed, listening to Sanchez's gentle snoring. She had told her love it would be after midnight. For a moment, she felt a slight twinge of conscience. Velvet Eyes would not approve. Edwin Forester's thin, aristocratic face came to her mind. *Lions and lambs* . . . well, Rosa had learned how to become a lion. Her gentle old husband was one of the lambs.

Guiltily, she glanced at him before tiptoeing out of the room. Poor old Sanchez, offering her marriage when the Don and his wife brought Rosa to the ranchero. He never asked or seemed to care who had fathered the child. As far as the old vaquero was concerned, the child was his, and

Turquoise loved him in return. On the whole ranchero, only her beloved señora and the old Don himself knew the secret of Turquoise's parentage. Rosa admitted to herself that she didn't love the child, either. When she looked at Turquoise, she saw Edwin Forester's aristocratic face.

Rosa passed the mirror in the darkened hall, stared at herself. Even in the shadows, she could see her thickening waist. Time was running out. All she had to offer was her fading beauty. She tiptoed up the stairs, down the hall.

Rosa hesitated with her hand on the doorknob. For just a moment, she remembered her Catholic upbringing, how much the señora would disapprove if she knew.

But hadn't Velvet Eyes done the same? Hadn't she been faithless with another man? Hadn't Rosa heard her say it herself that day in the study? But the señora had a good reason. Rosa gritted her teeth in anger at the old Don. *Si,* the old devil deserved what he was going to get. Even she, Velvet Eyes's personal maid, had not known how cruel he was to her beloved mistress. But when Rosa's lover had told her what he knew....

Very quietly, she opened the door, stepped inside, closed it behind her.

"Is that you, Rosa?" he whispered.

"Si," she answered, watching his silhouette against the bright moon as he rose up in bed. His hair, black as a bat's wing, hung down on his forehead.

Silently, she tiptoed barefooted across the Persian rug and climbed into his bed.

"We should stop," he said, "before we get caught—"

"We won't get caught," she answered, her lips seeking his hungrily. "Someday soon the old Don will die. Then we can figure out a way to get rid of my husband, and—"

"Don't talk," he said, cutting her off as if the subject was one he didn't want to discuss. "I've been thinking about you . . . wanting you. . . ."

His hot lips trailed down her neck, pulled her nightdress away to find her dark, big nipples.

She gasped at the touch of his seeking, greedy lips on her breasts, dug her nails into his shoulders. "I was afraid you and the other were both wanting that blond bitch—"

"Her? You think she could ever interest me? Make love to me the way you do? Why, even if I eventually marry, I don't see why things can't continue as they are."

He was lying about the blonde. Rosa sat upright in bed. "I thought someday you would marry me."

His hands pulled at her gown. "You have a husband—"

"Sanchez might die," she suggested. "He might—"

"We need Sanchez to help run this ranch." His hands ran down her thighs, sending delicious tremors through her.

"But I thought someday I might be your wife, and when the old Don is gone and the señora returns—"

His lips covered hers, his tongue forcing its way into her mouth as if he didn't want to hear what she had to say.

She, too, forgot her ambitions as her hands ran down his flesh to his hard, throbbing manhood. Her needs and his were all that mattered now. Lions, she thought, we're both lions. Sanchez and that pretty blonde were lambs.

He fondled her breasts. "I need you to search through his things. I'm looking for a letter, a note that might be hidden anywhere, maybe in his room."

"What's in the letter?"

"Don't ask questions, just bring me anything you find without reading it. Then you must ride to El Lobo for me."

She smiled in the darkness. "What excuse can I give?"

"You found out your mother is ill and must go to her, just like last time. But now, make love to me."

It would soon be dawn, she thought as she spread her thighs, let him ride her brutally, bruise her breasts with his bites. In only a few minutes, she would have to slip out of here, get back to her bed before anyone was up and around. But for now she gave way to the pleasure of his filling her, causing the exciting pain with his teeth.

He might have thought she would forget his promise, but she would not. Time was running out for her. She wanted to be more than the mistress, she wanted to be the wife. And while he made love to her, she planned how she would get rid of the threat of the beautiful blonde called Cimarron. . . .

Chapter Nine

Cimarron lay awake. It was almost dawn. Perhaps coffee was already being made in the kitchen. She grabbed a robe, opened her door just in time to see Rosa stick her head out of Trace's door, look up and down the hall.

Stunned by the sight, Cimarron stepped quickly back into her room, closed the door to a small crack, and peeked out. Rosa tiptoed down the hall.

Cimarron closed the door, leaned against it, her eyes shut. Trace and a married woman, wife to his *"compadre,"* as he called old Sanchez. She felt both indignation, pity for the old vaquero, and another emotion she was not quite sure of. For a moment, she almost labeled it "jealousy," and then snorted with derision at the thought.

She tried to keep from imagining Trace's lean body driving hard into the lush softness of the Mexican girl, gritted her teeth at the thought. Double damnation! Well, it was no business of Cimarron's that Sanchez couldn't satisfy the hot Spanish spitfire and she was sneaking into the foreman's bed at night. Certainly the virile cowboy was enough of a stud to satisfy any woman, any two women. He was as much of a stallion as that hot-blooded horse of his, Nightwind, that kept a whole herd of mares happy.

Cimarron wondered again who had fathered the beautiful little girl, Turquoise. She had known from the first that the swarthy old vaquero could not possibly be the father. But then, certainly the half-breed foreman couldn't either, not with the child's pale aqua eyes and porcelain-white skin. But Rosa's loose morals were not Cimarron's business, and she had never been one for malicious gossip or sticking her nose in other people's business.

She'd planned to get an early start on the ranch's books in the study this morning. Luis had told her they were in a jumbled mess with Señora Durango's leaving so suddenly last spring. His condescending manner when he'd offered her the job annoyed her as she dressed now. Luis was obviously one of those old-fashioned men who didn't expect women to have any brains at all. He probably thought she'd thumb stupidly through the accounts and give up. Well, she'd show him! She was not only smart, but she'd done a little bookkeeping for Uncle Ransford. Luis might think she was a stupid female, but she'd change his attitude.

She chose a blue crisp cotton with lace at throat and sleeves, foregoing a hoop for a flouncing ruffled petticoat, and pulled her long hair back with a bit of blue ribbon before going down to the kitchen.

Neither Rosa nor any of the servant girls were about yet. Cimarron knew her way around a kitchen. She was perfectly capable of starting the coffee, frying herself a slab of bacon and some eggs.

The scent of the cooking must have drifted back to the housekeeper's quarters, because Cimarron was just ladling her eggs and bacon onto a plate when Rosa stalked into the kitchen, still buttoning her dress.

"Gringo," she stopped, hands still on her buttons, "how dare you come into my kitchen!"

Cimarron considered again what she had seen upstairs, decided it was not her business. "I wanted to get an early start," she said coolly, "and I'm not used to sitting in a dining room, waiting for servants to bring my breakfast."

She reached for a large pepper mill on the stove to pepper her eggs, but Rosa jerked it out of her grasp.

"Such an impudent guest," Rosa said. "Helping herself to the most costly spices that I save for only the old Don. Don't you know how hard spices are to get with a war on?"

Cimarron was immediately apologetic. "Oh, I'm really sorry," she stammered. "I thought it was only pepper. I didn't think—"

"You should ask," Rosa held on to the pepper mill possessively, "not just help yourself, as if you were the señora herself. If you think to take her place, you are sadly mistaken, Gringo!"

"And if you think you can run me off the Triple D with your rudeness, *you're* mistaken!" Cimarron flared back, grabbing up her plate, a cup of coffee, and returning to the dining room.

As she pushed through the swinging door, she almost bumped into Trace, who grinned at her and took off his black hat. *"Buenos dias."* He winked at her. "Sounds like you've just made the mistake of tangling with Rosa."

"No, she made the mistake of tangling with me," Cimarron said coolly, annoyed with herself and him because she felt anger at the thought of the half-breed's making love to his friend's wife.

He looked puzzled at her cold fury. "If I'd known you got up so early, I would have invited you to ride out with me to see the sun come up."

She slammed her plate down on the table, ignored his attempts to pull out her chair for her. She jerked the chair out for herself. "I didn't know you could see the sun rise from your bed," she retorted before she could manage to control herself. What a liar! She knew what riding he'd been doing just before dawn.

But he looked puzzled. "Darlin'," he grinned crookedly, "I don't know what's put a burr under your saddle so early, but I like you better when you smile."

"Has it occurred to you I don't give a damn what you think?" She ate her food with quick, angry bites.

He frowned. "Texans don't like to hear ladies swear," he seemed to scold as he turned toward the kitchen. "Rosa!" he thundered, "Get me some steak and eggs out here!"

"You make me want to swear," Cimarron whispered

fiercely. "I don't like your condescending, domineering manner, Mister Cowboy! I don't carry your brand!"

He gave her a smoldering, possessive look. "Yes, you do, Wild One. I've branded you in a way no other man ever will. They say a woman never forgets her first man—"

"You just watch me!" she challenged, slamming down her fork. "You just watch me forget you! I might even decide to marry Luis."

He reacted with a start and his face was as forbidding as a west Texas cyclone. "You're mine, Cimarron. I haven't figured out what to do about you just yet, but you'll not marry Luis Durango."

Cimarron's mouth dropped open. "Why, you conceited jackass! How dare you tell me what I'll do!" She stood up so fast that her chair turned over just as Rosa came out of the kitchen with a steaming plate of steak and eggs and a pot of strong coffee.

Cimarron caught the look of utter surprise and bewilderment on the Mexican girl's face before Cimarron swept out of the room and went into the study.

She paced up and down, thinking about his impudence. The more she thought, the angrier she became. How dare he? Here he was sneaking servant girls into his bed and then telling Cimarron at breakfast that she couldn't marry Luis. Just who did he think he was, anyway?

She heard him say something to Rosa, leave the dining room. She held her breath but his booted steps passed the study and went out the door across the courtyard. She sat down at the desk, spread the ledgers before her, tried to look at them. But the figures swam before her eyes. All she could see was a moody, rugged face telling her she wasn't going to marry Luis if he asked her. The longer she thought about it, the madder she got, until she was doing a slow boil that picked up speed as she thought it over.

She was going to go out there and tell him off in a way that only a Texas girl could, and when she got through, his ears would be burnt to a crisp!

Grimly she marched across the courtyard toward the sounds of the ranch crew out by the corral. As she strode up, she saw Maverick start to mount a dun from the wrong side. She started to yell a warning, and even as she did so, she heard Trace yell, "No, Maverick, no—"

But the dun shied away, began to buck, the boy scrambling sheepishly out from under the flying hooves. "Sorry," he said, looking embarrassed as he stood and dusted himself off. "I keep forgetting—"

Sanchez wiped his leathery face with his crippled hand. *"Dios!"* he breathed, looking skyward as if imploring help. *"Hombre,* you got to learn to mount from the left side or get kicked to death."

Trace grinned from the top of the fence. "Or ride only Indian ponies, kid."

Holt led a blindfolded, nervous bay mare out. "Here, Trace, they say this one's a bad one."

Trace climbed down, ran a gentle hand over the mare's neck. "Horses are like women, Holt, they like to be stroked by a man who's an expert in the saddle." He swung up on the trembling bay. "Let her rip!" he ordered. Cimarron looked through the railing, so furious she could hardly see. She wanted to watch that horse throw the tough cowboy into the dirt and then stamp him into a smear in the dust.

The bay sprang into the air at the unaccustomed weight on her back, bucking as if she meant to jump over the moon.

"Stay with her, Trace!"

"Look at that sonovagun ride! You can shore tell he's part Injun!"

Hopefully, Cimarron watched through the railings. She wanted that horse to throw him in the dirt and stomp him.

Trace did ride like an Indian, she had to admit grudgingly. His hard, lean body was poetry in motion as the big bay sunfished, showing her rear hooves to the sky. Dust whirled up, the air smelled of horse and squeaking leather. Silver conchos gleamed in the sun. Cimarron ran her tongue over her upper lip, tasting the slight salt of her own perspiration, feeling the dust cling to her face. The cowboys shouted, waving their hats in the air as Trace rode the bronc down with the sure, confident manner of a top cowhand. Finally the mare quit bucking, did a slow, hesitant trot around the corral. When the bay snorted to a halt, Trace slid off, patted the lathered neck.

"There, baby," he crooned, "it's okay." The mare shuddered all over, whinnied at the encouraging voice.

Trace seemed to see Cimarron for the first time as he handed the reins to Maverick. "Just like I said, kid, mares are just like women, you have to dominate them, teach them who owns them."

He strode over to the fence, climbed it to face her.

Cimarron had never known such anger in her whole life. She had come out here to tell him off and he had just added insult to injury.

"Well, darlin'," he began, "glad you came out to see me ride, I—"

She swung as hard as she could, thinking how humiliating it would be for him to be slapped in front of his whole crew. Her hand made a sharp sound and left angry finger marks across his high-cheekboned face.

He caught her wrist with his left hand and held it in his steel grip, and the fury on his face was terrible to see. She was suddenly aware of the power, the strength of the man as he glared down at her, and for a moment she thought he would strike her back.

The cowboys fell silent. The corral was so still, she could hear Trace's labored breathing as he struggled to control himself. When his voice finally came, every word was bitten off in cold, bitter anger. "I told you never to do that, Cimarron. I ought to take you across my knee right now and spank your little bottom till it's covered with red handprints."

Maverick strode over. "Take your hands off her," the boy said, and his eyes flashed gray sparks. The white knife scar on his high cheekbone stood out on the dark face. Someday, Cimarron thought as she swayed in Trace's hard grip, someday the half-Comanche kid named Maverick would be an *hombre* whose name would make other men tremble.

Trace hardly glanced at him. "Don't mix in this, kid. Young broncs never challenge herd stallions."

Maverick glowered. "You can't treat her like that."

Helplessly Cimarron glanced from one to the other, then to the crowd of watching cowboys. Trace was a man, a big, lean man hardened by years on the range. Maverick was just a boy. Trace could kill him bare-handed if he wished.

"Please," she said, looking from one to the other, pulling on her arm that Trace gripped. "He's right, Maverick, don't mix into this." She had never felt so small, so fragile as she did now, gazing up at the brooding cowboy, the red mark of her hand still visible on his cheek.

The boy looked from one to the other, then backed away reluctantly. Holt gave her a dirty, sneering look. Sanchez and the others looked uncomfortable. No cowboy would stand by and see a lady mistreated, but on the other hand, they didn't mix in where a man and his own woman were concerned. The looks on their faces gave her to know they had already decided whose property she was.

Her wrist ached from the pressure of his fingers. She had not realized he was so strong. "Please, Trace," she whispered, "you're hurting me!"

Immediately he released her wrist, looked chagrined. "You shouldn't have slapped me, Wild One."

"I hated your remarks," she flared. "I know who you were talking to when you said that about breaking horses!"

He grinned ever so slightly. "Reckoned I deserved that. Personally, I wouldn't give a peso for a woman or a horse that didn't have a little fire and spirit to them."

"You're lucky Luis didn't hear you say that," she snapped. "He might have challenged you."

Trace rolled himself a cigarette. "No, Luis is lucky he wasn't here, darlin'. If he had been, the gallant gentleman might have felt duty bound to come to your rescue, and he's not much with a pistol unless he's standing close up."

Cimarron recalled watching Trace draw in the barn, remembering his speed and grace. If Luis had been here, her foolishness might have gotten him killed. "Where is Luis anyway? Is he out here?"

Trace lounged easily against the fence. "You must be kidding! Our handsome rake wouldn't get up this early to be in on the end of the world, right, boys?"

The cowboys guffawed and slapped their hats against their legs at the joke. She was annoyed that the disloyal men obviously liked the foreman better than the heir.

With an angry snort, she wheeled and marched back to the house, leaving the cowboys staring after her.

Double damnation! No, damn him, damn him, damn him! she thought as she marched up the stairs. Would he have taken her across his knee, spanked her bare bottom until it was red and stinging, as he'd threatened? She didn't doubt it a bit. He had almost dared her to marry Luis Durango, flung down a challenge to her. Again, she fantasized about becoming Señora Durango, with Trace begging to keep his job and her ordering him off the ranch.

As she went down the hall, she thought she heard a faint call from the room at the end. Concerned, she went to the old Don's door, knocked lightly.

"Come in, please."

The voice was deep, but it had a plaintive, lonely note that pulled at her tender heart. Cimarron had spent years caring for the preacher's invalid wife and the orphaned colts of the Schmidts' small ranch herd.

Cimarron went in. An old man sat up in the bed, propped by pillows. He had the hawklike profile of Spanish nobility and a mane of white hair. He raised his bushy white eyebrows at her like a regal, elderly lion.

Before either of them could speak, the tiny chihuahua bounced off the bed with a happy bark and dashed over to gambol around Cimarron's feet.

"You little rascal!" she exclaimed, leaning over to pick him up, "I wondered where you have been all morning."

"You surprise me, señorita," the old man said, and his voice had the deep ring of both Spanish accent and Texas drawl that vaguely reminded her of someone else. "Tequila is not usually known to be friendly to strangers."

"So I've heard," she laughed, putting the dog back on the floor. "I hear he has a taste for ankles when one least expects it."

He nodded, and the grim, hard mouth smiled a little. "Señorita, forgive me," the old lion said. "I am Don Diego de Durango, and you are?"

"Just call me Cimarron," she stammered, a bit uneasy before his penetrating dark eyes. "I'm a guest of your hospitality, señor."

"Cimarron," he smiled, "'wild one.' What memories that brings to mind, señorita. You know, one of my ancestors rode with the *conquistadors* when they brought the first cattle to Texas."

She leaned against a chair, smiled at him, liking the tough old man immensely. In his day, he must have been tough, as savage as . . . "And is that where your cattle came from, señor?"

"Si." He nodded. "The cattle escaped and multiplied. All a man needed in the early days was a land grant, the courage to fight Comanches, and the grit to go out and gather up the wild *cimarrones*. Hopefully, when my son inherits it, he will keep it growing as I have done. My ambition is to have a bigger spread than my friend at the Running W."

"Yes, Luis tells me you know Richard King."

He shrugged, stroking the dog's ears as it bounced back up on the bed. "We have a difference of opinion on which side to support in this war. But *si,* I know him as I knew Crockett, Travis, Bowie, Houston. They're all dead now, and I suppose I'll soon join them."

He sighed tiredly and the light seemed to go out of his eyes, as if he were severely depressed.

"I'm sure that's not true," Cimarron stammered.

He looked at her keenly, his head cocked to one side. "Señorita, you look familiar to me. Have we met before? Who are your people?"

"I'm sure we haven't," Cimarron answered quickly. It wouldn't do for him to ask nosy questions. For all she knew, he had seen her while visiting in Fandango. He might even be a friend of Uncle Ransford's.

"Strange," he mused, patted the dog. "I seldom forget a face. Perhaps I knew your parents. Was your mother Indian?"

"Hardly," Cimarron said, "but my father was." She had said too much already. She must get him off the subject. "I understand you were with the Texas Rangers, señor."

"*Si*. I was one of Jack Hays' boys. Mr. Colt owes the success of his revolver to us, you know." She could tell from his bemused expression that he was still searching his memory for the pieces of the puzzle that would tell him why her face was familiar. He sighed. "My wife was Indian, you know, Cheyenne. Ah, Velvet Eyes."

At the words, the small dog cocked his head inquiringly, whimpered softly. Cimarron felt tears come to her eyes at the pained expression on the old man's face. There is nothing so agonizing, she thought, as watching a strong man struggle to hold back tears.

She cleared her throat. "I have been lax about coming to visit you, sir, to thank you for extending the hospitality of the Triple D."

His rugged face was again alive with curiosity. "You have met my son?"

She thought of Luis, nodded. "He's very nice."

Now the old man's face really came alive. "I am glad you are here, señorita. I have about given up on my son's marrying. I fear to die without a grandson of my own, a fourth Durango to inherit this great empire."

Cimarron felt her face flush brick red. "You probably have many years to live, señor," she stammered.

He was at once contrite, leaning his elbows on his knees as he looked up at her. "Forgive me, señorita, that was clumsy of me. And don't feel you need to coddle me, lie to me. I have been a ranger, you know. I have fought by Sam Houston's side, killed Mexicans, renegades, and Comanches to hold my land."

She watched the tiny dog burrowing in under the coverlet until only his black shoe-button nose was visible. "I understand that, señor. I can see why anyone would love the Triple D."

The thought crossed her mind that she should tell him about her rape. Even as an invalid, the old Don was still in charge here. He wouldn't hesitate to order the moody cowboy tied to a wagon wheel, his shirt stripped off, while someone took a quirt to him.

But even as she considered it, she knew she would not. She had a mental image of the powerful body stretched helpless against the wagon wheel, blood running down his back. No, she couldn't do it.

The señor looked at her and nodded, as if he liked what he saw. "You will be staying with us long?"

Cimarron turned toward the door. "I—I don't know," she said honestly, her hand on the doorknob.

"I'll tell my son he's a fool if he lets you get away. There's something about you that reminds me of Velvet Eyes. Are you Cheyenne?"

She did not want to be told that she reminded anyone of the absent señora. "I really must be going," she said.

"Come back to see me, señorita," he said. "Some days I feel much better. There's to be a big party for me."

"Of course. We've missed you at dinner, Señor Durango."

The old man smiled. "You know, señorita, I haven't had much interest in anything lately, hiding out here in my room. I believe I'd like to have dinner in the dining room tonight with you and all the others. *Si!* That's what I'll do! When a servant comes to clean my room, I'll send word to make it an occasion in honor of Señorita Cimarron!"

Cimarron nodded. "It will be a pleasure to dine with you, sir. I'll look forward to it."

Then she turned and went down the hall to her room. She spent the rest of the day trying to make a decision. If Luis Durango asked her to marry him, should she? Of course, she should! Even the old man stood ready to give his blessing. She would be safe and secure as a member of this powerful family. How many women have grabbed at security, she thought, and cursed themselves for fools later? Could she learn to love the handsome Spaniard?

She still didn't have any answers as she went through the señora's clothes. *Moonlight.* That dress hung there and she had strange emotions as she touched it. Something about it tugged at her memory. It made her think of stardust, fog and wispy clouds. Cimarron selected a maize yellow dress with an off-the-shoulder neckline showing the swell of her bosom. She put on a hoop tonight, and the full skirt with yards and yards of fabric accentuated her small waist. There was even a small jewelry box in the wardrobe, and Cimarron selected a string of small, delicate pearls, knowing they looked like snowdrops against her tawny skin.

It would be wonderful to have money, she thought idly as she finished her primping. Fine clothes, jewels, servants to wait on her. But could money buy love? Luis was so handsome. Any woman would be proud to introduce him as her husband. And the age difference wasn't all that much. Fifteen years? A little more? Many Texas women were married to much older men. At least, he would be very experienced. She bit her lip in consternation, thinking her thoughts were unladylike. A respectable married lady wasn't expected to want a man in the carnal way. She was only expected to submit dutifully to his hot lust, produce children for him. All the same, she caught herself wondering what the handsome Spaniard would be like in bed. Would he be as virile, as ardent as the half-breed foreman? She blushed hotly at the thought as she went to dinner.

It was indeed a grand event with the old Don at the head of the table. He insisted on seating Cimarron in the hostess's place at the other end. Rosa looked pouty as a 'possum when she saw Cimarron sitting in the señora's chair. Cimarron smiled gently at the girl, knowing Rosa dared not make a fuss about the seating. But she had outdone herself on the dinner. The crystal and china were of the finest, reflecting the light of the great silver candelabra. The red wine tasted delicious, and Cimarron sipped it, giving Luis an approving nod. The rare roast beef told her why the Triple D was famous for its cattle. She had never seen such a huge roast. Everyone had more than they could eat, along with potatoes, fluffy homemade rolls, and tart, sand plum jelly. The little serving girl finally brought out Rosa's triumphant dessert, thick with chocolate and vanilla, full of eggs and rich cream from the ranch's own cows.

Cimarron hardly remembered the conversation, except that it was spirited and interesting, with much talk about whether the Comanche would hit the western settlements this autumn as they had in the past, and if the Triple D would find a market for its beef and fine horses when the war finally ended. The old man himself was in great spirits, telling exciting stories of the men he'd known who'd died at the Alamo, or with Fannin at the Goliad massacre. He told a funny story about Sam Houston's drinking, and a tale of Robert E. Lee when he was the colonel of the U.S. Cavalry stationed in San Antonio before the war started.

But it was Trace's face that kept taking her eye. He actually smiled tonight. She realized he was very handsome when he grinned, when the big, gentle eyes were shining with laughter instead of being darkly moody.

But finally the dinner was over. Sanchez helped Don Diego back to his room. Rosa and her child left, too. Cimarron, Trace, and Luis went into the study.

Luis poured. "Madeira, my dear?"

Cimarron nodded, seeing the sudden scowl on Trace's face at the endearment from the other man.

"Since you're pouring, Luis," he said, "I'll take the usual."

Luis wrinkled his nose as he handed Trace a small shot of tequila and some salt. "You hang around with cowboys too much," he complained.

"I like the crew," Trace said easily, draining the glass, pouring the salt on his fist, licking it off the way cowboys did. "But then, I wasn't schooled in Spain, I was raised in Texas."

"Believe me, it shows." Luis raised one aristocratic eyebrow. "Why, I'll bet you've never even looked through my magnificent library."

"Sure I have." Trace leaned easily against the desk. "You'd be just amazed what an education you can get in the study at night."

His eyes caught Cimarron's, and she choked on her wine, remembering the scene in the darkened room, the feel of his body heaving with passion as he entered her, the taste of his hot, sweet mouth.

Luis looked puzzled, shrugged, as if he did not quite understand what Trace was hinting at.

"Now, art is my subject," he said to Cimarron. "You know, I hoped to become a painter."

"Why didn't you?" Cimarron asked.

"Too lazy," Trace quipped, striding over to pour himself another shot of tequila.

For a moment, she thought Trace had gone too far. Luis's face mottled with color and his hand went to his pocket. She tensed, then sighed as Luis pulled out a silk handkerchief, wiped his face.

She put in quickly. "Luis, did you paint that portrait of your mother in the upstairs hall? It's lovely."

"Sí." He beamed at the compliment. "Sometime I would like to paint you, señorita, if you would do me the honor."

Trace groaned aloud. "I believe I'll go to bed. The manure is getting a little deep in here."

Luis whirled on him. "Watch your language in front of the lady!"

"I said 'manure,' didn't I?" Trace laughed easily. He snapped his fingers at the small dog, which accompanied him as he left the study. She and Luis were alone.

Nervously, Cimarron put down her wine glass, saw Luis sneak a preening look at himself in the big mirror.

"Señorita, it's very hot tonight," he said. "Perhaps we should go out on the veranda?"

She stood slowly, trying to decide what to do. She could suddenly decide she was tired, beg to excuse herself. Maybe he was only making idle conversation. Maybe it was supreme ego on her part to think he might be interested in a poor half-breed girl to add to this fairy-tale empire. Luis Durango was certainly as handsome and charming as any prince. And yet . . .

She scolded herself for her inner turmoil. "Of course, Luis," she agreed, her heart pounding a little harder. "It really is very warm for September."

They went through the open French doors, stood looking

up at the winking stars, at the Milky Way. The image of the spirit horse came to her mind as she looked off at the distant outline of hills. Of course, it had only been a figment of her imagination.

Luis was evidently nervous. He stood just behind her and rambled about how his mother had wanted him to be a doctor, but he had wanted to be an artist and now was neither.

"Perhaps you haven't missed your calling," she said politely. "Perhaps you were destined to be the best Don this ranch ever had."

She felt him brush slightly against her back. "Perhaps," he said. "But a Don needs a señora."

"Of course." She knew that was the answer he wanted, but she was suddenly shy, wanting to skirt the subject she thought he might be approaching. She babbled foolishly about how thrilled she was to be able to start a school for the vaqueros' children, about how she was looking forward to helping him straighten out the accounts for the ranch.

She stood turned away from him, looking out at the bubbling fountain while she chattered inanely. Cimarron felt his fine, manicured hands come up, rest on her bare shoulders.

"Señorita, if I may be so bold . . ." He was waiting to find out if she objected to his familiar touch. Like the perfect gentleman he was, she knew he would withdraw with a flurry of abject apologies if she so much as hinted she was insulted by his attentions.

Not like certain men, who took what they wanted. She closed her eyes, remembering the scene in the darkened study, Trace's brutal, demanding kisses.

She gave just the slightest nod of acceptance and she felt his hands tighten, heard a quick intake of breath. "Oh, Cimarron," he whispered in his cultured accent, "if you only knew how I've dreamed of this embrace since the first moment I saw you. . . ." His voice trailed off hesitantly and she knew he was too gallant, too refined to go further.

"Señorita," his hands tightened on her bare shoulders, "I know I haven't known you very long, but I think sometimes it's in the stars for people to meet long before they do."

She thought of stars. Of Milky Ways. Of Cheyenne spirit horses. Of Trace.

"I do, too, Luis," she answered encouragingly angry with herself at her thoughts as she turned around in the Spaniard's arms. She looked up into his handsome face, saw the desire there. Security. Safety. Power. Very slowly, she tilted her face up, closed her eyes as her lips half opened invitingly.

His breath was almost a sob as he bent to kiss her, and she could feel her breasts brushing against his fine broadcloth coat. She let him arch her against his body, his hands digging into her bare shoulders, his mouth claiming hers with a passion that surprised her.

This was it! This was what life was all about! This was love! She pressed herself against him, feeling the swell of her breasts crushed against his hard chest, the hardness of his manhood through her dress as he pulled her to him. Eagerly she answered his kiss, waiting for passion to sweep her, for her heart to pound with the thought of his making love to her.

But behind her closed eyelids as Luis kissed her, she suddenly saw the crooked smile, the moody eyes of the half-breed cowboy. She jerked away in surprise and dismay.

"What is it, my dear? Have I offended you?" His expression as he gripped both her hands was concerned, solicitous.

"No, not at all," she gulped. Surely if she were married, lying in this man's arms, she could blot out that brutal, passionate lovemaking from her mind forever, wipe out Trace's face from her thoughts, her memory.

Luis tilted her face up to his. "I suppose my passion surprised you, dear one. You must have been very sheltered, very innocent."

"Yes," she lied, "of course, that's it." Innocent. Sheltered. If he only knew she'd been loved by the man he seemed to hate. A man who'd had her writhing eagerly beneath his hard driving body, almost begging for his kisses. She wondered suddenly if she might be pregnant with the virile cowboy's child. If she were, what in God's name would she do? If she married Luis Durango right away, he would think it his. What a terrible trick. What an awful thing to do to a man. But even if she weren't carrying the foreman's child, a posse was relentlessly searching the countryside for her. Would the law dare go up against the powerful Durangos?

Luis kissed her again. "Cimarron, sweet one, I won't lie to you. I've been quite the ladies' man, never gave serious thought to marriage. But now, do I dare hope that someday you might consider. . . ." His voice trailed off and he brought her hands to his lips, kissed them gently.

"I—I'm not sure what you mean." She stalled for time.

"Cimarron," his words came out in a sudden rush, "will you—will you marry me?"

She closed her eyes to her doubts, pretended the face above hers was someone else's. "Yes, Luis," she whispered, "I'll marry you."

He gave a glad cry, kissed her again. "You won't regret this, sweet one, someday when we wed—"

"Someday?" she asked, puzzled. "Shouldn't we announce it? Marry soon?"

"Well," his voice grew hesitant, "it is perhaps not proper, with the señora and Dallas gone. I want everything done properly. That's why I think we should keep it secret for a little while until I can find the biggest ring in Texas, until I can find out what's proper under the circumstances, with no señora in charge. Of course, I've got to ask your papa—"

"My father is dead," she answered quickly. "I really don't have anyone for you to ask."

He gave her a piercing look. "I thought you said something about an uncle—"

"He's not really blood kin," she stammered. "It was just a family I stayed with is all."

"Then we will keep our little secret until all the plans can be made," he said as he held her hands, looking earnestly down at her. "But I have things I must change, must take care of."

It dawned on her that he might have a girl at one of the gambling palaces in San Antone, the kind of girl men kept but seldom married. He would want to break with her.

Would he want to marry Cimarron if he knew another man had already stolen her virginity? Yes, they needed to keep this engagement a secret until it was too late to stop the wedding. That cowboy thought he possessed her, and he might try to stop this marriage. "Certainly, Luis," she answered. "It will be our secret until you are ready to announce it to the world."

But later that night as she lay in bed looking up at the ceiling, she regretted her haste. She should have gotten to know Luis better before she accepted. She ran a dozen reasons through her mind as to why it had been a mistake to say yes to him. But it was the wee hours of the morning before she was ready to admit the truth even to herself. She didn't want to marry Luis Durango. When she tried to imagine herself making love to him, she kept seeing the face of that half-breed foreman.

Cimarron, you idiot! She sat up in bed, cursing herself for even daring to think of passing up an opportunity like that. Yet it wouldn't be fair to Luis, and it would be impossible for her. She imagined seeing Trace every day, talking with him, then going to bed at night with his employer. Luis was no fool. Just how long would it take him to figure it out? But the half-breed didn't want to marry her. He'd made it very clear that she belonged to him, that he enjoyed her body. But he wanted no permanent liaison, didn't trust women because of something that had happened involving Señora Ojos de Pana de Durango.

What an unlucky day it had been for her when her path had crossed his in the rain. By now she would have been in Galveston, figuring out a way to leave Texas for good. That was what she needed to do, leave Texas just like she had planned. What would she do for money? She thought of the small strongbox in the study desk downstairs.

No, she wasn't a thief. Cimarron wouldn't steal from the Durangos after accepting their hospitality. Somehow she'd manage without any money, maybe find a job cooking or cleaning on ranches along the way until she reached Galveston. She wanted to get out of here immediately. She couldn't look either one of those men in the eye tomorrow. The thought crossed her mind that with the bad blood already between them, they might even come to blows, to a killing because of her when Trace discovered she was to marry Luis.

Cimarron had to get off this ranch tonight, even if she didn't have any money. Quickly she gathered up a small bundle of clothes, slipped into a pair of mannish pants from Dallas's wardrobe. As she packed she thought she heard a noise downstairs, then shrugged it off. That dog, probably, wandering around the house. It took her only a few minutes more to gather up her clothes and put her pillows under the covers to make it appear she still slept if anyone checked her room.

Very quietly, she tiptoed down the stairs and went into the study. She took a pistol out of the gun rack at the end of the room. A desk drawer hung open as she tiptoed past it and she looked at it curiously, wondering. *She had to get out of here.* Quietly, she crossed the courtyard, passed the bubbling fountain, walked toward the stable. The Texas humidity seemed as hot as chili peppers. The scent of wildflowers drifted on the still air, and somewhere in the distance a coyote howled from a hilltop. It reverberated and echoed through the hills until it was lost in the distance. With longing, Cimarron turned and looked back at the big adobe hacienda, white and secure like a fortress. She knew what regret and what sadness tasted like at that moment. They tasted bitter.

Cimarron went into the stable, thinking again of the spirit horse. Did it really warn those of Cheyenne blood, as Trace said? Had she really seen such a thing or was it only her imagination?

The hay in the barn smelled sweet, was cushion-soft under her step. She'd have to steal a horse, as much as she regretted it. Nightwind nickered from his stall and she went over, stroked his velvet muzzle while he nibbled her fingers. "How are you, boy?" she whispered. "You okay?"

The horse seemed almost to move his head, whinny a warning. Puzzled, she stared at him. "Don't worry, boy, I won't take you," she crooned. "If I did, that ornery *hombre* would come after me like Satan coming up out of hell."

A figure stepped out of the shadows. If she hadn't put her own fist to her lips, she might have screamed.

As it was, she could only stare at him as he moved toward her, close enough to look down into her eyes. "Hell's bells! I thought it was you, sugar! What are you doing out here in the stable in the middle of the night?"

Chapter Ten

For a long moment, as Holt stared back at the pretty blonde, he thought she would scream. He started to clap his hand over her mouth.

But she recovered from her surprise nicely. "I might ask you the same thing," she retorted.

This kid had spunk, Holt thought with admiration. Before, he had just thought she was pretty, and most pretty women were soft, stupid.

He leaned against the stall door. "Well, sugar, you might say I've decided to move on."

"In the middle of the night?" she scoffed.

"Which brings us to another question," he said softly in his southern Missouri twang. "What's a house guest of the fancy Durangos doing wandering around the barn at night?"

He couldn't see her face but he could feel her tense. "I—I came out to bring Nightwind an apple."

"In the middle of the night?"

"Okay, so that's not what I'm doing," she admitted. "What are you doing?"

"I asked you first, sugar." The moonlight filtering into the barn caught the color of her long honey-colored hair and he imagined tangling his fingers in it, pulling her close to him. . . .

She seemed to consider her answer. If this gal had been prowling around in the house, it was a natural wonder they hadn't bumped into each other a few minutes ago when he was going through the desk in the study.

"Okay," she finally said. "I've decided to move on."

"In the middle of the night?"

"Will you stop saying that?" she flared, and he liked the spark in her eyes. Holt liked women with fire.

"So, sugar, it seems we're both leavin', sudden-like in the darkness. Which way you headed?"

She shrugged, reached for a saddle. "Haven't really thought about it, don't care, really. Maybe Galveston."

She sounded sad, despairing. The gal was in love with one of those two gents; the whole crew had been watching the show the last day or two, taking bets on which one would get her. Well, the boys was all wrong. Hell's bells. Old Holt was going to end up with her. "You aren't considerin' ridin' out by yourself, are you, sugar? With all them Comanches raiding around?"

"I can hardly advertise for a company of Texas Rangers to go along, can I now?" she scoffed as she led the sorrel out and started saddling it.

"Two of us would have a better chance." He considered stealing Trace's stallion, but even as he reached out to touch it, the horse snapped at his fingers.

"You big, black bastard!" he swore, jerking back. "Take my hand off at the wrist, would ya? If it wouldn't make so much noise, I'd shoot you!"

The girl whirled around. "It'd be stupid to take that horse," she put in quickly. "You know how much Trace thinks of him. He'd come after you."

Holt nodded as he led his own blue gelding out, started to saddle up. "You're right. I wouldn't want that half-breed on my trail. Anybody who takes anything of his would wish he hadn't."

She didn't say anything. Holt looked at the girl a long moment. "That may include you, sugar."

"Me? I don't belong to Trace!"

"Somebody forgot to tell him that, I'd say."

She flung her head up, spirited and wild as any mustang filly. "He's gonna find out if he doesn't already know about it."

Holt tucked the small strongbox in his saddlebags and swung up, the leather creaking in the silence. "You going my way?"

She looked confused, as if she didn't know or care which way she went as long as she got away from here. "I don't know. Which way you heading?"

He ran his hand over his unshaven face. "Well, if we head south or east, we may end up running into Rebel army patrols."

"So?"

"So, sugar, them Rebs is desperate for cannon fodder now with the war winding down! I already done my bit for the South. Nosiree, I ain't gonna be a draftee up on the front lines."

She swung up on the sorrel. "What do you suggest?"

He spat to one side. "If we go north, we still have to get through Confederate lines, and above that, Indian Territory, so that's no good. I say we head west!"

"West!" She sounded terrified. "Are you loco? That's Comanche country! Anyone can tell you aren't from Texas! You know what Comanche do to prisoners?"

"But don't you see?" He laughed triumphantly. "They wouldn't come looking for us in that direction, they'll figure we wouldn't be crazy enough to go that way."

She shrugged. "Why do you think they'll come looking at all?"

"Sugar," he drawled, "Among other reasons, you're riding a stolen Triple D horse. You know what Texans do to horse thieves?"

"You're right," she said, clucking to the sorrel. "Let's vamoose pronto."

He kneed his mount, walked his horse alongside hers quietly as they rode out of the barn. Naw, they probably wouldn't come after them over one stolen horse. But those two men would come looking for that blonde. And for Holt because of what he'd just taken from the house. . . .

It was stupid of him to take her along, he thought as they walked the horses away from the ranch. But on the other hand a gal like that would make a nice gift to El Lobo, who was going to be mad as hell at Holt for missing that shot. El Lobo had to answer to his boss right here. Giving the renegade the girl might make things right. The Comancheros' thirst for yellow-haired women was well-known. Even if he'd botched this job, Holt wanted to stay with the Comanchero. He'd gotten used to living the life of a midnight raider up in Missouri. . . .

"Okay, sugar," he said, "let's move on out!" They broke into an easy lope across the limestone hilltop. They would be many miles from here by daylight, and he didn't think even Trace could track them across this rocky ground.

He glanced sideways at the girl as they galloped through the moonlight. Her honey-colored hair blew out behind her, and she rode well, her firm thighs gripping the horse, her full breasts bouncing slightly. He imagined those thighs locked around him as they now gripped the horse, thought about the softness of her breasts.

Damn! He had to stop thinking like that. The thoughts made his manhood swell uncomfortably against the saddle. There'd be plenty of time for that later when the pair had put many miles between them and the angry swarm of riders who were bound to come from the Triple D tomorrow.

She glanced over at him, smiled confidently. Yeah, he saw the pistol stuck in her belt. The cocky little bitch thought she could take care of herself, that Holt would be no danger to her. After what he'd been through the last two or three years, taking that pistol away from her was going to be as easy as stealing from a collection plate. . . .

He winced at that image, immediately hearing the preaacher praying for Holt as he died, still clutching his Bible against the hole in his chest. *Lawrence, Kansas.* Sometimes, the memories kept him from sleeping. Sometimes he came up out of bed, gasping for air, smelling the flames from the burning church, the coppery scent of blood. . . .

The blonde rode a little ahead of him now and he watched her hair fly in the breeze, remembering the preacher's wife with yellow hair. She'd screamed and screamed and screamed. . . .

Holt needed a drink. Yeah, he'd be fine when they could finally stop and he could get to that bottle in his saddlebag. It was tucked in there right next to the moneybox from Luis's desk. Luck had not been running Holt's way in a long time, not since that night in Lawrence. . . .

He swore under his breath as his gelding ate up the miles. He'd muffed the job he'd been paid to come to the Triple D to do, so the guy had refused to pay him, had threatened to kill him when Holt tried to blackmail him. Holt had missed his one good shot at the target. Somehow, the man had sensed Holt up in the rocks and had jerked suddenly just as Holt fired. And the other one . . . well, that shot was just for looks, just to throw everybody off track, give the man an alibi so it would look like someone was trying to drygulch both of them. Holt had hung around, hoping to get in another shot, but his target was wary now, too wary.

Well, Holt knew when to cash in his cards and move on. And he'd cleaned out the little strongbox tonight. He was only lucky that damned little dog hadn't come down and barked at him. He could have killed the little devil with his pistol butt, but Tequila would have awakened the whole house first. And then while he was getting ready to ride out, the blonde had come out to the stable. Maybe Lady Luck was finally smiling on him. Holt had the money and the girl. When he put some distance between him and the ranch, old Holt was going to give that little blonde the kind of ride that would really tame her.

Both horses were lathered and blowing when they finally dismounted and walked a couple of miles to cool them out. Holt felt exhilarated as he glanced over at her. "I never thought I'd say this, but you look cute as hell in those tight pants."

"Forget it," she said, reaching down to touch the pistol in her belt reassuringly. "We need each other, Holt, to get away. But after that, we each go our own way, *comprende?*"

"Of course," he lied, licking his lips. He could see the tips of her nipples making an outline in her shirt as they jutted out. Damn, she must not have anything on underneath. He ran his tongue over his lips again, imagining how those firm nipples would taste to his eager tongue, his sucking mouth.

His groin ached so it was almost painful to walk. In a few more miles they would be out of the cedar, headed into the endless brush country where the mesquite would tear leather chaps right off a man's leg. Further west, he'd heard, water was so scarce you had to cut the tops off the cactus for a drink. He hoped the Comanchero were still up at Enchanted Rock. He tried to remember how many days' ride it was. "You from this part of Texas?"

She immediately stiffened, her guard came up. "What makes you ask?"

"Just a question, sugar, don't get your stinger out."

"Stop calling me that!" He could hear her bristle.

He'd take the starch out of her once they got far enough away. This little gal was hiding something herself. Years of surviving had given him the second sense that told him when someone else was on the run. It occurred to him it might be smart to slip the money into her saddlebags first chance he got, just in case the cowboys did catch up to them. With the horses cooled, they mounted up, rode steadily west through the September night. The Comanche moon lit up the Texas landscape like day. He could see why them damned Injuns liked to ride at night, he thought with a smile of understanding. It was cooler than the sweltering autumn days, and it led to mental terror among the settlers. No wonder Texans were a breed apart. It took blood like ice and guts of steel to stay on, building this wild frontier into a tame, civilized country when tonight's full moon might bring painted savages riding in to burn and rape.

That made him think of Lawrence again, and he heard the girl scream in his mind. "Ain't this a hell of a country?" he said, to silence the screaming. Damn, he needed a drink.

"You can take a Texan out of the Lone Star State," she said, "but you can't take Texas out of his heart."

He snorted in derision. "I agree with the guy who said, 'If I owned both hell and Texas, I'd rent out Texas and live in hell.'"

She looked at him. "Obviously, he wasn't a real Texan."

"Aw, sugar!" Holt laughed, "the place was settled by

renegades and outlaws! Isn't that what sheriffs write on a warrant when a guy disappears anyplace? 'G.T.T.'? 'Gone to Texas'?"

"You wanted by the law?"

He gave her a penetrating glance. "Are you?" Holt had said it in jest, but he saw the change in her face, the fear, the apprehension.

And the expression on her face, her yellow hair blowing about her face, made her look almost exactly like the young blond woman in Lawrence that night. The neighbor boy who rode with him, Frank James, told him he was asking for bad luck raping a preacher's wife. Holt had laughed, had enjoyed her anyway right there in the yard of the burning church, her husband lying dead with his Bible in his hands nearby.

Missouri was bloody border country, one family going with the North, relatives down the road declaring for the South. It was almost funny, now that Holt thought about it. Poor, barefooted country folks like his rushing to fight to save slavery when they'd never owned a slave, could never have afforded slaves.

The poor whites of southern Missouri was the ones who needed freeing, Holt thought bitterly as he rode along. Hell, slaves lived better than poor white farmers trying to scratch out a living on the rocky hillsides of the Ozarks. Holt could remember lots of nights going to bed hungry when there wasn't enough potatoes to go around. Biscuits and sawmill gravy. Damn, if he never saw another plate of that, he'd be in tall cotton. Sawmill gravy. Flour mixed with bacon grease, thinned with creek water.

Holt had been excited about the war at first, saw it as a way out, envisioned himself as an elegant soldier boy, wowing the ladies in a fancy gray uniform. He even got a pair of boots for his bare feet. And then the illiterate Missouri boy had found out that war wasn't parades and fancy uniforms and medals. War was terror and pain, and spilling your guts across your saddle as a cannonful of grapeshot caught you in the belly. Slowly, he realized that things weren't going to be any better for him when the war ended. Even if he got to keep the fancy gray uniform and the boots, when it was all over, he'd be back walking along behind a mule, trying to scratch an existence out of thin, rocky soil.

There was a rumor the guerrillas wouldn't be granted amnesty when it ended, like other southern soldiers. The government planned to hunt the raiders down like common outlaws. So a few months ago, Holt had left Quantrill. There was arguing. The group was breaking up anyhow. He and Frank and another Missouri kid named Cole Younger had left to go join up with Bloody Bill Anderson's raiders. Cole was so mean, he'd once tied several Yankee prisoners together and shot them just to settle a bet on how many bodies one Enfield rifle bullet would go through. Holt remembered now Frank and Cole was always talking about how they'd gather up their brothers, go into some kind of raiding together after the war ended.

There sure wasn't much of a way to make a living on the poor, rocky farms of southern Missouri. Holt had had enough; he lit a shuck for the Southwest, found his way to El Lobo. And the Comanchero had sent him to the Triple D to do a job for El Lobo's boss.

Holt and Cimarron rode all night and all the next day, barely stopping to grab a bite of cold food. It was late the next night when he finally decided there was enough distance between them and the ranch to stop to fry bacon, make coffee. Time enough for something else, too....

Holt watched the girl busying herself at the campfire. Sugar, he thought as he studied her, after supper, I got time for you....

In her haste to put distance between herself and the ranch, Cimarron had not given much thought to the man she accompanied. Now she took a good, long look at Holt as she bent over the tiny campfire, frying bacon.

A bitter taste of apprehension came to her mouth as she noticed for the first time that his holster was worn low and tied down. As she watched, he pulled out the pearl-handled Colt .44 and inspected it. The trigger and the trigger guard had been filed away. That pistol was meant to be fanned with the heel of the hand. A man could fire rapidly at a close target with that weapon. And only one kind of *hombre* needed to.

He walked over to where the saddles lay and took a bottle from his saddlebags. She watched him take a deep, greedy drink, the liquor running down both sides of his mouth.

He turned, held out the bottle with an unsteady hand. "Want some?"

"No, and you shouldn't drink so much, either," she said. "I've almost got some food ready." If he drank too much, the next thing he would want was a woman. . . .

She was afraid now, very much afraid, cursing her own reckless pride, the thought that she could deal with this *hombre* if he got any ideas.

He took another deep drink as he came over to the fire. "Don't boss me around, sugar. I've taken enough orders from my betters to last me a lifetime. I don't have to take orders no more, you hear me? I got money, the cashbox from the Triple D. You and me can have a big time."

Cimarron swallowed hard as she returned her attention to the sizzling skillet. She could feel his half-hooded, sleepy eyes studying her, and when she looked up suddenly he was staring at the cleavage of her bosom, visible in the low-cut neck of her blouse. Self-consciously, her hand went to her throat, fumbled with her buttons. She had her pistol, but somehow, way out here in the hostile, wild country with no one else around, a pistol didn't seem as much protection as it had when she had been standing in the barn. A little flicker of fear went down her back.

"You—you were the one I heard downstairs? You got into the desk?"

He smirked and nodded, seeming to enjoy her nervousness as he holstered the gun, squatted across from her. The flickering flames reflected little pinpoints of light in his pupils. Slowly he licked his lips, and she thought of a sidewinder they had ridden past just at dawn. Its yellow eyes had stared at her, expressionless and unblinking, as it reared its mottled head, its forked tongue darting in and out. This *hombre*'s eyes revealed that he was a little loco.

If she could just keep him talking, she thought, keep his

crazy mind off. . . .

"I—I don't think you ever told me where you were from, Holt," she said a little too brightly.

"Kansas, lately, southern Missouri before that," he answered laconically, pulling out a cheap cigar. He leaned over, picked up a burning stick to light it.

"Oh? Heard there was a lot of trouble in Lawrence last summer." She turned the bacon with a small fork.

"You heard right." He studied her in frank, impudent appraisal as he tossed the stick away, rubbed one grimy hand across his unshaven chin.

She looked down, intimidated by his eyes. She could see her own hands trembling, gripping the skillet handle and the fork. She had her pistol, but she'd have felt better if she had his Sharps rifle, too. And it was in his bedroll. Holt was between her and the gear. If she could keep him talking, keep his mind off. . . .

"We heard Quantrill's guerrillas killed a hundred people." Her words tumbled out too fast as she tried to build a fence of words between them. "Of course, that's bound to be wrong—"

"A hundred and fifty." He spoke very deliberately, and in her mind she heard the warning buzz of the sidewinder's rattles.

"My! That many?" She took a deep, shaky breath of the bacon smell. *She had to keep him talking.* "Heard they leveled the town—"

"We burned it to the ground," he said softly, the stinking smoke from the cigar curling up around his unblinking eyes.

Her pulse pounded so loudly, she was sure he could hear it over the crackle of the flames, the sizzle of the skillet. Very slowly, she looked up at him. "We?"

"We." He tipped his hat back, threw away his cigar. As she reacted, his hand snaked across, grabbed her wrist.

For a moment she froze, wincing in pain as his hand squeezed her wrist, preventing her from flinging the red-hot grease in his face.

Without thinking, she reacted in the only way she could. Before he could throw up his left one to stop her, she stabbed the small fork deep into the back of his imprisoning hand and screamed as she did so. He stumbled backward as she reached for her Colt, leveled down on him.

But he was staring at her, one hand cupped over the bloody one, his head cocked, as if he didn't really see her.

"Why do you always scream?" he asked. "Don't you ever stop screaming?"

He was drunk, that was all she could figure out from the words he babbled. The man moved toward her, blood from the back of his hand dripping through his fingers.

She cocked the pistol. "Don't come any closer."

He looked at her with mad, uncomprehending eyes, then back down at his bleeding hand. "I'm sorry I killed your husband," he mumbled as he moved toward her. "Frank said it was bad luck to burn the church. Is that why I keep hearing you scream and scream and scream?"

"That's far enough," Cimarron warned as he stopped, looked down at her. Something about her had driven him over the edge, she thought, the gun trembling in her hands. He was as loco as if he'd been eating Jimpson weed, the plant that sent livestock into a crazed frenzy. Indians thought the insane were touched by the Great Spirit, wouldn't harm them. Could she do less? Could she really shoot a man whose mind seemed to be wandering in the hazy past?

Even as she hesitated, her finger on the trigger, Holt reached out, jerked the pistol from her hand, tossed it away.

"Sugar, I'm not as crazy as you think," he snarled through clenched teeth as he grabbed her, jerked her to her feet. But his hooded, sleepy eyes told her otherwise.

She beat him on the chest as they struggled by the fire and tried to grab his gun. He slapped her repeatedly until her ears rang. "Sugar," he whispered, "you ain't gonna miss that husband, old Holt is gonna make you very happy."

She struggled, almost got away from him, but his hand caught the front of her shirt, ripped it open, spilling her breasts out to his view.

His eyes lit up and he licked his lips slowly, moving toward her as she backed away, her torn shirt hanging open.

"Come here, gal," he grinned. "Let me squeeze and love

them tits like they ain't never been loved before. We'll leave Lawrence together."

She shook her head as she backed away. She was so scared, her mouth hung open as she gasped for air to fill her lungs. Her naked breasts heaved with the effort, and he brought one hand up, rubbing his fingertips together as he advanced on her.

"Hell's bells," he smiled, making that reaching, obscene gesture, "I'm gonna take you out of this two-bit Kansas town. That preacher couldn't love you like old Holt can."

She could see the hard swell in his tight pants, and he grinned again, nodding as he saw where she looked. "You want it, don't you? Your husband won't try to stop us. I shot him when I burned the church, remember?"

Cimarron kept backing. The two horses stood unsaddled somewhere behind her. The gear was piled up near them. His Sharps rifle was in that bedroll. What a fool she had been! In spite of all her bravado, she was as soft as any other woman at heart, slow to pull the trigger on a crazy man reaching for her.

"Listen," she gulped, "Luis and Trace will be mad at you for doing this. One of them will kill you for it."

He paused, scratched his head. "I was supposed to kill him," he mumbled, "That's what I was paid to do and I missed my shot—"

"What?" Cimarron's face furrowed with puzzlement. "What did you say?"

"He's mad at me," Holt nodded. "Won't pay me, 'cause I didn't kill him."

She had to keep him talking. She backed away, her palms sweating. She had to keep his mind occupied until she could reach the bedroll. "Why?" she asked, "Why would he want you to kill him?"

"He's only third in line for the Triple D." Holt stopped, seemed to be thinking it over. "Two have to die before he inherits. Yeah, that's right, *uno, dos, tres.* Third in line."

What on earth was he babbling about? "Trace?" she stared at him unbelieving, glanced over her shoulder at the horses. *Only a few more feet. . . .*

He nodded. "That's right, sugar, third."

She only half heard him as she backed away. Another couple of steps and she would whirl and run for the bedroll. *Another step or two.* And then she stumbled backward over the unseen saddles and went sprawling onto her back.

Immediately he fell on her, tearing at her pants as she fought him. But he was stronger than she was, ripping the buttons, grabbing both pant legs and pulling.

He had her pants off now and fell heavily on her as they went to the ground. His hands gripped her wrists as he fell on her. Damn this saddle tramp! "You'll have to kill me first!" she shouted as she struggled, arching her body as he fought to stay on top.

"No, sugar, I'm not gonna kill you, not this time!" he murmured. "This time, you ain't gonna scream, you ain't gonna make me lose my temper just to keep you from screaming, are you?"

He gradually forced himself between her naked thighs as she fought him. One of his hands went up to pin her wrists above her head while his other went down to stroke her between the legs and unbutton his pants.

Cimarron trembled with both fear and rage as she felt his hot, naked maleness brush against her thigh.

His unshaven face ground against her breasts, his whiskers stinging like wind-driven sand against her fragile skin. "Oh, sugar," he breathed, "this is going to be even better than last time because you won't scream, will you? I don't want to have to cut your throat again. You weren't pretty with that blood smeared across your snowy tits!"

Cimarron's heart pounded so loudly she knew he could feel it with his lips as he nuzzled there. She felt his hand go down to touch the knife at his belt. Would this crazy man rape a woman dying in a pool of her own blood?

He grinned, looking at her with sleepy, hooded eyes.

He already has, she thought in terror, *he already has.*

"I—I'll let you do anything you want," she gasped, "just don't kill me! Please don't kill me!"

He laughed, took his hand away from his knife. "Sugar, that's real smart thinkin', not like last time. I didn't want to hurt you last time but you made me! You made me hurt you!"

"I won't this time!" she promised, gulping air into her dry mouth. "Oh, I won't scream, I promise!"

He ran his rough hand down her naked, silken thighs. "You want it, I know you do! I'm gonna ride you like the little unbroken palomino filly you are, and you'll want me. I won't have to use my knife this time because you won't scream! I keep hearing you scream in my head!"

She swallowed hard to keep from sobbing. Cimarron could smell the sour reek of his sweat, feel it dripping on her bare skin. His breath stank of cheap whiskey as his hot, wet mouth came down to cover hers. She gagged on the taste, the smell of him, his hot breath panting like some eager male animal. In the distance, she thought she heard a horse nicker and the sorrel whinny in return.

Indians! she thought, *Comanche riding in!* She wanted to scream a warning, but his mouth was on hers, his full weight crushing and bruising her soft breasts as he fumbled between her thighs, trying to force himself inside her unwilling dryness. *He would tear her; tear her until she bled.*

And now she fought him again, knowing it angered him. Cimarron was not some weak, cowering creature to lie here and let this brute rape her. He might kill her for her spunk, but she was going down fighting! And in her fury and her terror, she screamed, and screamed again.

"Damn you!" he snarled, and she felt him reaching for his knife, "Damn you! Why do you keep screaming and screaming?"

She fought her way out from under him, but he grabbed her again. She heard the sound of a man's boot stepping on a dry twig. Then the fire threw the shadow suddenly across both Cimarron and her attacker.

They both froze in place. *Comanche!* she thought in terror, seeing only the shape of a man in the firelight.

"Holt, get your dirty hands off my woman!"

Holt swayed on his feet, his hooded, half-mad eyes blinking, as if he didn't quite understand.

But Cimarron burst into sobs of relief at the sound of the

familiar, deep Texas-Spanish drawl. She ran toward him. "Trace! Oh, Trace!"

"Get back, Cimarron!" His strong arm caught her, held her against him a moment before pushing her to one side.

Holt went automatically into a gunfighter's stance.

Cimarron fell sobbing next to Trace's feet. She was naked from the waist down, her shirt torn to shreds. But she heard Trace's angry intake of breath, knew he had seen the bite marks, the bruises on her soft skin.

"Holt, you dirty sonvobitch, I'll kill you for this!"

She saw Trace's hand go to his holster, remembered how fast she'd seen him draw before, but he was faster now because of the black anger written on his features.

Holt's hand was a blur, slapping leather as he brought his pistol out, fanning the hammer with the heel of his hand. Nobody could shoot faster than a gunfighter fanning a Colt that way.

"Look out, Trace!" she screamed. Both pistols flashed as they roared. She closed her eyes against the light, clapped her hands over her ears to dim the sudden noise. She heard the bullet hit flesh, heard Trace cry out. Even as she stared unbelievingly, the half-breed stumbled, grabbing at his thigh as he went down.

"Trace! Oh my God, Trace!" She grabbed up his Colt. She'd kill the rotten skunk for shooting Trace!

And then, she realized Trace already had. Even as the hot pistol hung from her limp fingers, she saw the crazed gunman stagger, go down backward. A .44 slug will knock a man back a dozen feet when it hits dead center. Holt lay on his back, clutching both hands to his chest as she ran over and looked down at him, the pistol hanging from her fingers. Scarlet blood pumped out between his clutching hands with every beat of his dying heart.

He smiled up at her faintly. "Fannin' a gun's fast," he whispered, "but not accurate . . . never very accurate. . . ." Blood ran out of the corner of his mouth as he looked up at her, and she bit her lip to keep from weeping. His eyes were already starting to glaze over. "Don't scream anymore. . . ."

he pleaded faintly. "Oh, please, please don't scream anymore...."

Trace moaned and she came back to reality, threw the gun down, ran over to the fallen man, who pulled himself up on one elbow. "Stop crying," he commanded. "It's okay, just a leg wound. Did he ... did he hurt you?"

"No," she gasped, tearing away one of her sleeves to make a tourniquet. "He was just about to, that's all."

She ran back to Holt's body, hesitantly took his knife, came back over to cut away Trace's pants leg.

"Be careful, darlin'," he said half-jokingly, and she knew he joked to keep her from realizing how badly he hurt. "Do be careful with that knife. Some young ladies at Miss Fancy's would be mighty sad if you got too careless with that blade right where you're cutting!"

She stopped, glared at him, then resumed cutting the pants away from his upper thigh. "I ought to cut it off," she snapped, "make the young ladies' fathers sleep easier."

He laughed through clenched teeth, and she could only guess how badly he hurt. Quickly she assessed their situation. Trace had a bad thigh wound, but she had managed to stop the bleeding with her tourniquet. Now all they could do was wait for help.

"Trace." She wiped the sweat off his dark face, brushed the blue-black hair away from his forehead. "Where are the others? How on earth did you trail us?"

"Maverick and I found the tracks," he sighed, looking up at her as he lay with his head in her naked lap. "That little Comanche could follow a mouse's footprints across solid rock."

His head was warm on her bare thigh, but she never thought of modesty. The situation was too desperate. "Where's Luis? Where's the rest of the crew?"

He frowned up at her, tried to move off her lap, but he was too weak from loss of blood. "Damn!" he swore in his deep voice, "I get myself shot saving your virtue and you ask about the elegant aristocrat!"

"You can't save my virtue, remember?" she said gently,

stroking his face, knowing he was in pain. "You've already taken that."

"I never meant to force you, darlin'," he gasped, "I never meant to—"

"I know, I know," she whispered. "It doesn't matter anymore." She could see his upper thigh, a glimpse of his manhood in the ripped pants leg, and it occurred to her suddenly that she was as naked as the day she was born, but when she tried to move, he protested.

"Don't go, darlin'," he murmured, "don't leave me."

"I was just going to get you some water," she said comfortingly. She laid his head gently on the ground, went over to get the canteen and Holt's whiskey bottle. When she turned around, Trace stared at her with approval.

"Wild One," he murmured, "you're beautiful naked."

"Double damnation!" she scolded, grabbing up her pants as she came back over to the wounded man by the fire, "Even hurt, you think like a randy bull! I should have taken that knife a little higher!"

She knelt, gave him a drink. Cimarron sloshed it around as he sighed. There wasn't that much left. Her own mouth was dry as all west Texas. But she didn't drink, decided to save what little there was for him. If they didn't get help soon, Trace might not make it. She gave him a drink of whiskey. At least it would dull the pain. Then she pulled on her pants.

His eyes flickered open and he smiled faintly. "Like you better naked."

She didn't comment as she tied her shreds of shirt back over her bruised breasts and sat down on the ground and took his head in her lap. Already he felt feverish.

He might not make it through the night, as much blood as he had lost, the way the wound looked. And he was in this fix because of her. "Trace, where's the crew?"

"Coming," he gasped, reaching up to nuzzle his face against her breasts. ". . . Nightwind fastest horse so I came on. Lots of Comanche sign. . . ."

Comanche. There was no other word so frightening on the Texas frontier. And if those red demons found them before the cowboys did . . . She didn't want to think about what they would do to a helpless wounded man and a woman. If the braves were anywhere close, the echoing gunshots would draw them to this place.

Despairingly, she looked toward the horses. Nightwind stood patiently, cropping grass near the other horses. Maybe she could get Trace onto a horse. No, he was too heavy and too weak to mount without a lot of help.

He drifted into unconsciousness, and she had never felt so alone, sitting with his head in her lap with only the occasional snack of a burning branch in the small fire, an insect's chirp in the stillness. She jumped at every noise, thinking she heard Comanche sneaking up on her at the slightest breath of wind. Cicadas made their monotonous hum in the autumn night, the giant firelights lit the ebony darkness. The longer she sat listening, the more frightened she became. And as she became more frightened, she became unreasonably angry with Trace.

She hadn't asked him to mix into this. If he hadn't come along, she would have dealt with Holt somehow. She glanced over at the fallen body. Yes, she would have managed to get the drop on Holt and been on her way. But Trace had stuck his nose in. Now she was here like a small deer staked out to attract wolves. It wasn't fair. It wasn't fair at all!

She looked over at the horses again. Trace wouldn't be any worse off if she left him the canteen, the whiskey. His crew would show up in a couple of hours.

She heard the plaintive hoot of an owl and shivered. *Or was it an owl? Comanche were superstitious about owls, not so much so as the fierce Kiowa, but still. . . .*

Cimarron had never been so frightened. Damn Trace anyway! She hadn't asked him to stick his nose into this, and he'd be fine until his crew got here. *She would never again have such an opportunity,* she thought desperately. Money, all that money Holt had taken was in those saddlebags. This might be her very last chance to escape.

Gently she slid his head from her lap, gathered up all the guns, reloaded them, and laid them next to him, except for the one pistol she stuck in her belt. No one could blame her for saddling up and getting out of here. No one could blame her at all. What help would she be if the Comanche did show up?

Her panic justified her actions in her own mind as she quickly saddled Holt's blue horse. At least, she couldn't be accused of stealing a Triple D mount. She checked to make sure she had the money in the saddlebags as she mounted up. Someday she'd repay it, but right now that money and this horse meant freedom, a fresh start for her.

She sat the blue, looking down at Trace. Yes, he had guns in case a war party happened by. His crew would find him soon, she told herself.

His eyes flickered open, looked up at her. "You—you leaving?"

"Yes," she said. "I've got to think of myself. I've left you water, whiskey, loaded guns. Your men will find you soon. You'll be okay."

He nodded, his expression cynical. "Sure, darlin', don't you worry about me, I'll be just fine. Money's gone from the desk . . . suppose you have that, too. . . ."

"Holt stole it," she said. "I'll pay you back someday. I need it to make a getaway."

It occurred to her he could aim a gun at her, order her to dismount and stay, but he didn't. He just looked at her with those big, dark eyes."

"You've got to understand," she implored, "I would have managed to deal with Holt—"

"You were doin' such a good job of it, too," he whispered, a slight bitter smile on his lips.

"I didn't ask for your help," she snapped. "I didn't ask you to mix in. I've got to look out for myself first. You understand, don't you?"

"Sure, darlin'," he said, "I understand you're just like she was, looking out for number one . . . just a beautiful, selfish whore . . . somehow, I was beginning to think you might be different. . . ."

She couldn't bear to hear any more, couldn't stand the betrayed look on his face. She clucked to the blue and rode out, heard the hammer click back on a pistol.

"Come back here," he ordered. "Come back, you sassy little tart, or I'll blow you right out of that saddle!"

She tensed but kept her horse moving at a walk. She imagined what it would feel like to have a .44 slug hit her between the shoulder blades. It would knock her out of the saddle. She bit her lip, remembered the force of the slug knocking Holt backward, the hole in his chest big enough to put a fist in.

"Come back!" he ordered, "Come back, damn it!"

She heard his voice trail off in helpless frustration. He wouldn't kill her. She'd never really thought he would or she wouldn't have left him the loaded guns. The moody cowboy wouldn't shoot a man in the back, she thought, and he'd never shoot a woman.

She turned in the saddle and looked around. He had managed to raise himself on one elbow and was looking after her. She had never seen such hurt, such a betrayed look on a human face.

Double damnation! Damn! Damn! She reined in the horse, sat there a long moment. She had money and a good horse under her. If she turned back east, rode along the coast, she still might buy her way onto a ship. In front of her lay freedom and a fresh start. Behind her was a wounded cowboy she hated for raping her, a chance of being tortured by Comanche if a war party got there before the crew did. And there was always a rope back at Fandango.

He called after her. "What are you waiting for, darlin'? You've called my bluff! Go on! Get the hell out of here! That's what the señora would do, why should you be any different?"

With a resigned sigh, Cimarron turned the horse, rode back to the campfire, looked down at him. She couldn't read his expression as she dismounted. It was perhaps a mixture of surprise, of utter bewilderment.

She sat down on the ground, gathered him into her lap, hugged him against her breasts like a hurt child. "I don't need a second conscience," she scolded.

"You came back. You really came back...." He laid his

face against her breasts with a tired sigh.

"So I'm a fool," she shrugged, pushing the blue-black hair off his forehead. A disturbing thought came to her, something Holt had said.

"Trace," she said slowly, her face wrinkling with the effort, "in all the time I've been on the ranch, you never told me your last name."

He looked away, as if reluctant, as if he were hiding something. "Does it matter?"

She remembered again the dead man's words. Holt had come to the ranch to ambush a man. Two had to die. Well, the old Don was dying of his malignancy. No one would have to shoot him. And the bullet had missed Luis. Was he still in danger? Maybe it had only been the drunken ravings of a crazy man. But she had to know. "You hate Luis, don't you, Trace?"

"That's no secret," he gasped, "I'd like to see him roast in hell."

"Why?"

He ran his tongue over his cracked dry lips. "I—I can't tell you that . . . can't tell anyone. . . ."

Cimarron reached over, held the canteen to his mouth.

Third in line to inherit the Triple D. She remembered Holt's words. And her Spanish came back to her with a rush. *Uno, dos, tres.* One, two, three. Three. *Tres.* Trace. Oh, dear God, no!

But she had to know. "Your name," she asked, stroking his face as she put down the canteen. "Tell me about your name. What does it mean?"

He was fast sliding into blackness and didn't answer.

"Is it Spanish?" she asked again.

His eyes flickered open and he looked up at her, smiled as he nodded ever so slightly. "Nickname. She called me that. Trace . . . three . . ."

He was almost unconscious in her arms—she knew by the way he breathed, the way his face smoothed out. But she had to know, had to fit the pieces together. "Trace?"

She was not sure he heard her. He was fast sliding into darkness as he moaned slightly. She pulled him up against her breasts, comforting him, warming him with her body. "Trace? What's your last name? Tell me your name."

He only managed to gasp out three words before he slipped away into unconsciousness. Three words. And his voice was so low, she had to put her ear almost against his lips to hear. But when he said them, tears came to her eyes, ran down her face onto his.

"Trace," he gasped, "Trace Durango...."

Chapter Eleven

Cimarron stared down at the unconscious man in her arms. Oh, why had she asked? Sometimes there were things people were better off not knowing.

The fire threw up a little shower of sparks and she looked at the craggy shadows of his face in the firelight. Whatever feeling had been taking root in her heart for him withered and died. Cimarron had been raised in a parsonage. She could never give her love to a killer, and yet . . .

Something rustled in the bushes and she tensed. *Comanches.* But a gentle armadillo ambled into the edge of the firelit circle, turning its little snout toward her curiously. Its armored shell made little clicking sounds as it moved through the grass, stopped to dig for grubs with its long claws. She laughed with relief as it ambled away.

Oh, dear God, she was thirsty! She picked up the canteen, shook it. No, there was only a little, and Trace needed it. He stirred uneasily in her arms and she checked the bandage, loosened the tourniquet. He mumbled something and she leaned closer. "What? What did you say, Trace?"

His eyes never opened, but at the sound of her voice he moved ever so slightly. "No," he mumbled, "don't go . . . don't do this. . . ."

"I'm not going, Trace," she reassured him. "Remember? I came back. I didn't go after all."

"Liar!" He twisted in her arms, and she could only guess what he saw in his fevered unconscious brain as he began to swear, a long, tortured stream of the most terrible curses Cimarron had ever heard. "Whore! You whore... how could you, when we both loved you so?"

She tried to tell him again that she had never left, that she would not leave him, but she couldn't stop his struggles. If he didn't cease, he'd start that wound bleeding again. Cimarron looked toward his leg as he twisted and mumbled.

What kind of terrible, unseen demons did he fight? What horrible memories had his delirium unleashed? How could she soothe the angry, bitter cowboy? A thought came to her. She reached to take his hand in both of hers, and he gripped so hard that Cimarron winced with pain. She leaned over, kissed his lips. In his ear she whispered in Spanish, "I'll never leave you, Trace. *Yo te amo,* I love you. Do you hear me? *Yo te amo,* Trace."

It seemed almost like a miracle to her. He relaxed in her arms with a sigh. The frowning contours of his rugged face smoothed out. But he didn't let go of her hand.

He was still lying unconscious in her arms, still clinging to her hand when the Triple D cowboys rode into the camp a little after dawn.

Luis heaved a sigh of relief as he dismounted. "Señorita Cimarron, we've been so worried about you." He squatted by the fire, looked from her to Trace as the others dismounted. "How did all this happen?"

"Well," Cimarron began uncertainly, not quite sure what to say. Whatever she said, Trace would tell them the truth, and at the very least, she'd be in jail for stealing a horse. Oh my! She'd forgotten about the saddlebags of gold from the hacienda study. What a fool she'd been not to leave last night when she had the chance. Yes, she'd end up in the local jail, and when the sheriff checked with the one in Fandango....

But Sanchez saved her from answering as he strode across the circle and looked down at Holt's body. *"Dios!* This *hombre* is most dead!" He crossed himself reverently and she saw Luis look up and seem to see the body for the first time, and he crossed himself, too.

"Señorita," Luis asked again, "What happened?"

Trace's eyes flickered open, and contempt and pure hatred

crossed his features as he saw Luis Durango. She glanced from one to the other, seeing a resemblance for the very first time. The hard line of the mouths, the hawklike profiles, much like old Don Diego's.

Trace interrupted her thoughts as he grinned weakly. "Any you cowboys got a smoke?"

"Sure, boss!"

"Boy, howdy, are we glad to see you, Trace!"

The men clustered around, offering them both water from their canteens, rolling a cigarillo for Trace. Old Sanchez brought over a saddle, propped the foreman up, and lit the smoke with his crippled hand. *"Dios, compadre!"* the vaquero sighed, "we didn't really expect to find you alive after what we found a couple of hours ago at the Rocking R."

She saw the gallant Luis glance at her, shake his head ever so slightly in warning at the Mexican.

She looked from one to the other. "What are you trying to keep a secret?"

Luis shrugged, ran his hand through his gray-streaked hair. "Señorita, it is not something to tell a lady—"

"What happened at the Rocking R?" Cimarron demanded.

She glanced over at Trace propped up by the saddle. He paused with the cigarillo halfway to his lips. "The Rowlands are friends of Don Diego—"

"Were," Luis sighed. "I didn't see any point in the señorita's hearing the horrible details." He frowned at Sanchez, looked from Cimarron to Trace. "War party," he said. "Must have hit the ranch early last night. Never had a chance."

Cimarron automatically looked up at the sky, remembering last night's brightness. *Comanche moon.*

Trace swore weakly. "Anybody left alive?"

Sanchez took off his sombrero, fumbled with the brim. "We buried the man and the half-grown son. What was left of them, anyway. They'd been . . ." He looked over at Cimarron, hesitated, didn't finish. . .

Young Maverick squatted by the fire. "Livestock all taken. Might have been Comancheros involved. There were bootprints—"

"Comancheros this far east!" Luis snorted disdainfully, lighting a cigar. "Just braves wearing stolen boots off some poor dead Texan's feet!"

Trace glanced inquiringly at Maverick.

"That could be," the kid nodded.

Trace sighed, leaned back against the saddle, his face lined with weariness and pain. "What about the rest of the family?"

Luis fingered his mustache. "We found Mrs. Rowland's body a couple of miles from the ranch. That whole filthy pack of savages must have . . ." He looked over at Cimarron, didn't finish.

"What about those two little kids?" Trace said, trying to get to his feet.

Sanchez caught him to keep him from falling. "Right now, boss, you can't even stand up."

"*Si,*" Luis said, "we've got to do something about those poor little kids." He stood up. "I'll go after them myself, even if I get killed for it! I—"

"No." Maverick shook his head, regret in his eyes. "Believe me, Señor Durango, the trail is old. You know I'd be the first to want to go after them, knowing what my mother suffered, but that band is probably clear out in west Texas by now. Nobody can track them into their own lair deep in Komantcia."

Luis nodded, crossed himself regretfully. "I suppose you're right. But I'm willing to lead a rescue. Poor little tykes. God help them!"

Sanchez eased Trace back down. Trace said, "In case they're still around, we need to clear out of here."

Luis took a deep draw on his cigar, looked toward Holt's body. "A couple of you hands bury that *hombre.*" He looked at Cimarron. "What happened here, anyway?"

She had never felt so helpless as she groped for an answer. *What was it going to be like in prison?*

"Well—" But as she started to speak, Trace interrupted her. "Loco *hombre* abducted the lady at gunpoint when she caught him going through your desk, Luis."

"Holt has the money in his saddlebags," Cimarron blurted with a glance of gratitude toward the foreman. "He tried to . . ." She felt her face color as all the men turned toward her. "Well, you know," she finished.

"Si," Trace put in, "and while she was fighting him, I came along. Holt made the mistake of drawing on me."

Luis flicked a bug off the fine silk shirt. "Well, my dear, I'm glad you're not harmed. If I had been here, I would have whipped him like a dog, and then—"

"Oh, Luis," she smiled up at him warmly, "you're such a gentleman!"

Trace made a rude noise. "We can't stay here all morning listening to what the aristocracy *might* have done. We've got to get out of here."

Luis frowned, nodded. *"Si.* You men got that saddle tramp buried? Let's go!"

She watched Maverick kick dirt over the small fire as Sanchez and another cowboy put Trace's arms over their shoulders, tried to walk him to the horse.

His face contorted with pain.

Sanchez shook his head. "You can't bear to ride, *compadre*. You'll have to wait till we go get a wagon."

Trace gave him a stubborn look. "You just help me to my horse, old friend. We can't sit out here waiting for a wagon with Comanche in the area."

He should be ashamed of himself, she thought as she watched the old vaquero help Trace to the big black stallion. How could he look the man in the eye and talk about friendship when Trace was sneaking Rosa into his bed at night?

Luis came to her side. "Something wrong, Señorita? You frown so."

"No," she lied, "just tired. I'll be all right once we get back to the ranch."

He saddled her horse, offering his cupped hands so she could mount. "You know, Cimarron," he mused as he helped her up, "this whole thing strikes me as very strange. Did the dead man say anything, tell you anything before he died?"

"Why, no," she gulped, avoiding his eyes. She didn't know whether Luis suspected much of the plot against him, but somehow, she just couldn't bring herself to tell him of Trace's guilt. Not yet.

She saw the agony in Trace's gentle eyes as the men put him on his horse. His even white teeth caught his bottom lip and she winced, watching the pain on his face as he settled into the saddle.

Sanchez looked up at him. *"Compadre,* can you ride?"

He swayed a little in the saddle and Cimarron wanted to scream at all of them. *Can't you see how bad he hurts? No, of course he can't ride! That leg must be agony!*

Trace's dark face paled for a moment and then he straightened in the saddle. *"Si,* I can ride. I'm half-Cheyenne. Remember?"

Half-Cheyenne. The portrait of the young Indian girl came to her mind as they rode out. She remembered the very soft, gentle eyes of the painting, looked again at the suffering eyes of the half-breed hanging tight to his saddle.

Why had she not seen the resemblance before? Cimarron glanced again at Trace's large, dark eyes. They were just like the young girl's. *His sister,* she realized suddenly. *Velvet Eyes was Trace Durango's sister.* That only made the puzzle a bigger tangle to her. She thought about it all the way back to the ranchero.

Every foot of the ride must have been agony for the wounded man, she thought with sympathy and admiration. But Trace never cried out or complained. Luis, on the other hand, grouched the whole distance about the heat, how saddlesore he was, how bad the flies were.

Well, Cimarron thought defensively as she saw the crew exchange looks of disgust, after all, Luis was aristocracy, anyone could see that. He wasn't used to living the grind of an ordinary cowboy. And besides, the Spaniard was almost old enough to be some of these young cowboys' father. A man of thirty-nine or forty couldn't be expected to keep up this pace, especially if he were used to a life of ease and culture.

Trace's wound started bleeding again, and he swayed in

his saddle, more dead than alive by the time they made it back to the ranch.

The old Don, who seemed to be in remission, hobbled around, barking orders as they put Trace to bed. He sent Luis himself riding after the doctor.

Cimarron put a cold, wet cloth on the man's feverish face as he twisted and thrashed about.

The frail Don swore under his breath. "Just when we really need Rosa, she goes off to visit her family."

Sanchez pulled at his mustache with embarrassment. "But señor, how could she know when she left that we would come in this afternoon with a badly injured man?"

The white-haired Don nodded. "That's true, *compadre*. If she were my wife, I'd be worried about her riding off like that unescorted."

Sanchez's face furrowed with noticeable embarrassment. "Señor Diego, you know Rosa well. Does any man, least of all her husband, tell that hot-tempered girl what to do?"

Don Diego smiled. "You're right, *compadre*. If Rosa crosses paths with a stray Comanche, he'd probably run away from her fiery tongue."

Cimarron frowned at them both. "Get out of here," she ordered. "And señor, send one of the servant girls with plenty of hot water and bandages—"

"Señorita," he gestured, "this is not your job, one of the girls—"

"I'll take care of it," Cimarron said firmly, shooing them out. "Bring the doctor right up when Luis gets here."

They backed out of the room, and she took a pair of scissors, cut his dirty, bloody clothes away until he lay naked on his bed. Trace had the body of a Greek statue, she thought with awe, remembering a picture she'd once seen, studying every inch of him as he lay unconscious. She had known he was more man than she had ever met, but she had never really studied him before.

A girl brought water and bandages. It annoyed Cimarron the way the girl lingered, wanting to help. Why should she care if the girl's eyes seemed to caress the big half-breed, running over him as if she wanted very much to touch him?

He wouldn't be satisfying any little Mexican chambermaids for a long time.

The girl sighed again. "I'd be glad to replace the señorita looking after him," she said eagerly.

"Get out of here," Cimarron snapped. "I don't need any help; *gracias.*"

The girl fled, and Cimarron dipped a soft cloth in warm water and began to wash his lithe, sinewy body. *What a man.* She couldn't help but look at every inch of him as she washed him gently. As she washed across his chest, touched one of his dark nipples, he smiled ever so slightly in his sleep. Cimarron reddened in annoyance, wondering whether it was a servant girl, one of Miss Fancy's finest, or Rosa he dreamed of as she stroked him with the soapy cloth.

The leg wound looked bad but it had stopped bleeding. She changed the bandage and sat down on the edge of his bed. Cimarron was so tired, she almost felt like lying down next to him, snuggling up against him.

Double damnation! She jerked herself awake as she dozed off. What was she thinking of? What would people think if they found her snuggled down next to him? What did the maids already think about her insisting on caring for him? She ought to go on to bed and let the servants look after Trace, but she couldn't bring herself to do that.

He twisted restlessly in his sleep, mumbled something. Remembering what had worked before, she clasped his hand, stroked his feverish face. *"Yo te amo,* Trace," she said automatically without really thinking of the words, "I'm here. Take it easy."

She heard a scratching at the door and little Tequila scampered into the room, looked up at her, whining. She reached down to pat him. "Don't worry, this half-breed renegade's going to live to keep the girls at Miss Fancy's happy for many years yet."

Tequila promptly jumped up on the bed and burrowed in under the coverlet until only his little black nose was visible. He didn't come out again until Luis arrived with the doctor. Then he came out from under the covers snapping and growling.

Cimarron caught the dog. "I don't know what gets into him," she said sheepishly as the pet growled again at Luis. "Bad dog!" she scolded, "Bad, bad dog!"

Luis glared at the chihuahua as it cocked its head at him. "I heard the savages eat dogs," he laughed. "That little devil would only make a snack, but I'd offer the bread to make the sandwich."

Cimarron laughed, put the dog outside the bedroom, closed the door.

Dr. Hastings was red-faced, apologetic, slightly drunk. "Awfully sorry, miss. I was just having a little toddy to relax myself. Wasn't expecting to have to go on a call this late."

Cimarron glared at him. "If you were any more relaxed, you'd slide down the wall!"

Luis gestured consolingly. "Sorry, señorita, he's the best we can do."

"I'm afraid, that's all!" the man defended himself. "A rider just came hell for leather through town this afternoon. Comanches have been raiding again, hit near Austin. We never had things like that in Connecticut!"

Luis gave her a warning shake of the head. He was right, she thought, no use scaring the doctor more by telling him about the massacre at the Rocking R. He'd hear about it soon enough.

The doctor started to pull back the sheet and glanced uncomfortably at her.

Luis fidgeted. "Señorita Cimarron," he said uncertainly, "don't you want to step outside while the doctor, well, you know. . . ."

She yawned, too tired for false modesty. "What'd be the point? I stripped him and put him to bed myself."

Luis looked both horrified and annoyed. "You? A lady? With all the servants we have?"

She wasn't going to argue the issue, especially since she wasn't sure by his tone whether he was upset because she had dirtied her hands doing such menial work or whether he didn't like the idea of her seeing and handling the young stud's body.

"I'll go have a glass of Madeira while the doctor examines

him," she suggested.

"Good idea," Luis said, "I'll join you. It was a long ride. I should have sent a cowboy."

Dr. Hastings turned toward them, pulled at his yellowed mustache. "Perhaps a drink would clear my head—"

Cimarron frowned. "When you finish with your patient, doctor," she answered firmly as she and Luis went down to the study.

She was so tired. She stretched and yawned, suddenly noticed Luis staring. Cimarron looked down. Her torn shirt had parted as she stretched, revealing an expanse of pink-tipped breasts.

"Oh, excuse me, I had forgotten. . . ." Her face flushed crimson, especially at the sudden hunger in his eyes. Luis turned away abruptly, went to the door, called a servant.

"It's all right, señorita," he said smoothly, stopping to admire himself in the big study mirror, "you've had such an ordeal, and you're exhausted."

She stood up quickly. "Maybe I should go to my room—"

"No, no. The girl will bring you a shirt," Luis said. "I want to speak with you privately."

The servant girl entered with a flowing robe. Quickly Cimarron slipped it over her torn clothes.

"Now, good as new!" Luis said with a smooth smile. "Madeira, my dear?"

"I'd love some." She sank onto the leather sofa gratefully, looked around the room. "Seeing all these books reminds me that a couple of days ago the biggest worry on my mind was starting a school for the vaqueros' children." She laughed wearily.

He gave her a condescending look as he brought over a crystal goblet of wine. "I thought you were going to keep the ranch accounts?"

"I can do both."

"That's a lot of work for one little girl."

"Luis," she flared, standing up, "Don't treat me like a stupid child! I hate it when you insult me that way!"

He was instantly apologetic. "A thousand pardons, my dear. You see, I'm a gentleman of the old school. I've been reared to think fine ladies should be decorative, produce children. I spent too long in Spain, I suppose."

Idly she walked over to run her hand along the rows and rows of fine leather-bound volumes. "It's such a waste, Luis, all your fine books and little children who can't even read and write their names."

Luis shrugged, looked annoyed. "I think we've had this discussion before. It seems silly to me to educate future vaqueros and serving girls, but your wish is my command." He made a low, courtly bow.

She ran her hand along the row of books, looking at the titles. Shakespeare, Lord Tennyson, Chaucer. "I might educate a future poet," she said.

"Oh, really!" He sat down, crossed his legs.

She ran her hand further down the shelf. Broken Bones. Poisons. Infectious Diseases. "One of these children might even grow up to be a doctor."

At that, Luis laughed out loud. "You've sold me, my dear. Use the books, run a school. Anything that pleases you pleases me."

The old Don stuck his head in the door. "Ah, here you are. I thought I heard laughter. How's the patient?"

Luis jumped to his feet, instantly solicitous. "Come in, sir. Let me get you some wine."

Cimarron looked at Don Diego, thinking what a rugged, dignified cowboy he was. "Our patient's fine, I think," she said. "Dr. Hastings is with him now."

Don Diego nodded as he sat down and accepted the wine. "I was out in the courtyard, looking at the fountain, thinking...."

His voice trailed off sadly and Cimarron thought again about the faithless señora. About what emotional wreckage she had left behind her.

Luis lit a cigar. "Trace will be all right," he said gently to the old man.

The Don sipped his Madeira. "If only his sister would come home—"

"Everything's going to be fine," Luis said soothingly. "Why don't you go to bed now?" He went over, very gently assisted the old man to his feet.

"I believe you're right," Don Diego said heavily. He handed his glass to Luis, turned toward Cimarron. "You'll call me if there's a crisis?"

"Of course." She nodded encouragingly and caught the grateful look Luis gave her. "Now you go on to bed."

The Don paused in the doorway. "I'll go by his room, check on him before I retire." He studied Cimarron a long moment. "You're very much like my señora," he said softly. "I hope you'll stay."

Luis smiled, put the Don's goblet on a table. "Of course, she's going to stay. I'll insist!" He winked at Cimarron. The old man nodded, left the study.

They stood listening to his footsteps up the stairs. Cimarron looked at Luis with admiration as she drank her wine. "You're very kind and thoughtful."

He shrugged, took a puff of his cigar, looked slightly embarrassed. "My mother raised gentlemen."

She thought again of the portrait of the dignified old señora in the upstairs hall. The old Don's first wife, she thought, and then he had married a fiery young one who was faithless to him.

"Luis," she said without thinking, "Why does Trace hate you so? Is it over Velvet Eyes?"

His handsome face turned pale. "I-I haven't any idea what you're talking about," he said, but his eyes said he lied. His goblet clattered as he set it on the desk. "What has he said to you?" he thundered. "What has he told you?"

"Nothing!" she answered quickly, surprised at his sudden flash of temper. "He won't discuss her. Won't talk about her at all." She really should warn him Trace had paid Holt to try to kill him. But she couldn't bring herself to do it. At any rate, Trace would be no threat to anyone for the next few days.

Luis seemed to regain his composure. "It—it has to do with . . . it's a personal matter that I hope you won't bring up again. We must protect the old man, don't you see?"

She didn't, but she cowered a little before his anger. His expression, his actions had told her enough. Whatever was wrong between those two centered on the faithless Velvet Eyes. And the inheritance.

They heard a step and Dr. Hastings entered the study carrying his black bag.

Cimarron looked at him anxiously. "How is he, doctor?"

The man laughed, accepting the glass Luis poured with a grateful sigh. "Strong as the young stallion he is," he said. "It'd take more than that to kill that one."

"Oh, good!" Cimarron said with a rush of relief, "I was so afraid. . . ."

Luis gave her a searching look.

"He saved my life," she hastened to add. "After all, if it hadn't been for Trace . . . well, I'm grateful. Think how badly I'd feel if something happened to him."

Luis's face softened. "Oh, of course." Was that jealousy on his handsome features?

The doctor drained his goblet. "The old man looks good tonight," he said. "Just to see him, you'd never know—"

"Well, doctor," Cimarron said, "perhaps your diagnosis is wrong. When the war ends, Luis had said something about taking him back East to a specialist."

Luis sighed, shook his head. "I try not to get too hopeful, my dear, when he goes into remission like this."

"That's right," Dr. Hastings agreed. "With cancer, they seemed to have their ups and downs. Why, I've seen them look great and then, just like that!" He snapped his fingers. "They go downhill and die overnight."

Luis's face furrowed with grief. "Let's not even talk of the possibility of his death tonight. We've all just been through a terrible ordeal."

"I'm awfully sorry." The man held his glass out for a refill. "I forget how fond you are of him, Luis."

"As are we all," Luis said, taking the goblet from his hand. Instead of refilling it, he set it on the desk, took his elbow, steered him gently out the door. "I think you need some rest, Dr. Hastings," she heard Luis say from the front hall.

* * *

While Luis walked the old man out to his buggy, Cimarron gathered up the dirty goblets. With Rosa gone to visit her family, the house looked as if the servants were doing a slipshod job. The wilted oleanders in the vases should be replaced, she thought, but there might not be any blooms left. They had reached their zenith in the summer. Strange that Rosa would go off alone with all the Indian scare going on. If she were Sanchez, Cimarron thought, she wouldn't allow it. She thought about it a minute. Probably Rosa did what she wanted and her husband was afraid to speak out. It occurred to her that the Mexican might already know his wife was unfaithful but did not dare object.

She yawned. Every bone in her body ached with weariness, but she intended to sit by Trace's bed all night, every night until he was out of danger. And then, if Rosa still wasn't back, Cimarron would take over this household, snap all these lazy servants into shape. If there was one thing she knew, it was about housework, managing a home, and cooking. *Rosa*. Once again she remembered the girl coming out of Trace's room. She tried to tell herself the emotion that came to her was indignation. *Why then did it feel like jealousy?*

Luis came back into the room. "Sorry, my dear. Dr. Hastings was in worse shape than usual this evening."

"That old drunk!" She turned to blow out the lamp. "Is it safe for him to go driving off alone?"

"I thought about that so I put him up in the bunkhouse tonight," he said, standing in the lamplight. "I know he's a drunk, Cimarron, but he's a nice old man, and I'd feel terrible if anything happened to him."

Such a good person. She started to blow out the lamp. Luis stood in the light, studying her. She took a good, long look at Luis Durango, saw even more clearly his resemblance to the old Don and in a lesser degree to Trace. All the pieces of the puzzle fell neatly into place for her. One, two, three. Don Diego, Luis, and Trace. Grandfather, son, and . . . grandson.

Chapter Twelve

The Comanchero, El Lobo, squatted by the campfire, smiling with satisfaction as the new batch of weeping captives were herded into a pen near Enchanted Rock.

By the Holy Mother, the Comanche had helped bring in a promising bunch this time! Some would be ransomed by frantic relatives, some would be sold to Mexican silver and copper mines, and others, the savages would keep for slaves. He shook his head. Better to be dead than a slave in a Comanche camp. And the women. Ah, *si*. He pulled at his chewed-off right ear as he envisioned today's entertainment.

He stuck a cigar between his wolfish, prominent teeth. El Lobo. He liked his name. The Wolf was a good name for a swarthy, mixed-breed leader of the Comanchero.

El Lobo frowned, scatched his dirty beard. No, he was not the leader. He only took orders from the leader. It was not fair, not fair at all. El Lobo did all the work, took all the risks while the leader sat in that fine house and took part of the money from the sale of the stolen livestock, and captives' ransom. All the leader did was pick up gossip, send word as to where to strike. Well, this one was about to call a halt to the arrangement. Someday soon, the leader would be in for much shock when he needed El Lobo and the Comancheros. Would he be surprised! The Wolf and his savage pack of renegades were leaving Texas soon and returning to their stronghold in New Mexico.

With an oath, he wiped his sweaty, tangled hair. *Si*, that

one would be in for a heap of trouble then. He would really appreciate all that El Lobo had done for him. Why, the leader had never even had to come face to face with this bunch of Comanche. El Lobo and the messenger did it all. The messenger was due in today with yet more orders. The Wolf took a puff of the cigar, ran his tongue over his dirty fangs. Annoyed he looked up at the approach of his own second-in-command, accompanied now by a hatchet-faced chief, Pine da poi, which was Comanche for "whip owner."

"Ah, Pedro, how goes it?"

The short Mexican had one blind eye and walked bowlegged from years in the saddle. "Good, my general." He squatted by the fire respectfully. "Are you ready to inspect the captives now?"

El Lobo considered, listening to the weeping of the women, the screaming of the children. They were like sheep, he thought with annoyance, watching them crowd together in their pen near the base of the gigantic, round knob of pink granite. Enchanted Rock. The Indians thought it holy because it loomed up out of nowhere on the landscape. At night its hot surface contracted, creaking and groaning as the cool night air reacted with the heat. The savages even said it glowed at night, thought it haunted. . . .

The Comanche squatted down, his quirt whip hanging from his belt. "We want to scalp some of them," he demanded, scratching his privates. "We need the medicine of the scalp dance to insure the coming big raid."

El Lobo yawned. "Maybe later," he said. "Are there any pretty captives? Any rich ones?"

Pedro belched, his blind eye staring into nowhere. "Nothing very pretty this time. One who might be rich, judging from her jewelry. She was picnicking with a man, and when he saw the war party he jumped in the buggy and galloped it back to Austin."

"Such a brave Tejano to run for his life and leave the lady behind," El Lobo sneered.

Pedro's blind eye stared unblinking. "When you see the sow, you won't be surprised that he ran off and left her to save herself."

The Wolf smiled. That raid must have been a real surprise to the gringos, he thought. The citizens of Austin would never believe the raiders could be so daring. But the Comanchero were already planning their attack around Fredericksburg, just a few miles south of here. *Si,* they might hit other towns, too, like maybe Fandango.

El Lobo looked up at his lieutenant as he chewed his cigar. "But those two children we took in that ranch raid near San Antone are unusually pretty. I know a place in Mexico City that caters to rich gentlemen of . . . unusual tastes. We can sell that pair there."

Pine da poi shook his head. "No, some of our friends among the Kiowa saw them and want to adopt those two little ones to replace babies they have lost."

El Lobo started to argue. Damn! He hadn't raided the Rocking R just to pick up a few horses and cattle. The leader had mentioned those unusually pretty children, was already calculating how much that pair would bring in Mexico. El Lobo looked at the grim, hatchet-faced brave. The Kiowa and the Comanche had been close friends and allies for a hundred years. To offend the Kiowa was to anger the Comanche. He decided not to argue over the Rowland children.

Pedro scratched himself, frowned at a spotted dog lazing in the shade. "Fleas!" he grumbled in Spanish. "All these camps have dogs everywhere and the fleas eat me alive!" He pulled out his pistol, aimed at the spotted mongrel.

Whip Owner frowned blackly and El Lobo reached out and caught Pedro's pistol hand. "No, No!" he cautioned. "Are you loco? Do you wish to see us all massacred? If so, hurt a dog in a Comanche camp!"

Pedro's grimy face turned ashen as he looked over at Pine da poi glaring silently back at him. Very slowly, he put the pistol back in its holster, smiled sheepishly. "I keep forgetting. It is stupid to revere a dog because it is cousin to the coyote, their sacred spirit animal."

El Lobo glanced at the scowling brave. "Scratching fleas," he said softly in Spanish, "is much better than being staked out on an anthill."

The sound of a woman sobbing drifted on the September air. El Lobo felt his groin tighten in anticipation. The German areas of the hill country were more apt to provide the kind of women he liked.

"Any pretty ones? Any blond ones?"

"*Si* and no," Pedro grinned. "Some pretty ones, but the one who is blond is not pretty. In fact, she has an ugly face and the rump and legs of a palamino mare."

El Lobo took a puff of his cigar and winked at Pedro. "You know how I like to take a woman best. I will not even see her face. Just as long as she has yellow hair."

Pedro laughed. "Are you sure, my general? I have been making the men wait until you select the one you want before I turned them loose on the other females."

"We deserve to enjoy the women, too," Whip Owner argued in Comanche.

"*Si*, of course," El Lobo answered in a mix of border Spanish and the warrior's own tongue. He started to use sign language, remembered the Comanche didn't use it as well as the other Plains tribes, returned to border Spanish. "It is only fair. And after the men have enjoyed them all week, we will ransom them back to their frantic men. The ones too poor to be ransomed we will see or let the Comanche keep as rewards for their help."

Pedro stood up. "Shall I bring you the blond one now?"

El Lobo yawned. "No, later." He reached for a bottle of mescal. "Has the messenger arrived yet?"

"No, not yet. The sentries have seen the horse approaching, though." He hesitated. "My general, the men are eager to enjoy the captives. Is it all right if we—?"

"*Si*, of course." He waved Pedro away. "Share them among our men." He glanced sideways at the hatchet-faced brave. "And, of course, give our Indian comrades some of them. Just leave the blond one penned up until I take care of business."

"And after you finish with her?" Pedro asked.

El Lobo laughed. "Don't I always share with my men?"

Pedro and the Indian walked brisky toward the cage. In minutes, as El Lobo leaned against the rock smoking his cigar, he heard screams, female voices pleading for mercy in English and German.

Holy Mother of God, he wished they wouldn't take on so. The noise echoing through the vast emptiness annoyed his sensibilities. If he weren't so lazy, he'd go watch the fun. From here, he could see Pedro dragging a slim girl from the pen. Two other Comancheros caught a screaming older woman, pulled her out of the wooden cage, tore her clothes away. In minutes, the warriors had joined in, dragging the hapless captives out to share among themselves. He watched idly as one girl broke away from her captor, ran across the prairie. The men laughed at her vain attempt at escape, like cats playing with a small mouse. Hatchet Face ran after her. She shrieked when he tore her dress away.

Why do they make such a fuss, El Lobo thought with annoyance as he took another drink from the bottle. After all, that was what women were intended for. He could see the dumpy blonde cowering in the pen as she watched the violence and the rape of the others. This was the one deserted by her cowardly companion on the outskirts of Austin. She was too old for his taste, thirty or thirty-five, at least. And Pedro was right. She had a long, plain face and thick legs. But she did have yellow hair. With another few drinks of mescal, she might look pretty to him. He took another good look, laughed aloud. Well, maybe it would take more than a few drinks. . . .

Later, most of these same women would be ransomed back by their frantic families, but others would not. Some of the white men could not accept a woman who had been repeatedly raped by filthy Indians. And never in the history of Texas had a grown woman captive ever been returned by the savages without being raped first.

Some of those who were ransomed would be unable to face the curious, morbid curiosity of their friends and relatives. More than once, a ransomed woman had later committed suicide or lost her mind. El Lobo spat to one side. That was not his problem. His job was to make a profit from both ransom and selling guns and ammunition to the savages, taking cattle, women, and other booty in trade.

By the Holy Mother, it was hotter than the hubs of hell in this place. He slapped a fly on his greasy, bearded face, thinking longingly of his stronghold in the Sangre de Cristo Mountains. *The blood of Christ. Si,* the iron rich hills of New Mexico did glow red in the sunsets. And it was cool in the high, thin air. El Lobo was going back there in a couple of weeks whether the leader agreed or not. In fact, he might not even tell him the Comanchero were leaving. This war was winding down, any fool could see that. Soon the soldiers and all the men who had gone east would return to protect the ranches. Raiders would catch hell then from the angry Texans, the Rangers. But the Sangre de Cristo Mountains were more easily defended against attacks. It would take a good army to come into New Mexico after the Comanchero. Next year, when events quieted and Texans least expected it, the Comanchero would raid again.

A woman screamed and he frowned, watching her struggling on the ground. Four Comanches were holding down her hands and feet while another raped her. The sight of his humping over her pale naked body made the Wolf's groin throb with anticipation, and he looked toward the light-haired captive cowering alone in the cage.

Blonde women. Automatically, his hand went up to touch the scarred side of his head. There was no left ear anymore. That damned Cheyenne Dog Soldier had seen to that. El Lobo frowned, took a drink of mescal. He knew some of his men called him "half-ear" behind his back. They would not dare do so to his face. The right ear half-chewed off in a fight, the left one sliced away by that fierce Dog Soldier, Iron Knife. All over a pretty white girl . . .

It was a terrible weakness, he admitted, this thing he had for yellow-haired women. Someday, it was going to get him killed. It had already cost him his left ear, and if it had not been for the mercy of the little blonde, Summer Sky, it would have cost him his life.

He remembered the incident as clearly as if it had happened this morning instead of a half a dozen years ago . . . a white girl taken from a Butterfield stagecoach. She belonged heart, soul, and body to a fierce half-breed Dog

Soldier, Iron Knife, whom, it was said, had a long time before been known as Falling Star. . . .

El Lobo looked down at his left wrist, remembering the Rio Grande duel to the death over the girl. If he'd known how much she meant to the Indian, he wouldn't have tried to rape her and then offer to buy her from the warrior.

Half a dozen years ago, El Lobo had accompanied two Comanche chiefs, Buffalo Hump and Little Buffalo, and the Kiowa leader, Aperian Crow, up to parlay with the Cheyenne in the Indian Territory.

He tossed his cigar into the campfire now, remembering. The Cheyenne were camped very far east that season, up on the Arrowpoint the whites called the Arkansas River. Little Buffalo and Aperian Crow urged the Cheyenne to join them in warring against the whites, but Iron Knife had swayed his people against it. Buffalo Hump then decided to meet with the white soldiers at Rush Springs to discuss peace. But another group of soldiers had found Buffalo Hump's camp first and slaughtered the Comanche.

Well, because of that damned Iron Knife, the Comanchero had made no weapons sales there. Now the Cheyenne were somewhere up in Colorado, fighting vainly to protect their hunting grounds from gold prospectors. And just like their friends, the Comanche and Kiowa to the south, the Cheyenne were taking advantage of the lack of soldiers to spread death and destruction all through Colorado Territory and Kansas. Between them, the fierce Plains tribes had even managed to shut down traffic on the Santa Fe Trail.

El Lobo reached up to touch the scar where once he'd had a left ear. A Rio Grande duel . . . he'd been so sure he could win, because he was so skilled with the knife. Then he'd found out too late why the Cheyenne called the big halfbreed Cheyenne Iron Knife. They said the half-breed had been fathered by a chief called War Bonnet, and his mother was a German girl stolen from a Texas wagon train many years ago, one Texanna.

El Lobo looked down at his wrist again. It was his appetite for blond women that had cost him his ear in the Rio Grande duel. He had seen this Summer Sky, hungered for her, followed her down to the river while the warriors were in council. She had the longest wheat-colored hair he'd ever seen and eyes pale blue as a July afternoon. No wonder they called her Summer Sky.

He'd only meant to enjoy her a little, not realizing Cheyenne had such strong possessive feelings about females, not like the Comanche, where brothers often enjoyed each other's wives. Even now he could remember the feel of her full breasts, the cold water as he dragged her into the shallows. He had her on her belly, holding her face down in the stream, getting ready to take her from behind. But she had fought and screamed like a small panther.

And then suddenly, her Dog Soldier was pulling him away and El Lobo knew he was about to regret ever lusting after the Cheyenne captive.

And so there had been a Rio Grande duel. The chiefs tied the two men's left wrists together, armed them each with only a knife. The winner was to cut himself loose from the loser's dead body, take the girl. El Lobo was good with a knife, but the big half-breed was better. Only the mercy of the little blonde had kept Iron Knife from cutting El Lobo's throat. The brave had cut off the Comanchero's ear as a warning when he turned him loose. . . .

The sound of a horse approaching brought him out of his memories. He scratched like an old lobo wolf sunning himself on a warm day, looked up as the rider dismounted.

"Good to see you again," El Lobo smiled as he stood up. "We haven't seen each other in some time."

The Mexican girl nodded as she tied her mount to a twisted cedar tree. "There's been no need. You know what the leader expects, and your men have met him with the money regularly when he goes off the ranch."

He offered her the bottle of mescal, thinking how many times he had enjoyed her body when she had brought messages over the past couple of years. She was losing her looks fast, he thought critically, her body thickening, her face sagging. In another couple of years, no man would give her a second look. Even El Lobo did not feel himself quicken with desire when he looked at her, as he had in times past.

He watched her drink as he sat back down by the fire. "How are things on the Triple D?"

Rosa took another long drink, wiped her mouth. "My love will soon be the Don of the ranch, and then I will be the señora, and when Velvet Eyes returns—"

"*Si*, of course, but remember," he reminded her, taking the bottle himself, "don't get too impatient. There are still two Durangos, father and son, standing in our leader's way to the inheritance."

She frowned, and he noticed new small lines around her full mouth. "The old man will be gone soon. As for the other, well, my love tried to have him bushwhacked and the gunman missed. That loco one was not such a good shot."

He swore a string of filthy oaths. "I should have known better than give him the job. Is our leader angry?"

"*Si*. But I think he knows you did the best you could by hiring this Holt."

El Lobo nodded with a laugh as he drank again. "If you want something done right, you must do it yourself."

"Or get someone you can depend on to do it," she said, raising one eyebrow calculatingly at him.

He put his hand on her thigh. "I see trouble in your eyes. What else is happening on the Triple D?"

She put her hand on his hand, moved it slowly up and down her thigh, working the skirt up. "I have been thinking of loving you all this long ride. Can't we take care of business, messages, later?"

She leaned forward. He could see into the neck of her low-cut blouse. Her breasts were large, he thought as he looked, but beginning to sag. Still, they were inviting.

"You little *puta*." He pulled her to him with a grin. "Does he know you make love to me when we meet?"

She pulled his shirt open, ran her hand over the thick fur of his chest. "Probably. What scares me is that I don't think he cares. Sometimes I think he uses both of us."

El Lobo stood up, turned toward his tent behind him. "Are you hinting to return to New Mexico with me?"

She picked up the bottle, followed him into the tent. "Of course not. I have waited a long time to marry him, take a place of honor in the household as his wife."

He opened his shirt. "Has your old husband died?"

She took off her skirt, pulled the blouse over her head. "One thing at a time," she answered. "I'll deal with that problem when Don Diego and his son are gone. Then I will convince my love to send Sanchez away . . . or kill him."

"Sanchez has been on the Triple D for many years. I do not think our leader would do that." El Lobo took off his pants, stood looking at her naked body critically. *Si,* she was getting flabby, losing her looks. But still, she was good to a man, know how to satisfy him. If only she had yellow hair, he might steal her, take her back to his beloved Sangre de Cristos with him, make her his woman. As it was, willing Mexican girls with black hair could be picked up anyplace. He had several just like her, only younger, back at his stronghold.

Rosa came into his arms, placed her face against his hairy chest. "What are you thinking?"

"How desirable, how beautiful you are," he lied, gasping in pleasure as her sharp teeth found his nipple. His grimy hand went down to cup her big breast, ran his thumb across the dark rosette. Her wide mouth turned up and he ran his tongue across her lips, bit her tongue.

He put his hands on her bare shoulders, pushed her to her knees as he stood there. "You know what I like," he whispered. "Make me want you."

She complied and suddenly he felt his manhood swell, throb with anticipation at the touch of her warm mouth.

"Rosa, you know how I like to take a woman." He tried to push her to her hands and knees, but she resisted, pulling him down to the blanket.

"Not yet," she whispered, her voice husky with her own need. "Let me enjoy you first."

He lay flat on his back and she mounted him, riding him with an intensity that built and built. His hands reached up to pull her pendulous, sagging breasts down to his lips.

"My stallion," she whispered as the rhythm increased, "I'll ride you like a wild, dark stallion!"

He closed his eyes as his desire built, pretending she was

younger, prettier, pretending she had long blond hair. He put his big hands on her hips, grinding her down on his sword while she cried out, complaining that his brutal roughness bruised her skin.

But he satisfied her, as only raw, brutal mating could satisfy a bitch like Rosa. And after that, he forced her to her hands and knees, took her the way he really liked to take a woman.

Afterwards, they lay naked on the blanket, drinking mescal in the tent. A scream echoed through the camp.

She turned her head, slightly amused. "You have captives again?"

El Lobo laughed, lit a cigar. "You know I always let my men and the Comanche enjoy the Texans' women. They wouldn't ride with me if I didn't."

She sneered. "I know a woman I wish you would capture, turn over to your men."

"Oh?" He caught the troubled look on her face, the jealous tone of her voice. "You think your love dallies with another servant girl?"

Rosa sneered, brushed her dark hair back. "If it were only that, I could deal with it. This one is a guest of the Durangos who showed up in a mysterious way. Both the son and my love are loco over her. I see it in their faces. I fear she intends to take whichever one she wants, end up as señora of the ranch. But I will allow nobody but myself or Ojos de Pana to be señora of the Triple D."

"You may not be given that choice," he said, "if the new girl is very pretty. What messages do you bring from our leader?"

"Well, the Bar X has some fine-blooded horses that just arrived that you can steal. He says the raids need to be stepped up to make as much profit as possible. It is only a matter of time now until the war ends and the Texas men return. The last couple of years, the raiders could help themselves, the whole frontier was defenseless."

"*Si*, that's true," he smiled, remembering the burning ranches, the looting, the pretty women he had stolen and raped. "The Tejanos will come buzzing out at us like angry hornets when they get back to their lands and see what we have done. Only the mountains of New Mexico will be a safe haven for Comancheros then."

She nodded regretfully as she reached for her clothes. "That ends the profits, I suppose."

"Ah, the leader does not know the latest." He sat up, gestured with his cigar. "We still have big profits to make from the Comanche-Kiowa raid."

"What raid?"

"Even now, my old *compadres,* Little Buffalo of the Comanche, and Aperian Crow of the Kiowa are massing a thousand strong up along the Red River of the Indian Territory."

She looked askance. "What are your plans?"

He shrugged. "They, too, realize the Texans will be returning to protect their land, their women soon. They hope to sweep down across Texas in October, leaving death and wreckage behind them."

"In the long run, the savages can't possibly win."

He smoked his cigar. "You know that, and I know that, but poor, ignorant braves don't know that. Warriors are gathering in all the way from Komantcia in west Texas to the Kiowa forces in the Wichita mountains of southwestern Indian Territory. I know, because even now, I supply them with arms and ammunition for this."

"It is a big raid?"

"Believe me, Rosa, the biggest Texas ever saw. A thousand mounted warriors crossing the Red River to attack a bunch of frontier settlements and ranches that don't suspect they're coming."

"They'll be stopped."

"Who'll stop them?" He raised one eyebrow, cocked his head. "The forts are empty, the soldiers off fighting the Yankees. I tell you, they'll leave a bloody trail clear down the Brazos across central Texas. It will be remembered forever as 'the Great Outbreak of 1864.'"

"They probably won't get far enough east to destroy the Triple D," she answered. "So I don't care what happens to the gringos. But I don't think our leader had any idea this was about to happen."

"*Si.*" He frowned, scratched a flea bite, grumbling under his breath about the Comanche affection for dogs. If he were in a Cheyenne or a Sioux camp he'd put some of these scraggly mongrels in some squaw's stew pot. "That is one of my complaints about him, he leaves everything up to us. Why, he's never even met the Comanche who help him."

She pulled her blouse up over her shoulders. "He's afraid his identity will be discovered. Besides, with you and me doing all the dealing with the Indians, why should he ever have to meet the chiefs face to face?"

"I ought to be the leader; I do all the work," El Lobo snapped. "If I went back to New Mexico suddenly and you turned against him, he couldn't deal with the Comanche alone, they don't even know him."

"Which reminds me of the message." She leaned back on her elbows, reached for the bottle of mescal. "He's afraid the other ranchers might begin to notice the Triple D has never had any stock run off, barns burned. He would like you to make a token raid soon."

El Lobo licked his prominent fangs. "You mean, just enough damage and fire so the other gringos won't suspect he's in with us?"

She nodded. "He'll leave some of our poorest cattle out on our west range. Also, there is an old, seldom-used barn a couple of miles from the house. Your men can set fire to it. Then ride down to the house and make some noise, shoot a little so our ranchhands will think it's a real attack."

"Holy Mother, I don't like this." He scowled darkly at her. "Some of those hands are good shots."

"So?" she raised her eyebrows at him. "Keep out of rifle range and if the cowboys pick off a Comanche or two, so what? There's always more to do our bidding."

"Suppose I say no?"

She smiled, as if she held a secret too good not to share. "Remind me to tell you something before I go. I have a reason I think you will say *si,* something at the ranch you would like to have very much. On this one thing, I will double-cross my love. He would kill me for telling you."

El Lobo perked up immediately. "What is it?"

She smiled smugly. "I'll tell you when I am ready to leave, when I give you the details about your men raiding the ranch, what they are to do."

A woman screamed again, sobbed hysterically, and men laughed and hooted in derision. Rosa looked at him questioningly. "There is no one among them who might recognize me?"

"Don't think so. Only ranch we hit close to the Triple D was the Rocking R, and the damned Kiowa took those little kids to adopt while I was thinking where I could sell them. I think there's a couple of women from west of here, and oh, yes, we caught one ugly, middle-aged sow having a picnic outside Austin. Aren't you from Austin?"

Her lip curled with disdain. Obviously the word had evoked bad memories. "I was a maid in a rich household there. That was before Velvet Eyes took me home with her."

El Lobo stared at the girl's profile. "You still think someday the señora will return?"

Rosa smiled happily. "*Si,* when the war ends, danger is over, and the old Don is dead, surely she will come back to Texas. Then, if I can rid myself of Sanchez and marry into the family, we'll all live happily on the Triple D."

"What about her daughter, Dallas? Did she ever turn up or write home?"

Rosa shook her head. "No, Dallas ran away from that fancy school just before the war started. Personally, I wouldn't care if that half-breed has gotten married and never returns to Texas. She didn't like me very much."

He caught the jealousy in her voice. Obviously, the servant was very resentful of any attention the señora gave the beautiful, spirited daughter.

El Lobo yawned. "Would you like to see the captives?"

"Why not?"

"Come," he said to Rosa, "you will enjoy the entertainment the men are having with the captives." They went outside just as Pedro approached the tent.

"My general."

"What is it now?" El Lobo asked testily.

"That blond captive wishes to speak to you."

"Drag her up here, then."

But as she approached, Rosa stiffened suddenly, blinked, and then smiled largely.

Holy Mother of God, what now? "Rosa, what is it?"

"I'm going to enjoy this. I know this sow."

"You know her?" He looked from the weeping woman being dragged to his tent back over to Rosa's malicious, triumphant face.

"*Si,* I know her." Rosa snickered with delight. "You got a rich one, all right. Ten years ago, I was her personal maid. Lobo, that is Miss Emily Forester!"

Chapter Thirteen

Rosa had never felt such a thrill as she did now watching the fat, light-haired woman being dragged toward them, shoved inside the tent. They both went in, too, sat down.

El Lobo lazed back on his elbows. "Yes? What is it you want, gringa whore?"

"I demand to be returned to Austin at once!" Emily Forester was still haughty, demanding as ever, Rosa thought. The woman didn't look at Rosa, her attention was on the Comanchero leader. "Do you hear? I am from a very rich, important family, and you'll live to regret this!"

El Lobo made a face. "With your yapping, I begin to regret it already."

Emily Forester drew herself up arrogantly. "You don't know who I am."

"*Sí*, I do," El Lobo picked his teeth idly. "You are Emily Forester."

The woman's mouth fell open in surprise. Emily was ten years older than the last time Rosa had seen her, and the years had not been kind to the woman. She was even stockier, the long, horsey face appeared plainer, and the slight mustache was more pronounced now.

"Well," said Emily, "of course, I would have been surprised if you hadn't heard of me. After all, my family is influential, as well as very rich. Now I demand—"

"You'll demand nothing, bitch!" El Lobo retorted flatly, without a smile.

217

Emily looked more than a little disconcerted. She trembled as she ran her tongue along a quivering lip.

Somewhere outside, a woman begged for mercy in English. "No, please, don't—! My god, not with savages—!"

Rosa heard men roar with laughter, the sounds of struggle, of cloth ripping.

Emily glanced behind her toward the sounds outside. Fear now shone in the pale, turquoise-colored eyes. It seemed to be slowly dawning on Miss Emily Forester that her money and her family's influence might not do her much good in this situation.

Rosa stared balefully at the woman, remembering her weaker younger brother, Edwin. He might have married her if it hadn't been for his sister's lies. She gritted her teeth, recalling the humiliation of the chamber pot.

Emily still had not bothered to look at Rosa. Rich gringa women seldom noticed Mexican girls, except when they shouted orders, Rosa recalled bitterly.

Emily wavered before El Lobo as he watched her with the unblinking interest of a rattlesnake about to strike a rabbit. "I—I am rich," she blurted. "My family is very important."

El Lobo grinned, nodded. "Of course. I am counting on that ransom to finance my next shipment of guns. Who was the man with you at the picnic who ran to save himself?"

The plain face mirrored relief at his remarks about ransom. "That was my brother, Edwin. And he wasn't running away, he was going for help."

Rosa snickered at that, and the woman gave her a brief, cold glance of annoyance. "I'm not used to being laughed at by some camp-following Mex whore."

El Lobo winked at Rosa and she nodded slowly. Rosa had waited a long time for this revenge. She was in no hurry to rush the scene.

The Comanchero laughed. "So he was going for help! As I recall, the gringo fled like a squawking chicken before the cook's butcher knife."

Emily said a little desperately, "Perhaps he is having a little trouble getting the money together, but I'm sure it will get here."

"Maybe they think it over, decide you are not worth it." The swarthy renegade peered at her thoughtfully.

The homely face flamed. She who loved to humiliate others, to grind them into the dirt, Rosa thought, could not bear to be humiliated herself. "Of course they will pay—"

"If you didn't return, your brother would have more of the Forester money for himself, would he not?"

"My mother wouldn't allow that to happen." But she looked a little uncertain.

The sound of a woman weeping drifted to them, a woman crying, begging in English not to be raped again. Judging from the noise of the men, they were paying her no heed.

The richly jeweled, knobby hands brushed the thin hair back with a haughty gesture. "I demand you send a messenger to Austin that I'm unharmed, do you hear me! Mother will send the money."

"I've sent the messenger." El Lobo reached for the bottle of mescal, took a long drink, wiped his wet beard on his dirty sleeve.

"Oh, good. I was beginning to think . . ." Emily's lip twitched with a sigh of relief.

"Would you be willing to pay extra to rescue those who have no money?" he nodded toward the screams outside.

"Why should I?" She sniffed haughtily. "Those people are nothing to me, they aren't part of Austin society."

El Lobo held out the bottle to her. "Would you like a drink, Miss Forester?" His behavior was very polite, but Rosa knew him well enough to know he was enjoying a little game.

The woman acted as if she would refuse, her nose wrinkling in distaste. Then she seemed to think better of it, accepted the bottle, wiped the neck carefully before taking a small sip.

El Lobo looked up at her, grinning. "By the way, dear Miss Forester, I want to introduce you to this other lady, Rosa Sanchez."

"Oh," Emily's thin lips curled with disdain, "I'm afraid we haven't met. You see, in my social circle—"

"Oh, *si,* we've met." Rosa could no longer resist. "But I

suppose I meant so little to you, you wouldn't remember me. After all, what's one Mexican maid more or less?"

Emily Forester stared at her blankly for a long moment. Evidently, she was so used to faceless servants always at her beck and call that she never remembered any of them. "Is this some kind of joke? I don't think I know this girl—"

"Sure you do." Rosa stood up, looked the gringa in the eye. "Don't you remember the chamber pot? The frightened little Mexican peasant who had to clean up after you over and over? The one your brother got with child and threw out with no more thought than he'd give a stray dog?"

The dumpy woman stared stupidly at her. "I'm sorry, I don't...."

"Remember the chamber pot," Rosa said again. "Remember humiliating me, grinding me into the ground because I was poor and desperate and helpless." She made the deliberate motion of sticking her fingers down her throat. "Chamber pot, Miss Emily, remember, all over the fine new dress?"

The pale turquoise eyes widened with a sudden intake of breath. "You! Of course, I remember!" Her eyes looked into Rosa's now with hatred. "You ruined an expensive gown, wrecked my impression on a possible suitor! You deserve whatever these savages do to you!"

"Which is nothing." Rosa laughed harshly, sat back down next to El Lobo. "I'm a guest here. It is you who are helpless and desperate, Miss Emily. I'm an important part of the Comanchero operation in Texas."

Sweat stood out in small droplets in the slight blond mustache above the woman's thin lips. She turned, looked down at El Lobo lounging on his elbows. "You've sent a messenger. Don't listen to this woman. My family will send money to get me back unharmed—"

"I suppose they'll send money, which is more than I would do for a sow like you. And they will have to accept you, unharmed or not." El Lobo lit a cigar very slowly and shook out the match with a deliberate motion as Rosa watched. Emily Forester was evidently frightened now, her stocky body shook a little. "I—I'm a virgin," she stammered,

"Oh, please—"

"A thirty-five year wait for a man," Rosa interrupted, "that is about to be ended. By the way, you'd better hand over those rings now."

The woman's pale eyes widened. "But they're mine—"

Rosa smiled. "Give the rings to El Lobo. The others wouldn't hesitate to cut your fingers off to get them."

"Now, Rosa," the swarthy renegade grinned, showing his prominent fangs, "you're scaring this gentle lady." He held out his hand and the homely woman took off the rings, fumbling in her nervousness, and put them in his palm.

"Take them," she choked out, "just—just don't . . . well, you know. . . ."

El Lobo looked at the rings, stuffed them in his pocket. "Perhaps Miss Emily will be willing to do whatever necessary to protect her virginity."

The stocky woman brightened with hope. "I knew you'd see things sensibly, understand that the Foresters are influential—"

"Shut up, gringa bitch!" El Lobo took a deep puff of his cigar, studied the red-hot glowing tip. "And what would you do to protect your virginity?"

She looked confused, desperate. "My—my mother will be sending money."

Rosa watched the cat-and-mouse game. She had no pity, none at all for the arrogant woman. Rather she was looking forward to seeing her humiliated, groveling on her knees.

El Lobo looked from the glowing cigar back to the woman, as if contemplating something. "Your mother's money will be several days in coming. In the meantime, my Comanches love women with yellow hair—"

"Oh, please, God, no!" Emily lost all pretense at arrogance now as she went to her knees. "Not those stinking, filthy savages! Oh, please, I'll do anything!"

"Anything?" El Lobo demanded coolly.

"Anything!" Emily gulped, wiping at the tears flowing down her plain face.

Rosa smiled. The woman had no idea what was about to happen. She was about to be humiliated and tortured in ways that a sheltered, upper-class gringa did not even dream of. El Lobo would make the woman take part in all sorts of obscenity in the vain hopes of protecting her virginity. And finally, when he tired of her, he would rape her anyway. Then he would turn her over to the savages, the Comanchero, to enjoy her any way they wished before exchanging her for the ransom. She was not sure the arrogant Emily could withstand the ordeal without her mind cracking.

El Lobo stared up at the woman coldly. "Take off your clothes, gringa bitch."

"What?" Emily blinked, "What did you say?"

"I said take off your clothes." He grinned up at her, fiddled with the cigar.

The woman looked beseechingly toward Rosa. "Oh, please, can you talk to him? After all, you once worked for my family, and I would be so grateful—"

"Chamber pot," Rosa reminded her, "all I can remember is all those filthy chamber pots of vomit that I cleaned up after you."

El Lobo frowned at Emily. "I said take off your clothes, bitch."

Very slowly, the woman obeyed. Her knobby fingers trembled so badly, she had a hard time with the buttons.

Rosa stood up. "Oh, I forgot, Miss Emily," she said bitterly, "you're used to having a personal maid do little things like help you undress, aren't you?" She grabbed the front of the dress, gave it a hard yank.

The fabric made a loud tearing sound as Rosa ripped it off the pale skin. Emily looked terrified standing there in her lace underwear. "No, please—"

Rosa laughed as she reached out and ripped the delicate fabric from the thick body. The woman tried to hide herself with her hands, but the Comanchero ordered, "Take your hands away. Parade up and down for me like a fat palomino mare at the livestock sales."

The haughty woman turned her back and took a trembling step. El Lobo reached up behind her and pinched the skin of her fat, naked hip.

Emily screamed long and loud and whirled around, her

heavy pendulous breasts swinging like a cow's udder. "How dare you? How dare you?"

El Lobo shrugged. "Cattle usually carry a brand."

Emily was shaking now. "My mother will send money," she cried, "and when I tell her how this little whore of a servant watched without doing anything to help me, she'll fix you for this!" She shook with sobs, glaring at Rosa. "You'll be in a lot of trouble!"

"You just do that," Rosa challenged. "If you can remember anything when you leave this camp, you just tell the damned, uppity Foresters that the girl who emptied chamber pots waited a long time for revenge, but she got it! And by the saints, it was worth it!"

"Enough!" El Lobo was evidently wearied now and eager to get on with it. He reached down and unbuttoned his pants while the naked woman backed away, slowly shaking her head.

"No, my mother's sending money—"

He stood up, walked over to her, his swollen manhood visible in his open pants. He grabbed the woman and she screamed.

Rosa could have saved her even then, she knew. El Lobo would have left the woman alone if Rosa had asked him to. But all Rosa could think of was her revenge, the enjoyment of seeing the rich, arrogant woman humbled while she watched. Before it was over, Emily was even on her knees begging Rosa for mercy, for help.

Rosa spat in her face. "Sometime, somewhere, everyone gets what they deserve, gringa bitch! And I'm glad! Do you hear me? Glad I lived long enough to see you get yours!"

She laughed loud and long as El Lobo forced the fat woman to her knees, forced her to do things that for a proud society woman were unthinkable. And the things he did to Emily while Rosa watched were ingenious and terrible.

The woman was in a state of babbling hysteria several hours later when El Lobo tired of her, his sexual ideas exhausted. Then he turned her over to his Comanchero. Rosa watched with enjoyment as the Comancheros threw the fat woman down on the ground and took turns on her thick body. Then the Comancheros turned her over to the Comanche.

Rosa watched the brave called Whip Owner humping over the screaming, crying Emily. It occurred to Rosa that it was an interesting contrast, the pasty white skin beneath the dark, grimy body of the Indian.

Everyone gets what they deserve, Rosa thought with satisfaction. *Si,* God sees to it that they get what they deserve. Lions and lambs, she thought. Get a lion off its own property and it wasn't much, after all. Abruptly, her revenge seemed empty somehow. It was not as enjoyable to see the snobbish Forester woman humbled as she had thought it would be. She thought of her señora, Velvet Eyes. The señora would have tried to stop the rape and torture, she knew that. Rosa wondered if God was happy that Emily was finally getting what she had brought on herself.

Rosa had not been to Mass or taken communion in many years, she suddenly thought with an uneasy glance at the sky. Someday soon, she needed to talk to a priest. Someday, but not yet. . . .

El Lobo took another drink, looked sideways at Rosa. "You sick? You don't look like you feel well."

Emily Forester screamed again as the savages found some new way to hurt her, humiliate her.

Rosa frowned. "Will she survive all this?"

El Lobo grinned. "I won't let them kill her. After all, the rich family won't pay rewards for a dead body." He laughed coldly. "Her mind may crack, she may go insane. It's happened before. But her family won't even think of that, they'll pay to get her back."

"If her brother was in charge, they wouldn't. But I suppose her mother will." Rosa laughed uneasily. A tiny doubtful feeling starting to gnaw at her insides. "I must get back to the ranch. Pedro, bring my horse."

El Lobo leaned against a rock, watched her mount up. "You go so soon? You just arrived."

Rosa winked broadly. "How long can a woman visit her family without attracting attention?" She would not tell him the blond woman's frantic screams were beginning to fray her nerves.

"By the way, Rosa, what was it you were going to tell me about the raid on the Triple D? Something you thought I would be interested in?"

Rosa remembered. "There's girl at the ranch, a beautiful blond girl called Cimarron I wish you to steal when you come raiding."

"Cimarron." He seemed to savor the name. "'Wild One.' She is beautiful?"

Rosa nodded eagerly. "She is young, with long hair the color of dark honey. I promise you you have never seen such a woman."

El Lobo ran his fingers over the pink scar where he had no ear. "Does your leader know you tell me this?"

She frowned. "The leader and the son, too, are both so taken with this Cimarron, I feel they will finally fight each other to see who gets her. And that leaves me out."

He looked very interested. "I may lose some men trying to get her from the ranch house."

"So?" She raised both eyebrows. "You can always get more men. Besides, no one knows you are coming but our leader, and he will not be expecting you to take the woman."

"He will be furious with me, no?" He ran his hand through his beard, considering.

"He will be furious with you, yes. But he'll get over it. What can he do to you if the Comanchero are hundreds of miles away in New Mexico?"

"I don't know. . . ."

Rosa snorted with derision. "Are you a frightened steer to be so afraid, or the great snorting, pawing bull I know so well? After all, you do all the work. It is time you take charge of the Comancheros yourself."

"That's so." He nodded.

"Besides, you can pretend ignorance. Say later you didn't know he wanted her himself."

He laughed knowingly as she spurred her horse, started to ride away. "You are one cold bitch, Rosa. You'll get a front seat in hell someday for your sins."

His word disturbed her as Emily Forester sobbed and

begged in the background. Rosa turned to look. The savages had staked her out naked on the ground and . . . she did not think she cared to see any more.

Rosa reminded him of the date of the expected raid. "Just remember, it must look like the real thing for the cowboys and ranchers to gossip about."

He nodded, smiled. "I won't forget," he called as she rode off. "Not with a blond beauty waiting for me there."

Emily's screams reverberated in her ears as Rosa rode away. Velvet Eyes would be horrified, she thought. The señora was kind, gentle. She didn't know the meaning of revenge . . . but then, she didn't know about lions and lambs. . . .

Velvet Eyes, she thought. Had it really been ten years since the day she had met the señora in Austin?

Rosa had left the Forester's employment with a few coins Edwin had thrown at her and no letter of recommendation. She gave no thought to returning to the hovel of her parents. There was not enough food to go around there, and they would not want her back, anyway. She had only been one more mouth to feed while she was there, and now there would be two mouths.

For the next few weeks, Rosa had slept with men she met in low-class cantinas for a few pesos. But the higher-class male citizens of Austin wrinkled their noses at her ragged, dirty appearance.

She thought about going into prostitution or working as a serving girl in the cantinas, but there were too many young and pretty Mexican girls in those occupations already. And anyway, her belly was starting to swell noticeably on her thin frame.

In desperation by the end of the month, she was reduced to stealing and sleeping in doorways. The weather was turning colder. What she would do when the blue northers came in across the Texas plains, she didn't know. But as she was reduced to stealing food, she lived in fear of being arrested. She was not sure what the police would do to a poor

Mexican girl who broke the law.

Still, hunger was strong motivation, and when no one was looking, she grabbed food from stands in the open-air market. On several occasions, she stole a gentleman's wallet or a lady's purse. On that particular autumn day, a very fine buggy stood tied up before one of the stalls in the marketplace. As Rosa peeked around an adobe wall, a lady came out of the market. The lady was escorted on one hand by a handsome middle-aged Spaniard, and on the other, by a bowing and scraping shopkeeper. Enviously, Rosa watched the three walk toward the buggy. The shopkeeper placed an overflowing basket in the back.

"Now, Señora Durango," the shopkeeper said, smiling greedily, "can I get you anything else? Your wish is my command."

The woman paused, thinking. She was dark and beautiful. But she was not Spanish, Rosa decided as she studied her. The señor laughed. "Well, let's see, you bought gifts for our children, my brother, Sanchez, and the housekeeper. I don't think you forgot anyone."

The señora looked at the man. She had the most gentle eyes Rosa had ever seen. The woman dusted a speck from her rouge-colored riding outfit and said to the shopkeeper, "Señor, this will take care of the poor widow for a week or so, but there will be others."

The expensively dressed Spaniard looked adoringly at her and laughed. "You will spend all my money, my dear wife. I am rich, but I cannot afford to feed every starving widow in the world.

"No, Diego," the señora regarded him seriously, "we can't feed all the hungry, but we can feed a few. We can't change all the misery, but we can change a little."

Her husband smiled at her and patted her hand. "Ojos de Pana," he said softly, "the Church should consider you for sainthood."

The woman laughed. She had a deep, lovely laugh for a woman. "You, my husband, surely must know I'm no saint."

The señor laughed, tipped back his flat black hat. From where Rosa hid, she could see the gray in his hair and the lines in his face. He must be twenty or twenty-five years older than the soft-eyed woman, she thought.

"It's true." He winked at the shopkeeper. "Velvet Eyes has a temper, but she is a charming blend of angel and mischief. No woman could ever replace her in my heart."

The shopkeeper beamed and rubbed his hands together, "*Si,* Señor Durango, and she has given you an heir."

The señora put her finger to her lips and frowned. "I forgot something. The padre said there were children in his church without clothing."

Señor Durango moaned in mock despair and slapped his forehead. "Velvet Eyes, you will bankrupt me!" But his tone was light, good-humored. "We can't clothe every poor child in Texas."

"But—" she began.

"*Si,* I know, I know!" he nodded and winked at the shopkeeper who watched greedily. "We can't clothe them all, but we can clothe a few."

The señora nodded, her eyes so soft and gentle.

"Well, come then," the señor said, taking her arm and turning back toward the shop, "we'll get clothes for the *padre*'s orphans. Maybe my generosity will bring about a few candles lit for my soul."

The three turned and went back inside the store.

Rosa eyed the basket of food in the buggy. She didn't care if the food was bought for a hungry widow. She was hungry herself, wasn't she? If the rich lady wanted to help someone, Rosa was about to give her the opportunity.

If she hadn't been so greedy, she wouldn't have gotten caught. Rosa sneaked over and grabbed four apples from the buggy, hid them behind the wall. When the three still did not come out, she decided she might be able to steal the whole basket.

But the basket was heavy; it was all she could do to lift it. While she tried to carry it away, she forgot to watch the door of the shop. Behind her, she heard the shopkeeper shout, "Stop thief!" and the señora's cry, "She's stealing the poor widow's food!"

Quickly she looked toward the three and then down at the

basket. She could drop it and run, but she was too greedy and hungry. She stumbled away carrying it.

Behind her people were taking up the cry and chase. "Stop, thief!"

Desperately, she tried to run with the basket, staggering under its weight. As she stumbled with it, she realized the human cry was being taken up along the other shops. "Stop, thief!"

Now fear was stronger than hunger. She dropped the basket and started to run. People coming out of shops took up the cry. Buggies stopped along the street. Everyone seemed to be shouting, "Someone stop that girl!"

Frantically she dodged an outstretched hand and tried to cut through the open-air market. She crashed into a crate of squawking chickens. Baskets of fruit overturned everywhere bouncing along the cobblestones. Rosa glanced behind her as she ran. Her pursuers tripped and fell over the fruit, crashed into the crates of chickens.

But in the end, they caught her. A deputy grabbed her and dragged her back to the shop kicking and screaming.

"You little thief! Here she is, Señor Durango!"

Rosa fought like a cornered alley cat to get away, but she was weak from hunger. She could only imagine what terrors awaited her in the Tejanos jail.

A crowd gathered to gawk and gossip.

"What did she do?"

"She tried to steal from the Durangos!"

And now she stood panting and trembling before the beautiful dark woman. The soft eyes looked at her ever so gently. "You would steal from the poor?"

The deputy snorted. "I reckon I can make her wish she hadn't when I get through with her—"

The señora waved him to silence as her eyes searched Rosa's face again, looking both pained and bewildered. "You would steal from the poor?"

Surely no one but the Mother of God herself had such eyes, Rosa thought. She threw herself on her knees before the señora, really expecting nothing. "I am hungry and poor myself," she fired back, her eyes flashing.

Señor Durango shrugged. "My darling wife, let the police take her. She is a thief, a ragged *puta* like thousand of others—"

"But she said she was hungry."

The shopkeeper frowned. "She lies, no doubt, señora. Probably she will sell the food to buy wine."

The señora looked deep in Rosa's eyes. "Are you really hungry? Would you like a job?"

The señor clapped his hand against his forehead and groaned. "Velvet Eyes, we already have more stray people and pets at the ranch than we can feed. We can't take in every stray in the world—"

The señora smiled sweetly at him. "But my dear, we can take in a few."

Rosa stared back at her, hardly daring to hope. "You would not arrest me? You would offer me a job? Oh, señora, I would serve you all my days and be glad of the chance!"

The sheriff frowned, "Now señora, this little thief would probably steal all your jewelry and run off." He looked to the man. "Señor, can't you control your missus?"

The señor scratched his gray moustache and shrugged. "My wife has the face and soul of a saint, the guts of a Texan, and the stubbornness of a Mexican burro." He winked at Velvet Eyes. "I'm afraid that when she's angered, she also has the temper of a devil."

"I've just decided I need a personal maid." Velvet Eyes's chin went up stubbornly.

"You never had one before," Don Diego reminded her.

"Well, I will have one now!" There was a steely finality in her voice.

So Rosa had gone home with the Durangos and had been there ever since. Only those two knew the paternity of her child. Even the herd vaquero, Sanchez, did not know. Still, he offered marriage and she took it. Rosa had never told him who had fathered the child and in fact, he didn't seem to care. As the child Turquoise grew, she and Sanchez loved each other so much that she never told the little girl the man she adored was not her father. Sooner or later, the child must realize it, but why borrow trouble?

Velvet Eyes. Velvet Eyes. Why didn't you take me with you? I served you faithfully for ten long years, and I would have deserted my husband and my child to go back East with you and your Yankee captain.

Tears came to Rosa's eyes as she rode away from El Lobo's hideout. Perhaps when the old Don was dead, Velvet Eyes might return. And then if something happened to Sanchez, Rosa could marry her lover, really be a part of the Durango family.

Sanchez. Such a patient clod of a husband. She almost never let him touch her, except once two months ago when she thought she was pregnant by her lover.

Rosa frowned as she rode along. Everything had been going just the way Rosa had planned, and now this girl had showed up on the ranch.

Cimarron's pretty face and honey-colored hair came to her mind. That gringo *puta*. It would be obvious to a blind man that Trace and Luis had her on their minds. Well, El Lobo would take care of that. That long-legged blonde wasn't going to upset Rosa's plans.

Ten years. It had been a happy ten years for Rosa. *Sí*, everyone who knew Velvet Eyes loved her.

Rosa had thought the señor adored her, too. It was only after Velvet Eyes had run away that Rosa's lover had told her something that not even she, the señora's personal maid, had suspected. He told her that behind closed doors the old Don was cruel to Ojos de Pana, that he not only beat but humiliated her. Her lover hinted that the pair quarreled often in his presence. Rosa had been loath to believe it. She had been sure that the señor adored his wife. But Rosa's lover had insisted that secretly, because of jealousy, Señor Durango mistreated her. He said Velvet Eyes was too proud even to tell her maid and hid the bruises carefully. Well, no wonder the señora had run away with a lover, then.

The day before Velvet Eyes had left, she had disappeared mysteriously for the afternoon. When questioned, she had appeared to be hiding something. Rosa had thought she was off doing her usual charity. It hadn't even occurred to her that the señora might be meeting a lover, though her husband was old. As Rosa rode along, she remembered that scene in the study six months ago. Rosa and Trace had entered together and found the señora standing behind the desk with Luis. The old Don had gone for a couple of nights to the Rocking R, selling a bull to Mr. Rowland. Turquoise and the other children were off playing in the creek. The servants were taking a siesta. The señora appeared tense; she stared at Rosa and Trace. Then she had looked uncertainly at Luis, who stood behind her with his hands in his pockets.

"Where—where is my husband?" she had asked.

There was something about her tone that had made Rosa look up curiously. "Señora, the Don has gone over to the Rowlands about livestock. Remember?"

Trace had gone over to the table, poured himself a tequila. "We've been wondering where you were."

Velvet Eyes had bit her lip. *Never had she looked so small and beautiful,* Rosa thought now.

"I'm glad you two came in just now," she had said, "I wanted to say good-bye."

Trace had set his glass down noisily. *"Perdone?"* he'd asked, looking bewildered. He went over, slumped into a chair.

No one on the ranch had loved the señora more than Trace, Rosa remembered. The señora's voice had been as soft as her eyes. "I—I wanted to say good-bye. I'm going away. The señor and I argued over Dallas again yesterday morning. That's the last straw." The señora looked at Luis, and Luis shrugged, as if resigned to the fact. "There's a man, a captain I met when the Yankees held Galveston and I attended a party with the Don. The captain's returned for me. And maybe back East, I'll find Dallas, too."

Rosa had felt her mouth drop open. She glanced at Trace, who had half risen from his seat, looking stunned. "Is this some kind of bad joke?" He'd stared at her.

"No, it's no joke." The señora had tossed her head. "Many times when you thought I was out riding or doing good works, I was meeting my lover."

Rosa had felt horror-stricken. She couldn't believe these words from her beautiful señora. Of course the Don was not young, not virile anymore, but Rosa thought of the señora as a pristine saint, without the hungers of an ordinary woman. "I—I can't believe this."

Luis had looked pained. Trace's face had gone pale and he shook his head slightly, as if he could not understand what his ears told him. "No," Trace had said grimly, "No."

In the long moment of silence, Rosa had looked inquiringly at Luis. His face mirrored tension and pain. *"Sí. It's true,"* he'd said. "I followed her yesterday, watched them together. Just now I confronted her."

It was as if someone had announced that the Blessed Virgin was a whore. For a long moment, each had stared at the other as Luis's words sank in. The small chihuahua scratched himself on the sofa and wagged his tail, looking from one face to the other. In the silence, the dog's whimpering had sounded loud indeed.

Trace lit a cigarillo, his hands trembling. "What in the hell is this all about? You, of all women!" He had shaken his head as he stood up. "Wait until the old Don gets back to talk this over, and—"

"No!" Velvet Eyes had snapped, moving between him and Luis. "I'm supposed to meet the captain at Enchanted Rock. From there, we'll ride down across Mexico where the Yankees hold the coast and take a ship north."

Rosa had jumped to her feet. "Señora! Have you lost your mind? Your husband—"

"I don't care about that old man, do you hear!" Velvet Eyes had turned on her in a fury. "I don't care about him or any of you! I hate this ranch! I have always hated it! I can hardly wait to leave!"

Luis's face had contorted with emotion. "You don't have to be cruel to all of us, señora. If you're determined to leave, get your things and I'll drive you to meet this damned captain."

Trace's mouth had been a hard line as he tossed his cigarillo into the fire. "I don't understand all this! What will we tell the Don? Why don't you wait until he returns—"

"No!" she had screamed, her eyes dark with emotion. "I told the Captain I was coming! I don't care what you tell Diego! Tell him I returned to the Cheyenne. Tell him—"

"He'll never believe that." Trace's face had been a grim mask. "This is so unlike you—"

"I am tired of keeping up this façade of the saint, the loving wife for that old fool!" She'd almost screamed it at him. "I've talked Luis into driving me out to meet my love and don't any of you dare follow me! Rosa," she snapped, "go pack me a bag!"

"Señora! Please!" Rosa had wrung her hands. "If you are leaving, let me go with you."

"You have a husband and child," the señora had reminded her. "And I'm going clear to New York."

"I don't care about them. No one means as much to me as you do. Even in New York you will need a maid, someone to do your hair, look after your clothes—"

"There's plenty of maids in New York, why should I drag an ignorant Mexican girl along? They say the Irish up there work cheap; I'll get one of them." Velvet Eyes's tone was sharper than Rosa had ever heard her use before. "Rosa, do what you're told. Go pack my bag. I want to be gone before Señor Durango returns; he'd try to stop me."

Rosa hesitated looking from face to face. This could not be happening. Her world was falling apart. Everyone's world, everything on the huge ranchero revolved around the señora. Rosa could not imagine the Triple D without her. As she hesitated, the señora had whirled on her in a fury. "Do you hear me, stupid one? Now do as you're told!"

Tears had come to Rosa's eyes as she stumbled toward the door. She'd heard Trace behind her say, "Luis, you're going to drive her?"

Luis had sounded tired and defeated. "I've suspected for some time she was meeting this man, but I kept silent for love of Diego. I was foolish enough to think I could talk her out of going just now, but she won't listen. Perhaps it is better that she leaves before the old man comes home. Maybe we can protect him from this heartbreak if we tell him she returned to her Cheyenne people."

The voices had faded to a blur as Rosa ran up the stairs. Tears trickled down her face as she packed the señora's bag. It had seemed impossible to her that Velvet Eyes had taken a lover. Rosa would have sworn that the lovely Cheyenne loved nothing as much as her family and the ranch.

And yet . . . as Rosa had finished packing, she'd remembered that the señora had disappeared mysteriously only yesterday. When she had reappeared, her excuses for her whereabouts were flimsy, as if she was hiding something. So she had been meeting a lover all those times Rosa and the family had thought she was off doing charity work. Rosa never found out what had happened during the few minutes she was gone from the study. But she had reentered just as Trace lunged at Luis, swearing loudly. The señora stepped between them, holding Trace back from attacking the other man.

And as they struggled, he had turned his fury on her. "You *puta!*" he had raged, "you whore! How could you betray your husband in such a way!" Again he struck at Luis, who stood behind the señora.

The handsome Spaniard's face had contorted with anguish as he stroked his delicate mustache, but the other hand stayed in his pocket. "I'm sorry you had to find that out," he had said. "Old family skeletons are better off buried."

Trace had sworn again and thrown himself at the man as the slight woman struggled to stay between them. The señora had slapped Trace then, slapped him hard. Five red finger marks showed up across his cheek, as if they had been burned there with a branding iron.

Rosa had felt shock. Never had she seen the señora raise her voice, much less her hand to Trace.

He had stopped in his tracks, rubbing his hand across his cheek, staring in unbelieving horror at the woman. "You would strike me to protect him?"

"Someday, maybe you'll understand." The señora looked as if she were fighting to hold back tears.

Luis had played with a button on his silk shirt. "We never meant for you to find that out, Trace. But you will learn as you grow older that idols have feet of clay. Don't ever expect a woman to be faithful, and she won't disappoint you."

Trace had glared at Luis murderously. "You rotttten sonovabitch! I'll kill you sooner or later for this!"

Luis had stood with his hands in his pockets, his feet wide apart. His face crumpled. "No, you won't. Neither of us wants Diego to know our secret; it would break his heart. You'd have to explain it to the old man."

Numbly Rosa had walked over, handed the small bag to her. "Will you not reconsider, señora?"

The woman drew a deep shuddering breath. "No," she had said, "I want to be gone before Diego returns."

Rosa had looked wonderingly at Trace. What he had just heard, she could not even guess, but he looked like a man who carried the weight of the world's sins on his back. His shoulders slumped and he had gone over and leaned against the fireplace, as if his legs wouldn't support him. His dark face was almost pale, except for the red finger marks across his cheek.

"Yes! Go!" he had snarled. "Get out of here before your husband returns! Go break someone else's heart. The Yankee captain deserves what he's getting! I hope if you do find Dallas, she won't even speak to you when she realizes what a whore you are! Tell me, do you have a secret to tell her like you just told me?"

The señora had started to say something. She looked from Rosa to Trace. "I—I love you both," she said. "You will never know how much. Someday maybe, you'll realize—"

"Realize what?" Trace had laughed scornfully, tears in his eyes, "that you deserted us all for some uppity Yankee bastard?"

Luis had sighed, looking at Trace. "You're wasting your time, I've already used every argument I know to stop her." Then he spoke to the señora. "Dammit, Velvet Eyes, if you're going, let's go! I can't stand much more of this."

Trace had looked at him. "Why are you driving her?"

Tears had come to the other man's eyes. "I—I love her; I always have. The Don must know, but we've never spoken of it. Even though she's leaving with another man, I'll get her safely to him. I wouldn't want her driving across the hills alone."

Trace had looked at him almost sympathetically. "You poor, poor devil. She's left you no self-respect at all, has she?"

Luis had swallowed hard. "No, I'd do anything for her, even this." He took the señora's arm. "Come on, Velvet Eyes, he'll be waiting."

But she had turned back toward Trace. "Tell Diego—"

"You *puta!*" Trace had sworn, "I won't tell him anything! It would kill him to know what you're doing. If you are going, go!"

"He's right," Luis had sighed. "I hate being a part of this. Let's go meet that damned captain before your husband returns."

Little Tequila had scampered off the couch, growled at Luis, danced around the señora's feet. She leaned over and picked him up with her free hand. Tears had run down her face. "No, my pet, you can't go with me. Rosa, take him."

Rosa had gone over and taken the dog from her. As she brushed against the señora, she was very much aware of the sweet, haunting perfume Velvet Eyes always wore. Rosa choked back a sob. "You will not even take your dog?"

"No, I can't take him. Tell my husband . . ." her voice had trailed off as she looked at Trace. Rosa thought she had never seen such misery on two faces.

The señora had looked at him a long moment. "I pray that someday you will know how very much I love you, that you will find my message—"

"Get out of here, *puta!*" Trace's face had been dark with anger as he turned and looked into the fire. "I'll never trust another woman after this. You're all a bunch of faithless whores."

Luis had frowned. "Don't call her that. Even now, I'd kill any man who called her that." He looked toward Rosa. "When Diego returns, remember, she has gone back to her Cheyenne people. Later, we'll add to the story."

He had held on to Velvet Eyes' free arm as they went down the hall and out across the courtyard to the waiting buggy. Rosa had clutched the small dog to her breast as she ran to the French doors to watch the buggy drive away. "Can't you stop her?" she demanded of Trace. "Tell me what she said?"

"No, I can't stop her." His voice had been flat, devoid of emotion, but tears trickled down his face. "I-I can't tell you what she told me. I can't tell anyone. I only know that all women are faithless whores. None of them can be trusted. I'll never believe any woman after this."

And Luis wouldn't tell her either, when Rosa had asked him. He had returned from his errand almost in a state of shock.

Rosa couldn't contain her curiosity. Was the captain handsome? Would Luis tell her now what he and Trace had fought over in the study?

With a grimace, he described in detail the handsome man who had met the pair at Enchanted Rock. But no, he would not tell her what terrible thing had been said to Trace.

"It all happened a long time ago," he had answered sadly. "I'm sorry Trace had to find it out. Don't ask me again."

And Rosa never had, although she still wondered. Well, maybe the señora would tell her the secret when she returned to the ranch. Maybe even now, Velvet Eyes was tired of New York, eager to come home. But of course she had to wait for the war to end.

Rosa slapped her horse with the reins as she rode toward the Triple D. There was only one other problem and El Lobo was going to take care of it. He was going to steal Cimarron from the Durango ranch.

Chapter Fourteen

Nearly two weeks had passed since the incident involving the half-crazed Holt. Cimarron spent night after sleepless night by Trace's bedside while he mumbled in incoherent delirium. He seemed to sleep only when she held his hand and whispered in his ear, *"Yo te quiero, mi querido."* I love you so much, my sweetheart.

The weather stayed sultry and Trace began running a fever, so she spent hours sponging him, changing his sheets. For three nights he was in such feverish delirium and tearing so frantically at the bandages on his leg that she finally tied his wrists to the bedpost to control him. He thrashed about, and she stroked his sweating, naked body, murmuring endearments to him until he quieted.

Luis mumbled under his breath about her staying so much by the bedside, reminding her constantly that there were servants to do such dirty work. But old Don Diego seemed thankful for her help, and the crew, when they came to see about him, stared at her with new respect. She told herself that she looked after Trace with such devotion because he had almost lost his life rescuing her.

Rosa had been gone visiting relatives when they had returned with the wounded Trace, and she did not return for several more days. So Cimarron also took over the household and ran it in a much better-organized, more efficient manner, which brought nods of approval and smiles from everyone. She even considered cleaning Velvet Eyes' room, decided against it. Cimarron was not the señora here yet. Even old Don Diego seemed pleased, and his health appeared to improve in the changed atmosphere. Then Rosa returned and jealously took her position back.

Cimarron shrugged it off. There was no point in fussing with the sullen spitfire of a girl. If Cimarron decided to stay permanently, she would deal with that rude housekeeper. Cimarron had committed herself to marrying Luis, but she was having second thoughts about that. In the meantime, Trace Durango had not indicated any interest in her, although he was appreciative of her nursing care as he improved and was finally up and hobbling around. Sometimes she caught him watching her with a bemused look of curiosity that told her he still expected some trick, that he refused to believe she had no ulterior motive. When they talked, it was of minor things, carefully skirting anything of importance. Nor did she get any more information about the relationships in this tight-lipped household.

Now it was the last week of September, and the day of the old Don's birthday celebration. People would be coming from all over the country. No doubt everyone had heard this birthday might be the old man's last.

Searching through both Dallas' and the señora's things, Cimarron selected an off-the-shoulder peasant blouse with much lace and ruffling. Then she choose a bright-flowered skirt with flounces and many lace petticoats that emphasized her small waist. It was nearly noon as Cimarron pulled her hair back and tied it with a red ribbon.

She came down the stairs through the giant ballroom to stand before the mirror in the front hall, looking herself over as she heard the first guests arriving in the courtyard. She had not known she could look so pretty, Cimarron thought shyly. Never in her years in the parsonage had she had more than two dresses to wear, and they both had been drab and high-necked, as was expected of the foster daughter of a strict German pastor.

Maids and servants bustled about and there was a great air of confusion, of excitement. Cimarron offered to help organize the party. She received an icy look from Rosa, whose expression made no secret of the fact that she considered Cimarron a competitor for her position overseeing the household. But Cimarron was in too good a mood to let the sultry Mexican throw a damper on her spirits.

If Rosa didn't want her help, let the girl struggle with the preparations all by herself, Cimarron thought as she went through the French doors of the study out into the courtyard. Half the county must be gathering this afternoon, she thought with excitement as she looked at the crowd of buggies and riders. A small Mexican band was setting up under the paper lanterns on the big courtyard. This night there would be dancing.

Cimarron hugged herself with excitement. A real party! The kind she had always dreamed of. The only more exciting thing she could wish for was that the party be in her honor. Of course, that would never happen, she thought wistfully. A touch of sadness crossed her mind as she thought of the Longworths' party, which had surely been canceled. If only she could go back and change the past. She could never quite forgive herself for murder. Cimarron wondered suddenly if anyone might show up at the party who would recognize her. But checking casually with Luis, she decided it would be friends from this area, not anyone likely to know her. Because of the Indian problems, no one had been invited from so far away as the next county.

She came out into the crowd with trepidation, a little shy for a moment. Cimarron wondered if anyone might snub her, realize she was a poor waif who didn't belong in this elegant home. Then her chin came up proudly. Cimarron belonged wherever she was. No one would make her cower and cringe by snobbishness, she thought with a spirited nod of her head.

The old Don sat in a comfortable chair near the fountain, like a lord accepting homage from his subjects. People gathered to speak to him, ask after his health, give condolences on the señora's unexpected departure.

Women stood laughing in small groups, comparing notes on children and households, while their offspring ran through the crowd shouting and playing tag. Even little Turquoise and the other ranch children joined in, with Tequila dashing gaily at their heels. Cimarron smiled ruefully, wondering whom the little dog would bite before the day ended.

The scent of roasting meat came to her nose and her mouth watered. Over by the corral, she could see a firepit with two whole beeves roasting slowly while Sanchez and Maverick turned the spits.

She looked about for Luis and Trace. Just then, an elegant buggy pulled up out front and she looked at the beautiful, gaudily dressed young women in it. Trace limped forward to assist them down. Men laughed with awkward embarrassment as they looked at the pretty girls descending from the carriage to mingle with the cowboys. Cimarron saw indignant frowns on the faces of several dumpy housewives.

"Of all the nerve!" one huffed to another. "Can you imagine Miss Fancy's painted women showing up at a gathering of respectable people?"

The other woman raised her eyebrows critically. "They do say the old Don issued a blanket invitation to everyone in the county, being as how it's expected to be his last—"

"But you wouldn't think he would have included those hussies!" said the other, pursing her lips with distaste.

"Say," whispered a third behind her hand to a small group, "what do you think about Señora Durango running off last spring and going back to her people?"

"Well, what do you expect from an Injun?" the first said. "Even though we all liked her so well. . . ."

They looked up as Cimarron moved close, seemed to see her, changed the subject. She turned to look at the girls from Miss Fancy's as they moved through the crowd. Luis joined her and frowned as he looked that direction.

"I'm afraid the old man is very democratic," he complained. "He said *everybody,* but if it had been left up to me to issue the invitations. . . ." His voice trailed off as he took Cimarron's elbow and guided her across the patio to the old man and the crowd around him. In the background, the small band struck up a discordant, uncertain tune.

Luis looked her over admiringly as he elbowed his way through the noisy, laughing crowd. "I must say, Cimarron, my dear, you are easily the most beautiful woman here."

She smiled at him, but out of the corner of her eye she watched Trace bowing gallantly before Miss Fancy's girls, offering them glasses of wine. Cimarron gave Trace a withering glance and he winked slowly at her in a way that made the blood rush to her face.

And now Luis had elbowed his way through the circle around Don Diego. "Gentlemen," Luis said by way of introduction, "please allow me to introduce Señorita Cimarron, who is presently a houseguest on the Triple D."

The men all doffed their hats with a bow.

"Ah, a houseguest," one of them said knowingly, with a glance at Luis. "Then there will be an announcement soon?"

Cimarron felt herself blush prettily as Luis smiled. "I can only hope," he answered gallantly.

"Ah, señorita," said another, "you are the most beautiful woman in the hill country!"

"Señorita Cimarron, I am honored to meet you!"

As she nodded to each introduction, she heard one whisper hoarsely, "Luis, you are a greater fool than I think if you let this beauty escape you!"

Luis patted the hand of her arm still linked through his. "Gentlemen, you embarrass the lady!" But he smiled in obvious good humor, pleased that the crowd of ranchers was so taken by her.

She turned, reached down to the old Don in his chair. "Señor Durango, you look well this day! Happy birthday!"

The old man took her hand, kissed it. "You are such a polite liar. Ah, young lady, if I were twenty years younger, no, even ten, oh, well."

The crowd of men around him laughed and continued their talking of ranching, the war, and especially the Comanches plaguing the countryside. Cimarron kept her arm linked through Luis' but she looked over toward Trace. Even though he still limped, he was getting plates of food for the pretty girls from the notorious bordello. He must have felt her eyes upon him, because he turned and grinned at her.

Double damnation! How dare he be so friendly to those women! she thought with annoyance, then, very deliberately, turned back and engaged Luis in bright, animated conversation. She was as much upset with herself as she was with Trace Durango because she could put no name to the emotion she felt while watching him with the painted hussies. Was it indignation? Outrage? Jealousy? No, of course it couldn't be that, she told herself. It was just outrageous, that was all, that he should be so attentive, so friendly to those girls when there were other eager cowboys standing around who could easily get those girls a plate of barbecue, fetch a glass of punch.

Her mind wandered to the past several weeks. She had bathed every inch of Trace's hard, muscular body while he lay helpless and unconscious. In fact, on three nights, when he had been delirious with fever, writhing and pulling at the bandage on his leg, she had had to tie his wrists to the bedposts. Now she gritted her teeth at the memory of those sleepless nights of laving his feverish skin with wet rags, watching his naked body struggle against the bonds on his wrists. Trace had been helpless lying there naked, tied. Instead of sitting sleepless, wiping his writhing body over and over with wet, cool cloths, she should have turned him over to the servants.

Yes, that's what she should have done, she thought with annoyance as she heard loud laughter and glanced over to see Trace whispering into a pretty redhead's ear. Cimarron felt her blood pressure rising as she watched. The girls were evidently charmed by the young cowboy, all leaning close to hear his words, all looking at him with evident hunger.

Luis's glance followed hers. "I know it's annoying, my dear, for him to make a spectacle of himself like that before respectable people. But women like that are drawn to him. A lady like yourself would never. . . ."

The rest of his words were lost on her as Cimarron glared at Trace who now had his arm familiarly around the redhead's waist. No, a lady like herself would never, she thought and almost felt steam coming out her nostrils. Trace caught her eye, smiled knowingly again, and she knew that he, too, was remembering the hayloft, the study. Cimarron closed her eyes, not wanting to remember, but unable to stop herself. Once again she could feel his warm, sweet mouth invading hers, his hard body forcing hers to submit, accept him. She almost seemed to feel his hands on her thighs stroking her sensitive skin, his manhood surging deep within her as they coupled. . . .

"—my dear?" Luis inquired.

"What?" she started, "I'm sorry, Luis, I was— I didn't hear you."

He looked at her questioningly. "I was just offering you a chair, Cimarron, and asking if you would like a plate of barbecue?"

"Why, of course," she stammered, taking the chair next to the old Don. She felt herself flush under Luis's inquisitive gaze. If he only knew what she had been thinking. Why, she should tell Luis what Trace had done to her. She looked him over critically as the elegant Spaniard walked away through the crowd toward the barbecue pit. He was about the same height as Trace, a little heavier, and perhaps old enough to be Trace's father. They would be evenly matched if they ever did get into a fight, she thought. But at the same time, she knew she would never be the one to start a fight between them. They disliked each other enough as it was.

She stirred restlessly in her chair, only half listening to the old Don and the men discussing the price of beef. It was true. Texas had millions of cattle that couldn't be sent to the starving Southerners. The Yankees had controlled the Mississippi for over a year now, ever since Vicksburg had fallen. In desperation, some Texans had even tried swimming the beef across that big river and had drowned most of them. Listening, she heard one of the ranchers say Atlanta was now under siege, with Sherman expected to sweep completely across Georgia. The end of the war couldn't be far off.

Cimarron watched Luis get a plate for her and one for the old Don, then thread his way back through the crowd. The little band made up in enthusiasm what it lacked in skill, she decided, tapping her foot. She listened to the conversation of the ranchers. They were trying to figure how to get their beef to Yankee markets when the war ended.

She heard the old Don say, "... and Trace thinks we could just gather up everyone's stock and drive them north to the railroads."

"You mean, walk thousands of cattle all the way to Kansas?" The rancher shook his head. "That's loco."

"Maybe," another nodded, "but if there's any man in Texas who could start a cattle drive all the way up across Indian Territory to see them in Topeka or Wichita, Trace Durango would be the man who could do it."

She heard a murmur of agreement around her and she watched Luis moving through the crowd toward her in his fine silk shirt. Cimarron felt a little hurt that none of them suggested Luis. Why did everyone feel that damned foreman was the one with guts and determination in this family?

Why, if she told Luis what Trace had done to her, that noble gentleman would probably call the cowboy out, challenge him to a duel, or, at the very least, a fistfight. She glanced from Luis to Trace standing with the laughing girls from Miss Fancy's.

Si, she should tell Luis. But even as she thought it, she knew she wouldn't tell. It would ruin her chances with Luis, instinctively Cimarron sensed that. That elegant gentleman's pride would not let him accept used goods. Obviously Trace had no problem with the idea. One of Miss Fancy's girls laughed uproariously, and when Cimarron looked over with a frown, she caught Trace watching her.

Luis finally worked his way through the crowd and handed her and the old man steaming plates of barbecue and spicy Mexican beans.

She took a deep breath of the aroma, felt her mouth watering as she took the corn tortilla, folded it around a bit of meat the way Texans did, and took a bite.

But the old man frowned. "Luis, you didn't bring my any chili peppers. You know how I like chili peppers."

"But sir, with your stomach—"

"Dammit, at this stage, what difference does it make?"

The old man shook his white mane just like an annoyed lion. "Get me some peppers!"

Luis gave Cimarron a resigned look and started back through the crowd. The old man may be ill, she thought with amusement, but he's still top herd bull on the Triple D and he's not going to let anyone forget it. She imagined him as a young man thirty years ago. He'd be thinner, with blue-black hair falling down across his dark forehead under a flat black hat. In her mind, he looked like . . . no, that couldn't be right, she thought with confusion, and glanced again at the virile half-breed cowboy entertaining the whores.

Don Diego nodded to her. "You may think me rude, señorita, but I grow weary of everyone treating me like a sick, whimpering baby. I and my father before me have held this land against all comers, and I intend to be El Patron, the boss, right up until they throw Triple D dirt on me!"

Cimarron couldn't help but smile. She had grown increasingly fond of the spirited old man. "It's a wonderful party, sir," she said. "I'm having a good time."

"Good!" He pulled out a cigar, stuck it between his lips. "Do you mind if I smoke, señorita?"

She shook her head as she enjoyed the hearty ranch food. "Not at all, Don Diego."

He looked her over appraisingly as she searched through his pockets for a Lucifer match. "I like you, young lady, you have spunk and grit. The Durangos would benefit from that blood being added to ours."

She felt the blood rush to her face. "Señor Durango, please, you embarrass me—"

"Forgive me, señorita," he lit the cigar, leaned back, regarded her. "A rancher tends to think in terms of bloodlines. I'm not blind. I've seen how Luis and Trace follow you about. Have you decided between them yet?"

She looked about in utter confusion, embarrassment. "I— I don't know what you mean—"

"I'm sorry, my dear," he apologized again. "But I hear gossip, know that drunken doctor doesn't think I have long to get things in order. It's important to me to make sure things will be continued, that the Triple D will survive."

She looked toward Luis threading his way back through the crowd, tried to decide what answer the old man expected from her. She had underestimated the Don. He was as masculine, as dominating as . . .

"This reminds me of her parties." The Don smoked and squinted at her beneath his bushy white eyebrows. "Ah, we had lovely parties when Velvet Eyes was here! The ranchero was always full of people. I would like to see it that way again, hear Durango children running through the house."

For a moment, Cimarron considered asking him to explain all the questions in her mind, then decided against it. This was not the time or the place, and anyway, he might be as reluctant as everyone else had been to discuss it.

"Well, señor," she comforted him, "perhaps someday the señora will return from her people, and—"

He snorted, interrupting her as they both surveyed the noisy crowd and Luis threading his way through it. "I haven't said this to anyone else because they might think me loco." He fixed her with steely dark eyes. "Don't you realize, my dear, that Velvet Eyes is dead?"

Cimarron jerked around, stared at him. "What? What did you say?"

He took another puff of the cigar, sighed sadly. "Oh, I know what they all told me about her going back to her Cheyenne people so I wouldn't worry. It's not true, you know. Velvet Eyes is dead."

Even with all the talk and laughter and the discordant little band behind them, it was as if the two of them were all alone, because they looked only into each other's eyes.

"Surely, Don Diego, you are mistaken! Whatever would make you think—?"

"Because she is not here by my side." The old man patted the empty chair next to him. "It's very simple. My wife was the beat of my heart, the song in my soul to me, and I was the same to her. *Si*, we had a small argument the morning before she disappeared. But if she is not with me, it can only be because she is dead. Don't you understand?"

Cimarron swallowed back the lump in her throat, set her

plate in her lap, suddenly not hungry. She had never felt so sorry for anyone as she now felt for the trusting old man. It seemed so simple to him, she thought with pity. If you loved someone, you trusted without question. Why didn't he face reality? Of course it hadn't been the argument, it had been the handsome younger man. Would the Don be better off to know the truth? Was it better for him to think her dead than to know the faithless señora had run away with another man? How long did the old man have to live? She thought over the choice between the two as she watched the old man smoke, watched Luis walking toward them, decided it wasn't much of a choice.

Cimarron saw the chihuahua lurking behind a chair, but she didn't cry out her warning fast enough. With lightning speed, little Tequila dashed out, caught Luis's pants leg as he approached.

Luis swore mightily, jerking futilely at his pants leg. But his hands were full and he seemed to be unable to do anything about the small dog growling and tearing his pants.

Cimarron got up, rushed over to grab the chihuahua. Perspiration stood out all over Luis's handsome face and he muttered under his breath. "Little devil has torn these, too! This makes twelve! If it were left up to me, I'd—"

The old Don glared at him coolly as Cimarron put the dog down on the flagstones and it hopped onto the old man's lap. "You'd what, Luis?"

The Spaniard regained his composure nicely, handed him the plate. "You must admit the little rascal is a terror."

"Only to those he doesn't like." Don Diego took the plate. Tequila grabbed a bite of barbecue off it.

Luis glanced helplessly at Cimarron. "You can see how spoiled the dog is, what bad manners—"

"The señora loved him, and that's what counts with me," the old man said with stubborn determination, handing the pet a barbecued rib. Tequila cocked his head at Luis. He seemed almost to be challenging Luis, grinning at him as he took the meat, jumped off the Don's lap. Cimarron had a hard time holding back her smile as Tequila took the bone over under the oleander and settled down to gnaw it.

Luis sighed as he examined his torn pants. "The dog is spoiled rotten," he complained again to the old Don. "You really shouldn't allow him to eat off your plate and sleep in everyone's bed the way he does."

Don Diego dropped his cigar on the flagstone and ground it out with his fine, custom-made boot as he settled back to eat the plate of barbecue. "As long as I am Don of the Triple D, Tequila has the run of the place," he said firmly, "just like his sire and grandsire before him."

Cimarron saw the black look on Luis's face, saw him decide not to argue the point. She had a feeling the little dog better hope the old man lived forever. Not that she could blame Luis. Tequila certainly didn't seem to go out of his way to make the next Don like him.

The Don dug into the plate of spicy food with evident relish, biting into the hot peppers like a true Texan. The tortillas were piled high with chili, made hot and spicy, without beans or tomato sauce. To Texans, chili wasn't a dish, it was almost a religion, Cimarron thought as she handed her empty plate to a passing servant girl.

Luis leaned solicitously close to Don Diego. "Sir, you would like some wine?"

El Patron seemed to consider a moment. *"Si,* some Madeira would be nice. That imported brand you buy for yourself, Luis." He turned to Cimarron. "And you, my dear?"

"Of course, please." She nodded, watching Luis's tender concern for the old man.

"Fine Madeira coming up." Luis made a courtly bow, moved through the noisy, laughing crowd toward the house.

One of Miss Fancy's girls laughed uproariously, and both Cimarron and the old man turned to look at Trace's group.

"He certainly has a way with women, doesn't he?" the Don said before returning to his plate with gusto.

"Certain kinds of women," Cimarron said grimly, watching a painted blonde kiss Trace's cheek.

She felt the old man glance at her and back at Trace. "He has his mother's charm," he agreed. "I had thought perhaps you were interested—?"

"Who, me? No, I—" But as she opened her mouth to protest, a little group of men who had been standing talking now approached the old man.

"Señor Durango," one with missing teeth fumbled with his hat uncertainly, "we would like to speak with you."

"*Si*, Barlow," The señor put his plate on a nearby table. "How are things at the Bar X?"

"Not much better than at any of the others," a red-faced heavy man barged in.

Señor Durango frowned at the man's obvious rudeness. Cimarron saw the sudden fire behind his eyes, could imagine him as a young man. He had probably been a lot like . . .

"Señor, I will excuse your rudeness," the old man said coolly. "I don't believe we've met—"

"I'm from the Rocking R," the man huffed, "Rowland's brother. With them dead and my niece and nephew carried off by Injuns—"

"Of course," the Don said sympathetically. "I heard you were coming in to take over the ranch. You have my sympathy, sir. My men told me about finding the bodies."

The red-faced man frowned. "I've been trying to get a group together to go after them kids, but all these yellow bellies is afraid to go."

Don Diego glared at him. "If you are not a good shot, sir, I'd advise you not to call local cowboys 'yellow-bellied.'"

"Wal, in Austin, that's what we'd call men who wouldn't help kids."

Cimarron saw Don Diego look at the man's shoes. The ranchers all wore boots.

"You're from Austin?" the Don said. "What's the news from there?"

The other frowned. "Same as it is all over the hill country, Comanche raids. Why, a couple of weeks ago, they even hit the outskirts of Austin itself."

There was a murmur of surprise, and even Rosa, who was pouring coffee for the men, seemed to stop to listen.

"Austin?" One of the others scuffed his boot against the flagstones. "You mean, the Comanche raided there?"

The other sucked his teeth. "Couple picnicking on the

outskirts. The son got away, but they took the daughter of one of Texas's richest families, Emily Forester."

The name didn't mean anything to Cimarron, but it obviously did to the others. There was an excited buzz; even Rosa's eyes widened.

"Well, señor," Rosa said, standing there with her coffee pot, "usually, the family pays a ransom if they're rich and the hostage is returned—"

"She's already been ransomed," the man spat on the flagstones, "but they'd been better off to leave her with the Injuns."

Cimarron felt the same shock she saw on the other faces. "Surely, Mr. Rowland, you don't mean that—"

"Wal, the poor girl's mind is gone," he said. "No tellin' what them savages did to her. Miss Emily just keeps staring into space, saying the same words over and over like she's tryin' to let folks know something mighty important."

The Don leaned forward. "A name, perhaps?"

The man shook his head, and everyone seemed to stop talking to catch his words. In the background, Cimarron heard children running and playing tag, and the little band struck up again.

"Don't make no sense to nobody." Rowland shook his head. "Miss Emily just stares out the windows and says them words over and over. Somehow, everyone feels if they knew what she was talking about, it might give them some clue to all this raidin'."

"And the words are?" Cimarron prompted.

"Chamber pot," said Rowland.

"What?" Everyone looked at each other, puzzled. Rosa did a quick curtsey and walked away.

Cimarron tried to make sense of it. "Chamber pot?"

"Yep," Rowland nodded. "Her mind's gone, like I said, and nobody can figure out what she means by them strange words. No telling what them braves did to the poor thing."

Several of the men shook their heads in puzzlement and regret. "The Injuns is a caution, all right," one of them grumbled, "and it ain't just Texas Comanches. I heard the Cheyenne up in Kansas and Colorado is kicking up so much trouble, the Santa Fe Trail has been shut down."

"It's gonna be just like Little Crow's Sioux up in Minnesota two years ago when them savages went on a rampage and massacred hundreds," Barlow said. "That damned Lincoln stopped the army from hanging all but thirty-eight of them red devils. If they'd hanged them all, it would have sent a message to the others!"

The Don shook his head. "It's the way we've treated them," he said regretfully. "I suppose they realize this is a big chance to get even, with all the soldiers gone east."

Rowland frowned at the Don's kind words. "You sound like an Injun lover, Durango. I tell you one thing, any Injun, peaceful or not, stops on the Rocking R now that I'm runnin' it better be prepared to catch a load of buckshot."

"I don't know whether you will be able to keep that Rocking R going, Mr. Rowland," the old man said gently, "seeing's as how you're a city man. I'm sorry about the children, but we have no Rangers, no troops. In fact, if we even had enough cowboys to defend Texas, you wouldn't see things like that happening."

Rowland sucked his teeth loudly. "Are you saying we won't ever see them kids again?"

Don Diego sighed. "Probably not. They're either way off in the Staked Plains where no white man dares go or up in the Wichita Mountains in the Kiowa lands. It would take a thousand men to go into Indian Territory, bring those kids out, and we don't have that many."

"But in a couple of years, when the war's over," Rowland began.

Cimarron saw the looks pass between the other men.

Don Diego lit a cigar. "In a couple of years, my friend," he said softly, "it won't make any difference."

The man gawked at him, uncomprehending. "What do you mean by that?"

"I was a friend of the Parker family," the Don said, taking a puff of his cigar. "The Comanche took little Cynthia Ann back in 1836. The Rangers recaptured her four years ago."

"So? I heard that. So what?"

"So they should have left her with the Comanche,"

Don Diego sighed.

"Are you loco?" the man snarled, "Why, them savages—"

"Because by then, she was a Comanche herself," the old man went on, "married to a chief, Peta Nocona. They have to keep her locked up because she keeps trying to run away and go back to him and her sons. She had a baby girl, Prairie Flower, but I understand the baby died last year."

Rowland's red face went ashen, and Cimarron heard the murmur of sympathy from the others. "Are you sayin' my brother's kids'll become Injuns?" Rowland gasped, "That some red buck will take my niece and—"

"Please, señor," the old Don indicated Cimarron with a nod, "there's a lady present."

"Mr. Rowland," Cimarron said quickly, "you have my deepest sympathy on your loss. The Triple D crew found your poor brother's body while searching for me."

Rowland frowned at her, looked at the old Don. "That's just what a bunch of us been discussing, how the Triple D crew happened along so conveniently."

She heard the gasp run through the little group of men, saw some of them avert their eyes guiltily.

"What do you mean, sir?" Don Diego's mouth was a hard, grim line and his voice was a cold challenge.

Where was Luis? She saw him coming from the study with a tray of drinks. She looked around for Trace, but he was still visiting with Miss Fancy's whores. Sanchez and Maverick stood too far away, turning the barbecue spit as they roasted a whole steer.

"Some of us been talkin'," the red-faced man said. "It do seem more'n a coincidence that all the ranches in the hill country been raided except one."

The weathered face went pale, and the Don tossed the cigar away. "If you mean what I think you mean, sir, I hope you know how to handle a dueling pistol!"

Rowland's big mouth went slack. "You must be joking! You're living in the past, mister; dueling pistols? I suppose next you'll be slapping me in the face with a glove and calling in the seconds!"

The old man came to his feet suddenly, and Cimarron saw

the fire in his eyes as he did so. Once he must have been hell with hair on it, she thought, jumping up, grabbing his arm.

"Get off my ranch!" he ordered Rowland, jerking away from Cimarron. "You abuse my hospitality!"

She looked around for help, caught Trace's eye. Immediately the cowboy pushed his way through the crowd. She motioned to Luis, who handed the tray to a servant girl and shoved his way across the courtyard toward them.

"Didn't mean no harm," Rowland whined. "We all been talking, that's all. The Triple D has two half-breeds here; maybe one or both are in cahoots with—"

The Don struck the man then, with all the force of his weak, feeble arm, just as Luis and Trace pushed their way through the crowd. Trace grabbed the offender, pulling him away as Luis came to the elderly man and helped him back to his seat. "Sir, remember your health!"

Trace's wrath was terrible to see as he pulled the red-faced one away. "What'd you say, stranger, to make the old man so mad?"

"Just what everyone else is saying privately," Rowland blustered, pulling away from Trace's hand. "That it's funny as hell the Triple D ain't been raided yet, but maybe not, with a half-breed running things—"

He never finished. Cimarron clapped her hands over her mouth in dismay as Trace caught the red-faced man in the teeth with a well-placed fist.

Luis moved through now to grab the man. "How dare you?" he seethed. "Why, we've just been lucky, that's all. You men all know Trace, know he wouldn't be in cahoots with Comanche and Comanchero. And that half-breed kid, Maverick, we found wandering our west pastures—"

"Never mind, Luis," Trace grumbled, rubbing his fist. "Your loyalty is touching, but this city gentleman has obviously already made up his mind." He signaled one of the frowning Triple D cowboys. "The gentleman," he said with sarcasm, "was just leaving. Get his horse." Trace looked around the circle. "Anyone else want to make some groundless accusations?"

The band faltered to a squeaky halt and everyone's head

turned. Luis looked at Cimarron. "We can't allow his birthday party to be ruined," he said heatedly, waving at the band. "Start the music again! It was nothing, a little too much liquor." He smiled at the crowd as Rowland and several others left. "Go ahead, enjoy yourselves, *amigos!*"

"Oh, Luis," Cimarron sighed, "It was so awful—"

"Now I'm here, though," he bowed before her, smiling. "Everything's going to be fine. May I have this dance?"

She nodded, saw Trace watching them. He scowled and limped over to the sidelines as she went into Luis's arms. Trace was joined by several eager women who didn't look too concerned over whether he was able to dance or not.

Where were those girls when I was staying up night after night looking after that injured leg? Cimarron thought with a huff as she danced with Luis. Next time, that damned cowboy can set up his hospital room in Miss Fancy's Bordello. She had no doubt that he could have his choice of nurses there.

The party started again, with even more noise and laughter than before. It was dusk now, and the big harvest moon rose bright gold on the far horizon. Cimarron shivered as she looked at it, although the autumn night was warm. Comanche moon, she thought. I wonder whose ranch is being burned tonight? Whose women raped?

The paper lanterns around the courtyard were lit and the liquor flowed as the dancers moved out to the music of the band. Even little Turquoise dragged some small boy out on the flagstones, Cimarron noticed. The cowboys had taught Maverick to dance last night in the bunkhouse, she remembered, hoping he was having a good time. But she saw Maverick ask a rancher's daughter to dance, then saw the girl inspect his dark, half-breed face and shake her head curtly. Cimarron lifted her chin angrily, went over, danced with the half-breed boy herself. She burned with anger at the humiliation, the injustice of it all. Rowland had been too polite to include her in his accusation, but he might as well have. There were actually three half-breeds on the ranch.

The evening passed. Old Don Diego seemed to enjoy himself tremendously as he sat watching the dancers, and

Luis said to her. "Look at him! He's having such a good time!"

Cimarron smiled at him. "I'm so glad since . . . well, you know."

Luis crossed himself reverently, wiped his eyes. "Please don't remind me, Cimarron. I-I can't imagine life without him. He's such a grand old man!"

She felt touched by his concern. "Remember, the doctor might be wrong."

"Let us pray he is," Luis said as they danced.

She looked over, saw Sanchez pulling a reluctant Rosa out onto the dance floor, distaste on her face as she looked at the gentle vaquero.

Dr. Hastings has really helped himself to the wine and beer, Cimarron thought with disapproval as she saw him stagger past, very unsteady on his feet.

And the doctor wasn't the only one, she thought, pursing her lips tightly as she danced past Trace. He leaned unsteadily against the veranda railing, the little dog in one arm, a bottle of tequila in the other.

She could feel his eyes boring into her back, so she danced, laughed loudly, hung on Luis's every remark, as if she had never heard anything so clever.

When she looked around again, Trace and Rosa stood side by side, watching her. It was hard to say which face was the most annoyed. Trace might be jealous and Rosa obviously resented her taking Velvet Eyes's place as hostess, but Cimarron was having too good a time to care.

Midnight came on. Some families went home, but others stayed, and the party got louder and livelier as the evening progressed. Finally even the old Don excused himself, pleading weariness, but invited the crowd to stay and dance until dawn. He gathered up the little dog and went up to bed.

Cimarron had never had such a wonderful time. She danced with all the cowboys, this rancher, that shopkeeper, then back to Luis's arms again. She waited for Trace to ask her, but he did not. In fact, the cowboy seemed to study her with morose melancholy while he drank and watched.

Double damnation! He can't dance, he's limping on that injured leg, remember? But that didn't keep the women from flocking around him, she thought as she whirled by. There was a group of at least four women hanging on his every word, his easy charm. Why, he was actually smiling. He must be drunk.

It was the wee hours of the morning, but the band still played, couples still whirled to the music. Cimarron saw a few slipping away discreetly into the shadows to make love. Quickly, she looked around to make sure Trace was still in the courtyard. Had he slipped away into the shadows? She didn't see him anywhere. Suddenly she imagined him out on the grass with one of Miss Fancy's girls. Probably the girl wouldn't charge him one dime for the enjoyment of his virile skill. The redhead? That highly painted blonde? It was hard to check the faces and keep dancing.

Luis frowned down at her. "Whoever are you looking for, Cimarron? You keep looking around."

"Nobody," she stammered, but she couldn't stop herself from searching the sea of faces. Was he even now lying out there in the shadows with one of those girls panting eager and naked beneath his hard-driving body?

"His leg," she said without thinking as she danced. "If he isn't careful, he'll re-injure that leg."

"What?" Luis asked.

"Nothing," she gulped. She hoped he did hurt that leg if he were lying between that redhead's creamy thighs. Yes, she hoped he did hurt it again. If he were a horse, they'd have to shoot him.

"I don't know where your mind is," Luis said gently, "but I wish it were on me. I can tell you're not listening to the music, since you've stumbled over my feet twice now."

"I'm so sorry," she said, determining to pay attention. After all, Luis Durango was more handsome, more interesting, more . . . what? She relived the image of herself as Señora Durango with Trace begging her not to send him away from the ranch. As Texans would say, she thought doggedly, she'd send him so far away, they'd have to ship daylight to him.

The band broke into a Mexican folk dance now, the *jarabes,* and she had to concentrate to follow the quick jig steps as the guitar played and the gourds rattled. Even as she danced the fast steps, she looked around and couldn't find Trace. When the dance finished, both she and Luis were damp with perspiration, gasping for breath as they fell laughingly into each other's arms. For a moment, as he looked down at her, she thought he would kiss her, and she was not sure whether she wanted him to or not.

And then, ever the perfect gentleman, he regained his composure. "Señorita, I think the servants have made a fresh batch of punch and cookies. Shall I bring you some?"

"Oh, would you?" She fanned herself. "I'd be ever so grateful!"

Luis left and Cimarron stood gasping for breath, saw Rosa give her a scowling look as she came back, gathering empty plates and cups. Obviously, she resented Cimarron's behaving like the señora instead of helping with the work. But Cimarron didn't care. She had done enough housework over the years to feel like Cinderella, and she had never had such a good time before.

Double damnation! Where had that Trace Durango got off to? Why should she care? she asked herself. Well, she was worried about that injured leg. After all, she was responsible for his getting shot. . . .

Luis disappeared into the house. Cimarron glanced around. It was hot here on the crowded patio, she thought. Maybe a little cool air. . . .

She walked out into the deep blue shadows, around the side of the hacienda, out of the growing light of the paper lanterns. It was dark here with the giant oleander bushes around her. The blooms were all but gone now, one here and there wafting an exotic, haunting fragrance. That annoying thought came to her again and she reached for it, couldn't quite remember what it was. A cricket chirped away, unaware that a few more weeks a norther would sweep in and it would die. The orange and russet promise of October was just over the purple horizon.

Cimarron took a deep breath of the wildflower-scented air, wiped her perspiring face. Very faintly, she could hear the discordant notes of the little Mexican band floating on the still air.

Somewhere out near the bunkhouse, she heard a woman laugh. "You naughty boy!" the woman scolded, as if she didn't mean it, wasn't going to stop him from whatever it was he was doing.

She tensed, listening, imagining Trace in the woman's arms, his mouth invading hers hungrily. Cimarron shuddered, ran her tongue along her upper lip, remembering the taste of Trace's kiss devouring, dominating.

The woman laughed again. "If you ain't a caution, now, I told you not to touch me there. . . ."

Cimarron stiffened. Was it Trace? Just where was he touching the girl? She didn't want to remember, but she couldn't stop herself from recalling the stroking, seeking touch of his sure hands on her skin. Damn him! she thought savagely, damn him! She heard the woman laugh again, started to turn back to the courtyard crowd when she heard a limping step, knew with sudden relief that the woman lay in some other man's arms. Because as she turned, Trace Durango stepped out of the shadows, favoring his injured leg.

"Well, sassy miss," his voice was cold, bitter, "you've really been the belle of the ball tonight, haven't you, dancing every dance?"

He came up to her, a little unsteady on his feet, and she caught the scent of tequila, knew he was drunk.

"I—I came looking for you," she stammered, "I—"

"Well, darlin', you just found me." And before she could tell him she was worried about his leg, he grabbed her, pulled her to him. She started to protest, but his hands were already on her shoulders, sliding her blouse down. "Remember, you were supposed to say 'please Trace'?" He grinned down at her, "All evening, you've been asking me with your eyes, but I told you I wouldn't touch you again unless you begged me."

He was drunk, and the way he looked at her, she was a

little bit afraid. She decided to go back to the dance. She had to get away from this unsteady drunk. "Please, Trace," she protested, then stopped in alarm, listening to her own words.

"I thought you'd never ask," he said, and before she could protest further, his hot mouth came down to claim hers and he pulled her hard into the circle of his embrace.

Chapter Fifteen

Cimarron tried to protest that he didn't understand what she meant. But with his mouth covering hers, she couldn't speak. Her thoughts were in turmoil as his seeking mouth dominated hers, his tongue moving between her lips, caressing her tongue.

His hands were hot as flames on her bare shoulders, and her legs seemed to buckle under her. Without even realizing it, she leaned against him, her bare breasts pressed against his black shirt. Her nipples grew taut and sensitive as they brushed against his hard chest.

She tried to protest, but his tequila-tasting mouth only drove deeper into hers when her lips parted. His hands moved down her bare shoulders, one arm pulling her against him, the other hand coming around to stroke her breasts until she trembled with the sensation of his fingers touching her nipples.

Without meaning to, she moaned aloud. Against her mouth, he gasped, "I want you, too, darlin', I want you. . . ."

She couldn't stop herself from sliding her tongue between his open lips, touching, stroking the inside of his hot mouth with her darting blade. Cimarron knew by the way he trembled and pulled her hard against him that she had excited him almost to the breaking point.

Are you loco, Cimarron? she asked herself, are you some bitch in heat, eager to be taken by the first male who comes along? No, not any male, her body told her with mounting excitement, this male.

She couldn't restrain herself from pressing closer to his heat, feeling the hard maleness of him pushing against her body.

She shouldn't be here, she thought wildly, but she couldn't pull away. His strong arms lifted her, pulled her blouse down further until his hot, wet lips encircled her nipple, sucking, biting until she moaned and shook. Warm wetness smeared her dainty lace underclothing as she felt her eager body prepare itself for the mating.

His mouth nuzzled her breasts like a greedy child and the sensation made her insides tremble, wanting him . . . wanting him. . . .

"I—I've got to go back," she murmured, "I can't—"

"You asked me, remember?" he reminded her, and his wet mouth went up her neck, breathed warmly into her ear until she trembled with the feeling. "I want you, Wild One, I've wanted you since the first moment I saw you, and you want me, too, you know you do."

She tried to tell him he was mistaken, but her face turned up to his, accepting, no, demanding the caress of his lips. All her body could think of was lying on the soft grass under the oleanders with this cowboy riding her as hard and skillfully as he tamed a wild bronc.

"Trace . . ." she began, but he interrupted her, his breath coming in short, hard gasps.

"When I finish loving you, darlin', you'll do things you never dreamed of doing to a man, let me do things to you. . . ." His mouth covered hers again, his hands cupping her face as she swayed against him.

"Trace, your leg—"

"The hell with my leg," he swore as his hand cupped her breast. "You're going to do it to me, understand, Wild One?"

She had a sudden, clear vision of herself straddling his hard, lean body, riding him . . . riding him. . . .

Somewhere a million miles away, she heard Luis's voice calling faintly, "Cimarron, Cimarron, where are you?"

Trace swore under his breath as she stiffened, coming out of her tumultuous emotion. "Here, Luis," she called, pulling away from Trace, "I'm out here."

Trace glared at her in the moonlight. "You didn't have to answer him."

"He would have come looking, found us together," she said, jerking her blouse back up on her shoulders. Her breasts felt heavy without the support of his big hands. Under the bright cotton, she could still feel the heated moistness of his mouth on her nipples.

But when she turned toward the calling voice, Trace grabbed her arm. "That time in the barn, the study. Are you carrying my child?"

"I—I don't know yet," she fired back truthfully, "but you might as well know, if I am, Luis is wanting to marry me, and at least, the child would have a legitimate father."

If she had thought he would be angry, she was mistaken. For just a split-second, the cowboy's face was dark with emotion as he swayed drunkenly, then he threw back his head and laughed. "If anyone ever deserved a trick like this, Luis does!" Trace smiled bitterly. "Raising my bastard as his own, thinking it's his son is just what he deserves after what he did—"

"Cimarron?" Luis called. "Where are you?"

Had she expected Trace to ask her to marry him? Would she have said yes if he had? He was too bitter, too distrustful ever to give his heart and soul away completely, she thought, remembering him in those rare moments when he'd let down his guard as he loved her. That sensitive, vulnerable one was the man she hungered for now, but he was safely enclosed inside the hard shell.

Luis called again somewhere out there in the shadows. She didn't want to leave here. Her body wanted to spend the night on the soft grass in the moonlight in this cowboy's arms. But her common sense overrode her emotions. If she didn't move in the next few seconds, Luis was going to find them together and there would be trouble.

"Coming, Luis," she called back and turned to go.

Trace swayed on his feet. "You little *puta* tease," he muttered. "Start a fire, then run off and leave it burning without putting out the flames. Well, darlin', there's plenty of women at this party who want me to make love to them. I'll go find one—"

"Or two or three!" she snapped, angry with herself that the image of him in the arms of one of the pretty whores upset her so. "I'm sure even with an injured leg, you're stallion enough to service half a dozen of Miss Fancy's girls. They probably don't even charge you for it!"

He tipped the black hat unsteadily over one eye. "That's right," he nodded. "How'd you know?"

"I hate you for that!" Cimarron snarled, whirling away with a flounce of lace petticoats. "I'm coming, Luis!" she called, walking back toward the courtyard. "Here I am!"

Later that evening, she saw Trace with a bottle of tequila, the redheaded girl on his arm, the blonde on the other, heading for the shadows of the trees. Trace gave her an arrogant wink as he limped away with the girls, punishing her, she knew. Cimarron reacted with pain. Those two would put out the fire she had built in him. But what was she to do with the desire smoldering in her own depths?

Luis looked inquiringly into her face. "Are you ill, my dear? You look positively stricken."

"I-I'm tired, Luis," she lied. "I think I'm ready to call it a night. It was a wonderful party."

Luis nodded as they walked into the house, to the foot of the stairs. *"Si*, it was nice." He looked sad. "I wanted it to be the best party ever, since it is proably the old man's last. . . ." His voice trailed off and he swallowed hard, crossed himself.

She patted his hand. "You are a good person, Luis. Now go say goodnight to the guests. In the morning, I want to talk to you about the school for the ranchero children."

He smiled. "I thought you would forget about that silly idea, my sweet, but if it's important to you, it's important to me, too."

The next morning, Luis gathered up a few children and brought them to the house for her school. That evening she discussed it with him in the study. The two were all alone. Rosa and Turquoise had gone off to some vaquero's house to visit, the old man was in his room, and Trace and Sanchez were playing cards with the cowboys in the bunkhouse.

"Cimarron, you are wasting your time, I tell you." Luis paced up and down the study. "Why teach future vaqueros and housemaids to read? I declare, you are just like the señora. That is just what she was doing before—"

"Luis." Cimarron sat down on the fine leather sofa and spread her bright blue calico dress out around her. "Tell me what happened the day Velvet Eyes left."

She had never seen such pain in a man's face. "We don't discuss that around here. If Don Diego were to find out—"

"But you may tell me," Cimarron urged. "I know some of it already."

Luis went over to the desk, got himself a cigar with a trembling hand. "It was the most terrible day of my life," he said sincerely. "I hope I never have to go through it again. All of them, Rosa, Trace, the old man made me go over every detail about where I took her, what happened, what she said. But what we agreed to tell the Don were lies."

"Why did you help her leave?"

He lit the cigar, shook out the match. For a long moment, she did not think he would answer. When he did, his voice was a tortured whisper. "It was always an open secret that I loved her, would have done anything for her."

"Even driving her out to meet another man?"

His handsome face paled. *"Si,* that, too. I had no pride where Velvet Eyes was concerned. I had found out about her lover; perhaps I should have told the Don."

"Do you realize he's convinced she's dead?"

Luis started, and he whirled and looked at her. "What? Why would he think that?"

Cimarron shook her head slowly. "It's a foolish, naive feeling," she answered sympathetically. "But in some ways, he is a naive old man, seeing everything in black and white. Everything is so simple to someone with such old-fashioned ideals about love and marriage, I suppose."

"But why does he say she is dead?" The color came back to his face as he took a deep drag on the imported cigar.

"It's all so very simple to him." Cimarron shrugged. "He

loved and trusted her, she loved and trusted him. He is convinced that with a relationship like that, the only thing that could keep her from his side is death. If she is not with him, it is because she is dead."

Luis looked at her ruefully, nodded. "What an innocent idea," he said sadly. "I hope to God he dies before he finds out the truth."

"But he thinks her dead. That must be very sad for him—"

"Is it better for him to know that she ran away with a Yankee captain who was half his age?" Luis challenged, fingering a button on the exquisite white silk shirt. "If you care as much for the old man as I do, my sweet, I hope you will help me keep the truth from him."

"Luis, tell me about taking her to meet the lover."

He made an angry gesture of dismissal, paced the study, looking up at the mounted heads of wild animals along the high ceilings over the bookcases. "I've told Trace about it, I've told Rosa about it a dozen times. You must understand the whole thing is very painful for me."

"Then why did you help her leave?" Cimarron felt desperately sorry for the handsome Spaniard because of the pain in his eyes.

"I knew about the man, had followed her to the rendezvous. I argued with her to give him up and I would help her keep the secret forever to protect Diego." Cimarron looked at him a long moment, thinking how much he favored the old Don, favored him even more than he did his son.

"She asked me to drive her to the rendezvous," Luis said with evident anguish. He paused, as if not wanting to remember. "It was the most terrible day of my life."

She sympathized with this fine man caught in a moral dilemma. "What was the captain like?"

Luis shrugged. "Tall, sandy hair. Green eyes. From his bearing and manners, I'd say very rich, back East society. I suppose women would think him handsome. Velvet Eyes had met him at a party in Galveston while the Yankees still controlled that port."

"And after all this time, he sneaked back into Confederate

Texas for her?"

"If you had known her," he whispered, his eyes misty, "you would not find that hard to believe. But it was brave, wasn't it? The Yankee wore civilian clothes that day. If the Rebels had caught him, they would have hanged him for a spy. *Si,* it was reckless and brave."

Cimarron ran her hand over the lace of the full skirt spread out around her. "He must have loved her madly to take such a risk."

He looked at her thoughtfully, the smoke from his fragrant cigar drifting on the still air. "Every man who met her loved her madly," he said.

Including Trace? she thought, but she didn't ask. She didn't have to ask about Luis himself, it was mirrored in his eyes. She had never seen such grief, such pain.

"You painted the portrait of her?"

"*Si,* I painted the portrait just as I painted the one of my mother in the upstairs hall." Tears gathered in the distinguished eyes. "I loved her from the first moment I came back from Spain and saw her standing in this house. Velvet Eyes was that kind of woman. By my painting her, she belongs to me in a special way that she never quite belonged to anyone else. I captured her very soul on canvas, don't you see?"

It was quiet now, so quiet she could hear the fine leather of Luis's handmade boots squeak as he paced the floor, the big silver spurs jingling, jingling. "You can't even begin to imagine what it felt like to always love her, knowing she loved another man."

Trace, she thought suddenly. *She loved Trace.*

"And where did you take her to meet the Yankee captain?" she asked.

"Near the town of Wimberley. They planned to ride south into Mexico. If they eluded Confederate troops along the way, they could get a ship off the coast, go to New York. Have you been in Wimberley?"

"Once or twice." She almost said "delivering goods from my uncle's store," but instead she blurted, "I think it's near Jacob's Well, isn't it?"

"Si, that's the place." He turned away, crossed the floor to lean against the stone mantel. His hand shook as he tossed the cigar into the fireplace. "It was the worst day of my life." He came over and looked down into her eyes, and she knew he spoke the truth. "It was the worst day of my life," he said again and his eyes misted. "I had forgotten what happiness was until you came into my life, Cimarron. You are so very much like Velvet Eyes."

She wasn't sure whether she liked the idea that Luis was going to transfer his affection for the señora to her. It was almost like walking in a ghost's shoes.

"Luis." She stood up, took his hand. "What is Trace to you?"

He started as if she had struck him. "Why do you ask that?" he said guardedly. "What has he told you? Whatever it is—"

"Nothing," she answered truthfully. "Just like you, just like everyone in this damned house, he's told me nothing."

Luis was hiding something, she thought. She suspected from things she'd heard here and there that Luis was actually Trace's father, and yet . . . if so, why did the two hate each other so? Could Velvet Eyes be Trace's sister? Or was she just the old Don's half-breed wife, with whom Trace carried on with?

She waited. "Luis," she began, "tell me—"

"Don't ask, Cimarron," he answered sharply. "You're trying to open a Pandora's box of troubles that would only break someone's heart. Leave it closed and ask no more."

She dropped it then, leaving her questions unanswered. She only knew that Trace must be third in line for the inheritance. Was he Luis's son, illegitimate or not? Luis's younger brother? But she did not intend to leave it lie forever. Sooner or later, she wanted the answers to these puzzles everyone seemed so loath to discuss with her.

Luis offered his hand. "It's so much nicer outside on the veranda," he said gently.

She took his hand, let him lead her out to the courtyard by the bubbling fountain. The stars hung like chips of glass in the darkness. The Milky Way spread like snow from the lavender hilltops up into the pink-tinged clouds. The Cheyennes' Hanging Road to the Stars, she thought as she felt Luis's presence directly behind her. She stood looking down at the pool. There was enough light from the big moon to reflect their images in the placid water. Looking down, she saw both their faces, his hands coming up to her shoulders. She felt his fingers tense, as if waiting for her to protest. She closed her eyes, pretended he was someone else. When she didn't protest, he leaned over, pulled her hair away from the back of her neck, kissed the nape gently.

"Oh, *mi querida*," he murmured, "my love. I hope you don't think me forward, but this is something I've longed to do for a long time. I can hardly wait till we marry."

She made a small murmur of assent and his lips kissed the back of her neck again. He was handsome, rich, and powerful, she thought resignedly. Luis would protect her from the law, and if she were with child, it would have a secure existence. If she let him make love to her tonight, perhaps he might think the child was his.

"Cimarron, my sweet," he murmured against her hair, pulling her gently against him as his arms went around her waist, "what are you thinking?"

She looked down at the pool, saw both their reflections among the stars that seemed to float in the dark water. But in the water, she seemed to see another face, a moody, rugged face with large, distrusting eyes. She leaned over, swirled her fingers in the pool to destroy the vision. "I—I was thinking about us," she lied.

His arms pulled her more tightly against him. He held her so close she could feel his heart beating against her back, feeling his hard manhood swelling against her hips. "Cimarron," he whispered and she heard the desire, the suppressed passion in his tone. "I—I want to make love to you!"

She turned slowly in his arms. If he made love to her, he might feel more inclined to hurry the marriage, she thought as she looked up at him. Then why was she hesitating? There was no future with the scowling, distrustful foreman, none at all. She must look out for herself, for the child she might be carrying....

Still she hesitated, listening to a mockingbird that had been disturbed by the bright moon begin to sing to the coming day. Luis Durango was the only way out she could see to her dilemma.

"*Si*, Luis, I want to make love to you, too." She tried to give her most bewitching smile.

"Sweet one, pretty one..." He bent his head to kiss her, pulled her close.

Dutifully she turned her lips up to his. Surely this handsome Spaniard's kisses could make her heart pound faster, make her glad to become his wife.

He kissed her a little primly with his lips closed, and she sighed inwardly, wondering if this was the way all proper gentlemen kissed a girl. Somehow she was disappointed at the slight brush of his lips against hers. She closed her eyes, imagining the pulse-pounding, deep kisses of the half-breed. Maybe it wasn't considered ladylike to want a man's mouth to conquer hers, to thrust deep with his tongue as he did with his maleness, to hunger for him to mate with her like wild things coupling out in the shadows of the night....

He pulled back, tilted her face up to his with one carefully groomed hand. "You are so sweet, so innocent," Luis murmured. "There is so much to teach you."

If he only knew how much she had already experienced, she thought, looking down demurely. She had a feeling the Durango heir wouldn't want her if he knew. He was too proud, too arrogant to be second with a woman, especially second to a common cowboy. What would he say if he knew he might be getting another man's child in the bargain?

The thought worried her a moment, then it occurred to her that both men were dark and tall; they even resembled each other. If she bore him Trace's child, it would look so much like Luis that he'd never suspect. Was it a terrible thing to do to him?

She pressed herself against his chest so she could tell from his sudden change of expression that he felt her nipples through the fine silk shirt he wore. Then in seeming innocence, she moved so that her body pressed against him all the way down their bodies and legs. He looked a little disconcerted, but he did not pull away from her and she heard his breath quicken.

"Luis," she whispered, "I was hoping we could marry right away. There is so much for you to teach me. . . ." She let her voice trail off as she reached up, pulled his face down to hers, and kissed him with all the open-mouthed hunger that Trace had built in her the night before.

Luis groaned aloud and his arms went around her, jerking her against him so tightly she could hardly breathe. Now he kissed her the way she had expected to be kissed, his mouth forcing hers open almost savagely, his shaking hands pulled her dress off both shoulders.

Never had Trace treated her so roughly! She started to protest, then remembered she had brought this about herself to make him want her, to hurry up the marriage. She forced herself not to pull away, letting his mouth take hers so savagely he cut her lips. *She really was very innocent about men,* she thought in panic as she tasted blood from the force of his teeth on her lips. His hands cupped her breasts, squeezing so hard that she cried out, both afraid and surprised.

At that he pulled back, slapped his hand across his forehead. *"Mi Dios!"* he swore mournfully, "I completely forgot myself, señorita! Please forgive me, I never meant to insult you or imply—"

"It's quite all right Luis," she gasped, pulling her dress back up on her shoulders, wiping the blood from her lip with the back of her hand. Suddenly she remembered him mounted on the chestnut, using the cruel spade bit that tore its mouth, slashing its sides with his big Mexican spurs. What had she gotten herself into? With so little experience, she thought that all men were, deep down, like Luis, like Trace when he had raped her.

"No, it's not all right!" He wrung his hands together as he paced up and down the veranda. "I—I forgot myself, began to treat you like a common whore. Believe me, Cimarron, it will never happen again." He paused, took both her hands in his. "Will you forgive me?"

What else could she do? When she was his wife, how would he treat her? She had just seen a side of Luis that scared her a little. "Of course, I forgive you," she said quickly before she could give it more thought. "Men are so—so animallike in their passions." She looked away demurely, but she had seen the awakened hunger in his face, knew he wanted her in a way he obviously had not expected to.

"Cimarron." His hands went to her shoulders and once more he was the gallant gentleman. "Perhaps I could find a way to speed things up so we could be married right away."

"Of course." She should feel triumphant, knowing she would soon be mistress here, have the cowboy in her power. Somehow, she had never felt so miserable.

He kissed her cheek gently. "I'll arrange to announce it to everyone at once, maybe give a big party."

That sounded reasonable enough to her. She walked over by the rouge-colored oleander, took a deep breath of its haunting, exotic sweetness. "I love the fragrance of these. I know now why they were the señora's favorite flower."

"Let's speak no more of her or her flowers," Luis sighed. "The memories are too sad. When I'm Don here, I'll dig them all up, replace them with Cape Jasmine."

"I wouldn't want you to do that." She shook her head as she reached to break a blossom off, taking a deep breath. *The scent was suddenly so sweet, so heavy, that it was cloying, swirling around her like half-forgotten words to an old love song. And yet...* She sniffed it, trying to remember.

She tossed the bloom into the fountain, watching it float on the reflective surface. "Look, Luis," she whispered, "the pool has trapped a whole sky of stars. See the moon floating there."

Luis looked. "I see a Comanche moon," he said so softly that she had to strain to hear him. "There's nothing lovely about a harbinger of death and destruction. Do you know the Comanche never raid when the moon is in crescent with its tips upward?"

"I've heard that. But I don't know why."

"Legend says the moon overflows then, brings rain. War parties can be tracked in wet dirt."

"Well, in a few more weeks the blue northers will blow in and the Comanche will stay close to their campfires," she said, taking his arm as they went back to the hacienda. "The blooms are already mostly gone from the oleander."

He patted her hand that was linked through his arm as they strolled. "The northers never reach the south boundaries of the Triple D," he said. "Otherwise we couldn't grow it here."

He stopped just outside the French doors, took her in his arms again for a very controlled, almost passionless kiss. "This is an ungentlemanly thing to say, my sweet, but already I dream of your sleeping in my arms."

She reached up, gave him a peck on the cheek. What had she done? She tried to imagine herself spread out naked on Luis's bed while the handsome Spaniard made love to her. It would be his right, of course, as her husband. As his wife, she would have few rights at all; women couldn't even vote. Whatever he wanted, expected of her, she would not dare object. She wondered if his making love to her would be anything like . . . double damnation! Could she never get that cowboy off her mind?

At the foot of the stairs, he smiled down at her, kissed her hand. "You have made me a very happy man," he whispered. "I hope you will never be sorry."

She looked away from his eyes guiltily. She was already sorry, regretful. But she was not sure why. "It'll be a wonderful marriage," she said, and she was not sure whether she was reassuring him or herself.

"Oh, and Cimarron, I've decided to help you with your school. I'll pass the word among the help that your school has our blessings, so they'll let their children come."

Her doubts faded as she took both his hands in hers, looked up into his handsome face. "So sweet, Luis; *gracias.*"

The next day, Luis was more than helpful, making

suggestions, offering to look things up in his big library of books. Turquoise came into the room shyly, followed by a half-dozen other ragtag children of the vaqueros.

"Come in, come in," Cimarron motioned, "welcome to school. This is wonderful!"

The children peeked at her shyly, obviously not sure it would be wonderful, only following orders.

"Luis?" she asked, suspicion building in her mind, "did you pressure any of the parents?"

"Well, maybe a little," he laughed, fingering his pencil mustache. "Some of them thought it foolish, but I told them if the señorita wants it, Señor Luis orders it."

"I'm not sure you should have gone that far," she said grudgingly, "but once they see the children might improve their lives, how much fun it is, others will come."

And they did. The children must have gone out and told the others that the señorita was nice and the schooling not so hard after all, because the second day, even Maverick showed up, hat in hand.

"I know I'm not a kid, señorita," he mumbled, obviously much embarrassed, "but I'd like to learn to read. My mama taught me a little, drawing in the dirt with a stick, but I think I need to know more."

She pursed her lips. "Is it all right with Trace?"

"Yes, ma'm," he nodded. "The boss said he could spare me a couple of hours a day. Would you object to someone half-grown in your school?"

"I'd be happy to have you, Maverick," she smiled warmly, motioned him to a place on the floor among some of the little Mexican children. "Now, class, we'll count. *Uno, dos, tres. . . .*"

Tres. Trace. The thought of him made something in her chest squeeze so tightly she could hardly breath. The night she had stood with Luis by the fountain, her period had started. She wasn't pregnant, after all. She faced this with a curious mixture of relief and sadness. *Was she out of her mind?* Why would anyone want that moody half-breed's child? She could marry Luis now without a guilty conscience, and they would have children of their own. She should be very happy. But a tiny nagging doubt seemed to gnaw at her like a hungry mouse nibbling at a cake. She hadn't seen Trace since the party. As his leg healed he stayed out more on the ranch, rounding up cattle, doing little chores that seemed to keep him away from the hacienda so that he seldom took meals with them anymore or saw her. It finally dawned on her he was deliberately avoiding her. The old Don himself had a good day and then a bad one. Luis was right, the old man couldn't last much longer. The thought saddened her because she liked the feisty old fellow so much.

As for the sulking Rosa, she wasn't quite sure what to do with her yet. It occurred to her one day as she taught the small ones to read, that Rosa was hovering about the study too often, taking a very long time to dust and sweep. Then a thought occurred to her. That day after the children scattered to play, Cimarron cornered her.

"Rosa, I would be happy for you to come sit in my classes, if you wish."

The girl was immediately embarrassed, defensive. "I don't know what you're talking about," she said proudly. "I come in only to dust. I am educated already. The señora taught me to read and write my name."

Cimarron took a deep breath, feeling dreadfully sorry for the girl. "I didn't mean it that way," she lied. "I meant to help me with the children, help me with the school."

Rosa shook her dark hair back, now interested. "You ask for my help?"

"Si."

"In that case," the girl ventured, "perhaps I could take a little time to come in."

"I would be ever so grateful," Cimarron said hurriedly. So Rosa became a "helper," coming faithfully to the library in the afternoons. Cimarron aided the ignorant girl with her schooling, thanking her profusely for her "help."

She caught Rosa looking at her with troubled eyes. "Perhaps I have misjudged you," the girl said slowly. "You are very much like the señora. I wish now. . . ."

But her voice trailed off and Cimarron never found out what it was the girl wished. Luis and Trace both came into the study just then, and Cimarron saw jealousy cross the girl's features. Whatever it was that Rosa regretted, she evidently changed her mind and said no more.

Cimarron decided that if she couldn't win the girl over by the time of the wedding, she would ask Luis to find another position for Rosa so Cimarron could choose her own housekeeper.

And then one day, just after she had dismissed her little school, Tequila, who had slept happily on the leather sofa through every class, barked and went charging to the French doors. Curiously, Cimarron peeked around the door to find Trace leaning against the adobe wall outside.

"Have you been standing there eavesdropping all afternoon?" she asked easily as she went back in and started gathering up slates and chalk.

"A little while," he confessed, looking shamefaced, as if he'd been caught with his hand in the cookie jar.

She looked at him. "You could have come in. I'm teaching Maverick to read; I could teach you."

"For your information, I can already read," he fired back. "Believe it or not, I've read a lot of books from the study."

"Oh? Then what do you want?" She busied herself straightening furniture.

He moved up behind her. "You," he said simply. "I want you, Cimarron. I—I'm not talkin' marriage, but—it's you. I've tried, but I can't seem to get you off my mind."

She whirled around, both angry and indignant. "You aren't offering marriage? Just what are you offering, then? More nights of the barn; the sofa? Thanks, but no thanks. By the way, I'm not expecting your baby, after all."

She was amazed that his face looked disappointed. "Oh? Well, I can always try again—"

"Get away from me, you brute!" she snapped. "You just think you can grab me, take me any time you want?"

"We were good together. Don't you remember—?"

"You don't need to fill in the details," she snapped, confronting him, "I remember very well."

"You're all I think of." He took off his hat, twisted it in his hands. "You're the only woman I ever made love to that did that to me, darlin'."

Is there anything that tastes as sweet as revenge? "Even if you offered marriage," she flung at him, "you're too late! I'm going to marry Luis!"

He gave her a cold, hard look that made her shiver. "Over my very dead body, you will!" he vowed.

Chapter Sixteen

Don Diego de Durango sat in a chair looking out the window of his bedroom and sighed. He had been feeling so well as of late, he had begun to think that old quack of a doctor was wrong.

His mouth was a grim, hard line as he considered. They were all such fools to think they could keep it from him. Servants had loud voices when they gossiped with each other, and Don Diego had the light step of an old Texas Ranger. He'd heard the discussions, knew in spite of the cheery fronts everyone put on for him that Dr. Hastings thought the malignancy was slowly spreading. He wondered with detached curiosity just how long he had left.

No, he didn't want to die yet. He had fought Comanches, renegades, and outlaws. The beat of life was strong in him still, even though black depressions sometimes clouded his thinking. He hungered to live long enough to see his son finally marry, take over the ranch as he had himself when a Comanche arrow took his own father from this life. He nodded. Yes, he wanted to live long enough to dangle a couple of fat, pretty grandchildren on his knee. After that, he'd die content. And sixty-five wasn't so old, after all. Maybe the stupid doctor was wrong in his diagnosis.

His wife's pet, little Tequila, came through the door, hopped up on his bed, burrowed in under the covers until it disappeared from sight. "You'll get in trouble doing that yet," he prophesied. "Some maid's liable to gather you up with the sheets and put you in the washpot."

The tiny black button of a nose stuck out from under the blanket as the dog cocked his head at the friendly voice. Don Diego stood up from his chair a little unsteadily. "Come, Tequila, let's walk a little. I tire of sitting like an invalid all day."

The chihuahua accepted his invitation and trotted after him. Diego went into the hallway, stood looking at the dignified portrait of the old señora. His mother had lived to be eighty, but it didn't seem like he would last that long. Still, he thought, nodding, in the rough-and-tumble frontier of Texas, many men never lived to be thirty, so maybe he was lucky after all. No, he was not ready to die. So, secretly, he prayed for a miracle.

But last night he'd had another spell, and he knew in his heart his time must be running out. The vomiting, the running of the bowels, the sweating. Yes, the malignancy must be spreading. At those times he was depressed, dizzy, and could hardly breathe. The pain in his belly burned as if he had swallowed hot coals. He would get better after a day or two. About the time he thought the doctor must be wrong, it would happen again. The first time was only a week after Velvet Eyes had disappeared, after old Juanita, the housekeeper, had fallen down the stairs to her death. He knew Trace and Luis spoke of taking him back East to specialists when the war ended. But he'd seen the way they exchanged glances. No one thought he would live that long.

He walked off down the hall, thinking about the problem, the little dog trailing at his heels. Don Diego paused at her room out of old habit. The little dog looked up at him inquiringly, whimpering softly as it scratched at the door.

"You miss her, too, don't you, Tequila?" He opened the door slowly, went in. "They lie to us about her even as they lie to me about the seriousness of my illness. They think me too weak to take bad news, they try to protect me."

The dog jumped up on the bed, curled up with a contented sigh. Don Diego stood before the portrait.

Ojos de Pana. Velvet Eyes. It occurred to him as his eyes blurred with tears that he had never called his wife anything else in all the years of their marriage. Luis had painted this portrait only a year or so after she'd come to the Triple D. The dog in her arms was old Poco, Tequila's grandsire. A blind man could see by studying the magnificent portrait that the artist was in love with the subject. *Si,* he had always known it. But Velvet Eyes had never given her husband caught to doubt her. He would have trusted her with his life, with everything he owned, because he loved her so. It was one of those perfect unions.

He sighed as he stood before the haunting picture. That was why he knew they lied to him. Velvet Eyes loved him; she never would have gone away, not even back to her Cheyenne people. *Si,* they lied just as they all lied to him about his physical condition. Well, they meant well.

He moved unsteadily to the dresser, stood looking down at her silver hairbrush and mirror, the crystal perfume decanter. Idly, he took out the stopper, sniffed it. As he closed his eyes, breathing in the sweet, exotic scent, it was almost like having her in the room again. If he closed his eyes tightly and sniffed the fragrance, he could hear her light laughter, see her moving through the crowd at one of the many parties she gave.

Oh, Velvet Eyes, mi querida, *my sweetheart, I miss you so very, very much!* Tears overflowed his tightly clenched eyes, ran down his wrinkled cheeks. He sniffed the perfume again, and it was almost like an echo, a haunting refrain of romantic music eddying around him. Very slowly, he put the stopper back in the crystal bottle. It was not good to live in the past. Don Diego II had always been a tough, practical man. That was why his ranch survived and prospered while others gradually sank back into the soil along with their luckless owners.

No, he thought, looking lovingly at the dusty portrait, he would not tell anyone about the perfume he sometimes smelled late at night when the whole house was asleep. Sometimes he came awake, almost feeling her presence, hearing the rustle of her skirts down the halls. Then he would realize sadly that it was only the giant oleander bushes brushing against the adobe walls of the hacienda.

If you'll tell me, my darling, I'll see about it, he promised the portrait. I would want you to rest in peace. Is there something wrong? Something you know that I do not? Guiltily, he looked around, feeling a bit foolish communicating with a painting. But no, he thought stubbornly, it was not foolish. Never had two people been so close, never had two people communicated so beautifully. There was not another woman like her, unless it might be that fiery Cimarron girl who had come out of nowhere to dazzle Luis and Trace.

Si, that one was beautiful and spirited, too, he thought as he leaned against the cobwebbed post of the bed, nodding approvingly at the portrait. "You would like her, my love. This Cimarron would be a perfect wife for my heir. I never thought anyone could replace you as señora of the Triple D, but she is so very much like you. . . ."

Sometimes the portrait almost seemed to speak to him if he looked at it long enough. He really should straighten the frame, but it seemed almost sacrilege to touch it. Nor did he want anyone in here to clean, to handle her things. Many times he had come here in the past six months, drawn by some invisible magnet, as if the portrait called out silently to his soul.

He wished someone would be truthful with him. He was tough. He could stand the truth. It was the not knowing that gnawed at him like a cruel rat. *No, that was the tumor, the malignancy,* he thought, clutching his belly.

When his belly hurt, he tried to think of good times past, of the times he had made love to Velvet Eyes, of their children running through the house.

Dallas. Forgive me, my wife, he thought. You did not want me to send the girl to Boston, but I was a stubborn, foolish old man. As you said, maybe she should have been allowed to grow up here, marry a local cowboy. It was my own pride that sent her off to live with my friends, the Peabodys, put her in Miss Priddy's Academy. You knew she would not like it, so you were not surprised when we heard she'd run away. That was what we argued about the morning before the day you disappeared. But you would not have left me for so small a thing, I know. I swear to you that when the war ends, I will find our Dallas and bring her home where she belongs. And if I don't live that long, maybe Trace or Luis will.

The portrait almost seemed to breathe, to smile at him. The blossoms in her blue-black hair looked freshly picked. Even the painted dog seemed to move its tiny head, though it had been buried under the oleanders many years ago. She was trying hard to tell him something, he knew it. Or maybe he was imagining things because he was old and sick....

He had not been old and sick the day he had found his Velvet Eyes. No, he was a strong, mature man of almost forty years. And that fateful day, he had been riding with the Texas Rangers when they raided a Comanche camp. He closed his eyes, remembering. *Si,* it had been the year 1839, the year before the Comanche made a peace treaty with the Cheyenne. But at that time, the two tribes were still bitter enemies, fighting and raiding each other.

Don Diego had been a handsome, black-haired Spaniard, with only a touch of gray at his sideburns. His father owned the Triple D, one of the biggest ranches in Texas even then, but Don Diego liked to ride with the Rangers. That day they had attacked a Comanche camp, and the braves had scattered. When the Rangers rode in, they found a frightened Cheyenne captive girl in one of the tepees.

The Ranger captain shook his head in disgust. "Looks purty badly used," he told the others. "Look at the bruises on her. No telling what meanness them Comanche thought up to do to her."

The girl looked at them inquiringly, stood up slowly.

"Jesus!" One of the others spat to one side. "That's the purtiest thing I ever saw, I don't care if she is all bruised up."

Don Diego felt annoyance at the hungry way the Rangers looked at her from atop their horses. "Comanche are notorious for gambling women away, or trading them back and forth like a horse or a rifle."

The Ranger captain grinned and took a chew off a tobacco

plug. "Is it true a brave'll share his wife with his brothers?"

"It's true," Don Diego said reluctantly, looking at the girl, who now met his gaze bravely, proudly. "But he expects his brothers to share their wives with him, too."

One of the men guffawed. "My brother's got a good-looking wife, but I don't figure he'd cotton to sleeping with my fat old lady!"

The men laughed, and Don Diego dismounted and walked over to the girl who looked about wildly, as if to run away. She wasn't more than fifteen, he thought in disgust, looking at her injuries, maybe not more than fourteen.

Slowly he held his hand out. "I won't hurt you," he said in border Spanish and sign language.

The others slipped from their horses, came forward to surround her. Immediately, she shrank away.

"Get back, you're scaring her," he warned.

The captain looked her up and down appreciatively, pulled at his mustache. "I'd like to scare her," he laughed easily, "I'd give her the ride of her life."

Don Diego turned, glared at him.

"Hell!" the captain said apologetically, "it ain't as if she ain't second-hand goods. No telling how many Comanche bucks has used her since she was captured."

The girl looked back at Don Diego. She had a small face, full, passionate lips, and large liquid eyes like a deer's.

"Jesus!" said the other ranger, "what are we gonna to do with her?"

Don Diego told her in border Spanish and a smattering of Cheyenne that he would see her returned to her people.

For a moment, relief crossed her beautiful features. Then reluctantly, she shook her head, and her voice was as soft and velvet as her eyes. "My people would not want me back now. No brave would give marriage ponies for me."

The captain, who understood a little, said, "Why not? Why doesn't she want to go back?"

Don Diego hesitated. "I know the Cheyenne," he said slowly, "and she's right. They value purity in their women so highly that they keep chastity belts on them. No warrior would marry a girl, even a beautiful one, who's been used by half the males in an enemy camp."

The captain frowned. "Well, hell, Diego. What do we do with her?"

One of the rangers grinned, nodded. "Let's take her back to camp with us. We could use a cook and somebody to do the washing. And on cold nights, well, we'll share her. Seems she's used to being passed around."

A couple of the others laughed. "I get her tonight!"

The girl, who obviously didn't speak English, turned inquiring, trusting eyes on Diego.

He took a deep breath, trying to decide whether to tell her what the gringo men were offering. "She wouldn't be any better off than she was," he argued.

"Well," the captain laughed, "at least, we wouldn't beat her up, and there's not as many of us as there was of them Comanche bucks."

Anger built in Diego as the men laughed and joked. The girl turned soft, sad eyes on him, almost seeming to know now what was being said.

"I will belong to this one only." She squared her shoulders proudly, indicating Diego.

"Hey, Durango," one of the men caught her border Spanish, "looks like you're the lucky one. I'll trade you a good pony for her."

The girl came forward, put one small hand on his big arm. "You," she said with a nod. "I knew you were the one the first moment I saw you."

He was almost forty years old and the despair of his parents because he had never married. *Si*, there were many girls in the cantinas who winked at him, many high-bred Spanish ladies who wanted to share the rich ranch he would inherit. But no woman's eyes had ever called out to his heart before. Until now.

Diego felt the small hand on his arm, looked down into the proud bruised face. Somehow, he thought, a very long time ago in another life they had known each other, loved each other. And he had waited forty years for her to come into his life again.

He reached out, put his big hand protectively over her

small one. "I have no woman," he said in halting Cheyenne, "and I am a very rich warrior. If I knew where your father was, I would send many ponies to his tepee."

The girl blushed. Her lip trembled as she looked away. "My virtue has been taken," she answered. "No man would give any ponies for such a wife."

He put his fingertips under her chin, turned her face up to his. Her eyes were as big and deep as liquid pools. "Velvet Eyes," he whispered, "Ojos de Pana. You shall be my woman, and you are worth more ponies than even a rich warrior could give!"

He heard one of the rangers behind him. "What are those two palavering about?" he grumbled, "I don't speak Injun."

The captain cleared his throat, took out a handkerchief, and blew his nose. "It's just as well you don't, Myers. He just asked her to marry him."

"Marry him?" Myers said, "Why, I thought we was all gonna share her! After all, she'd been had by half the Comanche bucks in—"

Diego hit him then. His fist connected with Myer's jaw like the force of a hammer slamming into a side of beef. And when Myers staggered to his feet Diego hit him again and again, until the man spat out teeth and blood.

Then Diego stood over the fallen man, breathing hard and angry. "She's mine," he gasped out, "and only mine from this day forward. Any man says anything to insult her better stand ready to fight!"

The captain shrugged as he mounted up. "What'd Myers expect? Any Texan's gonna defend his woman."

Diego went over, swung up on his horse. He held out his hand to the Cheyenne girl. "Come, Ojos de Pana," he said. "We will go home now."

There was banked fire behind the softness of her big eyes. She reached up, took his hand, and he lifted her up behind him on the bay gelding.

He felt the heat of her against his broad back as her small arms went around his waist, her face pressed against his shirt. You old goat, he chided himself, you're almost forty years old and she probably isn't more than fifteen. But somehow, as he rode away with the girl snuggled against his back, he knew it was meant to be.

His parents were less than thrilled. They had expected him to select from the high-born girls of their rich Spanish friends. But even they came to see that this pair belonged together.

And what a señora for the Triple D she had made. From a scrawny, fearful girl child, she had matured into a beautiful woman. He had taught her to read himself, schooled her about table manners, about fine clothing. The ragged Cheyenne waif became the most elegant, wildly acclaimed hostess of any ranchero in the hill country. Everyone was eager to be invited to the Triple D as news of the beautiful señora and the wonderful parties she gave spread throughout Texas.

If he closed his eyes, even now, he could remember those first days, their eager, ardent lovemaking. And always, she slept curled up against his back, one arm thrown carelessly across his chest. Sometimes in the night he lay awake, enjoying the soft sound of her breathing, the warmth of her small, dark body against his own.

Oh, Velvet Eyes, my sweetheart. How can I live without you now when you were the beat of my heart, the song of my soul for so many, many years?

He sat down slowly in a shrouded chair, lost in the past. The past sometimes seemed more real to him now than the present. Maybe that was how one knew one was dying, Don Diego thought.

His father, Don Diego de Durango the first, had been killed by Comanche raiders right after Velvet Eyes came to the ranch. His strong-willed mother had lasted another ten years.

A few months after Diego married, Luis had come back from a Spanish medical school in some kind of hurried disgrace. It concerned a young lady, and it seemed that had he stayed in Madrid, her brothers would have challenged him to a duel. It had been important to Mother that Luis be a doctor, but he was too spoiled and lazy. Or maybe because he had no interest, Diego thought now, with regret. Luis had artistic talent, anyone could see that. He should have been allowed to study painting. But anyway, he had returned to the Triple D, even though he hated ranch life. Probably Diego should have given him an allowance and let him wander Europe the way so many of the spoiled nobility did these days.

Don Diego would admit it now, although before he would not even have admitted it to himself. Luis was more handsome, much younger than he, in fact, not many years older than Velvet Eyes herself. All these years, Diego had tortured himself with the fear that someday she might be unfaithful to him, leave him for Luis. But she never gave him cause to doubt her, and he came to rely on her, trust her as he did his eyes, his left hand that handled a gun with such skill.

No, she had not gone back to her people. He had asked many questions of everyone in the house. The answers they gave all seemed to be carefully rehearsed. Someone was hiding something from him, and he was too ill, too weary, too heartsick to figure out what had really happened. If he could only regain his health, he would have the truth, if he had to beat it out of those who lied to him. Now he lacked the strength to pursue the mystery, and even those he loved best would not give him straight answers.

Velvet Eyes, I miss you so, he thought as he stood up, took one last look at the portrait. He was not well, he thought, because he imagined that the portrait almost moved, almost spoke to him. The sweet, exotic scent of her perfume seemed to drift out of his memory along with the memory of warmth of her curled up in sleep against his back.

The perfume. He picked up the crystal bottle, considering. *Si,* he knew one who was worthy, who might appreciate it. He took it with him as he left.

I was lucky, he thought with a sigh as he shuffled from the room. So very lucky. How many men find such a love as I have had?

The little dog ran ahead of him down the hall as he returned to his room. He settled himself in his chair. The dog hopped up onto his lap. There was a timid knock at the door. He held Tequila close. "Come in."

The beautiful blonde entered and he smiled, waved her in. "I am so glad you came to see me, señorita. The time passes slowly for an old, sick man." Yes, he would give the perfume to this girl. Velvet Eyes would like that.

Her dark eyes met his levelly. Spirit, he thought, Spunk. *Si*, she was much like Velvet Eyes. She would be the perfect wife for the next Don.

"You are going to stay on the Triple D?" he asked.

"I don't know what I'm going to do." She shook back her honey-colored hair. "Although I certainly appreciate your kind hospitality. I came to ask about the black machine I discovered today in one of the rooms. What is it?"

Don Diego threw back his head and laughed. "It's one of those new sewing machines. I had it brought in past the blockade last Christmas as a gift for Velvet Eyes."

He could see the excitement in her eyes, and he thought again how lovely, how spirited she was. Which man would be lucky enough to capture her heart? They both wanted her. He'd watched quietly, waiting for her to make her choice.

"A sewing machine!" Cimarron said, "I've heard about the newfangled inventions, but I've never seen one. How does it work?"

"I'm not surprised you haven't seen one," he said. "There's probably only a few in the whole state of Texas, although they do say it will revolutionize dressmaking. You'll have to figure it out for yourself, young lady." He shrugged. "You run the thread through it somehow, then turn that little wheel on the side with your hand over and over to make the needle go up and down through the fabric."

She touched her chest. "Me? Oh, señor, I wouldn't dare touch something so rare, so valuable—"

"Nonsense!" he snorted, lighting a cigar. "It's just sitting there gathering dust. Velvet Eyes wouldn't mind, and I think you'll find many fabrics in the sewing room, too. Help yourself."

She was more than pleased, he could tell by the way her face lit up. He had a good memory for faces. Now, as he smoked, he studied hers. Somewhere from his past, a similar face nudged at his memory.

"Please, señorita, who was your mother?"

The girl was instantly tense, bit her lip as if afraid. "Why would you ask?"

He knocked the ashes off his cigar. "Something about you reminds me of some other girl I have known in the past...." He looked at her, trying to remember a Cheyenne girl who might have crossed his path somewhere long ago. "Your mother was Cheyenne?"

"No, my father." She hesitated. "Mother was German."

An image stirred, faintly. A German girl with light hair. "She was blond, too?"

"No, Texanna's hair was red-gold, like burnished coins, as I remember."

And now the face came back with clarity, in all its serene strength, its brilliant eyes the color of Texas bluebonnets.

"Of course," he muttered with a nod. "Of course, Texanna! I thought there was something familiar about you, young lady."

And now she leaned forward eagerly. "You knew her? You knew Texanna?"

He felt very, very old. When he had known Texanna, he had been recently married himself, the father of a new baby. And now, here sat Texanna's daughter before him. "*Sí*, I knew her."

"And?" She was pathetically eager to hear of her mother, and he wondered if perhaps she had never known her.

"I was with the Rangers who captured her away from the Cheyenne," he remembered. "The squaws were picking wild sand plums along the banks of the Red River. We probably wouldn't have even seen them if it hadn't been for the sunlight glinting off her hair."

"Her hair!" the girl said, her eyes bright. "Yes, when I was very small, Mama told me that was why my father kidnapped her in the first place. He was riding with a warparty through north Texas to attack the Comanche and paused at sunrise on a bluff overlooking the wagon train."

Don Diego nodded understandingly. "And he saw the sun

reflecting off that red-gold hair and fell in love with her. *Si,* I can imagine it. Texanna was one of the most beautiful women I ever saw in my life."

She frowned now. "Why did the Rangers take her?"

He pursed his lips ruefully. "It seemed like the thing to do at the time, poor, misguided fools that we were. We thought we'd found Cynthia Ann Parker. It didn't occur to us Texanna might be happy with her Indian chief. She had a young, fierce half-breed son with her."

"My brother, Falling Star," she put in.

"And she was expecting a baby. . . ." His voice trailed off as the impact hit him. "How old are you, Cimarron?"

"Twenty-two."

He nodded. "You were that baby. By the time we reached the town of Fandango, I knew we had made a mistake, tried to get them to return her to the Indians, but the others considered it unthinkable."

The girl sighed. "Too bad they didn't. I think Texanna was miserable back with the whites. She stayed five long years before War Bonnet managed to track her down and ride in after her."

"And your brother?"

"A saloon girl had been killed, I'm told," Cimarron said slowly, "and the town decided he had done it. They dragged him away to whip and lynch him."

"Remembering Texanna, I'll bet she didn't stand idly by or wring her hands helplessly."

Cimarron laughed. "You're right about that. The story is that she held off the whole town with a shotgun while she cut him loose from the whipping post. And about that time, War Bonnet rode in and carried them both off."

He looked at her quizzically as he smoked. "And you?"

Her lips trembled. "I was only five years old and sick that night. I'd been left with preacher Schmidt's wife while Texanna went off to rescue my brother. The mob was between me and Texanna, so they had to ride out without me."

Texanna must be dead, he thought. She wasn't the type to abandon her child. "And what happened to all of them?"

"I—I really don't know." She swallowed hard. "I suppose none of them are left. Anyway, they didn't come back, and the Schmidts raised me. Now they're dead."

"I knew your mother," he said with conviction. "She would have come after you if she could. And you've heard nothing of your brother?"

Cimarron shook her blond head. "No. Someday, I hope to find him. His name has probably changed by now. Mama told me a warrior's name is often changed when he grows up and does some brave deed."

"Well, the Cheyenne and the Arapaho are tearing up the frontier in Kansas and Colorado right now, just like the Comanche and Kiowa are doing here in Texas. Maybe someday we'll all be at peace and you can find your brother. In the meantime, you are welcome to stay on the Triple D forever."

"And use the sewing machine?"

"And use the sewing machine!" He laughed, feeling younger and more healthy than he had in weeks. The girl was like a tonic to him. He hoped his son had sense enough to recognize what a prize this girl was. He wondered idly if the children would have dark hair like their daddy's or blond hair like hers.

"What are you thinking?" she asked.

He laughed, took a deep puff on his cigar, patted the small dog asleep in his lap. "Nothing. Nothing at all. By the way, Cimarron, I want to give you this." He held out the crystal perfume bottle.

"Oh, I couldn't take that, it was hers." Her eyes widened as he offered it.

"I think she would want you to have it," he said as he pressed it into her hands. Because I'm sure you're going to be a member of this family, he thought. The only question now was which one she would choose—his son or . . . his baby brother?

Chapter Seventeen

Cimarron smiled back at the old man as she accepted the perfume bottle. Sometime soon, she would tell him she was going to marry Luis. But right now, for some curious reason, Luis wanted her to keep it secret.

Don Diego leaned back in his chair, eyes closed, still stroking the small dog that looked as sleepy as he did.

Very softly she tiptoed out, took the perfume bottle to her room, went back down the hall to the sewing room. Yes, it was still there, the small black thing on a tabletop. Maybe the only newfangled sewing machine in the whole of the Texas Hill country.

Cimarron was clever and determined. It took her only a few minutes to figure out how to run the thread through the machine. When she turned the wheel on the side with her hand, the needle went up and down through the cloth.

Double damnation! What would they think of next? Imagine a gadget that could help make clothes when now they were made by hand. This was going to revolutionize households. In her excitement, she turned the little wheel faster and faster, just to see the needle go up and down. Next thing you knew, some clever person would invent a way to wash clothes without a rub board or even figure out how to heat irons without placing them on a woodstove.

Eagerly she dug through the chests and boxes in the room. There were many yards of beautiful material, she thought, and she was clever. She could use an old dress as a pattern, take it apart and draw around it on the fabric so she would have something to cut by. Wouldn't it be nice if someone came up with ready-made patterns so one could pick and choose a dress style? Cimarron shook her head. That was just expecting too much. Wistfully, she looked at all the fabric, wishing she knew what dress styles were like back East. They had been full and spread over hoops when the war started, and she wondered if styles had changed much in the big northern cities?

She found a pair of scissors and some pins about the time she discovered the bright russet silk in a chest. Cimarron thought about it a long moment, remembering the clumsily made dress Rosa had worn. No doubt about it, that girl needed a new dress in the worst way. Cimarron frowned. Why should she bother? Rosa had done nothing to be friendly, nothing to warrant any effort on Cimarron's part. She considered a long moment, running her hand over the soft, fine silk. It would make a beautiful gown for herself and certainly it would be lovely with her honey-colored hair. Besides, she didn't know the sullen housekeeper's measurements. If she made anything for the girl, she'd have to guess the size. She looked over at the other fabrics, gingham and calico. Certainly one of those practical cottons would be good enough for Rosa if she decided to make the girl a dress.

Cimarron handled the russet silk a long moment, thinking. Then with a definite nod of her head, she made a decision, spread the fabric, and began to cut.

For the next two days, Cimarron almost hid out in the sewing room, telling no one what she was doing. She wanted it to be a surprise when she showed the beautiful russet-colored dress. She worked on the ranch books, too, but she did not skip her little classes in the study. Rosa attended, "to help with the children" and there was indecision in her eyes, some kind of inner turmoil.

Luis liked to sleep late in the morning and then go for a leisurely ride in the afternoons or into town to gamble or visit with other rich friends, Cimarron noted with a frown.

Well, he would change, lose that wild streak when they married. She noticed Trace was up before dawn taking care of the million and one jobs around the ranch and sometimes staying out past supper to see about some small detail. Cimarron began to wonder if Luis could run the ranch without the foreman, since she had already decided it was going to be impossible for her to have Trace around after they married.

The old Don seemed to be feeling better, and Cimarron wondered just how long that would last. Probably not until the war ended, but no one knew for certain just how much longer the South could fight. As for the rest of the world, Victoria still held the throne of England, although her beloved husband, Albert, had died in '61. The French had been in Mexico since 1863. Now Maximilian had been crowned emperor there. She wondered how long the patient Mexicans would put up with French conquerors.

But now a new problem occupied her mind. She discovered a problem in the ranch's books. She tried to catch Trace and tell him about it, but he only scowled. "Listen, I got a mare that's sick down at the barn; I haven't time."

"But the books don't balance—" she protested.

"You must not add any better than the señora did." Trace frowned. "That's just what she said a couple of days before she ran away."

His voice trailed off and they looked at each other, both thinking of Velvet Eyes. "Darlin', you probably just didn't add or subtract right. We'll discuss it when I have more time." He made a dismissing motion and took long easy strides out to the barn.

She started to mention it to Luis, but he was intent on taking her on a picnic down by the creek. As they took the basket out of the wagon, spread the luncheon under a tree, he said, "Maybe no sniper will take a shot at us this time." He patted the rifle in the back of the buggy. "Anyway, sweet one, this time I brought my carbine to defend us."

Cimarron frowned as she spread the Indigo blue skirt of her dress around her on the blanket. She started to tell Luis what Holt had said to her, that he had been the gunman hired to come in and drygulch the heir, decided against it. To tell would indict Trace.

"No," she said, "I don't suppose we have to worry about being shot at, Luis, but there is something I'd like to discuss with you."

He handed her a piece of fried chicken, a delicious hunk of homemade bread and rich butter. "You packed a nice lunch, Cimarron. I love layer cake and homemade pickles."

Cimarron took a bite. "Well, I had to catch Rosa out of the kitchen to do it," she laughed, biting into the crusty bread. "I think she would have been furious if she'd known I was going on a picnic with a Durango, or at the very least, that I dared cook in her kitchen without permission."

Luis scowled as he ate and drank the sweet, delicate wine. "Rosa is a problem. I think after we're married, I'll have to get rid of her, my sweet, find you a new housekeeper."

"I'm still hoping I can make her like me," Cimarron said as she ate. "It seems so cold just to replace her. Besides, you need old Sanchez."

"That's true, but I can't let her continue to mistreat you, my dear. Why, she acts as if she thinks she's the señora herself, although I don't know where she gets off putting on such airs. Something's made her very arrogant."

Cimarron had a sudden vision of the girl coming out of Trace's room. No wonder the girl felt she had a secure position. Cimarron thought as she ate the rich layer cake and reached for a white linen napkin. But she wouldn't bother Luis with that shocking bit of scandal. She had something more important on her mind. Now she sat watching Luis finish his lunch, then reach for the paints and easel he had brought along.

"I haven't painted in a long time," he beamed, "but your beauty seems to inspire me."

Troubled, she got up and went over to lean against a cottonwood tree while he set up his canvas. "Luis," she began. "I've found something wrong with the ranch books."

He looked at her over the top of the canvas. "What?"

"You know, you asked me to pick up where Velvet Eyes

left off—"

"Well, I didn't mean for you to take me seriously, my dear," he laughed as he got out his brushes and began to paint. "Actually, I figured, like most women, you really didn't know much about that sort of thing—"

"Don't insult me, Luis," she almost screamed at him. "I hate it when men treat me like a stupid female!"

He paused, looked at her. "My apologies, Cimarron," he said as he studied her a long moment. He went back to his palette. "Now if I can just catch the way your eyes flash when you're angry. . . ."

"I told you I found problems with the books," she said again as he painted. "You're just like Trace, you can't be bothered—"

"Of course, I can, my dear," he said smoothly, but she had a feeling he was only half listening to her as he painted. "You found some kind of error. Well, it's probably your addition, that's all."

She would shock him into listening to her. "Luis," she said, "what I'm trying to tell you is that someone is stealing from the ranch."

"What? What did you say?" She had his full attention now. His startled eyes looked into hers, his brush poised in midair. "Why, surely, Cimarron, you've just made some kind of mistake. Those are very serious charges you're making."

"I've gone back over them several times," she insisted. "The money and the cattle and horses the Triple D has sold over the past year don't always add up."

He tapped the handle of the paintbrush against his white, even teeth. "Oh, Cimarron, don't be so dramatic!" He hummed under his breath as he went back to his painting. "After all, a woman can't really be expected to do numbers correctly. I didn't expect you to really do the bookwork, I was just giving you something to do since you seemed so insistent on 'earning your own way.'"

"Luis, stop making fun of me!" She almost shouted this time. "I know how to do bookwork, I tell you, and the money and the livestock sales don't match up! Trace told me that just before the señora left, she mentioned something similar."

Luis looked at her strangely. "I hope you're not hinting that the señora ran off with some of the Triple D's money. The reproving expression made her feel guilty.

"I—I don't know who did it or is maybe still doing it." She looked away, unable to meet his eyes. "It does make sense, I suppose, that Velvet Eyes might juggle the books if she had decided in advance to take money and leave."

She paused. She didn't like her own conclusion. Somehow, everything she had heard about Velvet Eyes denied that she'd steal. But if she'd cheat on her husband. . . .

Luis shook his head. "Not the señora," he said. "No, I can't believe you would accuse her of such a thing." He looked annoyed and troubled as he resumed his painting.

"What about Trace, then?" she challenged. "Doesn't he handle most of the sales? Maybe he—"

"What a terrible thing to say! Trace and I don't like each other, but I can't believe he'd do that. Before this goes any further, maybe I need to examine the books myself," Luis said coldly. "My guess is you've made a simple mistake in addition or subtraction—"

"I don't think I have—"

"I'll check it myself," he said with finality, "and tell you later what I found. And Cimarron, have you mentioned this to anyone else?"

"No."

"Good. Then I suggest you don't." He looked at her for a long moment, went on with his painting. "If there's nothing wrong, it would be terrible to accuse him unjustly. On the other hand, if Trace has been selling livestock and pocketing the money, maybe I can lay a trap to catch him—"

"Somehow, I don't think Trace would—"

"You just now accused him, my dear," he reminded her, "and now you're having second thoughts. Make up your mind. But I'll look at the accounts and we'll discuss it later."

That was a real relief to her. She sighed and leaned back against the tree, letting her low-cut dress slip off one tawny shoulder. The breeze picked up a little, swirling her hair out around her face. Luis would take care of everything. She began to hope her figures were wrong. Maybe she should talk it over with the old Don. No, Luis had told her he would look into it.

"Beautiful!" Luis peered at her over his canvas. "You look beautiful, Cimarron, standing there looking out across the hill country, your hair blowing around your face. I think I'm going to be able to catch the very essence of your personality. I'll call it 'Cimarron, Wild and Free.'"

She laughed, reached to brush the blond tendrils from her forehead. "What are you going to do with this masterpiece?"

He put his brush down, came over, leaned his hands on the tree trunk, one on each side of her. "Don't you know, my darling?" he whispered. "It's going to hang over the great stone fireplace of the study for many, many generations to come."

"Oh, Luis, really," she scoffed, uneasy that his face was so close to hers. He was going to kiss her any moment, she knew that. She should be welcoming his kiss, she thought; after all, she had promised to marry him.

"Cimarron, my sweet," he murmured, "our grandchildren will stand in the study, look up at this portrait and say: 'Cimarron Wild and Free,' well, that certainly describes the old girl all right. She had spunk and grit and was not afraid to live life to the fullest."

"Luis—" She opened her lips to say something to discourage his kiss, but he leaned forward, kissed her, caught her lips half opened. His hands came off the tree trunk, embraced her. "Please, Cimarron," he gasped, as he kissed her again. "Oh, please let me—"

His kiss cut off his own words as he pulled her against him, his hands tangling in her long hair. They both still leaned against the tree and her legs began to buckle under his weight. They started sliding to the grass.

She should let him make love to her, she thought as she felt his hands warm on her shoulders. After all, she was going to marry him, and he was so handsome and so rich. Love with him should certainly be more exciting than the fevered mating of a sardonic cowboy used to saloon whores.

Luis's kisses became more feverish as his hands tried to work her dress down her shoulders. She wanted to be enthused, eager for his kisses, but even as she tried to pretend ardor, a face suddenly came to her mind, a dark, moody half-breed face . . . double damnation!

She pulled away suddenly, and Luis was immediately contrite. "Oh, my love, I've offended you! I'm so sorry to treat a lady like some common whore—"

"It's not that." She pulled her blouse back up, stood up, and leaned against the cottonwood. "I—I just think we should wait until we are married, that's all." She gulped, wondering if an experienced man would be able to tell on their wedding night that he was not her first. Perhaps she could fool him somehow. But could she? The thought unnerved her. This was a chance every unmarried woman in the hill country wanted, she reminded herself. She ought to be glad he wanted to marry her. But deep in her heart, she knew she had made a mistake.

"I-I think we should go back now." She took a deep breath, pulled her hair up with a ribbon, and tied it.

He shrugged, began to put his paints away. "Whatever you say, sweet one. I think I've enough done so I can work in my room on the portrait. And if not, I'll get you to pose for me again."

"Certainly." She walked toward the wagon, remembering his kisses, sadly wondering why they did not thrill her.

Late that night, she lay awake sleepless, considering her dilemma. She was sure many marriages lacked the heart-pounding excitement of the coupling she had experienced with Trace Durango; still, these marriages survived. Maybe she was expecting too much. The thought ran through her mind briefly that she might be in love with the half-breed foreman, and she laughed bitterly. He had raped, insulted and ignored her in the weeks she'd been at the Triple D. She'd have to be loco to love him.

And yet . . . she closed her eyes, tasting his hot mouth

dominating hers, his sure, skilled hands stroking her into submission as he would a nervous mustang. She jumped as she heard a scratching at the door, got up and opened it to Tequila. The brown pet hopped up on her bed and crawled under the covers until nothing showed but his shoe-button nose. "You little devil," she scolded, "someday, you're gonna get yourself in big trouble crawling under the wrong blanket or eating out of the wrong plate."

Tequila whimpered, hopped from the bed, scampered up into the chair by the French door, looked out.

Cimarron felt a shiver of apprehension run up her back. "What is it, boy?"

Curiously, she went to the French door, looked out. The bright Comanche moon lit the shadowy hillsides. And along the hilltop, the Cheyenne spirit horse ran again.

"Oh, no," she murmured. "It's a trick of my eyes, my imagination." But even as she stared, the wild steed galloped soundlessly along the distant crest, shaking its head, its long mane and tail streaming out behind it. Or was it only fog or wisps of clouds? The specter was as pale as moonlight against the dark velvet of the sky as it moved. *Clair de lune*. An image flashed across her mind of Velvet Eyes in her favorite dress gliding through the darkness.

Cimarron didn't believe in magic, in legends. There had to be a reasonable explanation for this, she told herself. But the small dog trembled and whined and she reached down to pat its head.

Even she could see from this distance that the running specter was in some kind of turmoil, of anguish. It shook its head wildly as it approached that point where the Milky Way touched the earth. Cimarron could feel its hopeless longing from here. It reared up on its hind legs, pawing at the sky. Bits of stars twinkled in its mane and fell away as it reared and plunged. Or were those comets? Meteorites? Falling stars? Again and again the ghost horse reared, attempting to run up the Hanging Road to the Sky.

"Go on!" Cimarron urged without thinking, "go on!" The little dog whimpered again as it watched. The phantom tried one more time, failed. Then, with a discouraged shake of its elegant head, it galloped away into the Texas hills, and there was only wispy gray fog and stars sparkling across the lavender shadows.

Something was holding it here. She thought. But what? Now she remembered Trace's comments about a warning, and she shivered again. The last time the spirit horse had galloped, she had ended up almost raped by Holt and Trace had been badly wounded.

Well, it was all nonsense, she thought stubbornly. She looked out the window again, saw nothing but an empty hilltop shining against the moonlight. The specter was only her imagination, after all.

But Tequila whimpered suddenly, bounced off the chair to the floor, trotted out the open French door. "Tequila, come back here!" she ordered in a hoarse whisper.

The dog looked over its shoulder at her and gamboled on down the staircase to the courtyard. Luis was right. Tequila was a spoiled, ornery pet. But Cimarron loved the little rascal. Somewhere nearby a prairie wolf howled, and she shuddered, thinking the tiny dog would only make one good mouthful. She heard his bark in the darkness below her. Darn that little rascal anyway! It would serve him right if a wolf did get him. Then she thought about how the sick old man would take the news, and that Trace would hold her responsible because she had let the dog out.

"Tequila . . ."

He barked again, a little farther out this time. Double damnation! In his zeal to reach that ghost horse, the little dog would end up too far away from the house. She imagined a big, lean wolf lurking out in the shadows.

"Tequila, come back here!" Clad only in her flimsy nightgown, she ran barefooted out onto the upstairs porch and down the stairs to the courtyard. She stopped by the bubbling fountain and strained her ears to listen.

"Tequila?" she whispered, walking to the big oleanders at the end of the adobe wall. "Tequila?"

"He's with me."

She started, gasped at the unexpected sound of another voice from the shadows. She didn't have to ask who it was.

She recognized the deep Spanish-Texas drawl.

She was suddenly very aware of just how flimsy, how sheer the nightgown was. She hugged her arms across her breasts as she tiptoed across the soft grass. "What are you doing out here?"

He leaned against the corner of the house, the dog in his arms. "Somehow, darlin', I think we've played this scene before." He leaned over and put the dog down, and it frolicked up to Cimarron, licked her bare toes.

She thought of the ghostly image. "You saw it, too?" she asked.

His face was shadowed. "Yes, it's running again tonight. I wish I knew what it meant."

She moved toward him. *Amethyst fog. Blue wispy clouds.* Why did she keep thinking of the señora? The señora was in New York. She had run away with a Yankee captain. Cimarron had listened too long to a grieving, sick old man. "We must be loco," she said. "Maybe we both imagine it. Nobody else seems to see it."

"Tequila does." He nodded toward the dog gamboling about her bare ankles.

"But why do none of the other people see it?"

"Because none of them are Cheyenne, darlin'. I told you it was a Cheyenne spirit horse." He stepped out of the shadows, and again he wore only trousers, and his black hair was tousled from sleep.

She felt the rhythm of her heart pick up. "I—I think I'd better go in."

"Come here to me."

Her body seemed to have a mind of its own. Even as she started to say no, her body moved through the darkness, right up to him.

His hands came up slowly, cupped her bare shoulders. "You're trembling. Are you cold?"

She would be a fool to admit it was because of his nearness, his bare-chested masculinity. "Yes, a little," she lied.

Silently, he turned her around, pulled her back up against him while his arms locked around her waist. His face was against her hair. She could feel the soft warmth of his breath on her neck even as she felt the heat of his big body against her back.

"How's your leg?" she asked.

"Fine."

"I—I ought to go in," she said, but she didn't move. It was funny how her back fitted against the contours of his big body. She stood there a moment, savoring guiltily the warmth of his strong arms around her small waist through the sheer nightdress.

He pulled her even tighter against him and the small dog sighed and lay down at their feet. "I come out here a lot," Trace admitted grudgingly, as if afraid she might laugh. "I like to watch Nightwind with his herd."

She looked off toward the south. Several hundred horses grazed peacefully, and on a ridge, outlined against the moon, the ebony stallion stood his guard.

"They're beautiful," she admitted, relaxing against him, knowing she should go back inside. "So wild and free." *Cimarron wild and free.* She remembered the painting.

As they watched, the great stallion galloped down off his ridge and nickered. A dainty palomino filly raised her fine head inquiringly, whinnied back, galloped out to meet the giant stallion.

"By the way," Trace said as they watched, "the old man's told me to give you that palomino filly, since she's the color of your hair. We call her Peso."

She turned her head, overwhelmed by the generosity of the gift. "I couldn't! She's worth a lot of money." *Peso,* she thought. My very own fine horse, just the color of the Mexican coin.

"The Triple D has thousands of horses," he said against her ear as they watched the two gallop toward each other. "The Don's orders were specific."

Nightwind met the palomino halfway, nickering, nipping at her.

"He'll hurt her!" Cimarron cried in alarm.

Trace's lips were warm against her ear. "No, darlin', he won't hurt her. He's going to make love to her."

She stared at the cavorting horse, aware now that one of Trace's hands moved down from her waist to caress the vee of her legs. The other came up to stroke her breasts.

Off in the distance, the black stallion nipped playfully at the filly's neck and the palomino turned coquettishly away from him.

"She's afraid," she whispered. "She'll run away."

Very slowly, Trace's arms opened, setting her free. "If she's afraid, then she'll leave."

Cimarron stood trembling, staring at the horses. The great stallion reared up on the filly now, taking her with savage fury. "He'll hurt her," she said. "He'll hurt her."

His voice was a whisper. "But she wants it. She's not running away."

What kind of tramp am I? she thought wildly as she stared at the plunging, snorting horses. There's no reason in the world I can't go back to the house. She took a hesitant step forward, stumbled, went to her knees.

"Cimarron? Are you hurt?" She heard him take a step.

"No, I—" She turned her body halfway back toward him, and when he stepped up to her, without thinking, she put her arms out and wrapped them around his legs. She had her face against his manhood, could feel the hard, pulsating heat of it against her face through the cloth. "Oh, Trace . . ."

His hands came down, tangled in her hair, turned her face up to his. "You'll have to ask for it, Cimarron, you know that." His voice was trembling with pent-up emotion. "You'll never again accuse me of rape."

Her whole being seemed to throb with wanting . . . wanting. . . . She didn't care about anything anymore but this overwhelming passion that was cresting, sweeping over her, pulling her under. It was ardor, hot desire for his body that she could not control.

"Aren't you going to leave me a shred of pride?" she sobbed. "I want you, Trace, you know that! Please, Trace!"

He reached down, swung her up in his arms, looked into her face. "Damn you, Cimarron!" he swore, "I've thought of nothing else but taking you again!"

His mouth covered hers, dominating, caressing while she sobbed in his arms. Off in the distance, she could hear the whimpering, the grunting as the big stallion finished subduing and mating his filly.

And now Trace kissed the tears off her face. "Don't cry, darlin'," he whispered. "It's all right. Don't cry!"

She felt the straps of her gown slide off her shoulders as she hung in his arms, and he hefted her so that his mouth nuzzled her nipple. Cimarron groaned aloud and he whispered, "Easy, little filly, easy! If you only knew how many sleepless nights I've laid awake remembering the taste of these!"

Her taut breast pushed up, urging him to taste still more before he turned her weight, bit her other nipple until she tingled, trembled all over.

"Trace, take me," she begged. "Take me now!"

With long strides, he carried her and laid her down on the fragrant wild flowers in the shadows of the tall bushes. Then he reached, caught the front of her sheer gown, ripped it away. "I want to see you," he ordered tersely, "I want to see if you're as beautiful, as desirable as I remember!"

She watched him unbutton his pants, step out of them. He stood there naked in the moonlight a long moment, the light reflecting off his lithe muscles, the sheen of his skin. He was as powerful, as masculine as the great stallion he rode. There was only a small scar from the leg wound. She thought of Greek gods. Many times in mythology some legendary God had mated with a mortal woman.

For a moment he looked down at her and she wondered why he hesitated. Without even realizing it, she held out her arms to him. "Come to me Trace, come to me, please. . . ."

He knelt and kissed the soft planes of her belly. "I want it to last for hours," he gasped. "I've waited so long for you to want me." She felt his hot, moist lips caress her skin, move gently down to kiss her trembling thighs. "Every inch," he promised, "I'm going to kiss every inch of that tawny skin."

Before she realized what he was doing, he turned her over, and his teeth were sharp, nipping at her small hips. She shivered with anticipation just as she had seen the palomino filly do, and his hands were beneath her, cupping her breasts, stroking, teasing.

Sooner or later, she thought, he would take her from behind, covering her, as Nightwind took his mares. But now, he rolled her over, loving and caressing her breasts until they were swollen and tender.

"Open your mouth, darlin'." She obeyed. His tongue plunged in deep. Automatically she sucked, wanting to take it deep inside her just as she longed to take his manhood.

Then he opened his lips, urging her to put her tongue inside, explore the depths of his mouth, then to taste his nipples in a way that drove him into a groaning, shuddering frenzy. "I—I was going to make it last all night, Wild One," he gasped, "but I can't stand anymore. I'm hurtin' now. Have to have relief!"

She was throbbing with eagerness too, surprised that a woman could ache from desire for a man.

She went down on her back, spread her thighs. She could feel the moisture between them even as his fingers stroked there. "Oh, Trace, for God's sake, please!"

"I—I might hurt you!"

"Hurt me!" She writhed under him. "Can't you see that's what I want! I want to be taken hard and ridden just like your stallion took that mare."

His fingers caressed. "You're small. I'm afraid—"

"You didn't worry about hurting me before!" She was angry with her need now, trying to pull him atop her.

"I thought you were a whore before," he said. His voice came in such a soft whisper that she wasn't sure she heard, but she thought he said, "And I didn't love you then."

She lay with her golden hair spread out like a fan in the moonlight under her naked body. Her pulse pounded in her ears with her need. She spread her thighs wide, looked up at him. "You said I'd have to beg and I'm begging. You've left me no pride, none at all. Trace, please...."

He hesitated only a split-second, his maleness hot and throbbing against the entry to her depths. Then he drove in so hard and deep that she gasped, almost cried out at the sensation.

"Relax, darlin'," he commanded against her ear. "Relax so you can take all of me. If you tense up, I'll hurt you."

She was being impaled against the ground by a sword, she thought, but oh, it was a wonderful, exhilarating impalement, even if it tore her apart. She took a deep breath, wrapped her long, slim legs around him, and felt him plunge into her to the hilt.

She moaned with the sensation, felt his hands go beneath her to cup her small hips, tilt her up so he could drive still deeper. The weight of his body rubbed against her swollen nipples, and she relished the feel of him grinding down deep inside her. Without thinking, she dug her nails into his lithe back muscles, urging him still deeper. And now again, she stood on the edge of a deep mental precipice, with the ground crumbling out from under her feet. Cimarron felt a turmoil of both fear and building excitement. Her own pulse pounded a deepening crescendo. She felt the sheen of perspiration as he rode her body.

The precipice of her mind seemed to be crumbling beneath her feet. If she relaxed and let it happen, she would fall unimpeded over the edge. It seemed a long, long way down, to some mysterious place that she had never been before. Did she trust him enough to let it happen?

"Trace?"

He seemed to catch the uncertainty, the fear in her voice as he covered her face with kisses. "Not yet, Wild One, wait for me, wait for me. . . ."

But she couldn't wait. Whatever was happening to her could no more be stopped than a stampede could be halted from rumbling across the prairie, than the fast current from Jacob's Well could be held back from tumbling into miles of black underwater caverns. Cimarron felt her nails dig into his back so hard she knew he must be bleeding, but she couldn't control or stop herself from urging his body still deeper as he coupled with hers.

She heard him gasp, stiffen. Then she could actually feel the maleness of him straining, spurting his lifeseed deep within her waiting body. At that moment she remembered no more, because the earth seemed to give way beneath her, and she fell from a dizzying height. For what seemed like forever, she fell head over heels, her arms and legs wrapped around the cowboy as he instinctively put his seed deep into her velvet place.

They say if you hit the ground before you wake up, you die, she thought as she seemed to fall into space, but she didn't care anymore. If it cost her life, this one time was worth it. Then she didn't remember anything, except the taste of his mouth, the scent of him, the heat of his damp skin on hers.

Very slowly, she came to, blinked. The stars above her stopped whirling, and she realized she lay wrapped about Trace. He couldn't have moved away if he had wanted to, so instinctively did her body want what his had to give. His face came up, his long eyelashes brushed across her face. "Are you all right, darlin'? I went crazy, I guess. Never wanted it so bad before. . . ."

Her body shuddered and gripped his convulsively. "I guess that went for both of us." She shook her head, as if to clear it. Was she some common slut, obligated by her own promise to marry one man, coupling with another out under the trees at night?

His hand trembled as he brushed small wisps of blond curls away from her face. "Damn!" he muttered. "I never met a woman who did it so well—"

"All I know is what you taught me." She smiled up at him, but inside, turmoil raged. She waited, waited for him to say he loved her.

But now that his hunger was sated, his face took on that guarded, moody expression she knew so well. "Have you let Luis make love to you?" His face was again dark, distrustful.

She didn't know whether to react with hurt or anger. Annoyed, she pushed him away, scooted out from under him. "Sure," she snapped, grabbing for the torn nightgown, "dozens of times."

He reached out to touch her face very hesitantly. "I'm sorry, Wild One, I shouldn't have asked. I guess I know better than that. It's just that I don't trust women. I expect the worst from them."

"Then you'll always find it." She stood up, shook her tangled hair back with angry gestures. Cimarron took a deep breath. He had marked her with the scent of his seed just as any great, rutting stag marks his female, yet he feared to trust her.

Suddenly she wanted to hurt him as he had hurt her with his question. She reacted with anger, grabbing the torn nightgown, walking away. "I just wanted you to see what you'd be missing," she flung back at him. "I'm still planning to marry Luis Durango!"

Chapter Eighteen

She was so hurt she reacted recklessly, grabbing up her nightgown, stalking across the courtyard. The tiny dog trotted at her heels. She wrapped her torn gown around her as she entered the house, thankful it was so late that no one was up.

She went into her room, closed the door, and stood leaning against it. Cimarron heard Trace come down the hall, stop at her door. She held her breath, waited for him to knock. If he did, would she be able to keep herself from throwing it open, falling into his arms? Would she surrender her pride, tell him she would take him on any terms he wanted, even if he didn't love her?

She didn't have to make that decision. He paused a long moment while she listened, then limped on down the hall to his own room.

Disappointed, she went over and lay down on her bed. After staring at the ceiling a few minutes, she decided she wouldn't sleep again this night. Every time she closed her eyes, she saw his face coming down to kiss her lips, felt his arms pulling her to him.

Double damnation! She got up uncertainly, wondered what time it was. It must be nearly dawn, she could see the faint glow on the drapes. She might as well get dressed. She put on the low-cut peasant blouse and bright skirt from the party.

Tequila hopped up on the chair, put his nose against the

glass of the French door, growled low in his throat.

"Now, don't start that again," she scolded as she put on her shoes and reached for a bright hair ribbon to tie back her long locks. "You can't possibly see any more Cheyenne spirit horses tonight, and I'll be damned if I allow you to take me on another wild goose chase outside that ends up under the oleander bushes with You Know Who."

She frowned as she tied the hair ribbon, remembering ... remembering.... What kind of woman was she anyway? She had told Luis she would marry him and yet, tonight, she had lain naked in wild abandon out on the grass with the moody foreman of the Triple D who offered her sex and passion. But he did not promise love, commitment.

Tequila increased his growling, jumping against the glass.

"Get down from there!" she scolded, coming over to pick him up. "It's just the sun coming up in the distance, stupid! You don't growl at the sun...." Her voice trailed off uncertainly as she stared out the drapes at the glow in the distant sky, and she questioned her own sanity for a split-second. Didn't the sun still rise in the east? But the glow was from the north....

Oh. God! The startling realization struck her full force. She dropped the dog, which scurried to the door, scratching and barking frantically.

Cimarron jerked the door open and ran into the hallway, and the chihuahua accompanied her, ran up and down the hall barking. "The old barn!" she screamed. "Everyone wake up! The old barn's on fire!"

Sanchez came to the bottom of the stairs in his long underwear. "What is it, señorita? Has something happened to the Don?"

"The barn, Sanchez!" she shrieked, gesturing wildly. "The old barn's on fire!"

He looked puzzled, confused. "Barn?" He mumbled sleepily. "My Rosa's missing. She's not in bed! Have you seen her?"

"She's bound to be in the house somewhere." Cimarron shook her head. "Go wake everybody up!"

Sanchez disappeared, and in minutes she heard the

clanging of the old bell by the back door as he sounded the alarm to awaken all the cowboys on the ranch.

Cimarron ran back to her room for her shoes. The old barn north of the ranchero, she thought, the extra storage barn where Trace had first made love to her. Stop it, Cimarron, you sentimental idiot, she scolded herself as she put on her shoes with quick, angry gestures. He didn't make love to you, he raped you there. And what had that been tonight? Was it love or was it only animal passion?

Her thoughts went to Rosa. Could the girl have been waiting for Trace in his room when he left Cimarron? She ran again into the hallway. Tequila galloped madly up and down the hall, barking loudly. Outside she heard shouts and bunkhouse dogs barking as the ranch came awake.

Luis stuck his head out of his door. "What's going on?"

But Trace came out of his room, gestured. "Old barn's on fire, Luis, get dressed! Let's ride!"

Even the old Don came out of his room, his eyes full of excitement. "What's happening?"

Trace brushed his hair back. "Fire at the old barn! The pasture's dry right now; if the fire spreads to the grass, we might lose the house!"

Luis stumbled out of his room. "Okay," he said, and Cimarron was impressed with his cool calmness. "Let's go see what's happening."

They all went down the stairs and out into the courtyard where the cowboys gathered, half-dressed, rubbing sleepy eyes. The breeze had turned out of the north and was picking up a little, Cimarron realized with alarm. If the fire spread to the dry grass, the wind might blow it this direction.

The little dog scampered around everyone's feet, barking frantically and adding to the confusion. Little Turqouise reached down and caught him up. "All you do is make noise, puppy," she scolded.

Sanchez joined the crowd. "Anybody seen my Rosa?"

Cimarron saw Trace and Luis exchange hostile glances, then Luis said, "She's bound to be in the house somewhere, Sanchez; maybe she got up in the night to get a drink."

"That's probably right," Trace said soothingly. He seemed

to be counting heads among the growing crowd of cowboys. "Get mounted, boys, let's get up there and see what we can do!" He glanced over at Cimarron. "You women get back in the house until we find out what's happening!"

Cimarron gave him a defiant scowl, picturing him lying in bed with Rosa only minutes after making love to her. Yes, he was probably enough of a stud to satisfy two women in one evening. Hadn't he done it before on the night of the party? "Don't tell us what to do!"

Trace looked puzzled. "You heard me," he said, "I—"

He never finished the sentence. A foaming, lathered horse galloped into the middle of the courtyard, the cowboy on his back slumped over the pinto's mane. Two arrows stuck at odd angles from the man's back.

Trace swore as he ran to him and caught the man sliding from the saddle to the ground. ". . . caught the night herd riders by surprise," he gasped, blood running scarlet from his pale lips. "Comanche . . . Comancheros . . ."

He was dead. Cimarron's eyes met Trace's across the limp body, and she saw fury there such as she had never seen before. The half-breed's eyes flashed dark sparks as he laid the man gently on the ground. Cimarron took her shawl and spread it across the cowboy's face.

He turned to Cimarron. "Now will you get back in the house or do I have to pick you up and put you there?"

"See here," Luis bristled, "you're not talking to one of your trampy whores—"

"We got no time for this!" Trace snapped with an angry gesture. "Mount up, *hombres*," he ordered, "and make sure you've got plenty of ammunition!"

One of the cowboys brought Nightwind around to the courtyard. The big horse seemed to sense the excitement and danger. He snorted and flung his head, and his nostrils flared scarlet as he danced and reared.

Trace swung up on the stallion and Cimarron looked up at the grim cowboy dressed in black, at the fury in his eyes, the hard set of his jaw. She knew what Death, what Grim Revenge looked like at that moment. "Let's ride!" Trace shouted.

Maverick started to mount. Cimarron called out just in time to stop him from mounting on the right side.

Luis snorted. "Damned Injun kid! You keep mounting our horses on the wrong side, Maverick, you're gonna get thrown from here to Kingdom Come!"

Maverick laughed sheepishly. "You're the ones mounting from the wrong side!" he shouted as he went around the horse and swung up on the left side. "Can I help it I can't break the habit?"

She had to admire Luis's cool bearing, his calmness. "You heard, Trace." He gestured to the cowboys. "Let's go kill Maverick's relatives!"

Maverick frowned, shouted to Trace. "I don't like this, boss, there's something wrong!"

Trace held the stamping, pawing stallion in check. "What? What, Maverick?"

Maverick shook his head. "This ain't the way Comanche work, no reason for them to burn that old barn—"

Luis frowned. "Are we gonna ride or sit and talk all day? Let's go!" He sawed at the chestnut's mouth savagely with the spade bit, racked its flanks with his spurs.

The old Don gestured for a horse, but Trace shook his head. "Somebody needs to stay with the women!"

"*Si*, you're right," the old man stepped back reluctantly and the crowd of cowboys rode out of the courtyard, leaving the frightened women standing there. Little Tequila struggled to get out of Turquoise's arms as he barked and growled.

Rosa came out to join them just then. Don Diego put his arm around the child's shoulders and frowned at her mother. "Where have you been, Rosa? Sanchez was looking for you!"

Cimarron thought, *I can tell you where she's been.* But she didn't say anything. The thought that Trace would leave her arms and go crawl in bed with the Mexican girl was too humiliating, too hurtful.

Rosa looked embarrassed. "I—I had to relieve myself, sir," she said, with just the right touch of humiliation. "One never expects to get caught in a position like that when all hell breaks loose!"

The Don chuckled and gestured to the frightened servant girls in the courtyard. "Everybody back inside! There's guns in the study! Can anyone besides me handle a gun?"

"I can," Cimarron volunteered, as she hurried to catch up with him. "I'm pretty darn good at it, too."

"Somehow, that doesn't surprise me," he said as he herded everyone inside. "Cimarron, it looks like it's up to the two of us if they get past our riders. The rest of you women can load!"

Inside the study, they overturned heavy tables and chairs dragged them in front of the French doors. One of the serving girls started to cry hysterically and another took it up. "The Comanches! We'll all be carried off by the Comanches!"

Cimarron went over and slapped her across the face. "Shut up! Do you hear me! Shut up! We need help! Screaming won't do any good! It'll only let the savages know where the women are if they get past the cowboys!"

The woman hushed immediately. In the sudden silence, the only noise was little Tequila barking frantically and a small baby crying in its mother's arms. Then the old man broke out a pane in the French door to shoot through.

In the moonlight Cimarron watched Rosa loading a rifle. The girl seemed unusually calm. Thank goodness for that, Cimarron thought appreciatively. She hadn't thought Rosa could be so calm, so helpful. Just goes to show, you never know what people are really like until you see them under stress.

In the distance they heard the echo of shots as the cowboys reached the old barn. The scream of a mortally wounded man drifted on the wind, and Cimarron froze, the rifle in her hands. *Was it Trace?* She had a momentary picture of him with a Comanche arrow in his chest, falling from the saddle. And then guilt flooded her because she hadn't even thought the dead man might be Luis.

Quickly, she knelt by the old Don, peering over the top of an overturned table. "Have they ever hit this ranch before?" she said, breaking out another pane of glass in the door to fire through.

"Not for more than twenty years. They killed my father in that raid." His eyes shone with excitement. She thought it a shame such a vibrant man would die of cancer.

"What do you think they want this far east?" she whispered, hefting the rifle.

"What do Comanche always want?" he asked. "Women, guns, and livestock!"

The horses, she thought. The big Triple D herd grazed only a few hundred yards away. She'd seen it when she was out on the courtyard with Trace. *Peso*. She hadn't even thanked the old man yet. The cowboys had caught their mounts, but the other horses still grazed much closer to the house than to the old barn.

Maverick's puzzled words came to her and she wondered suddenly if the whole thing were a trap, if the cowboys had been drawn away on purpose. But how would the Comanche know in advance the layout of the ranch?

If they rang the big bell the ranch used to call everyone in, they could get those riders back here fast, she thought. "Don Diego, I think we'd better—"

The sound of a hundred drumming hooves and shrieks like the tortured of hell broke the stillness. Cimarron never got to finish her words.

"Comanche!" Don Diego swore in Spanish. "Comanche coming in from the other direction!"

She saw them then outlined against the bright orange moon, twenty-five or thirty riders coming in hard to ride in circles around the hacienda. Each horse and rider was poetry in motion, moving at a hard gallop like one living, breathing thing. A hundred years from now, she thought with grudging admiration, Texans would still be complimenting horsemen by saying, "you ride like a Comanche." The bronze, painted bodies rode naked, except for breechcloths. The mustang mounts were mostly pintos, their bodies smeared with bright scarlet, ochres, and white paints for war medicine.

The old Don took a deep breath and aimed down his rifle sight as the horsemen swept by, riding in a circle around the ranchero. "Holy Mother of God," he said reverently, and pulled the trigger.

A bright splotch of crimson exploded across the rider's chest and he grabbed at the wound and fell from the handmade Indian saddle. Immediately, two Comanches rode in close, one on each side, lifted the fallen one, and carried him away at a gallop.

The Don shook his white head. "That's one of the differences between Comanche and your Cheyenne," he said to her. "The Cheyenne see nothing wrong with leaving dead warriors where they fall, but the Comanche will lose more trying to come back in to pick up their dead. We can use that to our advantage!"

Cimarron hadn't known that, but she realized that in the spot they were in, they needed every advantage they could get. "Trace will come back when he hears the shooting," she said as she aimed her rifle and squeezed the trigger. A skinny brave threw up his hands and fell from his running mustang.

The old Don glanced over at her. "You gonna marry him?"

She looked over at him, humiliated. "He—he hasn't said he loves me," she said truthfully, "but Luis has."

The old Don reloaded his Enfield. "I don't know what's eating that boy," he murmured as he pulled the trigger. "Been on the prod ever since the señora left."

A big, hatchet-faced Comanche on a fine gray stallion rode by, shot at them expertly.

"Must be a chief," the Don muttered, "look at that horse!"

She shot another Indian out of his saddle. A servant's baby began screaming at the noise of the guns, and Tequila barked frantically. Cimarron glanced over and saw Turquoise holding on to the little chihuahua that yapped and snarled to get out to the Indians. When she looked up she noticed that Rosa seemed to be watching her with a troubled expression as she loaded guns, handing them over with a calmness that surprised Cimarron.

"Comancheros!" shouted the old Don suddenly. "I see Comancheros riding with those savages!"

Over the shouts and shots and screaming, Cimarron whirled to look at the galloping horses racing back across the courtyard. Half a dozen now carried burning torches.

"Damn them!" the Don swore. "They'll try to fire the house next, drive us out into the open!"

She saw the big herd of Triple D horses being rounded up. The raiders were stealing them. Only one thing more they wanted, she thought, her mouth dry. They would try to take some of the women in this quick raid, then outrun the Triple D cowboys, who even now must realize that they were a couple of miles from the scene of the real action. Setting fire to the old barn had only been a decoy to lure the men away.

"Here they come!" The Don swore in Spanish as a rider galloped across the courtyard, carrying a burning torch. "If we don't get him, he'll toss it through a window, catch some furniture or the rugs on fire!"

Cimarron held her breath and aimed at the rider coming in at a full gallop, his dark body smeared with scarlet and yellow color. The flickering light of the torch he carried and the lathered, painted horse made him look like a demon galloping right out of hell. She squeezed the trigger and he went off the horse backwards.

The old Don gave her an admiring glance. "Good shooting, young lady!"

Two riders came in, tried to pick up the dead one at a full gallop. Cimarron aimed. "I'll take the one on the left," she said to the Don, "you get the one on the right."

"Done!" he exclaimed. Their two rifles cracked in unison and the two savages went spinning off their running horses.

"The roof!" Cimarron shouted. "They'll fire the roof!"

"Red Spanish tile, remember?" he reminded her. "But they'll burn the drapes and the furniture to smoke us out!"

"If we can just hold on a little longer, Trace will be riding back!" she shouted, choking on the acrid smoke of the rifles. She heard the tinkle of glass somewhere in another room, smelled smoke.

Rosa ran over. She didn't look calm anymore. "Señor, those devils have started a fire in the parlor!"

The Don swore mightily.

Rosa glared at Cimarron. "Here's what they're after!" she shrieked, her eyes wide, hysterical. "*Si*, they've heard about this blond one! They come for her! Send her out!"

"Rosa! Get hold of yourself!" The old man reloaded.

But the other women took up Rosa's cry. "*Si,* that's it, they want that gringo! Why should we die to save her!"

"That's loco!" Cimarron said, "How would they know—?"

"Word races through the war parties like wildfire when a beautiful yellow-haired woman shows up! Go out to them! I don't intend to die for you!" Rosa shrieked.

The old Don slapped her. "Nobody's going to die, Rosa, and we're not sending anyone out to those savages! Now get hold of yourself. Take a couple of these other girls and go put out that fire!"

The three crept away to do his bidding while Cimarron looked over at him, stunned. "You think what she says is true? You think they're after me?"

The old Don cocked his rifle, took down another racing brave, and coughed on the swirling smoke. "They're after any woman they can take! I don't deny that after the other night's big party, word might have spread of your beauty."

Cimarron was momentarily stunned. Could she be the cause of all this bloodshed, all this wreckage? She gritted her teeth and resumed shooting.

The Don looked around frantically for more cartridges, then seemed to remember he had sent Rosa off to put out the fire in the dining room. "Turquoise," he yelled above the echoing shots, the screaming baby, and the crying women, "bring me some more cartridges! These women can't do anything but cry!"

Cimarron glanced over and saw the little girl put down the dog, then run across to pick up cartridges. Tequila immediately charged for the nearest French door, barking and growling like a small wolf.

The old man laughed. "Those raiders would run if they knew our bad dog was trying to get out there to bite them!"

Cimarron tried to laugh, too, as she accepted a handful of cartridges from the little girl but her hand trembled as she took them. *Come on Trace,* she thought, *get back here—we need you! I need you!*

She ran her tongue across her dry lips, looking longingly out toward the fountain. Its cool water reflected the moonlight, the flaring torches and the hideously painted faces that regrouped out there. She felt a sharp pain, smelled the sweet scent of blood. She looked at her arm, felt the sticky warmth spreading down her skin before it occurred to her she'd been grazed by a bullet.

"Get ready, here they come again!" Don Diego shouted. "Who's that with them?"

For a long moment she strained to see through swirling puffs of rifle fire. Faintly, she heard the noise of the women in the dining room fighting the flames. She smelled the smoke. Then the wind blew a little of the haze away and she saw where the old Spaniard pointed.

"El Lobo!" the old man whispered in awe. "El Lobo himself! He's a Comanchero legend!"

The leader of this savage pack did look like a wolf, Cimarron thought, looking out at the swarthy man. The magnificent white stallion reared up, but the mixed-blood Comanchero on his back rode easily. Cimarron stared out at him, almost feeling that he saw *her,* because he stared at the house in that split-second that the magnificent white horse reared. El Lobo smiled a ferine, wolfish grin, his prominent fangs gleaming in the moonlight. Then he reined the horse around, riding a circle around the ranch house, the cartridge belts crossed over his massive chest reflecting the light. Cimarron shuddered as she stared back at the grimy, swarthy, bearded face, the tangled hair. *It's me,* she thought. *Somehow, he knows I'm here, he's come for me! Someone at the party told him about me and the fine herd of horses on the Triple D!*

Her heart pounded so loudly she could almost hear it over the shouts, the screaming women, the babies, and the barking dog. Tequila had left the study, she realized. She could hear the dog running through the house, barking frantically. If that little devil found an open French door, a broken window, he'd be right out there in the middle of those Comanches, she thought, and they'd kill him for sure. Oh, Trace, where are you? She pulled the trigger as the yelping braves made another rush at the house.

And then, as she feared, Tequila found his open window. She knew it immediately from his little bark of triumph. Her eyes caught Turquoise's as they both seemed to realize it at the same time. Tequila's bark sounded merrily from outside the house now.

"Oh, señorita!" Turquoise screamed, her small hands going to cover her mouth. "They'll kill him! They'll kill him for sure!"

"He'll have to look out for himself, honey!" she shouted with a sinking heart as she fired, "We can't stop to help him now—"

She glanced around. The child was gone. "Turquoise? Turquoise, where are you?"

She bolted to her feet, made a run for the front door. But she was already too late. Little Turquoise ran across the grass in the moonlight toward the galloping horses, shrieking, "Tequila! Tequila, come back!"

"Turquoise!" Cimarron shouted, but the child paid her no heed, obviously thinking only of the little dog already charging and snapping at the running horses.

Then the child was out there among the galloping ponies, and Cimarron lost sight of her in the swirling dust and smoke. "Turquoise! Come back here!"

Even as she screamed, she knew it was in vain. The child couldn't hear her over the noise and confusion. Even so, the little girl was thinking only of the beloved dog darting in and out among the rearing, snorting horses.

Cimarron hesitated only a moment in the doorway, her rifle still in her hands. Then the dust cleared for a moment and she saw the child standing among the charging, stamping steeds, looking about in terror. And she heard the surprised swearing of the Comancheros as the little dog raced in, attacking horses' legs, making them rear and buck.

For a split-second, Cimarron hesitated. Trace would be here any minute, leading the Triple D cowboys back to protect the ranchero. But a moment was going to be too late for little Turquoise. Cimarron would be going to a certain death if she ran out among those raiders. She heard the child crying, the frantic barking, and then she gave it no more thought. A child was in danger, and that was all that counted with her. Cimarron ran out among them, knowing she made a bright target in the flowered skirt, the white lace blouse.

She fired as she ran across the grass, took a rider from his horse.

From the house she could hear the Don's voice. "Cimarron, for God's sake, Cimarron, come back here!"

Not with a child's life on the line, she vowed silently as she ran, *not while Cimarron still lived, had any hope of saving the little girl.*

A rider thundered down toward her and she fired her rifle from the hip, not taking time to aim. She brought him down almost at her feet, the lathered horse thundering so close it brushed her arm, spinning her as it raced past.

The hatchet-faced Comanche on the magnificent gray stallion rode up and she pulled the trigger. He smiled with triumph as she pulled the trigger again, realizing with sudden horror that her rifle was empty. She grabbed it by the barrel, swung it at him. He reined his horse away, shrieking in triumph.

"Señorita! Help me! Help me!" the little girl cried.

Cimarron whirled around, dust clinging to her perspiring skin in the confusion. She saw her then. The warrior had the child, lifting her up before him on his gray stallion, the tiny dog snapping and worrying his dancing horse's hooves.

"I'm coming, Turquoise!"

She swung her rifle at the man, and he reined his horse away, hanging on to the screaming, crying child.

It was all dust and rearing horses, the smell of blood and flames, Cimarron thought in a daze. Away off in the distance, she thought she saw the Triple D riders coming in. But even her confused mind told her they were too far away. They would never get here in time. A Comanche dismounted, ran toward her with a bloodcurdling cry. *Not yet,* she thought doggedly, gritting her teeth with determination. *You won't take me yet!*

She swung the rifle by its barrel, putting all her lean, tall body behind the swing. The butt caught the brave in the belly and his face looked stricken. He made an agonized sound as he staggered and fell. But she lost her grip and the rifle went with him.

She heard a command barked in Spanish and the riders formed an irregular ring around her.

"Don't kill her!" She heard the command barked again, saw the leader, El Lobo, reining his snowy horse near her. She could smell him now, smell the rank scent of his dirty, hairy body as he rode close, saw the torches reflected in his wolfish eyes. "She's mine!" he shouted in triumph. "The yellow-haired one's what I came for!"

"No! Don't touch me!" Cimarron backed slowly away from him. But there were riders ringing her now, and she heard the shots from the Don's rifle, saw another rider go down.

"Let's get out of here!" The Comanchero shouted in broken Spanish to the hatchet-faced brave. "*Pine da poi*, take that herd out pronto!"

The swarthy leader rode down on her. She turned to run, but she was weary now. Her feet felt as if she wore iron shoes, and she had no weapon. She took about three steps before he caught up to her. She heard his horse, felt him reach for her. Then the sweating renegade swung her up, scratching and fighting.

"A wildcat, hey?" He leered as he dragged her up on the saddle before him, *"Bueno!* Good! I like women with a bit of pepper to them!"

Cimarron fought him as he pulled her against his dirty, smelly shirt, but his hands were like steel bands on her arms, hurting her cruelly as he held her. Somewhere she heard the echo of guns, the screaming of the little girl on the sharp-faced Comanche's gray mount, the barking of the little dog still charging about the horses' hooves.

El Lobo muttered a curse as he looked down at Tequila. "I'd kill you, little devil, if the Comanche wouldn't roast me for it!"

If she could only delay them a few more minutes. She fought him, clawed at his face, managed to get away from him, hit the ground running. But El Lobo rode his horse up behind her, swooped low like a hawk to grab her.

"You bitch!" he snarled, and blood ran from the scratch marks on his ugly face. "You bitch! You'll pay for this when I get you back to camp!"

He hit her then, clipped her along the jaw. The impact made her teeth slam sharply together, and she saw a double hazy image as she collapsed in his arms.

"To the west!" shouted El Lobo, waving his free hand. "Let's move out pronto!"

In a daze, Cimarron hung limply over his arm as he rode away, his hot hand squeezing her soft breast. As if from a great distance, she still seemed to hear the small dog barking, the pretty child on the other horse screaming for her papa. The last image that made an impression on Cimarron as she slipped into unconsciousness was how the galloping horse threw a distorted shadow along the ground as it ran, the giant silhouettes the war party made as they galloped west against the bright Comanche moon. *The spirit horse,* she thought, *I should have heeded the warning of the spirit horse.*

Chapter Nineteen

Cimarron gradually came back to reality. She knew many hours had passed because the sun was fully overhead in the October day. For a long time she was only half-conscious, aware that she rode slumped in a man's arms, his hand familiarly cupping her breast.

Her head ached from the crack on the jaw and the constant drumming of the horse beneath her. But finally, very slowly, she raised her head. A bearded, swarthy face surrounded by tangled hair leered down at her. "So you're awake?" he laughed with a nod. "I was beginning to think my little love tap had killed you!"

His sombrero slipped back and she stared up at him. His right ear looked as if it had been half chewed off in a fight, and where there should have been a left ear, there was only a pink scar.

"The child?" she gasped out, her throat dry and prickly as the Spanish Bayonet plants spiking up along the ridge to the west.

He laughed again and called out in border Spanish, "Pine de poi, she asks about the child!"

Cimarron heard the little girl whimper and craned to see Turquoise, dirty and weary-looking on the gray stallion behind the hatchet-faced Comanche. He snickered and made a vulgar gesture toward the little girl, showing what intentions he had for her.

Cimarron shuddered, only relieved that the child was too

young, too innocent to know what lay in store for captive females. At least they were safe as long as the Triple D cowboys were in hot pursuit. The renegades didn't dare stop to divide up the loot and rape the captives.

She shook her throbbing head to clear it, sat up in his arms. He ran his hands over her breasts boldly. She pushed them away, gave him a defiant look.

He grinned, showing yellow, prominent teeth. "Spirited! *Si!* That's the way I want them. Very spirited, so I can break them the way I like them!"

He put his hand on her thigh, worked it up under her skirt, and she dug her nails into the back of his hand. He cuffed her angrily. "Señorita, you got a lot to learn! You better be nice to El Lobo!"

After a couple of hours they called a quick halt at a stream to water the horses and eat tortillas wrapped around smoked beef jerky. Cimarron grabbed the little girl and they went out in the brush to relieve themselves.

"Are you all right? Turquoise, have they hurt you?"

"No, señorita." She wiped at the dried tears streaked across her ivory cheeks. "I'm sorry I got you into this. But at least, they didn't get Tequila."

"Cuss the little rascal anyway," Cimarron grumbled.

The child looked around. "Is there any chance of escaping?"

Cimarron looked the situation over critically. "Not in the daylight without horses."

"We could run—"

"They'd chase us down in five minutes and no telling what they would do to us then."

"I'm hungry. I want my papa."

Cimarron put a comforting hand on the little girl's shoulder as they turned back to where the Comancheros gathered by the stream. "I'll get us some food, dear."

She left the child in the shelter of a rock and went over to El Lobo, who was eating. "Don't we get anything?"

He nodded to tortillas and jerky spread on the rock next to

him. "Take some."

As she reached around him, he ran his hand boldly over her body. She jerked back, empty-handed. *So it was a game, was it? Well, if she was going to have to let him handle her to get food, she'd starve first.*

Proudly she lifted her head, started to walk away. Her eyes caught the beautiful child's pale aqua ones. And those eyes looked trustingly, waiting for Cimarron to bring her something to eat.

Cimarron gritted her teeth, went back, and reached around El Lobo to grab a handful of tortillas. She moved fast, but he ran both dirty hands across her breasts before she could pull away. The assembled riders guffawed loudly.

"Hey, she's hungry after all!"

"El General, at suppertime, can I take your place?"

"Enough!" El Lobo thundered, all business now. "We've got a long way to go, and those cowboys are not that far behind us. Pedro, did you leave them a little surprise?"

The one with the blind eye and bowed legs nodded. *"Si,* boss," he said in border Spanish. "I left three Comanche hid up in the rocks with good rifles back there along the trail. It'll take them several hours to get past those braves, and by then. . . ." He made a gesture, sliding one hand past the other to indicate that the raiders would be long gone.

"Bueno!" The leader stuck a cigar between his wolfish teeth, rubbed absently at his half-chewed ear. "Now let's vamoose! With a beauty like that one," he nodded toward Cimarron, "you know they'll be coming after us. Get a horse for the captives."

Pedro brought a barebacked sorrel horse around and motioned to the two.

"Eat up, dear," Cimarron cautioned the little girl, "this may be the only food we'll get for a while." They gobbled the last bites as the Comancheros grabbed them roughly, threw them up on the horse, tied their feet underneath the sorrel's belly. El Lobo took the reins, led the horse up next to his. "You better be a good rider, pretty one. If you slide beneath a running horse with those trim ankles tied together, you'll get stomped on."

The motley crew of ragged renegades laughed uproariously as El Lobo started off.

Cimarron gripped the horse's mane. "Hang on to me, dear," she whispered over her shoulder to the frightened child, "it'll be all right."

"I want my daddy," Turquoise sobbed.

"He'll come for us," Cimarron promised. "You know they'll come for us."

El Lobo grinned at her as he kicked his horse into a lope, signaled a couple of riders who took off along another trail. In a few minutes he signaled another bunch with a hand motion, and they rode off up another path. Finally, he signaled a group of Comanches, who galloped off in still a third direction, taking most of the stolen Triple D herd.

He looked back at Cimarron, chortled with laughter. "Like a covey of quail my raiders scatter, going in all directions to finally meet at our rendezvous point."

Cimarron kept her face immobile, concentrated on hanging on to the horse's sweating sides with her bare thighs, her fingers tangled in its mane. She could feel the small arms wrapped trustingly around her waist. Cimarron felt dizzy, her head still hurt. If she went under the sorrel's drumming feet, the little girl went with her.

She gave the renegade a scathing look. "They'll track you down, and then there'll be hell to pay!"

He threw back his head and laughed, chewing his cigar as they rode along. "The rocky limestone trails of the hill country leave hardly a hoofprint to be followed. That's why we have never been caught! Only Injuns are smart enough to track us, and they ride with us!"

All but two, she thought, remembering Trace and Maverick, but she didn't say anything. Now the band strung out along the trail and there was no time for talk, nothing to do but concentrate on staying on the horse's warm, sweating back.

Hours passed. The sun beat down even though it was the first week of October. The horse lathered as it ran. Raw sores began to gall her legs from the straddled position she rode in, and there was nothing she could do about it. The child sobbed softly against her back, but Turquoise followed her orders to hang on tightly.

Still, occasionally, Cimarron heard her murmur, ". . . my daddy, I want my daddy."

Old Sanchez, she thought, with warmth. Obviously no one had ever told the little girl any different. As far as she was concerned, he was the only daddy she had ever known and the only one she ever wanted. Turquoise never mentioned her mother, and Cimarron frowned as she rode along, remembering Rosa last night with her bald-faced lie. There was no doubt in Cimarron's mind that the sultry Mexican had been in Trace's room when the excitement about the barn fire started. Rosa was hardly the motherly type. What Turquoise needed was a plump, old-fashioned mama like her widowed friend Señora Rodriguez. Now there was a sweet, motherly woman who could love and properly care for a lonely little girl.

Cimarron's fingers clenched, hurting from hanging on to the tangled mane, but she dared not let go. She wondered if she would ever be able to straighten them out again.

What would happen when they reached the rendezvous? She didn't want to think about that. Cimarron had seen the way the Comancheros and the Comanches looked at her, yes, even at the innocent little girl. The only reason they hadn't been raped already was that there had been no time with the Triple D riders in hot pursuit only a few miles behind. *Trace and Maverick. Oh, where are you?*

Maverick dismounted and squatted down to look at the trail while the cowboys reined their horses in impatiently.

He looked up as Trace pushed his hat back, fidgeting. "What are you looking at, kid? I don't see anything."

"Come look." Maverick gestured. "You're part Indian, you should be able to read a trail as well as I do."

The lean, dark cowboy dismounted, and came over, the silver conchos on his black leather vest reflecting in the sun.

He knelt beside Maverick, studied the rocky limestone. "You're right, kid. I see the print now. Reckon I'm out of practice, haven't had to trail anyone in so long."

The handsome Luis leaned on his saddlehorn and peered down at them. "Well, I don't see anything, and we're wasting time. If we don't catch up with them soon, there's no telling what they'll do to Cimarron—"

"You think that's not on my mind?" Trace stood up abruptly, almost snarling at Luis. "But there's no point riding until we know which direction they took."

Maverick looked at the two men. They were both in love with her, no doubt about that. As he was himself. All the men had an eye for her, but he knew in his soul that one of these two would finally get her for his woman. He hoped she picked the half-breed Caporal. Maverick thought Trace's tough exterior was a mask to protect an *hombre* who was a little too tender, a little too sensitive for a Texas cowboy. It was the other one, the smooth, elegant gentleman, he didn't trust. And that one had been in a fury ever since this posse had started out. He grumbled to himself and snarled at everyone else.

Trace stuck his thumbs in his gunbelt as he stood up. "What do you think, kid? Is there any possibility they're Kiowa, or anybody but Comanche?"

Maverick studied the faint moccasin track, shook his head. "No, Comanche have short, broad feet. And they like fringe on the back of their moccasins just like they do on their leggings."

Sanchez looked from one to the other hopefully. "*Hombres*, what does that prove?"

Maverick frowned. "This moccasin was heavily fringed at the heel, I can tell by the print." He examined the horse droppings nearby. "Fresh. They're less than ten minutes ahead of us." He felt rage, a thirst for revenge building in him. Maverick had had only a brief glimpse of the raiders as they escaped, but he had seen the profile of the chief on the dark gray stallion as they turned and rode away. He would have known that hatchet-faced devil anywhere. Pine da poi, his father's brother.

"When we catch up to them," he snarled as he started to mount, stopping as he remembered about the gringo horses and going around to mount from the left side, "when we catch up to them, there's one of those Comanche I intend to kill myself, that big, hatchet-faced one. Don't let anyone beat me to him."

Trace swung up on the big black. "You're a little young to hate anyone as much as what I see in your eyes."

Maverick smiled grimly. "Two men in the world I want to see die slowly. One is Whip Owner, of the Comanche, and I want him to die by choking." He made the motion with his hands. "The other . . ." His voice trailed off uncertainly. Maverick had never met the white man he had vowed to kill.

The lean foreman nodded. "They say a Comanche lives in terror of dying by hanging or choking. Is it true?"

"It's true." Maverick relished the thought, could almost feel the pleasure of slowly garroting Whip Owner with the lash of the chief's own quirt. "They think a man's spirit escapes through his mouth as he dies. If he's hanged or strangled, his spirit is trapped in the dead body forever."

Trace gave him a long look. "You must have a good reason, kid, to hate a man that much."

Maverick reached up unconsciously and ran his finger across the knife scar on his dark cheek that Pine da poi had put there. *Annie Laurie's gray eyes smiled in his memory. Her Scotch-Irish face had been plain . . . except when she smiled.* "I got reasons," he whispered.

Trace studied him, seemed to see the anger in his eyes. "But why—?" he never finished. Trace glanced toward the nearby rocks and abruptly shouted, "Get down, *hombres!*" He dove off his horse to the ground, dragging Maverick with him. Both of them landed in the weeds as a rifle shot snapped close enough to hear the whine of the bullet.

"Take cover!" Trace yelled. "I saw the reflection off a gun barrel! There's a welcoming party up in those rocks!"

Maverick tasted the dust as he hunkered down next to the half-breed, and the Triple D riders spread out among the rocks. "What do you think, Trace?"

The Caporal frowned, motioning to the men to fan out.

"Reckon you'll all have to work at keeping their attention while I get up around behind them. Maverick, when we do catch up to them, do you have any ideas about taking Cimarron and the child out without getting them killed?"

"*Si,*" he whispered. "Trace, you and me, we're both half-breeds, dark enough to mix with those Comanche if we were dressed like 'em, smeared with paint."

Trace nodded, smiled. "And those braves up in the rocks have the clothes and things we need, right?"

Maverick spat to one side. "Looks like being Injuns may come in handy, after all, right, boss?"

Cimarron looked back as the rifle shots rang out, echoing through the hills until she couldn't be sure where they were coming from.

But El Lobo slapped his fine milk-white steed lightly with the reins, and the raiders moved on again. He looked over his shoulder, laughed loudly. "Seems like your *compadres* just found the snipers we left up in the rocks for them. That should keep them busy a few hours, and by then they'll have lost the trail!"

Cimarron began to pray harder than she ever had in her life. She was afraid for the cowboys coming after her, didn't want anyone killed to save her. But the child . . .

She couldn't bear to think what would happen tonight if the crew didn't get to them in time. No, she wouldn't think about that, she told herself stubbornly. She couldn't do anything about it yet, so she'd deal with it when she got there. All that mattered now was staying on this horse as it galloped along.

Tears came to her eyes and ran down her face as she tired, but the pace never slackened. The Comancheros and their fierce Indian partners rode northwest.

Another hour passed before the horses stopped at a shallow creek. She and the little girl were allowed a few minutes themselves and a quick drink of water before they changed to fresh mounts and rode out again.

Her thoughts went to the dark, moody cowboy. The most handsome one, the heir with the riches and power, was Luis. She must have been out of her mind to let her emotions run away with her, to go into Trace's arms with no questions, no bargaining for her charms. No doubt about it, all she had to trade on were her looks, and she wouldn't have them forever. If she wanted to be the rich, powerful señora of the whole Durango spread, she should have gone for Luis. But what difference did it make now?

Finally, the sun left a bloody trail of pink-splashed clouds and died along a western ridge. They rode into a camp, where all those who had broken off on other trails rejoined them. For a long moment, all she could think of was her relief that the miserable ride was over. Her legs and rear felt sore from the ride, her ankles numb from the rawhide thongs. She looked at the setting sun, over to the grinning face of the Comanchero, and a new dread came into her soul. She had kept her mind busy all day so she wouldn't have to think about the coming night, about what awaited her and the child in the Comanchero camp. The day had seemed to last forever as she rode the horse. Now she would have given anything to be back at the beginning of the ride, with the long hours ahead of her, hoping against hope that the Triple D riders would arrive in time.

El Lobo dismounted, sauntered over to her horse, cut the thongs from her ankles. She tried to avoid his waiting arms as she came off the horse. Her legs had lost their circulation and buckled under her as she slid down its side, and she fell into his arms.

Disgusted, she tried to push him away, but he laughed and deliberately rubbed her breasts against him as he held her captive in his embrace. "Still spirited! Good!" He looked down at her. "I was afraid by tonight you would have lost your fire, and I like my women fiery!"

"I am not your woman!" she spat at him.

"Are you not?" Very slowly, he rubbed her breasts against

his chest as she struggled to stand on her weak legs. "Who says otherwise?"

"I say otherwise!"

He turned her loose, let her stand. "Wait until tonight," he promised, with a slow, wicked grin. "My informant was right. You were worth riding all that way to steal!" He tipped his sombrero back, feet planted wide apart as he surveyed her. "But our leader will be furious! He ordered me to take a few poor cows, do a little damage. He didn't know I would steal his finest horses and his woman!"

She looked at him incredulously, feeling her mouth drop open. "Your leader? Who?" Her mind was in a whirl as she considered. *One of the cowboys? He had said informant. Who?* Slowly she turned and looked at the small girl, reached to lift her from the horse. *Could it be? No, surely Rosa wouldn't....*

Her mind went back to the days after Trace's wounding, when Rosa had been gone mysteriously. *And to whom did she inform?* She closed her eyes, remembering the girl at Trace's door. *And who on the ranch would think of Cimarron as his woman?*

She didn't have to ask. She saw the rugged half-breed's face as he marked her with his kiss, his seed.

Trace Durango. She was both furious and sad. Would he want her back badly enough to follow his Comanchero *compadres?* Or would he lead the Triple D crew in circles through the hills until they lost the trail?

Luis. Luis would keep looking for her. *Si,* Luis was her hope of rescue. But he wasn't the man Trace was, didn't seem to know horses and trails like the foreman did. Without Trace's full cooperation, Luis wouldn't be able to find her. How much help would the half-grown kid Maverick be as a tracker? For a long moment she surrendered to abject despair as she hugged the small girl to her.

"Señorita, are you crying?"

"No," Cimarron sobbed, looking away so the little girl couldn't see. "I-I got a fleck of dust in my eye on the trail. Everything will be all right, honey."

Bravely she took the child's hand, led her over by a

shadowy rock, and sat down. Whatever she did, she must not scare the child, must try to protect her. "Everything will be fine," she lied, "when the Triple D riders get here with your daddy leading the pack!"

"And Trace and Tequila?"

How could she tell her horrible suspicions to a small child? "I—I'm sure Trace will come, too, but they'll probably leave little Tequila at the house. He might bark and alert the Comancheros, and they'd all run away before your daddy could fight them!"

Turquoise beamed at her. With her ivory skin, soot-black curls, and pale aquamarine eyes, she was the most beautiful little girl Cimarron had ever seen. Someday, Turquoise would be a legend as the most beautiful woman in all the Texas hill country, Cimarron thought, and men would fight each other like rutting stags for her favors.

If she lived to grow up. . . . Cimarron looked around in despair at the renegades setting up camp, building a fire. They were obviously confident that no one could trail them into this thicket of willows and cottonwoods. The saddle horses grazed tied to a picket line and she saw only one guard posted with a rifle atop a giant boulder on the edge of camp. No, they didn't expect anyone to ride in and disturb their evening's pleasure.

Some of the men put up tents, began preparing food, roasting meat. Cimarron felt hunger gnawing at her belly. Darkness fell like a blanket over the camp. She and the child were motioned into line for a tin plate of roasted beef and beans, finished off with a cup of strong coffee.

Little Turquoise started to sit down in the big firelit circle, but Cimarron motioned her over to a shadowy place in the rocks to eat. "The less attention we attract to ourselves, the better," she said.

The child looked up innocently. "Why, señorita?"

Cimarron hesitated, not even wanting to think what lay ahead for them. "Just eat your food, dear." She patted the dark head gently.

The bearded renegades each got a plate and they scattered around the fire. They hunched over their food like wooly tarantula spiders munching prey. Cimarron kept her eyes on her plate, because every time she looked up, she saw curious eyes watching her. *She wouldn't look at them, wouldn't think about the men.* But she would still feel the hot glances, the eager looks. She felt like a small rabbit in a pen full of coyotes. When the animal pack finished feeding, their thoughts would turn to liquor, women.

Could she stall their intentions, delay them until the Triple D cowboys rode in? Suppose they had lost the trail? By submitting to mass rape herself, could she protect the child? If so, Cimarron would submit to their savage lust.

She could hardly eat, her heart was so full of dread and revulsion. But the men were in high spirits, gobbling and laughing, bringing out the strong mescal to drink. By listening to their talk, she knew they were sure they had lost the vengeful pack trailing them and had nothing to fear. If they had been worried, they would surely have posted more than the single guard she saw sitting up on the distant rock with his rifle and plate of beans.

The meal seemed to take forever, but it was still not long enough for Cimarron. All too soon, she saw El Lobo put aside his plate, wipe his greasy beard on his shirt sleeve, belch. He said something in a whisper to his lieutenant, Pedro, who laughed and looked over at her as he reached for a bottle, took a deep drink.

They all finished eating now and lounged around the big firelit circle, drinking. Pedro brought out a guitar, strummed a tune.

Cimarron looked around. All eyes had turned toward the females. If she was going to bargain to save the little girl, the time was now. She stood up on trembling legs, walked over to face the leader. "What do you intend to do with us? The Durangos will pay much ransom if you don't harm us."

The Comanchero leaned back on his elbows and his hat fell back, exposing his hideous ears. "They would pay much ransom and never know whether you were harmed or not. I've found women hesitant to tell what happened in our camp, and some of them lose their minds and can't tell anyway."

Cimarron took a deep breath, remembering the story of Emily Forester. *What had this animal done to her to destroy her mind so completely?* "My—my future husband is a Durango; he will kill you if you harm me."

El Lobo laughed, reached for a cigar. "I don't know which Durango we speak of, but I can tell you now our leader is surely already so angry at my double-cross that he will kill me if I don't vamoose from Texas."

She stared down at him. "I don't understand. Are you saying the Triple D expected to be raided last night?"

He smiled evilly, blew smoke. "I have already said too much, Yellow Hair. I don't believe my Comanchero will hang around to answer to his wrath. We long for our mountains anyway. I think we may clear out till his temper cools."

She felt a sudden surge of hope. "Then you will leave us for them to find?"

She spoke Spanish and the men laughed and nudged each other. She stood silhouetted against the fire, the scented cedar throwing up small showers of sparks in the darkness.

He looked her up and down very slowly as he smoked. "My men have waited all day for this," he said slowly. "They would be angry with me if I did them out of this treat."

Her throat was so dry and prickly she felt as if she had swallowed the thistles growing on the dry, acrid landscape. "The cowboys are liable to arrive to save us any time now, you'd best set us free!"

"We are terribly worried," he answered sarcastically, reaching for the bottle of mescal. "You can see how terrified my men are at this point of having the cowboys find us." He nodded toward the lazy, yawning mixed bloods and half-naked painted braves lounging around the big circle. "It would take a skilled Injun tracker."

The hatchet-faced Comanche snickered and said in Spanish, "I have used all my tricks, El General. None of those gringos can follow us. They are back there miles behind us wandering around in the hills trying to figure out which one of the false trails we spread is the real one."

El Lobo took a big drink from the bottle, let it run down

his beard, all over his dirty shirt. "Yellow Hair, how would you like to go back to my Sangre de Cristo stronghold with me? How would you like to be my woman?"

It took all her effort not to shudder at his words. She must not anger him. "The child?" she nodded back toward Turquoise. "If I say yes, what about the child?"

"What about her?" he smirked.

"If I let you do as you wish, you would spare the little girl?"

He laughed, slapped his knee. "I like your guts, señorita. You are in no position to bargain, yet you try to bargain anyway. That takes plenty guts!"

She glanced around the circle. All together, there must be forty or fifty men. She had a sudden vision of herself spead out naked, the ruffians holding down her wrists and ankles while they took turns enjoying her.

El Lobo smiled again, took another drink. He was toying with her, she knew, much as a bobcat plays with a small frantic prairie dog that has no chance of escaping its sharp claws. Maybe he was right, maybe she waited in vain for the cowboys to come to her rescue. But at least, perhaps she could sacrifice herself and save the child.

Pedro strummed his guitar again. El Lobo stared at her in the silence. "Do you dance, señorita?"

She nodded numbly. "Dance? Why, yes, a little. Why?"

He ran his tongue over his wolfish teeth slowly. "You will dance for our entertainment?"

Her mind raced like the frantic prairie dog trying to outwit the sharp-clawed cat. If she could get Turquoise out of their sight, maybe they would forget about harming her. "*Si*, I'll dance. But only if the child doesn't watch. Put her in one of the tents."

"Why? *Por que?*"

She winked at him wickedly, biting her lip to keep it from trembling. "Because the dance I do, no innocent child should see!"

The renegades sat up with sudden interest, began to whistle and cheer. The leader's eyes brightened with curiosity. "You are very bold to make such a statement." He leered at her. "I have seen some enticing Jezebels from both sides of the border dance to please me."

She cocked her head at him, smiling as she dug her nails into her sweating palms. "You haven't seen my dance," she said coquettishly.

El Lobo considered only a moment, his gaze going around his men who all seemed to be nodding approvingly. "*Si*, let her dance! We haven't see dancing since the last cantina!"

He frowned at the Comanche. "Whip Owner, toss the child in one of the tents until later."

"But I wanted to enjoy her myself!" Pine da poi frowned, looking as if he might argue, but the Comanchero glared at him and finally he obeyed.

Cimarron stepped into the firelit circle, her heart pounding harder and harder. She had given up all hope of saving herself. She only hoped that she could charm the men enough that they would turn their pent-up lust on her. Yes, she would let them rape her if need be to protect Turquoise. Maybe they would forget about the little girl after they had used Cimarron to sate their lust. Maybe there was the smallest chance Turquoise might crawl out the back of the tent, steal a horse, escape. . . .

El Lobo held the bottle out to her. "A drink, señorita, before you begin?"

"Of course. To heat my blood so I can heat yours." She flirted with him through her long lashes as she came over, took the bottle. The raw, strong mescal almost choked her, but she took several big swallows. If she were going to be raped by this pack of wolves, it would be merciful to be half-drunk, not to be aware of it as it happened.

The liquor ran out the sides of her mouth, down her neck and across her breasts in the low-cut blouse.

El Lobo stood up, pulled her to him. "Let's not waste a drop," he said, and his lips went to lick the spilled liquor off her neck, the swell of her breasts.

The crowd of renegades hooted and yelled encouragement. Cimarron laughed and forced herself not to recoil from the touch of his clammy wet mouth on her skin. "Not yet!" she teased as she pulled away from him, whirled back out into the circle. "I am going to dance for you in a way that

Salome would have envied!"

The crowd of men went wild, hooting and shouting vulgarities. More bottles were brought and passed around. Then the men fell silent as she moved out by the fire and Pedro began to play. Someone tossed her a pair of castanets, the little wooden clickers Spanish dancers wore on their fingertips, and she began.

Cimarron closed her eyes so she couldn't see the wolfish, hungry looks on the faces around the fire reminding her of what lay in store when the dancing ended. She stood very still, listening to the rhythm of the guitar as the liquor flowed into her veins, making her blood pound harder as her inhibitions melted.

Now, very slowly, she began to dance. And as she closed her eyes and swayed to the guitar, she became Salome, dancing to charm King Herod so he would give her the head of John the Baptist. She would dance in a way these animals had never seen before, she promised herself, letting her natural grace and rhythm take over. If it would save the child, she would dance in such a way that they would all want her as they had never before lusted for a woman and none would be satisfied with any but Cimarron.

Very slowly, she reached up as she swayed, untied the hair ribbon, shook her long hair out so that it hung about her shoulders. She caught the end of the ribbon in her mouth, pulled it through her teeth with a deliberate slow gesture. She flung it toward El Lobo who caught it to the cheers of his men, wadded it in his hand, stared back at her. His swarthy face was dark with hunger for her already, she thought, in a slight daze from the liquor. But she could make him want her more, oh, much more!

She began to dance about the circle to the guitar, clicking the castanets on her fingers rhythmically to the pulse pounding in her temples. Cimarron whirled and her skirts flew up, exposing her long legs. The men cheered, urged her on. She danced around, giving each man a hungry, deliberately tantalizing look that seemed to tell him she wanted only him. Instinctively she danced a ritual mating dance such as women of old might have used to tempt men.

A Comanchero swayed drunkenly to his feet, holding out a bottle to her.

Why not? she thought recklessly as she grabbed it, gulped it. With what was coming, it would be merciful to be half-aware. The liquor warmed her veins as she started dancing in earnest, and some of them clapped in time to her movements. Every gaze in camp was fastened on her swaying hips, she thought as she glanced up at the guard posted on the boulder. There was no guard visible up there now. Even he must have come down to watch her dance.

She let her blouse slip enticingly off one shoulder, and the men cheered, yelled vulgar epithets. She let it slip off the other side, whirling around the fire. She danced this way several minutes, clicking the castanets, tossing her long hair. But after a while, they began to get restless. "We want to see more of her than she shows us."

El Lobo shouted with a scowl. "Show us that tawny body, pretty whore, your teasing wears thin on us!"

There was a limit to how long she could stall them without giving them what they wanted, she thought in despair. And, very slowly, she took off the lacy blouse, tossed it aside, quickly shook her long hair down to cover her breasts, and began to dance again, eyes closed.

The rhythm and the liquor surging through her veins, made her more bold, less inhibited. *She was Salome dancing to please the king. She was a slave girl swaying to entice her masters in the palaces of Egypt or Greece. And she must please these men who held power over her body. She must please them to save the child.*

This thought alone gave her strength to reach for the button on the bright peasant skirt as the men stared. She heard them gasp collectively as she let it slide past her lace pantalettes, down her long legs to the ground, danced out of it. Next went the full lace petticoat as she whirled and twisted.

She was more than a little drunk, she thought as she danced around the circle, clad only in her long hair and her lace pantalettes. The men crouched closer, all holding their breaths, licking their lips. She would make them lust for her the way they had never wanted any other woman, she thought grimly as she shook her hair so that for the first time, her beautiful full breasts were clearly visible. She heard moans and breaths catching in male throats.

One man swore an oath, stumbled to his feet toward her, but another grabbed him, pulled him back, pushed him down. "Not yet, Miguel! We have all night! Let her dance!"

She looked around the circle, ran her tongue suggestively over her lips as she looked into each man's eyes. Then slowly, deliberately, she cupped her own breasts with her hands, danced around the circle offering their fullness to each in turn as her fingers stroked her nipples. She heard several groan aloud, and El Lobo's hand went down to touch himself between the legs. His tongue ran over his lips in a nervous motion.

He wanted her, she could tell it by the way his eyes darkened with desire. She danced and swayed to the guitar, running her hands feverishly up and down her own silken skin, over her own breasts and thighs as she danced for them. The circle was a blur of swarthy faces and brightly warpainted braves as she swirled dizzily. Once, she thought a warrior's face looked familiar to her. She would have sworn he had gray eyes, then knew it was only the liquor and the fear creating her wild imaginings. Another dark, moody scarlet painted face looked almost like. . . .

She was losing her sanity, beginning to imagine things, she thought as she closed her eyes, swayed to the rhythm. Her own vain hopes were creating familiar faces on the outlying edges of the crowd. Cimarron was tiring now. She could feel it as she danced, shook her long honey-colored hair that reflected the moonlight. She saw the painted, moody savage face at the edge of the circle again. *Trace,* she thought sadly, *he looks like Trace.* Cimarron closed her eyes, pretending she danced for Trace Durango.

That made it easier somehow, to pretend that she did not see the lusting, hungry eyes of the men surrounding her like the yellow eyes of a wolf pack closing in. *If she pretended she danced for her lover alone, it was easier somehow.* There was no ending to this, she knew with despair, except to be humiliated and raped by the eager male animals of this pack, but she would dance with her eyes closed, pretend she danced only for Trace Durango, and that he and only he would take her when the time came.

El Lobo shouted. "*Puta,* take the rest off! We want to see what it is we are getting!"

She had dreaded this and had stalled as long as possible, but now it must be. With trembling fingers she slid the lace pantalettes down her hips and slipped them off.

She felt the tears running down her face as the men moaned and babbled to each other in border Spanish of her beauty, her desirability. Her humiliation was complete. Like a harem slave dancing to please her master and his guests, she swayed, totally naked and vulnerable. She knew she was theirs to command, to do with as they wished.

But oh, she could make them want her, forget the child, forget everything but her! Maybe they would even fight each other for her favors.

And so she danced naked by the fire, clicking the castanets on her fingertips, shaking her head so that the long blond strands fell about her, covering her tawny body. She moved her hips to the music, writhed and twisted while the men groaned and whispered appreciative remarks to each other.

"Look at those long legs! With those wrapped around me, I wouldn't care if I died as I took her!"

"I get her before you!"

"I would pay big ransom if I was rich to own her!"

"But you poor Comanchero! You will be lucky if El Patron let you have her once!"

"He is fair! El Lobo will share her! But must we share equally with the filthy savages?"

"Shut up! They speak Spanish! You will get us all gelded and scalped!"

Her head felt dizzy and throbbing with the liquor as she swayed and writhed to the music, trying not to hear the ribald remarks from the men who watched her dance. *Si,* she was drunk, but oh, God, she wasn't near drunk enough for what she was going to have to endure this evening!

Had she imagined the familiar faces? Frantically, she opened her eyes as she danced around the circle. No, none of the savages looked familiar anymore. Only cruel, hungry Comanche and Comanchero eyes stared back at her. It must have been her own desperate imagination.

And then El Lobo swayed to his feet and stumbled out into the circle while his men shouted encouragement. "Me, the Wolf," he tapped his hairy chest, "I will dance with you."

She swallowed hard, forcing herself to smile invitingly at him as she danced tantalizingly close. He reached out, tangled his fingers in her long hair, pulled her against his sweating body.

With a flirting laugh, she unbuttoned several buttons of his shirt, saw the knife strapped inside to his chest, whirled away with a laugh.

He liked that. She could see it by the wide, wolfish gleam of his teeth. *"Si, puta,* undress me to entertain my men! I like that!"

How much longer could she stall, and what difference did it make anyway? She was only postponing the inevitable. Out of the corner of her eye, she looked over at the picket line of grazing horses. She might make a lightning run, jump on a horse's back, gallop away into the night like Lady Godiva. The element of surprise and their drunkenness might enable her to get away.

Hope rose in her heart as she thought about it while she smiled teasingly and finished unbuttoning his shirt as he tried to follow the dance.

No, she couldn't do that, she thought with finality, glancing toward the tent where the little girl was. Cimarron might escape, but there was no way she could take the child with her. For only a moment she was tempted, thinking of what lay before her this night if she didn't escape. But she couldn't do it. She couldn't escape and leave the little girl a captive here to deal with the angry, aroused men.

She danced close as El Lobo swayed unsteadily to the music. She reached out and unbuckled his belt while the men shouted encouragement.

leader needed no help with his pants. His breath came in deep, aroused gasps as he unbuttoned them, stepped out of them. He wore nothing underneath. He was a naked, hairy beast with his manhood jutting out before him as he licked his lips, moved toward her unsteadily.

Cimarron took a deep breath. She had run out of time. The whole pack would rape her now.

Chapter Twenty

Maverick had slipped up behind the lone guard on the boulder. Instinctively, he moved as silently as his Comanche ancestors. *Comanche. Enemy.* It was a word their old foes, the Utes, had given them from bitter experience.

This was a big gamble the Triple D cowboys were about to take to get Cimarron and the little girl out of the Comanchero camp. It had been Trace's idea for the two half-breeds to take the clothing of the Comanche snipers back at the rocks. The two had put them on and smeared themselves with warpaint so they could mingle with the group gathering around the fire.

Darkness fell. The Triple D riders hid, awaiting Maverick's killing the sentry to make their next move. The cowboys were outnumbered. Getting the two captives out alive depended on whether he and Trace could mingle with the renegades and warriors without being noticed.

Quietly, Maverick slipped up behind the sentry with a rawhide thong in his sweating hands. He had to kill the Comanche without his making a single cry to alert the others. The two captives' lives depended on what he did in the next few seconds. Below him, he heard the first strumming notes of a guitar, knew the Comancheros had finished eating. Now they would entertain themselves with drinking and rape. Maverick had to make his move fast, because time was running out for the woman and the child.

He took a deep breath, sweat making the scarlet paint

on his young body. He moved silently as the panther stalking its prey. The Comanche sentry stretched and belched, his attention on the people moving below him in the firelit camp.

Maverick tensed, taking the rawhide cord between his hands. His fingers trembled as he watched the sentry, remembered how much he hated the Comanche, what they had done to his mother. For this reason, he used the thong instead of a knife. *The spirit trapped in the dead body forever. It was a terrible retribution, but a fitting one for all Comanches. Annie Laurie, here's another one to pay for your death,* Maverick thought grimly as he crept forward.

He smelled the reek of bear grease and sweat as he looped the rawhide over the warrior's head and pulled tight. The warrior was strong and he struggled, grabbing in terror at the cord choking off his air, his spirit. For a long, heart-stopping moment, Maverick listened to his gasp, struggling to cry out. Then the sentry collapsed.

Without thinking, Maverick reached down and touched the body with his bare hand. "I count first coup on this man," he whispered in Comanche, then shook his head in annoyance. He was still half-savage after all, unable to free himself from his sire's customs. But his mind and his spirit were as white as his mother's Kentucky ancestors. She had seen to that.

From the boulder, he signaled the cowboys waiting in the darkness, then crept down to join Trace mingling with the men around the campfire.

The one-eyed Comanchero with the bowed legs still played the guitar. Maverick watched the hatchet-faced Comanche pick up the little girl, take her to toss her in a tent as Cimarron began to dance.

Whip Owner. Pine da poi, his own uncle. Maverick's hand went up to touch the knife scar on his dark cheek. His uncle had cut his face that night when Maverick had shown mercy to the tortured woman. Maverick had closed his eyes and cut Annie's throat when she begged him to end her agony. All because she had helped another prisoner escape. . . . Maverick had waited a long time for vengeance. Tonight it would be Whip Owner, if it cost Maverick his own life. . . .

Cimarron danced. Maverick heard the approving mutter of the males around him, commenting on her beauty, her desirability as she whirled in wild abandon. They would all rape her when her dance ended, Maverick knew that. He and Trace had only a few minutes to make their moves. It would be a long gamble to get Cimarron and the child out without harm. Trace's plan was that the cowboys would scatter the Comanche mounts, create enough confusion so the savages would think they were being attacked by a superior force, then scatter instead of fighting.

He looked across the circle at Trace Durango in his Comanche clothing, his bright warpaint. Only the large, sensitive eyes gave him away. He saw the anger on the other half-breed's face as the girl swayed and shed her clothes. Maverick caught his gaze, shook his head slightly. No matter how much it hurt Trace to watch the girl reveal her naked beauty before other men, he must not try to rescue her now. If he did that, it would wreck the plan. Still, he could tell by the hard set of the cowboy's face that he was enduring agony as he watched her whirl in wild abandon before the crowd of males.

No, Trace, Maverick willed him silently. You must not make your move yet, you must let her dance, even though it tears your heart out for others to see her body. The way the girl moved, she must be slightly drunk.

Once as she whirled, she seemed to catch Maverick's eye, recognize him. For a long heart-stopping moment, he saw her eyes widen, tensed as he awaited her cry. If she gave away the game now, the plan would fail, the renegades would grab Maverick and Trace. The whole plan depended on surprise, getting the captives out, then running off the Comanche horses.

He looked toward the picket line. Maverick had never really owned a fine horse, and there was one stallion there that took his eye. Not that he expected a poor half-breed like himself could end up with a fine-blooded stallion like that one. Dust Devil. *Si,* that's what he would call the dark gray if it belonged to him. He thought of the whirlwinds of dust swiftly across the Texas plains like tornados. *Si*, if he ...ed that stallion, he'd call him Dust Devil.

The girl danced completely naked now, and the men around him muttered, licked their lips, each eager for his turn with her. The Comanchero leader staggered to his feet and the girl unbuckled his belt, made motions for him to dance with her. The swarthy renegade stumbled out to the center of the circle, danced to the encouraging shouts of his men. Maverick glanced over at Trace's face as the leader took his pants off. If El Lobo raped her right out in the circle before everyone, there was no way to save her. Trace's face was dark with fury. Any second now, he would run out, attack the one-eared renegade, and the fight would be on. The girl's features were a mask of terror, but she continued to dance as the Comanchero swayed with her. He grabbed her up and carried her into his tent then, to take her there.

Now was the time. He caught Trace's eyes as the *hombres* yelled obscenities, passed bottles of mescal around. But Trace was already moving around behind the tent.

Quickly, Maverick looked around for Pine da poi, saw the hatchet-faced Comanche sneaking toward the tent where the little girl was. Obviously he intended to enjoy the child while no one saw him. This was Maverick's chance. He had waited a long time for this moment. He glided quiet as Death's shadow around behind that tent. Winding the rawhide around his hand, he ground his teeth in hatred for Pine da poi. Annie Laurie, he thought, this is for you. Someday, I'll get the white one, the husband who wouldn't pay the ransom, who left you to the mercies of my father and his four brothers.... Whatever happened in that other tent, Trace and Cimarron were on their own....

Cimarron didn't struggle as El Lobo carried her inside the tent. She lay stiff and wooden against his sweating, hairy chest. If she pleased him, she thought, pleased the others, maybe they wouldn't harm the child.

"Yellow Hair," El Lobo laid her on a blanket, "I liked your dancing." He stood looking down at her, staggering drunkenly. In the moonlight filtering through the tent, she could see his naked, aroused manhood as he swayed over her. "Have you ever been taken from behind, Yellow Hair?" he laughed, stroked his tangled beard. "That's how I like my women best! Please me and maybe I will not give you to the others. Maybe I will take you with me when I leave tomorrow for my mountains. You can be my woman."

She sensed that his enjoyment of her would be so terrible, she must postpone it. "But suppose the Durangos send ransom?" She felt her heart pounding in fright so hard, she was sure he could see it.

He squatted down beside her, laughed. "The one Durango will be angry with me that I've double-crossed him. And in this case, I don't think I would accept ransom anyway, pretty thing." His prominent teeth gleamed. "Only once before, up in the Indian Territory, have I seen a girl I desired as much as you, and I never got her." He scowled, ran his hand over the pink scar where an ear had once been. "That one belonged to a half-breed Dog Soldier who took my ear for wanting her."

She felt revulsion, terror as his dirty hand came down to paw her body. "I—I will try very hard to please you," she stammered, forcing herself not to withdraw from his groping hands, "if you will only set the child free, send her back to the ranch unharmed."

His hands cupped her breasts, squeezed cruelly as she flinched, determined not to cry out no matter how badly he hurt her. "You try to bargain with me, Yellow Hair? Be careful of my anger. Please me or risk my turning you over to my men, to the savages. The fat blonde from Austin I sent back for ransom didn't even have a mind left when they finished with her."

Emily Forester. He was speaking of Emily Forester. She felt her blood almost congeal in her veins at the image of what they must have done to that woman to terrify her into insanity. His hands stroked Cimarron's thighs and he ran his tongue over his lips as he leered down at her. Outside the noise increased as the renegades drank and gambled.

"Hear that?" El Lobo laughed. "My men await their turn at you. They beg that I take you out in the circle where they

...atch. How would you like that, pretty one?"

Cimarron swallowed hard, feeling her heart pound in horror. "No," she gasped, "oh, please, no, not that."

"Then please me," he commanded, and his hand went up to pinch her nipples. "Are you so frightened of El Lobo, then? I feel you heart beating hard under your breasts like a small, caged bird!"

She could only stare at his hard, jutting manhood as he stood up, looked down at her. "Get on your hands and knees, pretty bitch. You will please El Lobo in the way he likes best, and maybe I will not share you with my men."

Very slowly, Cimarron sat up, trying to decide what to do. There seemed to be no way out. She would have to submit to his indignities, do anything he demanded. It was the only way to protect the child. "*Si,*" she said as she got to her knees. "I—I'll do as you want."

He stared down at her, a drunken leer on his ugly features, completely intent on her naked body. He did not seem to see the warrior who came into the tent, stood directly behind him. *Oh, dear God,* she thought, *he expects me to submit to something involving the two of them, perhaps he will watch while the brave takes me. . . .*

El Lobo seemed to realize suddenly that she stared past his shoulder. He half turned, as if to see, and then, abruptly, the brave's big fist slammed down, caught the Comanchero in the side of the head. With a moan, El Lobo slumped to the floor.

Cimarron started to scream as the brave grabbed her, clasped his hand over her mouth. *Now the savage would rape her.* She panicked as she struggled naked in his strong arms.

"Dammit, darlin', stop fighting me," came the familiar deep drawl. "I can't fight all them and you, too!"

Trace. She collapsed in limp relief as he cradled her against him, only for a moment. Her arms went up around his neck. His pulled her hard against him, protecting her against his wide chest. For a brief moment, his lips kissed hers as he held her.

"Cimarron. Oh, darlin'! When I had to stand there

helpless with them jeering and grabbing at you—"

"Trace!" She felt tears running down her face as she snuggled against him, felt him kiss the tears away. She never wanted to leave the protection of his arms, she wanted to stay in their safety forever. But they had to get out of here. "Turquoise," she gasped, "the other tent—"

"I know, Wild One," he murmured, "Maverick's getting her out."

"I can't leave here naked," she protested as she pulled out of his arms.

"Here. Here's my leather vest. It's almost long enough to cover you. They think I stole it off a dead cowboy back at the ambush." He threw it to her, the silver conchos gleaming in the light. Cimarron slipped it on. The swell of her breasts still showed and it didn't quite cover her naked hips. She blushed inwardly, but there were more important things than modesty right now. She watched Trace cut open the back of the tent.

Cimarron looked from him to the unconscious Comanchero. "Are you going to try to take him with us?"

He nodded as he grabbed El Lobo by the shoulders and dragged him through the hole out into the moonlight. "There's something I need to discuss with this rattlesnake and when I get through doing that, I'm going to beat him bloody for putting his hands all over you."

She remembered what the Comanchero had said about double-crossing a Durango. Trace had better talk to him fast, get him to keep his mouth shut before Luis got a chance to ask El Lobo questions.

They moved quietly through the rear of the camp, Trace dragging the unconscious Comanchero. Back in the circle, she heard the noise, the complaining of the renegades.

"Isn't El Lobo finished with that female yet?"

"Someone go ask him if he will give us a turn."

"You ask him yourself! Would you dare disturb the Wolf before he gets done with a woman?"

Cimarron heard a moan and glanced down. The Comanchero was regaining consciousness, but Trace hadn't noticed. The disguised cowboy looked around, obviously

...ating on getting to the horses. At any moment, ...obo would call out. A movement off to the side caught ...er eye and she almost screamed, then recognized Maverick, also dressed as a warrior, carrying the little girl. *Of course she had seen them in the circle. They had watched her dance naked for the Comancheros.* Her face flamed at the thought.

"Almost there," Trace whispered, "Cowboys will run the horses off—"

She started to shout a warning but was a split-second too late. El Lobo came back to consciousness with a rush, scrambling away from the cowboy's hands while shouting for help. *"Hombres!* Help, *hombres!* Enemies!"

Trace hit him then with all the pent-up fury evident in his rugged face. The two men struggled and fought. Behind her, she heard noise and shouts as the renegades came alert to the danger. Shots and screams echoed through the camp as the cowboys charged in, shooting to scare the horses, stampeding the stolen Triple D herd through the camp.

Now the tied picket line of mounts bolted, and the scene was a confusion of shots, screams, and rearing, neighing horses. But still the two men fought behind her. Trace's fist hit solid as a hammer into El Lobo's teeth. "This is for touching my woman!" he snarled, "and this is for all the poor Texans you've killed!" His fist caught the Comanchero again with brutal force.

Luis ran up with two horses. "Señorita, are you all right?"

"Help him!" she shrieked, "El Lobo—"

A knife glinted suddenly in the Comanchero's hand as he reached into his shirt.

"Get back, Trace!" Luis yelled. She saw the moonlight glint off the derringer as Luis jerked it out and fired.

The swarthy renegade screamed, grabbed his fat belly, fell to his knees. For one long moment, his startled eyes looked into Cimarron's while the warm blood pumped out between his dirty fingers. Then he fell over on his face.

"Dammit, Luis," Trace swore, "I needed him alive!"

Luis shoved the gun back in his coat. "I save your life and you complain! I didn't have time to aim and just wound him! Of all the ungrateful..." His eyes stared at Cimarron's nakedness. She bit her lip in embarrassment, struggling to hide herself in the short vest. "Allow me, señorita," he said gallantly, taking off his coat. "Let me help you."

He slipped his coat around her shaking body, led her over to the horses. She looked up at him gratefully. "Thank you, Luis. I'm so glad you got here in time!"

Trace made a rude noise as he stalked over, grabbed the reins of his black stallion. "But you notice he didn't come walking right into the lion's den after you." He listened a moment as he mounted. "Sounds like the boys are right on time." He nodded off toward the confusion, the stampede of horses. "Let's get out of here before that mob figures out there's only a handful of us!"

Luis lifted her up to the saddle, crossed himself. "Señorita Cimarron," he said, "remind me to light a candle next time I'm in town to give thanks for your safe rescue."

Trace grinned. "Oh, are there candles at Miss Fancy's?"

"You're the authority on that," Luis sneered, mounting.

The three of them galloped out to meet the cowboys.

Maverick was already there, and Turquoise was handed over to old Sanchez's reaching arms. The riders raced through the night toward the east, driving the herd of Triple D and Comanche horses ahead of them.

Cimarron looked over at Maverick as they rode. "I knew I saw you in the circle as I danced."

He smiled at her, warpaint still smeared on his dark face. "I thought for a minute you'd call out, give us away. Trace was already about to run into the circle and rescue you. I could tell by his face he was loco over all those men watching you dance."

She flushed at the memory. Well, she had delayed the renegades, protected the little girl, that was all that mattered. If Trace thought she was a slut because of what he'd witnessed, she owed him no explanation. She thought about the dead Comanchero's words, wondered if she should tell Luis what she suspected about Rosa and Trace.

"Anyway," she said, "thanks, Maverick. Did you kill that Comanche chief?"

"*Si*. I strangled him very slowly. His spirit is trapped

forever now. I owed it to him."

She studied his tormented face. "Why?"

He shrugged. "Let's just say it was in revenge for a Scots-Irish girl named Annie Laurie McBride."

She stared at him curiously. "A Comanche captive?"

Grief marked his dark face. He nodded. "My mother."

She started to ask, saw Maverick's face become a cold, expressionless mask. Someday, he might tell his secret, but only to a very special girl, when he gave his heart away.

Cimarron sighed, looking now at the two men, Trace and Luis, who rode just up ahead of her. She was full of mixed feelings as they galloped through the night. Trace Durango was involved with the Comanchero somehow. What was she going to do about it?

Chapter Twenty-One

The Triple D riders reined up before the courtyard of the hacienda. Cimarron noted as Luis came around and helped her dismount that Dr. Hastings's buggy stood tied up out front.

Luis took a long look, crossed himself fervently. "Pray God something has not happened to the old man while we were gone. I want to be with him at the end. . . ." His voice trailed off as Rosa came out of the house with the doctor.

Rosa's face mirrored relief as she saw the group, hurried to them. "Oh, Sanchez, I've been so worried!" She tried to hug the little girl, who looked over at the old vaquero.

"Hug your mama," he said to the child.

Trace dismounted. "Dr. Hastings, is the old man—?"

"No, he's resting quietly now," he said, but his face was glum. "Made it through another crisis, but can't promise he will next time."

Luis grimaced, wiped a moist eye. "We all know it's only a matter of time, but we're just not ready to let him go. We love him so much." He went over, took the unsteady man's elbow, assisted him toward the buggy.

Dr. Hastings stopped to speak to Cimarron and she recoiled from the reek of liquor on him. "Glad to see you're fine, young lady, didn't really think they'd get you back."

"I'm all right." Cimarron retreated from his sour breath. "Turquoise and I were pretty scared, but thanks to this bunch of cowboys, we're all right."

The little girl looked around anxiously. "Tequila?" she asked. "Where's Tequila?"

At the sound of his name, the little dog bounced through the open French doors and across the courtyard. Barking happily, he danced around the child's feet.

Luis scowled. "Stupid, ornery mutt! If it hadn't been for him, the Comanchero wouldn't have taken the women."

Something stirred in Cimarron's memory as she watched the child play with the dog. "No, Luis, something El Lobo said made me think he had come looking specifically for me, that he came to this ranch to steal *me.*"

Luis's face mirrored horror. "What? Where would he get such information, why . . . ?" His voice trailed off as he looked at Trace, looked over at Rosa.

That look said a thousand things, Cimarron thought. Luis must know about that pair of lovers.

Trace pushed his hat back. "There does seem to be something strange about this whole raid," he admitted.

"Strange isn't the word," Rosa said, "with horses run off, men killed, and the attempt to fire the house."

Maverick nodded. "I spent time among the Comanche, remember? They can do a lot better job than they did here. They never bungle a raid so badly."

Luis fingered his mustache. "Perhaps they had inside help," he said significantly, looking around at Sanchez and the other riders.

Maverick flushed. "If you're hinting—"

Trace grabbed the boy's arm. "That wasn't aimed at you, kid. Luis is after me."

Cimarron broke in, tired and frustrated. "I can't believe this. We've all just survived a terrible experience. We're exhausted, nerves frayed, and we're going to stand out here and argue?"

Rosa gave her a long, searching look. "The señorita is right. I've got food ready; I even baked a cake with the little flour I have left. Let's eat."

Luis rubbed his hands together, took Cimarron's arm. "Sounds wonderful. Well, at least we got the horse herd back, even picked up a few fine ones from the Indians. Too bad that white stallion got away with the Comancheros, but now that gray stallion—"

Trace made a gesture of dismissal as they turned to troop into the hacienda. "You can get your greedy eyes off that gray, Luis, I've already decided who gets him."

Luis bristled. "That gray's a fine-blooded horse. I thought I might rebreak him for myself—"

"He's used to being ridden by warriors," Trace said, putting his hand on Maverick's shoulder. "He's accustomed to being mounted from the right side, Indian style—"

"So what?" Luis shrugged as he guided Cimarron toward the house. "I can rebreak him—"

"No need to," Trace said, and she saw him frown as he stared at Luis's hand on her elbow. "I figure we owe something to the kid here for riskin' his neck to help us."

"That's true," Luis answered grudgingly, smiling at Cimarron. "I was scared there for a few minutes that...." His voice trailed off significantly and she shuddered at the thought of what might have happened if Trace and the young boy had not disguised themselves and sneaked into the camp.

"So," Trace said, "I'm going to ask the old man's permission to give the Comanche stallion to the boy. How's that? A stallion as gray as a Texas dust devil for the kid with gun-metal gray eyes?"

Cimarron looked up at Luis, smiling. "That's a wonderful idea! Then Maverick won't have to worry about remembering to mount from the left side."

"Well," Luis answered grudgingly, looking at her, "I suppose the boy really is deserving, my dear."

Maverick looked around at all of them with a touch of wonder. "For me? You're giving that fine stallion to me?"

Trace clapped him on the back. "You earned it, kid, like you've earned a place here as long as you want it."

"I love this ranch," Maverick said soberly as they trooped into the dining room. "I feel at ease here."

Cimarron said, "What about Peso? Is she in the herd?"

Trace winked broadly. "Sure. Too many memories attached to that filly. I made certain she came back."

Maverick grinned. "It's good to be home."

Cimarron decided to ignore Trace's insinuation. She smiled warmly at the young boy. "Obviously you've got a home forever now, Maverick."

She looked around wistfully, wishing she could say the same. She was engaged to one man but in love with the other, and he just wanted to sleep with her. He would never love her, because of the scars another woman had left on him. What an impossible situation. What was she going to do about it? When the war ended, she could leave. Until then, she was stranded here. Later, her conscience told her, she must warn Luis about Rosa's and Trace's connections with the Comanchero. And yet . . . She went upstairs, washed, dressed, came back down to join the festivities.

Luis seated Cimarron at the table among the laughing, talking cowboys. It was obviously a very festive occasion for the whole Triple D crew to be invited in for supper. He sighed regretfully. "Excuse me, my dear, I think I'll go up and see how the old man's doing. Just to make sure he really is all right."

Rosa glared at him. "I told you he was."

Trace looked from one to the other of them as Cimarron watched. "Come to think of it, Luis, I think I'll go up with you. He'll want the details of our raid anyway, and I figure you'd give yourself too much credit."

Luis frowned at him, and the cowboys all laughed as the two men left the dining room.

Tequila hopped up in little Turquoise's lap, started eating off her plate.

Rosa put her hands on her hips. "You shouldn't let him do that, Turquoise. It's bad manners."

"The señora always fed him at the table." The child defended the dog hotly.

"But even Velvet Eyes didn't let him eat right out of her plate. Sanchez, can't you do something?"

Sanchez made a resigned, gentle gesture with his crippled hand. "Mind your mama."

Turquoise pouted a long moment, then obediently slid the brown pet off her lap. Tequila, in the meantime, took advantage of the hesitation to grab another half-dozen bites off her plate before she put him on the floor. The little dog immediately ran from chair to chair, sitting up and begging prettily, so that even the rough cowboys gave him tidbits off their dishes.

Cimarron smiled as she slipped him a small bite of roast beef. "You will be two feet wide and still only six inches high," she admonished him, "and too heavy for anyone to lift."

The prospect didn't seem to bother the dog at all. His little eyes twinkled as he cocked his head, licked his mouth, and sat up again, begging for another bite.

That afternoon she went up to visit the old Don, who seemed to be weak, but resting comfortably. "I suppose I keep hoping the doctor is wrong," he said, with a discouraged shake of his head. "About the time I get to feeling really good again, I have another spell. I guess sometime soon, one of them will get me."

"The war is almost over," she said comfortingly as she patted his hand. "Then we'll get you to a doctor back East who knows all the latest medicines. . . ."

His clear, dark eyes looked into hers and her voice trailed off. He did not believe he would last that long, she could tell by his depressed expression.

"It doesn't matter," he sighed, "although I keep praying for a miracle. Sometimes at night I think I hear my Velvet Eyes rustling down the hallways in that moonlight dress, and when I awaken, it's only the oleander brushing against the walls outside. I suppose I must be losing my mind as well to feel she is still about the place, trying to send me some kind of message."

If he only knew Ojos de Pana had run away with a lover to New York. When Cimarron left here after the war, went East, could she find that faithless wife, persuade her to return? What a trusting old man, she thought with pity as she held his hand and looked away so he would not see the tears in her eyes. To him it was very simple. To love was to trust.

She hoped fervently that his death came without his ever finding out what had really happened.

After a time he dropped off to sleep, and Cimarron went down the hall. Her thoughts were in turmoil as she tried to decide what she was going to do. Luis's door stood open, and as she passed he called out, "Cimarron? Can we talk?"

He motioned her inside. "It's not proper for a gentleman to entertain a lady in his bedroom," he began apologetically, "but we need to talk." He closed the door softly and led her across the elegant room to a chair.

She smiled at him as he sat down across from her. "Dear Luis, always the perfect gentleman."

He smiled, and for a moment she thought he would rise, take her hands in his, but he seemed to stifle the impulse. "You're a lady, señorita, anyone can tell that. I can do no less than behave chivalrously to you."

Then why did her heart yearn for the one who treated her like a harlot?

"Cimarron," his voice dropped to a whisper, "did that filthy Comanchero say anything to you? Tell you anything?"

She had decided she could never voice her suspicions about Trace. But she felt the guilty flush creep up her neck as she avoided Luis's eyes. "What—what makes you ask?"

He came over, sat on the arm of her chair, took her hands in his. "If you care about what happens to the old Don, to the Triple D, you should tell me."

His eyes were earnest, imploring, as he looked down at her. So noble, so caring, she thought, as her own filled with tears. It was right to tell. "Luis, I—I have reason to believe the Comancheros have one of their own here spying and reporting back to them."

His handsome face blanched. "No, I don't believe it!" He stood and paced the fine Persian carpet. "Did the Comanchero tell you that?" Luis regarded her keenly.

She ran the tip of her tongue over her dry lips, in a quandary as to what to do. How could she tell her suspicions about Trace? But she'd be as guilty as the Comancheros if she didn't attempt to stop the cowboy from his bloody endeavors. "El Lobo hinted that there was an inside man he'd double-crossed. I think they were both sharing Rosa. Luis, it—it has to be Trace. I saw her coming out of his room early one morning."

Luis looked stricken and swore in Spanish. "What has happened to honor and marital fidelity in this world? If old Sanchez or the Don were to suspect, there'd be real trouble!" He paced up and down. "I pray you're wrong, señorita, I just can't believe Trace would do something like that!" He fingered his mustache thoughtfully as he paused. "Oh, I'll admit we've had our differences, but I'll not condemn him until I've got indisputable evidence."

Cimarron shook her head. "I realize you expect the best from everyone, but I'm afraid the facts point toward him."

He frowned and she felt he did not want to believe what she told him. "Well, I'll investigate. Don't say anything to anyone while I try to find out what's going on, agreed?"

Cimarron stood up. "Agreed." She was doing the right thing, she thought as she crossed to the door. Then why did she feel so guilty? Quickly, she left the room, went down the hall toward the sewing room. She needed something, anything to keep her fingers busy so she wouldn't think about Trace. No wonder he looked moody and sullen all the time, with what he had on his conscience.

The half-finished russet silk dress lay across the little black machine. To occupy her mind, she went back to work on it. Tomorrow she would teach her little class again and visit the old man. Maybe Luis would find a reasonable explanation, maybe. . . .

As the hours passed, she made her decision. She would stay until the old Don died. He couldn't be abandoned twice. And when he was gone, she would leave. Trace's moody face came to her thoughts. She couldn't marry the one while she loved the other and that one did not love her, only used her to fill his masculine hungers. Well, he could satisfy those at Miss Fancy's. Those girls didn't expect commitment from him. But for Cimarron, love meant obligations. If he didn't care that much, he didn't care enough for her to stay. A woman who would settle for casual sex does herself no favors, she thought sadly. A man puts his brand on what belongs to him if it's important to him.

It was late afternoon. Her eyes and her back ached from sewing on the dress. Even her hand hurt from turning the little wheel of the machine over and over to make the needle move up and down. The thing was indeed a marvel, she thought tiredly as she held the dress up for a final inspection. Why, who knew what they would invent next?

The crispness of October lay gold and copper over the ranch. She heard the cowboys out by the corral laughing and joking, heard Turquoise running around the fountain, the little dog barking happily as they played. Cimarron didn't want to leave the Triple D, she thought; never had she loved a place so much.

Maverick had found a home here, why couldn't she? Because Trace was a Comanchero who didn't love her, and she wouldn't stay to be used like a common whore. If she couldn't have true love, commitment, and trust, she would go far away, try to pull the pieces of her life back together.

She heard a step out in the hall, then a hand on the knob. Rosa threw the door open. "You! What are you doing in my señora's sewing room? And you use her fancy machine!"

Cimarron paused, looked at the raging girl. "*Si*, I use the machine."

Rosa saw the fabric in Cimarron's hands as she marched over. "The russet silk señora bought to make herself a party dress! She'll want that when she returns! Who gave you permission—?"

"Señor Durango," Cimarron said calmly as she finished the last stitch, held it up admiringly. "Señor Durango said to help myself."

"You've been helping yourself ever since you got on this ranch!" Rosa snapped, confronting her. "Anything you want, you get!"

Cimarron thought about Trace, remembered Rosa coming out of his room. "No," she said, "some things I want I can't have. It doesn't matter. I'll leave sometime soon, and you can have him."

Rosa's expression grew hostile, guarded. "I don't know what you're talking about."

"Don't you?" Cimarron gave her a penetrating look. "You're different than I am, Rosa. I won't settle for less than marriage, complete trust and commitment."

A look of humiliation, doubt, crossed the other's dark face. "He will marry me, you'll see!"

"You already have a husband," Cimarron said, "so you're caught in a hopeless situation, too."

"Sanchez won't live forever," the girl said, "he's old, like the Don."

Cimarron looked at her thickening waist, the lines in her face, and she could only pity her. "But you haven't got forever," she said. "Do you think your lover will want you when you have gray streaks in your hair?" She pictured Trace laughing with one of Miss Fancy's girls on each arm at the barbecue. "He can have his choice of young, pretty women, as many as he wants."

She had hit a raw nerve, she thought with regret as she saw the stricken expression on the girl's face. Cimarron had touched something that obviously the girl herself had thought of many times.

"But you won't get him, gringa!" The Mexican girl put her hands on her hips in challenge. "You won't get him!"

"No, I won't get him." Cimarron stood up slowly, smoothed the russet silk of the dress lying over the machine. "He's made fools of both of us, I'm afraid."

The girl shook her head, as if dismissing an idea she didn't want to think about. Her gaze went again to the dress in Cimarron's hands. "You talk to distract me," she accused her, "I think I will go to the old Don, see if he really told you to help yourself to the señora's things, make yourself a dress from her fine silk—"

"But Rosa, I didn't make the dress for me." Cimarron picked up the beautiful garment, walked over to her.

The sultry face registered disbelief. "Then who do you sew for, gringa?"

It occurred to Cimarron that in her own way, Rosa was much like herself. Her childhood must have been one of poverty and loneliness. Maybe no one had ever really taught the girl about caring, so she didn't realize that what she did was wrong. How could she fault Rosa for going into Trace's embrace when Cimarron ached to do the same herself?

She was glad now that she had made this decision, this small gesture. "Rosa," she said, "I made this dress for you."

She held it out and the girl's mouth fell open. Rosa started to reach for it, then shook her head. "I'm only a housekeeper. I have no money to pay for dressmaking—"

"No, no," Cimarron said hurriedly, holding out the dress. "I made it as a gift from the señora's fabric. I think she would want you to have it."

The other woman's face registered disbelief and confusion. "Why—why would you do this for me? I have not had a kind word for you since you arrived. It's a trick! What do you expect to gain from me—?"

"Your friendship, Rosa," Cimarron answered almost in a whisper as she held the dress out. "And maybe as the years pass, maybe you will sometimes light a candle for me when you go to Mass, and think a kind thought for my memory."

Rosa's hands trembled and she seemed at a loss for words. She took a hesitant step, reached out a hand to stroke the fine silk. Her dark eyes looked questioningly into Cimarron's.

Cimarron nodded. "Take it. There's no strings attached, no obligation."

The girl took the dress very slowly, ran her hand over its folds. "I never had anything so fine in my whole life," she breathed. "I even married in one of my señora's used dresses, a nice one, but nothing like this."

Cimarron blinked back a tear, remembering the old dress of Prudence's she had been trying vainly to remake for a party that had never happened. She glanced over at the chests of fabric. Maybe she would make herself a dress. Then she shook her head. She had no heart for it.

Rosa ran her hands lovingly over the glistening, autumn-colored fabric and then looked at Cimarron with a troubled expression. "Perhaps I have misjudged you," she mumbled, "I think again now you are very much like Velvet Eyes—"

Cimarron laughed, trying to keep the tears from her eyes. "So everyone keeps telling me. But I will never be señora here, even though I love the Triple D as if I had lived on the ranchero always."

"My señora would have liked you." The troubled expression on Rosa's face worsened, as if she were fighting some inner battle. "Perhaps I have been wrong...." Her voice trailed off with a sob, and clutching the dress to her, she turned and ran out of the room.

The rest of the day passed in a blur. Cimarron was exhausted and went to bed early. Still, it must have been the middle of the night when she awoke with a start, listening. The house was as quiet as a tomb, she thought as she sat up in bed, holding her breath, listening. *Had she heard someone call her name?* It was a warm night for early October, and a breeze blew around the hacienda, rattling the roof tiles, making the big house creak and groan. She listened closely. It was only her imagination, but the wind seemed to whisper to her, "Cimmmarrron . . . Cimmmarron...."

A sudden gust of wind blew open the French doors leading out onto the upstairs porch. "Cimmmmarron," it moaned, "Cimarrrron...."

She must be losing her mind, she thought, shaking her head to clear it as she got out of bed, reaching for a light wrapper and slippers. She went over, closed the doors, leaned against them. No, it was just a bad dream brought about by the old man's comments about hearing skirts rustling through the house. She was tempted to go down the hall and see if the dress were hanging in the wardrobe. What would she do if it weren't? This was loco. She ought to go back to bed. Yes, that's what she would do. She'd get in bed, forget this strange dream and go back to sleep.

But as she started toward the bed, she bumped into the table and knocked over the perfume bottle. Cimarron took a deep breath and the scent came to her. First, it was so slight, she thought it was only her imagination, like the scent from a dried wedding bouquet that evokes memories of a past, happy day now gone forever. She took another breath. The sweet, exotic fragrance seemed to drift like wispy fog trailing on the night air. *Oleander,* she thought, realizing the fact she'd been groping for. *All the oleander on the ranch smelled like Velvet Eyes's perfume.* The hair raised on the back of her neck at the thought, but she was not really afraid. The fragrance, the whispering voice seemed almost to wrap her in a protective cocoon as she stood there in the darkness.

Without even thinking, she crossed herself, although she was not Catholic. "Velvet Eyes?" she blurted. She felt foolish then, calling out the name of a faithless señora who had run away with a lover. Whatever had made her think of Ojos de Pana? Curiously, Cimarron went out in the hall. It was so quiet, except for the breeze, that she could hear her own footsteps. She paused for a moment at Trace's door, wondering if he lay in there with the wife of his *compadre* in his arms.

The thought of his making love to Rosa made her wince.

"Cimmmmarron," the house seemed to sigh and whisper, "Cimmarrronnn. . . ."

She tiptoed down to the señora's room and opened the door. In the moonlight through the half-opened drapes, the portrait seemed almost alive. Cimarron stared at it. For a moment she would have sworn she saw the eyes blink, the portrait breathe. And the fragrance seemed so strong in this room that Cimarron gasped.

She turned, looked at the portrait again, decided only the scudding clouds crossing the bright moon made the portrait seem alive. *What was the woman in the portrait trying to tell her?* "Velvet Eyes, what is it?"

The frame still hanging crooked on the wall annoyed Cimarron's tidy soul. Automatically, she reached to straighten the dusty painting. But as her fingers reached out, the wind picked up outside, and a gust blew open the French doors. The crooked painting forgotten, Cimarron ran to close the doors. When she did, she heard the slightest whisper, "Cimarron . . . Cimarron. . . ."

"Is someone out there?" She went out on the upstairs porch, looked around. You idiot, she scolded herself, wouldn't they all laugh if they could see you talking to the wind, to portraits? The wind gusted again, slammed the door behind her. She tried to go back inside.

Double damnation! She was locked out. Now what? She imagined walking along the porch, banging on the French doors of each room to get in. She shook her head. She dared not disturb the sick old man, and she would be embarrassed to knock at Luis' door, tell him just how she had ended up locked out on the hacienda balconies. He would be so patronizing, so glibly understanding of a woman's clumsy stupidity.

Well, she sure wouldn't knock on Trace's door. Suppose Rosa was in there? As embarrassing as it was, she'd go down, knock on the glass where little Turquoise slept in a room of the servants' quarters. Maybe she could awaken the little girl, get her to let her back in the house without anyone's being the wiser. Yes, that's what she'd do.

Cimarron went down the outside steps, across the courtyard. The breeze stopped as suddenly as it had started, making Cimarron doubt her own sanity. Had she only imagined it had blown hard for several minutes, whispered her name?

She sat down on the wall of the fountain, watching the wavering moon floating on the dark surface like a gold dollar. October, she thought. The Comanche raids would reach their peak in the next several weeks, then things would calm down as the blue northers swept in across the west Texas plains. Even the Comanches hesitated to raid in the winter. When a norther blew in, temperatures plummeted without warning. It might be sunny and warm in the morning, freezing and snowing by afternoon. If Texas could just deal with the Indians a few more weeks, maybe by spring the war would be over and the soldiers would return to help the beleaguered settlers.

Cimarron took a deep breath and imagined she smelled the faint scent of a cigarillo, savoring the memory of the scent of tobacco on Trace as she reached out and trailed her fingers in the warm water, distorting the mirrored image of the Comanche moon.

She heard the sharp little toenails clicking across the flagstones and looked up to see the dog come around the corner of the adobe, dancing across the flagstones to bounce up on the wall beside her and lick her face.

"Was it you?" she laughed. "Was that crying voice only you whining to get in?" A sense of relief swept over her as she patted the little pet. Of course, here she was almost ready to believe in ghosts and it was only the dog that had gotten himself locked out, running from door to door, whimpering and scratching. Why, she had almost believed in her vivid imagination that something called out her name, that a portrait would try to communicate.

The dog panted loudly and Cimarron put him on the fountain wall, wiped perspiration from her own face. *"Si,* it is hot for October, isn't it, small one? Now, we need to slip around to Turquoise's room, see if we can wake her up."

But the dog had other ideas. Before she could stop him, Tequila jumped off the wall into the water paddling happily.

Cimarron laughed as she watched the fat pet swim. "You think they keep that fountain as a swimming pool just for you, don't you, Tequila? I'm hot, too, I wish I had the nerve to. . . ." She wiped her face again, watching the dog paddling merrily in the water. It seemed to look back at her as it swam, inviting her.

"Why not?" she thought recklessly, "after all, no one will see me! We'll both have a swim before we go in."

Quietly, she slipped out of her night clothes and slippers, stepped into the pool. The water bubbling from the fountain was only hip deep, and warm, and she joined the dog splashing and paddling about in the water. *Soon she would be gone from this place forever,* she thought, and tasted salt as the thought came to her. She would not think of that now, she would think only of the pleasure of this moment. She paddled to the other side, stood up. The slight breeze touched her skin like a lover's warm breath on her naked breasts and belly.

Memories came back to her, memories she couldn't stop of Trace Durango. She glanced toward the silent, sleeping ranchero, the quiet bunkhouse. She and the dog seemed to be the only two things awake on the whole Triple D spread as she played in the water like a child. Overhead, the white satin ribbon of the Milky Way stretched off into Forever. Stars sparkled like angels' beacons in the dark sky to guide those who had died tonight on a path on their way home to God.

The small dog swam over to the wall, scrambled out shaking himself, and water flew everywhere. Tequila barked inquiringly at her from his place on the wall.

"Be quiet, boy," she scolded as she splashed. "Next thing you know, someone will come out, and I'd feel silly being caught playing in the fountain like a small child."

"Darlin', you don't look like a small child from here." Trace Durango stepped out of the shadows, threw away his smoke as he walked over to the fountain.

"You peeping Tom!" She crossed her arms over her naked breasts, looked frantically toward her night clothes, but those lay on the flagstones by Trace's side of the fountain. She did the only thing she could. She dropped to her knees in the water, which was just deep enough to cover all but the uppermost swell of her breasts. "How long have you been spying on me?"

"Long enough to enjoy it," he said, coming over, sitting down on the wall next to the wet dog. "No need to be modest, Wild One. I've seen everything you've got to offer several times, remember?"

She felt herself flame with the memory. "A gentleman wouldn't bring it up."

"And would a lady be swimming buck naked in the Triple D fountain?"

"If you weren't always prowling around in the middle of the night, you wouldn't have seen me," she snapped, the water swirling as she moved. "Don't you ever sleep?"

His face was a study in sadness. "Not much anymore. Not since that day Velvet Eyes. . . ." His voice trailed off. Something was eating him, something deep and painful gnawing at his soul. "If I trusted you to understand. . . ." he began, broke off.

"Tell me, Trace." She almost reached out to him but stopped. In that split-second, she remembered about him and Rosa, about the Comancheros. *How could she care about such a man?*

But he had already retreated back into his shell at her hesitation. "I—I can't." His rugged face grew hostile, moody.

She shrugged. Her knees were beginning to ache. "Why don't you be a gentleman, throw me my clothes, and go away?"

He grinned, gave her the slightest shake of his head. "If I were a gentleman, I don't suppose I would have been standing out here watching you play Lady Godiva. That water does look good. Haven't played in the fountain in years." He started unbuttoning his shirt.

"You aren't coming in here?" she gasped.

"Darlin', you just watch me!"

Even as she shook her head, he stripped off his shirt, then sat on the edge of the wall to pull off his boots and socks. Then he stood and unbuckled his belt.

"I'll scream," she threatened.

"Go ahead," he challenged as he slid his pants off. "If everyone runs out, I'll let you explain what we're both doing out here in the fountain. Can't you just imagine Luis's face?"

"Very funny!" Cimarron snapped, backing away from him as he poised naked a moment in the moonlight before stepping into the fountain. She didn't want to look at the dark, muscled half-breed, but she couldn't seem to keep her eyes off him, remembering. . . .

She tried to scoot backward on her knees. It was hard to do. "You said you wouldn't touch me again unless I said 'please.'"

"So say it."

"No, go away." She looked past him at the grinning wet dog watching and wagging his tail as the two naked humans faced each other in the water. She had to get past Trace to get her clothes. For a moment she considered jumping out of the fountain and running around naked to Turquoise's window. Then she vetoed the idea in her own mind. She couldn't see herself wet and naked banging on the glass. Suppose Sanchez came instead of the child?

Trace waded slowly across the fountain to her.

"I'm not cheap," she said desperately, looking up at him.

"You think you can just take me anytime, anyplace, without promising me anything, making any kind of a commitment to me."

"If I trusted you, there'd be a commitment." He reached down touched her face.

"But you don't love me; you don't trust me."

He caught her naked shoulder, slowly pulled her to her feet. "I didn't say I didn't love you. But I don't trust you," he hedged. "I don't trust any woman. They're all a pack of cheating tarts."

She tried to pull away from his steel grip. "You've been hanging around with Miss Fancy's girls too long."

"At least, whores make no bones about what they are." He pulled her wet, naked body against him as they stood there in the hip-deep water.

She decided to pull away from him, jump from the fountain, grab her clothes, and retreat. Yes, that was what she would do.

The wet, naked length of him was like liquid fire against her skin as he pulled her against him so hard she could feel her nipples pressing into his wide chest. She looked up at him, feeling the pulse beat in his hard belly against her, feeling his manhood starting to rise.

"No," she gasped, "I want to go in. They'll be looking for us." She knew she babbled foolishly, but she couldn't seem to stop herself. "I want to get my clothes and go. Nothing's going to come of this and—"

"Cimarron," he tilted her face up to his with one hand. "Shut up. You know I'm going to kiss you, why are you trying to delay me?"

"I didn't beg," she reminded him.

"Then I will. Cimarron, you're driving me loco. All I can think about is you. I thought I would go crazy watching you dance for those renegades, that Cómanchero putting his hands on you, the others licking their lips in anticipation. Even Luis lifting you up on that horse."

She could feel the heat of him, the beat of his heart against her hands. "What are you asking me?"

He frowned, puzzled. "I'm asking you to let me make love

to you, please darlin'. . . ."

It wasn't enough, she thought, *she wouldn't settle for that.* But then his mouth came down on hers and she lost her resolve. "Oh, Trace . . ." Her arms went up around his neck and pulled his face down to her as he kissed her. She loved him. It was pure and simple. And nothing mattered more than that. Not even the fact that he might be one of the dreaded Comanchero. She loved him, and whether he loved her or not, whether he was good or bad didn't matter anymore.

Her mouth meshed with his, their bodies welded together with molten fire as desire swept them. Her tongue slipped between his lips, darting, teasing, promising, until he moaned and opened so that she could stroke the innermost reaches of his mouth.

His hands stroked her wet body until every fiber of her nerves and wet skin seemed to cry out for his touch.

The fountain bubbled behind them, the water lapped gently around their naked bodies as they kissed and caressed.

Trace's hands went to her small waist. "I'm going to take you right here, right now," he gasped and lifted her.

"Your leg," she whispered as she felt him part her thighs, "you'll reinjure that leg!"

"I'm not using my leg." His voice was low, husky as he grasped her small waist. So saying, he slid her onto his throbbing dagger as they stood there in the fountain.

Cimarron gasped at the sensation of his forcing his length up into her as they stood there. Then she sighed in surrender, brought her legs up to clasp his hips with them.

He let her lean backwards in his arms as her grip loosened on his neck and she arched herself. And when her body arched, he bent his head and she felt the heat of his mouth on her wet breasts.

She could feel him throbbing deep within her as he clasped her to him. "Let's finish this on the grass," she whispered.

For a moment, she thought he would refuse. His expression was so intense, she thought he would throw her on the wall, ride her quickly to completion. But he sighed heavily, withdrew. Swinging her up in his arms like a small, naked doll, he carried her to the shadows under the oleander.

The crushed wild flowers were scented and soft under her wet body as she spread her thighs, held up her arms to him. "Ride me," she whispered. "Ride me hard!"

"I like my women and my horses spirited," he gasped as he paused on his knees, looking down at her, water running down his body. "And I never break their spirits."

"No," she whispered as he came to her, "you only break their hearts."

But he didn't answer as he took her, deep and swift and sure. With a gasp of anticipation, she tilted her small hips up for his deeper penetration.

"No," he protested, with a gasp, "I'll hurt you, darlin'—"

"Then hurt me." She dug her nails into his muscular hips. "Then hurt me deep and good!"

He seemed to need no further urging, riding her, dominating her as he did the wild mustangs. Trace Durango was an expert with horses and women, she knew as his mouth teased her breasts, and then he rode her with an increasing intensity.

The feeling was building in her again, that dizzying, falling feeling, and she didn't fight it. She let it take her as she felt him shudder and drive one last time deep and hard into her very being.

"I love you, Trace," she whispered as she felt his body tremble with the effort of giving up its seed. "Oh, I love you so much!"

And as the earth slipped away from her, she thought she heard him gasp, *"Yo te quiero, mi querida,* I love you, my sweetheart."

She was not sure he said it, perhaps she only willed it so, she thought as they shared the feeling together for a long, heart-stopping moment. But he didn't repeat it, and she guessed that she had only imagined it because she wanted to hear it so much.

And finally, it was over. They lay on the grass locked in each other's arms. He raised up on his elbows, touched the tip of her nose with his fingertip. "You're quite a woman, darlin'," he admitted. "I never thought a woman could mean so much to me, make me feel...."

"Yes?"

He sighed regretfully, withdrew from her body as he seemed to withdraw from her emotionally. "Nothing," he said, "nothing." He rolled over on his back, put his arms behind his head, stared up at the sky.

Was he thinking of the señora? Rosa? There was no way she could know as she leaned on one elbow, looking down at him. Whatever it was that haunted him, kept him on the prod, was something she couldn't fight. The phantoms of his mind put too much conflict between them. Jealousy rose in her. Was there no way she could take his mind off the other love? Even while in her arms, had he been whispering "I love you, sweetheart," to some other woman?

She could get his notice! Impulsively, she leaned over, bit his nipple.

"You sassy little wildcat," he swore, pulling her down on top of him to kiss her lips.

She had his full attention now, she knew by the sudden intensity of his gaze, the way his nostrils flared as he breathed deeper. "You were ignoring me," she said. "I wanted your attention."

"You got it," he answered, reaching up to brush her hair back. "Now what else do you want?"

She almost said, "your love and devotion," but hesitated. She couldn't bear it if he threw his head back and laughed at her. "Your body," she tried to keep her voice light, "I want your body, you big stallion."

"Again?" His arms went around her as she lay on him, pressing her breasts flat against his wide chest. "You think I'm some kind of machine? Most men need a little rest before they can do it again."

"Oh?" she traced a path along his cheek with her fingertips and when they brushed against his hard line of a mouth, his expression softened and he kissed her fingertips. "How should I know that?" she asked innocently. "You're the only man I've ever had, and—"

"The only one you're ever gonna have," he said, so softly

she was not sure of his words.

"What did you say?" She waited, wanting him to tell her how much he loved her, wanting some kind of commitment.

"Nothing," he muttered. "Nothing." He rolled her over on her back, started to kiss and caress her skin. "You're beautiful, Cimarron, and passionate. Just the kind of woman every man dreams of."

He was kissing her all over, moving slowly down her body until his tongue flicked her navel, moving lower until his lips brushed her soft thighs.

She felt a surge of apprehension as his lips caressed along the inside of her thigh. "Trace, you . . . aren't going to kiss me . . . there?"

In answer, his lips touched her body where her thighs joined. She could feel his warm breath against her mound. "Trace, no. . . ."

But he paid her no heed, stroking the insides of her thighs with his fingertips, spreading them farther apart as his questing tongue moved closer, closer.

She started to protest again but realized suddenly that she couldn't stop him if she wanted to. She lay on her back with her thighs apart, and he was a big, strong male. He would do with her as he wanted and she wouldn't be able to stop him . . . if she wanted to stop him.

Somehow, her brain protested what his lips were doing, but it felt so good that she lay back in surrender, let it happen. His hands grasped her spread thighs, pulled her to his seeking lips. She felt her pulse, her heartbeat quicken. She trembled at the warm, moistness of his mouth caressing, stroking until she gasped for breath. Then his tongue was a hot, wet blade driving deep in her depths, and she caught the back of his head, pulling him still deeper. She cried out as she arched up and his mouth caressed and claimed her femininity. His big hands reached to cup and love her swelling breasts.

If she had felt desire before, the trembling release of falling over the edge of a precipice, it had been nothing like this. And when he finished with her and slid up to kiss her mouth, she could taste the essence of her on his lips and it excited her all over again.

She looked into his dark eyes, saw the unquenched desire there, ran her hand down to feel him, knew he was ready and able to service her again. Cimarron moved to place her head in his lap, and after a moment's hesitation, she kissed that which had given her so much pleasure.

She felt him gasp, surge with sensation at the touch of her mouth on him. "You don't have to do that," he said, but he didn't push her away.

He was built big, she thought as she kissed and caressed him with her lips. The musky male scent of him, the slightly salty taste of his seed excited her and she teased him with her mouth. Trace lay back with a sigh, tangling his fingers in her hair, pulling her face against him. "You better stop that, darlin'," he warned. "If you keep doing that, I won't be able to control myself. . . ."

His voice trailed off as she increased her caresses, suddenly wanting very much to take him this way. He seemed to fight it only a moment before he groaned and arched up. She felt the surge, the throbbing as she accepted him still deeper while her hands reached up to stroke his nipples.

And as he came, she drank his seed eagerly and deeply as he writhed under her and cursed. "Cimarron, damn you! Damn you, Wild One, for making me want you so much!"

Chapter Twenty-Two

Trace couldn't stop himself now, couldn't control his own primitive desires. As her seeking mouth took him, he tangled his fingers in her long blond hair, pulled the small face against his maleness. She seemed determined to exhaust him, take him completely. Finally he relaxed and let her warm lips love him, drain him as no other woman ever had. Cimarron was his now, all his. He knew that even as he pulled her up to kiss her mouth, tasted his own seed on her soft lips.

He had possessed her completely. *No, she possessed him completely.* No woman had ever loved him with such skill, no, not even the highest-priced girls of the bordellos. If he hadn't had the evidence of her virginity once smeared on his body, he would have sworn Cimarron was the most experienced goddess of love he'd ever taken. That was the trouble with women. He sighed as he laid her in the protective bend of his arm, her head resting in the hollow of his shoulder. They were all just tarts, climbing from one man's bed to another. They knew a man's weakness, used their bodies to take advantage of him.

Her hair tumbled across his chest like corn silk and her soft skin felt warm against his naked body as she snuggled against him. Instinctively, he reached out protectively to lay his other hand across her lean belly.

"I love you, Trace, *yo ti amo,*" she whispered. "Oh, I love you so much!"

He felt himself stiffen, draw away from her mentally. No woman had said that to him in six months. And the other had meant it in a different way.

I love you, Trace. The words echoed out of the past, and blew about in his memory like dead leaves of autumn before winter's icy breath. *I love you, Trace.* Velvet Eyes had lied even as Cimarron must be lying now. Women threw those words about so easily, just as men said "good morning." They didn't have to mean it to say it.

I love you, Trace. He didn't want to remember that day, but Cimarron's words had brought them back with a rush. Well, Velvet Eyes hadn't loved him, or the old Don, either. Otherwise, she would never have left them. She had betrayed Trace even as she betrayed his father . . . no, not his father. . . . That was the deepest, most bitter betrayal of all. He would never trust a woman again, and one cannot love deeply without trust, commitment. Cimarron had been trying to get through the locked, barred doors to his heart, his soul, but he had vowed never to let her. Those who opened up, who surrendered themselves to another person, got hurt too badly. No woman would ever do to him what Velvet Eyes had done to the old Don. But if there was ever one who might slip past his hard, angry facade, it was the blonde laying here in his arms.

Trace reached down, brushed Cimarron's hair back. She smiled faintly, snuggled closer to his big chest. He could see she was dropping off to sleep, secure in the protection of his strong arms. *Si,* if any woman could hurt him, destroy him, it would be the Wild One. But he would not let her, he resolved with steely determination. He would enjoy her body as he would a whore's, but never would he let her get too deep inside him where she could break his heart.

He sighed, looking up at the canopy of stars over them, listening to crickets faintly chirping from out on the prairie, Cimarron's rhythmic breathing.

He didn't want to remember the terrible day that Velvet Eyes had left, but the sharp fragments of memory remained, a bit here and there, like the shattered pieces of his heart. He recalled now that Rosa had gone up to pack the bag while the three of them, he and Velvet Eyes and Luis, stood confronting each other in the study.

Trace had stared at her. She had stood there, Luis directly behind her. "You're not serious! After all these years, you're not going to leave Father for some other man?"

Her dark, beautiful face was a mask of emotions that he could not quite decipher. "*Si*, Trace, as I told you, I'm going when Rosa gets back down here with my things."

Trace shook his head, studying her. There might be a gray hair or two in the ebony locks now as she approached forty, but she was still the great beauty Uncle Luis had painted many years ago. Yes, he could see why Don Diego de Durango had fallen madly in love with the Cheyenne girl less than half his age.

"No," he said, striding over to confront her. "No, you can't just sneak away while Father is gone. At least stay until he gets back and discuss this—"

"You're so young, Trace." She bit her lip, moved to stand between him and Luis who leaned against the desk, hands in his pockets. "All these years, it's been a facade. I—I never really loved Diego."

"But you've been married to him for twenty-five years," Trace protested as he confronted her. "It was a good marriage—"

"Was it?" she flared. "No one knows what goes on in a marriage but the two people in it. You have seen only what you wanted to see. Now, I've met a man, a Yankee captain—"

"You won't leave until you discuss this with Father," Trace said coolly, standing feet wide apart. He wasn't wearing a gun, it was in the rack at the end of the study. If need be, he would hold her here until the Don returned.

He looked at Uncle Luis, standing ill at ease, hands still in his pockets. "Luis, you don't intend to help her leave? Where's your loyalty to your brother?"

Luis shrugged. "My loyalty to Diego tells me to let her go and good riddance! Her mind's made up, Trace. I've already tried to talk her out of it. And she's right about the marriage.

If you hadn't idolized her so, you might have realized years ago that idols have feet of clay, that no woman can really be trusted."

Trace looked from one to the other. "What are you driving at?"

Velvet Eyes looked agonized but Luis sighed in resignation. "We've kept this secret too long. Velvet Eyes, you might as well tell him what I'm talking about."

She glanced from one to the other, back to Luis. Trace had never seen such pain on a face before. "Oh, Luis, don't make me tell him that, don't—"

"Tell him," Luis insisted. "Otherwise, he won't believe the rest of it. He's going to stop you from leaving with your lover."

"Tell me what?" Trace said, staring down at her, thinking how small, how vulnerable she looked. But a deadly black widow spider was small, too. "I can't believe all this I'm hearing. I—I can't believe you're running away with some man."

"You're so trusting, Trace," she said, and tears came to her eyes. "We've been rendezvousing all those times my naive family thought I was off doing charity work. I met him at a party in Galveston when the Yankees still held it."

He shook his head. "You've done this blatantly, right under the Don's nose, when he trusted you so much?"

She shrugged, glanced at Luis. "*Si*. That made it easy, you see. Yesterday, I rode out to make the final plans. If you and Rosa hadn't come in just now, we could have avoided this scene. I—I would have left a note of explanation someplace where you'd find it, understand—"

"A note? You cared no more than that? If I didn't hear it from your own lips, nothing in this world could make me believe what I'm hearing." A sinking sensation came to him, as if he were drowning. *Si*, it was true Velvet Eyes was often out on her little missions of mercy. No one thought anything about it. Last night at dinner, Trace had had a distinct feeling she was hiding something. But he had never suspected anything like this.

She had planned to wipe out twenty-five years of marriage

by just leaving a note where one of them might find it. "No," he shook his head stubbornly. "I don't believe you would be faithless to the Don. He worships and trusts you like the Madonna herself. Dammit! I don't believe—"

"You're a naive and foolish boy." Luis frowned. "My brother would be better off without her. That's why I'll drive her to meet this man. To protect Diego, we'll say she decided to return to her Cheyenne people. This isn't the first time the saintly wife has played the whore—"

"Watch what you call her!" Trace's eyes flashed. He doubled his fists as he advanced on the Spaniard, but she moved again to keep her body between them.

Luis sighed. "Tell him, Velvet Eyes."

She looked wildly from one to the other. "No, Luis, don't make me say that."

Luis's face was impassive as he stood there, hands in pockets. "He'll never believe you otherwise, won't let you go. Tell him."

Trace saw her hand tremble as she reached up to brush her hair back. "This—this is not the first man I have been unfaithful with." Her voice came so low, Trace had to strain to hear her.

"What? I don't believe you! You are a loved and trusted wife to a fine man, you wouldn't—"

Luis laughed. "Oh, yes, she would. All these years, behind Diego's unsuspecting back."

"I'll tell him," Trace snarled. "He'll call the man out, kill him—"

"I think you won't," Luis said. "Because you'll break my brother's heart."

Trace felt suddenly dizzy as he looked into the handsome sneering face, the agonized, gentle eyes of the señora. *And then he knew what Luis was hinting at.* All these years, Don Diego's dashing younger brother had lived on the Triple D. And Luis was Velvet Eyes's own age.

He could feel the rage building in him. "If it's you, Uncle Luis, I'll kill you myself!"

"Tell him, sweet one." The handsome Spaniard brushed against her rigid back.

She looked around at him in an agony of appeal, then back to Trace. "Luis came home from Spain only a few weeks after Diego and I married. Diego was old, but his brother was so young, so handsome."

Trace gaped at her. Any moment, he would awaken from this nightmare about the woman he adored, idolized. "Are you telling me you've been sleeping with Uncle Luis all these years? Why, my father—"

Luis nudged her, sighed. "Tell him, sweet one."

"Don Diego is . . . is not your father, Trace," she said wearily, tears running down her face. "I can only pray that someday you'll understand why I'm saying this—"

"I don't understand one damned bit!" Trace said grimly. "I walk in here, you start saying loco words that destroy me, destroy everything I hold sacred, talk crazy about leaving notes and disappearing! Then ask me to understand—?"

"Trace, please," she implored, glancing back at Luis, who nodded encouragement to her. "I—the man you have called 'Father' all these years is not. I—I was unfaithful to my husband from the first."

For a long moment, Trace swayed as the words struck him like a fist. She was bringing his world crashing down around him with a handful of words. "What—what are you saying?"

Luis smiled sadly. "Does she have to draw you a picture, Trace? You're too naive, too trusting. Stop idolizing women, putting them up on pedestals. None of them can be trusted, as you've just seen."

"When I tell my father—"

"But he isn't your father, *comprende?*" Luis smiled. "So stop calling him that. I bitterly regret what's happened, but I can't change it. She was beautiful, I was young. And her husband was old enough to be her papa. Now the three of us are going to keep this secret. What good would it do to hurt my brother with it?"

Trace nodded dumbly. He was too destroyed emotionally even to think. Luis was right. Trace would do whatever it took now to protect his father—no, he would not call him that now. He would call him the Don. And sooner or later, he would kill the younger brother who had cuckolded the old man with the faithless wife.

No, if he had not heard it from her own lips, Trace would not have believed any of this. She had a reputation for truthfulness. If she said it, it must be so. He blinked at Luis. "You won't try to stop her from leaving wtih this other man?"

Luis shrugged. "Not if she wants to go. She's broken my heart all these years; now the Yankee is welcome to whatever pain and pleasure she'll bring him. I'll pick up the pieces of my life and find another." He rubbed his hand across his eyes. "If there's a lesson in this, Trace, it's that a smart *hombre* doesn't trust a woman, let her break his heart. Enjoy them as you do a good wine, a cigar, but don't ever get involved enough so she can hurt you."

His heart was already broken. He could hurt no more than he hurt at this moment. The sharp pains in his chest must be caused by the jagged edges. *No, he had learned his lesson. His own mother was a whore. All women were faithless tarts. Women were not to be trusted, only used and enjoyed.* Trace looked at the pair, too agonized to speak.

The little dog, Tequila, bounded off the sofa. It danced over, growled at Luis, barked at the señora to be picked up. But she didn't move. In the silence, the only sound was the dog whining, dancing around the señora's feet.

Trace felt abruptly very weary. He was caught in a nightmare and couldn't awaken. If he didn't fight it, maybe it would pass and things would be as before. "You're going then, before the Don returns?"

Her eyes appealed to him. "*Si*, I—I'm going to meet my captain. Luis will drive me to the rendezvous."

"*I* should drive you so I could meet and kill the son-ovabitch! But you're not worth it!" The fury and the hurt surged in him as he realized the nightmare was reality. He would never again sleep soundly because when he did, he would see her lovely face, relive this agony time after time. "Then go, *puta!*" Trace snarled, "Get out of here before your husband returns, you faithless whore!"

"Trace, I . . ." Her voice trailed off and the small dog cocked its head, looked from one to the other. "I—I can't take the dog where I'm going, Trace; look after him."

He stared at her, laughed without humor. "You're walking out, leaving a pile of broken hearts, destroyed emotions, and you worry about a damned dog? *Si*, Señora Durango," he bowed coldly, "I'll look after your dog!"

She held out a hand to him and he slapped it away. "Trace, I pray that someday you'll find out why I did this, find out—"

"I know enough now, you whore!" he raged, backing away from her. "If you're going, get out before the old man comes back! Don't break his heart like you've just broken mine!"

Luis gave him a sympathetic look. "I'm sorry you had to find that out, Trace. We never really meant for you to know. I was more her age and it just happened—"

"For God's sake!" Trace raged. "Don't tell me the lurid details! I don't think I can stand any more!"

Luis shrugged, his face sad. "I've lived with it all these years. I—I never meant to betray my brother—"

"But you did!" Trace snarled, lunging toward him again. Again, Velvet Eyes fought to stay between them, struck Trace's face. Never before in his entire life had she ever raised her hand to him. He was as stunned by the act as he was by the sting of her fingers on his cheek. Tears came to his eyes. It must be true. She didn't love him or the Don. "Get out of here, *puta!* You destroy me with your unfaithfulness that I must now protect your husband from! Get off this ranch, you whore!"

He heard footsteps behind him and Rosa came into the study with the señora's bag. Trace rubbed his hand across his cheek. "You would strike me to protect him?"

There were tears in Ojos de Pana's eyes. "Someday, maybe you'll understand."

Rosa paused, looking shocked at what she'd seen. She came over, handed the señora the small bag. "Please, señora, you'll need a maid. No one does your hair like I can do! Please take me with you!"

The señora took a deep breath, shook her head. "No, Rosa, you have a family." She leaned over, picked up the whimpering dog with her free hand. "No, my pet, you can't go with me. Rosa, take him." She handed her Tequila.

The servant was almost weeping. "You will not even take your dog?"

"No, I can't take him. Tell my husband . . ." She didn't finish. Tears ran unchecked down her face as she looked at Trace. "I pray that someday you'll find out how very much I loved you. Are you ready, Luis?"

Luis gave a resigned shrug as he stood close to her. "If you still insist on going, I'll drive you there."

"Oh!" Rosa put her hand to her mouth in dismay, "I forgot to pack your favorite dress, señora, the moonlight one. Let me run back upstairs—"

"Never mind," the señora said, "when I finally need it, I—I'll come back for it."

Luis moved impatiently. "If we're going, let's go."

Velvet Eyes walked slowly to the door of the study, Luis right behind her. At the door she paused, looked back at Trace with obvious agony. Her small hands twisted the handle of the little bag. "I—I hope someday you'll understand," she said, "I hope the two of you will finally discover . . . well, just how much I loved you."

"Love!" Trace laughed coldly. "Don't talk to me of love, you cheating bitch! Get off this ranch and leave us to pick up the broken pieces of our hearts!"

Luis bit his lip, still standing with hands in his coat. "I regret having to be involved in this, but I'm determined to protect my brother. Diego would insist on calling him out, and he's too old for dueling."

"I'm not," Trace raged. "I'd happily put a bullet in the devil's heart!"

Luis wiped his eyes. "Diego's honor wouldn't allow you to take his place. We must protect him at all costs, so I'll drive her to meet this damned man. When I get back, we'll make up a story with all the details about how she returned to the Cheyenne."

The señora gave Trace one last agonized look, half raised her hand to him. "The letter is—"

But Luis nudged her. "Let's get this over with if you're determined to go. And for God's sake, don't write Diego any letter asking forgiveness, asking him to understand. He'd know then that we've lied to him. I feel like killing that damned captain myself!"

And then they were gone. Trace and Rosa went to the window, peered out as the buggy drove away. The little dog whimpered and whined in Rosa's arms.

Rosa turned to Trace, sobbing. "What was said while I was gone? Why is she going?"

He blinked back the tears, watching her lean over, put the small dog on the floor. It ran to the door, scratched frantically, wanting out, whimpering.

Trace watched it, drained of all emotion. "Nothing else was said," he lied. "Just what you heard. She's running away with some Yankee. We must protect the old Don from this knowledge."

"But why would she leave? She loved him so!"

"We only thought she did," he whispered. "We only thought she loved us all. But I'll never trust again. It hurts too much when they betray you."

The little dog whimpered again.

Trace came out of his memories with a start. He and Cimarron still lay naked under the oleander bushes. The wet dog whined a second time, jumped from the fountain wall, ran over to join them. The dog yapped, licking his face. Trace had been almost asleep, remembering. . . .

He loved Cimarron so much. He pulled her to him protectively, kissed her soft lips. Yes, he loved her, but he would not be hurt again, spend the rest of his life wondering if the children she produced were really his own. He couldn't give his love completely because he was too afraid to trust her with his heart. No woman would do to him what Velvet Eyes had done to his fath—to the old Don.

The breeze blew petals of blossoms that fluttered as they fell, lit on her bare breasts. He leaned over, blew them away, kissed her pink nipples.

She moaned and stretched, smiled up at him. "I love you," she whispered.

He hesitated, knowing what she wanted to hear, knowing he couldn't bring himself to say it. It made him too vulnerable. If she ever found out how much he really cared, she would use it as a weapon to hurt him. "We need to go in," he said brusquely as she sat up.

He saw the disappointment in her eyes as she shook her hair back, brushed the fallen petals from her naked body. "Of course," she said, and her voice shook a little. "We need to go in. The village doxie is finished satisfying randy males out in the bushes for this evening."

"Don't talk that way," he snapped.

"How was I?" she demanded, and anger built in her voice. "Was I as good as Miss Fancy's girls? You think I was satisfactory enough for her to offer me a job?"

He grabbed her wrist, jerked her close against him. "Don't talk like that! If another man touched you, you know I'd kill him!"

"But *you* can make love to anyone you want, isn't that right?" She stood up. "Curiosity is just eating me. Tell me, am I as good as Rosa?"

"Rosa?" He stood up slowly, looked at her in genuine puzzlement. How could she know about Rosa's attempts to seduce him? "Darlin', I don't know what the hell you're talking about! Rosa and I never—"

"You liar!" she almost shouted as she confronted him. "You bald-faced, double-dipped liar! I saw her coming out of your room early that morning before we had that run-in at the corral! And the night of the Comanche raid, I know she must have been up in your room!" Cimarron turned, stalked over to the fountain, picked up her clothes.

The little dog danced happily after Trace as he followed her in bewilderment and picked up his own clothes. "I swear, Cimarron, I've never made love to Rosa! She's married to my *compadre*. I would never—"

"Ha! Not unless you got the chance!" She pulled on her nightdress with jerky, angry gestures. "If you really cared about me, you'd ask me to marry you! A Texan always puts his brand on what belongs to him, what he values!"

"Cimarron," he hesitated as he pulled on his clothes.

"There's things you don't know about, things I can't tell you. If you knew—"

"I know when I'm being used! You think you can add me to your string of women, that I'll settle for the crumbs! Well, I want the whole cake!"

He pulled her kicking and struggling up against him. "I care about you," he insisted. "And you're mine in a way you can never belong to any other man!" His lips covered hers, kissing her even as she struggled and tried to pull away. She could fight him but she couldn't win. He was strong enough to dominate her, force her to bend to his will. Now he pulled her against him so hard she gasped for breath. His hot lips covered hers, forcing them open so he could plunge his tongue deep, reminding her that she was his.

He could taste the tears running down her face as he kissed her cheeks. She fought him like fury, but he twisted her arms behind her, held them pinned there as he lifted her to kiss her breasts in the loose neck of her nightdress. "You're mine, Cimarron," he whispered fiercely, as he tangled his other hand in her hair and forced her face up to his where she could do nothing but submit to his kisses. "Always remember that, Wild One. I've broken and tamed you for myself, and I'll kill the man who touches you!"

She cried openly now, the tears coursing down her cheeks as she surrendered, let him kiss her into submission. "So I won't be your wife," she whispered, "I'm just your slut! When you need me in your bed or out under the trees, you just snap your fingers and I'll come entertain you!"

"If you say so." He looked down at her, reached to brush the tears off her face. He couldn't, wouldn't tell her. She had too big a hold on him now. And in the long run, she would only break his heart. He pulled her up against him, kissed her deeply again while she hung almost limp and submissive in his arms. And he missed the untamed fire of her, the answering passion he had known before. He could feel her heart pounding hard against him, the shaking of her body as she sobbed.

He kissed her again, already wanting her, wanting the joyous coupling they had shared. No, wanting more than that. He hungered for that sharing of souls, that crest of passion that took a blending of spirits to achieve.

He pulled back and she looked up at him, cold and angry. She was stiff now in his embrace. "If you've had enough of me this evening, Mr. Durango, may I go in now?"

He sighed, nodded as he relaxed his grip, let her step away from him. What he really wanted to do was take her up there to his bed, make love to her again, and sleep the rest of the night with her curled up warm and safe in the protection of his arms. "*Si*, you can go in. By the way, I left the front door open. You aren't locked out."

Her nostrils flared with anger. "Why you—!" She grabbed up her slippers, stalked across the flagstones to the house, the small dog dancing around her feet.

Women! He watched her march to the house before he gathered up his clothes, dressed. He went into the study, got a bottle of tequila. He sat a long time in the darkness, thinking. He couldn't see any way out fo the dilemma. He had dealt with Comanches, gunfighters, panthers, and bad bulls. But the wild one with the yellow hair had him hesitant and mystified. He didn't stumble up to his room until he was very, very drunk.

He still hadn't made up his mind what to do about Cimarron at noon the next day as he went into the kitchen to get something for his pounding head.

Rosa frowned at him as she dished up food, put it on a tray. "What's the matter with you? You missed breakfast and it's nearly time for dinner. You sick?"

"You might say that," he sighed, getting himself a drink of water from the dipper. "That the old man's plate?"

"*Si*. Would you take it up to him? It's his favorite today, rabbit stew. Since he seems to be getting worse, I thought, well, you know. . . ." Her voice trailed off significantly and he nodded to show he understood. Rosa didn't seem to like the old man much anymore since the señora had left; maybe she held Don Diego responsible in some way. Ah, if his *compadre,* Sanchez, only knew that his wife . . . well, Trace wouldn't tell him. Trace could protect him from hurtful knowledge just like he could Don Diego.

Trace took a deep sniff. "Hmm. Smells good."

"Now don't you eat part of that as you go up," she admonished, waving a wooden spoon threateningly. "I save my best spices for him, since it's so hard to get him to eat. You others can make do with plain salt and chili peppers."

"Yes, ma'am," he said politely, taking the tray. "You've been extra good to him, Rosa. The señora would have appreciated it, as do we all."

Her face reflected inner turmoil. "Trace, we've known each other a long time. I've been thinking about her a lot lately. You never told me what was said while I was upstairs packing her bag."

His head hurt and he didn't want to think about his mother. "You were there that day in the study, Rosa, you heard the same things I did. There was nothing else of importance," he lied.

"But sometimes even when you think you know people well," she protested, "you don't really know them at all."

"How true." He thought again that he would never have suspected his mother of carrying on an affair with his uncle. "Nobody really knows what goes on in someone else's head, I guess, or behind closed doors."

"That's what I mean," she persisted. "I sometimes think she left because Don Diego was cruel to her."

Trace stared at her in astonishment. "I don't know where you got that idea. He adored her."

"But you don't know that for sure. She had to have some reason to leave," the Mexican girl said thoughtfully. "Perhaps behind closed doors, he mistreated her—"

"No, I don't think so. She—she had secrets we never dreamed of, Rosa." It was too painful to discuss anymore. "I'll take this tray on up to him now."

She raised her hand as if to stop him, then waved him on. "*Si*, go feed the old one, and by then I'll have dinner on the table for the rest of us."

He backed out of the kitchen with the tray, walked slowly up through the big ballroom. Little Tequila came out of the study, sniffed inquiringly as Trace passed him headed for the stairs. Then Tequila licked his chops and scampered happily along behind him.

Trace laughed in spite of his aching head. "No, no, little pet. This is special for the Don. Spoiled little dogs should quit eating off everybody's plate, anyway."

He thought about Rosa as he went down the hall. Faithless women cause so much pain, so much anguish to men who loved them. He sighed as he carried the tray into the old man's room. Of course Rosa cheated on Sanchez regularly. What Trace wondered was how Cimarron had figured it out. And just how much did she really know?

Chapter Twenty-Three

Cimarron sat next to the old Don's bed entertaining him and Luis with conversation as Trace entered with the tray, followed closely by the little dog.

She smiled as she stood up, took the tray from Trace's hands. "Ah, Señor Durango, here's your dinner tray. And it looks delicious. I can hardly wait for mine."

Luis lounged against a chair. "She's right, sir. Rabbit stew, your favorite. Looks like Rosa has outdone herself this time."

Cimarron made inane chatter with the old man as she put the tray on the bed. She didn't want to look at Trace after spending a sleepless night trying to decide what to do about him. He was either incapable of love or had been so scarred by past experience that he would never make a commitment. What else could she expect from a Comanchero?

Don Diego frowned and played with the spoon listlessly. "It looks good, but I'm still feeling bad from my last attack. I don't think I'm hungry."

Trace frowned. "You need to eat to keep up your strength. And it looks like Rosa has gone to a lot of trouble. Here, let me help you." He sat down on the edge of the bed, took the spoon, offered the old man a bite. But the Don shook his head, pushed the spoon away.

"I'm not so weak and sick I have to be treated like a baby! I'm still the boss here, and don't you forget it."

"I was only trying to help." Trace made a gesture of

annoyance as he stood up, moved over to look out the window.

Luis came to the bed, made a soothing gesture. "Trace is right, Diego." He gave Cimarron a nod as he took the spoon from the old man's hand. "Now, let me help you with this delicious stew—"

"You're as bad as he is," the Don snapped. "Just leave the tray and I'll eat it in a minute." His bushy white brows knitted together over his dark eyes. "Go on down and eat, all of you. I'll finish the stew in my own time."

Luis looked so hurt, so offended by the Don's sharp tone that Cimarron's heart went out to him. "You two men go on down to dinner," she said softly. "I'll stay here with Don Diego for a while. I'll bet he'll eat for me."

He ran his hand through his mane of white hair. "*Si*, maybe for you, señorita," he said with a charming smile as his left hand reached for a cigar.

Luis reached out as if to stop him, seemed to think better of it. "The doctor says cigars are bad for you—"

"By the Blessed Virgin's head!" the Don said as he lit it with a jerky, angry motion. "The fact that I'm dying is the worst-kept secret in the whole county, and you're worried about me smoking cigars?"

Luis made an agonized, helpless gesture and raised his eyebrows at Cimarron. "I was only thinking of what's best for you—"

"Never mind," Cimarron said hurriedly. "You and Trace go on to dinner. I'll sit here a while and see that he eats."

The two gave her grateful looks and left the room. The old man took the cigar from his lips and sank back on his pillows with a satisfied sigh. "Get that out of my sight. I'll eat it after a while."

"You should be ashamed of yourself," she scolded as she took the tray, set it on the floor by the bed. "You keep everyone shaking with fear of your temper."

He looked at her thoughtfully as he smoked. "But you're not afraid of me, are you, señorita?"

She smiled at him, shook her head. "I see a crusty old lion who likes to make everyone tremble with his roar. But I think inside you are as soft as feathers."

He threw back his head, laughed uproariously. "I like you, you know that, Cimarron? You've got grit, spunk. If God would grant me two wishes, one of them would be that you stay on this ranch forever."

She studied his hawklike profile, the hard mouth. Yes, she could see why this feisty old man had managed to hold his empire against wild animals, renegades, and Indians. "What would your other wish be?" she asked softly.

For just a moment, she saw the courage in his strong face waver. "I—I would ask for a miracle. That it's all a mistake, that I'm not dying after all, and will live to see my grandchildren riding across the lands of the Triple D."

She swallowed hard, blinked back the tears. What words of comfort could she give him? "Maybe it will finally turn out that the doctor is mistaken," she said.

The little dog lay on the bed and the old man stroked it absently while he smoked.

Cimarron patted his hand. "You really should eat," she scolded him softly.

He nodded. "For you, señorita, maybe I will when I finish my cigar. When one is old, depressed because he's dying, he does not feel obligated to do what pleases others if he doesn't feel like it."

She laughed. "I suspect, Don Diego, you always did exactly what you wanted to."

He grinned and the smoke curled around his head. "Mostly," he admitted, "except where Dallas and Velvet Eyes were concerned. I was always a slave to beautiful women."

Cimarron winked at him. "I suspect you are one of the last of the true gentlemen, Don Diego, one who really appreciates and idolizes women."

"*Si*, you understand me, Cimarron." He stroked the dog absently and smoked his cigar. "Like my wife, you also see through me. She said I was a white-maned old lion who roared a lot more than he bit. When everyone else trembled before the Don, she went her merry way, spending my money, doing as she wished. I could never say no to her, nor did I want to."

"And what was Dallas like?" she asked, looking down at the tray on the floor. If he didn't eat it soon, it would be cold and unappetizing. "I heard you sent her to school in Boston."

He sighed regretfully. "Dallas. It means 'spirited,' and she was. I shouldn't have sent her. Dallas was a tomboy, she loved the ranch, rode as well as any man. She could handle a gun, too. The señora was always afraid of guns, the noise, I think. She never learned to shoot. Velvet Eyes opposed sending Dallas off. We argued over it. In fact, our very last argument the morning before my wife disappeared was over that."

"And?"

His eyes grew moist. "Dallas kept writing, asking to come home. She was unhappy in that snooty, genteel school. She ran away from Miss Priddy's just before the war started and then we couldn't search because of the fighting. When it ends, I'll have police and sheriffs all over the country looking for her."

He crushed the cigar out in the ashtray on the bedside table. The dog stretched, shook himself all over.

"Don Diego," she looked toward the tray on the floor, "wouldn't you like to try some of that rabbit stew now?"

He sighed, leaned back against his pillows, eyes closed. "Not really; later. Maybe a glass of water, please."

"Of course." She got up, crossed the room to the water pitcher. He really did look very weak and ill, she thought as he lay back against the pillows. It wasn't hard to believe he was dying. And then Luis would control the ranch. She could have Luis and be señora of the ranch, too. But she knew she would never do that. She was in love with Trace. Should she leave the Triple D or take a chance that her suspicions about the Comancheros weren't true? Should she stay and gamble that he might finally care as much for her as she cared for him? The decision seemed overwhelming.

She poured the water, started back across the room. The little dog hopped down on the other side of the bed as she approached. For only a second she was puzzled and, then she knew immediately what the chihuahua was up to.

"Tequila! You bad boy!" she ran around the bed, put the water on the bedside table, grabbed the greedy pet. But Tequila still managed to gobble two or three good bites off the old Don's tray. "You shouldn't eat Don Diego's stew! Rosa would have fed you in the kitchen!"

She picked the dog up, but it didn't look as if it felt a bit guilty. Tequila licked his mouth and wagged his tail, looking back down at the tray.

Don Diego opened his eyes, gestured. "Let the dog have it. I'm not hungry anyway. I'd like to rest a while if you don't mind. . . ."

She put the dog on the bed where it promptly crawled under the covers with only the shoebutton nose sticking out. "Oh, well," she shrugged, leaning over to pick up the tray, "It's cold now, anyway. Don Diego, I'll take this to the kitchen, bring you another tray later when you awaken."

He didn't answer. The strong Spanish face relaxed as he dozed off, and she stopped in the doorway, studying him, thinking what a courageous old warrior he was, thinking how curious it was that he strongly resembled. . . . Tequila stuck his head out from under the cover, cocked it at her.

She laughed, snapped her fingers. "Okay, Tequila, I won't scold you anymore. Now come on down to the kitchen with me before you wake him up."

The chihuahua trotted obediently at her heels as she took the tray, went down the stairs. Rosa had evidently cleaned up the kitchen and was off in another part of the house. She could hear Trace and Luis talking ranch business as they smoked and had a drink in the study. Cimarron set the bowl of cold stew on the floor for the dog, got herself a dishful from the pot on the stove.

She was momentarily tempted by Rosa's pepper shaker of fine spices, then shook her head, remembering the war had made such things scarce and expensive. The old man deserved any kindness they could give him. Cimarron could make do with a little salt. It was hot in the kitchen, she thought as she looked down at the small dog. It nosed in the bowl of cold stew halfheartedly, finally walked away after one or two bites.

"You must be sick, puppy," she said jokingly, wiping perspiration from her face, "I never saw you turn down food before. Come on, let's go sit on the back porch where it's cool." She opened the screen.

The whole ranch seemed to be taking a siesta on this autumn afternoon, she thought as she sat down on the porch steps, took a bite of stew. Trace was right. Rosa's food was delicious. The old man had missed a treat by skipping dinner. After a while, when he awakened, Cimarron would try carrying another tray up to his room.

As she finished, she offered the empty bowl to Tequila to lick, but he whimpered and panted listlessly, turning up his nose at the treat.

"What's the matter?" she laughed, "I never saw you turn down food before, rascal. Are you sick?"

In answer, the pet whimpered, trembled, and staggered as it tried to walk toward her.

"Oh, my!" she said, suddenly concerned. "What's wrong with you?" She reached over, picked the dog up, put it in her lap. As she patted it, she examined it all over. Could it have been bitten by a rattlesnake? Be coming down with rabies? She felt helpless, not quite sure what to do. The strict German pastor had never allowed her to have a dog, and Aunt Carolina had never kept a pet. She said it would shed hair all over her carpet.

The little dog whimpered again, panting hard. Its eyes were dilated and it seemed to be having a hard time breathing. Now it climbed off her lap, stumbled out onto the grass, started to retch.

"Oh, Tequila, what shall I do?" she stood up, looked around as the dog vomited. "I don't know how to treat a sick dog." She felt helpless, frightened. She was quite fond of the little dog, knew the old Don adored it. She had a sudden feeling it might be dying as it staggered, vomited again. She picked the pet up, held it close. It panted rapidly and trembled. Snakebite? Rabies?

Maybe it was something Tequila had eaten. She had a sudden mental picture of the little dog gobbling from Don

Diego's bowl. Double damnation. The rabbit stew must be spoiled, and she had just eaten a bowlful. Everyone else in the house would be sick, too. It was hard to keep food fresh in warm weather. She sank down on the back step with the dog in her arms, awaiting the nausea, the pains from the tainted stew. It had smelled and tasted all right to her, but one couldn't always judge food that way. She'd heard of people actually dying from eating spoiled food. *Rabbit fever,* she thought. Rabbit fever was a dangerous sickness one could get from eating wild rabbits carrying that disease. She thought she remembered that Trace had shot these rabbits himself, but she wasn't sure.

Tequila looked a little better now that he had vomited. He wagged his little tail as she patted him, waiting for the nausea to overtake her. She wondered whether to throw the whole household into a panic by going in and telling them about it before she was sure. The dog whined, wagged his tail, obviously getting perkier by the minute.

"Are you okay now, Tequila?" she asked anxiously. "You gave me quite a scare there. Are you all right?"

The pet settled into her lap with a tired sigh, and she stroked it absentmindedly while she waited to see if she were about to become ill. Nothing happened. The dog's symptoms were very much like the old Don's, she thought idly as she stroked it. Maybe there was something in the old Don's room that brought about the symptoms. But what? Tequila didn't smoke cigars. Could he have chewed one up? People said tobacco was poisonous if one swallowed enough of it. The drinking water? She shook her head. As far as she knew, the dog hadn't drunk out of the old man's glass.

That brought her back around in a circle to the rabbit stew. Did she feel a tiny bit nauseated? Was it spoiled? She waited for the effects to hit her. Nothing happened as the minutes ticked by.

Obviously, that wasn't it either. She didn't feel sick and she didn't hear any activity from the inside of the house that indicated people inside were succumbing to food poisoning. Maybe there was just something spoiled in Don Diego's bowl.

A memory came back to her and she wrinkled her forehead, not wanting to acknowledge it as she patted the dog. Trace had brought that tray up, had urged the old man to eat it. She didn't like the horrifying suspicion that came to her mind, wouldn't go away.

Poison, she thought. No, that's crazy. There's no poison on this ranch. Trace won't even allow the men to poison coyotes, thinks it's not sporting. Besides, what motive would he have? She shook her head to clear it, ashamed and frightened that her mind was concocting such wild ideas.

The breeze came up suddenly out of nowhere, rustling through the oleander bush next to the back door. A green leaf of that exotic plant fluttered down and landed in her lap. And again, she smelled the very sweet, exotic fragrance. Was it her wild imagination that made the oleanders smell like Velvet Eyes's perfume? If she mentioned it to anyone, would they laugh or think her crazy? She brushed the leaf off her lap, trying to push the disturbing thought from her mind at the same time. She breathed, puzzled at the fragrance eddying around her like a whisper. The breeze blew past her again and another leaf fluttered from the bush, landed on her shoe.

Oleander. The word floated to her consciousness, almost as if someone whispered in her ear. She glanced around with an eerie feeling that someone stood behind her. But there was no one there. *Oleander,* the breeze seemed to sigh. She stood up slowly, took the little dog in her arms and went into the house. She put him on the floor, gave him a drink of water. He seemed to be recovered.

One of the little maids came into the kitchen with the dirty dishes off the dining table. "Carmel, did you eat stew for dinner?"

The girl nodded. *"Si.* It was good, wasn't it?"

Cimarron nodded. "Do you feel all right?"

The girl stared at her in puzzlement. "Fine. Everyone enjoyed the stew. Why, señorita, do you feel ill?"

"No," Cimarron answered truthfully, "I feel fine." She looked down at the little dog again. It wagged its tail weakly, lapped up the water. Now, why had the dog become ill?

Surely the stew wasn't spoiled if no one else was complaining of being sick.

She didn't know very much about dogs. Maybe dogs just got sick once in a while. She hoped it wasn't anything contagious to humans. She started to shrug it off. Tequila seemed okay now, sitting at her feet looking up at her. Old Sanchez doubled as the ranch's veterinarian. Maybe she'd ask him about Tequila's symptoms in case it ever happened again.

She thought about all the volumes of books in the study. Maybe there was a veterinarian book she could look in. The little dog trailed along behind her as she walked toward the study. As she entered, Trace shoved a book back on the shelf hurriedly, turned around with a sheepish grin. "I didn't hear you coming."

She looked around. Luis had left the room. "I thought I'd find a book on veterinary medicine," she said, looking at him curiously. "Didn't expect to find you in here in the middle of the afternoon. You always have work to do."

Trace nodded, looking a little like a guilty child caught at something naughty. "Just taking a break." He went over, leaned against the fireplace, rolled a cigarillo.

"Finding anything interesting?" she asked curiously, settling herself on the sofa as she watched him strike a Lucifer match on the stones. She wondered what kind of book a man like Trace Durango would read.

He cleared his throat. "Thought there might be a book on gun repair." He sounded a little too offhand. "Think I'll go see the old man, then go out to the corral. Did he finish his stew?"

The little dog leaped up in her lap, snuggled down. She remembered Trace's attempt to get the old man to eat. "No," she shrugged, "said he wasn't hungry."

Trace looked worried. "He's just going to waste away if we don't keep pushing food at him. I know he doesn't feel much like eating, but if we can just keep him alive till the war ends. . . ." His voice trailed off as he smoked and tossed the match into the fireplace. There was something about his expression that hinted he was trying to get up his nerve to say something. "Cimarron, about last night—"

"As far as I'm concerned, last night never happened," she answered coolly, avoiding his eyes, stroking the dog.

"There's lots of things I should tell you, Wild One—"

"Don't feel you owe me any explanations," she cut him off. "After all, I'm not the first easy slut you've tumbled in the grass just for the fun of it—"

"It's not that way at all," he flared, coming over to confront her.

"If you're going to see the old man, you should go on." Her voice was sharp and cold as icicles. She wanted to hurt him, strike out at him. "I may go ahead and marry Luis."

His expression was incredulous. "After last night, you'd marry him? What am I supposed to do, wait in the wings to keep meeting in the dark while the husband sleeps?"

"You should have had plenty of practice by now," she snapped, thinking of Rosa as she played with the dog's ears.

"Darlin', you're talking in circles. What's got your dander up? Has someone been poking you with cactus? I don't understand—"

"Go up and see the old man." She glared at him. "This conversation is ended."

"That suits me just fine!" He tossed the smoke into the fireplace, stalked out. She heard his boots stomping up the stairs.

Idly, she stared at the shelves where Trace had been fingering the books just as she entered. Gun repair. Somehow, that sounded phony to her. In fact, his whole attitude had seemed to be hiding something. She remembered his guilty look, the way he had turned quickly when she entered. Sliding the sleeping dog off her lap onto the leather sofa, she went over, ran her fingers along the books on that shelf. Shakespeare, Lord Tennyson, Chaucer. Broken Bones, Poisons, Infectious Diseases.

Shakespeare? She thought about it a moment. No, Trace Durango didn't strike her as the Shakespeare type. Tennyson wrote romantic poetry. That didn't sound like Trace, either. Maybe he hadn't been standing right here, maybe he'd been a little further down the bookcase.

Cimarron pursed her lips, thinking about it a moment. No, she was sure he'd been standing here. In fact, there were finger marks in the dust of the bookcase right along those books. Chaucer. No, even she couldn't really understand Chaucer, and she had more of a background in fine arts than the rough cowboy. Maybe he'd only been glancing idly through the volumes and nothing in this row had attracted his attention. Poisons. The book caught her eye. No, Trace wouldn't be interested in any of Luis's old medical books. She thought about it a minute, shook her head. The moody foreman just wasn't the type to allow his hands to poison varmints. He'd make the men use rifles, give the predators a sporting chance. She'd heard him bawl a man out for wanting to spread arsenic for coyotes. *Or was that an act for everyone's benefit?*

Curiously, she pulled out the volume. It wasn't as dusty as the others. Someone had handled it recently. Very slowly, she flipped through the pages, only half reading the print as her mind struggled with the problem of the moody cowboy. Just what was she going to do about him? Maybe she should marry Luis as she'd just threatened. But when she closed her eyes and thought of being kissed, caressed, the face that came to her was the half-breed Cheyenne's.

Double damnation! Annoyed with herself, she started to close the book, place it back on the shelf, but as she closed it, a word caught her eye. What was that? Curiously, she opened the book again, thumbed through it, saw nothing interesting. Maybe she had imagined the word she thought she'd seen. She reached to put the book back on the shelf but her hand stopped halfway up. She almost seemed to feel something brush against her hand, as if someone stood behind her, reached out to touch her. There was no one there. She looked over at the French doors. *A breeze,* she thought. But the doors were closed.

It was an eerie feeling. Cimarron took a deep, troubled breath. And she was surrounded by fragrance, the very sweet, exotic scent of perfume.

She hesitated, brought the book back down, flipped it open. The light was not terribly good here, she thought with annoyance. Cimarron took the leather-bound volume over to the desk and laid it down with its pages open. It was cloudy outside. The study seemed suddenly dark and ominous. She glanced up at the mounted and stuffed animal heads that appeared to glare at her.

I'll light the lamp, she thought, bending over to search the drawers for a match. Tequila sat up on the sofa suddenly, looking toward her. His ears cocked, staring at something intently. She whirled around, looked behind her. "What do you see?" she laughed, knowing there was nothing there. But the dog's gaze didn't waver.

A breeze came up suddenly through the study, flipping the pages of the open book over and over. She glanced around again to see if the French doors had blown open, because again she felt the movement of air. *Nothing. Nothing at all.* The doors were closed but the pages flipped over and over. A draft, she thought, of course, this is an old house, it's drafty. The dog whimpered, still gazing intently behind her. She looked, saw nothing.

"Tequila," she laughed, "I'm beginning to think either you're loco or I am." She reached to grab up the book, close it to return to the shelf. She wasn't interested in reading about poisons. She didn't know why she'd gotten the book down. But even as she grabbed the volume to close it, the word caught her eye again, the word that her glance had brushed when she'd started to put the book back on the shelf.

Oleander. That was the word. *Oleander.* She wrinkled her brow, puzzled as she took the book in both hands, stared down at the page. Now what were flowers doing in a book about poisons? Yes, it really was there. *Oleander.*

Curiously, she brought the book closer to her eyes, began to read in a whisper: "Oleander. Nerium Oleander L, is a member of the family Apocynaceae. The poisonous qualities of this plant were known to ancient Greeks. All parts of the oleander are poisonous, blossoms, stems, leaves. A single leaf is enough to kill a man. Symptoms of oleander poisoning are: depression, nausea, severe vomiting, stomach pain, dizziness, slowed pulse, irregular heartbeat, dilation of pupils, bloody diarrhea, paralysis of respiration and finally death."

She heard a noise, glanced up, startled. Trace Durango leaned against the door jamb. "Finding an interesting book?"

She slammed the volume shut like a small child caught with something naughty. "No—I," she stammered as she went over, slid the book back on the shelf, whirled around.

He laughed. "Well, you seemed so involved with whatever it was, I figured it must be interesting."

She glanced from him to the dog, which had settled down, its little head on its paws. Her mind was in such confusion that she found herself stammering foolishly. "A book, yes, an interesting book. I was trying to find something to read to the old man."

Oleander, she thought. *The old man doesn't have a malignancy. He's being poisoned with oleander. But how? And why? And more important, who?*

"Don't bother about going up to read to the old man," Trace said, "I just came from his room. He's asleep now. Sure doesn't look very good. I think I'll come back after a while, see if I can get him to eat some stew, since he didn't eat his dinner."

The thought that came to her made the hair rise on the back of her neck. "Trace, did you eat the stew for lunch?"

"Sure, didn't you?" He stuck his thumbs in his belt. "I must say Rosa outdid herself this time."

Rosa. Stew. Oleander. An image came to her mind, an image of a small dog eating out of the old man's bowl, getting ill, vomiting. But why would Rosa . . . ?

"I was afraid the old man wouldn't want it when I brought the tray in." Trace frowned. "But since it was his favorite and Rosa said she'd put in extra spices, well, I really did try to get him to eat." Trace looked at her a long minute. "Are you okay, Cimarron? You look pale."

"I-I'm fine," she gulped. *Trace*, she thought, *Trace and Rosa are in this together*. But how, and why? *Extra spices. The pepper mill.* She remembered how Rosa had grabbed it from her hand when she had tried to use it. She went over to the French doors, opened them to stare out at the giant oleander bushes. It had turned cloudy and cool, the wind whipping the branches back and forth. Even as she stared out at the courtyard, dead oleander leaves blew across the flagstones, whirled around her feet. And then the pieces of the puzzle fell neatly into place. *Oleander leaves. Dried oleander leaves ground up in the pepper mill.*

She heard Trace clear his throat behind her. "Are you sure you're okay, Cimarron? You look a little peaked."

She made a gesture of dismissal, turning back to study him. *But why?* she thought wildly. Why would Trace and his mistress plot to poison the old man when Don Diego's death would put the ranch into the hands of Luis, a man Trace obviously hated? That made no sense at all.

"You did eat stew at dinner?" she asked again.

"*Sí*, why?" He nodded, pushing the black hat back.

No, she thought, no; a man who rides a stallion with a hackamore to keep from hurting its mouth with a bit, the kind of man who wore no spurs, was too gentle to poison someone. She remembered the scene again in the hayloft, the time he had grabbed her arm, holding back an angry fury that frightened her. She didn't really know this man at all, she thought; she'd only been here a couple of weeks. How could she know what he was capable of?

She looked at her fingernails to avoid his dark, piercing eyes. "I asked about the stew because Tequila ate out of the old man's bowl and it made him sick."

She looked up quickly to catch his reaction, but he only shrugged, looked bored. "The little devil eats all sorts of things he shouldn't. The old man likes his food spicy, and it's probably bad for dogs."

How could he make such innocent remarks?

Trace went over to the sofa, picked up the sleepy pet, patted him. "Looks okay to me."

"It wasn't anything, really." She watched him flop down on the sofa with the dog in his arms. Was she relieved or disappointed that her remark hadn't produced more of a reaction? "But if there was anything wrong with the stew, it's a good thing Don Diego didn't eat it, wasn't it?"

Trace nodded as he patted the dog. "Yeah. Good thing."

Still no really big reaction. *What is the motive?* No one commits a crime without a motive, she thought, leaning against the French door. Why would Trace want to poison the old Don when that would put the ranch in Luis' hands?

She couldn't, wouldn't believe it. Cimarron closed her eyes, trying not to remember Trace bringing the tray in, urging the old man to eat. Had the two been poisoning him off and on for the past six months, getting people accustomed to the idea that the Don had a fatal malignancy so there would be no suspicions when he finally died? Was Dr. Hastings in on this?

She watched Trace stroke the dog. No, she thought, the doctor is just an inept, drunken quack. Then she remembered putting the oleander twig in her own mouth as she talked to the doctor, becoming slightly ill afterwards. She could remember Dr. Hastings's words now. "... pretty flower. You know, we don't have these in Connecticut...."

No wonder Doctor Hastings wasn't familiar with oleander poisoning. That drunken old bungler. She could feel Trace looking at her even though her eyes were closed as she leaned against the door.

"Cimarron?" he said with a frown. "You keep saying there's nothing wrong, but you act like you're in a state of shock. Are you sure you're all right?"

She took a deep, shuddering breath and there were tears in her eyes blurring his image as she opened them. "Trace," she said softly, "I've always wanted to ask you some things about the Durangos, the Triple D—"

"What kind of things?" His voice was tense, guarded. Trace stood up, pushing the dog off his lap.

"Oh, I don't know," she mumbled, watching his face, "the servants sure don't gossip much. None of the maids tells me anything."

His face became a hostile mask. "I've got to go, Sanchez is expecting me out at the corral—"

"Trace . . ." She plunged in. "Tell me about the Durangos."

"I don't know what you mean," but his smoldering eyes told her he did. He started edging toward the door. "There's nothing to tell." He was hiding something, she could see it in his eyes. "Who've you been talking to?"

She went over, confronted him, because she had a feeling he was about to shrug off questions he didn't want to answer and disappear out the study door. "Tell me about the old Don," she blurted before she lost her nerve. "Tell me about Don Diego, Luis, and you."

His face twisted with pain and indecision. "I can't, Cimarron. If the old man ever found out, it would break his heart—"

"What?" she insisted. "What is it you know, Trace?"

She saw the struggle on his face, knew he wanted very much to tell her. Then his expression gradually closed, and even his dark eyes looked at her coldly. Whatever it was, he didn't trust her enough to share it.

"Nothing," he answered. He tried to roll a cigarillo but his hands trembled so, he spilled the tobacco, and he flung it away from him in a fury. "Mind your own damned business, sassy miss! We don't need you sticking your nose in things here at the Triple D! I'll deal with everything in my own time in my own way."

She thought for a moment he would turn and leave the room, so she reached out, caught his arm. "Trace, why is it you hate Luis so? Is it because he'll inherit the ranch when the Don dies—?"

"Whatever gave you that loco idea?" He looked down at her. She could feel the pulse beating a rapid rhythm in his arm, saw his mouth harden.

She stared up at him in puzzlement. "Aren't—aren't you Luis's son?"

"Who told you that! It's a secret!" For a moment, she felt his arm stiffen, saw unleashed fury in his rugged face, thought he would strike her.

"No one," she blurted, letting go of his arm, backing away. "I—I somehow jumped to that conclusion. Isn't Trace a nickname for 'three'? Aren't you third in line for inheritance?"

He threw back his head and laughed coldly. "Is that why you've been cozying up to Luis, talking of marrying him? So you could be the señora of the Triple D?"

"No," she protested, "I only gave it a passing thought, I

never seriously—"

"You've outfoxed yourself, you greedy little tart!" he snapped as he spun away, stalked to the study door. "I was right not to trust you, you're just like the señora."

"So everyone tells me!" she fired back, still not understanding.

He glared at her, and she had never seen such distrust, such hurt in a pair of eyes before. "And to think after last night, I was seriously considering asking you—"

"Asking me what?"

"Nothing!" He spat out contemptuously. "I was right not to trust you, not to trust any woman. I'm looking for a woman who'd love me for myself, not so she could be queen of the big, rich Triple D!"

She shook her head. "I don't have any idea what you're talking about! And you've always lead me to think I'm just a tumble in the hay to you. Believe me, if I cared about a man, it wouldn't matter if he didn't have a dime."

He shook his head slowly, sadly. "No, darlin'. I can't believe you didn't make a greedy little plan to end up as señora here. Your only interest is in the inheritance—"

"But if Luis is next in line for the ranch—"

"Why do you keep saying that?" he raged. "I don't believe you really don't know who I am."

"Obviously I'm wasting my breath, but who are you, besides the most ornery, stubbornest *caporal* I ever met?"

He raised his eyebrow at her and laughed. "Okay, we'll play your little game," he sneered. "Luis Durango is the old Don's baby brother, the lazy, worthless *hombre* I'm going to throw off this ranch without a penny to his name when the old man finally dies. Then I can run things my way and don't have to worry about being blackmailed, forced to keep the secret."

"His brother?" She was bewildered and it must have showed on her face. "Who are you, then?"

"Trace," he smiled slowly, "Trace Durango. Tres means three in Spanish. It was a nickname Velvet Eyes gave me."

"A nickname?" she said irritably, "but—"

"Don Diego is the second in line," he said. "And me? Well,

my greedy little tart, I'm Diego de Durango the third!"

Her mouth fell open. "Trace, I had no idea—"

"It won't play, darlin'," he laughed bitterly, and he turned and stalked out of the house, slamming the big front door as he left.

Cimarron felt the tears rise and catch in her throat. She'd just had her suspicions confirmed. Don Diego was being poisoned and now she knew who had the best motive. *Trace,* she thought with anguish. *Oh, my God, Trace!*

Chapter Twenty-Four

She walked over, collapsed on the sofa. Now what was she going to do? The man she loved was poisoning his father so he could inherit the ranch. Strange, Trace never referred to him as his father. He always called him the old man or the Don. Nor did she understand his words about Luis and some secret. He was trying to confuse her, throw her off his trail so she wouldn't figure it out.

She fought an urge to run upstairs, gather up a few things and flee the ranch so she wouldn't have to be involved in this horrible drama. But she had to stay and do something quick if she wanted to protect Don Diego. Now that Trace knew she suspected him, he and his mistress would have to move fast. Was her own life in danger because she knew about the oleander? The thought both horrified and appalled her. Anyone who would poison a nice old man for an inheritance would certainly not stop at killing someone who interfered. She shook her head, remembering Trace's gentle lovemaking. No, Trace wasn't capable of murder. Then she remembered his moodiness, his unexplained melancholia, his fits of rage. She thought about the terrible Comancheros. Yes, maybe he was capable of it, after all.

What did she do now? It was unthinkable not to try to stop the pair from killing the old man. The sheriff . . . no, she couldn't go to the local sheriff. She told herself it was because the law might have a wanted poster on her, recognize her when she walked in. But that wasn't the real reason. Even if Trace Durango was a scheming killer, she couldn't help imprison or hang him. What did she do now?

She'd tell the old Don himself. Then she reconsidered. Just how did one go about telling a man his heir was trying to kill him for the inheritance?

What about Dr. Hastings? She shook her head. She'd have to get the harmless old quack sober enough to discuss it and that seemed near impossible. No wonder Trace kept saying he would take the old man back East to specialists. Surely he expected him to be dead before the war ended.

She'd asked Sanchez for advice. *How stupid of her,* she chided herself, wringing her hands. Sanchez was Trace's *compadre*. Not only wouldn't he believe that Trace was trying to poison the old Don, he probably wouldn't believe his own wife was guilty of adultery with his good friend. And even if he would believe it, did she really want to break that gentle old vaquero's heart by telling him of Trace's diabolical scheme, Rosa's cheating?

Maverick, then. Cimarron thought it over, changed her mind. Maverick, like the other wranglers, seemed to be coming under the magnetism of Trace's personality. Like the others, he'd follow Trace's lead right into hell. And besides, if Maverick would help her, what could a fourteen-year-old half-breed do? No white man would listen to him.

Luis. Of course when it came down to it, she was going to have to involve Luis to save his older brother's life. She had hesitated to involve a member of the Durango family. What would he say when she told him his own nephew was trying to kill Luis's older brother? Was Trace his nephew? Or was he his son? Luis hadn't had time to investigate the Comanchero thing and here she had something else to tell him. Would he listen or would he patronize her, she thought grimly, pat her on the head and tell her it was her crazy woman's intuition?

There were still some other pieces to this puzzle that didn't make any sense, she thought, knitting her brow. Trace had started to tell her something important, then obviously had not trusted her enough.

Well, no wonder. She stood up. Maybe he'd thought she

would go along, help him kill the Don. But he had a mistress who was helping. No, it was something else, some kind of terrible secret between Trace and Luis. And now she remembered the ranch books, the accounts she kept trying to balance that wouldn't balance. Maybe Trace had been selling the cattle off, pocketing the money. Maybe he had to gain control of the ranch before the shortage got so big that, Don Diego or Luis would notice.

Yes, maybe Luis could suggest some alternatives. She walked through the house, wondering where he might be. Maybe he was in his room. She went upstairs, tapped lightly at his door.

She tapped a second time before she heard his voice, drowsy and annoyed. "Yes? What is it?"

"Luis, it's Cimarron," she whispered hoarsely, looking up and down the hall to make sure no one saw her.

He opened the door, looking sleepy. Obviously she had disturbed his siesta. "Why, Señorita Cimarron. To what do I owe the pleasure of this—"

"Luis," she blurted, "I've got to talk to you. I think someone's trying to poison Don Diego."

"What?" His face showed horror. "What did you say?"

She looked up and down the hall. "We need to talk," she said. "I think someone's trying to kill Don Diego."

He stuck his head out the door, looked up and down the hall before pulling her inside his room, closing the door behind her. "I didn't want anyone to overhear us," he said, gesturing her to a chair. "Cimarron, I'm beginning to doubt your sanity. Every time I turn around, you've found another diabolical plot."

He gave her a penetrating look as he sat down across from her. "What have you found this time?"

She avoided his gaze, looked around. Everything about this room, from the oil painting on the wall to the fine oriental rug on the floor bespoke a refined gentleman of exquisite and expensive tastes. "You must believe me! Someone is trying to poison the old Don!"

He stiffened, stared at her. "You must be loco. There's no poison in this household. Trace won't even let the hands use it for wolves and coyotes."

"They're not using poison," she answered, "they're using oleander leaves, putting them in the old man's food."

His face paled and then he began to laugh. "I'm sorry to tell you this, my sweet. But that's the craziest thing I ever heard!" He stood up, went over to the bureau, got himself a cigar. "Señorita, you've been nibbling loco weed."

"Don't talk down to me, Luis, and stop treating me like a stupid, silly child! It's true, I tell you. Don Diego didn't eat his stew at dinner—"

"He didn't?" Luis paused as he lit the cigar. "I thought he was going to eat it after Trace and I left. If Diego doesn't start eating more, he's just going to waste away and the cancer will get him sooner—"

"Luis, that's what I'm trying to tell you," she almost shouted as her gaze swept the elegant room. A crystal vase of flowers, elegant furnishings, a small, silver derringer on the bureau. "The Don isn't dying of cancer."

"Oh, come now, Cimarron!" he scoffed. "No one would believe this wild hallucination of yours! If this is your idea of a joke, it isn't very funny!"

"The Don's being poisoned with ground-up oleander leaves! Little Tequila ate out of the old Don's bowl and got dreadfully sick a while ago."

Luis snorted. "I have to tell you, the little rascal is so hateful to me, I wouldn't mind if you told me he died, except it would grieve the old man so. Food spoils every once in a while, Cimarron, I remember that from my medical training. The rabbit was tainted or maybe carrying the dreaded rabbit fever, and so—"

"But nobody else got sick," she insisted, desperate to convince him. "Only Tequila, and his symptoms were the same as the Don's."

Luis blew smoke toward the ceiling, seemed to be weighing her words. She held her breath. If Luis wouldn't believe her, she had no idea what to do next.

"You keep saying 'they,' señorita. Just who do you think is behind this?" He gave her a piercing look.

She hesitated, caring so much for Trace. But she couldn't

stand by and watch him kill that nice old man. "Rosa," she sighed, "I think Rosa's grinding up the leaves in her pepper mill and sprinkling it on his food."

Luis stiffened, stared at her. "Rosa? Why, she's a trusted servant. She loves the old man. She wouldn't—"

"She's the mistress," she blurted, "and I think he's promised to marry her, make her señora of the Durango ranch when he inherits it. Then all she's got to do is kill off poor old Sanchez and everything's fine. No one will question the old Don's death. That bumbling doctor doesn't seem to know anything about oleander and no one will question his diagnosis when the Don dies."

Luis paced up and down the oriental rug. "You keep saying 'he.' Just who is the 'he' in this wild tale you've concocted?"

He gave her a thoughtful look and she stared deep into his eyes, hesitated. For a long moment, she did not think she could make this gesture of condemnation. "Trace," she sighed finally.

"Trace!" Luis snorted and made a gesture of dismissal. "Now I know you've been eating loco weed! Why would my nephew risk being hanged to get a ranch he's going to inherit eventually?"

"He's getting impatient." She thought it over. "And Luis, there's something else. Do you remember me telling you that I couldn't get the books to balance—"

Luis laughed. "No one expects a pretty thing like you to add figures. Didn't I tell you to forget it, I'd correct your mistakes? I figured you wouldn't be able to do it—"

"Stop that!" she snapped, eyes flashing. "Honestly, Luis, I'm not stupid just because I'm a woman. I tell you, the books don't balance! Someone's selling beef and horses off this ranch and pocketing the money. I think Trace knows I'm about to catch him at it. Maybe he's afraid I'll tell the old man."

He suddenly stopped smiling, seemed to consider. She breathed a sigh of relief. Finally he would believe her, take her seriously. Luis came over, sat down across from her. "Have you discussed this with anyone else?" he asked.

"Anyone at all?"

She shook her head. "No, I came to you first when I figured it out. I thought it might link up to the Comancheros. I didn't know who else to tell."

"Good girl!" He snubbed the cigar out in a crystal ashtray. "Your story begins to make a little sense to me, but still, I can't believe Trace would really—"

"And I'll tell you something else I suspect." She leaned closer. "I think he's mixed up somehow with the Comancheros. I think the raid was staged."

Luis's mouth dropped open. "Señorita," he said, "I better warn you you are making the most terrible accusation one can make in Texas right now. Why, if the ranchers in the surrounding area even suspected something like that, they'd lynch him without a trial. They might even be tempted to inflict a little Comanche-style torture on him after what all these frontier families have been through."

She shuddered, clasped her hands tightly together, swallowed back her tears. "I know that, Luis, God, how I know that! But don't you see how it all falls into place? The Triple D has only been raided once and the ranchers were saying at the barbecue they suspected the half-breed—"

"It might be that half-Comanche kid, the one called Maverick," he said stubbornly.

She looked at him. "I know you don't want to face the truth. But Luis, Maverick wouldn't have anything to gain. He's found a home here. Trace is teaching him to handle a gun. I know this is shocking to you, after all, a member of the family mixed up in something this sordid. No wonder you don't want to face it. But don't you see? If Trace is involved with the Comanchero, that gives him a way to sell off the livestock he steals—"

"I just can't believe Trace would do this." He shook his head, stood, paced up and down the oriental rug, big silver spurs jangling in the silence. "Besides, why did you think the raid on the Triple D was staged?"

"Because of what their leader, El Lobo told me."

Luis stopped, looked deep into her eyes. "And just what did he tell you?"

"Luis, he knew I was on this ranch. He specifically said he had come raiding because he knew a golden-haired girl was here. He said his messenger told him."

Luis banged his fist on the bureau and swore in Spanish. "That filthy . . . !"

"I figure Rosa is some kind of go-between," she sighed, "and she's jealous of me, thinks I might end up as señora here. So she thought she'd double-cross Trace, hand me over to El Lobo to remove me as a threat, and Trace wouldn't be able to do anything about it."

She had never seen such anger, such fury in a man's face. He sat down across from her. "I didn't want to believe it at first, but you seem to have it all figured out. You've convinced me, señorita. Now we've got to decide what to do. Are you sure you've discussed this with no one but me?"

"No one," she assured him.

"Let me think a minute." He stroked his mustache. "You understand this is such a shock to me to think my poor brother, Diego. . . ." His voice trailed off as he leaned back, tapped his fingers on the chair arm.

"I don't want to call in the law." She leaned forward anxiously. "I can't bear to think of Trace facing jail or even hanging."

"We can't just do nothing," the other said with annoyance. "Why, if that rotten pair managed to harm my poor brother. . . ." He paused significantly. "Do you have any ideas? Any suggestions at all?"

She shook her hair back, thinking. "I don't know what to do about Rosa, but I wish Trace would just go away somewhere. That way he wouldn't end up in jail and the old Don would be safe."

Luis frowned. "He'd never leave this ranch voluntarily," he grumbled. "I won't deny we've not always been on the best of terms because of . . . well, anyway, he doesn't like me. If something happens to Trace, I'm the one who inherits. For that reason alone, you couldn't talk him into leaving, even to save his life."

Cimarron frowned. "Who ends up with the ranch doesn't seem very important to me now," she sighed. "There's two lives hanging on this decision. I can't let Trace poison the old Don, but I can't let him go to prison, be hanged over all this, either."

"You love my nephew very much, don't you?" he asked gently, leaning back in his chair.

She couldn't keep the tears back, his voice was so warm, so sympathetic. *"Si,* very much, I know that must hurt you, Luis, knowing you were fond of me."

He turned his palms up in a gesture of acceptance, smiled weakly. "It always seems my lot in life to fall for women who love other men. What do we do now?"

"I—I don't really know," she wrung her hands, "but I'm willing to do anything to keep him out of jail, even if, in the long run, he hates me for it."

Luis cocked his head to one side. "You could love a man who would do cold-blooded murder?"

The tears overflowed and made warm, crooked trails down her face as she struggled with her inner agony. "I—I can't help it," she gulped, "I can't keep myself from loving him, even if he is a no-good killer."

Luis sighed, drummed his fingers on the chair arm. "I once hoped you might someday learn to love me, become my wife. I guess I thought I loved enough for both of us."

She glanced away so she didn't have to look into his hurt, accusing eyes. "Let's not speak of this, Luis, let's talk of what we must do next."

"I have an idea," he said slowly. "Frankly, it's proably not much of an idea, but it's the only one I can think of at the moment." He paused, shook his head. "No, I guess that's not very good, after all."

"What?" She gestured eagerly, "What's the idea, Luis? Anything beats standing by and watching him commit murder and getting lynched for it. What's your idea?"

He fingered his mustache thoughtfully. "Suppose I took Trace to the far edge of the west Durango range, gave him money and a horse, and told him to go somewhere else and never come back?"

"I don't think he'd leave willingly," she said slowly. "He loves this ranch."

Luis reached out, took her hand, squeezed gently. "I didn't say *willingly,* sweet one," he sighed. "But if he understood that we were on to him and the only other alternative he had was jail or a lynch mob—"

"Maybe he'd go then." She was so worried, so lost in thought, she hardly noticed Luis holding her hand. "You know him better than I do. He's one of the bravest *hombres* I ever met. He might be willing to stand up to a whole mob and try to talk them out of it."

Luis shuddered. "And if he lost the argument, they'd lynch him just for being a Comanchero, much less trying to kill the old Don. I fear to tell Diego. The shock of this will kill him."

Cimarron stood up. "I—I wasn't planning to tell him."

"How can we not?"

She thought a minute, her finger to her lips. "Suppose we tell a little lie to protect the old man? Suppose we just let him think Trace went west or went off to find Dallas, or Velvet Eyes, something like that? We could spare Don Diego's feelings that way."

Luis nodded an approval. "I think you have a good idea there. My poor brother has had enough unhappiness."

"I don't know what to do about Rosa, though." She pursed her lips.

"Let me deal with this scheming Rosa," Luis said grimly. "When I think that she deliberately handed you over to that terrible El Lobo, I think no punishment is terrible enough. But probably, I'll have to take command of the ranch until Don Diego is fully recovered, so I'll just send old Sanchez and his family off to our north or south ranges and get a new housekeeper here."

"She won't be punished that way!" Cimarron fumed.

Luis crossed himself. "God will punish the wicked in the long run; 'vengeance is mine, sayeth the Lord,'" he reminded her gently. "That way, I wouldn't have to hurt old Sanchez by telling him what his wife was up to. Besides, the faithless Rosa's liable to run off and join her lover after he leaves, so we couldn't punish her anyway."

Cimarron nodded, but still the idea of Rosa running away with Trace, sleeping in his arms, made her grit her teeth. *This is no time for jealousy, Cimarron,* she scolded herself. *Lives are at stake here.* Nor did she want to think of Trace's leaving forever and her not being able to see him again, never sharing his kisses, feeling his arms around her.

She blinked, trying not to remember the taste of his mouth, warm and sweet on hers, the feel of his hard body moving in rhythmic motion with hers, the ultimate sensation of him surging deep inside her body. . . .

"You're right, Luis," she sighed, "how do you think we should deal with this?"

He ran his hand through his dark, gray-streaked hair. "If he won't leave willingly, we'll get him off the ranch unwillingly—"

"I don't want him hurt," she interrupted fiercely.

He looked insulted, injured. "Señorita, he is my nephew. Even though we have had our differences about how the ranch should be run, I still care very deeply about him. You have my word as a Durango and a Spanish gentleman that I wouldn't do anything to harm one hair of his head." He held his right hand up.

"I'm sorry," she stammered, standing. "I—I'm just so confused, I don't know what to do next."

"I can understand." His handsome face grew melancholy. "To think that someone you love might be involved in something so terrible is unthinkable."

"And he had me so fooled," she said savagely, "with all this gentle fakery with the livestock, the way he seems to love the old Don so."

Luis sighed and stood up. "The best disguise for a ferocious wolf is inside the skin of a sheep," he said with a sad smile. "But I'll agree it's a great shock."

"So what do we do now?"

Luis fingered the collar of his fine silk shirt thoughtfully as he went to the French doors of the room and looked out. "Suppose we lure him out to the barn in the darkness, tap him on the head to knock him out—"

"I won't do anything to hurt him!" she snapped.

"Let me finish, please," he implored her. "Anything's better than having him rot in jail or end up swinging from a rope." His sigh was loud in the silence. "I'll get a horse, money, and supplies. Then I'll knock him out, throw him in the back of the wagon and drive him to the far western edge of the ranch. When he comes to, I'll tell him we're on to him and he'd better ride away."

"Suppose he refuses?"

"Do you think he'll refuse if I tell him I'll go to the sheriff if he comes back to the ranch?"

Cimarron smoothed a fold in her skirt. "Would you actually do that?" She had never felt so melancholy.

Luis shrugged. "I don't know, señorita. To protect my poor brother, I might. I'll do this tonight when everyone's gone to bed. That way, he won't be missed till morning. By then he'll be long gone."

She looked at him a long moment. "And just how do you propose to get him out to the barn to knock him out?"

Luis came over, looked down at her. "Cimarron," he said softly, "his life may depend on getting him off this ranch. That's why you're going to help me." He took both her hands in his, squeezed gently. "For his sake, for Diego's sake, I'm counting on you to lure him out to the barn late this evening where I'll be waiting."

"Oh, no—"

"If I try to take him by force, someone may get hurt," he said. "You know how strong he is, what a fighter."

She remembered Trace's muscular arms around her, the power of his chest and shoulders. "Yes," she admitted, "the only way he can be taken is by trickery. But he doesn't trust me, doesn't trust any woman. He won't fall for it."

"Can you blame him after the way Velvet Eyes ran off? It must have hurt him to find out she was a slut."

She gave him a searching, piercing look. "How do you know what she was, Luis?"

He stammered a moment, turned away. "If she would desert her husband for her lover," he said, "that tells you what she was. But all that matters now is what happens tonight. You're going to have to use your charms to lure the young man to the barn where I'll be waiting in the shadows to grab him. Can you do it?" He named the hour, after supper.

She walked over, opened the door. "I—I can do it." She stuck out her chin with fierce determination. "He'll hate and curse my memory, but if I can save his life and the old Don's, I can't worry about what he thinks of me."

Luis looked at her admiringly. "Such courage!" he said. "Until tonight."

"Until tonight, then."

"And señorita—"

"*Si?*" She looked back over her shoulder.

"If you believe in prayer at all, this is surely the night for it."

She swallowed hard. "You are a fine, reverent person, Luis," she said. "Perhaps I haven't really appreciated you before. I'll pray all evening and I hope you do the same."

He crossed himself, his handsome face etched with concern. "Cimarron, I'll pray over this like I never prayed before. Too bad we're so far from town. I'd go in and light some candles at the church."

She nodded, her heart aching. "We'll need all the help we can get to pull this off." She turned, went out.

Cimarron did pray about it all afternoon and finally, by evening, she had reached a decision. Maybe it was loco, maybe it was just plain foolish and stupid, but she had decided what she was going to do about Trace Durango.

When she heard the supper bell ring, she took a deep breath, started down the hallway. As she passed the closed door of Velvet Eyes's room, she was drawn almost irresistibly to pause there.

Did she hear a silent voice whisper her name or was it only her own sad sigh? She went in, stood before the magnificent painting. "I—I came to say good-bye," she blurted without thinking. "I'm going away."

When she heard her own voice echoing in her ears, she felt foolish that she spoke to a portrait and was glad no one else was there to hear her.

Did she imagine that the woman in the crooked frame was beseeching her, trying to communicate with her? Luis was right, she was having wild hallucinations. Cimarron turned to leave, paused. Turned back around. The eyes in the painting seemed to ask, to beg. Cimarron shook her head in annoyed puzzlement. It was only a portrait after all, why did she imagine it might be more?

Double damnation! Rosa had still not cleaned this room with its layer of dust, of cobwebs. The painting still hung slightly crooked, and that disturbed Cimarron's tidy soul. Even if she were leaving the ranch, it annoyed her that the portrait might hang there crooked forever. She reached out, very slowly straightened the big portrait on the wall. As she disturbed the painting, an envelope fell from behind the picture, fluttered to the floor.

Puzzled, Cimarron bent, picked it up. The envelope was sealed, and the dainty, feminine handwriting on the front spelled out "Diego." The scent of the perfume drifted to her nostrils from the paper. She stared at it in the dim light, glanced back up at the portrait. Was it her imagination, or did the portrait look both triumphant and at peace?

Stop that, Cimarron, she told herself as she fingered the envelope. *You do have a wild imagination. Now what should I do with this?*

She considered a long moment, then walked swiftly down to the old Don's room. He was asleep and snoring gently. Should she leave it for him to find? She considered a moment, then decided against it. If it were important, she didn't want to take a chance that Rosa or one of the other servants might pick it up. Well, she'd give it to the Don later. In the meantime, she was late for supper.

She stuffed the small envelope in the pocket of her skirt and went down to eat. The meal passed in a blur, she was so nervous. One of the servant girls served a rather burned and not very good roast and heavy biscuits.

Trace dropped one on his plate with a look of irritation. "These are as heavy as cannon balls. Where's Rosa tonight, Sanchez?"

The old vaquero rubbed his leathery face. "Some lady's having a baby, I think, so she went over to help. She said it might take all night. You know I don't ask what she does." He laughed good-naturedly.

Luis caught Cimarron's eye and nodded. She realized then that Luis had thought of some way to get Rosa off the ranch for a few hours. Of course, she thought, that was important. If Rosa went crawling into Trace's bed in the middle of the night and he wasn't there, she might alert the whole house to his disappearance. Cimarron wanted him to be far away by tomorrow morning where no one could hurt him. *Would Trace forgive her for her part in this?* Whether he did or not, she was determined to follow through. She went up and took the old man a tray herself to make sure the food was served off the regular roast. Although, with Rosa gone for the evening and knowing Cimarron suspected him, she didn't think Trace would dare try anything alone.

When they adjourned to the study, Luis yawned. "I think I'll turn in early," he said, standing up.

Trace went over, poured himself a glass of tequila. "I don't know why you should be tired." He sounded annoyed. "You weren't out there helping us shoe horses today."

Luis said, "While you're busy insulting me, Trace, you might remember to be a gentleman and see if the lady would like some wine."

Trace glanced inquiringly at Cimarron, who was too nervous to swallow anything. "No. No, thanks," she said.

"Luis, you don't need to correct my manners," Trace said, pouring a little salt on the top of his fist to go with his drink. "One elegant nonworking gentleman is about all a ranch can support."

Luis gave Cimarron a resigned look, shrugged. "I don't feel like taking offense tonight," he said. "I think I'll go on to bed."

Sanchez yawned. *"Si.* Me, too. Come, little one," he said to Turquoise who sat on the floor playing with the dog. "Let's go to bed."

"Not yet, it's too early," the child protested.

"Daddy says," Sanchez reproved her. The child stood up and went over and hugged the old vaquero. He ran his crippled hand through her black hair.

"Yo te amo," Turquoise whispered, "better than Mama."

Sanchez clucked disapprovingly as he put his arm around her shoulders and they started from the study. "Good thing your mama isn't here to hear you say that. She would be terribly hurt."

"No, she wouldn't," the child said stubbornly. "She really doesn't like either one of us very much."

"Hush! That's not nice." Sanchez's voice drifted to them in the study as the pair walked back to the servants' quarters. Cimarron took a deep breath, watched the little dog rolling on its back on the floor, watched Trace drink his liquor. Abducting Trace had seemed like a good idea early this afternoon, but now she wasn't sure. She wasn't even certain she could lure him out to where Luis waited. The handsome Spaniard, of course, was supposed to go up to his room, then out the French doors onto the upstairs porch and across the courtyard to the barn.

Would Trace hate her for the trick she was about to pull on him? How would he feel toward her tomorrow? She had made a decision about her own destiny when she had left Luis's room, but now she wavered, wondering about that. But no, she was going to follow through because she loved Trace Durango. She admitted it to herself as she watched his rugged, moody face. There would never be another man she cared for as deeply as she cared for him. He had stolen both her virginity and her heart.

Trace Durango, she thought fiercely, looking at him, *I love you so! I can only hope when it's all over, you'll forgive my trickery, understand why I did it.*

He must have felt her intense gaze, for he looked up abruptly and their eyes met. He fiddled with his glass a moment, looked away. "We need to talk, Cimarron. I can't seem to get you off my mind. You're driving me loco." He set the glass down on a table, came over, caught her wrist.

She felt herself tremble in the heat and hardness of his grip. "You mean you want me to lie down on the sofa and spread my legs for you like one of Miss Fancy's girls?"

He jerked as if she'd struck him, and for a moment she thought he might slap her. "Don't talk like that," he snapped, "that's not what I mean at all. I—I need you,

Cimarron. I never thought I'd say that to a woman; it hurts my pride. But I'm saying it now."

She looked into the big, gentle eyes, wondered how he could deliberately, cold-bloodedly try to poison a fine old man. And yet, she loved him more than security, more than riches, more than life itself.

"Trace," she pulled away from his grasp, "if you were going away, would you take me with you? Would you care that much for me?"

He cocked his head at her, ran his hand through the blueblack hair that always seemed to be hanging on his forehead. The lamplight gleamed on the silver conchos of the black leather vest. "What kind of loco talk is that? I expect to stay on the Triple D until I die of old age and they pile its dirt on my coffin."

She wasn't going to pursue her questioning. Cimarron had already made her decision. Let the cards fall where they may, she told herself as she looked back at him. I'm willing to take a gamble on whether he really loves me or not, and if he doesn't, well, I'm no worse off than I was when I arrived on this ranch only a couple of weeks ago.

"Cimarron," he put his hands on her shoulders, "I don't know what all this crazy talk is about me leaving the Triple D, but what I want to talk about is us."

She heard a maid go by in the hall and pulled away from him. It was late. Everyone was settling down for the night. "There's people still up, Trace, someone might overhear. Let's go out where we can talk."

"Sure." They went though the French doors, the little dog trotting along behind, its nails clicking on the flagstones of the courtyard.

He started to take her in his arms, but she looked up at the upstairs windows, pulled away again. "Suppose someone's watching?"

"So what if they are?"

She gave him her most flirtatious glance, looking up at him through her long lashes. "Let's go out to the barn, check on old Nightwind and Peso."

He acted as if he might protest, then shrugged and took

her arm. "Why not?"

The moon was big and orange tonight, with wisps of red clouds floating across its surface.

"Comanche moon," Trace mused. "Somewhere those savage devils are gathering at this very moment, deciding where to rape and burn and torture tonight."

She shivered at the thought as they entered the barn. She supposed he'd said that to throw her off the track, not knowing she was on to him. What kind of cold-blooded *hombre* supplied rifles and cartridges to the war parties in exchange for money? No wonder he'd managed to come through rescuing her all right. His men had probably recognized him, refrained from shooting. And what would he do when he left here? Would he rejoin his Comancheros, ride openly with them now?

Cimarron leaned against a pile of hay, thinking what it would be like to live among, ride with the savage Comancheros. It would be a terrible, hard way to survive. But if it was the only way to stay by the side of one you loved, it was worth it. Putting her hands in the pocket of her skirt, her fingers found the crumpled, forgotten envelope. Double damnation! She had forgotten to go back up to Don Diego's room. Well, she'd give it to Luis, let him give it to the old man.

Nightwind nickered, and she went over and patted his velvet nose. Tequila looked up at her and wagged his tail.

"Darlin', I ought to be mad at you," Trace said softly, and she turned inquiringly to face him. He looked down at the pet gamboling around her feet. "First you steal my dog."

His hands went to her shoulders, pulled her to him as the stallion nuzzled her back. "Then you steal my horse."

She looked up into his eyes, her senses dizzy with his nearness. She could smell the sweet scent of hay, the tequila on his breath.

"And then you steal my heart," he murmured and his lips came down on hers in tender domination. His hands pulled her against him so hard, she had the feeling he was trying to pull her inside him, make her a part of him.

Her hands went around his neck as she kissed him fiercely,

steeling herself in her resolve about what she was about to do. Trace Durango was a wild, free thing, like the big wolves that ran the endless prairies of the Lone Star State. If the law didn't hang him, they'd throw him in jail. An untamed spirit like Trace was never meant to be caged, she thought, he'd die of a broken heart if he had to spend any part of his life in prison.

"Forgive me, sweetheart," she murmured against his lips, "I hope someday you'll understand. . . ."

His hand went to the open neck of her blouse, caressed the swell of her breast as he kissed her hair. "I don't know what you're talking about, darlin', but I don't care anymore. I want you, *comprende?*" His voice was angry as he admitted surrender. "I don't trust you, but I want you bad. You're like a fever in my blood. All I can think of anymore is taking you in my arms, loving you. . . ."

His voice trailed off as he pulled her to him again, and she ran her hands up and unbuttoned his black shirt so she could stroke his nipples.

He gasped with desire. "I'm gonna carry you up in the hay, darlin', make love to you like I did that very first time when I made you mine!"

She could feel his hard manhood pressing against her, eager for entrance. She felt the sudden warmth, the moisture at the joining of her thighs as her own body responded to the thought of his loving her. They made love so well together, she thought as she kissed the corner of his mouth, brushed her fingertips over his nipples while her own breasts strained against the tight fabric of her blouse. Yes, they made beautiful love together, rhythmic, graceful, like two dancers who anticipate each other's moves.

She regretted deeply what was going to happen, but it was the only way, she knew. Trace would call it betrayal and might hate her for it, but she loved him enough to risk his hatred if it would save him from the law.

He made as if to swing her up in his arms, but she pulled away playfully. "Not yet." She tried to sound coy. "You may be eager to get me up in the loft, but I'm going to enjoy just standing here kissing and teasing you a little."

His hand pushed down the front of her blouse, stroking her nipple while his other hand went to cup her small bottom. "Very well, sassy miss, we'll tease each other and see who surrenders first."

Her body actually ached from wanting him, she thought with surprise as she felt his fingers encircle her nipple, stroking so lightly she gasped at the sensation. For a moment, she forgot why she had brought him out to the dark barn as she enjoyed the touch and taste of him. She could already imagine the hot velvet stroking of his tongue on her body, the stroking, seeking, sucking of his mouth on her. The thought made her tremble with anticipation, even though she knew the lovemaking would never take place.

"Darlin', are you cold?" He cupped her small face with his two hands and then pulled her up against him, sheltering her slim body with the strength and warmth of his big one.

"Trace," she whispered, unable to stop herself from jealous curiosity. "About Rosa—"

"What about her?" he murmured. He didn't seem to be listening as he held her close, kissed, caressed her ear.

The sensation of his wet, warm tongue probing its recesses made her suck in her breath. "Do I—I mean, am I better at this than she is?"

He looked down at her, obviously amused and puzzled by her question. "Darlin', I don't know what the hell you're talking about. But then, any man who claims to really understand women is a fool, I reckon."

"I won't be angry if you tell me," she insisted. "I saw her coming out of your room that morning—"

He kissed her again, cutting off her questions. "Are you loco? Rosa is married to my *compadre,* I would never—"

"I hate it when you insult my intelligence by lying to me!" She looked up at him, eyes filling with tears. "Are you going to stand there and deny you've made love to her?"

His face flushed a little in the moonlight. "Well, she did hint one time she was available, but I never—"

He was going to lie about it, she thought sadly. What difference did it make now? She wished he trusted her enough to level with her. She heard Tequila lying by her feet start to growl softly, and she looked over Trace's shoulder to see Luis lurking in the shadows.

She almost screamed a warning, then remembered in time. She reached up, cupped the dark, rugged face in her hands, pulled it down for her kiss. "I want you to remember, Trace, that I love you! No matter what happens, no matter what you think of me tomorrow, remember that I loved you enough to risk your hate."

His hands came up to clasp her shoulders, arch her yielding body against the hard planes of his. Her eyes flickered open. His were closed, lost in the kiss. She heard Tequila growl slightly again as Luis moved closer, and the black stallion behind her nickered and moved in his stall restlessly.

Forgive me, darling, she prayed as Luis came closer, *Oh, forgive me. I'm doing this for your own good.*

But Trace's Indian blood must have sharpened his instincts, warned him of approaching danger. He pulled away from Cimarron suddenly, half whirled to meet the intruder. "What the hell—?"

She saw the reflected flash of Luis's derringer as it came down and caught Trace across the temple. The half-breed stumbled and went down with a groan.

Tequila started barking. Horrified, Cimarron sank to the barn floor, gathered the unconscious man into her arms. "You didn't have to hit him so hard!" Her fingers went to brush back the black hair and touched warm, red blood.

Luis dropped the derringer in his pocket, kicked at the small dog that scampered under the protection of a pile of hay. "I hit him as lightly as I could, señorita. I didn't expect him to sense me standing behind him and whirl around. It's that damned Cheyenne blood in him. He would have made a fierce warrior."

"And don't kick the dog!" she snapped as Tequila scurried away.

"I'm sorry, Cimarron. I was so afraid his barking would bring people running." Luis leaned over, threw the unconscious man across his shoulder, and laid him in the back of the wagon that was already hitched and standing around to the side.

Cimarron fought down her feelings of despair. Was she really doing the right thing? Of course she was. "I'll saddle his horse," she whispered.

"Hurry up," Luis ordered tersely as he threw a blanket over the unconscious form. "I don't know how long he'll be out, and when he comes to, there'll be hell to pay!"

She ran back to the barn, led the big black horse out, saddled it with shaking fingers. Then she took a deep breath, wondering if she were doing the right thing. She was going to follow her heart. *Sí,* it was right. She loved Trace Durango more than anything in this world, and she had made her decision this afternoon. Quickly, she led out the golden palomino, Peso, and saddled her, too.

Luis sat on the wagon seat, stamping his feet nervously, jangling the big spurs. She led the two horses out, tied them to the back of the wagon. "What's this? He won't need two horses?"

"I thought I'd go with you to the west boundary—"

"No, Cimarron." He shook his head. "It's too dangerous out on the western border. I'm taking a big chance myself. I might run into a Comanche raiding party out there somewhere. Now you go back in the house and go to bed. You'll not only be safe, you will look completely innocent if there's any questions as to what happened to Trace."

But she came around the side of the wagon, giving him a stubborn look as she climbed up on the seat beside him. "I'm going along." She looked over at him. "What are you going to tell people about his disappearance?"

His elegant face wrinkled into a frown. "We'll tell everyone he went off to try to find his mother among the Cheyenne. Or, since Rosa is also gone, people will think they ran off together, which is a perfectly good excuse if she should decide not to return."

She grimaced. "You know he had the nerve to act innocent when I asked him about Rosa?"

Luis shrugged, sighed. "What did you expect from someone rotten enough to try to poison his own father? Now, go in the house, Cimarron, and let a man handle this—"

"Stop treating me like a child!" she almost screamed at him. "I'm going to see this thing through so I can make sure he's all right when we leave him."

Luis looked as if he might argue, and she snapped at him, "I warn you, Luis, if you try to keep me from going along, try to take me back to the hacienda by force, you'll see kicking and screaming enough to wake up folks at the state capital! My name isn't 'Wild One' for nothing!"

"All right, all right." He made a placating gesture, slapped the reins against the horse's back, and the wagon pulled away. "Although, as a real gentleman, it worries me to endanger a lady. I won't draw an easy breath till I get you back here to the ranch safely."

She didn't say anything. She wasn't coming back to the ranchero with Luis. She had made her decision this afternoon. She was going with Trace Durango, because life without him wasn't worth living. Whatever hardships lay in his future, she was going to share it. And if tomorrow he hated her, wouldn't take her along, well, she'd saved his life, anyway. She didn't care who got the ranch, it wasn't as important to her as he was.

Cimarron looked around as they drove away with the two horses tied on behind. "What happened to Tequila?"

Luis snorted. "I probably scared him into running back to the house when he tried to bite me and I kicked at him. Little devil almost alerted Trace and ruined everything!"

"Kicking Tequila wasn't part of the deal," she complained. "Don't ever touch him again, or I might lose my temper and kick *your* shins."

"I'm sorry I upset you," he soothed, "it won't happen again, my love. But he's such a nuisance."

She settled back on the wagon seat and didn't look behind her. She would feel guilty if she thought about the unconscious man under the blanket back there. He had trusted her and she had betrayed him. No, not betrayed him, she was saving her love's life.

Cimarron brushed her hair back, listened to the wheels squeak as they drove away. "Tequila is a feisty little devil, isn't he? He probably did go back to the house when you scared him."

It was a cool night. Cimarron shivered a little and shoved her hands down in her skirt pockets, found the crumpled envelope again. "Oh, Luis, I found something this afternoon, forgot to give it to Don Diego."

"What is it?" He glanced over as she brought the envelope out.

Cimarron shrugged. "Just a letter or something. It fell out from behind Velvet Eyes's portrait when I straightened the frame."

Luis peered at it as she held it up. Then he shrugged and yawned. "I'm afraid that's nothing important, my dear. Have you opened it or shown it to anyone?"

"No." She felt a little crestfallen at his lack of interest. "I forgot about it, but I figured you could give it to the Don later."

Luis's tone reflected disinterest. "It's not anything important, Cimarron, only an appraisal of the painting's value for estate purposes. Every painting in the house has one in the frame. I'll put it back there when we return to the ranchero."

"Oh." She stuffed it back in her pocket, feeling very much the fool. Luis's tone indicated he thought her a stupid, hysterical female for attaching some importance to the envelope. She watched the low-lying silhouette of the ranchero as they drove away toward the west. The moon hung bright and full, throwing ghostly shadows as Luis clucked to the horse and the wagon picked up speed.

October, she thought with a shiver, *the waning days of the Comanche moon.* Soon the blue northers would blow in and the warriors would settle in for a quiet winter. Maybe by next spring the soldiers and the ranchers would be home from war to protect the frontier.

She heard Luis clear his throat. "Sweet one," he stammered, "I know this is not the time and place to talk of this, but you know how I feel about you, have felt about you since the first time I saw you."

"You're right, Luis," she said tersely, keeping her eyes straight ahead of the brown ribbon of road lapping across the endless hills. "This isn't the time or place."

"Just remember," he said a little desperately, glancing over at her, "now that Trace is leaving, I will be the one to finally inherit the Triple D when the Don dies, although I pray he has many years ahead of him." He crossed himself reverently. "You'd promised to marry me. Remember you still can, and have all the power, money, and prestige that goes with the Durango empire—"

"Let's not talk of it now," she snapped. "Later."

You're a fool, I suppose, she told herself as the wagon moved away from the ranch at a fast clip. A very handsome, polished gentleman has offered you a life of ease on a silver platter. But she was going with Trace Durango, no matter the hardships or the poverty that lay ahead as he rode away to an uncertain future.

For only a moment she glanced back toward the solid comfort of the sleeping hacienda. They drove along in the moonlight, straight into Comanche country. "Luis," she said, "I've never had the nerve to ask before. Just what was Velvet Eyes to Trace?"

He glanced at her sideways. "What do you mean? I figured you knew she was his mother."

She felt her mouth drop open. "His mother? I had begun to think she might be his sister or his sweetheart?"

"Well, she was only about sixteen when she had him."

"But the portrait with Tequila makes her look still only sixteen."

"That's not Tequila," he said, "I should know, I painted it. That's Poco, Tequila's grandfather."

Now she had a whole new bunch of questions, but it was too late to ask them. She craned her neck to look back at the ranchero fading into the night behind them.

Then she turned around, her chin up in stubborn determination. It was too late for regrets, for second thoughts. There was no turning back now. The cards were being shuffled tonight by Fate. She'd take the hand she'd been dealt, play it, and hope the queen of hearts was high and there was no joker in the deck.

Chapter Twenty-Five

Luis Durango glanced at the beautiful blonde beside him on the wagon seat as she held up the envelope.

Damn! Cimarron had finally found the incriminating letter, quite by accident, after he had searched frantically for it all these months! He forced himself to feign casual disinterest and not grab it from her hands. Even though his heart pounded with relief and excitement, he dared not make her suspicious until they were far away from the ranch.

Velvet Eyes' note. Luis watched Cimarron stuff it back into her pocket, obviously disappointed that he had shrugged it away. If she only knew how he had searched for that envelope she now held! Every drawer, closet, box, and cabinet on the entire ranch had been ransacked several times, without results. He'd explored Velvet Eyes' room but hadn't found anything. And her accusing eyes looking down from the portrait made him so uneasy, he'd not gone in there again. No, she wouldn't hide it in her room, knowing that was the first place he'd look. He'd even investigated the old barn. In fact, the day he had come to the old barn and found Trace there, Luis had intended to search it again.

How like clever Velvet Eyes! She must have realized he would never think to look behind the portrait he had painted himself. In fact, he had begun to doubt that there *was* any note, that that was Velvet Eyes' revenge. *Si*, the Cheyenne would plan that type of vengeance, making him sweat and worry, spend the rest of his life looking for an incriminating letter that didn't exist. The last six months had been a nightmare for him as he searched, fearing someone else would find it, tell the law.

When he got this stupid girl away from the ranch, he would take that note and destroy it. Then it would be her word against his. Luis had already planned how he would buy her silence. *With Trace's life.*

The hours passed and they drove west. He had not planned to bring her along. She would try to interfere with his plans. But she was a stubborn little thing.

He glanced down at his big Mexican spurs reflecting the moonlight. Mustangs could be broken for a submissive ride, and so could beautiful, spirited women.

She dozed off as the time lapsed and leaned against his shoulder. Very gently, he put his arm around her, let her rest her head against his chest as he drove.

His groin ached with the feel of her soft, warm body against his, and he looked down into the beautiful face and wished he could stop the wagon right now, carry her over under the scrubby mesquite, and make love to her.

Si, he would be kind and gentle until she was his legal wife. Once the *padre* said the words, she would be his body and soul. Everything on the Durango spread carried the Triple D brand, and she would be no different. On their wedding night, he would send all the servants away, and heat the branding iron in the fireplace of the study.

He felt his manhood swell painfully at the images of their lovemaking. She could beg, but who would be there to hear her? With no servants around to stop him, he'd rip the white wedding dress from her ripe body and tie her up. It would be exciting to hear her scream and beg when he put that glowing iron on her creamy hip, branding her as Luis Durango's forever. Then, if she still fought him, he would treat her just like a mustang with the sharp spurs and the cutting bit. When that satin, ivory body was smeared with its own blood, when the pretty bottom was crisscrossed with red welts from his quirt, she'd submit, all right, do anything and everything he demanded of her.

Among other things, Luis wanted his own sons to build his empire, and he had now found a dam worthy of the fine Durango bloodline. *Si,* he would see she produced a son for him every year, for he would mount her before she was even recovered from childbirth. With a baby continually in her arms and one in her belly, not to mention the nursery full, he wouldn't have to worry that his wife might end up in some other man's bed as had the married women he himself had been with. He looked down at her, thought wistfully of Velvet Eyes, the only other woman he had ever dreamed of marrying, in spite of all those sluts he had taken to bed.

Velvet Eyes. His heart twisted with bitter regret. He had loved her from the moment he came back from Spain and found his older brother Diego married to the young Cheyenne beauty. Many women had fallen prey to Luis's smooth charm and he had expected that Ojos de Pana would too.

But Ojos de Pana was faithful to Diego. She didn't even seem to see young Luis when he flirted with her, and once, when he tried to embrace her, she'd slapped his face sharply and threatened to tell her husband. That would not do. He had temporarily ceased his attempts at seduction. If Diego got mad and ran him off the ranch, Luis was not sure how he would support his expensive tastes. He wasn't really equipped to hold down a job, and besides, he didn't want to work. Let Diego kill himself over the ranch he had inherited from their parents when they died. The oldest son had gotten everything. His mother might have spoiled Luis, but she had known enough to leave the ranch to the responsible one and tell him to look after his baby brother. Not only had Diego gotten the ranch, he'd gotten the world's most desirable woman for a wife.

Velvet Eyes. Luis had never made love to the exquisite Cheyenne beauty, not even once. His brother's faithful wife had rebuffed him totally. He felt the tall blonde close to him as he drove and remembered. Luis had been the black sheep, the spoiled handsome son of a doting mother who had sent him off to medical school while his hardworking, older brother sweated to keep the Triple D running. But medical school had been too much work. When his grades were too poor and he was dismissed, Luis decided to become an artist. But that also took hard work and dedication. What he really liked to do was hang around the cantinas of Madrid, drinking and laughing with other rich, idle gentry.

Luis frowned as he drove along, swearing silently in Spanish. There had been the incident of a powerful Spanish father who had paid him to paint a portrait of his shy, homely daughter who was destined to be a nun. Luis had seduced her without a speck of remorse. However, there was regret when her brothers found out about it and came looking for him. He'd barely gotten out of Spain with his life. So he had come back to Texas, and his big brother had made a place for him, tried to teach him ranching.

Cimarron stirred against his shoulder. "Trace," she murmured in her sleep, "Oh, Trace . . ."

With a surge of jealousy, Luis wondered if Trace had already taken the beauty's virginity. Luis was vain and unsure of himself. He didn't like taking another man's leavings, and worse than that, if she were experienced she might compare Luis's lovemaking to his nephew's. He preferred to seduce virgins, so the girls would have no one with whom to compare him.

He ran his hand up under her breast so he could brush his fingertips against it while pretending to merely support her weight against him if she should awaken suddenly. Automatically, his other hand went to touch the little silver derringer he always carried in his pocket.

Si, he had carried it that day, too, the day Velvet Eyes had disappeared. As he drove west, he looked down at Cimarron asleep against his shoulder. Luis had thought he could never love again as he had loved Velvet Eyes. He had been wrong. This blonde's personality was very much like Ojos de Pana's. The thought pained him as he remembered that day, six months ago, the scene in the study. He'd walked in unexpectedly, caught Velvet Eyes with the account book open on his desk. When she raised her head and looked at him, he knew she had discovered his evil doings.

"Even when I followed you yesterday, Luis," she said softly, "I could not, would not believe what I saw when you met those Comancheros with the cattle." She looked back down at the scrawled numbers. "Now I know why the figures haven't made any sense lately. Numbers don't lie."

Luis shrugged, moved around behind her. "So? Diego has more than he needs. And it's hard to live on the allowance he gives me when I have such expensive tastes."

"I'll tell him what I've just discovered the minute he gets back." Her dark eyes flashed as she faced him, one hand still on the incriminating ledger. "I should have told him before, when I only suspected you. But I hesitated to come between my husband and his worthless baby brother until I could prove your guilt."

He reached into his pocket, pulled up the derringer where Velvet Eyes could see it. "Reconsider, my pretty one. Do you think I'd hesitate to kill to keep my secret?"

She eyed him coldly as he dropped the derringer back in his pocket. "I'm not afraid of you, Luis. I should have told the Don long ago how many times you tried to seduce me. But again, I hesitated to break his heart by telling him the truth. I'd hoped you'd reform. But this is the end. I'll tell him when he returns."

"Suppose you disappear?" Luis said, hoping to scare her. "Suppose they all thought you'd run away with a man?"

Velvet Eyes laughed, but she didn't move away from the desk. "My family would never believe that unless they heard it from my own lips."

"Perhaps that, too, could be arranged," he said, his mind busy. Luis wanted everything the Don possessed: his position, his ranch, his money, and yes, his woman. Luis hated his brother as he hated Diego's son. Every time he looked into Trace's face, he was reminded that Diego possessed Velvet Eyes, that he had sired a son to carry on his name. When he saw Trace, Luis always thought of Velvet

Eyes in Diego's arms, and it tortured him.

They heard Trace and Rosa talking as they came down the hall toward the study. Velvet Eyes jerked toward the sound as if she might cry out a warning, then looked toward the gun rack at the far end of the room.

"Don't even think about it." Luis pressed the derringer against her back through his coat pocket. His voice was cold but his fingers sweated. "You are getting ready to leave with a lover, a Yankee captain you met while on a trip to Galveston with the Don. And I think your son could even believe he was fathered by me—"

"I won't do it!" she said as the approaching footsteps echoed in the hall.

"*Si,* you would do anything to protect them," he whispered through clinched teeth. "I have two bullets if you don't. One for each of them. What have I to lose?"

And so the tragic little scene had been played out. He had not realized how brave Velvet Eyes was, how far she would go to protect her son. But it had been all she could do to stay between Luis and Trace. If there'd been a struggle, Trace might have managed to take the derringer from him, but not before Luis shot him. And Velvet Eyes didn't dare call out a warning. Trace couldn't have run to the gun rack before Luis killed him. It was preposterous that the two had believed the señora's words. But after all, they could not know she was under duress, and Velvet Eyes had always been known for her truthfulness.

They had left the study, she carrying the small travel bag, he holding her arm, appearing to assist her but in reality making sure she didn't run. The two in the house could not see that his other hand held a pistol. Luis couldn't miss if he fired this close to the woman's body. As they climbed into the buggy to leave, Velvet Eyes had turned to him, her lips trembling. "Was—was my performance satisfactory?"

He smiled as he patted the derringer in his pocket, clucked to the horse, and drove away. "You're quite an actress, my dear. Don't look back, I think Trace and Rosa are watching from the house. I thought for a minute there I was going to have to kill your angry son."

"Why do you think I put so much into my performance?" she answered bitterly, "I would do anything to protect him and my maid, you know that. That lie you forced me to tell him was despicable, Luis."

He chuckled as they left at a fast trot. "I thought for a moment, as we crossed the courtyard, you might take a chance on screaming a warning so that Trace would run for the gun rack."

"I thought about it," she answered, "but I knew you were desperate, that you might panic and shoot me. What are you going to do with me, Luis? Instead of holding me as a hostage, why don't you let me go and run away? If you'd promise never to return to the Triple D, I don't think Diego would report you to the law."

He winced as he looked down at the petite beauty. *What was he going to do with her?* He'd thought no further than escaping an armed confrontation with her son. Leave this ranch? Leave the luxury and prestige of the Durango empire? There was only one answer to his dilemma. Sighing, he headed the buggy toward Wimberley.

"Why don't you answer me, Luis?" There were tears in the magnificent dark eyes. "You've made my son hate me, made him think I'm a whore. God will punish you for what you do, Luis. Why did you force me to act this charade? Don't you realize I suspected you, that I would leave incriminating evidence behind?"

He fingered his mustache, thinking. "You lie out of desperation," he thought aloud, a little frightened now. Velvet Eyes was known for her truthfulness. What was it Trace always said about her? If Mother says it, you can take it to the bank.

"Do I?" she smiled mysteriously. "But you're not sure, are you, Luis? Even if you never find my letter, even if it doesn't really exist, you'd live in fear that Cheyenne vengeance might come full circle, that someday someone might find it." She frowned sadly. "It was rotten, what you made me say."

He thought about the possibility of a letter as they drove. "I needed leverage against your stubborn son and your worshiping maid, Velvet Eyes. If he thinks we share a terrible secret about his parentage, he'll be under my control, will do anything I want to protect his father from finding out. I'll involve the stupid Rosa, too."

Velvet Eyes wiped at a tear trickling down her dark skin. "You will go too far, Luis. How long can you steal from your brother before he figures it all out?"

Luis frowned and concentrated on the road ahead. "I underestimated you, didn't think you were clever enough to discover the shortage of funds. I didn't realize you had trailed me to the rendezvous with the Comancheros. If I hadn't walked into the study unexpectedly just now, I wouldn't have discovered that you knew in time to stop you from telling Diego."

She smiled, calm and serene. "Well, I've protected my son and my maid, and their lives were far more important than what Trace thinks of me. What happens now?"

He hesitated, looked over at her. "Velvet Eyes, I've always loved you, you know that, always wanted you. I'm better looking than my brother and much younger. Think about taking me as your lover. I don't want to kill you."

She shook her head. "I've never been unfaithful to Diego, I never will, not even to save my own life." She gave him a long, piercing look. "I promise you this, Luis, if you persist with this evil thing you do, I will seek revenge, destroy you somehow."

He snorted with laughter as they drove northwest. "Brave words from one who is helpless, at my mercy."

"Remember, I'm Cheyenne," she warned, "and although I've embraced the Church because of Diego, I still believe in the tribal, ancient ways. Somehow, I'll make you regret this evil thing you do, punish you in some ironic way."

He smiled at her as he whipped up the horse. "I don't believe in barbaric hocus pocus!"

She seemed to think about it a long moment as she studied him in the afternoon light. "My people believe in spirit magic, Luis, that one can return from the dead to protect or seek revenge. You are a handsome, vain man. Guard your looks well, my brother-in-law, for there is where your danger lies. What most you value is what you will lose if you anger the Cheyenne spirits. It will come full circle, through someone carrying the blood of my people."

He did not answer, although he felt suddenly uneasy. They drove a long time, until they were at the destination near Wimberley. But at the last, he wavered, could not bring himself to do it. He forced her out of the buggy, walked over to look down at the deep, forbidding water.

Velvet Eyes looked into the dark depths, then looked at him, her eyes brave, unwavering. "So this is where it all ends? You're a coward, Luis, a killer of women. Remember what I said to you of Cheyenne spirit medicine, of Indian vengeance. You won't get away with it!"

He studied the swirling water and his artistic hands trembled as he turned back to face her. She had known him better than he knew himself. Of course he could not do it. He loved her too much. "Velvet Eyes," he grabbed her shoulders, "reconsider. You don't want to die. We can have a fine life together."

She lifted her chin bravely. "And what must I do to save my life?"

Luis had never felt so torn by conflicting emotions. He was risking all he owned, all his stolen wealth, but he loved this woman so. "Why do you ask? You know what I want! Your word is good, I'll take your word if you give it. Promise you won't tell what you know to anyone or interfere with my plans. Promise that you'll become my woman."

She shook her head stubbornly. "And next you will ask my help in killing my husband and disinheriting my son so you can own and control the Triple D?"

He hesitated, thinking how small her shoulders were in his hands, how fragile she was. "I've always loved you, wanted you. But you're right. I'm greedy, Velvet Eyes; I want it all, you, and the ranch, and the Durango fortune."

"Then kill me if you can work up the courage," she said simply, looking up at him with those soft eyes. "Kill me, Luis, for I promise you this. If I leave this place, if you let me live, I will do everything in my power to stop you and protect my husband and son from your ruthlessness."

"No," he begged, pulling her to him. "No, my darling, I

don't want to kill you." He was weeping openly now as he tried to kiss her and she struggled. "I love you, don't you know that? But I can't let you tell and have my brother throw me off the ranch! I've never worked. I've always had money. I wouldn't know what to do if Diego made me go. Please, Velvet Eyes, I love you—"

She tried to twist out of his hands, and they fought and stumbled in the loose rock on the edge of the hole.

"Please, my darling," he begged, weeping, as they battled, "please, I'll let you live! Only love me—"

Her foot slipped as they struggled and she went off backwards. He heard her head strike the rock as she fell. Frozen in horror, he looked down at her floating on the water's surface, gazing up at him with dead, sightless eyes. Before he could move, the current caught her, pulled at her, dragged her down. The last thing he saw were the big eyes staring up at him accusingly. The current caught her in a whirlpool, pulled her out of sight forever, took her down, down into the bottomless depths of Jacob's Well. . . .

Luis trembled now looking at Cimarron sleeping against him as he drove through the darkness. Trace had not stirred since they'd left the barn. Would this beauty be willing to die for her love as Velvet Eyes had done? He shuddered at the memory. Everything had been going according to plan until this girl came along. First, he'd tripped old Juanita, the housekeeper, sent her falling down the stairs to her death. Even Rosa didn't know about that. But it had been important to place Rosa in the kitchen so she could cook. Poor Rosa. She was so ambitious, so greedy, so stupid. And she was fast losing her looks. It hadn't been hard to dupe her into the plot, make her think her beloved señora had run away to escape the old Don's cruelty. Luis had been very convincing as he told Rosa the proud señora had confided to him that the Don secretly mistreated her. Then Rosa had been willing to help Luis poison his brother. That time he had spent in medical school had been useful, after all.

Tonight he would hand Rosa over to the Comancheros as

a gift, make his nephew a slave of the Comanche. With that weapon, he could force Cimarron to marry him, do what he wanted, especially since he'd had one of his informants start searching into her background, found something interesting in Fandango. . . .

Cimarron had given him quite a scare this afternoon. He'd thought at first she was on to him. Luis had almost collapsed with relief when he'd found out she thought Trace was the guilty one.

Rosa. His mistress had been sent off this afternoon to bring his Comancheros and Comanches to the meeting place. Little did Rosa know he intended to hand her over to the new second-in-command, Pedro, as a gift. The ugly blind-eyed one had always lusted for her and the white stallion. Now Pedro would have both. Luis had grown tired of the stupid, uneducated girl in the past six months.

Cimarron awakened, looked around. "Is it much farther?"

"No, my dear," he assured her. The Comanches would be waiting just up ahead at the rendezvous in the grove of trees. They would geld their new slave, of course, to make him obedient and tractable. But Trace wouldn't be needing his manhood anymore. After all, Luis would have his woman.

Cimarron looked over at him and he thought he'd never seen such beauty, not since Velvet Eyes. He'd used the small sketch of the blonde to paint a giant, magnificent portrait. When he was Don, the painting would hang over the fireplace. "You know, Luis," she said, "I don't understand how Trace could have found out about oleander. I'd think it would take someone with medical training."

"I guess he found it in the library. After all, that drunken old quack from Connecticut didn't know, either," Luis said. Cimarron was more clever than he had thought, to figure out about the pepper mill.

She sighed. "If it hadn't been for Tequila getting a bite off the old Don's tray, I guess the Don would have died and we'd all have blamed the malignancy."

"*Si*, if it hadn't been for the dog, it would have worked out according to plan." *Damn that mutt!* What terrible thing could Luis think to do to the chihuahua for almost ruining things? Whatever torture he decided on for Tequila wouldn't be enough. And Luis still had to go back to the ranch and finish poisoning his brother.

"I still haven't figured out how Trace knew which ranches to raid. I suppose Rosa carried the messages."

He shrugged casually. "Probably Miss Fancy's whores told him which rancher had come into money, who had bought a fine new horse worth stealing." That and the gambling tables of San Antonio were where Luis got his information.

"But I don't understand about Holt, the gunfighter."

"What do you mean?" He looked over at her as the wagon moved up the road toward the grove of trees. That loco Holt. He should have known better than let El Lobo recommend him.

"He said he'd been brought in to kill the heir, but he must not have known who the heir actually was, since he took a shot at you."

"Probably not." That loco fool had missed Trace. That was the reason Luis had refused to pay Holt and they had argued. The other shooting had been staged so Luis would have Cimarron as a witness. He hadn't expected Holt to double-cross him, steal the cash box and the girl. Thank God Trace had killed the gunman before he could blab.

Cimarron sighed. "I wouldn't have thought Trace would get double-crossed by his own Comanchero when they staged the ranch raid."

Luis laughed. "There's no honor among thieves, they say." Wasn't that the truth! El Lobo must have wanted the blonde bad to chance Luis' wrath. But he'd managed to kill him before he could tell anything. Handing Rosa over to the ugly Pedro was her punishment for double-crossing Luis.

"When Trace's sister, Dallas, returns, what will you tell her?"

"Well, she hasn't been heard of in four years; maybe she's dead and will never turn up." In fact, Luis was counting on it. He didn't want to have to fight the spirited Dallas over the inheritance. But surely she was dead. Anyway, he'd worry about that problem in the future. He had all the trouble he could deal with right now.

Luis pulled into the grove of trees, heard the bird calls signal each other. *Good. The Comanche were waiting.*

Cimarron frowned. "Why are we stopping here?"

"I thought this was far enough."

"I hope you brought enough supplies to last him a while," she said worriedly.

"Of course." Trace wasn't going to need much as a slave of the Comanche. And Luis wanted that stallion for himself. He'd geld that black devil, take his savage Spanish bit, his quirt, and his spurs to that big horse.

He came around to help Cimarron from the wagon seat. Foolish girl, he thought as he put his hands on her small waist, lifted her down. He knew what she was planning, had as soon as he had seen her bring Peso out. Cimarron thought she was going to leave with Trace.

"I just hope we're doing the right thing." She looked up at him with those dark eyes as he put her down.

"Of course, we are, my dear." The right thing for Luis Durango. He took her arm and they walked over to a boulder and leaned against it.

He could see the worry on her pretty face in the moonlight. "I—I'm dreading this," she said. "He's going to hate me for my part in this."

More than you know, my sweet. "Everything will be fine, Cimarron," he assured her. "Trust me."

"Luis." She hesitated, bit her lip. "I—I'm not going back to the ranch with you. I've decided to go with Trace. I love him, I can't help it. I'd rather live poor, on the run with him, than be your señora and have all the luxury of the Triple D. I'm sorry to hurt you, but there can be only one man for me."

Tears came to his eyes, and he blinked them away. "You're very much like Velvet Eyes," he murmured. "Such a woman is very rare. I never had one care so much for me."

Her face clouded. "I—I'm sorry, Luis. I just can't give you my love."

There was no need for pretense anymore, now that they were far away, now that he had her in his power. He put his hands on her shoulders. "Then I'll just have to take what I can get, won't I? You're not going anyplace, Cimarron, except back to the Triple D with me, to become my obedient, submissive wife."

She looked up at him, puzzlement on her face. "No," she shook her head, "You don't understand, Luis—"

"No, it's you who don't understand, my sweet." He smiled down at her, tightened his grip on her shoulders. "I'm going to do you just like I did my nephew. For six months I've blackmailed him with a lie to keep his mouth shut. I'm going to hold something over your head, in this case, Trace's life, to insure you do as you're told."

She looked up at him, obviously not comprehending. "Is this some kind of joke?"

He nodded, caressing her shoulders with his hands. "The joke's on you, sweet one. By the way, I've had someone do some investigating. I know there's a beauty named Cimarron Heinrich missing from the town of Fandango. There was something about a stabbing—"

"You rotten snake!" she swore, trying to pull out of his hands, but he grabbed her, dragged her back to him. "What's this all about? Are *you* the guilty one?"

He twisted her arms behind her so cruelly that she cried out. "Of course!" he said. "And even now, my mistress, Rosa, brings the Comanche to rid us of my half-breed nephew."

She looked up at him, stunned. "You and Rosa?"

"You and your stupid cowboy should have trusted each other, confided in each other more. Trust is what love's all about. In that, Velvet Eyes and Diego could have given you both lessons."

She tried to pull away from him, but he held her pinned against the rock, her hands held behind her while he ran his free hand over her breasts. "Trace will kill you for touching me!"

He smirked and continued his stroking, enjoying the feel of her satin skin. "We are already surrounded by Comanche, my sweet." A bird call echoed through the woods. "Hear that? It's a signal. Now we'll make a deal. You go back to the ranch, keep your mouth shut, and marry me."

"Never!" she gasped defiantly, struggling to break free of

his caressing hands.

"I don't think you mean that, sweet one." He smiled at her, pulled her blouse down so he could enjoy the sight of her beautiful breasts. They were full and creamy, the nipples pink as delicate rosebuds. "After all, your lover's life is going to depend on what kind of obedient wife you make. If you make me angry, I'll send a message to the Comanche, tell them to torture the slave."

Her mouth dropped open and she ceased her struggling. "No one could be so cruel! Besides, why would you want me, knowing I love Trace?"

He tilted her face up to him and she didn't fight him. "I can be ruthless, cruel, when I want something badly, and in this case, I want the ranch, and you. . . ."

"But I love Trace—"

"But you'll be my submissive wife, let me make love to you anytime I choose and bear heirs for me. If you love Trace enough, you'll do that, and in return, I'll see the Comanche don't mistreat their slave too badly over the years." He would tell her about the gelding later, gloat over it to her.

Her face was a frozen mask of emotions as he ran his hands over her ripe body. She cringed but didn't try to push him away. "You'll go back and kill your own brother?"

He shrugged, enjoying the softness of her. "How else would I get the ranch? Mama thought she was so smart, leaving it to Diego, but I'll get it and run it my way."

"I'll tell the law, I'll tell everyone in the county what you did—"

"No, you won't, sweet one. Remember Trace's life depends on whether you make me happy, keep me satisfied. And later, I'm going to watch you destroy that letter in your pocket, because, you see, I'm sure it contains damning evidence against me."

Her eyes widened. "The letter! You acted as if it weren't important."

He smiled, relishing the shock on her pretty face. "I didn't want to make you suspicious until we were too far from the ranch for you to alert anyone, call for help."

He pulled her closer. "Now let's see how submissive you

can be, how much you can please me," he murmured. "You'll let me make love to you to protect him, won't you?"

She trembled in his arms, swallowed hard. *"Si,* Luis. I hate you, but to protect Trace, I'll do anything you want."

"That's a good girl, I knew you'd see it my way." He tilted her face up, forced her mouth open with a savage kiss. She was stiff and wooden in his arms. "You're not pleasing me, sweet one," he murmured. His fingers dug into her waist until she flinched. "Please me, if you love him."

She relaxed a little in his arms and he ran his hands over her eagerly, his blood hot and pounding in his temples. He had dreamed of forcing her to submit to him since the first time he'd seen her, and now, it was all coming true. He ran his hands down to stroke her small hips, grew excited at the idea of taking his sharp spurs to her, his quirt, the terrible Spanish bit. He'd do things to her he wouldn't even dare do to a whore, but she would be helpless as his wife, submitting to protect Trace.

"Make me happy, sweet one," he commanded, and her arms came up slowly, hesitantly around his neck. He crushed her to him, kissing her so savagely he could taste the blood as his teeth cut her lip. He forced his tongue into her mouth, holding her head so she couldn't move away while he caressed the insides of her lips. Later at the ranch he would force her to take his manhood that way and she wouldn't dare object. It was the ultimate surrender, the supreme domination. The thought excited him to a fever.

He lifted her now, set her on the boulder, pulled her blouse still lower to expose her lovely breasts completely. "You are more desirable than I ever imagined," he gasped as his greedy mouth sought the rouge-pink crests.

For only a moment, she stiffened. Then, as if seeming to recall, she brought her hands up, pulled his face against her breasts. *"Si,* Luis, I—I'll make you very happy!"

She was weeping inside, he could tell from the way she trembled, but he didn't care. If he couldn't have her love, he'd settle for her body.

He put his hands on her thighs as he kissed her nipples, pushed her skirt up. Running his hands impudently up and down her bare thighs, he looked up at her and saw the pure hate in her eyes. He didn't mind. He wanted her badly enough that he didn't care if she hated him. She would be his captive love slave, submit to him anytime he demanded it, in any way he wanted her. If she hesitated, he would only need to remind her of the Comanche's prisoner whose life depended on her behavior.

The bird call echoed through the woods, closer now. Luis sighed. His manhood ached with need for relief, but the coupling with this beauty would have to wait until the business was finished.

He ran his hands over her breasts again, bent his head to kiss her bare thighs. Later, he would kiss and caress her depths, make her forget the cowboy. Surely she was as passionate as she appeared. He was eager to find out. He gripped her thighs so hard that she winced.

"You must remember to please me," he reminded her, and she dutifully pulled his face against her breasts, bent her head to kiss his hair. "Please, Luis," she whispered, "Don't hurt Trace, I'll let you do anything to me. I'll do anything you demand, just let him go."

His groin ached to mate with her. The frustration made him bite her breast, and she whimpered but she didn't pull away. "See, my dear," he murmured, "you're already learning to be submissive, to please me." He moved his lips across her nipples wishing he had time to take her now. But it must wait. The Comanche were assembling to receive delivery of their new slave.

Chapter Twenty-Six

Trace came back to consciousness gradually. For a long moment, he blinked, trying to decide where he was, what had happened. His hand brushed away the blanket covering his face. He stared up at the stars, the bright Comanche moon.

A wagon? Puzzled, he looked around. Yes, he lay under a tumble of blankets in the back of a wagon stopped in a grove of cottonwood and willow trees. His own horse and the palomino, Peso, stood saddled and tied to the tailgate, looking back at him.

His head ached. He ran his hand up to his temple, felt dried blood there. *What had happened? Where was he?*

He tried to remember the sequence of events that might have brought him here. All he could recall was standing in the barn, kissing Cimarron. He had intended to ask her to marry him tonight. In fact, this afternoon, she had interrupted him in the study while he was searching for a proper poem for the occasion. When she'd caught him by surprise, he'd been too embarrassed to admit he was reading poetry, had quickly slipped the volume back on the shelf.

Cimarron. Her image came to him, the feel of her warm, yielding body against his, the taste of her mouth, the sweet scent of hay ... a noise ... Tequila growling a warning. When Trace had whirled around, he remembered only pain and light exploding in his head. Then he knew the sensation of falling ... falling....

Where was she? Suppose whoever hit him had hurt her?

Trace struggled to sit up in the wagon, found himself dizzy, his head aching. *Cimarron. He had to find her, help her.*

The soft sound of two voices came to him faintly on the autumn breeze. He looked over the wagon side at the figures leaning against a boulder, talking. He concentrated hard to focus his eyes. *Luis and Cimarron?*

Yes, that's who it was, all right. They stood only a few yards away and Luis had his arms around her, caressing and kissing her while they talked.

Trace stared unbelievingly for a long moment. But she wasn't resisting Luis's caresses. Damn her! He realized suddenly that the whole thing had been planned. The sultry blonde had led him into a trap. Luis had been waiting for him in the barn. Damn the tricky little bitch! He'd been a fool even to think of marrying her. *Well, Trace, my boy, you knew better, you know women aren't to be trusted. Why did you let down your guard?*

She's just like your mother, after all. He didn't want to think about that, how Luis had been using Trace's knowledge of his paternity for the last six months, blackmailing him to keep his mouth shut about Luis's activities. If his fath—no, if Don Diego ever found out his wife had been unfaithful, that the son he loved had been sired by his younger brother, the shock would kill that fine old man. Trace had let himself be blackmailed to protect the Don from the knowledge.

Damn Luis! He watched as the handsome Spaniard caressed the blonde. Wasn't it enough that he'd seduced Rosa, had been sleeping with her for months? Trace knew about it, but Luis had blackmailed him to keep his mouth shut. Besides, how could he tell his *compadre,* Sanchez, that his wife was a faithless bitch? Now it appeared Luis was adding Cimarron to his list of conquests.

A bird call echoed through the shadowy trees and Trace tensed, realizing it was not a bird of the hill country, especially calling at night. But he knew who would use a bird call as a signal. The hair on the back of his neck went up in prickles of fear as the chilling realization swept over him. *Comanches.*

He watched Luis lift Cimarron to sit atop the boulder. The pair seemed oblivious to anything but their lovemaking. Trace watched Luis pull down her blouse, exposing her full breasts. On the breeze, he picked up Luis's faint words, "You're more desirable than I ever imagined." Even as Trace watched, torn by jealousy, the Spaniard's mouth moved across her firm pink nipples.

And Cimarron clasped his head to her breasts, murmuring, *"Si,* Luis, I—I'll make you very happy!"

Why that cheating little tart! Trace clenched his teeth, his head aching, his heart torn as he watched Luis push her skirt up, stroke her bare thighs. Trace almost shouted, *No, she's mine!*

Even as Trace watched in unbelieving anguish, Luis pulled her to him, seemed to be whispering endearments in her ear as he ran his hands familiarly over her thighs.

In his rage, Trace had to fight to control himself as Cimarron tilted her head back for Luis's kiss.

Shaking with jealous rage, Trace felt for his pistol. He'd kill them both for this betrayal. The strange bird call echoed through the trees again.

His hand went to his waist in vain. The holster . . . Frantically, he felt for it, then remembered. Of course he hadn't gone armed walking out with a beautiful girl to the barn to steal a few kisses. Trace held his breath and his temper while he watched them kiss and caress in the moonlight. A Comanche war party was in the area, yet Luis and the girl he kissed were so lost in each other and their lust, they didn't even seem to hear the signals. Luis might not even be armed, and Trace's big Colt was in the gun rack back at the study.

What to do . . . He sat up, started to call out a warning to them. Then he gritted his teeth, watching Luis kiss her beautiful breasts, move to kiss her creamy thighs.

Damn her to hell! Damn them both! They deserved the torture of the Comanche. Trace's Indian blood made him light-footed as a panther. He slipped out of the wagon, untied the two horses at the tailgate. Glancing back at the two entwined in each other's arms, he had to fight his anger at the betrayal. He wanted to turn and run to them, jerk Luis away from her, hit him with all the force he could put behind a hard-driving fist. Yes, that mouth that was kissing her breasts should be cut to shreds by pounding blows, the handsome face should be smeared with Luis's own blood.

No, no time for revenge, Trace thought as he sneaked out of the wagon and tiptoed away leading the two horses. His own Cheyenne blood made him sense the presence of the Comanche war party when no gringo would have known it. Let the Comanche do his revenge for him when the savages surrounded the unsuspecting pair of lovers. No one could think up tortures like the Comanche. Trace intended to clear out of there, and in a few minutes the faithless pair would be screaming their lives away staked out naked by a campfire. Oh, they might let Don Diego ransom Cimarron, but of course, all the braves would rape her first. Never, in all the history of the frontier, had a grown white woman ever been returned by Plains tribes without being raped first.

Well, hell, she deserved it for breaking Trace's heart. And Luis . . . the Comanche had been known to cut off a man's maleness, shove it down his throat while they tortured him to death in other ways. Luis deserved that for all the women he'd seduced, Cimarron, Rosa, Velvet Eyes. The thought of his mother caused Trace anguish as he moved as silently as his Cheyenne warrior ancestors, tiptoeing away leading the two horses.

For six months now, ever since Velvet Eyes had admitted that Trace had been fathered not by her husband but by his baby brother, Luis, the handsome Spaniard had used it as ammunition against Trace. Yes, Trace knew Luis was stealing livestock. He'd figured that out by the figures in the account books. He'd known Luis was seducing Rosa, too, but the blackmail made Trace helpless to do anything about it.

So Luis and Cimarron were about to be captured by the savages and get what they deserved. Trace led the horses a short distance away before he mounted Nightwind. Leading Peso, he rode along the trail headed back east. He wasn't sure if the war party were watching him. But this he knew, if he could reach a straight, level place in this twisted trail and put Nightwind into a gallop, there was no horse in Texas fast enough to catch him. He'd make it back to the ranch and be rid of that conniving, cheating pair forever.

His head still ached and his mouth tasted as fuzzy as an old saddle blanket. Nightwind picked his way quietly along the trail at a walk. Up ahead, Trace could see a level place gleaming in the moonlight. If he could reach that point, no war party could catch the fleet stallion on the straightaway.

He took a deep breath to still his pounding heart, and then, on the breeze, his keen Cheyenne nose picked up the slight scent. *Comanche,* he thought, and had to fight himself from panicking, kicking the stallion into a lope here and now. He must not alert the braves to the fact that he knew they were out there watching him.

No one but an Indian could have caught the smell, read it. The rank, rancid scent of old sweat, buffalo dung, and bear grease. It was Comanch, all right, not Kiowa. The bear was a Kiowa spirit animal. They would never kill one, or smear themselves with its fat. Once you smelled a Comanch, you never forgot the scent. To Trace, it smelled like rotten Death.

He was afraid now as he forced the stallion to keep to a walk, afraid as only a man who had seen the tortured victims of Indian raids could be. It was a Texas legend that sometimes when the Rangers overran a Comanche camp, they mercy-killed the writhing, screaming lumps of white flesh that had once been human beings.

He glanced back over his shoulder. The pair of lovers were so involved with each other that they hadn't noticed him leaving or the skulking forms moving through the shadows. *Good enough for them!* he thought grimly. They deserved what the warriors would do to them.

But abruptly, he remembered Cimarron's dark eyes looking up into his, her mouth yielding beneath his own as he made love to her under the oleander bushes back at the ranch. Another face came to him, the face of Emily Forester as the Rowland brother had described her. Trace could only imagine what the Comanche must have done to the woman to drive her into blank, mindless insanity. . . .

He looked ahead. Only a few more yards and he would be on the straight, level stretch where he could whip the stallion up and outrun the red devils. They wouldn't kill Cimarron, he thought, she was too pretty, her golden hair too highly valued. Some chief would take her for his own, as had happened to Cynthia Ann Parker. When her soft, tawny body was lying under some savage male as he used her, he might not care if her mind was destroyed. As long as that warrior could enjoy her ripe body. . . .

Could Trace go back to the old Don, look him in the eye and lie convincingly, tell him he did not know what had happened to the missing pair? Besides, there were only two saddle horses, and three people. They would never be able to unharness the old wagon horse in time. That old horse was slow as Christmas besides.

The bird call echoed faintly through the trees again as the Comanches moved up, signaled each other. He turned to look behind him at the pair still kissing by the boulder. *You're a fool even to consider going back, Trace Durango, you won't be able to get them out before the war party surrounds the area. You'll only be killed trying.* He saw his mother's face before him suddenly, and the good, noble countenance of old Don Diego. Everything they'd taught him came back ringing in his ears. *What sets a man above an animal is the fact that he has a conscience, that he knows right from wrong. And what Trace Durango was doing was wrong.*

He took a deep breath, reined in the stallion, turned him slowly around. His only chance to save them was the element of surprise. If he rode in at a hard gallop, brought them out riding double before the war party realized what was intended, they had one slim chance of outrunning the Indians. But he was counting on the element of surprise and two fine-blooded horses to save all three.

He settled himself in the saddle, tensing with readiness. Then he brought his reins down hard across the startled stallion's flanks, and the horse bolted ahead as Trace screamed out, "Comanche! Watch out! Comanche!"

The black snorted and raced back toward the boulder, Peso running easily along beside as they galloped to an almost certain death.

"Comanche!" he shouted as he rode forward, saw Luis and Cimarron's startled faces as they pulled apart, looked toward him. He had a split-second to make his plans as he galloped into the circle, saw warriors running toward him. Trace would throw Luis the reins of the other horse while reaching down himself to lift Cimarron up before him on Nightwind. The odds were impossible, he knew, and the pair didn't deserve his help, but he was a man, not an animal and he couldn't ride away and leave them to the terrible tortures of the Comanche.

Luis didn't seem to understand what he was shouting. Trace thought with horror as he galloped up. The handsome Spaniard stood looking up at him, not moving, even as the savages ran out of the woods around them. He heard Cimarron scream. Then he was surrounded by the skulking braves as a dozen hands reached up, dragged him kicking and fighting from the stallion that reared and plunged in confusion.

A warrior screamed in agony as the black's hooves flashed like steel hammers, catching the man in the head. He went down, rolling in pain under the horse that stomped him into a shapeless mass. Trace shouted encouragement to the horse as he screamed and fought his captors himself.

Everything seemed to move in slow motion, as in a dream, Trace thought as he struggled, a dream where one fights and tries to run away, but there are dozens of hands reaching out to stop him, pull him back.

He thought he must be losing his mind as he fought the grabbing hands and they struggled near the wagon. He imagined he saw a small head poke out from under the blanket, awakened by the noise and shouting.

But Cimarron screamed, "Tequila!" and the little dog charged out of the wagon, barking and snapping among the horses, causing them to rear and buck. The dog was a tiny tiger among the Comanche, dashing here and there, biting ankles while the braves shouted and shrieked.

Luis snarled. "Cimarron, catch that damned dog before he makes our friends mad enough to take it out on us! Dealing with Comanches is tricky business!"

Trace stopped struggling as two strong bucks held him prisoner. He stared unbelieving as Cimarron gave him a guilty look before running to obey Luis, snatching up the barking, snapping chihuahua.

She paused before him, holding the dog against her breasts as the warriors pinned his arms. "Trace, you don't understand. This wasn't the plan at all! I didn't know—"

"I understand!" he snarled at her. "I understand I've been betrayed because I went against my better instincts and finally trusted a woman. What a fool I was! I even rode back to save you two from the Indians!"

Luis leaned against the boulder and smiled. "Don't waste words on my stupid nephew, my sweet," he said. "He doesn't know lies from the truth anyway, or he would never have believed what I forced Velvet Eyes to tell him, then used to make him do as I wanted. He was scared I'd tell his father what Velvet Eyes had said."

Trace felt his face go ashen. "But you're my father. Velvet Eyes said—"

"It is amazing what you can force a woman to say when you have one of these in her back," Luis said, bringing a little silver derringer out of his coat pocket. As he handled it, the barrel reflected the bright moonlight. "Especially when you've told her if she doesn't, you'll kill her precious son and maid."

He must have misunderstood what his uncle had said, Trace thought as he struggled to break away from the braves who held his arms pinned back. "What—what do you mean?"

There must have been fifty Comanche braves gradually forming a ring around them. Luis gestured and the whole group moved into the woods to a nearby clearing where a large bonfire burned. Trace fought, but his captors dragged him along, and the circle formed again in the clearing.

"Just what I said," Luis sneered, "you were stupid to doubt your mother."

But Trace could only stare in shock at his uncle. "You're not my father? Are you saying you forced Velvet Eyes to lie? That she never slept with you?"

"Velvet Eyes was the most faithful wife I ever met," Luis admitted. "I tried all those years to get her in my bed, but she loved her husband." Luis looked around the circle, obviously puzzled. "Where are my Comanchero? I see no one but savages, and I don't know them."

Trace gasped with surprise. "*Your* Comanchero?"

"*Si*, I'm their leader. That's why I had to kill El Lobo, I was afraid he might confess to you. . . ." He looked around again, spoke to a warrior. "Where are Pedro and his *hombres?* They were to be here."

"Gone," the brave answered in border Spanish. "Gone from my people." He used the sign language signifying the Comanche tribe, the fluid backward movement of the arm meaning "snake." "Gone home to their mountains. Pedro take white horse, go. Say come back other times."

Luis' face turned an angry red. "What is this foolishness of their going without my orders? That leaves me alone to deal with these savages, and they don't really know who I am—"

Trace laughed coldly. "Then I reckon you might be in a little trouble, unless Rosa arrives to identify you." Trace looked around the circle, thinking the crimson war paint reflecting in the campfire made the braves look like demons from Hell. He snarled at Cimarron. "And to think I rode back to try to save you, not knowing you were here to meet with them!"

He struggled again to break free, and a big Comanche brave struck him, knocked him to his knees. With a strangled sob, Cimarron put down the dog, ran over to throw her arms around Trace. He looked deep into the teary brown eyes as she embraced him. "What's your game now, darlin'?"

Cimarron held him close, looked up into his smoldering eyes. "Trace," she gasped, "I've been such a stupid, blind fool to be duped by Luis. If I had only trusted you, told you what I suspected—"

Luis snorted. "You're both a pair of fools!" He faced them, hands on his belt. "If you both hadn't been so suspicious, so afraid to trust each other, neither of you would be in this fix now. Love is trust, stupid ones. If you love someone, you trust them. Velvet Eyes should have taught you that."

A man came into the firelit circle and Cimarron gasped at the majesty of him, the eagle feathers in his black braids, the rich beadwork on his costume. The others made way for him respectfully, but the tiny dog growled. She grabbed up Tequila and fell to her knees beside her love, who was still held by two big braves. There must be fifty or sixty warriors in the circle, she thought. For the first time she noticed the crimson and ochre war paint on their faces, the deadly lances in their hands. Her heart pounded so fearfully, she was sure all could hear it.

The leader folded his arms, looked around at the three, and spoke regally to Luis. "Are you the *hombre* the Spanish girl carries messages for? We have never met."

Haughtiness and disdain were all too evident on Luis's aristocratic features. "Of course, I am."

The Comanche's frown deepened. "Be careful of your tone, white man, when you speak to Peta Nocona, chief of the Nocona band. Blame me not for taking caution. With the Comanchero gone back to their own land, I have only the word of the girl as to the identity of her secret leader."

Cimarron hugged the little dog to her, afraid yet curious as she stared at the chief. So this was the legendary Peta Nocona, husband to Cynthia Ann Parker who had been recaptured by the Texas Rangers and returned kicking and screaming to her white family. The whites said she had left two half-breed sons with the Comanche.

She looked around, trying to figure out a plan, a way of escape for her and Trace. It was hopeless. There must be fifty warriors here, all painted for war.

Peta Nocona looked from one white man's face to another. "One of you is the leader of the Comanchero, the other the good, strong slave we are supposed to take away tonight. I will know if you speak the truth, Spaniard, when the girl comes over from our other camp down the creek."

Cimarron looked up at him and back to Trace as the chief's words sank in. "No!" she screamed, "Luis, you lied! You said we were going to take Trace out, exile him from the ranch. That's why I brought Peso, I was going with him!"

The chief looked at her admiringly. "The yellowhair is a gift for me? I have wanted no other woman since the Tejanos carried off my beloved Naduah, the one the whites call Cynthia, four winter counts ago."

Luis looked uneasy, angry. "No," he said, "she's mine. I bring you the slave as a gift, and the golden horse, Peso."

"No!" Cimarron screamed. "I'm not your woman, and how dare you give him my horse?"

"You rotten bastard!" Trace struggled to his feet, trying to charge Luis, but the warriors grabbed him. "She's mine! And the black stallion's mine!"

Luis smiled, fingered his mustache. "I'm going to geld your stallion and ride him myself. If gelding doesn't gentle him, I'm looking forward to using my big Mexican spurs, quirt, and a Spanish bit on the ebony devil!"

"You filthy—" Trace fought to break away from his captors.

"And as for your woman," Luis laughed, "when you're sweating and slaving for the Comanche, I want you to think often about me making love to her, putting my sons in her belly. All these years, I had to see that image of the woman I loved married to my brother."

"I won't let you make love to me!" Cimarron shouted, her face hot with anger. "Do you hear me? I'll never—"

"Never's a long time, sweet one," Luis smiled. "Remember what I told you a while ago while I kissed you? If you are obedient, submissive to my attentions, you buy protection for Trace."

Trace looked from her to him, puzzlement on his face. "What's he saying? He was forcing you to make love to him a while ago when I saw you—"

"I was trying to protect you, Trace," she wept. "I would let him do anything to me to save you. I love you, I've always loved you."

Luis laughed. "I'm sure she means it, nephew. But even if her heart belongs to you, I'll enjoy her body just the same. She will make a beautiful Señora Luis de Durango when we go back."

"But I love Trace! Don't you realize that?"

"It doesn't matter, sweet one." He shrugged ruefully. "You see, I want you bad enough to take you any way I can. As long as I can make love to you, force you to produce sons for me, I don't care who rules your heart. By the way, I'll tell you now, my sweet. Trace isn't the one who's been sleeping with Rosa; I am."

She felt suddenly sick as she turned slowly, looked into Trace's eyes. "Then you were telling me the truth?"

His eyes were a gentle caress on her face. "I've loved only you since the first moment I saw you, Cimarron. But I was afraid to trust you, afraid to love you, afraid you were like my mother—"

Luis laughed, a hard bitter laugh. "She's *exactly* like your mother, you poor, blind fool! You should have listened to Don Diego. He alone believed and trusted Velvet Eyes, and he never doubted her love."

Trace looked at Luis, confusion evident on his rugged features. "But that day in the study, Velvet Eyes said—".

"I told you she would have said anything I told her to say, stupid blind one." Luis took the derringer from his pocket, hefted it in his hand. "Do I have to draw you a picture? Like your clever blonde, your mother had discovered the shortage in the account books and my involvement with the Comanchero. She was going to tell the Don. I knew if I let her do that, he'd kick me off the ranch, and I have no skills, no way to hold a job. I'm used to money and an easy life."

"Then when she slapped me to protect you—"

"Velvet Eyes was protecting you, my stupid nephew," Luis grinned. "If you had attacked me, I would have shot you down and she knew it. The other lie was my idea, the one about me being your father."

Trace's face went pale. "She—she lied about that?"

"With a gun in her back? Of course, she did. I knew you would do anything I told you if you thought that, afraid I would tell the lie to my brother."

"You made me think my own mother was a whore," Trace said grimly, "when in reality, she—"

"When in reality, she was the faithful wife your father

always knew she was. I tried to get her to help me kill him, marry me, and take over the ranch. She wouldn't do it, even to save her own life."

The horrible realization of his words echoed around the circle, and with a terrible scream of vengeance, Trace broke free of his captors and charged across the circle. Cimarron could only clutch the growling dog and watch Trace attack.

Trace growled low in his throat like some terrible avenging animal as he lunged toward the Spaniard. He saw the flash as Luis brought the derringer up, fired at him. The first shot went wild as Luis's hand shook. The second shot caught Trace on the right shoulder as he leaped for the man. The pain burnt across his flesh like a smoking branding iron, but his momentum carried him forward.

He craved vengeance, and all the hounds of Hell, much less a bullet, couldn't have stopped him as he lunged and they went down, rolling and struggling in the dust.

Luis broke free, swayed to his feet, threw the empty derringer at him. It struck a glancing blow off Trace's chest and he gasped at the impact, staggered.

Luis looked around the silent circle of warriors. "Stop him, do you hear? Stop him!"

But the great chief held up a restraining hand to his watching men. "Let the gringos fight it out. If he is indeed the powerful leader of the Comanchero, he can win this fight. Besides, seldom do we get such entertainment."

Luis stumbled backward as Trace advanced on him. He looked around at the Indians. "I am the Comanchero leader, *comprende?* And I say seize him!"

But Peta Nocona shook his head. "I will take the word of Pedro, or Rosa, or the winner of this fight as leader, for surely the powerful chief of the Comanchero can win."

Trace staggered to his feet, reaching up to touch his bloody, throbbing shoulder. "So it's just you and me facing off, Luis, like two stallions fighting for control of the herd, the right to rule this stretch of prairie."

Luis stopped backing, seeming to realize the disadvantage Trace was up against with his injured shoulder. *"Si,* and the stallion who rules the herd gets to mount the filly, right?"

His big spurs gleamed in the firelight. He nodded toward Cimarron who watched from the sidelines, still clutching the dog. "They tell me Comanche sometimes geld slaves to make them docile. I'll see to it myself before I ride out of here with your woman, your horse. They both need a lesson from my spurs, my Spanish bit, my quirt."

The images the words brought to his mind made Trace frown with fury as he advanced on the other.

"Watch out, Trace," Cimarron screamed from the sidelines, "don't you see he's trying to make you angry enough to lose your judgment?"

Trace nodded, trying to bridle his cold rage. "I know what he's up to, darlin', but fighting bare-handed, he's a coward. He's going to think he's tangled with a scorpion."

Luis's eyes looked into his, confident and cruel, as he reached down and unbuckled his big Mexican spurs. "But I'm not bare-handed, nephew. I'm wearing those razor-sharp spurs you always complain about, remember? You've seen what they can do to a horse, let's see what these wheels of death can do to a man!"

Cimarron shrieked imploringly to the chief. "Make them fight bare-handed! Take those spurs away!"

But Peta Nocona only grunted. "If your man's a good fighter and deserves to keep you, let him take those weapons away from the handsome one!"

Now it was Trace's turn to back away. Apprehension and fear made a hard knot in his belly as he retreated from the knife-sharp wheels, big as silver dollars in Luis's hands. Yes, he'd seen Luis cut a horse to ribbons with those spurs and had held his protests for fear of the secret Luis might tell Don Diego.

He glanced around helplessly. There was not even a limb within reach that he might use for a club. The firelight reflected red on the spurs as Luis advanced menacingly. *Soon,* Trace thought, *soon the spurs would be red with blood.*

"Come on, cowboy," Luis snarled, beckoning to him as he advanced. "Come on! When I get through with you, even your woman won't be able to recognize your face!"

"No!" Cimarron protested, putting down the dog as she scrambled to her feet. She tried to run forward, throw herself between the two combatants.

"Get back, Cimarron!" Trace ordered. When she didn't move, he signaled the chief. "Keep her out of this! She's the prize for the winner!"

"And that's going to be me!" Luis grinned as a warrior caught Cimarron, dragged her kicking and screaming to the sidelines, where she sobbed and fought to get away.

But her movement had diverted Luis's attention momentarily, and Trace took advantage of the fact to charge. He had to get one of those spurs! He dived for the other man and their hands locked on each other's wrists as they grappled.

Luis's face gleamed with sweat close to his as they struggled for possession of the spurs. "Remember, cowboy, when this is over, remember how I'm going to enjoy your woman. When we finish this fight, I'm going to geld you with one of these. If you're a slave, you won't need your manhood anymore!"

Trace's wounded arm ached, but he managed to twist one of the spurs from Luis's hand. Now they crouched, facing each other in the circle of braves, each armed with a flashing wheel of death.

Trace brought his down with a slashing motion, but he was still weak from the bullet wound. Luis caught his wrist and they fell in a tumble, rolling near the fire. And when they finished rolling over and over, Luis was on top.

His handsome face was ugly with anger and cruelty as he clasped Trace's left wrist, slowly bending it backward toward the flames. "You'll drop that spur, half-breed! No man can endure the kiss of fire on his knuckles!"

Trace heard Cimarron scream again, knew she struggled to break away and come to his aid. But the Comanche holding her was strong.

Very slowly, Luis forced Trace's hand backward toward the fire. Trace gritted his teeth, tried to throw him off, but his uncle was as tall and heavier than he. Now he felt the heat of the fire on the back of his hand as Luis gradually forced it back.

"You're gonna drop that spur," Luis snarled through his teeth. "Then I'm gonna cut you to pieces with the other one!"

Trace was weakening. His head still ached from being cracked across the skull in the barn. The flames scorched his knuckles now as Luis forced his hand slowly down toward the campfire.

"Scream!" Luis ordered, "Damn you! Scream and beg! Maybe I'll show mercy!"

"Not if you burn it to a charred stub," Trace gasped through clenched teeth. His hand was a mass of agony. *Blood will tell,* he reminded himself over and over, *blood will tell.* And the blood of generations of Cheyenne chiefs and old Diego de Durango coursed through his veins. Trace Durango was true to his bloodlines. He vowed not to cry out, no matter what torture Luis inflicted on him.

He struggled, but still Luis's hand forced him slowly, inevitably into the flames. Trace bit his lip to keep from screaming, tasted his own blood, knew what hell was really like as the crimson flames licked the back of his knuckles.

Dimly in his torture, he could hear Cimarron's weeping, the small dog's frantic barking over Luis's hard breathing, the murmur of the Comanche warriors at his show of bravery.

"Scream!" Luis commanded, his eyes bright with sexual arousal at the pain he inflicted, "Scream like a squaw birthing a baby!"

Trace bit his lip to hold back the cry as the fire touched his hand. He made one last, heroic effort, twisted out from under Luis, came out on top.

Trace still held the spur, but his hand was a mass of pain. He held the other's right wrist, started forcing it back toward the flames. "Now, *you* scream, Luis! Like a squaw in childbirth!"

Big droplets of sweat stood out on the aristocrat's face. His eyes widened in fright as he seemed to realize what Trace intended. His hand was nowhere near the flames yet, but already he was screaming. "No! No! For God's sake! No!"

"Then drop it!" Trace commanded, bending Luis's hand back. "Turn loose and drop it in the fire!"

Luis began to sob and slobber as he opened his hand, let go of the spur. It tumbled with a clinking sound into the fire, unavailable now to either of them. Trace still held the other spur, but Luis clutched that burned left hand, wrenching it away from Trace.

"Enough of this!" Peta Nocona shouted, signaling his warriors who rushed forward to drag Trace off the fallen Luis. "We are out of time! Some of my warriors intend to ride out before dawn to join with the Comanche and Kiowa who attack the settlers to the north." He looked at Trace, nodded. "Whoever you are, Comanchero or not, you have proved your bravery. We will give you a horse and set you free."

Trace staggered, clasping his blistered left hand in his right one. "What—" he gasped, "what about my woman? Does she go with me?"

Peta Nocona seemed to consider as Luis got to his feet. "She came with the other as his woman, she will leave that way."

"Never mind, Trace," Cimarron sobbed, "I'll go with Luis! This is your one chance, your only chance for freedom, don't you see?"

But Trace shook his head, even though he was weak and wounded and knew he didn't stand a chance against the other. "No," he gasped stubbornly, "I'll stay and fight to the death before I let him take you!"

Luis swung around, leering coolly. "Then get ready to die, cowboy. No woman is worth your life, not even that one! But if you put that kind of value on her, I'll enjoy her twice as much when I take her tonight!"

Cimarron clasped her hands to her mouth, freeing the snarling little dog from her grasp. "No, Trace, do you hear me! I'll go with Luis!"

The chihuahua raced across the circle and Luis kicked at it savagely. It yipped as the heavy boot caught it, threw it to one side. Trace saw the look dark as thunder on the chief's face as the little dog dragged itself pitiful and whimpering back to Cimarron's arms.

Luis laughed as he moved close to Trace. His powerful

arm with the spur flashed down, tearing the black shirt to shreds. The blood spurted red and warm as the wheel of death cut through the fabric, leaving a scarlet trail across Trace's powerful chest.

Trace gasped at the stinging pain as Luis's arm flashed again. The shirt tore away, cut to ribbons, leaving his dark body naked to the waist, smeared with blood and sweat.

He staggered backward, shaking his head to clear it, threw his hand up instinctively as Luis brought the spur down across Trace's palm, cutting it to the bone. But now Trace gripped Luis's wrist with the bloody hand. The blood ran down both their arms, smearing the silver spur as they fought over it, then dripped to mingle with the Texas soil.

Luis's face was close to his as they struggled for possession of the weapon. "I'm gonna ride your woman with these tonight," he promised, his white teeth gleaming with excitement at the thought. "I'm gonna ride her and cut her to pieces with these spurs. You think of that while you carry burdens like a mule for the Comanche!"

The thought enraged Trace. He was so weak that he hovered near unconsciousness, but he could not quit. In his mind's eye, he saw Luis mounting the creamy, silken body, heard Cimarron cry out in pain....

Not while Trace Durango lived! This was a fight to the death, and Luis would have to kill him to make good that promise. Not while Trace Durango had the strength to lift an arm to stop him!

Rage built in him as they fought and meshed, struggling for possession of the sharp spur. His valiant body was slowly failing, he could feel it, but he ran on sheer heart and courage now.

Luis's face was suddenly afraid, desperate at such bravery, such determination. "I'll geld you!" he swore. "You'll be a gelding, not a stallion! I'll cut your face to ribbons!"

"You've just pronounced your own sentence!" Trace snarled, and with his last bit of strength, he wrenched the big spur from the Spaniard's hand. In that split-second as Trace brought the spur down, he saw the firelight flash on the silver, and Luis screamed in terror.

Trace put his last strength behind his blow, and the spur caught Luis's handsome face at an angle, cutting deeply from his hairline down across his nose and cheek. The face was an unrecognizable, bloody scar, laid open to the bone.

Luis screamed like a woman, clasped his hands over his torn face and stumbled away. "You've maimed me! My face! You scarred my face! It's her vengeance! It's Cheyenne spirit magic!"

Trace swayed on his feet, looked down at the bloody spur in his hand. The elegant face was now forever scarred. "It's over," he whispered, "she's safe!" His hand unclenched and the bloody spur fell to the ground with a clatter that could be heard over Luis's agonized screaming.

He wasn't sure whether he was going to be able to walk across that circle to claim her, but he would try. She was his prize. He'd won her.

Trace smiled at Cimarron as he staggered, saw the sudden horror in her face, heard her scream a warning. A shadow fell across him suddenly and he tried to turn to protect himself, knew his injuries made him move too slowly. He threw up his hand to deflect the shadow that came down. He wasn't fast enough, and the club caught him across the head, sent him falling to his knees.

He tried to catch himself, but the light slowly faded, and the only sound he heard was the roaring in his ears from the blow. As he went down, half-conscious, he remembered the taste of gritty dirt in his half-opened mouth.

Chapter Twenty-Seven

"Watch out, Trace!" Cimarron screamed as she saw the Mexican girl, Rosa, suddenly run up behind him with a club in her hands.

Trace stared back at Cimarron as if he didn't comprehend her words, then turned, tried to throw up his hands to protect himself. *But he was hurt and weak,* she realized in that split-second before Rosa's club clipped the side of his head. He fell to his knees, reached toward Cimarron as if asking for help, fell on his face in the dirt.

Rosa went to Luis and tried to comfort him, but he slapped her away, screaming. "He's cut me! He's scarred me for life! I'll be ugly!" He slapped at her again. "Get away, *puta,* I don't want you!"

Cimarron put down the dog, ran over to gather up the half-conscious Trace in her arms. "Trace! Speak to me! I love you! I love you!"

She heard a movement, looked up into the face of Peta Nocona. "You remind me of my own golden-haired one," he said softly. "For this reason alone I grant you safe passage through Comanche country. You may ride out."

She hardly dared hope as she looked up at him, cradling the hurt man in her arms. "You're letting us go?"

But the chief shook his head. "Only you, Yellow Hair. The man turned down his chance to leave, and I have much reason to hate the Texans. I heard you claim the palomino mare as your own. Take her and leave this place."

She glared up at him defiantly, still cradling Trace in her arms. "And what if I won't leave my man?"

"You would share his slavery?" He gave her a long, searching look. "Think, Yellow Hair. Take your horse and go in peace."

She had never before faced such a decision. Cimarron looked over at the moaning, bloody Luis and Rosa, who was trying to doctor his torn face. They were both oblivious of the little drama being played out between her and the chief.

Freedom, or slavery with Trace. Her decision to make.

Trace stirred, gestured weakly. "Darlin', this is your chance, your only chance. Take Peso and get the hell out of here! Do, you hear me, get out while he'll let you go!"

The chief gestured impatiently. "Hurry up, woman. My men are ready to leave this place. A thousand strong, the Comanche and Kiowa gather to follow Little Buffalo and Aperian Crow."

Trace gasped. "The final push? The big raid?"

Peta Nocona nodded. "We make one last attack, sweeping toward that which whites call Elm Creek on the Brazos. It is our final chance to drive back the whites before their soldiers return from the war to the east." He looked at Cimarron. "Choose, woman."

Cimarron looked from one to the other in an agony of indecision. *Freedom alone, or slavery with Trace.*

Trace tried to push her away. "Do you hear him?" he gasped over the moaning of Luis in the background, "Get out of here, darlin'! You're loco if you don't go!"

Cimarron looked down at him, reached gently to touch his smudged face. She had already made her choice. Cheyenne courage coursed proudly through her veins. It was her heritage from her father. And her other half was pure Texan, for she was the daughter of strong, serene Texanna.

"I've made my decision," she whispered, lifting her chin bravely to look the fierce Comanche in the eye. "I'll stay with my man!"

Trace shook his head, tried to push her away in protest. "Are you loco? You'd give up your life for me?"

"Your mother left her home for you," she said calmly.

"Am I not the woman Velvet Eyes was?"

Tears came to Trace's eyes. "You're just like her, darlin', just exactly like her!"

Peta Nocona shook his head in disbelief. "You love this cowboy so very much, then? You would accept the terrible slavery of the Comanche to stay by his side?"

Luis seemed to hear for the first time. He shoved Rosa away roughly. "The blond one's mine, chief! I demand you keep your part of the bargain! The deal was you take the cowboy into slavery!"

Cimarron looked up at him and gasped. Luis's face was a thing of horror, with a slash across it that cut clear to the bone. The wound would heal into a terrible, livid scar. Women would shudder now when they looked at him. He staggered over, stood looking down at Trace with angry vengeance in his eyes.

The tiny chihuahua raised itself weakly, limped over and attacked Luis's boots again. Luis laughed as he leaned over, picked the small dog up by the scruff of the neck, held it out to the Comanche leader. "Here, chief, someone told me Indians eat dogs! I make you a gift of this little devil! I hope you impale him on a stick and roast him alive while I watch!"

Rosa gasped in horror. "No, Luis!" she protested, "My God, not to Comanches!"

Cimarron heard the gasp of shock and dismay throughout the warriors as others translated the Spaniard's words. Rosa ran over, tried to take the whimpering dog from Luis's outstretched hand.

Then the Comanche chief's voice rolled out like ominous thunder. "Do no harm to the small warrior, Tejano! Put the cousin to our spirit animal on the ground most carefully!"

Luis pushed the protesting Rosa away, offered the whimpering pet again by the scruff of the neck. "No, you don't understand, chief, I want you to eat him! Kill him!"

"Luis, please!" Rosa screamed, "You offend them!"

Peta Nocona's face went livid with anger. "You think we are Cheyenne or Sioux? The coyote is our spirit animal! Comanche do not harm his cousin, the dog!"

Luis's eyes blinked in his ravaged face as he seemed to

understand he had committed a terrible error. Very slowly, he put the small dog on the ground. It ran over, jumped into Cimarron's lap, licked her face.

She hugged both the dog and the injured man to her.

Now the chief faced the Spaniard with the scarred face. "You offend the Comanche," he said coldly. "I begin to wonder if you are really the Comanchero leader we have obeyed so long—"

"And will keep obeying," Luis snarled arrogantly, "You hear me? I am leader of the great Comancheros, and you are nothing but a pack of ragged, dirty savages—"

Rosa tried to grab his arm, "Luis, please, be careful what you say—"

"Peta Nocona," Luis shouted, "I give the orders, remember that! I'm leaving with the blond one. I order you to geld this cowboy, keep him in slavery. I make you a gift of the girl, Rosa. Do whatever you want with her."

Trace tried to struggle to his feet, but he was hurt badly, too weak to challenge Luis again.

Cimarron held him close, wept in protest. "Luis, no! I'll go with you, be your wife! Do anything you want! Just ask them to give Trace his horse and let him go!"

Luis laughed coldly. "I want both his horse and his woman, my dear. I intend to geld that stallion, too. Remember, as long as you are a dutiful wife, I'll send messages to the Comanche not to kill him, only work him hard, but the gelding order stands."

Rosa looked desperately from Cimarron to Luis. "But you promised if I helped you poison the cruel old Don, you would someday make me señora of the Triple D."

Luis guffawed, stuck his fingers in his belt. "You! You dirty Mex peasant! Surely you didn't think you could ever be more than just my mistress?"

Her face was a mask of hurt. "I—I thought you would kill Sanchez for me so I could be your wife—"

"Kill Sanchez?" Luis snorted, "I need him to run the ranch! But sometimes, when Cimarron is heavy with child, I might still sleep with you now and then. Tonight, when we get back to the ranch, I'll want you to finish off the old Don for me."

Rosa shook her head slowly as she advanced on him. "I'm not sure of anything anymore. I helped you only because you told me Don Diego was cruel to my señora, that if he were dead, she might return—"

Luis shrugged impatiently, scorn on his torn face. "You're such a stupid, ignorant peasant! Velvet Eyes will never return, never, do you hear me, never!"

Rosa gestured imploringly. "Of course, she will, when we kill her cruel husband. That's why you told me she ran away with the Yankee captain."

Luis wiped at the congealing blood on his face. "She's dead, do you hear me?" he shouted. "She refused me, and she was going to tell Diego of my stealing."

Cimarron gasped at his words and clasped Trace to her. But Trace managed to get to his knees, his face distorted by inner turmoil. "What—what did you say?"

"She had my derringer in her back when we all played out that little scene in the study. She was protecting you two idiots that day!"

Rosa blinked, stared at Luis, horror etched on her features. "You—you killed Velvet Eyes?"

Luis nodded, fingering the deep cut across his features. "I loved her, but she wouldn't have me. *Si.* I—I killed her. She's lost in the depths of Jacob's Well!"

Cimarron closed her eyes, trying not to imagine the ghastly scene. "Oh, dear God!"

Trace gave an agonized cry as he tried to scramble to his feet, but Rosa's scream carried clearly. *"You killed her? You killed my señora?"*

The great Comanche chief shrugged impatiently, motioned toward the painted warriors mounting up in the background. Others still stood around him holding the long Comanche lances. "It is almost daylight," he intoned. "Some of my braves ride now to join the combined Comanche-Kiowa forces sweeping seven suns from now across north Texas. Rosa, you are the only one of these gringos we have dealt with. I trust you. Tell me, which one did the Comanchero order me to take away as a slave?"

Luis gestured toward Trace. "It's him!" He turned his horribly scarred face toward the Mexican girl as Cimarron gasped in protest. "Tell him, Rosa," Luis said. "Then you and I and Cimarron will ride back to the Triple D."

Tears ran down Rosa's face as she looked at Cimarron, and Cimarron appealed silently with her eyes.

Rosa nodded, seemingly in shock. "Gringa girl, you love Trace so much you are willing to go into slavery with him?"

"I will!" Cimarron declared.

"No!" Both Trace and Luis protested.

Luis whirled on Rosa. "Tell the Indians, Rosa. Let's get back to the ranch."

Cimarron saw the look on Rosa's face, an expression of deep regret, of sorrow and pain.

"The gringa made me a dress," she said softly. "She is, after all, much like my poor señora, kind, loving. God forgive me for being so greedy, so blind—"

"Rosa," Peta Nocona gestured, "which one?"

Cimarron held her breath, stared up into Luis's sneering, confident face. *Capitivity with the Comanche or a love slave to this monster? Whatever it took to protect her injured lover or to stay with him, she'd do.*

Luis frowned. "We're wasting time, Rosa, tell him!"

Very slowly, Rosa turned and pointed an accusing finger at Luis. "That one!" she shouted. "That one deserves the slavery of the Comanche!"

"You *puta* whore!" Rage replaced the startled expression on Luis's face as he ran over, jerked a lance from a warrior's hand. In two strides, before anyone could move to stop him, he stabbed Rosa through the chest, impaling her against the ground while Cimarron screamed and the little dog barked.

"Seize that Tejano!" Peta Nocona's face was terrible to see as he gestured toward Luis. "I should have known he was not the real leader of the Comanchero. The real El Patron would not kill a trusted messenger!"

Cimarron wept as she ran over to gather the dying girl into her arms. "Oh, Rosa! Rosa!"

Warriors seized Luis, dragged him away. Cimarron could hear him screaming, "It's a mistake! I tell you! The girl lies!

She lies! I tell you! It's a mistake!"

Rosa's eyes blinked open. Blood made a crimson, crooked trail from her lips. But she managed to smile as she looked up at Cimarron. "You are much like Velvet Eyes," she murmured. "You and your cowboy deserve to be happy."

Frantically, Cimarron pulled at the lance. "I'll get you back to the ranch! I'll get you to a doctor—"

"Don't! Don't pull it out. It hurts so much." Rosa grimaced. "I'm dying, I know that . . . I've been such a greedy fool . . . so afraid of growing old . . . God will punish me . . . lion and lambs . . . Tell Sanchez . . ."

She went limp in Cimarron's arms, and Cimarron wept. "No, Rosa, we'll get a doctor, I'll . . ." Her voice trailed off as she looked down into the still face. Rosa Sanchez would never have to worry about being old and ugly, about losing her beauty. She had just run out of time.

Peta Nocona came over, touched Cimarron's shoulder. "My men will put her in the wagon along with your hurt cowboy and the little brown warrior."

She wiped at the tears in her eyes, looking up at him, hardly daring to hope. "You—you're going to let us go?"

He nodded and jerked his head toward Luis who still shrieked and protested in the background. "We were told by Rosa that the leader of the Comanchero had ordered us to take away a slave, and we have done so. Pedro will tell us next year if we have done well." He shrugged. "Of course, by then, it may not matter. Our slaves do not always survive that long."

She stood up slowly, watched the warriors carry the lifeless body to load in the wagon beside the injured Trace. She looked at Peta Nocona, almost understanding, sympathizing with him. "It's futile for the Indians to attack the north Texas settlements," she said softly as she walked with him to the wagon. "Soon, there'll be more whites on your hunting grounds, always more, like a great wave sweeping the tribes away."

"I know that," he answered sadly, putting his arm around the shoulders of a young boy standing by the wagon. "Our Cheyenne and Arapaho brothers fight even now north of here to force the miners out of the Shining Mountains. We cannot win in the long run, but we must try." He looked down at the boy. "My other son is dead, so when I am gone, my son Quanah will carry on."

Cimarron looked at the young half-breed as she climbed up on the wagon seat next to the small dog. He stared back at her with the deep blue-gray eyes of his Texas mother. "I think," she said, "the white world will have cause to remember a chief called Quanah Parker."

Peta nodded. "Have you—have you seen my woman? My little girl?"

Cimarron shook her head as she gathered up the reins. "No," she answered, "but those who have say she grieves, that she is a Comanche in every way but skin color." She would not tell him the rest of it. Word had come that the child, Prairie Flower, had died last year.

The young boy frowned. "When I am chief, I will make the Texans sorry they took my mother and my baby sister!"

She looked into his fierce, determined eyes. "I'll bet you will at that." Then she clucked to the horse, moved out.

The two horses were still tied to the back of the wagon. As Cimarron pulled away toward the east, the little dog turned back and barked at the warriors mounting up to ride away. Scrappy to the last, she thought, smiling at the pet.

Trace groaned, raised up on one elbow. "Got to warn the settlers," he gasped. "Nightwind's the best horse in Texas . . . I'll ride to warn them. . . ."

"No," she said softly, glancing down at the blanket-wrapped body lying next to him. "It'll take an Indian, all right, to get through those lines, and a good horse, but you're too badly hurt. Maybe I—"

"No," Trace struggled to get up as she kept the wagon moving to the east. "You don't know the trails, wouldn't know which way to go—"

"Then those poor devils are on their own and God help them," Cimarron said grimly as she kept driving. Behind her, she heard Luis's voice echoing faintly, still protesting as they tied him on a horse and started away from the rendezvous. Hooves drummed like thunder as the Comanche, painted for war, rode away north. Dawn touched the sky a misty pink in the east. The whites will not soon forget the Comanche moon of this October, she thought with a tired sigh, wishing she could help them. She glanced down at the man, and at the little dog curled up next to her on the wagon seat. Trace was hurt and she didn't know the trails. God help the ranchers and farmers on the upper Brazos, she thought, because they were going to need a miracle.

Tequila sat up suddenly, his ears pricked forward. And then the horse's ears went up. The two horses tied on behind nickered at the sight of the approaching rider.

She saw the war paint, the feathers, and looked around frantically. A Comanche warrior rode into view. She wondered if he would know she was under the protection of the great chief of the Nocona? Would the brave believe her and let her go in peace?

He must be with a war party, she thought as the Indian on the gray horse approached, because in the distance behind him, she could make out the form of another mounted man. *Could she find a gully, some rocks to hide the wagon? No, too late! He had seen her.* He waved a hand and shouted.

Her heart pounding, Cimarron looked around for a weapon. A stick! A rock! Anything to protect her injured love! But as she started to jump down, grab up a rock, little Tequila cocked his head toward the rider. Then, very slowly, his tail started wagging.

She stared at the approaching Comanche, looked in shock at the tiny dog as its tail wagged furiously. It yapped a welcome. "Tequila? Have you lost your mind?"

"Cimarron!" the Comanche shouted. "Hey, Cimarron!"

She collapsed on the wagon seat, staring at the horseman and the young gray stallion he rode as he galloped up. "Maverick? Double damnation! I thought you were part of a war party!"

Trace roused himself, struggled to his knees. "Maverick," he gasped, "We've got to warn the settlers. . . ."

Maverick frowned as he leaned over the wagon, looked at Trace. "What happened?"

"Never mind," Cimarron said, "I'll tell you later. Why are

you dressed like that?"

He grinned, showing even white teeth in his dark face. Only the steel-gray eyes gave away the secret behind the garish paint. "I thought I might have to sneak through their country alone looking for you two." He nodded toward the other rider coming up fast. "Sanchez is with me. Where's Rosa and Luis? What's going on? The whole country is full of Comanche!"

Cimarron hopped down off the wagon seat. "Never mind all that right now, we'll explain later. Do you know the Elm Creek area of the north Brazos river country?"

"Like the back of my hand," he nodded, suddenly serious. "Remember? I lived with the Comanche."

Trace climbed unsteadily from the wagon. "I see what your plan is, Cimarron. Maverick and I did it before." He looked from her to the boy. "Maverick, I'll need war paint, buckskin clothes." He untied Nightwind.

Cimarron got down from the wagon seat, untied Peso. "If you two think you're riding to warn the settlers without me, you're crazy!"

Trace frowned at her. "You know how far it is to Elm Creek? No, you can't go! I won't put you in danger!"

"Double damnation! I'm going along!" she declared stubbornly. "If you won't let me, I'll follow you!"

Maverick shook his head. "Trace and me speak a little Injun, we can mix among them if we have to, but with that light hair you can't slip past the war parties."

"I said I'm going," she said stubbornly. "Steal me a rifle. I'm a good shot, can ride as well as any man. If we run into a war party, tie me up, pretend I'm a captive."

Trace grimaced. "I don't like this idea—"

"You can't stop me!" she declared with spirit.

He gave a searching look, swallowed hard. "You know, you're just exactly like my mother!"

Maverick fingered the scar on his cheek. "Why don't you both go home and let me do this? I got no family to mourn me if I don't get back."

Trace reached out and put his hand on the boy's shoulder. 'You got a family, kid, I promise you that. But I'm going along, Maverick . . . Durango."

Tears came to the boy's eyes at Trace's words. For a moment he couldn't speak, then he cleared his throat. "The settlers have only one chance, since they're outnumbered. If someone can kill the chiefs, the braves will think it's bad medicine, call off the raid, and head home."

Cimarron sighed. "The settlers don't know that."

Trace looked at her. "But we know it," he said significantly, glancing off at the vaquero riding up.

Sanchez reined in, dismounted. *"Dios!* We been looking for you. What happened?"

Cimarron put her hand on his sympathetically. "There's much to tell, *compadre."*

The Mexican pushed his sombrero back with his maimed hand. "Are you all right? Have you seen Luis or my Rosa?"

Cimarron bit her lip, squeezed his arm compassionately. "Pull yourself together, dear Sanchez." She paused, nodded toward the blanket-covered form in the back of the wagon. "We must ride to warn the settlements of a Comanche uprising. Luis is a victim of the Comanche and Rosa . . . well, Rosa was killed by a Comanchero."

Agony contorted the old man's face. He started to uncover the body, but Cimarron caught his hand. "No, Sanchez, you don't want to see. I can only tell you that your Rosa died bravely, saving our lives, and at the last, she asked me to give you a message."

Tears ran down the leathery face as he leaned against the wagon and wept. "A message? My Rosa thought of me at the last? I—I never thought she cared!"

Cimarron hesitated, looked into Trace's eyes. She knew then that neither of them would ever tell anyone the whole story. It would break Don Diego's heart and it would break Sanchez's heart, too. They would bury Rosa in the russet silk dress in the family plot. She had wanted so badly to be a Durango. It was an ironic ending, but a just one.

She tried to remember Rosa's last moments. She had said something about "lions and lambs." Cimarron searched her memory. There was a Bible verse about lions and lambs lying down together. Yes, that must be what Rosa had meant. Cimarron would see to it that there was a little marble gravestone with a lamb on it.

Rosa had tried to tell her something about Sanchez. What was it? She had started and never finished. "Tell Sanchez. . . ." she had said. *Tell Sanchez what?*

Would God forgive her for what she was about to do? Maybe it *was* what Rosa had meant to say. Cimarron swallowed hard. In her heart, she knew it was right. "Rosa said, 'Tell Sanchez I love him, tell him my last thoughts were of him.'"

Sanchez took out a bandana, wiped his eyes, gave her a brave look. "Thank you, señorita, thank you for those kind words. It'll make it a little easier for me, knowing she loved me after all."

He tied his horse on behind the wagon, climbed up to the wagon seat beside the dog, and pulled away.

Maverick kicked his horse into a trot, started north.

Cimarron looked into her love's eyes and knew they would keep the secret of their knowledge, except that they must now tell the old Don that Velvet Eyes was lost in the trackless, underwater caves of Jacob's Well, a victim of the Comanchero. But then, hadn't he said all along that she would never have left him, that she must be dead? He had loved and trusted her without hesitation.

Trace reached over, touched Cimarron's cheek. "All these months, I've hated my mother, not realizing she gave her life to save me. She loved me and Father, after all."

"And you are his true son," Cimarron whispered. "His health will gradually return, and we'll never tell him about the poison. He'll think he was granted a miracle."

"No, we won't tell him about his brother's plot, it would only grieve him." He took her in his arms, looked down into her face. "I can't believe you loved me enough to take slavery over freedom."

She kissed his lips. "Trust me," she whispered. "I would have given my life for you." She felt the envelope in her skirt pocket. "Later, my darling, when we have time, there's something I must show you."

Maverick turned in his saddle, yelled back at them. "Hey, you two, get mounted! We've got a long ride ahead!"

Trace nodded at him, then turned back to her. "When this is all over, if we make it back, will you marry me?"

She took a deep, shuddering breath. "I—I can't, Trace, you see, there's something you don't know about me."

"Whatever it is, it won't matter," he said fiercely as he kissed her. "All that matters is that I love you, trust you as I never have any other girl."

"You say that now, but when you hear it, you won't want me. It's—it's something terrible."

"Try me, darlin'." He kissed the tip of her nose. "There's nothing in your past so horrible that it could stop me from marrying you. I want you by my side forever!"

She knew then that she had to trust him not only with her heart, but with her life. But still, she hesitated a long moment before she took his challenge. "Not even when I tell you I'm wanted for murder back in Fandango?"

Chapter Twenty-Eight

Carolina Longworth stared at the invitation the messenger had just delivered. It was certainly on the finest of paper, she thought enviously as she seated herself on the threadbare sofa of the tiny rented house. Now, just who would be inviting the Longworths to anything that required such expensive stationery?

Her hands trembled a little as she tore it open, quickly read the elegant handwriting. "Girls!" She jumped to her feet. "Patience! Prudence! Come here! We've been invited to a ball! Do you hear me? A ball!"

Patience stuck her head around the door, rubbing her reddened hands on her apron. "Prudence isn't home yet. A ball? Did you say a ball? For pity's sake, we don't know anyone who can afford to give a fancy party. Nobody invites us to anything anymore now that we've lost our money. All those fancy friends of yours, Mother, turned out to be fairweather friends."

Carolina waved the invitation triumphantly. "At last, someone who counts has seen the Longworths for what they really are! This invitation is from the Durango ranch. The Longworths are going to take their rightful place in high society!" She was so excited, she jumped up, whirled around the room, pretending to waltz. "As I always said, what goes around comes around."

Patience scratched her fat waist. "What kind of ball is it? Why are they giving it?"

"It says a 'surprise ball,' so who cares?" shrugged Carolina. "Why, we'll be the envy of Fandango when I tell it. Isn't it lucky that when our house burned in the Comanche attack, we managed to save those new gowns we'd had made for our party?"

"That's about all we saved," her daughter grumbled. "Why, sister and I never worked so hard in our lives as we have since that ungrateful Cimarron ran off. She did a lot more work around here than we realized."

Carolina frowned. She didn't want to think about that day. There had been too many unanswered questions. She hoped her ungrateful niece was scrubbing floors or waiting tables in some low cantina. "Yes, it was too bad we had to call off our party last September, but this is going to make up for it. Imagine, an invitation to the Triple D ball! Oh, I'll make sure everyone in town knows we're invited so I can rub it in on those who weren't. That's the best part of being popular, you know. Money and popularity are the most important things in the world. High society, here we come!"

She thought again. "This is a chance to talk to the Durangos about renewing our note. It's due in a couple of weeks, and if they don't renew, I guess we won't even have this dump to live in."

Patience put her hands on her ample hips. "Why, this is too awful for even that horrid Cimarron, and you know she's not used to the best like we are."

"That's right," Carolina nodded. "Always remember, Longworths are better than anybody just because we're Longworths!" A thought occurred to her. "Oh, Patience, are you going to be able to get into that ball gown? You've gained so much weight—"

"I haven't gained as much as sister has, for pity's sake," Patience said defensively. "With her having to work in the business because we can't afford help anymore, she keeps stuffing herself full of crackers."

"We've only got a little time to starve some of that off you girls." Carolina started making plans as she rubbed her hands together eagerly. "This is my chance to approach Don Durango about renewing the note, and you girls finally get to meet that rich, handsome heir."

Prudence burst through the front door. "Guess what? There's a big ball at the Durango ranch. The mayor's wife came in the store to rub it in and everyone laughed when she asked if we'd been invited. Maybe we should have treated people a little better when we had money."

"Well, guess what?" Carolina's eyes gleamed with malicious glee as she waved the paper under her daughter's nose. "The Longworths got invited, too! We're all going to the ball, girls!"

The three of them clasped hands and danced around in a circle. "The ball! The ball! We're going to the ball!"

Patience stopped, frowned at her work-reddened hands. "I'll never get my hands pretty. That damned Cimarron."

"My hateful niece never really appreciated all the Longworths did for her," Carolina said. "Why, we gave her our old clothes, and the leftovers from our kitchen—"

"Even Cimarron wouldn't live here," Prudence said woefully, looking around.

"Well, of course, we deserve better just because we are Longworths." Carolina nodded. "But this invitation proves what I always say—"

The girls sang out in unison, "What goes around comes around. That's what you always say, Mother."

Carolina nodded smugly. "That's right, girls. Now, let's start making plans—"

"I wish that Cimarron was here so she could stand and watch us drive away to the ball, leaving her behind—"

"I've prayed and prayed that cousin would get what she deserves," Prudence said. "It wasn't fair she was smarter and prettier than us. I've been so mad that we had to call off our own party because of Daddy's terrible accident."

Carolina patted each of her fat, homely daughters on the shoulder and sighed, wondering if she could add a switch of false hair to their thin locks and starve enough off them to get them into those gowns. "Just think, girls, maybe you'll each meet a rich husband at the ball."

Prudence's prominent teeth stuck out over her bottom lip. "Maybe we'll even get a chance at the heir himself."

Carolina sighed and took a good, long look at her two daughters. Besides being homely, they were stupid and clumsy. She had always secretly envied her sister Texanna her beautiful, graceful daughter....

"What do you suppose ever happened to her?" Pru asked.

Carolina shrugged. "Who cares? That ingrate! Neither she nor her mother appreciated everything I did for them." Carolina brushed back a wisp of hair, frowned as she reread the invitation. "Strange, there's a note at the bottom, and I'd swear the handwriting looks familiar."

"What does it say?" The girls asked in unison.

"Something about bringing Señora Rodriguez with us to the party. How would they know that old Mex's name?"

Patience registered disgust. "Isn't that the one who was Cimarron's friend? Why, who'd invite her anywhere? She doesn't have any money or influence."

"Now girls," Carolina said, "you know high society people wouldn't invite someone poor to a party. Somehow, they heard she works at parties, that's all."

Prudence brightened. "Sure, they want her to come work serving the party, washing dishes. I wish I knew where our hateful cousin was, I'd like to see her at that party, too."

Her sister clapped her hands with glee. "Yeah! Wouldn't you just love to dance by and see Cimarron in some old rag of a dress serving the table while we have a wonderful time with the handsome, rich men at the party?"

"Well, Pru," Carolina said, "next time you're going that way, tell the Rodriguez woman we'll pick her up. She's poor and needs the work, so she'll go. I don't think she gets enough to eat half the time. Now, girls, we must start on our diets and make plans. This is the Longworth family's chance to make an entrance into real society. Someone has finally seen us for what we really are."

Patience did a little dance around the floor, making the furniture shake. "Oh, I can hardly wait to tell everyone in town we've been invited."

Pru's face lit up maliciously. "Yes, won't it be fun to tell those who aren't invited? Nothing's more important than being popular, unless it's being rich!"

"Now, girls," Carolina smiled sweetly. "You're supposed to pretend you didn't know they weren't invited when you tell. That way, you can still hurt their feelings without looking like you did it deliberately."

They all giggled in unison at the prospect.

And now, at last, it was the night of the ball. Carolina could hardly control her excitement as the buggy reined up in front of the elegant Durango hacienda. It had been a long drive, but it was worth it. The ranch was even more lavish, the family evidently even more wealthy than she had ever dreamed.

She glanced over her shoulder at her two fat daughters, combed and powdered like two prize pigs in the back, and Señora Rodriguez sitting quietly in her patched dress. Even though bright, big-flowered prints were all the rage, she wished the girls had chosen some other fabric. They looked like two large, overstuffed sofas. At least, her own gown of reseda green was more elegant.

"All right, girls, here we are! Now step out carefully, I wouldn't want you to trip and fall in that courtyard before all these fancy people standing around."

The girls squealed in unison at the rich splendor.

"Don't do that," she admonished. "You're Longworths, remember? Don't sound like two pigs caught under a gate. Speaking of hogs, stay away from the food."

Ransford tied up the buggy reins, stepped from the carriage. "Just try to keep them from it," he complained. "We're trying to make silk purses out of . . ." His voice trailed off as he took out his watch, checked the time.

He came around to help her from the buggy and she frowned at him. She'd had the strangest suspicion ever since that day she'd come home and found him with the sewing scissor stuck in his chest, just narrowly missing the heart. Ransford had told the flimsiest story she'd ever heard about trying to help Cimarron with her sewing and falling on the scissors. He'd said it must have frightened Cimarron badly, maybe she had even thought him dead and she'd run away in a panic.

He looked at her as he helped her from the carriage. "What are you thinking, my love?" he asked sweetly.

"I was just wishing you wouldn't use so much bay rum." She glowered at him. "I don't know whether real society men use bay rum." No, she hadn't believed that cock-and-bull story of his for a minute, but to save face, she'd had to pretend she did. How humiliating it would be to think that her husband, who had lusted after her sister, Texanna, might have tried to take advantage of Texanna's half-breed daughter. No, it was just too humiliating. She was scared the town of Fandango didn't believe it, either. If the sheriff wouldn't have arrested her, she would have taken those scissors to Ransford herself, only she had in mind a better place to cut the randy storekeeper.

Carolina looked around at the fine carriages pulling up before the hacienda, the crowds of well-dressed people. Oh, yes, this was definitely where she belonged, mixing and mingling with the cream of society. Carolina's father had been a poor tailor, but she'd always been ruthlessly ambitious to move up the ladder. Her own family had never appreciated her efforts to tell them how to behave.

She looked at her clumsy daughters clumping across the flagstones past the fountain. Was there any chance the Durango heir might be attracted to either one of them? Well, stranger things had happened, and the Longworths were getting desperate financially. Besides burning their fine home, the Comanches had cleaned out the store. All that coupled with their extravagant life style made it imperative that they get the loan renewed. If, by some miracle, young Durango might be interested in either one of her girls, his father might erase the debt.

As she started across the flagstones on Ransford's arm, she turned back to Señora Rodriguez standing there quietly by the buggy. "I'm sure you're supposed to go around to the servants' entrance," she snapped. "I'll find out."

But no, there seemed to be some mistake. When a servant opened the door to them and Carolina asked, the girl said she had instructions to bring Señora Rodriguez right in the front with the guests. Carolina tried to argue with the girl. Obviously, the Durangos were expecting some rich, influential Spanish lady of the same name. Surely, the Durangos didn't want a common servant coming in the front door. But no, the girl insisted she had her orders. That Mex was ushered into the front hall along with the fine guests, where she stood looking shy and afraid.

The home almost took Carolina's breath away. It had the finest carpets, paintings, the most expensive furnishings she'd ever seen. Matter of fact, she thought, it made the pretentious home she had once owned in Fandango look like a shabby shack.

And speaking of shabby . . . she glanced quickly at her two daughters' gowns, then down at her own reseda green. Compared to the fine dresses the other guests were wearing, she began to feel like a country hick. In her own little town, she had thought she was such high society. Maybe being high society in a little town wasn't such an accomplishment, after all. She looked to see what the other men were wearing, realized immediately that Ransford's vest was too bright, his hair too greased. Carolina felt conspicuous, miserable. She'd never been on the receiving end of snobbery before, she thought, as she saw wealthy women look her over, sweep past her in their magnificent gowns. She hadn't realized how much it hurt.

"Mama," Patience whispered hoarsely, in a voice that carried, making all the elegant people turn around and smile. "Mama, look at that buffet table! Did you ever see such food? Look at that fancy cake!"

The people around them laughed and Carolina felt her face flush. "Be quiet, Patience, try to act like you have a little class!"

"That's right, sister," Pru nodded. "Remember we just barely got into these dresses. You eat very much, your buttons will pop off, leaving you standing there in your camisole!"

"Well, if we can't eat, and nobody talks to us, and no fellows ask us to dance, what do we do all evening?"

Carolina sighed heavily. She already knew it was going to

be a miserable evening. There was much laughter and talking as the people milled around in the big room under the giant chandelier. She hardly saw anyone she knew, and her two daughters were the fattest, homeliest, and worst-dressed of the entire group of young ladies. A band played at one end of the big room, and near the band stood the most beautiful little girl Carolina had ever seen. The child had black curls, ivory skin, and pale turquoise eyes. She held a wiggling chihuahua dog in her arms and it struggled to get down, barking madly.

A handsome, older Spaniard with a mane of white hair and a flowing mustache made his way through the crowd toward them. He wore an elegant, Spanish-cut suit of the finest fabric. "I think that must be old Don Diego de Durango himself," she whispered nervously to Ransford, and mentally practiced her curtsy.

As she watched, the tiny dog leaped from the little girl's arms, hit the floor running and dashed through the forest of legs toward them. Carolina could follow his path by the frantic barking, the ladies' squealing, the gentlemen's exclamations as the dog growled and nipped a path across the room. Carolina stared in dismay as the little dog raced up to Ransford and bit him on the ankle.

"Land o' Goshen!" Ransford howled, dancing around, kicking at the dog. The dog nimbly avoided the kick and tore Ransford's pants as it bit his ankle again.

The old Don hurried up. "Tequila!" he shouted. "You little rascal! You aren't supposed to bite our guests!" He leaned over, picked up the pet. The tiny dog growled at Ransford, tried to get away from the old man. Obviously, it would have liked nothing better than to bite him again.

The old Don handed the dog to the little girl as she ran up. "A thousand pardons for my dog's bad manners! Here, Turquoise, take this bad boy!"

The dog growled again at Ransford as the little girl took it, hugged it to her.

The aristocratic Spaniard bowed low. "I am Don Diego de Durango the second, and welcome to our small party. You are of course, the Longworths? I knew you from the description."

Surely he was not trying to insult them, although there was just a touch of scorn in his voice. Carolina bent her head in acknowledgment. If this was a small party, she'd like to see what the Don considered a big one. Oh, wouldn't it be wonderful to have this kind of wealth? And this fabulous home! Why, it was almost as large as a castle. She could hardly wait to see the prince.

Ransford smiled uncertainly. "That was your dog, señor? But of course, what a cute dog! He was just playing, I'm sure! And now, sir, I want to present my lovely daughters."

Carolina had to punch Patience's arm to get her mind off the buffet table so she could be introduced. Prudence almost fell as she tried to curtsy daintily.

The gallant old man glanced behind Carolina. "And who is this you brought with you?"

Carolina frowned, glanced over her shoulder at the shy Mexican widow. "Oh, I brought along Mrs. Rodriguez, as I was instructed. I suppose someone can direct her to the kitchen—"

"The kitchen?" He threw up his hands in horror. "Oh, my instructions definitely aren't for the kitchen."

Carolina gasped. "Surely she isn't a guest!"

The Don smiled. Even as Carolina watched in disbelief, he bowed low before the shy woman, kissed her hand. "You have a powerful friend in this household, Señora Rodriguez," he said. "My instructions are to introduce you to our foreman, Sanchez. He's little Turquoise's father."

The widow blushed, and anyone could see by her gaze as the Don pointed at a leathery-faced vaquero in the crowd across the room that she thought he was a handsome *hombre*.

The old Don turned to the child, smiled at the little dog still growling at Ransford. "Dear, take Tequila over to the buffet table and let him enjoy himself."

Prudence gasped at her elbow. "Oh, Mama, isn't that the most handsome man you ever saw in your life?"

Carolina turned to see where her daughter pointed and had to admit the girl was right. The young man was tall, lean, and somewhere in his middle twenties. Even if he hadn't been dressed in an expensive black outfit, he still would have made any woman's heart beat a little faster.

Don Diego turned to follow their gaze. "Oh, yes, my son, Diego de Durango the third. We call him Trace."

Patience's mouth dropped open. She looked as if she were trying to catch flies. "The heir!" she said. "We finally get to meet the Durango heir!"

Carolina almost moaned as people around her tittered at her fat daughters' open-mouthed gaping at the young man. She must have been crazy to think he might be interested in either one of her two homely, dull-witted girls.

"Señor Durango," Ransford blurted, "I'd like to talk to you about our bank note. . . ."

The Don frowned at him, then looked back toward Sanchez elbowing through the crowd. "I don't mix business with pleasure, Señor Longworth. Besides, my new daughter-in-law handles our bookkeeping. I've decided to let her make the decision on whether to call your note."

Pru's face fell. "Daughter-in-law? You mean, that handsome young man is married?"

"*Sí*. They were married this morning by the priest from San Antonio. This ball is in celebration." He nodded with satisfaction. "The girl is the most beautiful woman you can imagine. She came to us out of nowhere and we're all in love with her! Somehow, I think you might know her. . . ."

There was a fanfare of trumpets and all heads turned toward the staircase.

"As a matter of fact," the Don gestured, "I believe she's about to make her grand entrance now. I insisted on hiring a French dressmaker, although she offered to make the ball gown herself. It's that new shade of deep pink called Solferino. I think you'll agree it blends well with the Durango family rubies and diamonds."

Carolina had never felt such envy. Her daughters had no chance at the handsome heir and his money. Well, they probably wouldn't have had much of a chance anyhow. The new wife must have everything, beauty, elegance, breeding to have landed a catch like that.

Wistfully, she listened to the blare of trumpets, saw all the heads turn admiringly as the Durango heir made his way to the foot of the stairway to await the entrance of his wife. Carolina had never seen such adoration on a man's face as he looked up the stairs. *Oh, to have a man look at her only once that way,* she thought sadly. *Oh, to be loved and cherished, as this woman obviously was!*

The girl stood at the top of the big stairway, her face shadowed. But Carolina gasped in awe at the dress. "That has to be the finest dress in all Texas," she said without thinking, gaping at the deep pink moire spread wide over the hoop to accentuate the tiny waist.

The old Don smiled. "If it isn't the finest, I've been cheated," he said. "The fabric was imported at great expense just for her. And she's more than welcome to anything my money will buy." He gave Ransford a long look. "The girl has a real talent with scissors, I understand. Now, excuse me please, I must make the annoucements." The old man moved through the crowd to the stairs.

The light reflected off the sheen of the fabric, the sparkle of the rubies and diamonds around the girl's tawny neck. Her earrings alone must have been worth a fortune.

Enviously, Carolina heard the admiring murmur of the crowd as the handsome young man awaited the girl in the shadows at the top of the stairway.

Prudence said, "That dress makes mine look terrible."

Patience nodded. "And look at that ruby bracelet and the jewels in her hair!"

Carolina blinked, only half listening as the girl started to descend the stairs. "She's breathtaking," she sighed, "like Cinderella arriving at the ball."

Prudence moaned. "And oh, what a prince she got!"

The orchestra struck up entrance music and the crowd started to applaud. The applause became louder and louder as the girl came down the stairway toward the outstretched hand of Trace Durango. Carolina heard Pru and Patience start to clap their beefy hands, and automatically, she did the same. The girl continued down the stairs, the lights reflecting off the Durango rubies around her throat and entwined in her upswept blond curls.

The applause grew and the crowd around them murmured appreciatively of the girl's beauty as she descended the stairway. Carolina gasped, stopped clapping. *Why, that girl looked like . . . no, of course it couldn't be.*

But about that time, Ransford choked and started coughing. Then Prudence cried out as if someone had just stepped on her big foot. "Mama! Mama! That girl looks like—"

Patience gasped, "No, it can't be!"

But it was. Even as Carolina blinked again, unwilling to believe what her eyes told her, she knew exactly who that was coming down the stairway.

Chapter Twenty-Nine

Cimarron took a deep breath as she slowly descended the stairs, the Solferino pink moire dress shimmering in the lights. Below her was a sea of admiring, friendly faces. She looked around anxiously. *Had they come? Yes, there they were.* How provincial they looked, her two cousins in big-flowered fabric that made them look even fatter. She looked at Aunt Carolina's dress, thinking that that shade of grayish-green was a bad choice for someone with pallid, washed-out coloring, even if it was stylish. *And then they saw her, too.* She knew the instant the Longworths recognized her from the stricken looks, the open mouths.

But she saw the old Don moving through the crowd toward her. She looked now for only one face, the face of her husband. He smiled up at her as he stood awaiting her at the foot of the stairway.

Trace, my only love. She reached the last step, and he reached out to take her arm, put it through his, patted her hand. "Señora Diego de Durango the third, you are the most beautiful, most desirable woman in this room."

"As my husband, you are, of course, partial." She smiled with pleasure as they waited for the old Don to join them.

Trace brought her hand up and kissed her fingertips, and the giant jeweled wedding ring she wore flashed in the light. "I mean it, darlin'," he whispered in his deep, Texas-Spanish drawl. "Every man here envies me tonight. And by the way, I think your relatives have arrived."

For just a moment she tensed, and his hand covered hers protectively. "No one can hurt you anymore, Wild One. You have the Durango heritage, money, and power behind you. And God help anyone who tries! They'll answer to me!"

"That's right, isn't it? I keep forgetting this ball is for me." She brightened as she straightened her shoulders regally. "And to think, once my highest ambition was to attend a tiny party in a little country town."

He smiled back at her reassuringly as Don Diego came forward to take her other arm. They led her over in front of the orchestra. The old man beamed at the crowd. "It is my pleasure to announce that my son was married this morning to this beautiful creature, with my blessings. Join me in honoring her, welcoming her to my family!"

Cimarron hugged him, kissed his cheek as the crowd applauded. Then she and Trace moved through the crowd of guests, nodding and acknowledging the congratulations, the comments on the beauty of the bride.

When she had finally trusted Trace enough to tell him of her past, he had investigated and found out what Luis had obviously already known. She wasn't wanted for murder, after all. Ransford had protected himself by keeping the secret.

They walked over to join her relatives, and she wondered now why she had ever been so impressed. The Longworths weren't really very high class, Cimarron thought. They were, after all, just cruel, pompous small-town hicks.

"Hello, Aunt Carolina. Welcome to Triple D ranch," she said coolly.

She thought for a moment her aunt might faint. In fact, the whole Longworth family stood with their mouths hanging open.

"H—hello, Cimarron," Aunt Carolina finally blurted. "Speak to your favorite cousin, girls."

Patience and Prudence gaped at her. Cimarron thought she'd seen more intelligent expressions on Durango cows.

"Cimarron," Prudence finally said, "is this ball really in your honor? You mean, you married the heir?"

Cimarron winked and smiled, a little too sweetly. "You

know what your mother always says, girls, what goes around comes around. I remember there was once some question over whether I might attend a cheap little party. People are saying this is the finest ball Texans ever saw."

She looked over at Ransford, a little afraid, because of his expression, that he might collapse of shock.

"Land o' Goshen, h—hello Cimarron," he mumbled sheepishly. "How's my favorite niece?"

"Never been better! Sorry to hear of your accident," she said, wrinkling her nose at the smell of bay rum. "You should learn to be a little more careful with sharp things. Who knows, next time it might be a knife."

He turned three shades of crimson and gulped. "I—I'll remember! Now, dear niece, about the bank note—"

"We'll discuss all that later," she smiled, enjoying herself. "And while we're at it, we'll discuss the virtues of being humble and apologetic."

Aunt Carolina gasped. "Please remember I was dear Texanna's sister."

"I remember everything, dear aunt, everything you ever did to both of us. I'll think about it." It was strange, she thought, she didn't even really hate the Longworths for hurting her anymore. The small-town cruel snobs weren't worth the trouble.

And then she spotted her old friend standing shyly behind the Longworths. "Señora Rodriguez!" She threw her arms around the Mexican widow. "I'm so glad you came! I have a handsome *hombre* named Sanchez who wants to meet you."

Her old friend hugged Cimarron. "My friend, I'm so glad to see you! I thought it surely was a mistake that I was brought to so fine a house—"

"No mistake! You deserve it for what Fandango has put you through!" Cimarron turned, motioned. "Sanchez, here's the señora I have invited to meet you."

He came through the crowd, shyly, hesitantly, his eyes on the shy widow standing next to Cimarron. She looked from one to the other, smiling as she made the introductions. It was easy to see they were attracted to each other.

Good, she thought. It was time for Sanchez to cease his

mourning for the dead Rosa, time for him to marry again. And her old friend would make a wonderful mother for little Turquoise. She knew now it had been right not to tell the old vaquero anything. Rosa had earned his respect and silence by her bravery. And there was no reason to hurt the innocent with the truth.

The orchestra struck up a melody. Sanchez made a courtly bow to her friend. "If the lovely lady would care to dance and then see the ranch. . . ."

Mrs Rodriguez took his arm, her face bright with pleasure. "It has been a long time since a handsome *hombre* asked me to dance! I wouldn't miss it for the world!"

The pair moved out onto the floor and Cimarron smiled at Trace's father. Don Diego had gradually recovered from his illness, and Trace and Cimarron had vowed never to tell him what his beloved baby brother had attempted. And poor, blundering Dr. Hastings had returned to Connecticut now that the war was over.

The mourning period was ended. The Durango family had made a pilgrimage to Jacob's Well to throw oleander blossoms on the dark surface of the water, to say prayers for the gentle Cheyenne woman who had died to protect those she loved. The dignified Don Diego would survive his grief, and someday there would be grandchildren for him to enjoy.

The half-grown Comanche boy joined them then, and the Don put his arm around the boy's shoulders. "Oh, you haven't met my adopted son. This is Maverick Durango. He was one of the heroes of the Elm Creek uprising."

Ransford's eyes widened. "Land o' Goshen! I heard a trio rode up to the Brazo country to spread the alarm. Heard the uprising was stopped before it really got started because someone shot and killed the chief, Little Buffalo."

Maverick smiled modestly, winked at Trace and Cimarron. "I had some help from Cheyenne friends."

Trace tapped his foot to the music. "Excuse me, please," he said, "I want to dance with my beautiful wife." He pulled her out on the floor. They danced together as beautifully and rhythmically as they made love, she thought dreamily as he whirled her out under the great chandelier and people made way for them.

She heard the murmurs around them. "What a stunning dress she has!"

"And what a handsome couple they make, him with that coal-black hair and hers so honey blond!"

She danced and smiled up at her beloved.

He looked down into her eyes. "Wild One," he whispered, "what are you thinking?"

"How much I love you," she answered, snuggling closer in his arms as they danced. She wanted to give him an heir as soon as possible. Now, since she was half-German and half-Cheyenne and Trace was half-Spanish and half-Cheyenne, the future baby would be one-quarter Spanish, one-quarter German, and ... "Double damnation!" she said aloud, "Another darn Cheyenne half-breed!"

"What?" he looked puzzled. "What did you say, darlin'?"

"Nothing." She smiled up at him, thinking how happy old Don Diego would be when she produced a grandchild.

Trace whirled her around, glanced toward the buffet table. "That Tequila!" he laughed. "Look at him!"

She looked. The fat little chihuahua sat up prettily, waved his paws in the air, and Turquoise gave him another bite from the table. "That little pig!"

"Speaking of which," Trace nodded, "look who else is enjoying all the food."

Cimarron giggled in spite of herself. Since no one seemed to have asked them to dance, both Longworth girls stood with plates heaped high by the ornate wedding cake, gobbling as if afraid someone might take their food away from them.

People stared and chuckled at the pair, while Aunt Carolina, Uncle Ransford, and the handful of Fandango society looked mortified and out of place in the elegant company.

Maverick approached with two plates full of delicious food as the pair left the dance floor. "Here you go, brother and sweet sister-in-law. And I'll get you some wine."

Cimarron took a bite of the meat, the delicate cake. "Mmm. I never had anything so good before." She accepted a crystal goblet from the tall boy as he returned.

Trace took a glass. "Let's toast!" He clinked his glass against the others. "Here's to half-breeds," he said, "And to a love waiting out there somewhere for our Maverick!"

The steel-gray eyes smiled. "If she's as sweet, as beautiful as your lady, I'll drink to that," he said as he sipped. "Now here's my toast." They waited expectantly. "To Cimarron Durango, the Wild One who has finally been tamed, and to Trace Durango, who has his work cut out for him to keep her tamed! And here's to the Triple D's fourth generation!"

Cimarron blushed and held up her own glass. "In that case, we'd better drink to Cheyenne passion." She winked boldly at Trace, promising with her eyes.

His smoldering gaze caressed her as he drank and refilled his glass. "And this toast is for my Cheyenne princess, who reigns over both my heart and the whole Durango empire."

"Hear! Hear!" Maverick said as he drained his goblet.

The party seemed to go on and on, she thought, deliriously happy. Never could she even have imagined so much fine food and wine, so much dancing. She was the center of attention, of everyone's admiration. The women wanted to compliment her gown. All the men asked her to dance. She saw her two homely cousins staring enviously from the sidelines, but no one asked either of them to dance.

Finally, at midnight, Trace and Cimarron went out onto the veranda in the night air to see the full moon. The tiny dog followed them out through the open doors and hopped up on the wall surrounding the bubbling fountain.

The scent of wild flowers came to her on the gentle breeze that caressed her perspiring skin. The oleanders were in bloom again, and she looked at the magenta and pink blossoms and thought of the gentle señora who had loved them so. Laughter and music echoed faintly from the house through the open French doors.

"Now that the war's ended," Cimarron said, leaning against Trace's broad chest, "we must try again to find your sister and my brother."

The dog cocked its head, staring into the distance. She looked quizzically at the chihuahua. Tequila's comical ears went up and he watched something in the distance intently. But this time, there was no mournful howl.

Cimarron looked down at the tiny dog staring so earnestly into the darkness.

"What on earth do you think you see?" she asked.

Trace started to answer, and then they saw it, too.

Across the hilltops, silhouetted against the moon, came the galloping, ghostly phantom. Cimarron held her breath and watched, hardly daring to breathe. It was as haunting, as mysteriously beautiful as she remembered.

Always before, the specter had galloped to the edge of the sky where the Milky Way met the earth, hesitated, and kept running. But as she held her breath to watch, the vision of sparkling light and stardust never stopped. It galloped madly, purposefully off the edge of the horizon and up the ghostly trail of clouds called the Milky Way.

For only a moment they saw it, a flash of light as it poised in midair along the midnight black of the world and then started up the snowy path of clouds. Only one brilliant flash, and it disappeared into the darkness.

"The Hanging Road," Cimarron murmured, remembering the Cheyenne legend of heaven. "She's made it, Trace, she's gone forever now. The spirit horse has run the very last time."

Tears came to Trace's eyes. "Maybe we don't see what we think we see," he whispered. "Maybe it is only a comet's trail flashing across eternity. . . ."

"You're Cheyenne. You don't believe that anymore than I do. Velvet Eyes couldn't leave until she protected those she loved, until she was avenged. Now she may look on the face of God."

She felt him slip his arm around her, and her own eyes were not dry as the sparkle of light moved up the Milky Way. It blinked once and then faded into the vast blackness.

"Good-bye, Velvet Eyes." She could not stop the tears that ran down her face. "Oh, good-bye . . . good-bye."

Clair de lune. Moonlight. There was no use in going to look. Somehow, she knew the dress would be gone. There are some things that cannot, should not be explained. That's how legends, how fairy tales are made.

She said, "We will tell no one of this. What we have seen is sacred to the Cheyenne."

He swallowed hard. "No, we'll tell Father. I think he will understand and be comforted."

Trace could call him "Father" again without hurting. They both trembled on the edge of tears. After they had foiled the Comanche raid on north Texas, the two had opened the envelope and read Velvet Eyes's last message.

My Darling Diego,

If you are reading this, I am dead, but I have left this letter hidden in hopes that you will discover it in time to protect yourself and our beloved son from evil.

Knowing Luis is your adored baby brother, I have never told you how he has attempted to seduce me and plotted against you. This afternoon, I followed him to his rendezvous with the Comanchero. Seeing Luis with them is the final piece of the missing puzzle, because I have suspected for several days that he is stealing livestock and trading with those renegades. I think he plots to take over the whole ranch, maybe even do away with you and Trace.

As I write this late at night, you are at the Rowlands' ranch. I don't know what to do until you return so I can tell you what I've found out. Tomorrow, I'll go through the ledgers one more time to get facts and figures to give you when you return. I dare not tell Trace, I fear to cause a confrontation between him and Luis. As you are Don of this ranchero, the final decisions of the Triple D are yours, my darling, and I await your return with eagerness. Our small argument this morning over Dallas was only because we are both sad over her disappearance. It does not change our love for each other. My thoughts are of you tonight, my only love, and our beloved children. *Yo te quiero, mi querido.* Ojos de Pana.

When Trace read it, he had put his head on his arms and wept great, gasping sobs that seemed to cleanse his moody, bitter soul. "She gave her life to save mine," he had whispered again and again. "Oh, Mother! Mother!"

Then he and Cimarron had carefully destroyed the note. Its contents could only hurt the old Don. And after all, justice, a terrible Cheyenne justice, had been done.

Here tonight in the courtyard the sky was dark again, the spirit horse gone forever up the bright star trail.

Trace took a deep, shuddering breath, looking skyward. "Velvet Eyes is at peace now. *Hena-haanehe,*" he whispered in Cheyenne, "That's the end. It's over." Then he took Cimarron in his strong arms and kissed her. "But for us, darlin', this is only the beginning."

"*Yo te amo,* I love you," she whispered in Spanish and English. Her arms went around his neck and she kissed him deeply, thoroughly. There was no wine as intoxicating as the taste of his lips.

His hands held her waist with gentle tenderness. "To really love is to trust, and I give you my heart, along with my name. *Yo te quiero, mi querida.* I love you, sweetheart."

His tongue flicked against her lips, searching, exploring. She felt him take a deep breath, and his warm hands clasped her shoulders, pushed the rose-pink moir down until he could caress the swell of her breasts.

Cimarron felt the excitement building in both of them at what was to come. She could never get enough of the taste and feel of his hard body. "But what about our guests?" she murmured.

Trace's eyes smoldered with banked passion as he swung her up in his muscular arms, turned toward the outside staircase. "They're all still having such a good time, they won't even miss us, darlin'. We have the first of many nights awaiting us upstairs."

She laid her face against his jacket, looking into his eyes. As she reached up to touch his lips with her left hand, the jeweled ring caught the light. "I love you, my husband."

He kissed the tip of her nose as he carried her across the flagstones to the foot of the outside stairway. The little dog hopped down off the wall and tried to follow them, but Cimarron waved him away. "No, you little rascal," she laughed, "you can't go with us. Go on back into the party. Beg some more food off the table. Go have some fun!"

The chihuahua barked happily and scampered back through the open French doors as Trace carried her up the stairs. "I'm not sure you should have told the little devil that," he cautioned. "You know what he likes to do best—"

She heard a bark drifting above the faint music, through the open doors. Then a familiar voice wailed, "Land o' Goshen! Somebody help me! That damned little dog . . . !"

Cimarron listened, looked up into Trace's eyes as she put her face against his shirt and giggled. "I think you're right. I'm afraid Tequila has just bitten Uncle Ransford."

"Naughty Tequila! Remind me, darlin', to give him an extra treat at breakfast. But right now, I'm going to make love to my wife!" He didn't put her down as he kissed her, carried her into their room, kicked the door shut.

He laid her on the bed, undressed her gently. "You look beautiful naked," he said, "wearing nothing but a king's ransom in rubies. Remind me to buy you some more." He leaned to kiss her breasts and she caught the blue-black hair and pulled him toward her as her passion built.

She shook her hair loose so that it covered her with its golden glory. "Oh, Trace," she said as his lips caressed her, "make love to me in ways I can't even imagine."

"I've got a lot of imagination," he murmured as his lips moved across her breasts. "And all night to do it."

"No, dear one," she gasped as she felt his lips caress her, felt her own body ache with hunger. "We've got the rest of our lives!"

"That's not long enough," he answered as he kissed her again. "Not near long enough!" He took her in his arms and began to make love to her.

It would be a long, wonderful night, she thought. He kissed her, murmuring endearments, and her own ardor built as she embraced him. Then he entered her, and the rhythm of love began. They moved together, coupling in a graceful movement of desire and fulfillment. She held him tightly as the ecstasy increased to a crescendo. Her last conscious thought as she went over the edge and fell into darkness was that he was right. *A lifetime was not long enough. But it would have to do.*

To My Readers

My grandmother was born in the Brazos River country not too many miles from the area of the Comanche-Kiowa raid of 1864. What I have told you of Texans voting against seceding, the lynching of protestors at Gainesville, the slaughter of Union-sympathizing Germans at Nueces, and La Lux Del Llano, the light of the prairie, has been carefully researched. Matter of fact, the mysterious light also turns up here in Oklahoma when atmospheric conditions are right.

I attended college in the Texas hill country and did a little cave exploring in the area, but I was never loco enough to swim into Jacob's Well. Yes, it really does exist, on the Cypress Fork of the Blanco River in western Hays county. It is notorious enough to rate a story in the July, 1981, *Reader's Digest,* entitled: "Ninety Feet Under." Those who have survived the descent say that at the bottom, one has to take off one's scuba tanks and swim through a tiny, eighteen-inch hole to enter into what has been described as a giant underwater cave big enough to park a fleet of 747 airplanes. Depending on whom you ask, the death toll stands between nine and sixteen. Jacob's Well is on private property and has security guards to keep would-be divers out of its deadly depths. Efforts to seal it have failed.

In the story you have just read, the town of Fandango and the Durango ranch are fictitious. The rest: the beautiful hill country surrounding Fredericksburg, the Devil's Backbone, the Enchanted Rock are tourist attractions not far from San

Antonio and Austin.

Any Gulf Coast gardener will reaffirm the toxicity of the flowering oleander. Don't eat honey that might have been made from the nectar of this poisonous blossom or even roast a hot dog on one of its branches. The flowers and leaves can be lethal.

Maybe it's ironic that the town named for Peta Nocona, Nocona, Texas, is now a leading producer of cowboy boots. His half-breed son, Quanah, became the fiercest war chief the Comanche ever produced. The Texans respected and admired him enough to name the county seat of Hardeman county in his honor. Quanah, the last chief of the Comanche, his mother, Cynthia, and his little sister, Prairie Flower, are all buried at Fort Sill cemetery in Lawton, Oklahoma, near the Kiowas' sacred mountains, the Wichitas.

The "Great Outbreak" ultimately involved not only the Comanche but the Kiowa, Navaho, Cheyenne and Arapaho. Hundreds of Comanche and Kiowa warriors attacked the Elm Creek area of the Brazos river in October of 1864. Little Buffalo and twenty of his braves died, while eleven whites and eleven ranches were victims. When Little Buffalo was killed, the Indians decided it was a sign of bad medicine and fled. Kit Carson battled the Comanche later that year up in the Panhandle, and his subordinate, Captain Pfeiffer, attacked the Navajo in Canyon de Chelly and destroyed them so completely that they never made war against whites again.

It is a fact that in the "Great Outbreak" raid, the Comanche-Kiowa took seven women and children hostages. A brave black man, Britt Johnson, whose wife and children had been stolen, went deep into the heart of Comanche country and bargained successfully for the captives' return. All but one small girl. The Kiowa refused to give up little Millie Durgan, because she had been adopted into the family of Chief Aperian Crow.

Many years later, an old Kiowa woman, Saintohoodi Goombi, was identified as the missing Durgan girl. But the woman had no memory of her life among the whites and no interest in renewing friendship with them. She had married a warrior, produced a family, and spent the rest of her days among the Kiowa, dying in 1934. She is buried in Rainy Mountain Indian cemetery near Mountain View, just north of the Wichitas. That Kiowa stronghold above the Red River is about a hundred miles from my home in the Cross Timbers region of central Oklahoma.

The Cheyenne and Arapaho, warring against the miners and gold prospectors coming into western Kansas and the Colorado Territory, would clash with Colonel Chivington and his Territorials in 1864 at an obscure place called Sand Creek. Chivington, as you recall, had destroyed the Texas regiments at La Glorieta Pass, near Santa Fe, leaving the Texas frontier open to Comanche attack.

Yes, the colors of women's dresses in this story are authentic. All those I named, russet, indigo blue, reseda green, dove gray, clair de lune, and solferino pink were popular colors of the 1850s and 60s. Solferino pink was named in honor of Napoleon III's 1859 battle at Solferino, Italy. For this information, I am most grateful to the book *Calico Chronicle, Texas Women and their Fashions,* by Betty J. Mills, published by the Texas Tech Press.

To the Cheyenne, a story is a possession, like a pony or a blanket. None but the owner may tell it, share it with his friends. When tales are told at night around the campfire, it always ends this way: "That is my story. Can anyone tie another to it?" Then another Teller of Tales stands and begins to weave his magic. Sometimes the stories go on all night. Always the storyteller asks: "Can anyone tie another to it?"

Oh, yes, Ancient One, I can tie another to the tale I have just told. All the threads I leave unfinished I'll tie onto later as I weave my legends of the West. The story of Cimarron's big brother, the Cheyenne Dog Soldier who stole a Boston debutante off a Butterfield stage, has already been told in my first book, *Cheyenne Captive*.

Ten years will pass before Maverick, now the tough trail boss of the Triple D, will again cross the path of that other Comanche half-breed, Quanah Parker. Both have vowed vengeance for the deaths of their white mothers. But each will take a different road, one choosing his white heritage, the other, the red. Quanah will lead his warriors against the entire U.S. Cavalry. But Maverick searches relentlessly for only one man, the coward who failed to ransom his gentle mother. God help anyone who comes between him and his revenge! But what if that someone is a passionate beauty with flame-colored hair?

Cayenne is a red-hot pepper Texans use to spice up their Mexican food. What a perfect name for fiery Cayenne McBride! The stubborn redhead is on her own quest and will reward the man who helps her with her virginity. How can this innocent know that she is only being used for the lean cowboy's vengeance as she succumbs to his Comanche caress?

I'll save your spot by the campfire as I begin to weave this tumultuous romance of two maverick hearts caught between love, loyalty, and revenge a long time ago in the West. Come slip back in time with me....

Yo te amo,
Georgina Gentry

I read forty-six books to bring you authentic background for *Cheyenne Princess*. Many of these are rare or out of print, so you probably could not get them. But I will always recommend interesting books at the end of my novels that you might find at your public library. The ones I depended on most were:

Comanches, the Destruction of a People, by T.R. Fehrenbach. Publisher: Alfred A. Knopf, Inc.
The Comanches, Lords of the South Plains, by Ernest Wallace and E. Adamson Hoebel. Publisher: University of Oklahoma Press.
Lone Star, a History of Texas and the Texans, by T.R. Fehrenbach. Publisher: American Legacy Press.

Now you can get more of HEARTFIRE right at home and $ave.

Preview Four Brand New ZEBRA Heartfire Romance Novels...

FREE for 10 days.

No Obligation and No Strings Attached!

♥

Enjoy all of the passion and fiery romance as you soar back through history, right in the comfort of your own home.

Now that you have read a Zebra HEARTFIRE Romance novel, we're sure you'll agree that HEARTFIRE sets new standards of excellence for historical romantic fiction. Each Zebra HEARTFIRE novel is the ultimate blend of intimate romance and grand adventure and each takes place in the kinds of historical settings you want most...the American Revolution, the Old West, Civil War and more.

FREE Preview Each Month and $ave

Zebra has made arrangements for you to preview 4 brand new HEARTFIRE novels each month...FREE for 10 days. You'll get them as soon as they are published. If you are not delighted with any of them, just return them with no questions asked. But if you decide these are everything we said they are, you'll pay just $3.25 each—a total of $13.00 (a $15.00 value). **That's a $2.00 saving each month off the regular price.** Plus there is NO shipping or handling charge. These are delivered right to your door absolutely free! There is no obligation and there is no minimum number of books to buy.

TO GET YOUR FIRST MONTH'S PREVIEW... Mail the Coupon Below!

Mail to:

HEARTFIRE Home Subscription Service, Inc.
120 Brighton Road
P.O. Box 5214
Clifton, NJ 07015-5214

YES! I want to subscribe to Zebra's HEARTFIRE Home Subscription Service. Please send me my first month's books to preview free for ten days. I understand that if I am not pleased I may return them and owe nothing, but if I keep them I will pay just $3.25 each; a total of $13.00. That is a savings of $2.00 each month off the cover price. There are no shipping, handling or other hidden charges and there is no minimum number of books I must buy. I can cancel this subscription at any time with no questions asked.

NAME _____

ADDRESS _____ APT. NO. _____

CITY _____ STATE _____ ZIP _____

SIGNATURE (if under 18, parent or guardian must sign)   2176
Terms and prices are subject to change.